Henry Parry Liddon, John Octavius Johnston

# Life of Edward Bouverie Pusey, Doctor of Divinity, Canon of Christ Church

Regius professor of Hebrew in the University of Oxford. Vol. 4

Henry Parry Liddon, John Octavius Johnston

**Life of Edward Bouverie Pusey, Doctor of Divinity, Canon of Christ Church**
*Regius professor of Hebrew in the University of Oxford. Vol. 4*

ISBN/EAN: 9783337318192

Printed in Europe, USA, Canada, Australia, Japan

Cover: Foto ©Raphael Reischuk / pixelio.de

More available books at **www.hansebooks.com**

# *Life of*
# *Edward Bouverie Pusey*

### DOCTOR OF DIVINITY
### CANON OF CHRIST CHURCH; REGIUS PROFESSOR OF
### HEBREW IN THE UNIVERSITY OF OXFORD

BY

# HENRY PARRY LIDDON, D.D.

D.C.L.; LL.D.; LATE CANON AND CHANCELLOR OF ST. PAUL'S

EDITED AND PREPARED FOR PUBLICATION BY THE

## REV. J. O. JOHNSTON, M.A.
PRINCIPAL OF CUDDESDON THEOLOGICAL COLLEGE

AND THE

## REV. ROBERT J. WILSON, D.D.
LATE WARDEN OF KEBLE COLLEGE

AND THE

## REV. W. C. E. NEWBOLT, M.A.
CANON AND CHANCELLOR OF ST. PAUL'S

*IN FOUR VOLUMES: VOL. IV (1860—1882)*

*With Portrait and Illustrations*

# LONGMANS, GREEN, AND CO.
### 39 PATERNOSTER ROW, LONDON
### NEW YORK AND BOMBAY

### 1897

# PREFACE TO VOL. IV

ALLUSION was made in the preface of the last volume to the general divisions under which Dr. Liddon proposed to arrange his biography of Dr. Pusey. Naturally he regarded that long life chiefly in its relation to the Oxford Movement. It would fall, he used to say, into four parts, to be entitled the Preparation, the Movement, the Struggle, the Victory. If in such a scheme the third volume could be described as the Struggle, the present may be taken with equal propriety to represent the Victory, although it must be admitted that to a considerable extent it is still only a record of conflict and endurance. Yet when this volume begins, a great victory has already been won on behalf of the principles for which Dr. Pusey had so painfully struggled.

In the dark years between 1846 and 1860, Dr. Pusey was engaged in convincing his fellow-countrymen that, in spite of all assertions and appearances to the contrary, the teaching which specially characterized the Tractarians was true

to the traditions of the English Church. Already
by the year 1860 the soundness of this claim was
beginning to be acknowledged on all sides; and
Catholic teaching was emerging once for all from
under the dark clouds of suspicion and obloquy
which the defection of so many friends had caused
to gather round it. Indeed, so completely had the
honesty of the Tractarian position been vindicated,
that Dr. Pusey found himself able, without forfeiting
the growing confidence in his sincerity, to make open
proposals for reunion with Rome, which, ten years
earlier, would have been regarded as the last act of
treachery. And as time goes on the Victory, to
which Dr. Pusey's patient endurance so materially
contributed, becomes more and more apparent : and
to-day the Archbishops of England in addressing
' the whole body of Bishops of the Catholic Church '
are able to assume, as part of the undisputed
heritage of the English Church, such doctrines as
the Apostolical Succession and the Sacrificial Aspect
of the Holy Eucharist, which fifty years ago were
generally branded with all the discredit that belonged
to the hated word Tractarian.

During the latter part of his life, other work of
a most urgent kind mainly occupied Dr. Pusey's
attention. In the strange outbursts of controversy
about Absolution in 1873 and 1877, we have indeed
echoes of an old conflict; but as a rule he is now
engaged far more in repelling attacks on the position
which hitherto all Christians had held in common, than in laying claim to a neglected portion of

the Catholic deposit. The air was full of hints, and doubts, and open denials suggested by the misunderstandings and mistakes which not un-naturally accompanied the early growth of modern science. On all sides men, in their wish to be loyal to truth, were in danger of sinking down to blank infidelity under the influence of the hasty assertions of unscientific science, and in consequence of a loose and unintelligent hold of the fundamental truths of Religion. Especially was this the case in our Universities. The changes made by the First University Commission had practically deprived the Church of its ancient inheritance; and there were many who supposed that the faith of the Church would be as short-lived as its endowments.

To the great effort to save souls in the midst of this general unsettlement and to keep them in the Faith, Dr. Pusey devoted nearly all his later years. The Ritualistic controversy which raged throughout the whole period interested him only indirectly. His whole heart was engaged in defending the Faith not only against open attacks, but also against the unwise counsels of those Churchmen who seemed to imagine that some kind of advantage could be gained by making a present to opponents of this or that unpopular portion of the Christian creeds. From the vantage-ground of the full Faith of the Catholic Church, and with his wide knowledge and clear insight into the limits of any possible range of Physical Science, he was able not only to steady and reassure many troubled minds, but also to make timely contributions of permanent value to the cause of Christian apology.

But besides the change in the character of Dr. Pusey's later work, there was a yet greater change in the feelings of Churchmen towards him. The vindication of the Tractarian position naturally involved the restoration of its chief living champion to an influence wider and deeper than he had ever exercised before. His age, character, and history gave to the utterances of this period a moral weight which was quite unique; and on questions on which all Christians were agreed, his words commanded unusual attention and respect throughout the Church. In the University pulpit especially, where he addressed his hearers as ' My sons,' the attractive force of the claim which that title implied was deeply felt, and his solemn counsels and earnest exhortations carried with them the authority of a revered parent or of an aged prophet.

Dr. Liddon died before he had reached this portion of his own loving memorial to Dr. Pusey. His only contribution to this volume is the touching description of Dr. Pusey's last days and of his deathbed. The rest has been compiled by one of the editors, and for many reasons it was a task of no little difficulty. The events described are quite recent; many of the actors are still alive, and a large quantity of material is still unavailable : this period could not therefore be treated with the same fullness as the earlier years. It must further be remembered that the chief controversies are still unsettled, and some of the most delicate situations preserve their form unchanged to the present day. The compiler has therefore aimed at restricting the narrative as closely as possible to the personality of Dr. Pusey himself, and presenting clearly his attitude towards these modern controversies in the form with which he had to deal with them. So far as possible, nothing has been admitted with which he was not directly concerned. At the same time it was found necessary to omit many interesting questions with which Dr. Pusey was in some way connected, as a brief reference to them would have been unintelligible, and a sufficiently full account might have seemed tedious.

The volume was written in the hope that it would receive throughout that careful revision at the hands of Dr. Wilson, the Warden of Keble College, to which the other three volumes owe so much. Here especially his intimate knowledge of the whole period, his ripe judgment, and his sympathetic appreciation of the minds of Dr. Pusey and Dr. Liddon, would have made his assistance particularly valuable. But when he had only partly revised some of the early chapters, he was called away to his rest on May 15th last. At the request of Dr. Liddon's literary executors his place was taken by the Rev. W. C. E. Newbolt, Canon and Chancellor of St. Paul's.

Throughout, the editors have freely used the collection of letters which Dr. Liddon left behind him, and they can only repeat the thanks which were expressed in the preface to the first volume. They have assumed that these letters were entrusted to Dr. Liddon to be quoted with all due discretion. When they have had any hesitation, they have applied for permission before inserting them in this volume : and if by any chance any documents have been used for which such permission should have been asked, they desire to apologize for the unwitting inadvertence. Special thanks are due to Cardinal Newman's literary executor for his ready permission to print letters.

The most obvious of the many omissions of this volume is the neglect of almost the whole of that side of Dr. Pusey's work which was devoted to the counsel and direction of those who came to him in theological or spiritual difficulties. He never spared time or trouble in assisting any who applied to him ; and with the truest sympathy he placed at their disposal all the resources of his knowledge and his wide experience. It has been found quite impossible to do justice to this aspect of his many-sided ministry in the pages of a biography which has already reached such large dimensions ; but it is hoped that at an early date it may be possible to issue a volume of his theological and spiritual letters.

For the valuable Bibliography the editors are indebted to the skill of Mr. Falconer Madan, M.A., of Brasenose College, Sub-Librarian of the Bodleian. He compiled it several years ago at Dr. Liddon's request, and has recently revised it throughout and very kindly corrected it for the Press. Besides its general value and interest, the Bibliography will be found to supplement the Life on many points which were unavoidably omitted.

The editors feel it a great happiness to be allowed at length to complete this great work. From the first Dr. Liddon was determined that the story of Dr. Pusey's Life should readjust the balance of those partial histories of the Oxford Movement which had appeared before 1882, and should cause his great friend to stand out in Church History in his rightful place. This aim was admirably fulfilled in his own work in the first three volumes; and it is humbly hoped that in this last volume all defects of narration will be overlooked in recognition of the honesty, the insight, the courage and the patience of this most loyal son of the English Church.

It is specially appropriate that these last sheets should pass to-day to the printer's hands. On this day fifteen years ago Dr. Pusey died at Ascot; and eight years later on the same day Dr. Liddon was buried at St. Paul's Cathedral.

'Requiem aeternam dona eis, Domine,
Et lux perpetua luceat eis.'

J. O. J.

W. C. E. N.

*September* 16, 1897.

# CONTENTS OF VOL. IV

## CHAPTER V. 1866-1867.

## CHAPTER VI. 1869-1870.

## CHAPTER VII. 1865-1872.

## CHAPTER VIII. 1866-1872.

## CHAPTER IX. 1870-1873.

## CHAPTER X. 1873.

## CHAPTER XI. 1873-1877.

## APPENDIX A.

## APPENDIX B.

---

# LIST OF ILLUSTRATIONS.

# THE LIFE

OF

# EDWARD BOUVERIE PUSEY

## CHAPTER I.

THEOLOGICAL LIBERALISM IN OXFORD—SERMONS ON
THE NATURE OF FAITH—THE NEW PROFESSOR OF
GREEK—PROPOSED INCREASE OF ENDOWMENT FOR
THE GREEK CHAIR—PROSECUTION OF PROFESSOR
JOWETT—ENDOWMENT OF THE CHAIR.

THE new University *régime* which was inaugurated in
October, 1854, represented of course far more than a change
in the outward arrangements of Academical life. It was
coincident with the dominance of a new spirit in the
thought of the University; and with this spirit it was
obvious that the Church was now bound to reckon. The
danger of uncontrolled and unbalanced reasoning on the
facts of Revelation had long been anticipated; and it had
for many years been leavening a small section of English
thought. But at this time it threatened to attain a power and
prominence in Oxford which suggested the gravest results
for a later period both within and without the University.

The Tractarian Movement has generally been described
as an attempt to effect a 'High Church' revival, by reasserting those portions of the Church's teaching which the
popular 'Evangelicalism' was in danger of overlooking. This

indeed was its immediate and most obvious result ; but the Tractarians were not ultimately concerned with the deficiencies of Evangelicalism.  They were chiefly thinking of the assaults of ' Liberalism ' upon the institution and faith of the Church.  They were convinced that the only adequate protection against such assaults was to be found in strengthening a position which Evangelicalism had not thought it worth while to occupy.

Cardinal Newman has told us that these fears filled his mind during his foreign tour in 1832 and 1833 ; ' I had,' he wrote, ' fierce thoughts against the Liberals.'  The letters of that date from Keble, Newman, Froude, Rose, Perceval and all who took part in the ' Association of Friends of the Church,' show that they were keenly alive to the reality of this danger.  But the ordinary Englishman was far from being aware of the principles and tendency of the Liberal school of theology.  He heard proposals in Parliament and elsewhere for abolishing Irish bishoprics, and for strange changes in English Cathedrals; but he knew nothing of the theological and ecclesiastical presuppositions which underlay these changes.  Newman alluded to this connexion between ' Liberal ' theology and some of the Parliamentary measures of 1832 in a retrospective passage of the Advertisement to the third volume of the ' Tracts.'  ' Irreligious principles and false doctrines which had hitherto been avowed only in the closet, or on paper, had just been admitted into public measures on a large scale.'  Already in 1835, the practical questions had fallen into the background, but the question of theological principle was becoming more apparent.  The subject is discussed by Newman at the close of that year in a lengthy Tract (No. 73) 'on the Introduction of Rationalistic Principles into Religion '; at the end of this Tract he calls attention to the ' subjectivity ' of Evangelicalism, which he considered its great weakness, and which, to his mind, rendered it useless as a defence of Church doctrine.  The concluding paragraph is sufficient to explain what Newman meant.  While exposing Rationalism, he was looking round for traces of its spirit nearer home. He says that the Evangelical appeal to the heart alone shared the fatal defect of one-sidedness that belonged also to that exclusive appeal to reason against which the early Evangelicals had nobly revolted. ' I will conclude by summing up in one sentence, which must be pardoned me if in appearance harsh, what the foregoing discussion is intended to show. There is a widely spread though variously admitted school of doctrine among us, within and without the Church, which intends and professes peculiar piety, as directing its attention to the *heart itself*, not to anything external to us, whether creed, actions, or ritual. I do not hesitate to assert that this doctrine is based upon error, that it is really a specious form of trusting man rather than God, that it is in its nature Rationalistic, and that it tends to Socinianism. How the individual supporters of it will act as time goes on is another matter,—the good will be separated from the bad, but the school, as such, will pass through Sabellianism to that "God-denying Apostasy," to use the ancient phrase, to which in the beginning of its career it professed to be especially opposed [1].' The following year witnessed the first skirmish of the coming struggle in the agitation which sprang up against the appointment of Hampden as Regius Professor of Divinity.

Pusey, too, it will be remembered, had in early days been painfully brought into contact with the same spirit in the German lecture-rooms. The words have already been quoted [2] in which he describes the moment during his stay at Göttingen in 1825, when he first realized the condition of theology and religion in Germany, and was able to anticipate the future of English Academical thought. ' This,' he reflected, ' will all come upon us in England, and how utterly unprepared for it we are!' In his first book on the causes of the rationalistic character of German theology, he traced it mainly to the decay of belief, to the absence of any vigorous healthful religious life in German Protestantism, to what he called its 'dead orthodoxism.'

---

[1] ' Tracts for the Times,' No. 73, p. 53.    [2] Vol. i. p. 77.

In writing this book, he had his eye on the condition of
the English Church. 'I feared,' he explained to Rose,
'lest people in England were verging towards Rationalism . . . lest cold dry views on the one hand, and especially
a decayed Pietism on the other, might find their parallel
among us and bring in Rationalism here also[1].' In
speaking thus he is expressing his dread of that attitude
of mind which allows Reason to limit the possibilities of
Revelation, instead of confining itself to its legitimate work
of testing its evidence and understanding its moral weight.
Tractarianism attracted him at first perhaps by its life
and reality, and, throughout, his interest extended always
beyond the assertion of doctrine as doctrine, to the restoration and extension of everything that could win souls to
the Christian faith and thereby establish them in practical
holiness.

The influence of Newman, and in his own way of Pusey
also, during the twelve years between 1833 and 1845 did
not a little to check this spirit of Rationalism, and to prepare the Church to resist it if it should grow stronger.
Many of the ablest and most highly cultured minds found
refuge from this tendency in the fuller restatement of
the whole Catholic creed which the Tractarians set before
them; and it was a common saying when the Heads of
Houses were taking their measures against Newman, 'You
may crush Tractarianism, but then you will have to deal
with Germanism.' This was very soon found to be true.
After the Academical overthrow of the Tractarians as a
party in 1845, and the consequent suspicion and discredit
which fell on them, a new and more vigorous school of
Liberal Theologians began to gain a wider influence in
Oxford. Dean Church has left an interesting sketch of
the differences between the Oxford Theological Liberals
before 1833 and after 1845. Whateley was the representative
of the earlier, and Stanley of the later school[2].

'The older Oxford Liberals were either intellectually aristocratic, dis-
secting the inaccuracies or showing up the paralogisms of the current

[1] Vol. i. p. 177.      [2] 'The Oxford Movement.' p. 338.

orthodoxy; or they were poor in character, Liberals from the zest of sneering and mocking at what was received and established, or from the convenience of getting rid of strict and troublesome rules of life. They patronized Dissenters; they gave Whig votes; they made free, in a mild way, with the pet conventions and prejudices of Tories and High Churchmen. There was nothing inspiring in them, however much men might respect their correct and sincere lives. But a younger set of men brought, mainly from Rugby and Arnold's teaching, a new kind of Liberalism. It was much bolder and more independent than the older forms, less inclined to put up with the traditional, more searching and inquisitive in its methods, more suspicious and daring in its criticism; but it was much larger in its views and its sympathies, and, above all, it was imaginative, it was enthusiastic, and, without much of the devotional temper, it was penetrated by a sense of the reality and seriousness of religion. It saw greater hopes in the present and the future than the Tractarians. It disliked their reverence for the past and the received, as inconsistent with what seemed evidence of the providential order of great and fruitful change. It could not enter into their discipline of character, and shrank from it as antiquated, unnatural and narrow [1].'

Tractarianism was sufficiently definite to have been crushed by direct attack; but it was difficult to find any weapons to wield against this new foe. 'Germanism' in fact in those days was by its own nature peculiarly able to evade assault. Its weapons were questionings, hints, doubts, suspicions, undigested and exaggerated criticism and distorted historical analogies. The perils to be apprehended from it were those which are always incident to a period of transition. Questions involving entirely new considerations had to be discussed at length : the whole evidence, and the methods of dealing with it, had to be tested by laborious study before any conclusion could be reached. But in the meanwhile the negative hints, which in the mind of the critical theologian are sometimes balanced and checked by strong personal faith, would be working havoc in the minds of the simple, or the indifferent, or the impatient. To arrest at least for the moment the destructive

---

[1] With this estimate of the later Liberalism should be compared the words of a private memorandum by one of its leaders, Archbishop Tait: ' The great evil is that the Liberals are deficient in religion, and the religious are deficient in liberality.'— ' Life of Archbishop Tait,' i. p. 325 (3rd edition).

action of this unscientific and untested criticism, it seemed best to set forth the faith of the historic Church both in its corporate fullness, and in its inner reality as apprehended by the soul through grace. It was felt advisable to utter a serious warning against two great dangers—the danger of seeking for faith by a mere intellectual process of reasoning and study of evidences, and the danger of mistaking the reasoned apprehension of fragments of the Christian Creed for self surrender to the completeness of the Revelation of God[1].

In view of such anxieties as these, and feeling the great need of protecting the rising generation of University men, Pusey availed himself of the opportunity of setting forth the origin, nature, and conditions of Christian faith in two sermons which he was called upon to preach before the University in the Michaelmas Term of 1855. The theme of the former of the two sermons is given in the following words :—

'Faith, from first to last, is the gift of God to the soul, which will receive it. God prepares the soul, with its will, not without it, to receive the Faith. God stills the soul, that it may listen to the Faith ; God flashes conviction into the soul, that it may see the truth of the Faith ; in those who through His grace persevere to the end, God seals up the Faith in the soul, that it may keep the Faith which it has received, unchanged, undiminished, unadulterated, the source of life and love and holiness, until faith is swallowed up in the blessed-making sight of Him Whom, unseen, it believed[2].'

The Scriptural evidence of this truth, that all faith is the gift of God, Pusey places in contrast with the language in which it is often assumed ' that the province of Reason is antecedent to that of Faith,' and with the aggressions of natural intellect in regard to things above nature.

'Reason, unaided, cannot even penetrate into the sphere of the objects of Faith ; nor can it, in any case, discern their substance or measure them by earthly laws. But Reason, healed, restored, guided, enlightened, by the Spirit of God, has a power of vision above nature, and can spiritually discern a fitness, and correspondence, and harmony

[1] Preface to Pusey's University Sermons, vol. i. p. x.
[2] ' All Faith the Gift of God,' pp. 6, 7.

in the things of God which, through faith, it has received and believed [1].'

' Intellect, penetrated by the Spirit of God, irradiated by His light, kindled by the glow of Divine love, reflects to after-ages the light which it has caught, illumines mysteries, guards truth, unfolds our spiritual nature, orders the whole sum and relations and proportions of Divine and human knowledge. But intellect, unenlightened by Divine light, intuitive as it may be in human things, is blind in Divine.' . . . 'All its natural knowledge cannot decipher the very alphabet of the supernatural [2].'

The temptation, then, of a highly intellectual age is to imagine that a grace which is wholly the gift of God can be commanded by the power and secured by the grasp of the natural intellect: to forget that 'humility, simplicity, candour of soul, integrity of the will, are the true, because the faithful, recipients of Divine knowledge.' For ' God set free the intellect, not by overpowering arguments addressed to itself, but by bursting the bonds whereby it was held, and removing the scales whereby the light, which should enlighten it, was excluded.' ' He imparted to faith, what learning helped not, and ignorance hindered not, to receive.'

But ' since faith is the gift of God through grace, whatever injures grace, weakens Faith. Faith may live on for a time without love, and become what is called an historic Faith. But Faith without love has no root. For we are "rooted and grounded in love." It is the last judgment of God upon the soul which *will* not live as it believes, that at the end it believes as it lives [3].'

Having shown in the former of the two Sermons how faith is, at every stage in its increase, the gift of God, and how the knowledge of Divine things lies wholly beyond the dominion of the natural intellect, Pusey goes on in the latter Sermon to teach the essential unreserve and self-surrender of the true act of Faith.

'Faith, whether in God or man, is an implicit, full, unswerving reliance in the Being Who is the object of Faith. If it is not absolute or perfect, it is not Faith.' ' Faith is one and indivisible.' ' Whatever touches Faith in God in one point, touches the whole spiritual being.'

---

[1] ' All Faith the Gift of God,' pp. 16, 17.
[2] Ib. pp. 23, 24.  [3] Ib. pp. 33, 34.

' He who rejects any one revealed truth, does not hold whatever other truth he does not part with, out of submission to the authority of God Who has revealed it, but because it approves itself in some way to his own natural mind and judgment.  What he holds, he holds of himself, accounting it to be truth, not as Faith [1].'

It follows that the denial of revealed truth which begins at one point is ever tending to spread to the whole fabric. The proverb ' nemo repente turpissimus ' finds its analogy in the progress of theoretic unbelief.  ' This is a characteristic of all who have parted with Faith, that they began with some one point.  They parted, as they thought, with one point of Faith ;  the event showed that they parted with the Faith itself.'  This general statement is copiously illustrated by Pusey from the history of heresy.   In case after case—

' The form of heresy was different ; the principle was the same. Man trusted his own conceptions of what a Revelation from God should be, what it were fitting for the Infinite God to do and be, rather than submit blindly to what God had revealed of Himself, that, not trusting in his own light, he might receive, pure and unmixed, the light from God.'  Men ' make their own notions the criterion of the Mind of God ; not the revealed Mind of God the corrective of their own thoughts [2].'

The tendency which he has thus traced in the past, Pusey then characterizes in its modern forms : in the inclination 'to remove from religion all which is austere,' 'all which shocks our sensitiveness or our taste, or our ways of thinking, or which requires a decided submission of our minds': in the drawing ' distinctions, what is to be really matter of Revelation, and what not' : in the assertion that ' our Lord and His Apostles " accommodated themselves " to the then prevailing notions in matters which (it is assumed) do not affect the centre of religion ; i.e. in part they taught the Truth of God, in part they countenanced human error.' Lastly, the fore-assured failure of all attempts to bring Revealed Truth within the limits which natural reason might have devised for it, is shown by pointing to the

[1] ' Real Faith Entire,' pp. 44-53.          [2] Ib. pp. 66, 72.

'one overwhelming, heavy, impenetrable cloud' which as a matter of fact weighs on all which we see of God's creation, 'the mystery of evil in the works of God, Almighty, All-wise, and All-good, can neither be explained, nor softened, in any system of religion or irreligion.' And in the face of that unintelligible mystery,

'It were against reason to require, as a condition of our belief, that we should understand anything bound up with the existence of evil.' 'Since the existence of evil is absolutely inexplicable, it is an unreasonable cavil to except against the extermination of the Canaanites, or the eternity of punishment, or any doctrine of the Atonement, as contrary to the attributes of God. For since we cannot in the least understand how the existence of evil at all is reconcileable with the attributes of God, plainly we cannot understand what is a part and consequence of what we understand not.'

'Meanwhile, one Unfailing Light there ever is in our remaining darkness, to which, if we cleave, our darkness will be light around us. Truths of God wear a very different aspect as we scrutinize, speculate, theorize, criticize, or as we love, adore, reverence, hearken, obey.' . . . 'Only fix steadfastly in thy heart what God Is, and what thou [1].'

The two Sermons set forth very impressively the preacher's conviction as to the rightful use and the unwarrantable assumptions of Reason in regard to supernatural Truth: they show clearly and powerfully how he would bid the intellect bear itself in the presence of God's Revelation. And it is almost impossible to read them without a deep sense of the solid strength of the position which is thus taken up. They explain how vitally important Pusey considered that position to be, and how it was involved in all those great conflicts which, under varying conditions and ways, claimed so much of his time and labour during the rest of his life.

It was clear at various points in the course of the sermons that Pusey had in mind certain dangers which were prominent and threatening at that very time. He spoke as having before him—as expecting that many of his hearers would have before them—certain recent publications: and the Notes and Appendices added to the Sermons when

---

[1] 'Real Faith Entire,' pp. 85, 86.

they came to be printed made it clear what these were. Foremost among them was an Essay on the Doctrine of the Atonement, published in that year (1855) by the Rev. B. Jowett, the Professor of Greek, in his Commentary on St. Paul's Epistles to the Thessalonians, Romans, and Galatians. This Essay Pusey subjects to severe and detailed criticism in one of the notes to his two Sermons. He shows how very inadequate its statements are as to the very centre of Christian Faith in the Atonement and the Person of our Lord.

Incidental allusions in letters show the depth and strength of Pusey's conviction in regard to the character and tendency of Mr. Jowett's theological teaching. He was indeed among the most conspicuous, able, and effective representatives of a school which Pusey felt himself bound to meet with unqualified opposition : a school whose influence he judged to be most gravely harmful. Any act which seemed to show indifference to such views, or which might be regarded as an encouragement to the opinions which Mr. Jowett had published, would have seemed to Pusey a betrayal of the trust he held in Oxford for the religious welfare of the University and its students.

While these most serious questions were occupying Pusey's mind he was called to consider the proposal that the University should be asked to vote £300 a year for the increased endowment of the Regius Professorship of Greek, to which in 1855 Mr. Jowett had been appointed. This proposal was the beginning of a long, confused, unhappy conflict. Until that date, the stipend of the Professor of Greek had been only £38 a year. This had been felt for many years to be quite inadequate. In fact when Dean Gaisford was Professor, the Dean and Chapter of Christ Church had sent a petition to the First University Commission and requested that, in case of any further diversion of their revenues to University purposes, and in case no other provision was made for the Professor of Greek, some of their own property should be allotted to that Professorship when it next fell vacant. This offer the

Commissioners had declined, without however making any provision for the Chair. But now when it was proposed that the University itself should provide the increased endowment, and when Mr. Jowett's labours as Professor were made the ground of the increase, other considerations, academic and religious, had to be taken into account. From an academical point of view it is necessary to bear in mind that the Professorship of Greek was founded by King Henry VIII, and endowed by him, as were also the other Regius Professorships ; and the Crown still retained the right of appointment. A serious constitutional question therefore would arise as soon as it was proposed that the University should provide the money for increasing the endowment of a Crown appointment—a question which had been already raised successfully against the proposal of the First University Commission to vest the appointment to all newly created professorships in the hands of the Crown. Ought not the University, it was asked, to have some voice in the appointments, for which it provides all or a large part of the funds? Besides, there was another of Henry VIII's Professorships, that of Civil Law, almost as poorly endowed as the Greek Chair. Ought not both the cases to be considered together? Moreover, from the point of view of the religious character of the University a far more difficult question arose. The University Statutes still required that its Professors should not teach anything contrary to and inconsistent with the doctrines of the Church of England. Did not the University wish to maintain this requirement of the Statutes? Oxford was still regarded as a Church University : would it not appear that the Church was indifferent to the theological teaching of the clergy, if the University seemed to bestow a mark of favour on one of its clerical Professors who contravened the teaching of the Church?

Probably the judgment which will rise in most minds when first glancing back at this episode, without considering to the full all the conditions of the moment, will be that it would have been best to acquiesce in the measure, as an act of justice, and to let any one who would make what controversial advantage he could out of it. But as has been shown the proposal was by no means a simple one. To avoid serious misunderstanding it would have been necessary to set it forth in some form which would safeguard the rights of the University over the use of its own money, and which would be consistent with the still surviving tradition of the religious character of that body. The early form of this proposal ignored all these difficulties. Pusey never diverged from the line of endeavouring to increase the stipend. He conscientiously voted against all proposals which ignored the serious character of the academical and religious opposition; but he laboured throughout, more strenuously than any of the Professor's friends, to discover a scheme which would give substantial justice to all the interests that were involved.

The first mention of the matter in Pusey's correspondence is in a letter to Keble, written in May, 1858 :—

'It is proposed,' he writes, 'to endow the Regius Professorship of Greek with £300. There is no doubt that it will pass Council. It is the Professorship, not the Professor, which is endowed ; i.e. the terms of the notice are, that the Professorship be increased. But I cannot, in my own mind, separate them. . . . It seems to me that we should be declaring ourselves indifferent as to Professor Jowett's misbelief if we make the grant.'

At the same time it is clear that Pusey was fully aware that to oppose any scheme for providing a reasonable income for one who was well known to be working very hard with his pupils would be liable to misconstruction. He thought therefore of moving for a Committee to report to the Council on Professor Jowett's book, as had been done in Ward's case : and he was also considering various ways in which the endowment might be justly increased without prejudice to the University and without risk of harm to the cause which he had at heart. One plan which he suggests to Keble in a letter, apparently of May 24, 1858, is that the consideration of the matter 'should be deferred until the whole case of the Regius Professors be considered.' 'Civil Law,' he adds, 'is almost as poorly endowed.'

The proposal came before the Council early in June, 1858; some members opposed on the religious ground. Pusey reserved that point, but urged the constitutional difficulty about the relation to the Crown. His anticipation as to the immediate issue was not fulfilled, for the motion was lost by a decided majority.

The question came to the front again in the Michaelmas Term of 1859 :—

### E. B. P. TO REV. J. KEBLE.

Stanley is agitating the resident Masters to memorialize the Council to endow Jowett until his Professorship shall be otherwise endowed. This is, of course, a personal act of favour to Jowett. . . . If a grant is made to him, we pledge ourselves to indifference as to religious belief for the future. It is possible that the grant may be stopped in Council; but Scott and Jacobson are supporters of it, on the ground that we must separate the Professor from his creed. 'He works well as Greek Professor, therefore he is to be endowed.' . . . I think that the only alternative of a controversy like the Hampden one would be to let it go by default, and assent to the principle that the University takes no notice of any heresy or unbelief in its secular teachers.

In answer to this letter Keble writes on November 8, 1859 :—

'If I were in the Council, I think I should certainly start what I call the Constitutional objection to this grant, viz. that it is not good to increase the influence of the Crown in the University, and that if we increase a Professor's stipend, we ought to have some check on his appointment. On which ground I should object to augmenting your stipend as much as Jowett's.'

In the event of defeat on this point, Keble was inclined to assent to the proposed increase of the endowment of the Professorship; but he would at the same time have signified openly, and if possible put it on record, that

'This grant on the part of the University must not be understood as implying any favourable judgment of the theological views of the present Professor as expressed in such and such passages.'

The proposed grant was again rejected on November 14 ; but it was clear this was not the end.   Early in the January of 1860 Pusey writes again to Keble :—

'The Jowett business much perplexes me. . . . I should have no objection to the endowment if it could be made apparent that it was not personal.'

He suggests that the increase might be made in one of the following ways :—

' If Government were asked whether, if the University would endow the Chair, they would adopt the precedent as to the Chairs endowed by Colleges, and place the appointment in the hands of certain high officers of the Crown, instead of the Prime Minister only, with e.g., the Chancellor of the University.   The same might be proposed as to the Regius Professorship of Civil Law, which is only £100 per annum.

' Another plan might be to take into consideration the whole subject of the endowment of Professors.   If Jowett's endowment came as part of a batch, I should not think it so mischievous.   It would not be a personal vote.   But now it is simply a vote of honour.'

During the Easter Vacation Pusey entered upon a long correspondence on this subject with Mr. Gladstone, as a member of the Government.   He laid before him the following scheme which might, as he thought, find favour with the University, and in regard to which he hoped it might be possible for Mr. Gladstone to obtain a ' primâ facie' opinion from Lord Palmerston ;—that the University should provide for the increase (to £600 a year) of the endowment of the two scantily-endowed Regius Professorships, those of Civil Law and of Greek; that, in consideration of the great increase in value thus conferred upon these two Chairs, the Crown should in their case appoint always, not on the single recommendation of the Prime Minister, but on the recommendation of Boards, on which the University should be represented.   Mr. Gladstone entered with much interest into the suggestion, but felt that, as a member of the Ministry, he could hardly venture ' to form individually a definitive opinion on a plan relating to Crown appointments which the head of the Government might afterwards disapprove.' Early in the following Term Pusey steadily pushed forward his proposal, and brought it at last in a definite shape before the Hebdomadal Council. It was generally welcomed; and the Vice-Chancellor advised him to send a draft of the plan to Mr. Gladstone, unofficially, but 'in the name of an influential Committee,' with the request that it might be communicated to Lord Palmerston. 'No one to whom I have mentioned the subject,' Pusey writes, 'has expressed any disagreement from the plan. It has received the concurrence of leading persons of different parties.' The matter was, however, delayed by the near approach of the triennial election of the Council.

At an election in the Michaelmas Term of 1860 among the Professors returned to the Hebdomadal Council were Dr. Hawkins, Dr. Pusey, and Dr. Stanley, the number of votes being equal for the second and third[1]. In the reconstituted Council Stanley tried again to force on the separate endowment of the Greek Professorship, and quoted the Bishop of Oxford as sharing his views. Pusey immediately appealed to the Bishop, giving a brief history of the dispute up to the moment.

E. B. P. TO BISHOP WILBERFORCE.

Christ Church, October 31 [1860].

Dr. Stanley having quoted to me your Lordship's name, as wishing Professor Jowett's chair to be endowed, I wish to state to you how matters now stand.

The majority of Council resisted the vote of a direct and personal augmentation of Professor Jowett's income, partly on the ground that, since his endowment came from the Crown and the Professorship is in its nomination, the duty, if any, lay on the Crown. The University is not bound to augment Crown patronage. But the deeper ground was, that since Professor Jowett is a sceptic, denying all which a Socinian

---

[1] In the course of this Term the University was stirred by a keen contest between Mr. Monier Williams and Mr. Max Müller for the Boden Sanskrit Professorship. Pusey had written strongly to Keble in favour of the latter; and his name appears (with those of the Bishop of Oxford, Sir F. Rogers, Mr. R. W. Church, Mr. Keble, Mr. Jowett, Dr Stanley, Mr. M. Arnold, Mr. Burgon, and Mr. Liddon) in the long list of Mr. Max Müller's supporters. Mr. Monier Williams was elected.

denies, it would be very evil for the University to do any act which should look like personal favour to Professor Jowett.

However, to avoid heart-burnings, I proposed last time in Council that we should inquire of Lord Palmerston whether he would recommend to the Crown to allow the nomination of the two ill-endowed Professorships of Civil Law and Greek to be vested in a Board in which Government should have the majority, but the University be represented (after the pattern of the Boards formed by the Oxford Commission), provided the University would endow. Lord Palmerston assented to the principle. I proposed, accordingly, last Monday to carry on the negotiations. Nothing remained but to settle the Boards, about which there would be no difference of opinion. I hoped that, the question being thus removed from the Professor to the Professorship, the Professorship might have been endowed, and Professor Jowett might have had his £400 a year, and the University not have been committed in any way to any personal approbation of Professor Jowett.

The whole might have been completed in the present term, and the salary, if it was thought well, might have dated from its commencement.

In this state of things, Professor Stanley gave notice that he should move that Professor Jowett's chair should be endowed at once with £300 per annum, until it be permanently endowed. This, while it offers to Professor Jowett less than my arrangement would give him, would effectually defeat mine. For if the University, without conditions, endows the chair with £300 per annum, it would have nothing to offer to Lord Palmerston as a ground for vesting the nomination in a Board.

The only real object of Professor Stanley's motion can be to make the vote one of confidence in Professor Jowett.

Has your Lordship read the article on Neo-Christianity in the last *Westminster Review*, in which the reviewer clearly, though painfully, shows that the writers of the Essays teach the same as themselves, the human origin of the Bible and its absolute want of Authority?

I doubt whether Professor Stanley is to be moved. But I write this to your Lordship that I may know what to say if your name should be quoted against me.

The Bishop replied that in his conversation with Dr. Stanley he had entirely misunderstood the question, that he considered Pusey's proposal in every respect far the best, and would greatly lament any vote which implied confidence in Professor Jowett as a teacher of theology.

Stanley's motion was again rejected; and before the end of 1860 Pusey was able to tell Mr. Gladstone that his own plan had been passed by the Council, and to send it to him in a printed form.

In regard to this plan Pusey hoped that ' it may both put an end to heart-burnings, and be for the permanent good of the University'; Mr. Gladstone thought it ' both liberal and wise'; Sir George C. Lewis wrote to Lord Palmerston: ' So far from seeing any objection to the proposed arrangements, I think them very advantageous;' and at last, after another long delay, Lord Palmerston wrote to Mr. Gladstone the following letter :—

94, Piccadilly, April 14, 1861.

My DEAR GLADSTONE,

I am perfectly ready to agree to the Oxford plan for improving certain Professorships, the only point, as far as I understand the matter, with regard to which my concurrence is required, being the change proposed to be made with respect to the Regius Professorship. It is proposed that a University element should share in the choice of the person to fill such Professorship. I am quite willing, as First Lord of the Treasury, to concur in such an arrangement.

Yours sincerely,

(Signed) PALMERSTON.

Rt. Hon. W. E. Gladstone.

This letter Mr. Gladstone forwarded to the Vice-Chancellor. 'wishing a happy issue to the proposals.' But while these negotiations were going on, this matter of University policy was gravely complicated by the outburst of an agitation which was felt through the whole Church of England. This arose out of the publication of a volume of collected 'Essays and Reviews,' of which a fuller account will be given in the following chapter. To this collection the Professor of Greek had contributed an essay on the interpretation of Scripture. His essay in itself seemed to many to make his theological position still more untenable, while its association with writings which gave yet deeper offence intensified the opposition to him. The whole volume was causing the greatest excitement throughout the country, and was threatened with synodical condemnation by the Convocation of Canterbury; two of its contributors were being prosecuted in the Ecclesiastical Court of Arches,

at the very moment when, on May 7, 1861, Pusey's plan
for augmenting the two Professorships was submitted to the
Convocation of the University. It was vigorously opposed
by the Provost of Oriel. who reminded the University that
the Statutes forbade any Professor to utter anything ' quod
Fidei Catholicae adversatur.' Pusey defended the scheme
and claimed that it was framed in such a manner as to
preclude personal considerations. Stanley thanked him for
his advocacy of the compromise. On a division, however,
the proposal was defeated by ninety-one votes to seventy.

The issue of the debate was more than a heavy disappointment to Pusey. Certainly he had worked hard in the
matter ; Stanley more than once publicly thanked him for
' his indomitable perseverance in pushing the question
forward.' But the majority against the plan was swelled
not only by several Liberals who, while they sympathized
with the Greek Professor, objected to this particular method
of increasing his stipend, but also by not a few of Pusey's
own nearest friends. Some of them were determined. even
before the publication of ' Essays and Reviews,' not in any
way to endow the Chair of Greek so long as it was held by
Jowett ; and there were many others who, without any clear
realization of the difficulties with which the question was
encumbered, were beginning to lose their trust in Pusey
because the plan which he proposed did not at first sight
commend itself to them.

Keble was far too clear sighted not to perceive the
damage this adverse vote would inflict on the Church and
the difficulties in which it involved Pusey. Writing to
Liddon, who had voted with the majority, he says, ' You too,
and all of us ' . . . are ' bound in equity to consider the
pressure which lies upon persons trusted with government,
and which, in more cases perhaps than not, forces them
to adopt the least of two evils instead of what is abstractedly
best.' In the same letter Keble showed how completely he
himself trusted Pusey's action in proposing a scheme which
would involve the increased endowment of the Greek Chair,
and how much he regretted the failure of that scheme :

'Whatever you do,' he adds to Liddon, 'beware of taking towards him a suspicious or aggrieved tone. . . . As things are, the grievance, I should say, is much more on *his* side.' The sequel will show how true this estimate was. Had Pusey's scheme been carried in May, 1861, all the events described in the rest of this chapter would never have happened, and all the bitterness that ensued from them would have been avoided.

As it was, Pusey felt very deeply that in a critical moment he had been deserted by many from whom he might reasonably have expected support; and he wrote to Liddon :—

'For myself, I am minded (though I shall do nothing hastily) to resign my seat in Council, and retire from the politics of the University. I have enough to occupy me in the "Commentary"[1]. I have given up for some time the hope of doing good in Council. I cannot even prevent evil.'

It seems clear that his whole heart had been set on the compromise. Had it been accepted, it would, without showing any partiality towards Professor Jowett's teaching, have provided the increased endowment to the Professorship and thus have settled this troublesome matter.

But if Churchmen would not vote for Pusey's plan, still less could they accept Stanley's proposals. On the same day that Convocation had thus defeated Pusey, a meeting of the Congregation of the University was held, at which was promulgated a form of Statute for the augmentation of several other poorly endowed Professorships, which, being entirely in the gift of the University, were free from the special difficulties of the Regius Professorships. Professor Stanley took this opportunity for a renewed effort, and moved, as an amendment, to add the Regius Professorship of Greek to those mentioned in the Statute. The

---

[1] The Bible Commentary, in connexion with which he brought out his work on the Minor Prophets, was always regarded by Pusey as the best antidote to a lax theology. In expressing his gratitude at the prospect of a Commentary on St. John from the hand of Keble, he writes (Oct. 12, 1862) : 'I am sure that the development [i.e. unfolding] of Holy Scripture is the way to meet heresy and rationalism.'

proposal was obviously too grave to be taken in a thin
meeting after a session of nearly three hours; the debate
therefore was adjourned to May 16, when Pusey spoke
against Stanley's motion on the ground that, by isolating
the Professorship of Greek from the other poorly endowed
Regius Professorship, it made the grant too much of
a personal matter. He was quite ready to vote for the
increased endowment of the Greek Chair, but only because
of its claim as a poorly endowed Professorship. Stanley
on the other hand with singular infelicity laid the main
stress on the extremely valuable work of the Professor
who then held the chair. Stanley's motion was thrown
out. In the same term Pusey again brought forward
a proposal to request Lord Palmerston to insert a clause
into the New University Bill, which would facilitate any
proceedings in connexion with the endowment of the
Chairs of Greek and Civil Law. This further scheme was
laid before Convocation on June 6, and again rejected.

Once more the matter came before Congregation in the
form suggested by Stanley. On November 20, 1861,
a Statute was promulgated proposing the increase of the
stipends of the Professor of Greek, and of six other professors, to £400 a year. The Statute was introduced by
Stanley in a long speech, which was not calculated to
pacify opponents, inasmuch as it laid far more stress on
the personal claims of the Professor because of his valuable
work than on the claims of the Professorship because of its
poverty. In consequence of this form of advocacy Pusey
felt obliged to oppose the measure not only on constitutional, but also on the more personal theological grounds,
again expressing his regret that his own efforts for a neutral
course had been unsuccessful. After a very long and rather
hot debate the matter was adjourned. It was resumed on
Tuesday, November 26, and the Statute was rejected by
ninety-nine votes to ninety-six [1].

On the following day an article appeared in the *Guardian*

---

[1] It is thus stated in *Guardian* for Nov. 27. Another authority says
ninety-eight to ninety-five.

in opposition to Pusey's attitude on this question; the writer asserted that

'It has been felt by many of those most averse to Professor Jowett's theological teaching, and we confess to a participation in the feeling, that substantial justice required that he should receive an adequate remuneration for his labours as a Professor, notwithstanding that as a writer he has taken a line which they would be among the last to defend.'

This article was criticized by Pusey in a letter, which is valuable as stating at length the grounds on which he felt constrained to oppose the endowment in spite of the seeming claim of justice. He was well aware of the obloquy to which his action exposed him. He laid much stress on the question of patronage, and on the Christian character of the University, which was implied, as in other ways, so expressly in its regulations with regard to Professorships. This, it may be mentioned, is a point which must especially be borne in mind when, thirty years after the event, and under greatly altered conditions, we endeavour to estimate the controversy. He further urged that it seemed 'an uncalled for confidence in all future Prime Ministers to endow' the Greek Chair tenfold out of the funds of the University, and then to place the nomination, without reservation and without check, in the hands of the Prime Ministers; and he contended that the precedents which had been adduced for such a course were imperfectly analogous. 'But,' he went on to argue—

'though this was a real objection to the proposed plan, of course, that which lay nearest to the hearts of Christians was the conviction that by making a *direct* grant to Professor Jowett we should have been endorsing his religious scepticism. Others may be able to separate the Professor from the writer; we could not. . . .

'As a Christian University, we are just as much bound to regard the *Faith* of Christ as His laws. We pray God weekly that "true Religion may ever flourish and abound" among us. Our Statutes inculcate the performance of our ordinary professorial duties; but they inculcate as solemnly, that none of us "directe vel indirecte doceat, vel dogmatice asserat, quod fidei Catholicae vel bonis moribus ulla ex parte adversatur." But the University does not restrain this to our direct teaching in our offices. It does not mean that Professors may use all the weight which their office gives them to disseminate scepticism or misbelief, to " sow doubt broadcast " through the land, provided they throw a veil over it in their Chairs. It does not so limit its prohibition. It speaks not of *lectures* but of *Professors*, and what it forbids in one place it forbids everywhere.'

In the same issue of the *Guardian* with this letter appeared a second leading article entitled 'One Word more about the Greek Professorship.' The writer fully recognizes that there is in the view taken by Pusey, and by others who had spoken in the same sense, much that is natural and plausible ; but he goes on to urge what had already often been urged by others :—

'It seems to be admitted that Mr. Jowett cannot be formally challenged by the University, notwithstanding that the University Statutes are so clear against unsound teaching.' ... 'It seems to us, we must say, an unfit course for a body like the University, when an instrument of direct attack is unavailable, to resort to the employment of indirect means of discouragement. If it cannot turn him out of the Professorship it is not indeed to be asked to favour him, but it ought not to withhold what his Professorship gives him a title to.' ...

In accordance with this argument, the Professor's friends had often demanded that the definite charge of heresy should be preferred in the proper court, and Pusey recognized the force of this claim. He himself was anxious to endow the Chair in spite of the opinions of its occupant, if it could have been done without any appearance of partiality and with due regard to the University's patronage. But many others still steadily refused to put on one side their hostility to Professor Jowett's opinions and to vote for the increased endowment while he continued to hold the Chair ; and so long as Pusey was unable to command their votes, he could not secure the passing of his own plan for augmentation ; while at the same time he was bound to oppose Stanley's proposals, because to him they always savoured of partiality. In the circumstances Pusey thought there was nothing to be done but directly to challenge the orthodoxy of the Professor. If that were to succeed, the idea of an increased endowment would for the present be withdrawn : if it failed, he could not imagine that there could be any reasonable ground for continued opposition on the part of even the most conservative of his friends. This conviction is expressed in a letter to Keble on Feb. 4, 1862.

The best course therefore seemed to be to prosecute Professor Jowett in the Vice-Chancellor's Court, on the ground of those passages in his Commentary and in his Essay which appeared to contravene the authoritative teaching of the Church of England. Accordingly in the earlier part of the ensuing Long Vacation Pusey gathered together the chief passages on which such a prosecution might be based, and sent them to a solicitor, that they might be put into form, as a Case to be submitted to the Queen's Advocate, Dr. Phillimore. The process of drafting the Case proved long ; and it was not, apparently, until late in September that it was laid before him. His opinion bears date October 12, 1862, and is to the following effect. With respect (1) to the Doctrines of the Atonement, Satisfaction for Sin, Vicarious Suffering of our Saviour, he finds that

'the writer in these' (passages quoted from the Commentary) 'and in other passages, and, as it seems to me, by the whole tenour of his argument, does contradict the doctrine contained in the Thirty-nine Articles and the Liturgy, and set up another and a different doctrine in the place of it.'

Similarly, with respect (2) to the Inspiration of Holy Scripture, he finds that passages in Professor Jowett's Essay are 'certainly at variance with, and contradictory of the doctrine of the Church of England as contained in her formularies,' according to the recent judgment of the Dean of Arches in the suits which arose out of 'Essays and Reviews': and with respect (3) to the Three Creeds he finds that language in the Essay 'plainly contradicts' the Eighth Article. Dr. Phillimore further gave it as his opinion that the Vice-Chancellor would be bound to admit articles containing charges of heresy, or of preaching doctrines contrary to the Church of England, against any

Professor resident in the University, and could be compelled to do so by *mandamus*.

On receiving this opinion Pusey sent it at once to Keble.

REV. J. KEBLE TO E. B. P.

Oct. 13, 1862.

It has struck me whether as things are [i.e. since it has been decided to try the suit], it might not be advisable to withdraw the opposition to the endowment of the Greek Professor (except as to getting a check on the Crown appointment), since it will be superfluous if we succeed before the judges, and void if we fail. And if it could be so, it would surely, I think, lessen the exasperation. Tell me, please, what you think of this.

Pusey answers :—

' I spoke to ·—— and —— about your suggestion of withdrawing the opposition. The line which they were disposed to try was to adjourn the discussion until these proceedings should be terminated.'

But the dominant theme of Pusey's letters to Keble at this time is the difficulty of securing such promoters for the prosecution as Dr. Phillimore had suggested. He ' thought that there had better be three, of no pronounced party, and residents ' : and Pusey writes on Nov. 6, in much disappointment about the general reluctance to take up the task.

E. B. P. TO REV. J. KEBLE.

Nov. 6, 1862.

It is the old story, ' who is to bell the cat ? ' Here, in Oxford, we seem to be so familiar with our evils as to acquiesce in them, sleeping in the snow, which is death. . . . And now Bp. Colenso is striving to make a position in the Church for his unbelief. And then the Church would be (God forbid) dead. I used to maintain and do maintain, that the Church must bear with much, for fear of worse evils. But she must not bear with this naked denial of our Lord the Atoner, and of God the Holy Ghost Who spake by the Prophets. . . . I never felt so desponding as I do now, not at people's attacks (these we must expect), but at the acquiescence in them on the part of religious men.

Keble's answer is prompt and characteristic.

REV. J. KEBLE TO E. B. P.

Nov. 8, 1862.

Your last note troubles me greatly : but I suppose what you mean by saying that if this Dr. Colenso is borne with, there will be ' no Church ' means that eventually it will lead to such and such consequences, not that it will formally unchurch us at once. I still hold to my old *mumpsimus* that the Prayer Book being what it is we cannot be unchurched by mere abuse or default of discipline. I see the great τόπος to frighten us from proceeding is to be 'the effect of persecution upon ingenuous youth,' and the great instance appealed to is the success of the Tractarians in consequence of their being persecuted. Perhaps this had better be dealt with somehow. I think the persecution was but too successful against us.

In answering this letter, with a hearty assent to its interpretation of his meaning, Pusey informs Keble that Dr. Ogilvie, the Regius Professor of Pastoral Theology, 'has consented to be one to present the articles.'

In order to support Pusey, Keble wrote a letter to the *Guardian* of Nov. 12, which is perhaps his fullest public statement of the sympathy with which he viewed this prosecution.

REV. J. KEBLE TO THE EDITOR OF THE 'GUARDIAN.'

SIR,

The correspondent who in your last number so earnestly depre-cates any such proceeding will, I trust, forgive my pointing out one or two flaws (as I conceive them to be) in his reasoning, such as ardent writers are very apt to overlook. First, his view seems to me altogether narrow and onesided. He confines his anxiety to one set of persons—young men who happen now to be, or lately have been resident students in Oxford ; and he implies that if the measure prove unpopular or exasperating to them, that will be such and so great an evil as no benefit in any other quarter can possibly compensate for. But those who are proposing to put the Statute in motion, have tried, no doubt, to enter into the mind of its framers—into the old academical feeling on such matters; and may be pardoned surely for the step they are taking, whatever present discomfort it may cause, if on the whole it seemed calculated to protect the University and the Church, and the souls committed to the charge of them both, from 'desolating opinions' such as these are allowed to be ;—to protect them, I say, in the next and following generations, and all over Christendom ; even though, as your correspondent seems to intimate, the present set of students must be given up to them as incurable, a thing that can hardly be taken for granted.

Next, he writes as if the intended movement were one in which the whole governing body of the University is called on to take part, instead of being as I suppose it formally is, a private suit, which any member of Convocation has a statutable liberty to promote. This cannot but make a good deal of difference in the quantity of 'heart-burnings, discord, and interruption of the work of the place,' which must needs be anticipated. If, indeed, as is reported, the friends of Mr. Jowett, and tolerators of his 'desolating opinions,' are on the point of renewing the controversy of last year, there will be little or no additional disturbance caused by an attempt to bring the affair to a constitutional and legal issue. Generally, I think, that has been the course recommended by such as were most anxious to keep the peace when parties ran high and could not be quieted. 'The law is open and there are deputies : let them implead one another.'

Thirdly, I cannot read in the recent history of Oxford troubles the warning which it is said to convey, that interference by authority tells only in promoting the cause which it is intended to quash. The present condition of the University, by the 'Member of Congregation's' own statement, is a direct instance of the contrary. Why are these over-liberal opinions (as he and I agree in considering them) so rife in that once faithful body? One reason unquestionably is that there in an especial manner the hand of authority has been busy in discouraging, and as far as might be silencing and banishing, those who had been first to sound the alarm, and to take arms for securing the 'Holy Place' (for so it then seemed to many) from such desolation as is now apprehended. I do not say that there was no offence given or any wrong wilfully done. I simply state the notorious fact. To make good your correspondent's reasoning, the opinions for which Dr. Newman was censured ought now to be prevailing in Oxford. The 'Member of Congregation' fairly sets forth, as I imagine, the ordinary conversational topics on his side of the question. But he will pardon me for thinking that it will need some stronger argument to withhold serious men from an effort which in their mind is even necessary in order to settle no less a question than this :—

Whether the University of Oxford now is, and means to be hereafter, a believer in the Bible or no ?

J. KEBLE.

During the Christmas vacation of 1862–3, Dr. Heurtley, the Margaret Professor of Divinity, undertook to be a second promoter, overcoming, for conscientious motives, what was clearly an extreme reluctance and distress : Pusey himself, undertook to be the third promoter : and on Jan. 1, 1863, he writes to Dr. Heurtley :—

'As you say, nothing but absolute sense of duty could make me move in this sad case. Like all decisive movements, it may occasion some to take more eagerly the wrong side. So people say now, that Arius or Eutyches or Nestorius ought not to have been condemned. I believe that such things only elicit the evil which lurks within already, and which is just as fatal when lurking within as when it comes out. There has been no time in the Church when its teachers would have been allowed to deny such truth as Professor Jowett has denied; and every publication is in advance of the other. The second edition of his Commentary (although some offensive language was dropped) denied truth more dogmatically than the first; and the Essay denied more truth yet. We have waited long, and have been disappointed. But after all, prosecution is not persecution. I have courted prosecution when people have denounced me on hustings, &c. There is real persecution in that against which one cannot defend one's self. To have it adjudged by law whether one is teaching according to the doctrine which one has professed, is no hardship. I should have hailed it gladly.

They are terrible times. Mere infidelity there always has been and always will be. But this claim of Bishop Colenso, Professor Jowett, and others that this teaching is to be part of the recognized teaching of the Church of England, is a claim that the sheep should be destroyed by the shepherd.'

Some doubts which had been suggested in regard to the security of the grounds for the third charge having been settled by the decided opinion of the Queen's Advocate and of Dr. Swabey, the formal proceedings in the Chancellor's Court began on Friday, February 13, 1863, before the Assessor, Mr. Mountague Bernard. On that day Mr. Pottinger, who appeared for the respondent (Mr. Digby Latimer appearing for the appellants), applied that the case might be adjourned for a week; and, this having been granted, he announced his intention of entering a protest against the jurisdiction of the Court, and of taking every possible objection to the citation as to matter and form.

On the following day, February 14, there appeared in the *Times* a leading article which gave rise to a prolonged war of letters. The article began by maintaining the 'almost ludicrous vagueness and irrelevancy' of those passages in the University Statutes upon which the Queen's Advocate had held that the impeachment could be founded: it went on to discuss the incompetency of the Court to decide on questions of such moment, and the possible abuse of ' this rusty engine of intolerance': it dwelt on the theological differences of the three Promoters, and the curious coincidence by which this suit was beginning on the same day on which Dr. Hampden in 1836, and the

Tractarians in 1845, had been attacked.   In its concluding
paragraph occurred the following sentences :—

'We do not for one moment impugn the motives of those who have
taken upon themselves to denounce him (Professor Jowett).   On the
contrary, we believe their motives to be the highest that can actuate
short-sighted men with a rooted distrust of the power of truth to abide
the ordeal of free inquiry.   It is not of motives, but of consequences,
that we would speak. . . . The old attempt to set up the interests of
religion and piety against those of truth and justice will fail, as it has
ever failed. . . . The question, then, arises whether the College to
which he (Mr. Jowett) belongs and the cause of education in Oxford
are to be sacrificed to the *odium theologicum* of a few infatuated
dignitaries. . . . We may pity Dr. Pusey and his co-prosecutors, for
they know not what they do, but we trust, for the sake of interests far
higher than they seem to discern, that the deadly blow which they are
now aiming at the peace of the Church of England will not be suffered
to take effect.'

This was hard language and really begged the whole
question at issue.  Pusey thought therefore that it ought not
to be left unanswered.  Accordingly he addressed to the
Editor of the *Times* the following letter, which appeared
on the 19th of February.  It may be here cited almost
in its entirety : for it gives a careful presentation of the
grounds upon which he was acting.

### E. B. P. TO THE EDITOR OF THE 'TIMES.'

I never have (he wrote) distrusted, nor do I distrust, the power
of God's truth to abide any, the most searching, inquiry.   I have now
for forty years, as a duty, read more anti-Christian writings than any
probably of your readers, and I have observed during that period that
all deeper thought and criticism uniformly tended to the support of
the Faith or to bring men back to it.   But it is one question whether
truth will stand (which, being Divine, it will, of course) ; it is quite
another whether all individuals are judges of truth, and whether they
are so sure of being led into truth that it should be matter of indifference whether they are taught truth or error.   If this were certain, it
would, of course, be needless to have any teachers at all.   It is true,
beyond all question, that God's truth will stand ; but it is true also
that individuals, to their own great loss, are led away by their teachers
from it.   You have yourself, at different times, clearly stated the
principle that so long as the Church of England remains what she is
her ministers are bound to teach what they have professed they will
teach.   I cannot imagine anything more demoralizing than that

clergymen should profess their belief in great fundamental truths, and assert the contrary; that they should affirm to God, as the mouthpiece of a congregation in prayer, what they should contradict in their sermons or their writings. No sect in England would tolerate this. It is a matter beyond the question even of theological truth. . . . It would be the destruction of all trust between man and man, it would make our worship of God a mere piece of acting, if we were to teach one thing in church, another out of it, or contradict in the pulpit what we had said in the public prayers.

Yet there has been of late a most large and systematic claim put forth that we clergy not only should inquire, but that, although our inquiries should, unhappily, in the case of any of us end in the loss of our faith, we should still continue to act as clergy. A claim has been made to affix new meanings to words, and so to subscribe our formularies in senses which they will not bear.

It is impossible, then, to look upon Professor Jowett's teaching otherwise than as a part of a larger whole—a systematic attempt to revolutionize the Church of England. The publication of the 'Essays and Reviews' was a challenge to admit that teaching, as one of the recognized phases of faith, in the English Church. All which was said of the 'courage' of the Essayists implied this. To leave the challenge unnoticed would have been to acquiesce in the claim. The subjects on which we are told, on high legal authority, that there is evidence that Professor Jowett has distinctly contravened the teaching of the Church of England are great and central truths. They are—the doctrine of the Atonement, the Inspiration of Holy Scripture, the agreement of the Creeds with Holy Scripture. Painful, then, as it is, to have to act against one with whom, in this place, we must needs be brought into contact—painful as are many other consequences of an appeal to law—yet I hold myself bound by my duty to God, to the Church, and to the souls of men, to ascertain distinctly whether such contradiction of fundamental truths is to be part of the recognized system of the University. Now, if the question was to be tried at all, it could be tried only in the Chancellor's Court, since resident members of the University, who are not by virtue of any office subject to any other jurisdiction, are prohibited by its statutes from suing, or following any suit, in any other court except in the Court of Appeal. Prosecution is not persecution. It would be an evil day for England when it should be recognized that to appeal to the majesty of justice is to contravene truth and justice. I have left unsaid in this letter much which I might otherwise have said, because, as the subject is now before the Court, I hold it to be a duty to abstain from saying anything except as to the abstract principle.

The correspondence which followed this letter straggled on for five weeks, finding its way into various fields, more or less remote, more or less interesting; and it would be a wholesome study for any one who is inclined to enter too readily into newspaper controversy.

On Friday, February 20, 1863, the case was resumed in the Chancellor's Court of the University of Oxford. The Proctor for Mr. Jowett entered his protest, both on historical and practical grounds, against the jurisdiction of that Court in a 'spiritual' charge of such a character. He further contended that a Professor appointed by the Crown was not amenable to the University, citing the case of Pusey's suspension in 1843 by the Vice-Chancellor alone, as a proof that a Regius Professor could not be tried before a court. The Court was adjourned for another week for the decision of the Assessor on these points. On February 27 Mr. Mountague Bernard gave his judgment that Regius Professors were liable to the jurisdiction of the University, and that the Court in which the proceedings had been taken was the only court that could be open to the Promoters of this suit. But since there was no precedent for such a prosecution, he was not certain whether the Court had jurisdiction in cases of this character. In this uncertainty he refused to admit the protest against his jurisdiction, but at the same time refused to admit the articles on the part of the Promoters. The Promoters could, however, appeal against his decision, if they desired to do so, to the Court of Queen's Bench, which might issue a *mandamus* to enforce the hearing.

Before making any such appeal the promoters thought it good to ask the Opinion of the Queen's Advocate (Sir Robert Phillimore) and Mr. J. D. Coleridge (afterwards Lord Chief Justice) on the Assessor's decision and the probable fortunes of an appeal to the Court of Queen's Bench. The Opinion was equally adverse on both subjects. They considered that the decision was incorrect, inconsistent, and without precedent ; at the same time, although the Court of Queen's Bench had power to compel the hearing of the charge, it would probably be very reluctant to interfere in a matter which was one of Academical discipline. In the light of such an opinion the Promoters intimated to the

Vice-Chancellor on May 8 that they did not intend to carry the suit any further.

Pusey had done all that he could to obtain a legal decision on the responsibility of the University for the teaching of Professor Jowett, and had failed; he had now to decide on his own future attitude towards the increased endowment of the Greek Chair.

E. B. P. TO REV. J. KEBLE.

St. Mark's Day, 1863.

. . . . The next question is as to the endowment—Ogilvie wishes me to persevere in opposing it. I am inclined to desist, on the ground that the Assessor has ruled that offences against faith are not to be punished. We might have disputed that decision, and do not. People have so hopelessly confused the question of endowment as if it were a mere matter of paying a person for his labours (which labours almost all the tutors do avail themselves of) that, having failed of the greater, I am inclined to give up the less. I should be regarded as a mere persecutor, debarring another of his pay, while I have a large professional income myself. But what think you? I hardly think it tact to resist. We have been defeated, although illegally. Having so failed, it seems to me like a petty vexatious matter to withhold an income from him. The greater seems to me to involve the lesser. I am inclined to vote against it in Council out of deference to those members of Congregation who returned me ; and then in Congregation to state why I remain neutral, acquiescing in the decision that although the Statutes have a moral, they are, during the Assessorship of Bernard, to have no punitive force, and that we are in the state of Israel under Judges, when every one did that which was right in his own eyes. But I should like to know what you think.

Keble, who had contributed £100 towards the expense of this fruitless endeavour to obtain a legal decision from the University, wished still to make some kind of definite protest against Mr. Jowett's teaching while giving up all opposition to the endowment of the Professorship. 'I do think it hard,' he wrote, 'for Oxford to be injured and the world scandalized, by its going about, as of course it will, that our general feeling is "Let such teaching have its way."' On the other hand, other friends were still unconvinced and persisted in trying to force Pusey into renewed opposition to the endowment, although he said that it had now become 'hopelessly a bad battle-ground.'

Before the end of 1863, Pusey had introduced into the Hebdomadal Council another measure for the endowment of the Greek Chair. This scheme, after referring to the duties of the Chair, contained in deference to Keble's suggestion the following clause, dealing with its present occupant 'modo ne Academia de scriptis ejus (quoad fidem Catholicam tractaverint) judicium tulisse censeatur.' On February 4, 1864, this statute was passed in the Congregation of the University. It was supported by Stanley, who had now become Dean of Westminster, as well as Pusey and Liddon, while Professor Heurtley, one of the Promoters of the recent suit, spoke against it. Pusey's speech explains the point of view from which he was now again supporting the increase of the endowment. After referring to the separation between himself and his friends on this question, he said :—

'I am not going to throw the slightest doubts on the wisdom or legality or justice of the decision which summarily dismissed the indictment which we were in this House often challenged to prefer, and which at last we found it our bounden, though most painful, duty to prefer. We acted according to our conscience, and the Judge acted according to what he thought best for the University. I have now to speak only of the results of his judgment. These are, that it is ruled that every professor or tutor is left wholly to his own conscience what he shall teach on any matter of faith ; provided that, if a tutor, the Head of his College do not interfere with him ; or, if a professor, he do not teach things contrary to the Catholic Faith in his lectures. We, the professors, are thrown back the more upon our subscriptions, because there is no judicial authority except as to our public lectures. Any professor may print defences of Atheism, Deism, Socinianism, or of any other of what used to be called "blasphema dogmata," if he thinks it in harmony with his subscription. Any tutor may do the same, if he is not withheld by the recollection that the Statutes require him to be 'religione secundum doctrinam et ritum Ecclesiae Anglicanae sincerus.' It seems to me then that the act of endowing the Greek Chair cannot be construed into any indifference as to the religious teaching of our professors, since it has been judicially pronounced that they are free to teach whatsoever they will, only not *ex cathedrâ.* And if so, all those grounds, so often urged in this house, have their full force. So long as the grant seemed to imply indifference on the part of the University to what was believed to be denials of the faith, a great principle was at stake which had to be maintained at any cost. Now that this issue is removed, I believe from my inmost heart that we shall best consult the interests of the faith by removing an occasion of heart-burnings, which indispose some minds to the faith. Not that I hope for any great results. For we are at the beginning of a deepening and widening struggle for life or death, for the life or death of the University as a place of religious learning, for the life or death of the Church of England as an instrument of God for the salvation of souls. And this struggle must give occasion for fresh heart-burnings and misunderstandings. But what we can do for peace and love, that we are bound to do, leaving the result with Him with Whom are the issues of life and death.'

The Statute was submitted to a crowded meeting of Convocation on March 8, 1864, exactly a month after the decision of the Judicial Committee of the Privy Council on the two suits connected with 'Essays and Reviews.' Churchmen throughout the country had been summoned by Archdeacon Denison and others to oppose Pusey's measure, and it was rejected by 467 votes to 395. The Senior Proctor had greatly excited the hopes of the Promoters of the statute by using in a moment of confusion the customary formula for announcing the success of a measure, '*Majori parti placet.*' A perfect tumult of applause preceded the correction of the mistake, and a yet louder tumult from the other side followed it. It was generally known that the Privy Council Judgment in favour of the 'Essays and Reviews' greatly influenced this adverse vote.

Some of Professor Jowett's friends seemed now to despair of any increase of endowment from the funds of the University: and they had sufficient influence in high places to induce the Government to consent to a plan which would provide the additional money for this Crown Professorship out of the funds of the Church. On April 11, 1864, the Lord Chancellor, Lord Westbury, introduced into the House of Lords a bill for endowing the Greek Professorship with one of the many Canonries which was in the gift of the Crown. This strange proposal had first been submitted to the Hebdomadal Council at Oxford, and had received the

approval of all that body, except four, among whom were
Pusey and Heurtley.  Pusey saw in the measure 'an ex-
ceedingly clever move,' but under the circumstances one
of the worst scandals that was possible.  He wondered at
the blindness of the Conservatives who could vote for it;
to himself it was but the firstfruits of the action of those
'wise young men who (three years before) thought they
saw further than the old veterans.'  For the moment the
Lord Chancellor's bill was defeated; it passed a second
reading, but on May 13, on the order for going into
Committee, the previous question was carried against the
Government, by a large majority.

It was extremely unadvisable to leave the matter in this
unsatisfactory state.  Pusey deeply deplored the incurable
short-sightedness of his own friends in the matter; although
he most cordially agreed with their reasons for opposing the
endowment, yet in his mind they were clearly outweighed
by other considerations.  He saw that in the rapidly
altering state of the University those reasons did not constitute a valid argument for withholding the immediate
endowment of the Chair; he felt that in spite of them the
Professor was unfairly treated.  Little as he liked the
office, he felt it his duty to make another attempt to remedy
the grievance, in order if possible to prevent the renewal
of the Government measure and the continued charge of
unfairness.

But at the same time any proposal of the kind was made
far more difficult by the intense strain of ecclesiastical
feeling at the moment.  'Essays and Reviews' had just
been condemned by the Convocation of Canterbury, after
two of the writers had been acquitted by the Judicial Committee of the Privy Council; and there was widespread
alarm and distrust about the teaching with which Professor
Jowett's name was associated.  Accordingly Pusey found
himself separated from all those who had hitherto been
with him in his continued support of the claim of the Greek
Chair.  It was of course no great matter of surprise that
Archdeacon Denison vehemently attacked him both in

private correspondence and in public speech ; he declared
that ' of all things that have occurred in our time to shake
our faith and confidence in man, and to show how remarkably
this time is a time of expedients rather than of principles,
of contrivances and management rather than of faith and
patience, nothing has occurred to compare with this act of
Edward Bouverie Pusey.' But now Bishop Wilberforce also
wrote on October 24 one of his most urgent letters, praying
Pusey to desist from his attempts, and assuring him that
in the present circumstances of the Church his effort was
fraught with 'extreme evil' and was aiming 'a very deadly
blow at the truth of God.' Pusey however persevered,
defending his intended action on every ground. And
even Keble began to waver in his support : he was afraid
lest, if Pusey was successful, the University should appear
to be in yet greater antagonism to the Church, by having
endowed the writer of one of the Essays which the
Convocation of Canterbury had so recently condemned.
Yet Pusey still persisted in his effort. On October 31,
he warmly supported in Council a renewed proposal to
raise the stipend to £400, with the guarding clause ' modo
nec Academia scripta eius, quae ad fidem Catholicam
pertinent, comprobasse teneatur, neque rectae fidei Pro-
fessorum horum incuriosa esse censeatur.' This was again
defeated, and Pusey was filled with astonishment at the
inconsistency of his Conservative colleagues, who would
accept without safeguard a measure of the Government
which disposed of Church property for the use of the Professorship, while they rejected a carefully guarded plan
which disposed of University funds for a University. purpose.

E. B. P. TO REV. J. KEBLE.

October 31, 1864.

When Lord D[erby] consulted the Council as to the endowment
with a Canonry, only four members were found to dissent. of whom
Heurtley and I were two. The Conservatives, who have thrown out
this measure, to a man supported it. I read to the Council a statement of the Archbishop of Canterbury : ' I trust that the Jowett affair
will be settled before Parliament meets again. It is most important

'that it should be so. Indeed, I feel so strongly about it, that if it
'comes on again, the Archbishop of York and I shall come down to
'vote for the measure,' but it had no effect.    On their part it is
'straining at a gnat after swallowing a camel.'    No good can come
of it.    It makes me more and more sick of the Conservative party.
They seem to me to sacrifice everything to their wretched Conservatism.    We shall see what comes of the motion for a Committee
which is to come on next Monday, but I have ringing in my ears,
'Quos Deus vult perdere, dementat prius.'

The motion for a Committee of the Hebdomadal Council
to inquire into, and report upon the endowment of the
Professorship was more fortunate, and Pusey was appointed on the Committee.    On November 10, he wrote
to Mr. Gladstone to say that the Committee had agreed
to recommend to the Council the resumption of the proposals which Pusey had so warmly supported in 1861, and
which had been rejected chiefly by the votes of his own
friends.

But in the event he was to have a more direct relation to
the endowment than he expected.    Before the Committee
was appointed, Mr. (afterwards Professor) Freeman had
maintained in a letter to the *Daily News* that the Dean
and Chapter of Christ Church held certain lands under
conditions which made it obligatory upon them to augment
the emoluments of the Greek Chair.    This was no new
assertion.    It had been made repeatedly, but sufficient
evidence for it had never been produced.    Soon after
Mr. Freeman had revived it, some fresh evidence in its favour
was discovered.    The Dean and Chapter, however, were still
convinced that no legal claim could be made against them,
and submitted the matter for the opinion of Counsel.
Sir Roundell Palmer and Sir H. M. Cairns decided in
their favour, and maintained that no legal obligation
lay upon Christ Church to increase the stipend beyond
the sum that had been paid for so many years.    But
rather than rest under the slightest suspicion of unfairness,
the Dean and Chapter decided that 'on grounds of general
expediency' and under the great difficulties of the case,
they would raise it to £500 a year.

E. B. P. TO THE RIGHT HON. W. E. GLADSTONE, M.P.

Christ Church, Feb. 21, 1865.

. . . The Dean's letter to the V. C. announcing that we have agreed to raise the Greek Professor's stipend to £500 per ann. will be printed to-morrow, together with the Opinion of the Attorney-General and Sir H. Cairns, that we are under no obligation to do so. Half of us, however, thought that as we have estates which West-minster gave up in order to be free from the duty, we were under a moral obligation to provide adequately for him. Had I known that we had these estates, I should never have troubled you and Lord P[almerston] and Sir G. Grey with those negotiations. I in-quired very many years ago in Gaisford's time about it, but could learn nothing. And the list of estates, tithes, &c., given in Rymer as belonging to Westminster before they gave up those of which we now have some, did not contain any of ours. King James I and Charles I when they annexed stalls to the Divinity and Hebrew Chairs, ignored any duty of Christ Church to augment, unless indeed Laud may have wished to make the Hebrew Chair manifestly theological.

We do not say that we augment the Professorship of Greek out of our incomes (for there was no other way), but they can very well bear it.

It was then in unavoidable ignorance that I made the application to you. It is said that they did not know at the State Paper Office anything of the document which completed the evidence. I am so thankful that the question is now at rest.

Thus after nearly six years of very painful controversy, this complicated and unfortunate question was settled. At this distance of time and under the altered conditions of University life, it is very hard to understand and appreciate the motives which actuated the refusal of a scheme which at first sight may appear as a mere act of justice. The danger for us now in reading the story is lest we should regard the Oxford of 1860 as having already laid aside its old religious character; it must not be forgotten that it was still largely a body bound by the 'Articles of Religion,' and that it still contained many who twenty years earlier had suffered greatly at the hands of the Liberals for alleged faithlessness to them. The detailed account of this painful controversy is at least a matter of justice to Pusey's memory. There is no incident in his life which is more frequently remembered against him, and hardly one which suffers more from incomplete remembrance.

# CHAPTER II.

'ESSAYS AND REVIEWS'—ECCLESIASTICAL PROCEEDINGS — THE OXFORD DECLARATION — CORRESPONDENCE WITH THE REV. F. D. MAURICE AND DEAN STANLEY.

ALREADY in the account of the troubles about the Greek Professorship, allusion has more than once been made to the volume of 'Essays and Reviews' which was published in February, 1860. Before describing the proceedings to which this volume gave occasion, it may be desirable to summarize briefly its contents.

It consisted of seven Essays, which had been written without any internal relation to one another. Dr. Temple, the Head Master of Rugby, wrote on *The Education of the World* in terms against which no direct charge on the score of orthodoxy was raised; Dr. Rowland Williams reviewed *Bunsen's Biblical Researches;* Professor Baden Powell contributed an Essay on *The Study of the Evidences of Christianity;* the Rev. H. B. Wilson, one of the 'Four Tutors' who publicly assailed the arguments of Tract 90 in 1841, took the opportunity of a review of some addresses delivered at Geneva, to speak on *The National Church;* Mr. C. W. Goodwin wrote on *The Mosaic Cosmogony;* the Rev. Mark Pattison described *The Tendencies of Religious Thought in England, 1688-1750;* and Professor Jowett concluded the volume with an essay on *The Interpretation of Scripture.* The note 'to the Reader' at the beginning of the volume described the book 'as an attempt to illustrate the advantage derivable to the cause of religion and moral truth from a free handling, in a becoming spirit, of subjects peculiarly liable to suffer by the repetition of conventional language and from traditional methods of treatment.'

The Essays differed very widely in ability, learning, and reverence ; and, in spite of the claim for mutual independence and the limitation of the responsibility of each writer to his own Essay, the book was read as a whole in the light of its more startling portions. All the writers were popularly, though untruly, assumed to hold the same opinions, and the volume was interpreted as a concerted attack upon Revealed Religion. No doubt the Essays contained some good and true statements which, when duly qualified, have since been generally accepted, as well as others which were neither good nor true. But these thoughts, besides being new, were also stated in some cases recklessly and crudely, and in such a manner as to suggest irresistibly, to the inexperienced general reader, conclusions hostile to the Christian Faith. That such a supposition was not without justification with regard to some of the Essays may be gathered from the words of one who was the most conspicuous champion of the book as a whole. Writing before the great outburst of indignation, Stanley, who was then Canon of Christ Church and Regius Professor of Ecclesiastical History, says in a letter to the editor of the *Edinburgh Review*, for whom he was preparing a review of the volume :—

'Wilson's [essay] has committed the unpardonable rashness of throwing out statements, without a grain of proof, which can have no other object than to terrify and irritate, and which have no connexion with the main argument of his essay. Powell's is a mere *réchauffé* of his (to me) unintelligible argument about miracles. . . Goodwin's is a clear, but offensive, exposition of the relations of Genesis and geology. Williams is guilty of the same rashness as Wilson— on a larger scale—casting Bunsen's conclusions before the public without a shred of argument to prepare the way for them or support them [1].'

Dr. Tait also (the Bishop of London), who was afterwards the most prominent opponent in Convocation of the proceedings against the book, was bound to admit that

---

[1] ' Life of Dean Stanley,' ii. 34, 35.

he did not wonder at the outcry and alarm, for the clergy had been effectually frightened by 'the folly of the publication of "Essays and Reviews," and still more of Stanley's ill-judged defence of them in the *Edinburgh* taken in connexion with "the madness of Bishop Colenso."' He says, 'I deeply deplore, indeed execrate, the spirit of much of the "Essays and Reviews[1]."'

In this case, as in the matter of the Greek Professorship, the altered relations between the Church and the Universities, and the enlarged experience of the Church during the last thirty years, might at first sight suggest the greater wisdom of leaving the book alone, on the part both of the ecclesiastical authorities and of Churchmen in general. Such a course was rendered impossible alike by its enemies and its friends. The *Westminster* and *Edinburgh Reviews* on one side, and the *Guardian* and the *Quarterly Review* on the other, compelled attention to it. Public feeling was too deeply aroused on both sides ; six large editions had already made the book known all over England, and the mass of Churchmen were seriously alarmed. It was generally felt that the Bishops were required to take some active proceedings against the Clergy who held such teaching : minds were too agitated for calm argument, even had such argument been possible. To many simple Christians, who had been educated in a narrow tradition with regard to Holy Scripture, it seemed that if the Bible could not be trusted in the exact sense in which they had always understood it, everything was tottering. Yet the Essays were of a character that did not admit of refutation by any ready argument or by a simple statement of the orthodox Faith. This was well brought out in a letter from Pusey that appeared in the *Guardian* of March 6, 1861.

### E. B. P. TO THE EDITOR OF THE 'GUARDIAN.'

A correspondent of yours mentions me with others (I know not whether excluding or including me) who are called upon, by their position, to answer the unhappy 'Essays and Reviews.' The subject

---

[1] 'Life of Abp. Tait,' i. 325.

has been in the minds of many of us. The difficulty has arisen, not in providing definite answers to definite objections, but in giving systematic answers to a host of desultory attacks on Revelation, its evidences, the Bible which contains it, and the truths revealed. The well-known passage in the unbelieving *Westminster Review* states the extent to which the truth has been attacked : it did not fall within its objects to notice the guerilla, pell-mell character of the attack. But look at the list :—

' Now in all seriousness we would ask, what is the practical issue of all this ? Having made all these deductions from the popular belief, what remains as the residuum ? In their ordinary, if not plain, sense, there has been discarded the word of God, the creation, the fall, the redemption, justification, regeneration, and salvation, miracles, inspiration, prophecy, heaven and hell, eternal punishment, a day of judgment, creeds, liturgies, and articles, the truth of Jewish history and of Gospel narrative, a sense of doubt thrown over even the Incarnation, the Resurrection and Ascension, the Divinity of the Second Person, and the Personality of the Third. It may be that this is a true view of Christianity, but we insist, in the name of common sense, that it is a new view' (p. 305).

An attack may be made in a short space. If any one cannot rest on the authority of the Universal Church, attested as it is by prophecy, nor again, on the word of Jesus, he must take a long circuitous process of answer. But already, if books we must have, these would need to be books, not essays. What could be condensed into essays upon— 1. Revelation ; 2. Miracles ; 3. Prophecy ; 4. The Canon ; 5. Inspiration ; 6. Our Lord's Divinity and Atonement ; 7. The Divinity and Offices of God the Holy Ghost ? But beyond this, there is the miscellaneousness of their random dogmatic scepticism. The writers, in their own persons, rarely affirm anything, attempt to prove nothing, and throw a doubt upon everything. If any of us had dogmatized as to truth as these do as to error, what scorn we should be held up to ! They assume everything, prove nothing. There is only here and there anything definite to lay hold of. One must go back to the foreign sources of this unbelief, to find it in a definite shape which one could answer. I have made a list of the subjects on which I should have to write on my own special subject, the interpretation of the Old Testament. Some, indeed, admit of a short answer. . . . Yet these are but insulated points, easy to be defended because attacked definitely. But when their range of attack extends from Genesis to Daniel ; when one says that credible history begins with Abraham (Williams, p. 57) ; another, that there ' is little reliable history' before Jeroboam (Mr. Wilson, p. 170 ; of course contradicting each other as to the period between Abraham and Jeroboam) ; another denies the accuracy of the Old Testament altogether according to our standards of accuracy (Prof. Jowett, p. 347), asserting that, ' like other records,' it was ' subject to the conditions of a knowledge which existed in an

early stage of the world' (ib. p. 411),—that 'the dark mists of human
passion and error form a partial crust upon it' (Wilson, p. 177),—that
the truth of the unity of God in Scripture only gradually 'dispersed
the mists of human passion in which it was itself enveloped' (Jowett,
p. 286); when contradictions between the Kings and Chronicles are
vaguely assumed (Wilson, p. 178, 9—Jowett, 342, 7); when it is
asserted that prophecies of Jeremiah, Isaiah, Amos, failed (Jowett,
p. 343); and implied that God could not predict the deeds of one of His
creatures by name (ib.); that when Nahum prophesied, there were
human grounds to anticipate the destruction of Nineveh, which he
prophesied (Williams, p. 60); or that Micah, in prophesying the
Birth at Bethlehem, meant only a deliverer in his own times (p. 68);
that 'perhaps *one* passage in Zechariah and *one* in Isaiah (it is not
said which) may be capable of *being made* directly Messianic'
(Williams, p. 69); and that 'hardly any, probably none, of the
quotations from the Psalms and Prophets in the Epistles is based on
the original sense or context' (Jowett, p. 406); when the genuineness
of the Pentateuch (Williams, p. 60), of much of Isaiah (ib. 68, Jowett,
p. 313), Zechariah (Williams, p. 68), Daniel (pp. 69, 76) is denied;
when it is asserted that the aspects of truth in the Book of Job or
Ecclesiastes are opposite or imperfect (Jowett, p. 347), that actions
are attributed to God in the Old Testament at variance with that
higher revelation which He has given of Himself in the Gospel (ib.),
when Abraham's sacrifice of Isaac is attributed, not to God, but to
'the fierce ritual of Syria' (Williams, p. 61), not to speak of the
temptation in Paradise (p. 177), the miracle of Balaam's ass, the
earth's standing still, 'the universality of the deluge, the confusion of
tongues, the corporeal taking up of Elijah into heaven, the nature of
angels, the reality of demoniacal possession, the personality of Satan,
and the miraculous nature of many events' (Wilson, p. 177), or the
Book of Jonah (Williams, p. 73),—how can such an undigested heap
of errors receive a systematic answer in brief space, or in any one
treatise or volume? Or why should these be more answered than
all the other attacks on the same subject, with which the unbelieving
press has been for some time teeming? People seem to have trans-
ferred the natural panic at finding that such attacks on belief could be
made by those bound to maintain it, to the subjects themselves; as
if the faith was jeopardied because it has been betrayed. With the
exception of the still-imperfect science of geology, the 'Essays and
Reviews' contain nothing with which those acquainted with the writings of unbelievers in Germany have not been familiar these thirty
years. The genuineness of the books impugned, the prophecies, whose
accomplishments in themselves, or in our Lord, is so summarily denied,
have been solidly vindicated, not in essays, but in volumes. An
observation on the comparative freedom and reasonableness of 'the
Conservatism of Hengstenberg' and Jahn (Williams, p. 67) is, I
believe, the only indication given in the volume, that much which the

writers assume as proved, has been solidly disproved.   Some volumes
have, I believe, been already translated.

But in spite of these difficulties, the public excitement
demanded some immediate re-assurance.   In consequence
of a great number of appeals for guidance, and not a few
vehement protestations and indignant remonstrances, a
meeting of Bishops was held in London in February, 1861,
to consider the opinions contained in the volume, and
the steps which should be taken with reference to it.
Their deliberations resulted in a public Letter, drawn
up by Bishop Wilberforce, which was signed by twenty-
four Bishops, including Bishop Hampden and Bishop Tait,
as well as the Bishops of Oxford, Salisbury, and Exeter.
Without mentioning the book in this document they
unanimously expressed their sorrow that any clergyman
should in any way deny the Atonement or the Inspiration of Holy Scripture, and confessed their inability to
understand how such opinions could be held 'consistently
with an honest subscription to the Formularies of our
Church.'   They reserved, however, the consideration of any
proposals for further action.   A few days after, on March 13,
a petition was presented to the Archbishop of Canterbury,
signed by 8,500 clergy, requesting the Bishops to take some
judicial proceedings in the matter.   The book was consequently under discussion in both Houses of Convocation
for some time, and it was decided that there were sufficient
grounds to proceed to a Synodical Judgment upon it.
But, on July 9, all such proceedings were indefinitely
postponed because the Bishop of Salisbury had instituted
legal proceedings against one of the writers on the ground
of his Essay.   The respondent in this suit was Dr. Williams,
the Vicar of Broad Chalke.   Another suit was soon after
commenced by the Rev. James Fendall against Mr. Wilson,
for certain passages in his Essay.   Bishop Hamilton's action
in instituting the suit against Dr. Williams was warmly
supported by Pusey, who was at first as sanguine about
its results as he was convinced of its necessity.

It was but another instance of Pusey's singular confidence in the interpretation which a Court of Law would place upon our Formularies. It will be remembered that his objection to the action of the 'Six Doctors,' in 1843, was not that they had condemned him, but that he had been condemned unheard; and he vainly endeavoured to remedy this injustice by a suit in another court, and even desired that Bishop Bagot should institute a friendly action against him. Later again he appealed to Bishop Wilberforce to prosecute him so as to test his teaching in what seemed to him at that time the most suitable way. Whatever may be thought of this method in the present day, Pusey was convinced that it was the most direct method of carrying out the discipline of the Church with regard to doctrine. His confidence in the employment of this weapon was apparently the result of the firm conviction that his own was the only legitimate interpretation of the Formularies. He had not sufficiently realized the subtlety of the methods of legal interpretation. Even the startling results of the Gorham Case had not as yet opened his eyes. This is expressed, early in the proceedings, in the following letter to Bishop Hamilton :—

E. B. P. TO THE BISHOP OF SALISBURY.

Pentire, Newlyn, June 22 [1861].

I can only conceive one of two issues of the prosecution, either (1) the condemnation of Dr. W., or (2) even if it could not be proved to the satisfaction of a judge that Dr. W. were more than a relater of Bunsen's theories, still a condemnation of these theories. . . . I wonder that persons . . . do not see that the question is not about the clergy but about the people : that it is not whether A. or B. shall be interfered with or let alone, but whether our English congregations are to be taught these things by our clergy.

The suits against the two Essayists were adjudged by Dr. Lushington on Dec. 15, 1862, in the Court of Arches, on very narrow issues. Many of the articles of the accusation which had been handed in by the prosecution had been rejected for various reasons by the judge: so that the case was far less complete than it had been at first. The Bishop of Salisbury might have appealed to the Privy Council against their rejection; but he, not unnaturally, shrank from the responsibility of recognizing that Court by himself invoking its decisions; he therefore contented himself with allowing the suit to proceed in the Court of Arches on the four remaining charges only. On each of these Dr. Lushington decided against the respondents, and they without hesitation appealed to the Judicial Committee of the Privy Council. The cases were argued in the latter part of June, 1863, before the Lord Chancellor (Lord Westbury) and three other Law Lords, besides the Archbishop of Canterbury (Dr. Longley, formerly Bishop of Ripon), the Archbishop of York (Dr. Thomson), and the Bishop of London (Dr. Tait, who, as Fellow and Tutor of Balliol, had joined with Mr. Wilson in 1841 in urging the authorities at Oxford to take proceedings against Tract 90).

The exact charges which were under consideration before the Privy Council can be briefly stated. Against Dr. Williams it was alleged that in certain passages of his Essay he had maintained that the Bible was not the Word of God nor the Rule of Faith, and, further, that he had described Justification by Faith as being no more than the peace of mind and sense of Divine approval which comes of trust in a righteous God. The other Essayist, Mr. Wilson, was charged with having in effect stated that the Bible was not necessarily at all, and certainly not in parts, the Word of God, and with having in effect denied a future Judgment and an eternal state of rewards and punishments.

While the matter was under the consideration of the Judicial Committee, the minds of Churchmen were further agitated by the works of Bishop Colenso, for which he had been sentenced to deposition by the Bishop of Capetown in December, 1863. Before the Judgment was delivered, it was generally understood that the verdict of the Ecclesiastical Court which had been adverse to the respondents. would be reversed, and grave fears and anxieties prevailed. ' Dearest friend, forgive me,' Keble wrote to Pusey on January 28, 1864, after apologizing for delay in writing, ' I fear more troubles are coming on, and I shall be even forced to write to you more punctually. I mean about the Courts, Capetown, &c.' Pusey was not at that moment so anxious about Capetown, but he had already made up his mind as to what ought to be done, if their worst fears about the Privy Council were realized.

E. B. P. TO REV. J. KEBLE.

[Christ Church], Jan. 29, 1864.

The domestic case is very grievous. We must try for two points : (1) to get the Bishops to reaffirm the doctrine or doctrines which the Judicial Committee denies, if it does ; (2) organize a systematic annual agitation for a new Court of Appeal, and not rest, so long as we are here, until it is granted. We shall have the Low Church with us now. The *Record* inserted a letter of mine, signed 'Senex,' praying that the decision of the Privy Council might not be against God's truth, or the like. (I told the Editor privately who Senex was, yet he put it in, I hear.) However, we shall know next week the form of the decision. Only Jelf tells me, that the lawyers all shake their heads about the impending decision.

At the same time he penned a series of long and anxious letters to the Bishop of London, pointing out the evil consequence which would ensue if the doctrine of the Essayists was pronounced to be justifiable.

The long-expected Judgment was at last given on February 8, 1864. The Judges began and concluded their decision by emphatically stating that they were compelled to found their Judgment on 'the meagrest disjointed extracts,' contained in the reformed Articles as they came from the lower Court. They stated. as had been already asserted in the Judgment in the Gorham case, that they had no power to decide doctrine ; they could but examine the plain grammatical meaning of the extracts and see whether they were in conflict with the true construction of the Articles and other Formularies of the Church of England. They further maintained that to justify a condemnation in a suit of this character the contradiction between the extracts and the Formularies must be direct. On these principles they held that the charges against Dr. Williams and Mr. Wilson were 'not proven.' Dr. Williams was charged with saying that the Bible is not the Word of God : the Judges found no such statement in the extracts before them, and therefore acquitted him. Mr. Wilson was charged with contradicting the Articles and Formularies by holding that the Bible was not written under the Inspiration of the Holy Spirit, and that it was not necessarily at all, and certainly not in parts, the Word of God. The Court held that this charge involved the proposition that it was contrary to the Articles and Formularies of the Church of England to 'affirm that any part of the canonical books of the Old and New Testaments, on any subject whatever, however unconnected with religious faith and moral duty, was not written under the Inspiration of the Holy Spirit.' Since this proposition could not be found by the Judicial Committee in the portions of the Articles and other Formularies that were cited, the charge was held not to be substantiated. As regards the second charge against Mr. Wilson, it was held that he had said nothing that denied a future judgment or eternal happiness, although he had expressed a 'hope' that 'a judgment of eternal misery may not be the purpose of God.' The Court was unable to find any such distinct declaration of the Church on the subject of the Eternity of final Judgment as to require them to condemn such a hope as 'penal.'

Pusey and his friends saw that if the appellants were ready to accept the interpretation which the Court had put upon their language with regard to Inspiration and Justification by Faith, their language was harmless enough. But it was felt to be extremely desirable to take immediate action with a view to the explicit assertion of the belief of the Church about Inspiration and the future state, and also with a view to ascertaining the exact legal force of this finding.

Immediately on reading the decision, Pusey poured out all his thoughts about it to the Bishop of Salisbury, which he summarized in the following letter to Keble.

E. B. P. TO REV. J. KEBLE.

[Christ Church, Feb. 10], Ash Wednesday, 1864.

I wrote to the Bishop of Salisbury last night, expressing my own opinion that Dr. Williams had been acquitted by his words being taken in a sound sense. If he accepts the acquittal, he virtually withdraws what he said, and in regard to Inspiration, accepts a statement which, in its obvious meaning, is sound. In regard to the 'Merits of our Lord,' by accepting the acquittal he would accept the literal meaning of the words, that 'we are justified for His Merits,' which, unless he have any reservation, is a statement of the true faith. I suggested to the Bishop that as this was his own case in his own diocese, it might have a good effect to put forth something of this sort in a Pastoral.

With regard to Mr. Wilson, I said that I thought that what the Judges said on Holy Scripture *might* bear a possible sound construction, although, I fear, not theirs.

But in regard to that awful doctrine of the Eternity of Punishment their Judgment is most demoralizing in itself and in its grounds.

As to its grounds, it puts an end to all confidence between man and man, between the teachers and the taught, and it teaches people dishonesty on the largest scale. For if our English word 'everlasting' is not to mean 'everlasting,' because some have explained away the meaning of αἰώνιος, then one is not bound to the received meaning of any word whatsoever. Then the second Article might be consistent with Arianism, for 'Begotten *from everlasting* of the Father' might only mean 'a long time ago,' but 'in time'; and we have no word to declare that Almighty God is eternal. This is an extension of the old argument, 'If there is no everlasting death, there is no statement of any everlasting life.' One class of heathen did not believe their supreme god (such as he was) to be eternal, but to be the active principle, developed in time, out of ὕλη.

But on the same principle, every heresy would be admissible which took the received terms in new senses, and we might be inundated with every heresy.

If 'everlasting' might mean 'long enduring,' 'grace' might, of course, equally mean what the Pelagians called it, God's 'favour,' or it might mean His 'help through our natural powers.' And this is, in fact, a far-spread perversion of words which the new compromising school of unbelievers adopts. They mean by 'Inspiration' God's suggestions to any uninspired mind, and by 'Revelation' the understanding of God which they suppose us to acquire through our natural faculties. If 'everlasting' is to be taken in any other than its legitimate English sense, because it is not so defined, so may any other. An Act of Parliament may define its words, but words cannot be defined in Prayers or Theological statements. Do you not think that you could work up something of this sort for the Bishop of Exeter to write? He would like what you would write better than what I should. It would be of great value, if some of the Bishops would begin by speaking.

I have asked Cotton to try to stir up the *Record*. *We* have no organ, now that the *Guardian* is liberalized. . . . I am going to write to the Archbishop of Canterbury ; and would not you write too ? For the most formidable thing of this Judgment (as it appears on the surface) is, that the two Archbishops, while objecting to the Judgment on other points, do not object to this, which makes it seem as if they concurred. Surely Archbishop Longley cannot doubt that it is the doctrine of the Church.

Both Archbishops had openly dissented from the rest of the Judicial Committee on the subject of Inspiration ; and Pusey was right in thinking that the Archbishop of Canterbury (Dr. Longley) could not have consented to the language of the Judgment on the subject of Eternal Punishment. Appeals from the Bishop of Exeter, Keble, and Pusey brought the following private assurance from the Archbishop, which was printed in the *Guardian* in the middle of March.

Lambeth Palace, March 4, [1864].

I wish it to be generally understood that, in assenting to the reversal of the Judgment of Dr. Lushington on the subject of Eternal Punishment in the case of Mr. Wilson, I did so solely on technical grounds ; insomuch as the charge against him on this point was so worded that I did not think it could be borne out by the facts.

The Eternity of Punishment rests, according to my mind, exactly on the same ground as the Eternity of Blessedness ; they must both stand or fall together ; and the Church of England, as I maintain, holds both doctrines clearly and decidedly.

At the same time Pusey and Keble were representing to Bishop Phillpotts the great value of a short Pastoral Letter addressed to his diocese on the subject. They were deeply convinced that the practical results of this Judgment would be extremely serious with regard not only to the faith but also to the life of large numbers of people. So far as the matter was affected by the Judgment of the Judicial Committee of the Privy Council, Pusey and Keble appealed to Mr. Gladstone in the hope of enlisting the aid of politicians in reforming the Final Court of Appeal for ecclesiastical cases. Mr. Gladstone's answer fully acknow-

ledged the unsatisfactory nature both of the Court and of
its decisions, but did not, to Pusey's great disappointment,
hold out any hope of effectual assistance.

On such matters as Inspiration and the Doctrine of Everlasting Punishment, Pusey had great hopes that it would
be possible to unite the Low Church and High Church
parties. In the Gorham and Denison Cases such a hope
was out of the question; but the defence of the doctrines
which were now assailed seemed likely to be of the deepest
common interest. ‘We shall have the Low Church with
us now,’ he said to Keble. Even before the decision he had
written to the *Record*, and within a few days of the
Judgment he sent two other letters to the same paper.
In the former he gave expression to ‘the pent-up longings
of many years,’ and made an appeal for ‘one united action
on the part of every clergyman and lay member of the
Church.’ He had long anticipated the coming of a time
when the pressure of the common enemy of unbelief
would draw closer into one band all who love their
Lord as their Redeemer and their God, and the Bible
as being indeed the very Word of God. He laid great
stress on the wide practical evil and loss of souls that would
result from any seeming doubt about Everlasting Punishment. His special wish was that in some way or other
there should be a general reaffirmation of belief on that
subject.

‘ There is more than one way of doing it. It is for others to think
which should be chosen. But we should not rest, we should give no
rest to men, nor (they are God's own words) ‘ to God ’ until it is made
plain that the Church does faithfully and lovingly warn the wicked of
the doom which their Redeemer, Who died that they might not die
eternally, says He shall pronounce on those who to the end reject His
long-suffering mercy.’

He was greatly displeased at the position taken up by the
*Guardian* with reference to the Judgment; both he and
Keble declined any longer to read it, and ceased to use
it, as before, as a medium of communication with their
friends.

His appeal to the *Record* brought him many warm expressions of sympathy and promises of help. The most interesting reply was from his cousin Lord Shaftesbury, whose last letter to him had been written in a tone of severe remonstrance for neglecting to defend the Faith,— one of the duties of his academical position which his correspondent considered that Pusey had forgotten.

LORD SHAFTESBURY TO E. B. P.

Grosvenor Square, Feb. 26, 1864.

You and I are fellow-collegians and old friends.

Time, space, and divergent opinions have separated us for many years ; but circumstances have arisen which must, if we desire combined action in the cause of our Common Master, set at nought time, space, and divergent opinions. We will fight about those *another day ; in this* we must 'contend earnestly for the faith once delivered to the saints'; and it must be done together. Now your letter to the *Record* shows (at least I think so) that you are of the same mind as myself. We have to struggle not for Apostolical Succession or Baptismal Regeneration, but for the very Atonement itself, for the sole hope of fallen man, the vicarious Sacrifice of the Cross. For God's sake, let all who love our blessed Lord and His perfect Work be of one heart, one mind, one action, on this great issue, and show that, despite our wanderings, our doubts, our contentions, we yet may be one in Him. What say you ?

Yours truly,

SHAFTESBURY.

Rev. E. B. Pusey, D.D.

Pusey at once replied with characteristic warmth :—

E. B. P. TO LORD SHAFTESBURY.

Christ Church, Oxford, Feb. 28, 1864.

MY DEAR SHAFTESBURY,

I thank God for your letter, and for the renewal of old friendship. I always sought to live in peaceful relations with those who love our dear Lord, and adore His redeeming mercy. Those few lines in the *Record* express what has for these thirty years been the deep longing of my soul, that we should understand one another, and strive together against the common enemy of souls. This soul-destroying Judgment may, with, I fear, its countless harm, be over-ruled in God's mercy to good, if it binds as one man all who love our Blessed Lord, in contending for the Faith assailed. I have ever loved the (to use the term) Evangelical party (even while they blamed me), because I believed that they loved our Redeeming Lord with their whole hearts. So now I am one heart and one mind with those who will contend for our common Faith against this tide of unbelief.

Yours affectionately,

E. B. PUSEY.

I only had to-day your letter dated Feb. 26.

I had thought to write to you the letter which I afterwards sent to the *Record,* but I thought it best in the end not to ask you to own me again, till you should be so minded.

But beyond all other results of this common anxiety, the most important to Pusey was the complete establishment of the most friendly relations with Bishop Wilberforce. During the Denison Case it will have been noticed that from time to time friendly and confidential communications were passing between them: in 1857 and the following years the Bishop never failed to enlist Pusey's help and advice with regard to the Courses of Sermons which he arranged at St. Mary's and St. Giles', Oxford, for the under-graduates. On two occasions they seemed to be in momentary danger of taking different sides about the endowment of the Greek Professorship; but those dangers soon passed away. The prominent action which Bishop Wilberforce took with regard to 'Essays and Reviews' from the very first, both in the *Quarterly Review* and in Convocation, made it natural that Pusey should appeal to him about the best practical course to pursue at this crisis. On Feb. 13, five days after the Judgment, he wrote to the Bishop urging the necessity of some action.

E. B. P. TO BISHOP (WILBERFORCE) OF OXFORD.

Christ Church, Feb. 13 [1864].

One can hardly think of anything for the hidden blasphemy of that Judgment which declares that to be uncertain which our Lord taught, and for the loss of countless souls which it will involve, if not repudiated by the Church. For nothing, I suppose, keeps men from any sin except the love of God or the fear of Hell. And the fear of Hell in most cases drives us to seek God and to know Him and to love Him. It is most demoralizing in its virtual denial of faith and on the principles on which it is based. I am going over with Liddon the two Judgments to see what truths are thrown open between them, that it may be seen what has to be reaffirmed. As it is, the moral effect of the Judgment was briefly stated in the *Times—*

'the teaching of the Essayists is recognized.' Without some combined effort to repudiate that Judgment the Church of England will be destroyed or will become the destroyer of souls.

On February 21 the Bishop wrote to Pusey, enclosing two documents which had been drawn up by W. R. Fremantle, one of his rural deans and afterwards Dean of Ripon, and Woodford (afterwards Bishop of Ely). One was a proposed declaration of belief in 'the Divine authority of the Canonical Scriptures as being the Word of God, and in the certainty of the Everlasting Punishment of the wicked'; the second was a Memorial to the Queen praying her to issue a Commission to inquire into the constitution and practice of the Judicial Committee of the Privy Council. The Bishop joined in the wish for a Commission, but earnestly begged Pusey to serve on a committee which would, as a first step, take action with a view to the affirmation of the impugned doctrines by all except 'the tainted section' of the Church. Pusey at first signed both the papers, but on second thoughts he doubted the wisdom of any attempt to obtain a Royal Commission on the Courts. He feared that after a year's delay they would only obtain an unsatisfactory answer, and by that time people's energies would have cooled down.

The Bishop in reply could not agree that it was inexpedient to have a Commission on the working of the Final Court of Appeal, but he added : 'What I am most anxious about for the present is that you should do your utmost to weld together for this purpose the two great sections of the Church, High and Low ; and that at all events the protest and declaration should be numerously signed.'

A large number of graduates came to Oxford on February 25 to vote on some extensive changes in the Examination Statutes. This was regarded as a favourable opportunity for concerting some common action such as Bishop Wilberforce desired, and Pusey was appointed a member of a representative committee [1] to which was

---

[1] It consisted of Archdeacon Clerke, Dr. Cotton, Archdeacon Denison, Rev. W. R. Fremantle, Dr. Leighton, Dr. J. C. Miller, and Dr. Pusey.

assigned the delicate task of drawing up a Declaration which was to unite and satisfy the many diverging interests, all alike hostile to the Judgment.

The Declaration, which the Bishop had suggested, was altered by the committee until at last it assumed the following form, in which it was hoped that sufficient care had been taken to exclude evasion without going beyond the Formularies of the Church of England [1] :—

'We the undersigned Presbyters and Deacons in Holy Orders of the Church of England and Ireland, hold it to be our bounden duty to the Church and to the souls of men, to declare our firm belief that the Church of England and Ireland, in common with the whole Catholic Church, maintains without reserve or qualification, the Inspiration and Divine Authority of the whole Canonical Scriptures, as not only containing but being the Word of God ; and further teaches, in the Words of our Blessed Lord, that the "punishment" of the "cursed" equally with the "life" of the "righteous" is "everlasting."'

The following letter, in which Pusey sent a copy of this Declaration to his Diocesan, describes an interesting example of the extreme difficulty of uniting for a common purpose those who are separated by great differences of opinion on other points :—

E. B. P. TO BISHOP (WILBERFORCE) OF OXFORD.

Feb. 28, 1864.

The Warden of All Souls and I had a conversation with Archdeacon Randall, yesterday, and he seemed satisfied with our explanations. Our idea in this Declaration was to unite as many as possible. You will observe, if you look, that we declare our belief, not, in the doctrines, but that the Church of England in common with the whole Catholic Church maintains them. The expression 'firmly believe that,' was put in to satisfy Dr. Ogilvie. He said that he would sign the Declaration with those words, and would not without. Heurtley, we hoped, would follow him. We had then the alternative of my standing alone in a document issuing from Oxford, as the one representative of the Theological faculty, or of acceding to his proposal. It is very sad that people stickle so much, each for his own form of words, but I have found it in the experience of some thirty years. I said to Archdeacon R. that we could strike them out, but with the loss of the one or two Divinity Professors who would sign it.

---

[1] On the terms of the Declarations, see two letters from Pusey, published in the *Guardian* of April 13, 1864, p. 347.

For the omission of the reference to the Privy Council, we had two classes to look to. Mr. Fremantle wrote first, privately. Evangelicals, Erastians, and timid people were against any direct reference to the Privy Council, even in the very modified form in which the paper was drawn up. Dr. Miller of Birmingham adhered uncompromisingly, [? on behalf] of those whose adherence he told us would secure hundreds of signatures. Dr. Wilson, Mr. Venn, Mr. Auriol, demurred, and it was transparent, that they feared lest, in shaking this Judgment, they should shake the Gorham Judgment too—which of course they would. Then, too, timid people like Heurtley and the Dean of Exeter, Lord Middleton, would not sign even a seeming Protest.

What then we hoped by this measure was, to lay a broad basis for future operation and to strengthen the hands of Convocation. I trusted that this Declaration would show that the misbelievers were but a small body, whereas I believe that the Privy Council passed their dishonest Judgment, believing it to be a large one. We owe it also to show to the people of England, who might be seduced to sin by being thus taught to disbelieve Hell, that the great body of their clergy believe it.

In regard to the word 'plenary inspiration,' it was the received term of my youth. I proposed at first 'that the whole Canonical Scriptures are the Word of God,' but Dr. Miller thought that it would not convey our full meaning, although he owned that Colenso and others, by substituting the formula 'contains the Word of God' for '*is* the Word of God,' show how much lies in that word 'is.' Archdeacon Hale suggests 'the authority of the whole Canonical Scriptures as the inspired Word of God,' which I will propose to the committee to-morrow, please God. But Dr. Stanley and Professor Jowett own an 'inspiration' of the Scriptures, but a 'fallible inspiration.'

The opinion of the Archbishop ought to be elicited before the circulation of any Declaration. The use made of his name is terrible. The unbelieving party are parading it. Dr. Stanley (in answer to my expressing a difficulty as to preaching in Westminster Abbey) writes to me, 'I can understand that you might feel your relations altered towards the Church itself, whose highest tribunal and *whose two Primates* have delivered a Judgment which you so much deplore.' This language and the unexplained fact will drive hundreds to Rome.

The Warden of All Souls, who is not in Oxford to-day, has the sketch of a letter which your Lordship suggests; but the committee thought that it had no authority to write to the Archbishop or to address him, having been appointed for a different purpose. I would have written, but (I think that probably by some accident) he did not answer the letter which I have already written.

It would be easy, I think, to settle to send the Declaration to his Grace, but owing to the interruptions of the proceedings on Thursday, the committee received very limited powers. Perhaps this could be repaired to-morrow week, when I suppose that there will be another gathering on the question of the endowment of the Greek Chair.

I have a very cordial letter from Lord Shaftesbury (my cousin), from whom I have been separated for many years, proposing union in very warm earnest terms.

But the work of the committee was successful at least in drawing men together. 'The Declaration is wonderfully uniting all but the Rationalists,' was the report that Pusey sent to Bishop Hamilton on March 1. At the same time he was cheered by a letter from Archbishop Longley, telling him that he was waiting for the presentation of the Declaration as the most suitable moment for a public assertion of his belief in the doctrines with which it dealt. But the Archbishop was unable to await the presentation, as it would unavoidably be two months before the signatures could be collected and arranged. Therefore, on March 14, he issued a Pastoral Letter to his clergy, in which he discusses the doctrines on which the Judgment had touched, and especially asserted his firm conviction that 'the Church has no more sure warrant for belief in the eternal happiness of the saved than it has for belief in the eternal suffering of the lost.' He explained that his concurrence in the Judgment on this point was caused only by the obscurity of Mr. Wilson's language. In the following month the Archbishop of York also issued a Pastoral Letter to the same effect.

During March the 'Oxford Declaration' was the subject of a great correspondence. It was most violently attacked by many who, for varying reasons, felt unable to sign it, and Counsel's Opinion was taken on both sides as to the legality of such a Declaration. On one side Dr. Stephens and Mr. Traill maintained that 'it is not consistent with the obligations under which the clergy have placed themselves . . . to sign the Declaration'; while another opinion, which bore the signatures of Sir Roundell Palmer and Sir H. M. Cairns, asserted that 'it is not in any way unlawful for clergymen, either singly or together, in their preaching or otherwise, to affirm' the words of the Declaration. On legal grounds then the Declaration might proceed; but it was attacked for a very different reason by the Rev. F. D. Maurice in the columns of the *Times*. The lengthy correspondence is too important to be reproduced in any shortened form :—

### REV. F. D. MAURICE TO THE EDITOR OF THE 'TIMES.'

London, March 4, 1864.

SIR,

A document has appeared in the *Times* which purports to be a protest proceeding from certain divines in Oxford and presented for signature to all the clergy of England.

The protest is apparently occasioned by the decision of the Privy Council in the cases of Dr. Williams and Mr. Wilson. Yet I question whether any of the laymen or ecclesiastics who pronounced that decision would object to the mere terms of this protest. Dr. Williams and Mr. Wilson themselves might, I conceive, sign it with as much sincerity and good faith as Dr. Pusey and Dr. Miller.

For a sense—and by no means a non-natural sense—might be given to the words of that protest which would utterly prevent Dr. Pusey and Dr. Miller from signing it with any sincerity or good faith. If by declaring their belief in the inspiration of Canonical Scriptures they exclude men of this day from God's inspiration, they must contradict the letter and spirit of the thirteenth Article. If by affirming that the Bible *is* the Word of God they mean to deny that any other and higher meaning is to be given to the expression 'Word of God,' they must refuse St. John's Gospel a place among the Canonical Scriptures; they must set aside the creeds of the Church; they must place themselves on the level of M. Rénan.

The second clause of the protest seems to affirm that the word 'eternal' or 'everlasting' in the Scripture applies as much to the punishment of the wicked as to the life of the righteous. If that is what the clause means, every one must accept it who accepts our Lord's teaching in the twenty-fifth chapter of St. Matthew's Gospel.

If it means anything else—if it means, for instance, that God's punishments are not to be effectual, that eternal life is not the life of the eternal God, that eternal punishment is not the punishment of losing that life, that righteousness is not to prevail over evil, that God's purpose is to keep man for ever and ever in evil—it should say what it means.

Seeing that the protest is intended, I presume, to protect the Church from ambiguities, it should not itself offer an excuse for all possible ambiguities.

F. D. MAURICE.

### E. B. P. TO THE EDITOR OF THE 'TIMES.'

Christ Church, March 7, 1864.

SIR,

Since Mr. Maurice in his strictures on a Declaration (now in circulation among the clergy of England), as being ambiguous, speaks of me, you will I am sure think it fair to insert my answer. I shall not follow him into controversy on sacred subjects, but shall confine myself to the point that the Declaration is not ambiguous.

He alleges that 'Inspiration' in Article XIII ('works done before the grace of Christ and the Inspiration of the Spirit') is used of the ordinary gifts of God's grace, and that the expression 'the Word of God' is used by St. John of our Divine Lord. But every one knows that the meaning of words is determined by the context. In the statement that 'the Church of England maintains without reserve or qualification the Inspiration and Divine authority of the whole Canonical Scriptures as not only containing but being the Word of God,' the word 'inspiration' clearly does not mean the ordinary gifts of God's grace to all Christians, else the writings of Christians who have the grace of God, would be Holy Scripture (which is absurd). Nor can it mean by the word of God, 'God the Word,' both because there is no question as to the meaning of 'the Word of God' in the Articles referred to, and it would be senseless and blasphemy to say that the Holy Scriptures are God the Word. Dr. Lushington stated in his Judgment, that 'God's Word written and "Scripture" are in Article XX plainly identical' (p. 15). Wishing to adhere strictly to our Formularies we employed the expression 'the Word of God' as being used of Holy Scripture seven times in the Articles.

In regard to the other statement of the Declaration, Mr. Maurice says—' It seems to affirm that the word eternal and everlasting applies as much to the punishment of the wicked as to the life of the righteous.'

The language of the Declaration is, not 'applies to' but 'is.' It further teaches, in the words of our Blessed Lord, that the punishment of the 'cursed' equally with the 'life' of the righteous, is everlasting.

I should have thought it impossible for any one to say that such a statement is 'ambiguous' or to doubt its meaning.

For the rest I keep my promise not to enter here into Mr. Maurice's theology.

Your obedient servant,

E. B. PUSEY.

### REV. F. D. MAURICE TO THE EDITOR OF THE 'TIMES.'

London, March 8, 1864.

I am not aware that I troubled the readers of the *Times* with any discussion about my theology. I commented on a document which was put forth under the sanction of distinguished names, which was published in your columns, and which all the clergy of England are invited to sign.

This document, being put forward as a protest on behalf of our Articles, used the word 'inspiration' in a sense which I thought was very likely to interfere with the sense given to it in one of those Articles. I am most strengthened in that conviction by Dr. Pusey's letter in the *Times* of to-day.

He says that I spoke of the 'ordinary gifts of God's grace.' I never used the phrase. It is his own. I should not consider that an ordinary gift, which the Article says is necessary that we may do good works. That Dr. Pusey and the authors of this Declaration call it by that name is a proof to me how little they are in harmony with the author of the Article or of the Collect which we repeat in our Communion Service, and how far we shall go wrong if we follow their guidance. They wish us to think the only full—'plenary' I suppose, means full—inspiration is that which they find in letters. The inspiration of life is only 'an ordinary gift.'

I do not for a moment suppose that Dr. Pusey confounds the Living Word with the letters through which He may speak to us. But I think he ought very seriously to consider whether the language of his Declaration of faith may not involve others in this confusion. The compilers of the Articles have carefully guarded against it. If they speak ever so many times of the Scriptures as 'the Word of God' they had begun with an Article 'on the Word or Son of God.' But this Declaration is the supplement to the Articles. It is to remove ambiguities from them.

Dr. Pusey wishes that we should give the fullest, strictest force to our Lord's words respecting punishment. He cannot wish it more than I do. The punishments of God I find in Scripture are always said to serve the ends of righteousness. So long as they last, to whomsoever they are supplied, I believe they are witnesses that He does not wish His creatures to continue in unrighteousness.

### E. B. P. TO THE EDITOR OF THE 'TIMES.'

As before, I will not trouble you with any theological controversy. Mr. Maurice charged the Declaration with being ambiguous which, if true, would have involved a grave moral fault. He grounded his charge on what certain words—'inspiration,' 'the Word of God'—might mean, apart from their context. My answer was that there could be no such ambiguity in that context. There can be no doubt what the meaning either of 'inspiration' or of 'the Word of God' could be in the sentence—'Maintain, without reserve or qualification, the inspiration of the whole Canonical Scriptures as not only containing but being the Word of God.' Plainly, it means such 'inspiration' as constitutes that which was written under its influence 'the Word of God.' Mr. Maurice ignores this statement and reads me a lecture on my use of the familiar theological term, 'the ordinary gifts of God's grace.' Any operation of the grace of God on the soul is plainly supernatural; 'the ordinary gifts of God's grace' are stupendous gifts of His love. Yet they are ordinary, in that they have been for above eighteen centuries and are given to every one who has asked for them and has been or is a Christian, not in name only but in deed. A gift which has been given to every faithful Christian since our Lord left this earth must be different from that which, under the New Testament, was given only to Apostles or companions of the Apostles. God has raised up men whom He 'endowed with singular gifts of His Spirit,' but He has not, since He removed St. John from the earth, raised up one whose spiritual gifts could entitle what he wrote to be called Holy Scripture.

Any question, however, as to the ambiguity of the Declaration is removed by Mr. Wilson's letter to the *Daily News*. Mr. Maurice said :—

' Dr. Williams and Mr. Wilson might, I conceive, sign it (the protest) with as much sincerity and good faith as Dr. Pusey or Dr. Miller.'

Mr. Wilson answers, in effect, that he would not sign it if he could, and could not if he would. He would not, because he believes it to be directed against the decision of the Judicial Committee : he could not, because it states explicitly what he does not believe.

Mr. Wilson, in reinforcing his own opinions by an extract from a Rotterdam pastor who denies eternity of punishment as inconsistent with the attributes of God, shows the depth and breadth of the question at issue. We do not believe in the same God. God Whom we adore in His awful and inscrutable justice and holiness, these writers affirm to be cruel. The God whom they acknowledge we believe to be the creature of their own minds, not the God Who has revealed Himself to man.

### Rev. F. D. Maurice to the Editor of the 'Times.'

... I do not know what Mr. Wilson has written respecting the new Declaration of Faith; but like him, I never would sign it. My reasons are these :—

1. An irresponsible self-elected committee has no right to frame a new test for the Church of England.

2. The test is not an honest one. It means more than it says. If a man does not accept it, he is told that he denies the inspiration of the Scriptures, that he rejects the Word of God, that he will not receive the express declaration of the Spirit. If he does sign it, he is told that he has committed himself to a condemnation of the decision of the Privy Council ; to a special notion about inspiration which I for one believe to be dishonourable to the Word of God, to the notion that God condemns men to everlasting sin which I for one hold to be an accursed notion.

3. Because the adjuration prefixed to this Declaration that ' for the

love of God' we should put our names to it, received a very lucid explanation from the recent decision of the Oxford Convocation. It means 'Young clergymen, poor curates, poor incumbents, sign, or we will turn the whole force of religious public feeling against you. Sign or we will starve you! Look at the Greek Professor! You see we can take that vengeance on those whom we do not like. You see that we are willing to take it, and that no considerations of faithful and devoted services will hinder us.' This is what is called signing 'for the love of God.' I accept Dr. Pusey's own statement, tremendous as it is. I say that the God whom we are adjured to love, under these penalties, is not the God of whom I have read in 'the Canonical Scriptures,' not the God who declares that He abhors robbery for burnt offering.

In my turn I will implore and even adjure. I call upon the richer incumbents of London and of all parts of England, upon the learned members of cathedral establishments, upon those in the Universities who are not yet pledged, to protect their younger and poorer brethren from this moral force—a phrase which means to these theologians, as it meant to the Chartists, the threat of physical force.

I call upon the bishops—not only upon those who have made themselves responsible for the whole or any part of the Privy Council decision, but upon all who are not prepared to surrender their own functions to any self-created committee, to say whether they think that the Church requires a new test, whether they think that we are obliged 'for the love of God' to subscribe one.

### E. B. P. to the Editor of the 'Times.'

Mr. Maurice from a charge of ambiguity in the recent Declaration goes to a charge of dishonesty. 'The Declaration,' he says, 'means more than it says.' Before, it was to be capable of opposite senses, so that Mr. Wilson or Dr. Williams were to be able to sign it. Now that Mr. Wilson has declared that he could not sign it, Mr. Maurice says, 'Neither could I.' Where, then, is the alleged ambiguity? Now he alleges that it is expressed so clearly as to admit of no doctrine of Inspiration short of what it states, and that a doctrine which Mr. Maurice believes to be 'dishonourable to the Word of God.' How one mind could bring all the successive charges which Mr. Maurice had alleged I cannot understand.

Further, Mr. Maurice imputes blasphemy to the belief which he rejects. The Declaration is to 'commit men to the notion that God condemns men to everlasting sin.' This blasphemy Mr. Maurice well knows that no one holds; it is of course contrary to the Being of God that He should be the author of sin. Very few in England (whatever they may think or wish as to man) do not conceive of Satan as remaining, of his own free will, fixed in evil. Our Redeemer declares the endless punishment of the wicked; the addition that 'God would condemn man to everlasting sin' is Mr. Maurice's.

In this life too God maintains in being persons who persevere to the end unchanged in sin, yet He does not thereby 'condemn them to sin.'

From allegations of dishonesty and of blasphemy Mr. Maurice goes on to charge oppression upon those who take part in the Declaration. viz. that they wish to impose a new 'test' and to make an oppression of it. This is childish as well as unjust. Any one who knows anything of the habits of mankind knows how very many concurrent grounds there always are against signing anything. Some 'never sign at all,' some take exception to this expression, others to that; some think such a statement not to be called for; others that it is of no use, &c. When, then, there may be so many reasons why a person may not have signed it, it cannot of course be assumed that any given individual clergyman did not sign it because he did not agree with the truths contained in it. The very idea, then, of 'a test' is gone. A Declaration would only be a 'test' if there were any authority which could require any party to declare his assent to or his dissent from it. I *do* believe that the 'Declaration' will have a great moral effect on the country. I believe the Bible to be very dear to the people of England, and that they will be much reassured to find that their clergy do as a body, with one heart and one mind, receive the Bible as the infallible Word of God, not as 'containing that Word' only. For if the Bible contained the 'Word of God' only, who could say where in the Bible that Word was to be found? Each would find it according to his own bias in what he liked. One would find it in this saying, another in that; and the negative tastes of any two persons might combine to find it nowhere.

Mr. Maurice excepts against our 'asking other clergymen to join us for the love of God.' This arises from our opposite convictions. What else could they do who feared lest people should be encouraged to disbelieve the Bible and Hell and that they were in risk of losing their faith and their souls?

Thus for the moment the controversy ended. Pusey's conviction of the extreme gravity of the question at issue explains why he expressed himself throughout the whole controversy on 'Essays and Reviews' with a warmth which he uniformly repressed on all other occasions.

At the same time Pusey was carrying on another correspondence with Dr. Stanley, who had recently left his Oxford Professorship for the Deanery of Westminster. The Dean had a sincere desire to 'enlarge' (as he called it) the Church of England, and felt it his duty to give, to every preacher of eminence within the Church, the opportunity of addressing the mixed congregations that assembled in the Abbey, on the subject of the truths which they all held in common.

Pusey was among those who received an early invitation to preach. Stanley had from the first held aloof from 'Essays and Reviews' and declined to contribute to the volume; but he had in public warmly defended its writers and fervently expressed his thankfulness for the decision of the Privy Council. 'That the Church of England does not hold— (1) verbal inspiration, (2) imputed righteousness, (3) eternity of torment, is now, I trust, fixed for ever [1].'

The points on which Stanley differed from him were necessarily at the moment painfully prominent in Pusey's mind, both because of 'Essays and Reviews,' and also because he was at that moment specially harassed by the complexities of the controversy about Professor Jowett at Oxford, which had already laid him open to so much misunderstanding from friends who could not appreciate his tolerant attitude towards the endowment of the Greek Chair. He was greatly perplexed about his answer to the Dean's invitation. He first wrote neither accepting nor declining, but calling attention to the importance of the questions on which they differed, and calling Stanley's attention to a criticism of his Lectures on the Jewish Church, in the book on Daniel.

E. B. P. TO DEAN STANLEY.

Christ Church, Feb. 23, [1864].

... We are at a critical moment. I, as you may have heard, have joined those, whether Evangelicals or others, who think it necessary that the Church should in some way reaffirm the doctrines upon which doubt has been thrown by the late Judgments. Your friends, I hear, are rejoicing in it. So there we are in direct antagonism. Some to whom I owe great deference say to me 'I confess that I should feel a shock at your preaching at the Abbey at this juncture, and I think that this would be the feeling of many people.' It gives an appearance of unreality if people, who are at that moment in active antagonism on what they believe to be of vital moment, unite as if there were nothing at issue between them.... I believe the present to be a struggle for the life or death of the Church of England, and what you believe to be for life I believe to be for death ; and you think the same reciprocally of me.

I fear, then, lest in accepting a personal token of confidence from

---

[1] 'Life and Letters of Dean Stanley,' ii. 44.

you, in offering to me what has never been offered to me before—the
privilege of preaching to all those souls in the Abbey—I should be
confusing people's minds. . . . People might ask what *do* those people
think to be truth?'

The Dean replied by stating the grounds on which he
had made the offer, and renewing it 'in the name of our
common Christianity and our common Church.' With
regard to the decision of the Privy Council, he wrote
as follows:—

DEAN STANLEY TO E. B. P.[1]

Feb. 25, 1864.

I regret, but cannot be surprised (after what I have often heard you
say), that you should be displeased at the recent Judgment, which to
me appears so wise and just. But I cannot see that this divergence
makes any difference in my position, or in yours, with regard to these
sermons. I can understand that you might feel your relations altered
towards the Church itself, whose highest tribunal and whose two
Primates have delivered a Judgment which you so much deplore.
But as to any action within the Church, I cannot recognize any further
difference than may have been occasioned by the divergence which
existed between us at the time of the Gorham Judgment, and which
was expressed by many in terms at least as strong as those which you
use on the present occasion.

I confess that I was startled and pained by your letter of adhesion
to a newspaper (you will forgive me for saying what I am sure you
must often have heard said by others) of so scandalous a character as
the *Record*. . . .

With regard to the theological differences to which you so kindly
allude, and especially to the note which you mention in my 'Lectures
on the Jewish Church,' I will only say that I have said there nothing,
in principle, beyond what you yourself said formerly in the book on
German theology.

Pusey was unwilling to stand aloof from any scheme
designed to bring home the truth to the souls of people
who are seldom within its reach. On the other hand, he
dreaded lest he should appear to countenance indifference
by allowing himself to be mixed up with those whose
teaching he so profoundly distrusted. He therefore wrote
again to Stanley to ask the names of those with whom he
would be associated if he accepted the proposal.

<hr>

[1] 'Life and Letters of Dean Stanley,' ii. 162.

E. B. P. TO DEAN STANLEY[1].

February 28, 1864.

Can you tell me who the other preachers are whom you propose to invite to preach at the Abbey? I know that you sympathize most with those most opposite to my belief. And yet this is not the case of persons preaching incidentally in the same church. It is a cycle of preachers—one system, one whole. You appeal to me kindly in the name of 'our common Christianity.' Alas! I do not know what the common Christianity of myself and Professor Jowett is. I do not know what single truth we hold in common, except that somehow Jesus came from God, which the Mohammedans believe too. I do not think that Professor Jowett believes our Lord to have been Very God, or God the Holy Ghost to be a Personal Being. The doctrine of the Atonement, as he states it, is something wholly unmeaning. Of his heart, of course, I do not speak; I only speak of his writings.

For yourself, my dear Dr. Stanley, you say that you have said nothing in principle beyond what I said in my books when I was twenty-eight. Would to God you did not!

I wrote to the *Record* because I wanted to unite with the party who take it in, and to whom I had access through it. I dare say it has said many a hard thing of myself and my friends; no one can suppose that I endorse these things.

But I must, and do, join heart and soul with those who oppose this tide of Rationalism. Nothing, of course, but the deep conviction that the souls of the young and the faith were imperilled would have induced me to unite in the prosecution of Professor Jowett.

The Dean told him the names of the other preachers and renewed his request, saying that the Archbishop of Canterbury would have preached, but he was engaged. 'I venture,' he added, 'to express my surprise that you should scruple about preaching in the same Church with the Archbishop and myself, and not scruple about making an ally (without a word of justification) of a newspaper which notoriously violates the first principles of truth and charity every week.' Pusey was as perplexed as ever, and wrote again for the advice of Bishop Hamilton and Keble. 'One's feeling says,' he wrote to Keble, 'If God did but speak through one to six consciences of those 3,000! Then comes one's fear of seeming indifference. . . .'

Keble had not yet been invited to preach[2], but he had

---

[1] 'Life and Letters of Dean Stanley,' ii. p. 163.

[2] He and Liddon were asked after

Pusey declined: see their letters in 'Life and Letters of Dean Stanley,' ii. 159, 165 sqq.

already made up his mind in his own case: if the Dean were to ask him, he should decline, for the same reasons as caused him to decline to preach at Oxford. But he found it very difficult to decide what Pusey should do. At last he wrote to say that 'having such countenance as that of Archbishop Longley, he should think that Pusey could say "yes" without scandal.' But before his opinion reached Oxford a letter from Bishop Hamilton had caused Pusey to send a final refusal.

E. B. P. TO DEAN STANLEY[1].

March 5, 1864.

I trust that I have not caused you inconvenience by the difficulty which I have had in making up my mind. It would have been a glad office to me to preach to those 3,000 if so be that God would have spoken through me to one soul effectively. But I dare not. I think that one of the great dangers of the present day is to conceive of matters of faith as if they were matters of opinion, to think all have an equal chance of being right, which involves this—that there is no faith at all. The essence of your scheme seems to me to be to exhibit as one those whose differences I believe to be vital; and so, although it is with a pang that I relinquish the offer which (differing so much from me) you kindly made me, of speaking God's truth earnestly to all those souls, I cannot with a safe conscience accept it.

To the outside world it might have seemed that Stanley's courteous invitation could have been accepted with a similar courtesy. But Pusey felt that such a judgment would only be passed by those who regarded all doctrinal differences as matters of unnecessary detail. However greatly he might prize each opportunity of preaching for the salvation of souls, he could not face the grave danger of seeming to regard as indifferent distinctions which he for his part believed to be vital. It was no consolation to him that other good men, who were at one with him on the question at issue, did not share his apprehensions. As Keble said in reply to the invitation which Stanley sent to him a few days later, ' Were I to accept it, it would be in discomfort and fear, lest by seeming to bear with doctrines which you avowedly uphold, and which I believe in my

<hr>

[1] ' Life and Letters of Dean Stanley,' ii. 164.

heart to contradict the foundations of the Faith, I should cause harm which would far outweigh any good which one might do by preaching.'

Meanwhile signatures to the Declaration were pouring in from all sides. Altogether eleven thousand Clergymen signed it. In presenting it to the Archbishop on July 12, the Committee stated that they knew from the letters which they had received that there were some thousands more of the clergy whose faith the Declaration expressed, but who were deterred from adopting so novel a course of remonstrance by 'various natural and legitimate considerations.' But it was far more than a mere demonstration with no ulterior issues: as a united expression of the faith of the great body of the clergy it carried considerable moral weight, while it was an assurance to the Bishops of the very general support which they would receive in any measure that they might devise for guarding what was believed to be the faith of the Church on these points. In the next month it was followed by a Synodical condemnation of 'Essays and Reviews' by both Houses of the Convocation of Canterbury. It seemed at length that the clergy had taken the only practicable courses for protecting those positions which appeared to be assailed. But important as the Synodical Declaration was, it is not necessary in this connexion to trace its history at any length, as Pusey was not directly concerned in it.

The harmony of feeling which drew together the bishops and clergy belonging to both the great parties of the Church was the most cheering aspect of this sad discussion. It was in vain for Bishop Thirlwall to maintain that the 11,000 signatures added nothing to the weight of the opinion of Dr. Pusey. Dr. Tait, the Bishop of London, who was the chief opponent of the Synodical condemnation in the Upper House of Convocation, felt otherwise[1]. He saw clearly what powerful weapons this Declaration and condemnation were when representing a coalition of two such forces on the basis of the deep convictions which they

[1] 'Life of Archbishop Tait,' i. 325 (3rd ed.).

held in common; and in a private diary he puts on record his interesting yet singular conviction that it is part of his vocation to resist the tendency of the Evangelical party to coalesce with the High Church for the purpose of resisting the spread of Broad Church teaching. Such a coalition would undoubtedly have greatly changed the lines of the policy according to which he was prepared to direct the fortunes of the Church of England.

# CHAPTER III.

### 1861-1865.

A WIDELY-SIGNED Declaration of faith from the clergy
and a Synodical condemnation of ' Essays and Reviews ' by
the Convocation of Canterbury seemed at the moment
to be the only possible course in order to allay the
popular anxiety.  Although Newman and Pusey had long
anticipated the opening of these questions, ordinary Churchmen were filled with painful surprise at such ' free-handling '
of the truths of Scripture by clergymen.  They did not
understand such an academical treatment of religious
truths, and they looked with justifiable alarm at the
statements and tone of the Essays : not unnaturally they
needed to be assured that the clergy as a body also
repudiated them.  Whatever opinion may be held as to
the wisdom of the proceedings which have just been
described, it is easy to understand how imperatively some
immediate action was demanded so as to calm the widespread excitement of simple minds.

At the same time it was equally obvious how inadequate
any such action would be as a controversial reply to the
many difficulties which this volume presented for the first

time to the minds of religious readers in England. The belief of the Church in the truths which God has revealed to us is independent of any discoveries which criticism may make with regard to the Bible; but attacks upon that belief, which are made in the name of scientific Biblical criticism, cannot be finally disposed of by the voice of the Church in Declarations and Synodical condemnations. They demand the patient investigation and careful study of years. Not unfrequently it is found that a startling statement, which at first sight was supposed to be hostile to the faith, contained an element of truth which only needed to be disentangled from the falsehood, or exaggeration, or misrepresentation with which its original statement was encumbered; when sifted and brought into its right relations with the rest of the truth about Holy Scripture, it finds its home in the general body of the Church's thought.

Few people in 1861 had any idea of the many years of steady work which a belief in these principles would entail on the students of theology. This is true both of many of the Essayists and also of many of those who attempted to answer them. As was wisely said at the moment :—

' Several of the writers have not got their thoughts and theories into such order and consistency as to warrant their coming before the world with such revolutionary views. But there has been a great deal of unwise passion, and unjust and hasty abuse ; and people who have not an inkling of the difficulties which beset the questions, are for settling them in a summary way, which is perilous for every one. However, I hope the time of protest and condemnation is now passing away, and the time of examination and discussion in a quieter tone beginning [1].'

In this examination Pusey felt called upon to take his share. His position as Regius Professor of Hebrew seemed to prescribe the defence of some parts of the Old Testament as his special contribution, and this he at once commenced with characteristic thoroughness. Early in 1862 he began

---

[1] 'Life and Letters of Dean Church,' p. 157 : To Dr. Asa Grey ; March 28, 1861.

to prepare his Lectures on the Book of Daniel, and in the Easter Term of that year he had delivered four of them. The rest were delivered at intervals as they were ready: they were finished in November, 1863, and published in the following autumn.

He selected the Book of Daniel because Dr. Williams had asserted that recent criticism had proved that the book was written at a very late date; and Pusey was convinced that if he could show this assertion to be untrue, it would shake the confidence of the younger students of theology in other supposed critical triumphs. But another and far deeper question lay immediately behind the question of date:—

'I selected the book of Daniel because unbelieving critics considered their attacks upon it to be one of their greatest triumphs. The exposure of the weakness of some ill-alleged point of evidence has often thrown suspicion on a whole faith. The exposure of the weakness of criticism, where it thought itself most triumphant, would, I hoped, shake the confidence of the young in their would-be misleaders. True! Disbelief of Daniel had become an axiom in the unbelieving critical school. Only they mistook the result of unbelief for the victory of criticism. They overlooked the historical fact that the disbelief had been antecedent to the criticism. Disbelief had been the parent, not the offspring, of their criticism, their starting-point, not the winning-post of their course [1].'

These Lectures therefore contained no dispassionate academical discussion of the date, authenticity, and authorship of the Book of Daniel. They materially differed from such an 'introduction' as an ordinary expositor would now prefix to a commentary on a portion of the Bible. 'Essays and Reviews' and the serious harm that was resulting from such methods of handling the Old Testament, and especially from the hints thrown out which tended to disparage the value of prophecy, are throughout present to his mind. The whole discussion is focussed upon the question of the definitely predictive character of the book. Arguments are carefully marshalled to show that it must indisputably contain predictions, because trustworthy scientific criticism cannot

[1] 'Daniel the Prophet,' by Rev. E. B. Pusey, D.D., Pref. p. vi.

assign any date to it so late as the events which the writer
treats as being still in the future.  He refused to regard the
minuteness of some of the predictions as giving the slightest
warrant for a suspicion of their authenticity; he pointed
out that this feature rendered them all the more in harmony
with the rest of Scripture.  With elaborate care he argued,
from a comparison of all available materials, that not only
the character of the Hebrew of the book exactly suited the
traditional date of composition, but that the form of
the Chaldee, in which language six of its chapters are
written, excluded any later period from consideration.  He
maintained that the minute, fearless touches, involving
details of customs, state-institutions, and history, belong to
one who must have lived in the period which he described ;
and that the passages which appeared to present historical
difficulties are really, when considered in the light of full
knowledge, indications of an accurate and familiar acquaintance with all details which could belong only to a contem-
porary, as Professor Ramsay has triumphantly shown in
the case of the writer of the Acts of the Apostles.  Further,
he maintained that the theology of Daniel was exactly
what would be expected from a Jew living during the
Babylonian captivity.

Throughout the book the reader is presented with a most
remarkable collection of varied knowledge, handled with
great skill.  Pusey indeed was determined to make the
defence as thorough as possible.  He resented most deeply
the manner in which some English writers had transcribed
from foreign critics arguments against the ordinary view
of the Bible, not only without showing any independence
of thought, but sometimes even betraying their failure to
understand the argument that they reproduced.

If his opponents could be satisfied to make use of such
poor work as this, Pusey for his part, in writing his lectures,
determined to give of his very best for the defence of his
own belief.  He read every work that had been written
against the traditional account of the Book of Daniel, and
spared no pains of research to discover facts which would

throw light upon the difficulties which seemed to crave for solution. In this volume, as in the 'Commentary on the Minor Prophets,' he thus noted carefully every recent theory; and his scholarship throughout is marked with the usual characteristics of thoroughness and trustworthiness. At the time one or two writers ventured to impugn his knowledge of Hebrew; but some very pointed retorts to them in the postscript to the preface of the second edition showed clearly the side on which the ignorance lay. Pusey, in fact, is now allowed, by those whose extensive knowledge of Semitic literature renders them competent judges, to have been a sound and accurate Oriental scholar, and to have had an exact and idiomatic acquaintance with the usage of Hebrew words, even if they feel unable to accept his critical conclusions. These lectures on Daniel are acknowledged not only to be replete with learning, but also to sum up with masterly ability the conservative position with respect to this part of the Bible.

Exception has often been taken to the tone which he adopts towards the opposing position. It must, however, be remembered that his eye is not fixed upon individual exponents of a school of criticism, but upon the form of thought out of which that school first sprang. He had ever before him those forms of German unbelief with which forty years earlier he had become painfully familiar at Göttingen, and from which these theories originally emanated; and he saw, behind the first English skirmish with these old German foes, the whole advancing host of Rationalism. Whether rightly or wrongly, he desired by strong language to awaken English readers to the vital questions involved in the controversy, as he understood it. Some of the Essayists, as clergymen, had gained a reputation for boldness by raising questions which, as a matter of fact, insinuated to many minds an unbelief which they did not openly state. Pusey could see no frankness or candour in such a proceeding, and he desired to tear aside the veil which hid from the public eye the source of their arguments and the issue to which he was convinced that they would ultimately lead, and to stamp it all as 'unbelief.' He did not mean that all who held this position were 'unbelievers'; he allowed that many honestly thought it possible to combine such criticism with a firm hold of the Faith. But he wished to point out that in his opinion they were on an inclined plane, and must eventually either discard their criticism or surrender their belief.

It must frankly be admitted that since 1864 the tone of the best Higher Criticism has changed; as a rule, it is no longer characterized by reckless and unfounded assertions to the same extent as in those days. But Pusey dealt with an earlier and cruder form of it, in which his accurately trained mind could find no trace of scholarly research, and his deep reverence for God's revelation heard no answering echo. And he spoke of it according to what he saw and heard. Undoubtedly we are now accustomed to listen to the confident hope which speaks of the time when the terms of reconciliation between the New Criticism and the Old Faith may be stated without compromise and without surrender. But thirty years ago, at any rate, there was good reason for the very gravest fears. In his anxious yearning over souls, Pusey could not allow himself to forget, even if others ignored, 'the absolute and entire loss of faith in all Revelation among many of the younger disciples of the new school[1].' As one after another fell away, Pusey saw that there was 'death in the pot' that contained the wild gourds of the young prophets. Now the young prophets are engaged in casting in the meal; time will show whether they have succeeded in healing the pot. *Adhuc sub judice lis est.*

As Pusey brought his public Lectures on Daniel to a close, he endeavoured in other ways to influence the younger members of the University. With this view he commenced at his own house a series of informal meetings of undergraduates and Bachelors of Arts to discuss difficulties which had been raised about the Old Testament. At these *levées*, as they were sometimes called, he invited

---

[1] 'Lectures on Daniel the Prophet,' Preface to the second edition, p. lix.

his guests to send in notice of the difficulties which they felt ; and at the next meeting these were dealt with, partly in the form of a lecture and partly in the way of question and answer. The following were among the subjects which were chosen—'the Mosaic account of the Creation,' 'the Deluge,' 'the Plagues of Egypt,' 'the hardening of Pharaoh's heart,' 'the influence of Egypt on the Mosaic system,' 'Dr. Colenso's work on the Pentateuch,' and 'the date of the Book of Joel.' The first of these meetings was held on November 4, 1863.

Pusey used also for the same purpose all his turns for preaching in the University pulpit. He felt that in many instances the young had to be won again to Christianity. It was believed at that time that a fashion prevailed among the more talented young men to regard unbelief as a mark of intellectual power [1], and it seemed necessary to restate the most central truths of the Faith with careful explanation of their full meaning. As he says himself, he 'essayed to teach his young audience first principles of faith, or he dwelt on doctrines that had been represented as incompatible with Revelation, or on subjects which from early experience he had felt to be of value as evidence of faith.'

In pursuance of this purpose, on October 13, 1861, he preached in reply to Mark Pattison's essay in ' Essays and Reviews ' : he agreed with him that the Evidence writers of the seventeenth and eighteenth centuries were not convincing, but pointed out that their real deficiency lay not so much in the fact that they appealed to Reason, as in the fact that they endeavoured to discover in the intellect alone all the grounds of the living faith of a Christian. The intellect could of necessity at its best only show that there is a probability that Revelation is true.

' Men might act prudentially on such grounds as these; they might cultivate some moral virtues, act as good heathen, to escape the risk of Hell. But the inmost soul (whether it can analyze the grounds of its faith or no) knows that these are not its grounds. Such a conclusion, after a balance of probabilities, is not the Divine faith of which

[1] Pusey, ' University Sermons,' vol. ii. pref. p. viii.

Scripture speaks, which God gives, which Christians have. . . . Faith, by its certainty, sees Him Who is invisible. . . . This was the promise as to the Gospel, not "opinions," or "views," not uncertainties, or a hesitating belief, which it should be 'the safer side' to accept, which the contradictions of the world could browbeat ; but *knowledge*, a certain, personal knowledge of God and of Christ, a knowledge given to us by God, not collectively only, nor to the first disciples more vividly than to us, but individually also ; a knowledge which God should infuse, with His gift of faith, into the soul [1].'

Again, six months later, by the appointment of the Vice-Chancellor, he preached on the motto of the University, '*Dominus Illuminatio Mea,*' and set forth God as the only source of all knowledge, whether in Reason or in Revelation. These were followed by a series of Sermons on the evidential value of the predictive element of the Old Testament, especially with regard to the prophecies about our Lord, and His Atonement and His Kingdom. Against all depreciation of the reality of these predictions, Pusey at great length set forth the fact that the prophecies were uttered before the events and that subsequent history most remarkably fulfilled them. He was very much impressed by the convincing power of this evidence beyond all other kind of argument, and he pleaded earnestly for its prayerful consideration as a remedy for the intellectual unsettlement of the day.

'Man cannot give faith : man cannot demonstrate faith into the soul ; he can but meet argument by argument, and little comes of it. "Rarely, very rarely," said one of much experience, "have reasonings or discussions subdued or brought back wandering hearts." The prophetic word is powerful, more powerful than any exposition of it ; for it is the Word of God ; it breathes with the Spirit of God, it burns with the love of God. It will lead you, for God will lead you through it. Only give up your whole heart to Him Who made you in His Love. Say to Him, "My God, I believe, with my will, whatsoever Thou hast revealed. For Thou art the Truth. Thou canst not deceive, nor be deceived ": and pray to Him.

I knew the inmost heart and mind of one of the clearest intellects of my day, who, in his youth, was beset by the difficulties of a more powerful philosophy than any of these things which are circulating among you, and who thought it impossible that he could ever again

---

[1] 'University Sermons,' ii. pp. 12, 13.

believe a miracle. By God's mercy, in order not to pain his parents, he entered a church, and there heard again some of the narratives of our Redeemer's life. It flashed upon him, "but for the miracles, this sounds like true history." So he prayed to God the sceptic prayer, that "if He concerned Himself about His creatures, He would hear him." God heard the prayer, the best which, in that state of unbelief, His creature could make, and, through the study of the prophetic word, led him to acknowledge the miracle of Divine wisdom in prophecy, and so gave to him the light of faith.

Only seek with thy whole heart, without reserve, without withholding anything[1].'

Another sermon dealt with the doctrine of the Atonement ; another on Everlasting Punishment, in the Michaelmas Term of 1864, and another in Septuagesima, 1866, on ' Miracles of Prayer,' in reply to Professor Tyndall. In all these he had in view ' that strong tide of half-belief, misbelief, unbelief, which has so largely occupied every sort of literature.' He longed to set forth to the young—' my sons[2],' as he touchingly calls them—some of the truths on which he lived, and which he feared that they might, in a moment of loyalty to supposed truth, be led to sacrifice. These dreary years of struggle for the truth are comparatively uninteresting to describe ; they must have been yet more wearisome to Pusey as he lived and fought each moment, throwing up continuously new lines of defence. In his sermons alone, of the records of this period, do we find the brighter side of the clear faith, the strong courage and the great thirst for souls which stimulated and sustained him in the conflict.

To the same kind of work belongs also the valuable Paper which he read at the Norwich Church Congress on October 5, 1865. He had for many years been maintaining that watchful interest in the progress of physical science which he continued until the end of his life. While other people talked of sympathizing with scientific progress, he

---

[1] 'University Sermons,' ii. pp. 74, 75.
[2] In his later sermons, this was the common title by which he addressed the undergraduate members of the University. The earliest use of it appears to be in the sermon on ' Christ the Light of the World ' (vol. ii. p. 130), preached about 1864.

read the scientific books whenever he found that the faith
of believers was imperilled by them. He saw also most
clearly the necessity of warning eager but short-sighted
Christian apologists against the serious and constantly
recurring temptation to adjust, without due caution, the
interpretation of Scripture to the latest phase of scientific
teaching. He had been corresponding with Newman on
the subject in 1858.

REV. J. H. NEWMAN TO E. B. P.

April 11, 1858.

As to Geology, I am the worst person to consult possible, and so
I think is any co-religionist of mine—and for this reason—because so
little is determined about the Inspiration of Scripture, except in matters
of faith and morals. There is an old traditional feeling in favour of
many views, which may not in the event prove more tenable than that
of the sun going round the earth. I think that in Galileo's time
a shock was given to the Catholic mind which never can be repeated.
And then, too, I cannot help thinking a lesson was given to ecclesiastical authorities, which they will never forget, of not *seeming* to mix
what in fact they did *not* mix up, questions of theology and questions
of science. Then, on the other hand, I have a profound misgiving of
geological theories—though I cannot be sure that facts of considerable
importance are not proved. But in the whole scientific world men
seem going ahead most recklessly with their usurpation on the domain
of religion. Here is Dr. Brewster, I think, saying that, 'more worlds
than one is the hope of the Christian,' and as it seems to me, building
Christianity more or less upon astronomy. I seem to wish that Divine
and human science might each be suffered in place to take its own
line, the one not interfering with the other. Their circles scarcely
intersect each other.

Again a few days later Newman writes :—

REV. J. H. NEWMAN TO E. B. P.

April 21, 1858.

... I quite feel what you say about Buckland's 'Reliquiae.' It has
made me distrust every theory of Geology since : and I have used your
words, 'Why take the trouble to square Scripture with facts and
theories which will be all changed to-morrow, and we obliged to begin
over again?'

While preparing his Paper for the Norwich Church
Congress, Pusey had another opportunity of consulting

Newman when he met him at Hursley on September 12[1]. After this talk Newman still wrote anxiously on the subject, 'fearing lest neither people's minds nor the subjects themselves were ripe for discussion.' But Pusey knew how greatly people were distressed by the supposed contradictions between Geology and the Bible, and he thought it was a good time to make clear the distinction between what is of faith and what is not. ' People are uncomfortable about all these allegations of Lyall and others, and would be glad to have a way out of them consistently with the truth of Holy Scripture.' He felt that he could show that physical science could have nothing to say against the Bible.

Had Pusey cared for popularity, he would have been much flattered by his reception at the Church Congress at Norwich. From that large assembly of Church-people he received a welcome which was far more than the ordinary kindly greeting to those who are at the pains of addressing a meeting. Reiterated bursts of cheering were intended as the meet recognition of one who had suffered, on behalf of the Church, an amount of misunderstanding and calumny which falls to the lot of few. The Paper which he read on the occasion was of marked importance: if its positions are commonplaces in theological thought now, they were then far in advance of what was ordinarily held by either scientific or theological students. It was the product of a period in which he thought himself able to see the possible reconciliation of divergences which were widely regarded as permanent. Within the Church of England the attacks on the Faith seemed to be uniting ' High ' and ' Low ' Church. Pusey's ' Eirenicon,' with regard to the relation between the Church of England and the Church of Rome, was at that moment being issued from the press ; and this address was another and, in the event, a far more successful ' Eirenicon,' to reconcile the supposed antagonism between the Bible and Physical science. To appreciate Pusey's untiring labours, it must be remembered that

[1] This meeting is described at length in the next chapter.

this work in reply to 'Essays and Reviews' was being
written at the same time as the 'Eirenicon,' and that he
went up to the Norwich Congress whilst preparing for a
journey to France with a view of ascertaining the attitude of
some French Bishops towards his proposals for Reunion.

His Paper began with warnings against the over-hasty
adoption of any scientific theories, however closely they
might seem to fit the Biblical record, and also against the
fear of any scientific facts; at the same time he warns
students of the Bible against being 'too positive, in matters
not connected with the centre of Revelation, as to any given
interpretation of any insulated statement.' 'The right interpretation of God's Word will never be found in contradiction
with the right interpretation of His works.' But there may
be faults on either or both sides: either the theologian or
the physicist, or both, may misinterpret the facts of their
own science. 'It is uniformly not in the facts, but in the
theories founded thereon, that the alleged contradictions
lie.' This thought he illustrates at great length with regard
to the Scriptural statements and the scientific facts in connexion with the first chapter of Genesis, the account of the
Deluge, and the unity of the human race. He concludes
with a review of the past history of the relations between
Revelation and Science, and a statement of their right
attitude to each other.

'It belongs to the comprehensiveness of Revelation, as coming from
Him Who is Infinite, embracing and enveloping man in all his faculties,
incorporating itself in his history, traversing his paths, rolling in its
own orbit around God, but reflecting His light in turn on everything
of man, the least as well as the greatest, that it should seem liable, in
its long and intricate course, to impinge upon some other truth of
God or man. People have watched it, thought a collision inevitable,
expected its extinction; but like Jesus, it passed through the midst
unharmed. They were but nebulae, which seemed to oppose its way.
True! we cannot divide Holy Scripture or Christianity, polypus-
like, so that one part might be cut off, and the rest remain in the same
life as before. It is one whole; and as, in that beautiful system of our
nerves, one prick at an extremity runs through the whole and may
carry death, so it would be with the Gospel, if it were possible. But
we who know in Whom we have believed, know that it is not possible.

Attack after attack has fastened upon it, now here, now there, and people have looked on wondering, as they did at St. Paul at Melita, looking when he should have fallen down dead suddenly; but he had shaken off the beast into the fire and had got no harm. As in St. Paul's case, the poison might reach from one of those extreme points which Christianity puts forth even to its centre, if it had not a Divine life. But we, who are of it, know that it has an invulnerable life which cannot be reached, for it is upheld by God.

This, then, is our attitude toward any researches of any science; entire fearlessness as to the issue; awaiting that issue, undisturbed, whenever it shall unfold itself. . . .

Faith can afford this. For it has its own separate sphere, the home of its being. Physical science and faith are not commensurate. Faith relates to that which is supernatural; science, to things natural; faith *rests* upon what is supernatural; science, upon man's natural powers of observation, induction, combination, inference, deduction; faith has to do chiefly with the invisible; science, with this visible order of things. Science relates to causes and effects, the laws by which God upholds His material creation, or its past history. It is purely material. Faith relates to God, His Revelation, His Word. Faith has the certainty of a Divine gift; science has the certainty of human reasoning. Faith is one Divine, God-given, habit of mind. It is one and the same in the well-instructed peasant as in the most intellectual philosopher, perfect, solid, unshakeable. What really lies outside the peasant's faith, cannot really touch the faith of any, however intellectual. Faith lives above the clouds of human doubt, in the serene sunshine of the Eternal Light; and, contemplating Him, the Cause of all causes, the Truth of all which is true, the Life of all that is, is sure that there is a solution of any thing which seems for a time (if so be) insoluble. Lightning and storm gleam far below. For it rests secure in the bosom of its God.'

From different sides Pusey received the warmest thanks for his Paper. The feelings expressed by all are as briefly summed up as possible in the following short letter from the distinguished Linacre Professor of Physiology at Oxford, whose opinion Pusey valued highly :—

PROFESSOR ROLLESTON TO E. B. P.

Feb. 12, 1866.

I am very much obliged to you for your Norwich address. I wish all writing on the subject had been in the same spirit of caution and courage: and I hope it will be widely read, as it will prevent much mischief being done to the cause of Revelation, on the one side by its foes and on the other by its friends.

At the same Congress Pusey spoke at a meeting in favour of having all sittings in Church free and unappropriated. His words on that occasion explain the principle which led him, many years before, to make great sacrifices that he might give £5,000 anonymously to build churches in Bethnal Green, and, in the following summer, to spend the Long Vacation in caring for the cholera patients in the same neighbourhood.

' I have taken the greatest interest in this society on the ground that it is pre-eminently a Gospel society. It declares and maintains that we are all one in the Eyes of our God, and insists on the Church that her special heritage is the poor. I never can see a poor religious man without feeling the utmost reverence for him, and his patience, his whole character, his self-denial, his endurance, are to me the most stupendous proofs of the stupendous grace of God. I never see a religious poor man without expecting, by the mercy of God, to see him far above myself in heaven. I say this society is especially a Gospel society, because its object is the poor, and it requires only one word to ask you how much we are indebted to the poor. From Whom had we the Gospel? He Who gave it, He Who redeemed us, and He Who died for us, was a poor Man, so much so that ancient writers whenever they found the word "poor" in the Old Testament,—for example, " Blessed is the man who considereth the poor and needy"— they asked the question, "Who is this poor—Jesus?" Whom did He send out as His disciples?—the fisherman, the tent-maker, the tax-gatherer. Who converted the world but the poor? Century after century the Christians were simply the poor, and they conquered the conquerors of the world. One thing, however, I can say to you, because I can look further back than perhaps all but some two or three of you, and that is : that though there may be a "day of small things," still a great change has in the present century begun. When I was a boy myself, my lot was cast a good deal in the West of London, and I never saw there the face of a poor man. The first I saw was when I went to hear the most eloquent preacher of his day, Bishop Heber. I did not see him, but I saw what was far more blessed to me than that—a poor man standing in the midst of the congregation, with tears streaming from his eyes, as touched by the message which produced them. That must be some fifty years ago, and through all that time I have never forgotten the face of that poor man. . . . I am afraid it would be too true to say that the largest heathen city in the world is the city within a hundred miles of this place, because no heathen city in the whole world has anything like its population. . . . I may say my greatest interest in coming to this place is yourselves—and I wish to say,—and my name has been made a bye-word for things with which I am little concerned,—to tell you of the deep interest which, in a life now reaching towards the age of man, I have ever felt in the poor, and the deep interest I have in this society, because it restores the Church to be the mother of the poor, and restores to her her great, her noblest heritage, without which she would be as nothing, without which she would be disclaimed by her Lord—the poor [1].'

It will be seen that in all these various ways of Lectures, Sermons, *Levées*, and Papers, Pusey was endeavouring to make solid contributions to the defence of Christian doctrine. But his mind was naturally occupied at the same time with the old question of the constitution of the Final Court of Appeal for ecclesiastical cases. The decision of the Judicial Committee of the Privy Council in the two suits connected with 'Essays and Reviews,' recalled the attention of Churchmen to the constitution of that tribunal which had as a matter of fact acquired the right to declare the legal interpretation of the doctrinal Formularies of the English Church. The agitation against the Court that followed upon the Gorham case has already been described [2]: it was renewed with yet greater force in February, 1864, and with far greater hope of success. In 1850, the decision was practically on a point which separated the two great parties of the Church from one another: on the present occasion they were prepared to act in harmony. Immediately after the decision, Pusey opened a correspondence with Mr. Gladstone both about the Judgment itself and also about the constitution of the Court.

E. B. P. TO RIGHT HON. W. E. GLADSTONE, M.P.

Feb. 18, 1864.

As for the Judicial Committee, we have the highest Court in Ecclesiastical matters advocating a 'non-natural' sense being put on words, and acquitting Mr. Wilson by aid of such non-natural sense. On this I have written more at length in the *Record* of to-morrow, if they put it in. On this principle, a non-natural sense might be put on every doctrinal term, 'faith,' 'grace,' even 'God.' It seems to me an utterly unprincipled Judgment, which the judges would have reprobated in any Civil matter.

[1] From a Report of the Free and Open Church Conference, given in the *Norfolk Chronicle.*
[2] See vol. iii. chapters x and xi.

But what is to be done? It would be far better that all Courts should be abolished, and men left to their own consciences and Subscription, than that the law should be thus profaned to teach them to cheat their consciences. . . .

I hear that the Bishop of Oxford wished that the Bishops should be excluded from the Judicial Committee, so that it should be a merely Civil Court, without having any plea of having an Ecclesiastical sanction. I am not satisfied that it would be best. For if it is done at the wish of the Church, then it is the Church who wishes her doctrines to be defined by persons who never studied them and, I fear, too often do not believe them.

There might be more hope of justice if the Bishops were equal in number, but then this must be without possibility of packing them.

After the Gorham Case, one thousand Clergymen, members of Convocation memorialized that the Supreme Court of Appeal should be the Provincial Synod. This is the only Ecclesiastical Court of Appeal.

The truth might have more chance than it has now if all the Law-Lords sat, with or without an equal number of Bishops.

A change of the Court of Appeal would be good, even if it should do nothing more than prevent this flagitious Judgment being final. For the Judgment of this Court of Appeal would not be binding on a new Court.

I have not ceased to be hopeful, although I see it to be a struggle for life or death of the English Church. There is much more faith among the young men now than there was a few years ago, so that God the Holy Ghost has not forsaken us.

But it is a perilous crisis, and the principle adopted seems to be ' Part with those who believe most and retain those who believe least.' God be with you.

Our new Eccl. Hist. Prof. will be a great gain [1].

Mr. Gladstone was fully alive to all the difficulties of the case. He felt doubtful whether the main objection to the Judicial Committee lay in the fact that the Court had to deal with defendants as criminals, or in the fact that judges who were not trained theologians were set to try theological cases. He, however, preferred what was called the Bishop of Oxford's plan of improvement, by which the judges would be all laymen and therefore would not seem to commit the Church by any of their decisions.

A few days later Pusey received from Bishop Wilberforce,

---

[1] Referring to Dr. Shirley, who succeeded to the Chair of Ecclesiastical History, when Dr. Stanley became Dean of Westminster.

as has already been stated, a draft petition to the Queen, expressing a belief that the Judicial Committee is ill-adapted as a Court of advice to Her Majesty in appeal from the Ecclesiastical Courts, and praying that a Commission may be appointed to inquire into the matter. Pusey did not believe in the wisdom of a demand for a commission. In writing to Liddon he expressed his objections to the proposal.

E. B. P. TO REV. H. P. LIDDON.

Monday [Feb. 22, 1864.]

... The result would probably be, that we should have an unsatisfactory answer after a year, and that then people's energies would have relaxed. ... Then, of course, the Chancellor would not like the implied censure on his own Judgment, yet he must be a member of the Commission.

*The* radical evil of Law Judges is their bias to acquit the accused. In their own Courts, where they understand the law, this tends only to a rigid construction of evidence, which may be right. But in Theology, which they do not understand, it leads to a lax construction of the Formularies, which lessens on each occasion the sum of that doctrine, which the Clergy are required by law to believe.

After the Gorham Case, one thousand Clergy of our Convocation memorialized for the substitution of the Provincial Synod.

I am inclined now to wish that the Prayer should be, either that the Judicial Committee should be changed, or that the subject should be referred to Convocation if it is necessary that the Queen should give leave for any measure being devised. ...

But as a preliminary step Pusey thought it good to get a legal Opinion on the exact force of the Judgment which had just been pronounced. He submitted a Case to Sir Roundell Palmer and Sir Hugh Cairns, asking fifteen questions as to the meaning of the Judgment. He desired to know how far the Court gave its sanction to certain conclusions which were certainly contrary to the faith, and which seemed logically to result from the words of the decision. After waiting three months the following brief Opinion was the only answer :—

'We are of opinion that the Judgments of the Privy Council in the recent cases of Dr. Williams and Mr. Wilson, do not, by necessary implication, or otherwise, furnish the means of determining in the abstract any of the legal questions raised by the present case.

'We understand these Judgments merely as deciding that, in those particular cases, there was no offence against the law pleaded or proved, unless the exact propositions stated by the Lord Chancellor could be deemed to be embodied in the formal and dogmatic teaching of the Church of England, so as to be rigorously binding upon every clergyman : which they were held not to be.  But it would be most unsafe, and, in fact, impossible, to attempt to derive from those decisions, any rule for the determination of other hypothetical cases, each of which (if it should ever assume a practical form) must depend upon its own circumstances.'

To this the following postscript was added in consequence of the vagueness of the expression 'exact propositions.'

'We understand the Lord Chancellor to have, in substance, founded his Judgments upon a negative answer to the inquiry whether every Clergyman of the Church of England was strictly bound to affirm the following propositions :—

1. That every part of every book of Holy Scripture was written under the inspiration of the Holy Spirit, and is the Word of God.

2. That it is impious or heretical to entertain or express a hope, that even the ultimate pardon of the wicked, who are condemned in the day of Judgment, may be consistent with the will of Almighty God.'

Such an Opinion limited indeed the harm that the Judgment might effect; but still Pusey felt it intolerable that a decision on doctrine, even in such vague terms, should issue from a Court of Final Appeal not purely spiritual. To his mind the contention that in a suit with criminal consequences no other decision could be expected, provided only one further reason for agitating for a change.  He wrote for Keble's advice in the matter.

E. B. P. to Rev. J. Keble.

June, 1864.

What do you think of having a society for agitating the change of the Final Court of Appeal, or joining any existing society on condition that they would do so? . . . I am afraid that the Low Church would leave us on any definite plan which would put more power into the hands of the Bishops; and the High Church, as you say, are so strangely apathetic. . . .

We have to take care not to show misgiving about the Church of England, else people will go off like a landslip.

But at this moment Pusey's health broke down under
the strain of his varied work. The Judgment about
'Essays and Reviews,' the excitement and correspondence
about the Declaration, the labour of bringing out the
Lectures on Daniel, the many anxieties as to the Greek
Professorship, and constant work in connexion with the
business of the University were too great a strain even
for him. It seemed for the time that his health was
seriously injured, and his doctor ordered him to leave
Oxford. He found a retreat at Ascot Priory, which, as will
be seen, he often revisited, and where the invigorating air of
the pine woods always refreshed him. 'I find,' he told
Keble afterwards, 'the smell of the pines refreshing to the
brain. One does not find out until one is poorly, how that
common gift of smell refreshes the brain, please God.'

It was in this weak state of health that he sent to the
Press, with a strongly worded Preface, the Opinion which
Sir Roundell Palmer and Sir Hugh Cairns had given
about the bearing of the recent Judgment. This Preface
he sent in proof to Keble, explaining that he 'wrote it
on the idea that unless one said strong things about the
unprincipled character of this decision, and of any future
probable decision, one might just as well write nothing at
all.' 'I went,' he explains half humorously in another letter
in which he adopts some of Keble's modifications of his
language, 'as near to incurring the penalties of libel and
treason as I thought I might without sin.' His letters show
very evidently the overstrain of the time : he is desponding
and lonely. This feeling of depression was no doubt
increased by Liddon's long illness, on whom at that time
he largely depended for keeping himself in touch with the
younger High Churchmen.

In the early days of September, 1864, he issued this
pamphlet under the title of ' Case as to the Legal force of the
Judgment of the Privy Council, *in re* Fendall *v.* Wilson ;
with the Opinion of the Attorney-General and Sir Hugh
Cairns, and a Preface to those who love God and His
Truth.' The Preface certainly justifies Pusey's account of

it, as containing severe expressions. Its aim is to show
the diversity of interpretations that were given to the
Judgment. For very varying reasons Roman Catholics,
Broad Churchmen, and others were triumphing over the
supposed loosening of doctrinal bonds in the Church of
England, while others, who feared the consequence of the
Judgment, were correspondingly depressed. But this
legal Opinion, Pusey contended, had removed the causes
alike of triumph and of fear. The Attorney-General and
Sir Hugh Cairns had explained that the Judgment neither
denied the Inspiration of Scripture nor the belief in Eternal
Punishment; it only stated exactly what it stated. Nothing
must be read into it, although its first aspect was so threatening. Pusey pointed out that there was no hope of ever
getting a better Judgment, because if these cases must be
criminal the bias of the Court would be of necessity in
favour of the accused. The Court had no training
in the theological meaning of the words which it was
called upon to interpret, and, legally, the words of the
Judgment, which seemed to convey so much, admitted
only the minimum of meaning of which they were capable;
at the same time the principles of interpretation on which
the Judgment was based were, he thought, beyond words
deplorable. The Judicial Committee had agreed, as he
understood, to take words in a non-natural sense, and
to give any possible meaning to a word which was not
clearly interpreted in the Formularies. It was intolerable,
so Pusey argued, that the truth should thus be endangered;
such policy overlooked the value of the Church as securing
the stability of the State; and would probably rend the
Church in twain. The present idol of the Church physicians
seemed to be to sacrifice everything to comprehensiveness,
and to let the Church comprehend the nation by becoming
an aggregate of all the unsanctified opinions of the world,
'a Pantheon of all its idols.' The principles enunciated
by the Lord Chancellor would make Articles, Creeds,
Prayers, Scripture a mere superficial mirror in which any
one, instead of seeing the truth of God, was to see only the

reflection of his own mind. It was a time, Pusey claimed, when every minister and member of the Church, who had any love for his Redeemer, or for the Word of God, or for the Truth as it is in Jesus, should unite as one man to cast off this Anti-Christian tyranny of the State.

He concluded with a few practical suggestions to keep alive this desirable object in men's minds.

'Pledges have been the fashion; and a general election is at no great distance. Let Churchmen, on the principle of the Anti-Corn-Law League, league themselves for "the protection of the faith." "The Church is in danger," has been, and will again be, a strong rallying-cry. And now the peril is not of some miserable temporal endowment, but of men's souls. Let men league together to support no candidate for Parliament who will not pledge himself to do what in him lies to reform a Court which has in principle declared God's Word not to be His Word, and Eternity not to be Eternity. And let them support persons, of whatever politics, who will so pledge themselves. Let men bind themselves not to give over, but to continue besieging the House of Parliament by their petitions, and beseeching Almighty God in their prayers, until they shall obtain some security against this State-protection of unbelief. Better be members of the poorest Church in Christendom, which can repel "the wolves which spare not the flock," than of the richest, in which the State forces us to accept as her ministers those whom our Lord calls "ravening wolves." Withal see we to it, that we pray God earnestly day by day to stem this flood of ungodliness, and to convert those who are now, alas! enemies of the faith and of God.'

These were strong words; but Keble as well as Pusey felt that they were very urgently needed. The troubles of the times, the apparent concession to unbelief, and the taunts of Roman Catholics, rendered calmness almost impossible. Manning and the *Westminster Review* united to give the same interpretation of the Judgment: and the fear of secessions to Rome and the threatening dominance of Liberalism in the Church of England caused Keble to give his full approval to Pusey's vehement language. He wished that a paper of his own should be circulated with it, and desired that the two papers should be said to stand to each other pretty much as letters which have crossed.

'But be sure,' writes Keble, 'I will try to be a sort of armour-bearer or trumpeter for you in the fight which, as you say, is too plainly coming. . . . I expect that the *safe* party, who will shake their heads at us, will be more numerous than any other. God grant they may not ruin us.'

The correspondence that passed at that time between them betrays the strength of the feeling that moved them both ; they were entirely at one on this as well as other questions. Whenever he heard any one speaking disparagingly of Pusey's actions, Keble would say emphatically, ' Remember I am a " Puseyite " of the very deepest dye.'

The *Times* attacked Pusey's Preface as 'inflammatory' and his proposals as 'threatening.' Keble takes this opportunity of joining openly with Pusey. In the *Times* of September 22 he completely identifies himself with him in his present anxieties, and sets forth the worthlessness of the assumptions which were lulling a number of Churchmen into a false security with regard to the principles of the Judgment. In the following passage, Keble forcibly exposes the dangers involved in silent acquiescence.

Rev. J. Keble to the Editor of the 'Times.'

Sept. 20 [1864].

1. It is assumed that the wrong done by the sentence, be it great or small, is confined to Dr. Williams' and Mr. Wilson's parishes, and that others, therefore, need not be concerned ; which, to those who count faith in the Bible and in eternity to be more than a matter of life and death, is as if the guides of public opinion were to say, ' It is only Mr. Briggs and his friends who are damaged ; why such an outcry about bringing his murderer to justice ? '

2. Men talk as if the practical effect of the Judgment would be limited to that special form of words which the two defendants respectively used ; as if there could be the smallest doubt what a learned counsel's reply will be when some Bishop shall hereafter ask whether he may safely refuse institution to any one simply holding and teaching the uncertainty of Eternal Punishment, or denying this or that portion of Canonical Scripture, acknowledged genuine, to be the Word of God ?

3. It is assumed that the disparagement attaches only to those two doctrines, as if our Creed were not a structure, no part of which will bear displacing ; as if all evidence properly Christian did not fade or vanish on the doubt or denial of Inspiration and all sanctions properly Christian on the doubt or denial of Eternity.

4. It is assumed that the interpretation of the legal conditions

upon which benefices are held cannot possibly involve a question of orthodoxy.

5. It is assumed that our objection is to the substance only of certain decisions and not, as the truth is, to the composition also of the Court itself, and to some of the rules or principles by which it is apparently bound, as, for example, that a theological word is not to be taken in its known theological sense, unless that sense be laid down in terminis in the Formularies themselves; and again, that when the judges differ, the minority should be denied permission to explain its dissent, which is contrary, I believe, to the practice of her Majesty's civil courts.

6. It is assumed that (since the Court avowedly takes no cognizance of doctrine) we are to be content to do without any doctrinal court at all.

7. After we have been lulled by the first five assumptions into a belief that our dogmatical position is not affected by the Judgment, it is assumed that we had better remain quiet, because the Judgment is but a step in an inevitable process which will rid us of dogma altogether.

8. It is assumed that the disadvantage of moving in this affair is so great and apparent as at once to overweigh the sad and palpable scandal which our seeming apathy is causing all over Christendom, and which is sure to be felt more and more both by the friends and enemies of the Church.

Pusey thanked him warmly for his letter, which he could not help contrasting with his own, ' Yours so calm, mine so fiery.' But Keble replied, ' I have been a little worrying myself that I did not more distinctly express sympathy with your *wildness* in my *tame prose*. But there will be opportunities.'

While it was not difficult to agree in protesting against the Judicial Committee, the constitution of the Court that should be proposed in its place was, of course, a matter on which it was far more difficult to reach a decision.

E. B. P. TO REV. J. KEBLE.

Sept. 25, 1864.

I hope that the Bishops of Salisbury and Oxford will not be satisfied with the mere striking out of the ecclesiastical element of the Court. For whatever is done would be done at the mere instigation of the Church; it is one thing to be under a bad government, and then, being under one, to desire that it should be made worse in order that one might say that one had nothing to do with it. It might have been better to be under a mere civil court than under the pseudo-ecclesiastical court on the ground that we, the Church, had nothing to do with the establishment of a civil court; but if we ask that the pseudo-ecclesiastical court be turned into a mere civil court, we have to do with it. We have seen that the tendency of the Law Lords is to lay open all doctrine. To acknowledge the supreme court and to ask that it should consist exclusively of the Law Lords, would be to ask that they alone should have supreme control of all doctrinal causes, and so lay open anything and everything they please. It would be a sort of vote of confidence in them. The State is quite satisfied with the present constitution of the Court. If it is amended, it will be amended to please the Church. But we cannot be the parties to obtain the alteration and then turn round and say we have nothing to do with it. We should be shutting our own eyes. Our Bishops must be cognizant of what passed through Parliament.

I sent to Liddon for the Bishop of Salisbury a sketch of a court such as we have often talked of, in which the facts should be determined by Law Lords, but any interpretation of the Formularies should be by the Spirituality.

At the same time Pusey was in correspondence with Mr. Justice Coleridge who had invited him to suggest some better alternative for the Final Court; and his attention had been called to the extreme difficulty of devising any tribunal which, while it possessed a theological knowledge sufficient to investigate the meaning of doctrinal statements, had also sufficient legal experience to decide upon the evidence. A few days later, a meeting of the chief movers in this matter was held at Rev. W. Upton Richards' house, 158, Albany Street, to concert some plan of action. Pusey asked Liddon to go to this meeting with him: 'I hope you will be there; you are quite old enough to be an Arch-conspirator.' It was seemingly the first occasion on which Liddon was thus invited to the inner and informal councils of those who were generally recognized as advising the actions of Churchmen in such matters. He was unable to go: but Pusey met there Keble, Lord Richard Cavendish, George Williams and others. It was decided to form an Association for the Reform of the Final Court of Appeal, and to draw up a Paper indicating the aims which Churchmen might put before them without committing themselves as yet to any one scheme. But it was found very difficult to work, and to enlist other workers, except on more definite lines. The various schemes are all referred to in the following letter :—

E. B. P. TO REV. J. KEBLE.

Oct., 1864.

Do you know whether the Bishops of Salisbury and Oxford have come to any understanding about the Court of Appeal ? I am come not to mind much what the Court is, so that it is not the present. A change of the Final Court of Appeal not only annuls the legal form (whatever it is) of that opinion, but it is a censure on the non-natural interpretation of that Court in the late case.

Of the plans, that of the Bishop of Salisbury, to refer any explanation of doctrine to the Upper House of Convocation, is the plan of most faith, for their wrong decision (synodically) would go far to commit the Church to heresy. Indeed, I suppose that the minority would in such case have to renounce communion with the heterodox majority.

The Bishop of Salisbury's plan would be following the old authorities at least as to the decision of doctrine. The Bishop of Oxford's would not be unsafe if some six or eight sees were to be named, e.g. the two Archbishops, Bishops of London, Durham, Winchester, and the three senior bishops.

I do not know that even the plan of leaving it with the Judicial Committee, enlarged, would matter, so that it be not left under the influence of the Lord Chancellor, and they be restricted to saying ' non-proven ' *without giving any theological reasons.*

Do you think that, in the case of a Conservative Government, —— would join with others in telling Lord Derby that the support which they would give him would depend upon his not nominating Neologians to high ecclesiastical preferment ?

At the Bristol Church Congress in the same month Pusey and Keble agreed to open the subject during the discussion on Church Synods, on the afternoon of Tuesday, October 11. Both of them were now more decided in favour of the Episcopal Synod as the right Court for doctrinal trials, even if the facts of the case should be submitted to a civil Court. Keble argued at Bristol that *a priori* the present Court would have been thought excellent in that it combined both the civil and the ecclesiastical element, but practically it had not turned out so. As a matter of fact, he maintained, it was an infringement of the Bishops' rights. But still his statements were not clear enough to get general support for his newly

formed Association; he knew well the price that they
would have to pay for more definite proposals. ' In nearly
all quarters,' he writes on October 15, 'the same thing is
said, " Be more distinct," and when we are more distinct
in our own senses we shall find all abounding in *their*
several senses also.' At another meeting of the Committee
of the Association on November 23, Archdeacon Denison
endeavoured to make the Association more definite, and
carried by a majority the adoption of the formula 'No
Bishops in the Court of Appeal.' This was passed against
the wish of Pusey and Keble, and it also met with the
disapproval of Mr. Gladstone, and was subsequently
withdrawn.

E. B. P. TO RIGHT HON. W. E. GLADSTONE, M.P.

Feb. 21, 1865.

. . . Our Court of Appeal Amendment Association has gone back in
part to what I always wished it to be, an Association to obtain redress
of the grievance, without prescribing the way in which it should be
redressed, which belongs to the Legislature or to Convocation, as far
as it advises the Legislature, not to us. I could accept much which
I could not ask for. I care not how many experiments are tried and
fail, until we come to something bearable at last. I only deeply care
about not acquiescing in a known and tried evil.

When Convocation met in February, 1865, the reform of
the Court of Appeal was brought forward by the Bishop
of Oxford, who had been in correspondence with Mr. Gladstone about it for four years. It was frequently debated in
both Houses; evidently so important a question did not
admit of being hastily settled. Those who were dissatisfied
with the action of the present Court were numerous enough;
but no one could see a remedy. It seemed more reasonable
that statesmen should formulate the practical remedy for
grievances under which the Established Church was
suffering in an intensified degree in consequence of recent
legislation. In this state of opinion Pusey could only hope,
as he tells Bishop Wilberforce, that a few more decisions of
the Lord Chancellor might increase the present distrust, so
as to make reform absolutely imperative.

# CHAPTER IV.

1865.

IN the Preface to the 'Case as to the Legal Force of the
Judgment of the Privy Council *in re* Fendall *v.* Wilson,'
Pusey had described the attitude of the Roman Catholics
towards this decision in the following terms: 'While
I know that a very earnest body of Roman Catholics
rejoice in all the workings of God the Holy Ghost in the
Church of England (whatever they think of her), and are
saddened in what weakens her who is, in God's hands,
the great bulwark[1] against infidelity in this land, others

---

[1] This expression was taken from
a private letter from 'one of the
deepest thinkers and observers' in the
Roman Church ('Eirenicon,' Part I,
p. 7). Its likeness to a well-known
passage in Newman's 'Apologia,' App.
p. 27 (1st ed.), in which the Church of
England is spoken of as 'a serviceable
breakwater against errors more fundamental that its own,' gave rise to a
widespread impression among Roman
Catholics that Pusey was quoting
Newman. In fact, in a first review
of the 'Eirenicon,' in the *Weekly*
*Register*, the words are attributed to
him. Newman, who himself thought
the expression must have come from
De Maistre, at once disclaimed the
authorship in a letter to the editor of
the *Weekly Register*, dated Nov. 19,
1865; he did the same also at length in
his 'Letter to the Rev. E. B. Pusey, D.D.,
on his recent Eirenicon' (London,
1866), pp. 11-13. Strange as it
may appear, Pusey with characteristic
sentiment had never read the part of
the 'Apologia' in which the words
occur: 'I could not go through the

seemed to be in an ecstasy of triumph at this victory of Satan.'

There were no doubt at that time serious internal differences which marred the apparent harmony of the Roman Catholic Communion in England ; whether, however, their opinions with regard to the Church of England exactly corresponded with Pusey's description may be doubted.   Still, it was inevitable that the attention of Roman Catholics should be directed to this open allusion to their diverging judgments.   Hence, a few weeks after the appearance of this pamphlet, Pusey received a friendly communication from Dr. Manning intimating the early appearance of a public reply to it.

REV. H. E. MANNING TO E. B. P.

Bayswater, Nov. 6, 1864.

MY DEAR FRIEND,

In a few days Longman will send you a copy of a Pamphlet which I have addressed to you.

It contains, I fear, many things in which I cannot hope for your assent ; but nothing, I trust, which can give you personally any pain. It cost me no effort to write to you, and of you, with respect and affection, in which, during all these years, I have never varied towards you.

We live in times when those who count God's Truth more precious than all the world, ought, for that Truth's sake, to speak out charitably but intelligibly.   You will not find, I trust, any controversial spirit in what I have written.   I do not believe in it : and if I knew how to say what I believe without paining those who do not believe as I do, I would never use other words.

I hope you and your family are well in health.   It is so long since I have heard of them, that I do not know how to speak or ask about them.

Believe me, always,<br>My dear friend,<br>Yours affectionately,<br>H. E. MANNING.

parting over again ; so, by force of the pain, I stopped short, and whatever you said, I have not seen it ' (P. to N. Nov. 18, 1865). But for twelve months this mistake had no little influence on the tone and drift of the controversy that ensued, especially as it was commonly said that Manning was included among those who were in an 'ecstasy of triumph.' (See Manning's 'Letter to the Rev. E. B. Pusey, D.D.,' pp. 6, 43.)

Manning's Pamphlet [1] claimed to be a sketch of the true Roman Catholic view of the Church of England and its troubles. The writer denied that he belonged to either of the two classes which Pusey had mentioned; rather, according to the faith he had received, he regarded the Church of England as under the influence of the Holy Spirit, not merely like the whole human race, but more especially because, like the Dissenting bodies, it was made up in the main of baptized people who were, to a very great extent through no fault of their own, outside the true Church. In the English Church, he said, the Holy Spirit gives grace to individuals, as He did before the Church was founded; but in saying this, no Roman Catholic would affirm that the English Church had 'the character of a Church.' Manning allowed that any authoritative denial of any portion of the 'fragmentary truths,' which he recognized as still existing in the Church of England, was to be deplored; although Roman Catholics watched with satisfaction every change, social and political, which weakened the hold of the English Church on the country (p. 29). Far from being any bulwark against infidelity, the Church of England had floated, he maintained, with the flood of unbelief, and was itself a source of unbelief because of the truths which it rejected.

The whole tone of the pamphlet was distinctly polemical; and in spite of Newman's question, 'Why should you answer him?' Pusey reluctantly thought it necessary to reply. He commenced his answer in the form of a Letter to Keble, defending the English Church against Manning's account of it; but while he was wearily arguing over the old ground to show that the Thirty-nine Articles diverged in language rather than in meaning from the decrees of the Council of Trent, he suddenly changed his plan. He determined to drop entirely the tone of an apology, and to make his answer a plea for re-union

---

[1] 'The Workings of the Holy Spirit in the Church of England,' a Letter to the Rev. E. B. Pusey, D.D., by Henry Edward Manning, D.D. (London, Longman, 1864).

between the Church of England and the Church of Rome [1]. He explained his reasons for this change in a letter to Newman about twelve months later when the book had been for some weeks in circulation.

E. B. P. TO REV. J. H. NEWMAN.

Nov. 6, 1865.

I see that my Letter has two aspects. First and originally it was a defence. I know not whether you ever saw Archbishop Manning's Letter [2] to myself. It denied us everything, except what in a greater degree Dissenters had too—I mean everything living and substantial and operative, except as far as God does not deny grace to any. I answered it unwillingly, but it was put upon me, and I did not like to refuse, the less because Manning (as he then was) had singled me out. My plan, in the Articles which lay down doctrine, was simple enough. It was to say that there was divergence of language (where there was) and not, I believed, of meaning. Then came Art. xxii, and the difficult class of subjects mentioned in it. In writing this, the thought came to me of making it an Eirenicon. I meant by this to point out or suggest what we could accept, if it could be made quite clear that, in accepting this, we did not accept what lay beyond it. I hoped that the Roman Church might agree to lay down that it required thus much as matter of faith, and not more. Such an authoritative explanation would be something wholly different from unauthoritative explanations, such as those of Milner. But in order to explain what we want, we ought to explain why we want it. It would be an unmeaning thing to ask that it should be defined, that nothing more was of faith touching the Invocation of Saints than what is given in the Council of Trent, as explained by Milner, without saying why we desire this. We should be asked, naturally, 'Why do you want us to make any new decrees? The Church does not make decrees on matters of faith, without a reason; what reason have you to give for what you ask?' Now if, as I believe, the system in regard to the Blessed Virgin is the chief hindrance to reunion, and if a declaration by authority that something which does not necessarily involve this (as the Council of Trent with Milner's explanation) is alone of faith, would remove that chief hindrance to reunion, then an intelligible ground is given for the request.

As soon as the work of the October term of 1864

---

[1] No notice is taken here of the work of the A.P.U.C., which had been founded in 1857, and which was at this time addressing the authorities at Rome on the subject. (See 'Life of Cardinal Manning,' ii. p. 279 sqq.)

Pusey's work was completely independent of this Association.

[2] Since writing the Letter Dr. Manning had been made Archbishop of Westminster in succession to Cardinal Wiseman.

was over, he applied himself to this task of replying to Manning.

E. B. P. TO REV. J. H. NEWMAN.

Christmas Eve, 1864.

. . . I am writing an answer to Dr. Manning, yet one which I hope that you will not much dislike, considering that I am where I am. I have long felt that although there are some things, e. g. Indulgences, which I cannot in the least understand, our difficulties are mostly in the practical system rather than in the *letter* of the Council of Trent. If Rome could authenticate all which she allows individuals to say in explanation—I mean, if a Council of the Roman Church would say, 'Such and such things are *not de fide*,' as well as what is *de fide*—the greatest difficulty in the way of the reunion of the two churches would, I think, be gone. The Council of Trent seems to me to have drawn the line as to the minimum which is to be believed: the English Articles seem to me (speaking generally), especially Art. xxii, to condemn a maximum, as not being to be believed. So we are at cross-purposes. Only, while there is no explanation on the Roman side, what is the practical system of the Roman Church everywhere would become the practical system here, in case of the reunion of the Churches. My letter is, in fact, a reawakening of Tract XC, which, though its principles have sunk deep, is not much known by the rising generation.

Newman in reply pointed out that in his opinion Pusey's expectation of a declaration on the part of the Roman Church as to what is not *de fide* was unreasonable, as limiting the future guidance of the Church in matters as yet undefined.

REV. J. H. NEWMAN TO E. B. P.

Jan. 4, 1865.

. . . You indeed want the Church to decide what is *de fide* and what is not; but, *pace tuâ*, this seems unreasonable. It is to determine the work of all Councils till the end of time. How, e. g. was it to be expected that Perrone's *doctrine of Intention* (as opposed to that of Catharinus) should be *explicitly* declared by *St. Paul* to be *not de fide?* No one on earth can draw the line between what is *de fide* and what is not, for it would be prophesying of questions which have [not] yet turned up. All we can say is that *so much* actually *is de fide*; and then allow a large margin of doctrine, which we accept as *de fide* implicitly, so far forth as God by His Church shall make it known. All one can say is that, till God illuminates the Church on a point, the children of the Church are obliged, and so are at liberty, to go by their best judgment either way; e. g. St. John Damascene (?) may speak of the Holy Ghost as proceeding only from the Father, till the fuller truth

H 2

is made known through the Divinely appointed channels of teaching. It seems to me unreasonable then to ask for more than *liberty* to hold what is (though not defined) contrary to the *general* belief of the faithful. You are not bound to believe that the Pope out of General Council is infallible, but I don't see how you can exact from us a dogmatic definition that it is not a point *de fide*.

Pusey had hoped that more was possible than Newman would allow. He had hoped that the Roman Church as a body might be willing to decree what individual Roman writers had frequently and readily admitted.

E. B. P. TO REV. J. H. NEWMAN.

Christ Church, Oxford [Jan. 5, 1865].

I certainly did think that in a subject which had long been before the Church, as Purgatory, the Cultus of the Blessed Virgin, Indulgences, she might decide what is not *de fide* as well as what is. Of course one must always trust God for the future. But, as you know, the practical difficulty of the Church of England is much more as to things not defined to be *de fide* than as to the letter of the Council of Trent. But then, supposing the Church of England to be willing to accept the Council of Trent *provided* the acceptance of it involved no more than its words go to, how would she escape accepting all the rest, against which the chief objection lies? I mean, supposing the Council of Trent could be authoritatively so explained, as Du Pin did to Wake, how could she avoid having the whole system contained in the 'Glories of Mary' made her system? For by virtue of the authority ascribed to the Pope (although this, I suppose, is no where settled as *de fide*), he would appoint Bishops and they ordain Clergy, who would teach it. And so the distinction between what is *de fide* and what is not would come to nothing. I cannot imagine being in the Church of Rome and then criticizing or not receiving anything proposed to me. I cannot imagine how any faith could stand it.

This correspondence revealed a serious divergence between Pusey and Newman as to what could be done. While no doubt explanations as to the limits of dogmatic teaching in the Church of Rome might tend towards reconciliation, the power of unlimited future definition which Newman acknowledged to lie in the Church would render such negative explanation valueless for any formal action such as Pusey contemplated.

Pusey's line of apology naturally would take two directions. He would, in the first place, restate the real doctrine of the Church of England, somewhat in the manner of Tract XC, and then with a view of emphasizing his demand for the rejection of all that was not *de fide*, he would proceed to point out how largely the popular Romanism differed from the authorized dogmatic standards. In carrying out the former part of his task, he would inevitably be using many of the arguments of Tract XC; and just at that moment Newman sent him a letter from a correspondent who asked permission to reprint that Tract. ' I don't wish,' adds Newman, ' to give him the leave that he asks. Can you give me your opinion?' The following was Pusey's reply :—

E. B. P. TO REV. J. H. NEWMAN.

[Dec. 29, 1864.]

If Tract XC is reprinted at all, I should like to reprint it ; and it might suit well to reprint it now that I am anew reawakening people's minds to it. I had forgotten that it was out of print. I should like to reprint it. You know that I am in the odd position of not being responsible to any one Bishop; but besides, times are so changed that none of our Bishops would feel called upon to interfere now. They are content to leave things to God's providence, as I so wished them to do twenty years ago.

He explained the circumstances in which he wrote more fully to Mr. Copeland, who was himself engaged in preparing a history of the Oxford Movement.

E. B. P. TO REV. W. J. COPELAND.

Christ Church [Jan. 17, 1865].

What we want at Oxford is to be left to ourselves. The extreme Rationalists are doing their worst. They say, ' If you believe this and that, you must believe *that* and *that*.' In other words, ' If you are Christians, you must be Catholics'; so they are giving us a good crop of able young men, i. e. God overrules their unbelief to make these consistent in faith. There is rest at present from any anti-Roman or anti-Tractarian controversy, which the presence of a R. C. College or Oratory at Oxford would be sure to awaken.

Whether my Letter to J. K. in answer to Manning will reawaken that controversy, I know not. The Low Church know now that they want us ; but whether that will overcome their horror of ' Popish errors,' I know not. However, I am giving hints of terms of reunion of 'Ανατολικὴ Δυτικὴ 'Ημετέρα. I think that I shall send it you to look at before it is published. The beginning is only the old story which we have told so often :—Tract XC over again, which made me ask dearest N. to let me republish Tract XC.

Newman gave Pusey leave to publish the Tract when he pleased, and Pusey sent it and Keble's 'Letter to the Hon. Mr. Justice Coleridge on Catholic subscription to the Thirty-nine Articles' at once to the Press, while he was writing an historical preface to be prefixed to both.

E. B. P. TO REV. W. J. COPELAND.

[Plymouth, Jan. 25, 1865.]

Tract XC and J. K.'s defence are in the Press. . . . I am writing a Preface, the object of which is to account for people's so mis-understanding Tract XC. It runs into history; but will not interfere with yours, because I do not use any MS. documents, nor go into detail. The only points I want to make out are the promptness of dearest N.'s explanation, and of the condemnation by the Heads. . . . I mean to say, that had the four Tutors or the Heads waited for an explanation of the Tract, they could not have acted as they did, whatever else they might have done. I want to rehabilitate Tract XC, because an exposition of this sort, as being true, is essential to our position, and yet the obloquy on Tract XC is a grave scandal to our principles. Dearest N. has rehabilitated himself as honest ; I want to show that the Judgment was precipitate.

Copeland helped Pusey greatly in the historical Preface.

E. B. P. TO REV. W. J. COPELAND.

Christ Church, Oxford [Jan. 30, 1865].

What a mass of facts you have, of which I know nothing ! I shall be so glad to see your History. What I am doing is very simple. I want to show why Tract XC was misunderstood at the time. . . . It is like an old world, long hid by a cloud, and the cloud parting. . . .

As Tract XC was the scapegoat, I am satisfied that that interpretation of the Articles will not be thoroughly cleared till the mud is washed clean off from Tract XC. People look with suspicion upon it, as on a thing which has been everywhere spoken against.

Copeland pointed out the difficulties which surrounded the historical account of the Tract, and reminded him of the correspondence between Newman and Maurice on the subject two years before.

REV. W. J. COPELAND TO E. B. P.

Farnham, Feb. 5, 1865.

Great care and accuracy indeed will be needed in touching the old *vexata quaestio*, now that more than ever K.'s lines are realized, all

> 'Round about the battle lowers
> And mines are hid beneath our towers.'

We rustics often say about this time of year 'Rooks smell gunpowder,' so I hope do you, especially as *incedis per ignes*, and we may all be shaken out of bed some fine morning, as by the Erith explosions!

But the historical Preface to Tract XC needed more time for preparation than the reply to Manning allowed him. It was therefore put aside to await an opportunity of more leisure. But at this time Pusey was able to do Newman a favour by means of which he relieved himself also from a serious anxiety about the proposal to build a Roman Catholic College at Oxford.

During the year 1864 Newman had purchased the site of the old Oxford Workhouse, a valuable plot of ground of about eight acres, and report said that a handsome Roman church was to be built there. Pusey wrote in great distress to Copeland as to one who saw more of Newman than he did himself, and pointed out the consequence of this plan, if it was carried out.

E. B. P. TO REV. W. J. COPELAND.

Christ Church, Oxford [November 6, 1864].

... From the R. C. point of view, I have marvelled at the forbearance, that something of this kind was not done before. It is, of course, a declaration of war against the High Church party. For there are next to no Roman Catholics here. It can only be directed to win our young men. If the annihilation of the English Church is to be [the] stepping-stone for Rome to recover England, this would be tangible. It would be Monsignor Manning's policy. *Now* we are happily without any controversy except with the unbelievers. The Evangelicals somehow never took root here. The antagonism to the Tractarians has ceased, because men see that we are fighting against the common foe. Controversy against 'Popery' as [well as] Tractarianism is over. But a R. C. establishment (of whatever nature, for I know not what is intended) would revive all the Ultra-Protestant antagonism, necessarily. For if they are on the aggressive, people must take the defensive, and will probably take the offensive also.

Our people will be sickened as you were; and so Oxford would be
again left to those who have no sympathy with the R. C.s, and who will
be forced into antagonism with them. A High Church body there
always will be, while the Prayer Book remains: but, of course, whatever makes Ultra-Protestantism rampant and weakens the High
Church emperils the Prayer Book. I believe that, all over the
country, the High Church is stronger than even in those outwardly
flourishing days, but I dread the confusion into which Oxford would
be thrown. The 'Liberals,' those of the laymen who believe nothing,
are triumphing already at the prospect. They find themselves pressed
by us, and so are glad of the diversion.

As you still talk familiarly over these things with dearest N[ewman],
I wish you would talk over this side of the question with him.

A fortnight later Newman writes to explain his intentions. Young Roman Catholics were beginning to go to
Oxford; the land was offered to him, and his Bishop put
the Oxford mission into his hands. He intended to do his
best to found an Oratory at Oxford, as at Birmingham,
though he did not intend to come himself. He had no
plans, but promised that he would not be a party to any
measures different from those which would flow from the
principles of the 'Apologia.'

In reply, Pusey repeated all the fears that he had
expressed to Copeland; and Newman explained to him
that his 'fellow-religionists' were in a great fright about
the admission of their sons to Oxford, and the establishment of the Oratory in Oxford was a compromise between
forbidding Roman Catholic students to go to Oxford and
establishing a college for them. And as regards the fears
of harm to the English Church from his occasional presence
in Oxford, Newman adds: 'I perfectly understand that
there are persons who would think that my coming (ever
so little) to Oxford would tend (so far forth) to weaken the
dogmatic teaching of the Church of England; but I should
not agree with them.'

When he heard that the University had been intending
to buy the ground which he had secured, Newman offered,
through Pusey, to sell to the University all but two acres,
which would suffice for his own purpose. But a meeting
of Roman Catholic Bishops on December 13 came to such

an unsatisfactory decision that Newman offered to sell the whole plot of ground to the University—an offer which was accepted by the Convocation of the University on February 9, 1865.

Meanwhile Pusey continued to work at his reply to Manning. He thus reported the progress which he had made in the last birthday letter that he was able to write to Keble.

E. B. P. TO REV. J. KEBLE.

Christ Church, Oxford, St. Mark's Day [April 25], 1865.

I have finished my printed Letter to you. It is chiefly a defence of ourselves against Manning, explaining our Articles in the old way, excepting against the large R. C. quasi-authoritative system, under the head of Art. xxii, and then speaking hopefully of ourselves, and, as we trust, our office of reuniting Christendom, following in the wake of Du Pin and Archbishop Wake. Liddon has seen it, for I wished a second eye to see what I was addressing publicly to you. He wished me to say more about the doctrine of the Immaculate Conception; so I am making an Appendix, and am going to town to-morrow to examine the votes which the 500 bishops gave. There were some very remarkable opinions given against making it a dogma—especially the Archbishops of Rouen, Paris, Salzburg. All the Professors at Maynooth were against it, and the R. C. Archbishop of Dublin.

I am writing on purpose to-day to express my thankfulness for the many and great mercies which God gave us through giving you to us to-day, and my hope for their continuance.

Your affectionate and grateful,
E. B. P.

As usual, however, new fields opened before him, and the completion of the book was again and again delayed.

E. B. P. TO REV. W. J. COPELAND.

St. Lawrence Dene, Ventnor, I. W., July 24 [1865].

. . . As for my Letter to J. K., first I got immersed in the 'Pareri dell' Episcopato Cattolico[1]' and read through all the answers of the Bishops to the Pope about the Immaculate Conception, and lately I have got into the last Encyclical. What a strange way they are driving on! The last result of the *Dublin Review* is that the Pope is personally infallible as to facts too, not connected with faith or morals, and that,

---

[1] 'Pareri dell' Episcopato Cattolico sulla definizione dogmatica dell' im-  macolato concepimento della B. V. Maria.'

however he utters his pronouncements. Bellarmine is left far behind. So his Italian government is to be matter of faith too, and that the Pope never did anything wrong to the Greeks.

The Letter was at last completed early in September, and Pusey at once wrote to ask if Newman would accept a copy of it.

E. B. P. TO REV. J. H. NEWMAN.

Sept. 4, 1865.

At last my book is finished. I think that I said that it was meant to turn out an Eirenicon. They seem to be aweful times everywhere. Would to God we were not spending our strength, but could fight against the common foe of souls and of the faith.

But now as to sending it to you. I have not, in all these sad years, sent you anything which had any controversy in it. And in this too, though I have been reviving the mode of conciliation of Du Pin and Wake, I have had to deprecate the Ultramontanism, which, in the *Dublin Review*, goes beyond Bellarmine as to the Infallibility of the Pope and the large development of the system as to the Blessed Virgin. There is, of course, no declamation: it is simply historical, I believe.

But now the object of this note is to say, unless you should otherwise read it, I should not send it you. I should be sorry that you should have anything of mine from the booksellers ; but still more sorry to be the occasion of your writing anything against it by bringing it under your notice. . . .

I am going early next week to see Keble.

Ever yours most affectionately,

E. B. P.

It was a pleasure to Pusey to find that Newman was willing to accept a copy of his Letter. He seems to have had every confidence that it could not give offence.

REV. J. H. NEWMAN TO E. B. P.

The Oratory, Birmingham, Sept. 5, 1865.

I shall be much obliged by your sending me your book. Somehow, outright controversy is more pleasant to me than such uncontroversial works as are necessarily built on assumptions, which pain me.

For myself, I don't think I have written anything controversial for the last fourteen years. Nor have I ever, as I think, replied to any controversial notice of what I have written. Certainly I let pass without a word the various volumes which were written in answer to my Essay on Doctrinal Development, and that on the principle that truth defends itself, and falsehood refutes itself : and that, having said my say, time would decide for me, without any trouble, how far it was true, and how far not true. And I have quoted Crabbe's line as to my purpose (though I can't quote correctly) :—

> 'Leaving the case to Time, who solves all doubt,
> By bringing Truth, his glorious daughter, out.'

This being so, I can't conceive I could feel it in any sense an imperative duty to remark on anything you said in your book. I dare say there is a great deal in which I should agree. Certainly I so dislike Ward's way of going on, that I can't get myself to read the *Dublin*. But on those points I have said my say in the Apologia, and, though I can't see the future, am likely to leave them alone. A great attempt has been made in some quarters to find (censurable) mistakes in my book, but it has altogether failed, and I consider Ward's articles to be important attempts to put down by argument what is left safe in the domain of theological opinion.

But while I would maintain my own theological opinion, I don't dispute [with] Ward the right of holding his, so that he does not attempt to impose them on me : nor do I dispute the right of whoso will to use devotions to the Blessed Virgin which seem to me unnatural and forced. Did authority attempt to put them down, while they do not infringe on the great Catholic verities, I think it would act, as the Bishop of London is doing, in putting down the devotional observances of the Tractarian party at St. Michael's [Shoreditch] and elsewhere. He is tender towards free-thinkers and stern towards Romanizers. 'Dat veniam corvis, vexat censura columbas.' Now the Church of Rome is severe on the free-thinkers and indulgent towards devotees.

Pusey's Letter to Keble [1], generally called his First Eirenicon, was, as has been said, primarily a reply to Manning's attack upon the English Church, but also far more than a reply. It was a vindication of the claims of the English Church to be a portion of the Catholic Church in doctrine and Sacraments, and a detailed exposition of those portions of the Roman system which in Pusey's mind compelled the continued separation between England and Rome. In the earlier part, the ground is not new : it is a vindication to a Roman Catholic of the Thirty-nine Articles which had been so often vindicated five and twenty years earlier in reply to Evangelicals. He points out the doctrinal

---

[1] 'The Church of England, a portion of Christ's one Holy Catholic Church and a means of restoring visible unity. An Eirenicon in a letter to the author of " The Christian Year," ' Oxford, 1865. There was another title on the back of the binding of the book, 'The Truth and Office of the English Church.'

affinities between them and the decrees of the Council of Trent, and shows that Manning's charges against the teaching of the English Church are untrue in some cases, while in others they are equally forcible against the formal teaching of the Council of Trent.

In working out this point he had the further object of showing that the divergence between the formal teaching of the Church of England and the Church of Rome is not so wide as is commonly taught. The mass of objections against the Roman Church in the mind of an ordinary Englishman relate, Pusey points out, to that 'vast system as to the Blessed Virgin which to all of us has been the special "crux" of the Roman system,' and to the popular teaching about Purgatory and Indulgences [1]. This teaching is not to be found in the formal Tridentine decrees. It existed indeed, and had been strongly attacked, when those decrees were drawn up; but the Council tacitly allowed that it was not *de fide* by saying nothing in defence of it, in spite of the objections raised against it. This teaching was, however, now in common use by Roman priests. and put forth as certain truth in books which have the sanction of her Bishops and by writers who have been canonized. He proved this point by lengthy quotations of extreme statements on these subjects from well-known writers who are held in high esteem in the Roman communion. The quotations must needs have been very distressing to many Roman Catholics; they went beyond the decrees of the Council of Trent, but no restriction or prohibition had been issued with regard to them, and popularly they were part of the formal teaching of the Roman Church.

Pusey thought that it would be a great advance towards reunion if such statements were authoritatively asserted to be not *de fide*, and not necessarily to be taken into account in discussions about reunion. He alleged as a precedent for such explanations the overtures which Du Pin and others made to Archbishop Wake in the eighteenth century, when he proposed a union between the English

---

[1] pp. 101–205.

and Gallican Churches. Du Pin's 'whole plan seems to be an anticipation of our dear friend's Tract XC.' Then he alluded to the hopes of reunion entertained in later years by 'the profound and pious Möhler,' on the basis of the recognition by each side of its own great mistakes, and to the hopes which the Ultramontane Count De Maistre entertained for the Church of England in the time of her profoundest lethargy. After unsparingly pointing out her faults, De Maistre still said of her, 'Cependant elle est très précieuse sous d'autres aspects, et peut être considérée comme une de ces intermèdes chimiques, capable d'approcher des élémens inassociables de leur nature.'

'And now God seems again to be awakening the yearning to be visibly one, and He Who alone, the Author of Peace and the Lover of Concord, must have put it into men's minds to pray for the unity of Christendom, will in His time, we trust, fulfil the prayer which He Himself has taught. . . . A plan which should embrace the Greek Church also would facilitate what English Catholics most desire—authoritative explanations. Cardinal Wiseman, in his memorable letter to Lord Shrewsbury, laid down as a principle, 'We must explain to the utmost[1].' The Church of England and the Council of Trent have long seemed to me at cross purposes. In some cases, at least, the Council of Trent proposed the minimum, of [sic] which it would accept, but left a maximum, far beyond the letter of the Council, to be thereafter, as it was before, the practical system of the Church. The Church of England in her Articles protested against that maximum, the practical system which she saw around her; but, in many cases, she laid down no doctrine at all on the subject upon which she protested. She made negative statements to show against what she protested, but set down no positive statement to explain what, on the same subject, she accepted. . . . It may be that the Church of England might offer such explanations of the Thirty-nine Articles as the Roman and Greek Churches would accept, such as are suggested by Bossuet, or by the Commonitorium of Du Pin; or, according to the precedent of the Council of Florence, the Thirty-nine Articles and the Council of Trent (which was so largely directed against errors of Luther) might pass away and be merged in the Eighth General Council of the once-more united Christendom[2].'

The Letter concludes with a glowing picture of the dangers through which the Church of England has kept the Faith, of her present vigorous life, and the manifold proofs

---

[1] Letter, p. 31.    [2] Eirenicon, Part I, pp. 266-268.

of the 'organic working of God the Holy Ghost in her.'
It is not, he maintained in opposition to Archbishop
Manning's statement, a question of grace acting only in
individual souls ; it is the operation of God the Holy Ghost
upon the Church as a whole. The pages in which this is
worked out are specially valuable, but do not admit of
condensation. They are a stirring apology for the English
Church. combining a loyal and affectionate review of her
present condition with a statement of his hopes for the
work which it may be the Will of God to accomplish
through her in the future.

The Eirenicon was hardly out of Pusey's hands when he
unexpectedly met Newman at Keble's house at Hursley.
It must have seemed to Pusey as an omen that his hopes
of reunion between the Church of England and the Church
of Rome would be realized.

He writes to his brother :—

E. B. P. TO REV. W. B. PUSEY.

[Sept. 14, 1865.]

Strangely, I met J. H. N. at dear J. K.'s this week on my visit on
my return from residence at Oxford. He is deeply lined. It is the
first time I have seen him since he came to me at Tenby, when I was
ill [in 1846]. We talked comfortably about past, present, future [1].

Newman has given a full account of the meeting in
the following letter to the late Sir John Coleridge, which
was published in Keble's Memoirs [2].

REV. J. H. NEWMAN TO SIR JOHN COLERIDGE.

Rednall, Sep. 17, 1868.

It was remarkable, certainly, that three friends—he, Dr. Pusey, and
myself—who had been so intimately united for so many years, and
then for so many years had been separated, at least one of them from
the other two, should meet together just once again ; and, for the first
and last time, dine together simply by themselves. And the more
remarkable, because not only by chance they met all three together,
but there were positive chances against their meeting.

---

[1] 'Mrs. Keble being ill, we three
dined *tête à tête* together, a thing
which perhaps we never did before
in our lives.' J. H. N. to Rev. G. D.
Boyle. Sept. 15, 1865.
[2] 'Memoirs of Rev. J. Keble,' pp.
528–530 (2nd ed.).

Keble had wished me to come to him, but the illness of his wife, which took them to Bournemouth, obliged him to put me off. On their return to Hursley I wrote to him on the subject of my visit, and fixed a day for it. Afterwards, hearing from Pusey that he, too, was going to Hursley on the very day I had named, I wrote to Keble to put off my visit. I told him, as I think, my reason. I had not seen either of them for twenty years, and to see both of them at once would be more, I feared, than I could bear. Accordingly, I told him I should go from Birmingham to friends in the Isle of Wight, in the first place, and thence some day go over to Hursley. This was on September 12, 1865. But when I had got into the Birmingham train for Reading, I felt it was like cowardice to shrink from the meeting, and I changed my mind again. In spite of my having put off my visit to him, I slept at Southampton, and made my appearance at Hursley next morning without being expected. Keble was at his door speaking to a friend. He did not know me, and asked my name. What was more wonderful, since I had purposely come to his house, I did not know him, and I feared to ask who it was. I gave him my card without speaking. When at length we found out each other, he said, with that tender flurry of manner which I recollected so well, that his wife had been seized with an attack of her complaint that morning, and that he could not receive me as he should have wished to do, nor, indeed, had he expected me ; 'for Pusey,' he whispered, 'is in the house, as you are aware.'

Then he brought me into his study and embraced me most affectionately, and said he would go and prepare Pusey, and send him to me.

I think I got there in the forenoon, and remained with him four or five hours, dining at one or two. He was in and out of the room all the time I was with him, attending on his wife, and I was left with Pusey. I recollect very little of the conversation that passed at dinner. Pusey was full of the question of the Inspiration of Holy Scripture, and Keble expressed his joy that it was a common cause, in which I could not substantially differ from them ; and he caught at such words of mine as seemed to show agreement. Mr. Gladstone's rejection at Oxford was talked of, and I said that I really thought that had I been still a member of the University I must have voted against him, because he was giving up the Irish Establishment. On this, Keble gave me one of his remarkable looks, so earnest and so sweet, came close to me, and whispered in my ear (I cannot recollect the exact words, but I took them to be), 'And is not that just?' It left the impression on my mind that he had no great sympathy with the Establishment in Ireland as an Establishment, and was favourable to the Church of the Irish.

Just before my time for going Pusey went to read the Evening Service in church, and I was left in the open air with Keble himself . . . . We walked a little way, and stood looking in silence at the church and churchyard, so beautiful and calm. Then he began to converse with more than his old tone of intimacy, as if we had never been parted, and soon I was obliged to go. . . .

He wrote me many notes about this time ; in one of them he made a reference to the lines in *Macbeth* :—

> ' When shall we three meet again?
> When the hurly-burly 's done.
> When the battle 's lost and won.'

But the newspapers gave their own account of the meeting, to Pusey's great annoyance.

E. B. P. TO THE EDITOR OF THE 'GUARDIAN.'

Christ Church, Oxford, Oct. 9, 1865.

I much regret having to obtrude upon the public my own private feelings, but the statement which you copied from some local paper (inaccurate in every particular, except that I spent some happy hours with my friend Dr. Newman) is so intensely painful that I cannot help myself. The statement is, that Dr. N. and myself were '*reconciled after twenty years.*' The deep love between us, which now dates back for above forty years, has never been in the least overshadowed. His leaving us was one of the deep sorrows of my life; but it involved separation of place, not diminution of affection.

Pusey saw good reasons for attempting to get as wide a hearing as possible for his plan of reunion. Rumours of an approaching Council at Rome seemed to suggest that the favourable moment for decisive action had arrived. He wrote hopefully about it to Mr. Gladstone :—

E. B. P. TO RIGHT HON. W. E. GLADSTONE, M.P.

[Sept. 19, 1865.]

The Bishop of Brechin wished me to have it translated into French and German, which I am about to have done so soon as I find the translators. We want to have a hearing with the non-extreme party before the Synod at Rome next year. I read through the correspondence with the Pope published in the ' Pareri dell' Episcopato Cattolico ' on the Immaculate Conception. There seemed to be many moderate men then : but, alas ! the Episcopal life is short, and fifteen years may have removed a good many to their rest. My hope, however, is not in many, but that it is God the Holy Ghost, the Author of Peace and Lover of Concord, Who is putting into people's hearts to wish to be one.

With the same purpose a journey to France was pro-
jected to bring the Eirenicon under the notice of the French
Bishops.

E. B. P. TO REV. J. H. NEWMAN.

[Early in October, 1865.]

I think I shall try to present my book myself to some French Bishops.
Alas! what a short-lived generation the Episcopate is.   I find that the
Archbishop of Rouen, who replied to the Encyclical, is paralytic, at
least so I was told, at Rouen.   I have a wish to see some Bishops
myself, and I think I shall try to use this short interval before the
Oxford term to see whom I can.   I want to know what they would
think of giving us the same terms as Bossuet or Cardinal de Noailles
would.

He accordingly started for France as soon as he could
get away after reading his Paper at the Norwich Church
Congress.   He left Poole for Cherbourg on Wednesday,
October 11, and returned to England on October 20, having
crowded no little work into those ten days.   He wrote an
account of his earliest visits to his son Philip from Paris.

E. B. P. TO PHILIP E. PUSEY.

Paris, Monday [Oct. 16, 1865].

So much time was lost by not coming on Monday . . . and subsequently by the difficulty of getting to the Bishop of Coutances, whom
I thought likely to be one of the most favourable[1], that I am come here
thus late, having followed the Bishop from Coutances to Avranches,
and then to St. Michel.   He was most kind, and gave me his blessing.
Then the Bishop of Rennes being out, I saw his vicar, who spoke
kindly.   From the Bishop of La Val I got a rebuff, so I did not try
Le Mans.   Yesterday, being Sunday, I saw the Bishop of Chartres for
a short time.   He was kind but not encouraging.   It was near service
time, so I did not see much of him.   To-day I went with my letter to
the Archbishop of Paris[2], who, wisely, never allows an answer to be
waited for; so I must wait at home to-morrow to see whether there is
any appointment.

[Tuesday.] I am staying at home, partly for an answer from the
Archbishop, to know whether I am to see him.   I think that very likely

[1] He judged from the official replies
to the inquiry of Pius IX in regard
to the doctrine of the Immaculate Conception, which are published in the
'Pareri dell' Episcopato Cattolico
sulla definizione dogmatica dell' im-
macolato concepimento della B. V.

Maria,' and are very frequently quoted
in the 'Eirenicon.'

[2] Monsignor Georges Darboy, who
had been appointed Archbishop in
1863. He was afterwards murdered by
the Communists, on May 27, 1871.

I may not. For, since the rule here is to tell the Archbishop beforehand why one wishes to see him, he may think that I have told him all
I have to say, and not thinking it practicable, may send me an answer
through some chaplain.

He wrote a full account of his journey to Bishop Forbes
as soon as he reached home, on the following Friday.

E. B. P. TO THE BISHOP OF BRECHIN.

[October 20, 1865.]

MY DEAREST FRIEND,

The first stone is, I trust, laid on which the two Churches may
be again united—when God wills and when human wills obey. I had
two most interesting audiences with the Archbishop of Paris, who
seemed to be of a very far-sighted, moderate, and comprehensive mind.
He seemed entirely to recognize our position, thought that there were
faults on both sides in [the] Reformation, accused no one. The upshot
was that he thought that there might be union on the basis of the
Council of Trent, *but* explained. The custom at Paris is that one has
to explain beforehand why one wishes to see the Archbishop. So
I wrote him a letter (with which he was evidently well satisfied, and
of which he spoke kindly), saying what we wished—that our difficulties
lay rather in things outside of the Council of Trent than in its letter,
and gave as an instance the system of the most holy Mother of God,
and asked whether it could not be laid down that nothing was of faith
except what the Council of Trent declared, that it was good and useful
to, &c. He said that the formulizing of a new article of faith was a very
grave matter, but he saw no reason why it should not be. He thought,
on the one hand, that there must be a reaction after the death of the
present Pope ; on the other, he thought that the English nation would
be more ready to come to terms when it had had some reverses.
I asked him definitely at the end of the first interview, 'Do you, then,
think that it would be a practical matter to work for—the reunion of
the Churches on the basis of the Council of Trent explained?' He
said, 'Yes.' I told him that I had been advised to have my book
translated into French. He said, 'Do ; the subject ought to be considered.' He anticipated that there might be some stir, but said that
if there was he would defend it. If I understood him right, he thought
it might perhaps be put into the Index, but he did not think that a great
evil. I was not always certain of his French, for my hearing is not as
good as it was ; but of the main outline I am certain. He said that
the conciliators were always successful in the end, that people did not
wish for extremes. He spoke with great admiration of the English
character, said that the Church stood in need of the Anglo-Saxons,
that the French were impetuous and went full tilt at their object ; but
that the English would always beat them—for they kept their end in
view, and then moved or did not move, just when and how they saw

that it would advance their end. I first called on him on Tuesday. On his saying that he had watched our Movement for twenty years with great interest, and asking me the title of my book, that he might send for it, I took it him; and yesterday he told me that he had *parcouru* it, but that he meant to study it, that he would write me his opinion of it. He had before proposed to me a continued correspondence. He said that dear J. H. N. would be the person to frame the terms of conciliation[1]. Evidently he has the thing at heart.

Bishop Maret, upon whom I called, was out; but after this hopeful interview with the Archbishop I did not try any more. I had before been received most kindly by the Bishop of Coutances, who left an official meal to see me. He said, to my surprise, that he thought that the Pope would have great difficulty in conceding in Europe the Communion in both kinds, or the marriage of the clergy. It was his own remark. I had taken it for granted, that, since they were matters of discipline, there would be none, and so had not mentioned it. The Bishop of Rennes was giving a Retreat: I saw his vicar-general, who was also very kind, and advised that we should send our propositions to Rome, that they would be considered by able theologians, and that, even if they missed, no harm would be done. Then I saw the Bishop of La Val, having meant to go round by Le Mans, Angers, Orleans, Blois to Paris. But La Val was so discouraging that I thought I would not go any more to unknown Bishops. La Val's line was that I was kept back by mere secular grounds: I answered, 'God alone knows the heart, Monsignore[2]'; to which he said that there were very few Gallicans in France, that he had never been one. So I went to Chartres. He [the Bishop] was very kind, but still had the same idea, that submission was the only line: but as he was going to Church, I could not say as much as I wished; and I could not say so much on my side to those Bishops for fear of wounding them. I went to the Cathedral at Chartres for the Evening Service, and there, while service was being chanted, I observed little children being taught to kneel before and kiss something which I did not see. Peasants went up to it and knelt and prayed before it. I looked afterwards and found that it was a handsomely-dressed Madonna with brilliant glass eyes. At Rouen I saw a whole range of tablets (double) the whole length of the church: 'I called upon Mary and she heard me.'

---

[1] 'The Archbishop of Paris asked me whether my " relation " to you continued, and asked me to give you his "respectful and affectionate "—the substantive, I am sorry to say, I forget.'— E. B. P. to J. H. N., Oct. 30, 1865. 'His idea was that should, by God's blessing, the English Church desire explanations, you would be the person to draw up such explanations as the Roman Communion might give and we receive.'—E. B. P. to J. H. N., Nov. 1, 1865.

[2] To this Dr. Liddon adds the note: 'Dr. Pusey told me that he had also replied to the Bishop of La Val that "At my age, Monsignore—sixty-five— this world can have little to promise for any of us."'

The Archbishop [of Paris] was surprised and pleased when I told him that we acknowledged the Primacy. He owned that the relations to Rome involved in the Supremacy were very different from what they were · instanced the pallium, which was not sent at first—that Bishops at first were confirmed by their Metropolitans only (just as we think), &c. I said that the Supremacy touched us only in its consequences. He asked 'What?' I: 'If the Pope appoint our Bishops, they our Clergy, then we have the whole practical system taught us and our people.' He: 'A Concordat might be come to, though with difficulty, by which the Bishops might be elected by the other Bishops, or in other ways, or nominated by the Queen, "*quoique Protestante.*"' He acknowledged our Succession and the grace of our Sacraments. I can hardly be mistaken in thinking that he acknowledged that we are a branch of the true Church, *enté sur le tronc, qui est Jésus Christ*, and that we had the *sève*, since we had life. Certainly I heard nothing to lead me to think that he was speaking of this as our view of the case, and he seemed to me to be speaking of his own belief about us. There was not a word in the two hours expressing any wish about my joining them: but the whole was encouraging in the plan of working for reunion. He said that the book struck him as very conscientiously written, that he was glad that I had so worked out the part of the Immaculate Conception, that it was evidently a *chose qui vous touche.* When I spoke of the first stone being laid, I meant the fact that the Archbishop of Paris is so thoroughly interested in it.

Now for a little question of detail. Parker raised the question to-day whether it would not be better to give all the extracts from the 'Pareri' in the originals. As far as I recollect, those which are not French are Latin, except one Italian and one Spanish. Parker thought it would look more authentic. Of course French priests could read Latin, but this would make a difference between the German and French translations. The Germans cannot read French. And one should miss the French laity. The Archbishop of Paris said that effective movements came from below. What say you?

Your most affectionate,

E. B. P.

I quite agree as to dropping all allusion to Manning.


On his return to England, Pusey learnt the manner in which his book had been received at home. No other work that he ever issued had been welcomed with so much general favour in the Church of England. Letters of hearty approval poured in upon him. An old friend, who had been somewhat alienated from Pusey of late, wrote as follows :—

ARCHDEACON CHURTON TO E. B. P.

Crayke, Oct. 10, 1865.

I believe a week or ten days may have passed since I had the great pleasure of receiving 'from the Author' a copy of the 'Truth and Office of the English Church.' It would, however, have been *impossible* for me to write a mere acknowledgment of what the post had brought me till I had read it. Two other copies had been ordered before yours came; and I have only delayed, till the intervals of daily duties allowed me to read through, what I never have willingly laid down since I first opened it. Thanks, my dear Pusey, a thousand thanks, for the instruction, the comfort, the uplifting of heart and mind, which have attended me throughout the perusal of this admirable volume! I know not how to select where all is so good, so close to the point, so *un*redundant—to coin, in your own way, an Anglo-Saxon compound! But, what is most of all full of hope and comfort, it seems to me so wonderfully to combine, what none surely hereafter can question, such hearty love and loyalty to the 'English Church,' and such a firm trust in the Providential purposes, for which we humbly believe she is still preserved among us, with the utmost scope for those Catholic aspirations after Reunion, which, we will not doubt, are also for the wisest and most beneficial reasons and objects reviving in the present age of the Church, and, if sustained with patience by wise and faithful men, must in the end bear fruit, and restore some of those things that are fallen. I have no doubt you will live, D.V., to see some reward for your excellent labour in this—and perhaps even greater than you have seen before.

Two English Bishops also sent their warm expressions of approval.

BISHOP [HAMILTON] OF SALISBURY TO E. B. P.

Palace, Salisbury, Oct. 10, 1865.

Most heartily do I thank you for the copy of the 'Eirenicon.' I am always deeply touched by your kind thought of me—but more than this. Having read it, I can thank you for it as God's good gift to our Church in our present distress. Both Churches, viz. the Roman and English, are in practice far below their fixed standards; but what every one must, I think, feel after reading your book is that we are by God's mercy emerging from the low atmosphere of our past practical system, and that Rome seems to be more and more substituting the evils of her practical system for the higher teaching of her Canons.

BISHOP (ELLICOTT) OF GLOUCESTER AND BRISTOL TO E. B. P.

Clifton, Bristol, Nov., 1865.

Again let me thank you for your valuable, your truly valuable and timely volume. I have read very attentively a great deal of it.

I must be honest—so I won't say that former fears as to the possibility of union are yet wholly removed. But this I can honestly say, that your book has completely prevented me ever throwing obstacle or opposition in the way of a union between Churches. At present, then, thanks to your Christian learning, I stand 'at gaze'—fears still, but *some* nascent hopes in my heart.

With all kindest regards,

Yours thankfully and affectionately,

C. J. GLOUC. AND BRISTOL.

A later letter on the same subject must also find a place here :—

DR. DÖLLINGER TO E. B. P.

München, 30 Mai, 1866.

VEREHRTER HERR UND FREUND,

Oxenham meldet mir, dass Sie geneigt seien, in den Sommerferien nach Deutschland zu kommen. Thun sie diess ja, besuchen Sie recht bald München, und steigen Sie bei mir ab, wo zwei Zimmer zu Ihrer Verfügung stehen. Wir können da in aller Ruhe Dinge, die Ihnen wie mir am Herzen liegen. I am convinced by reading your Eirenicon that inwardly we are united in our religious convictions, although externally we belong to two separated Churches. There can be no fundamental difference of opinion between us. Über die religiöse Lage Deutschlands überhaupt kann vielleicht Niemand Ihnen besseren Aufschluss geben als ich. Wenn Sie meine Einladung annehmen, machen Sie mir eine grosse Freude. Über Ihr treffliches Irenicon würde ich Ihnen schon lange geschrieben haben, wenn das, was ich darüber zu sagen hätte, nicht zu viel für einen Brief wäre.

Totus tuus,

I. DOELLINGER.

At first every opinion was favourable. 'I do not hear of any expression of disapprobation,' Pusey writes, 'even among those who do not sympathize with it.' But Newman's silence troubled him. At last, at the end of a month, a letter from W. G. Ward gave him an opportunity of writing in the hope of drawing some answer from Newman.

E. B. P. TO REV. J. H. NEWMAN.

Christ Church, Oxford, Oct. 30 [1865].

I never was more at a loss than as to the probable reception of this book. But the idea of a reunion on the basis of the Council of Trent seems to be fairly launched ; though, as you will have seen, my own position is rather not to object than to receive [sic]. I mean, e. g., that I believe in some purifying dealings of God after death, rather than

have any definite belief about Purgatory.  However, the book does
seem to be allowed of or received in quarters where I did not expect
it.  I believe that God the Holy Ghost could alone have put into
people's hearts to pray for reunion ;  and so that He will bring about
what He teaches to pray for.  And I hope that this book may be
a help.

Ward is going, he tells me, to write strongly against it.  He calls it
an ' attack.'  But unless one states our difficulties, they cannot be
met ;  and I have stated them only historically.  Ward tells me,
' I hear from undoubted authority that he [you—I of course have not
named you] is quite earnest on the same side [as Ward], viz. that your
book is not really an ' Eirenicon,' but peculiarly the reverse.'  I hope
this is not so.  There are so many who could not conceive themselves
separated for half an hour, of their own will, from the Church of
St. Augustine and the Fourth Century, whose whole intellect would go
along with it.  Why should there be irremediable difficulty now ?

Newman's answer was a great disappointment.  He
seemed to ignore the fact that Pusey had not recklessly
quoted extreme Roman statements ; but that he had taken,
as the basis of his hopes of reunion, a supposed willingness
on the part of the Church of Rome to dissociate herself
from such teaching as was clearly not in accordance with
her authorized dogmatic standards.  If he had felt himself
bound to give instances of that teaching, it had been
only with the hope that they might be disavowed.  Not
unnaturally, however, his intentions in making the quotations had been misunderstood.

The Oratory, Birmingham, Oct. 31, 1865.

It is true, too true, that your book disappointed me.  It does seem
to me that ' Irenicon [1] ' is a misnomer ; and that it is calculated to make
most Catholics very angry—and that because they will consider it
rhetorical and unfair.

How is it fair to throw together Suarez, St. Bernardine, Eadmer and
Faber ?  As to Faber, I never read his books ;  I never heard of the
names of De Montfort and Oswald.  Thus a person, like myself, may
be in authority and place, and know nothing at all of such extravagances as these writers put out.  I venture to say the majority of
Catholics in England know nothing of them.  They do not colour our
body.  They are the opinions of a *set* of people—and not of even

---

[1] It was thought interesting to retain the spelling which Newman almost
uniformly adopts for this word.

them permanently. A young man or woman takes them up, and
abandons them in a few years. The simple question is, How far ought
they to be *censured*? Such extravagances *are* often censured by
authority. I recollect hearing, more than twenty years ago, instances
of books about the B. V. M. which Pope Gregory XVI had censured.
I think I am right in saying that very superstition about our Lady's
presence in the Holy Eucharist has been censured—I think Rogers
told me this in 1841, writing from Rome. Nor is Cornelius à Lapide
implicated in it—he says not that the Blessed Virgin is present in the
Holy Sacrament, but that, since she was our Lord's Mother, what *was
once* her flesh, being *now* His, is there. It is no longer hers when He
appropriated it. Moreover, he says this, commenting verse by verse
on a passage of Scripture commonly interpreted of her, and thus (with
various success, as all commentators are wont) making something out
of each verse, as it comes, to the purpose. He is not propounding
a doctrine, but interpreting a chapter.

Then again, I thought no one but V.-C. Wynter[1] would confuse
Intercession with Invocation. Suarez speaks of Intercession. I have
tried to find your passage of him, with doubtful success—but I cannot
believe that he enunciates the proposition, without there being some
explanation of it, ' No one is saved who is not *devout* to Mary.' But
it may be quite true, nevertheless, that Mary's *intercession* is a necessary part of the economy of Redemption, just as Eve co-operated in
Adam's fall. It is in this point of view that St. Irenaeus calls her
Advocate—whatever the Greek word was in his text. As to Eadmer
or St. Bernardine, of course where the religion was *established*
throughout a people, and Hail Marys were said every hour, for a man
to *reject* such a devotion would be an act so grave, especially if he still
kept the *faith* (which, of course, such writers supposed, for devotion,
not faith, was the need of their day), that I think it would be something
like rising up against his own means of salvation. And if you cannot
put Suarez, a theologian, in the same boat with Italian preachers and
spiritual writers, much less is Faber to be taken as his interpreter.
Suarez teaches dogma, and dogma is fixed. St. Bernardine is devotional, and devotion is free.

Then, as to these excesses, so there are excesses in statements of the
doctrine of Eternal Punishment. I don't suppose either of us would
think it fair or sober in a *Westminster Review* to quote St. Ambrose
or St. Hilary on Eternal Punishment, add to *their* passages quotations
from the Puritans, Wesleyans, from Dr. Cumming or Mr. Spurgeon
(or say from St. Alfonso or any Italian preacher), and to argue from
the vulgarities or profanities of such Protestant preachers, against the
awful doctrine itself.

An Irenicon smoothes difficulties: I am sure people will think that
you increase them. And, forgive me if I do not recollect what you
have exactly said, but I do not think you have said definitely *what you*

ask as a condition of union, in respect to the cultus of the Blessed Virgin. This would be something *practical.* Do you wish us to deny her Intercession? or her Invocation? or the *forms* of devotion? or what? Had this been clearly done, people would have thought you practical—but forgive me if I say that your pages read like a declamation.

If I am not mistaken, you gave this reason last February, why you wished me not to come to Oxford [1], that it would cause a renewal of the attacks on our doctrines—yet you are doing the very thing yourself. And you said that since my day, those who agreed with you in Oxford had *ceased* to attack Rome, and this was a characteristic mark of the difference in the Oxford party when *I* belonged to it, and *now.* Yet this is what people are saying against your book, viz. that it is an *attack.* The *Guardian* of last week says, à propos of what you profess to bring out in your pages on the cultus of the B. V. M.: ' It is language which, after having often heard it, we still can only hear with *horror.*' Is this the effect which an Irenicon ought to produce on the mind of a reader? What can the *Record* or an Exeter Hall Tract do more than excite horror?

I will not go on to other subjects. Bear with me, because you have asked me: and I should have to answer for it, if I did not speak out.

Ever yours most affectionately,
JOHN H. NEWMAN.

If Newman viewed Pusey's argument in this way, it was not to be supposed that less friendly Roman critics would be won by the book. But Pusey's immediate concern was to clear himself from the charge of speaking peace with his lips when he had war in his heart. It was a charge repeatedly brought against him throughout the whole controversy.

E. B. P. TO REV. J. H. NEWMAN.

Nov. 2 [1865].

Kindest thanks for your letter. I had no idea of attacking anything. I thought that I had avoided everything like declamation. I do not recollect using a single epithet, or anything but a statement of what I thought important facts. I meant merely to put out what are our difficulties. I did not, as a mere presbyter, wish to put down formally what I thought should be the formula of union, nor had I any idea of wishing to interfere with others' devotion, or that anything should be condemned. What I wanted, I thought I had explained at the beginning of p. 100, 1, that that should be declared to be alone *de fide* which the Council of Trent had laid down on the subject of Invocation.

[1] See page 104.

I mean that if the explanation of Milner, which I quoted in p. 100, were laid down authoritatively, so that all besides should be left as pious opinion, an immense step would be gained.

I certainly meant to put down nothing except what I thought was taught by writers of weight. In St. Bernadine and Eadmer (quoted by Liguori, &c., as St. Anselm) I took, as I thought, favourite authorities in St. Liguori (Glories of Mary), the Month of Mary, &c. Suarez also I took from Liguori. In fact, I *thought* that I had so far only put together what I found together in a favourite book of one canonized.

Faber I took as being, I thought, one of the most favourite books (to judge from the sale) of the present day, and, in regard to the Holy Eucharist, he cites St. Ignatius.

I thought 'There it is; if any of it is disowned, it is a gain.' I thought that everything was published under authority, so that nothing could be likened to the ravings of Spurgeon, who represents nobody but himself, and belongs to himself and to nobody [else].

I thought that none of the system of the B. V. had been *de fide*, and this is what I wished to be said by your authorities indirectly. I did not want you to deny her Intercession (which of course I never doubt, or indeed that of any of the Saints), 'or her Invocation or the forms of devotion.' It would be simple impertinence in us to prescribe terms to you. We have only to look to ourselves. The character of an Italian or Spaniard is different from that of an Englishman or German. But, after the doctrine of the Immaculate Conception had been so long a pious opinion, it has been declared to be *de fide*, and many bishops said that it was so held among their people. So, I thought, and much more, might any of those points which I set down, because there would be no counter-tradition about them, whereas, on account of the doctrine of the transmission of original sin, there was a good deal, I thought, on the doctrine of the Immaculate Conception. Forgive me, the last thing which I should wish to do would be to dispute with you. I only want to explain what I meant. The Pareri showed me that a good many of your bishops had a tender feeling towards those not in their communion, and thought of the bearings of fresh Articles of Faith upon them. So then, in view of the Synod of next year, I was not sorry, since I wrote at all, to say what are our difficulties, lest any of them should be made matters of faith too. But then too I wished to show that our difficulties lay outside the Council of Trent, and, as I thought, outside what is *de fide* (the Immaculate Conception is a perplexity), and so I thought it no attack, since I was mostly speaking of things not *de fide*, as I believed, but which, as things stand, individuals of us, if we joined the Roman Church, must receive.

Well, I hope the explanation is not worse than the book. It is a great sorrow to me that you should think the book an attack.

Newman's reply is somewhat more sympathetic than his last letter.

REV. J. H. NEWMAN TO E. B. P.

The Oratory, Birmingham, Nov. 3, 1865.

I think I quite gathered from your book what you bring out so clearly in your note of this morning.

My great anxiety is, that I fear the substantial framework of it will not be taken in by the mass of readers, but they will go off upon those other portions of it which are so much more easy to understand.

If I am led to publish anything (of which I have no present intention) I should treat the book simply as an Irenicon, as you wish.

Pusey could not be content without more fully explaining why his Eirenicon was bound, in some portions at least, to have the appearance of an attack.

E. B. P. TO REV. J. H. NEWMAN.

Nov. 6, 1865.

If parts of a family are at variance, the fault must be either wholly on the one side or on the other, or divided. The more I smooth down difficulties, the more I should leave our position as unreal, unless there were something behind. A defence, of necessity, involves some fault on the other side. But I hoped that it was no real attack so long as it did not relate to matters declared to be of faith. At the same time, it is a real practical subject. I have said more than once that I cannot conceive how any faith could stand the leaving one system which it had once thought Divine, and criticizing anything in the system to which it had submitted as being alone Divine. I felt that had anything driven me from the Church of England, I must have and should have submitted myself to the whole practical system, such as it is taught in the book with which we are most familiar, Liguori. A lady to whom I said something of this sort appealed—now many years ago—to you; she wished to join the Church of Rome, seeing that she could receive the Council of Trent and the Creed of Pius IV. I said that she ought not to join it unless she could receive the practical system as taught by Liguori. She sent me your answer, in which you said, ' Dr. P. is quite right ; a person ought not ' (I forget the exact words, but in whatever way you would express joining the Church of Rome) ' unless he can receive the system taught by Liguori.' You said to me twenty years ago, ' I do not go as a reformer.' True ; one could only go as a little child, leaving behind everything which one had been taught. While then I approximated, wherein I could, to the Roman system, it seemed to me both honest and the only way not to mislead, to state what to my mind were the real difficulties. Others may dwell on the Supremacy. To me and to all of us the

Supremacy, as I said to the Archbishop of Paris, would be indifferent but for its consequences. On his asking 'What?' I said that the appointment of our Bishops from Rome involved the appointment of all our teachers, and consequently the authorized teaching of that which was just our difficulty.

If you could read through what I wrote, you will have seen another motive in all that which I wrote about the system as to the Blessed Virgin. It seemed to me that, on the principles and with the object upon which and with which the Immaculate Conception was made matter of faith, any other popular belief might be made matter of faith. Here was already a fresh difficulty in the way of the reunion of the Eastern Church as well as of our own. Many of your Bishops felt this : I hoped the more that if they thought that it would be a difficulty to the English Church, they might the less decree anything in the Synod of next year.

One more thing must have gleamed through, that the Roman Church had its perils as well as we have, and that perhaps we might help in averting those perils.

All this, my dearest N., is not mere controversy. . . .

I am, as you see, in this dilemma : if I do not state difficulties, I seem unreal ; if I state them, I seem controversial.

Keble was as anxious as Pusey with regard to the effect that the Eirenicon might have on Pusey's relations with Newman.

REV. J. KEBLE TO E. B. P.

Nov. 8, 1865.

. . . I believe you have been in communication with dear J. H. N. since your book came out. He wrote to me, but he has not said I might send you his letter, and perhaps it is as well not, for it vexed me in two ways : (1) he seemed to me to take a very unpleasing view of the book, wondering how it could call itself an εἰρηνικόν, and almost out of temper with it : and (2) it disappointed me after I had been led by your letter to hope that the moderate R. C.'s would take it as it is meant and sympathize with it. I wrote to him pointing out that in fact his own statement, that ' Suarez, &c. was not to be charged with maintaining the *Invocation* of S. Mary as essential because they taught her *Intercession* to be so,' was in fact an instance of difference between formal and popular R. C. doctrine as taught by you : and that, so far he was conceding your ground for hoping that something might be one day said or done to moderate the excessive worship of her. Indeed he himself said that in the time of Greg. XVI several books were condemned in that sense. And altogether his sayings in this very letter seem to me to confirm yours, to the effect that while born R. C.'s are not to be held committed to all these extreme ideas, it will be a hard fight for any convert who wishes to keep clear of them. Poor dear fellow, I do hope he will not waver in his friendship for you. He said he had no thought of writing on this matter. I have not told him a word of your good news from France, supposing it strictly confidential. It will be a great pleasure when you can spare me the letter which gave dear Bp. Forbes such comfort. God be thanked for all.

As soon as the Eirenicon was published, Pusey wrote to Keble about the plan of reprinting Tract XC.

E. B. P. TO REV. J. KEBLE.

[About Oct. 21, 1865.]

Now that this work is done, I think that it would be a good opportunity for [re]publishing Tract XC. My explanation of the Articles in my Letter to you, is Tract XC in substance over again. People are now prepared for it. I think that my historical Preface will remove a good deal of prejudice and your Letter to J. C.[1] still more. Liddon agrees with me, that the sort of slur on Tract XC is a great hindrance to the Catholic interpretation of the Articles.

Have you anything to alter in that Letter to J. C.? For, since it was not published, it is fair to omit or alter anything.

Keble was willing to leave the matter entirely in Pusey's hands.

REV. J. KEBLE TO E. B. P.

Heather Cliff, Bournemouth, Nov. 8, 1865.

I cannot see how to adapt that poor Pamphlet of mine to the present improved state of things without really writing it anew. If it is worth reprinting at all, it must be merely as a document to illustrate our condition and proceedings in that emergency. As at present advised, I would leave it at your service to come out whole or in part.

Before the publication of the Tract, Pusey explained to Newman that the Preface was only historical, and that he had purposely not submitted it to him in order to 'leave him freer.'

E. B. P. TO REV. J. H. NEWMAN.

Nov. 13, 1865.

The failure of the Eirenicon in your eyes makes me anxious about my Preface to Tract XC. I had made it simply defensive of Tract XC on the historical side. In so doing, I have quoted largely from your letter to Jelf, because it was the explanation which the Heads ought to

---

[1] 'The Case of Catholic Subscription to the Thirty-nine Articles considered, in a Letter to Hon. Mr. Justice Coleridge by Rev. J. Keble,' privately printed, 1841.

have waited for.  I have, of course, not cited any expressions which
you have since retracted.  I have sent it to Copeland, asking him
whether there is anything which he thinks you would not like. . . .
I would ask to send it to you, only I thought that it would leave you
freer that you should not have seen it, and that Copeland's seeing it
would be the same.

Newman was very glad that Pusey should have taken
this course.

REV. J. H. NEWMAN TO E. B. P.

The Oratory, Birmingham, Nov. 14, 1865.

. . . I feel very much your kindness in respect to Tract XC.  Of
course the historical is its weak side, or rather it does not attempt it ;
and it is the most important side, for it is the question of the matter
of fact.  I recollect Keble suggesting something to be written on it
at the time : but nothing was done—because I had promised to keep
silence about the Tract.  It is impossible that I can dislike anything
you do about it : my own view of it has been expressed so clearly,
that, though your own differed ever so much, there could be no
mistake—but besides, I am far *more* than safe in your hands.  And
after all, I have nothing to do with the Tract now.

The change in public opinion since 1841 was so great,
that the republished Tract was received without any dis-
favour.  By March, the first edition of 3,000 was sold.  There
had been some criticism of the details of the history, but
Pusey was satisfied.

E. B. P. TO REV. W. J. COPELAND.

Christ Church, Oxford [Lent, 1866].

The result of this history as to Tract XC, rather shows that
it is *not* premature to publish all.  For Hawkins alone of the Heads
bristled up a little, and his bristles are gone down.  Plumptre was
quite satisfied.  Indeed it shows the marvellous change, that one
can publish Tract XC, and all its history, without the slightest
commotion.  Only we were then in the prime of life, younger than
our persecutors ; now, I am an old man.

But the correspondence about the Eirenicon was still
going on.  Newman, as Keble said, seemed to allow that
the natural course for any convert to Romanism would be
to accept their whole popular system ; only he wished to
distinguish the Roman practical system which he accepted
from the local colouring of that system which he rejected.

REV. J. H. NEWMAN TO E. B. P.

The Oratory, Birmingham, Nov. 10, 1865.

. . . It is quite true that I said, and I should say still, that it is a mere doctrinaire view to enter a Church without taking up its practical system—and that, as represented by its popular catechisms and books of devotion. In this sense I hold by 'the system' of St. Alfonso Liguori. But I never meant to say that therefore in all matters of detail I hold by him. I ever use his moral theology, but I do not hold by his doctrine of equivocation, nor is it held here in England. I hold by his numerous spiritual books, but I do not accept and follow views which he expresses about the Blessed Virgin ; and even though I looked upon him as a dogmatic authority, which he is not, I should not therefore feel bound, unless I thought right, to take his anti-Augustinian doctrine of Predestination. The practical 'system' remains quite distinct from the additions or colour which it receives in this country or that, in this class, in this school, or that.

Nor will any French divine, or German (though *not* a convert), more than myself, criticize or reject the 'practical system' (in the sense in which I have explained it)—nor is there anything which such a divine is disposed to criticize or abandon, which I should not be ready to do the like with, if I thought fit, myself, *though* a convert.

In reply, Pusey maintained that he had only quoted accredited books, and had only objected to doctrines and practices which he thought a Roman convert would be obliged to accept, although not formally *de fide*. He felt the personal attack which a writer in the *Month* had made on him, because Newman sometimes contributed to that paper ; but from Roman Catholics in England he expected little, because they were so intent on making conversions. 'But I want,' he adds, 'not to let the end of the Eirenicon sleep. I have been wondering whether you could draw up something which I might put before the English Church, as terms to offer.' Newman counselled delay : he wanted to 'get up' the book, and thought that Pusey should wait to see what his opponents had to say in reply.

REV. J. H. NEWMAN TO E. B. P.

Nov. 14, 1865.

In a word, you should have all the case before you. All this takes time, but in so great a step as you have taken, time must not be grudged. Did I write anything, it certainly would not be at once, but after I had seen what others said—nor could I write without a great deal of thought and of advice; and the advice at least I could not get in a moment.

Pusey's only reason for hurrying was that he wished to get a hearing, before the Council, which was expected in 1866, could affirm the Temporal Power or the Infallibility of the Pope to be *de fide*. Newman reminded Pusey that in an Allocution delivered on the Feast of the Annunciation in 1862, the Pope had declared the Temporal Power to be not a dogma of faith but a necessity of the time, and assured him that there was no fear of Papal Infallibility, except in so limited a form as practically to leave things as they were.

REV. J. H. NEWMAN TO E. B. P.

Nov. 17, 1865.

... It is impossible that there would not be the most careful conditions determining what is *ex cathedrâ*, and it would add very little to the present received belief. ... Have you thought of Mgr. Dupanloup? He (entre nous) was gravely opposed to the issuing of the Syllabus, &c., and much disconcerted at its appearance. Don't repeat it, but he said, 'If we can tide over the next ten years, we are safe.' Perhaps you know him already. You should have seen Père Gratry in Paris; I mean, he was a man to see.

Two days later Newman wrote in a yet more friendly way.

REV. J. H. NEWMAN TO E. B. P.

The Oratory, Birmingham, Nov. 19, 1865.

... I am much surprised and much rejoiced to see yesterday's article on your book in the *Weekly Register*. I hope you will like it. I have not a dream who wrote it.

If they rat next week, it will be very provoking. I am not easy about it, for not long ago they would not insert a review of a book *because* it was *not* according to Ward, who *is* according to Manning, who *is* according to the Pope. But this review, though not against the mind of the Pope, is certainly contrary against Ward and Manning.

It has surprised me so much that I said to myself, Is it possible that Manning himself has changed? He is so close, that no one can know.

On the other hand, I know some, if not most, of our bishops are against the *Dublin*—and it really looks as if they were taking up the matter, and that we should have some permanent change in the *Register*.

I am sure you should not be in a hurry in what you propose to do.

This review in the *Weekly Register* was by Father Lockhart. With some diffidence and all deference to higher authority, he suggested that Reunion on the lines mentioned by Pusey was better than perpetuated schism. In reply, Pusey wrote to thank the editor, and reaffirmed his convictions that the great body of the faith was held alike by both, and that the Council of Trent demanded nothing which could not be explained to the satisfaction of English Churchmen, if explained *authoritatively*. As regards the Supremacy he said, 'We readily recognize the Primacy of the Bishop of Rome ; the bearings of that Primacy on other local churches, we believe to be a matter of ecclesiastical, not of Divine law ; but neither is there anything in the Supremacy in itself to which we should object.'

Both these statements were severely criticized. The former was said to go even beyond the statements for which Mr. W. G. Ward had been deprived of his degree and others had been suspended by their Bishops. Pusey wrote a second letter to the *Weekly Register*, dated December 6, 1865, in which he pointed out that he did not claim as did Ward, to hold all Roman doctrine, because that would include the popular system as well as what is formally *de fide*, and would also imply the acceptance of doctrine on the sole authority of Rome. He explained what he intended as follows :—

'On comparing my belief with that expressed by the Council of Trent, I thought that its terms, as explained by some individual doctors, yet of authority among you, did not condemn what I believed, and did not require me to believe what I did not believe. I thought that the Council of Trent *so* explained for the Church of England, might be a basis of union. If I may sum up briefly, I think that not only on the whole range of doctrine, on the Holy Trinity, and the Incarnation, but also on Original Sin and Justification, and all the doctrines of grace, there is nothing to be explained ; that on the Canon of Scripture, the Holy Eucharist, and the Anointing of the sick, there is what has to be mutually explained ; that on what I suppose you will account points of lesser magnitude, as those alluded to in our XXII Article, there will be need not only of explanation, but of limitation, what is to be *de fide*.'

His words about the Supremacy gave great offence even to his friends. But he explained in the letter just quoted that the Supremacy, as defined by the Council of Florence, was very vague and does not necessarily involve the appointment of Bishops, the sanction of Canons or the carrying of *all* appeals to Rome.

Lockhart's review was apparently severely handled by his superiors: Pusey heard that Archbishop Manning had bidden him to write on the other side and to set forth the difficulties of Reunion; and another letter which Pusey received from a Roman Catholic alluded to the treatment of Lockhart as a 'fierce tyranny which would hinder an expression such as his, and which calls to account every one who would venture to steer clear of Ultra-isms.'

Pusey sent the correspondence to Keble, who replied as follows :—

REV. J. KEBLE TO E. B. P.

B[ournemouth], Nov. 24, 1865.

. . . I am very thankful for the particulars that seem to be coming out as to the way in which R. C.'s receive your book. And J. H. N., as I had hoped, is coming round. How strange it is that he should entirely forget your having written entirely on the defensive: as though you had been challenging H. E. M. and not replying to his challenge. But one can see that he is not altogether easy in his position. And all the world can see that at any rate Rome has now no special right to twit us with our unhappy divisions.

It will be noticed that Newman did not at first feel called upon to publish anything in answer to the Eirenicon, at any rate for some time; but for several reasons he was induced to change his mind. The question of Reunion was at that moment before the Roman authorities both in England and Rome. The Association for the Promotion of the Unity of Christendom had addressed a letter to Cardinal Patrizzi early in the same year, and the reply to it had been decided on at Rome at this time. This reply was now expected in England, and was, as we know, hostile to the Association, which had fallen under the grave displeasure of Dr. Manning. Newman's name had also been connected with the Eirenicon through the correspondence in the *Weekly Register*. Dr. Manning moreover had just become Archbishop of Westminster in succession to Car-

dinal Wiseman, and it may well have been that Newman
considered that silence on his part might be misinterpreted,
especially in the peculiar relations in which he stood to
the new Roman Archbishop[1]. Early in December he
wrote to tell Pusey that he was preparing an answer.

REV. J. H. NEWMAN TO E. B. P.

The Oratory, Birmingham, In fest. Concept. Immac.
[Dec. 8.] 1865.

You must not be made anxious that I am going to publish a letter on
your Irenicon. I wish to accept it as such, and shall write in that
spirit. And I write, if not to hinder, for that is not in my power, but
to balance and neutralize other things which may be written upon it.
It will not be any great length. If I shall say anything which is in the
way of remonstrance, it will be, because unless I were perfectly honest,
I should not only do no good, but carry no one with me: but I am
taking the greatest possible pains not to say a word which I should be
sorry for afterwards.

I hope you found nothing to annoy you in Lockhart's second
article.

Pusey's reply gives some idea of what he had to pass
through at the time.

E. B. P. TO REV. J. H. NEWMAN.

Christ Church, Oxford [Dec. 9, 1865].

As you said of me [with regard to the re-issue of Tract XC], I am
safe in your hands. This discussion is taking too wide a range, for me
to wish you to be silent. As for me, I am in a moral Bay of Biscay.
I have no idea, when I wake, what the post will bring me. One day
I have an assurance that Bishops, whom I did not dare hope it of,
have recommended and expressed their satisfaction as to the Eirenicon.
Then come those two letters of A. Gurney's (alas! an Universalist);
then the *Globe* says, either my degree ought to be taken from me, or
Ward's restored. I do not know which he wishes. Then I see
a kindly review of me from Dr. Guthrie, a Presbyterian. Then
Lockhart presses me not to say that I do not believe the Supremacy
to be of Divine right; and some of my friends, urging that John Bull
will be mad about the Supremacy and pressing me to say something:
you blame what I have said about the system as to the Blessed Virgin;
some blame me, as if in my letter to the *Weekly Register* I have
retracted it.

I do not expect any personal attack except in the papers. What
alone I apprehend is any Protestant demonstration which shall check

[1] 'Life of Cardinal Manning,' ii. ch. xiv.

things or discourage your people.  Else things work on more hopefully
If the leaven works on undisturbed, and people pray, all will be well.
It was curious to see a Birmingham paper owning that the project
of reunion 'really seems to have attracted more attention than would
be thought possible by those unacquainted with current Theological
literature.'

I am going to France again, to see some whom I had not seen before ;
but I shall not go unless there be some lull.  If the wind does not rise
higher, what there has been will only prove a favourable breeze.

Newman only remarks on the mass of criticisms which
Pusey had mentioned—'Don't be persuaded by Lockhart
to meddle with the question of the Pope's jurisdiction.  He
either has it by Divine right or has not—and the consequences are serious either way.'

A long 'philosophic and very candid' review in the
*Times*[1] of December 12, the day on which the reissue of
Tract XC appeared, spoke favourably of the Eirenicon,
and evidently saved Pusey from a good deal of trouble.

E. B. P. TO REV. W. J. COPELAND.

Christ Church, Oxford [Dec. 15, 1865].

. . . What a time of railroad speed we live in !  One seems to live
years in weeks.  That five-columned respectful review of the Eirenicon
in the *Times*, seemed to me to betoken (1) that there would be no
Protestant reclamation, else the *Times* would not have committed
itself; (2) that the proposal for union was making an impression, else
the *Times* would not have troubled itself ; (3) that it meant quietly to
put a wet blanket upon it.  So I discharged another letter to the *Times*
which it courteously put in, in big print.

On Tuesday morning I hope to sail for France and see more
Bishops.

Pusey started again for France on Tuesday, December 19,
having been carefully advised by a friend of Newman's as
to the best course to follow.  At Paris he had another
interview with the Archbishop, and saw some others,
including Père Gratry, 'who received me most lovingly,' and
the Bishop of La Rochelle.  The next day he went to
Orleans and saw Mgr. Dupanloup ; on December 22, he
went on to Marseilles.  He stayed there a week, working

---

[1] This was from the pen of Dean Church ; see Church's 'Occasional Papers,'
vol. i. p. 334 (Macmillan).

at a University sermon for January 28, at some examination
papers, and at the Commentary on Nahum. On December 30, he went to Biarritz, and on January 3 and 4, 1866,
he had two long interviews with the Bishop. On January
10, he writes to a Cambridge friend who was having the
Eirenicon translated for foreign circulation.

E. B. P. to Rev. G. Williams.

[Pau, January 10, 1866.]

I have had three very happy interviews. I do not like to name
names, but one very eminent Theologian ended a discussion of one
and a half or two hours in which I spoke freely, with the kiss of peace,
owning me as a true brother; and an Archbishop, whom I had not
before seen, did the same twice, after my asking for and having his
benediction. A good priest, to whom he introduced me as a Catholic,
rather opened his eyes, to know whether I had been actually received.

On January 13, he is at Bordeaux, going to dine with
the Archbishop, and to 'talk with him as long as I like.'
He returned through Paris [1], reaching Oxford on January 18.

The only full account of this visit was sent to the Bishop
of Brechin [2]: generally he speaks of it as 'deeply interesting,'

[1] In this connexion, although belonging to a later period, may be
quoted a characteristic story which is
told in the 'Lettre Pastorale de Mgr.
François Lagrange, Evêque de Chartres, à l'occasion de son entrée dans
son diocèse,' Paris, 1890, pp. 27,
28 :—

'Si ces fils, séparés ou égarés,
n'ont pas ou n'ont plus la foi, peut-être ont-ils, Dieu seul le sait, qui seul
voit le fond des cœurs, la bonne foi ;
c'est-à-dire la sincérité, qui fait ce
qu'elle peut et ce qu'elle doit pour
croire ? Ce mot éveille en nous un
souvenir que, dans l'effusion de ce
paternel entretien, nous demandons la
permission de rappeler. Il nous arriva
un jour de nous trouver seul en wagon
avec le célèbre docteur Pusey. Nous
demeurâmes stupéfaits de voir cet
homme, qui avait franchi des abîmes,
arrêté aux portes de la vraie Eglise
par ce que nous appelions des broussailles : mais il était empêtré là. Après
la discussion, voyant que nous prenions
notre livre de prière, il nous demanda

de réciter l'office du jour avec nous.
O providence ! c'était l'office de la
Chaise de saint Pierre, dont précisément il venait de contester l'institution
divine, tout en reconnaissant qu'elle
était indispensable à l'Eglise. Quand
nous eûmes fini, nous le vîmes, ému
par la beauté de cette belle liturgie
catholique, joindre les deux mains,
baisser la tête, fermer les yeux, et
laisser échapper de grosses larmes
que, silencieux et respectueux, nous
regardions couler. Tout à coup,
élevant la voix, il dit, "Je crois explicitement tout ce que je sais révélé,
et implicitement tout ce qui l'est."
Ce n'était pas encore l'acte de foi
catholique, c'était toujours l'esprit
privé se substituant à l'autorité constituée : n'était-ce pas là au moins la
bonne foi ? Combien il eût mieux
valu pourtant que ce puissant esprit
eût pu être amené à la lumière totale !'
[2] When Bishop Forbes died, nearly
all Pusey's letters to him were returned,
and were probably destroyed.

and 'theologically more satisfactory than the other.' He gave a few details in a speech at an English Church Union meeting on June 13.

'I assure you that people in England will be extremely astonished if I am able to show (as I hope soon to do) how much that is popularly supposed to be *de fide* with Roman Catholics is not *de fide* with them. I will only give one instance. I saw a theologian, and one of the most eminent. We talked for two hours about the Council of Trent, and about our belief as it is expressed by those whom we considered to be the most genuine sons of the Church of England. The result was that point after point he was satisfied; and the interview ended in his saying, "I shall salute you as a true brother." As to Supremacy he said, "I do not know where it is to be found stated in what the Supremacy consists[1]." It has been said that I have lived so much among old books that I do not know that the modern practice is very different from what I had gathered from those old books. As regards Appeals to Rome, which formed so large a portion of the quarrel at the Reformation, this theologian told me that there is now scarcely such a thing known as an Appeal. He stated that those things which the Church of England disclaimed were no essential parts of the Supremacy; and I may add that a very eminent French theologian said to me, "If other matters are settled, the Supremacy will make no difficulty." ... He left me saying, "This does not touch our consciences; if other matters were settled, the question of the Supremacy could be easily arranged by a *concordat*[2]."'

In France, at any rate, Pusey had no difficulty in winning a sympathetic and appreciative hearing from leading theologians[3].

---

[1] In one of his interviews with the Archbishop of Paris, Pusey asked him whether he should omit or retain in the French and German translations what he had said about the popular system. The Archbishop replied, 'Retain them, both on the general ground which you mention, of not seeming to wear two faces and saying things in England which you do not say here: and also they are *your* difficulties: of course I do not agree with them: but you have stated them fairly and it is well that they should be considered' (Pusey to Newman, Jan. 26, 1866).

[2] Speech of Pusey at E. C. U. Meeting, June 13, 1866. Cf. the *Guardian*, June 20, 1866, p. 647.

[3] At this time also Pusey took great interest in the foundation of the Eastern Church Association, and in the visit of Prince Orloff, and the discussions about Reunion with the Eastern Churches. He also contributed a valuable introductory Essay to the Rev. J. G. Lee's volume of collected 'Essays on Reunion.' One point carefully elaborated in this paper was a vigorous protest against the project of union with the Scandinavian bodies of Christians, which was being ingeniously pressed forward by the Editor of the *Colonial Church Chronicle*. 'With them,' he maintained, 'intercommunion might be too easily restored, because we have everything to lose by it and nothing to gain.'

# CHAPTER V.

1866-1867.

AS soon as Pusey returned from his second visit to France, in the middle of January, 1866, he received a copy of the printed Letter[1] which Newman had told him he was preparing. It would be out of place here to recapitulate the details of the line of argument taken in this reply, for it is now well known that they were dictated by the difficulties which arose from the internal dissensions of the English Roman Catholics, not less than by Pusey's project of Reunion. But so far as concerns Pusey's book Newman explained that he felt obliged to answer it, partly because of its allusions and supposed allusions to him, and partly because it treated Faber and Ward as if they were representative English Roman Catholics. With regard to these well-known writers, Newman said that however much they might be personally respected, 'the plain fact is, they came to the Church and have thereby saved their souls ; but they are is no sense spokesmen of English Catholics.'

[1] 'A Letter to the Rev. E. B. Pusey, D.D., on his recent Eirenicon,' by John Henry Newman. London, Longmans.

Newman's gravest charge was aimed at the way in which Pusey dealt with the practical system of the Roman Church on the subject of the Blessed Virgin. He objected that Pusey did not state his own opinion or that of the early Fathers on this subject : and that the quotations which he held up to reprobation were nearly all taken from foreign books, sometimes from books which Newman himself had never seen, and which contained sentiments quite unfamiliar to him until he read the Eirenicon. 'I do not,' he says, speak of these statements as they are found in their authors, for I know nothing of the originals, and cannot believe that they have meant what you say ; but I take them as they lie in your pages. They seem to me like a bad dream. I could not conceive them to be said[1].' At the same time he complained that Pusey had given only a one-sided view of the Roman teaching about the Blessed Virgin, in a manner which was little suited to win the sympathy of Roman Catholics. 'There was,' he said, 'one of old time who wreathed his sword in myrtle ; excuse me—you discharge your olive branch as if from a catapult[2].'

Rarely has rhetorical skill been more ingeniously employed than in this half-playful banter. The expression about 'the catapult' lives in memory more easily than the rest of the controversy ; but its injustice is generally overlooked. Pusey had certainly laid bare without reserve the serious defects in popular Romanism ; for, as has already been said, it would have been useless to approach the question of Reunion without frankly stating the great obstacles which some Roman teaching had put in its way. But Newman's epigram cleverly diverted attention from the fact that the sting lay in the obstacles themselves and not in their enumeration. However, in acknowledging the Letter, Pusey contented himself with assuring Newman that, except in direct quotations, he had no personal reference to him in the Eirenicon. He added that he had habitually looked upon him as an exception to the

[1] 'Letter to the Rev. E. B. Pusey,' pp. 119–121.     [2] Ibid. p. 9.

rule that 'converts' go further in the way of extreme opinion than old Catholics. 'I got your "Letter,"' he adds, 'on my return from the cathedral, where in celebrating the Holy Eucharist I had been praying for union.'

This led Newman to explain that he had honestly intended in his Letter to meet Pusey's challenge that members of the Church of Rome should come forward and say that they did not accept the extreme statements about the Blessed Virgin which Pusey had quoted. But in doing this, he had had to state his 'whole mind,' and explain the points in the 'Eirenicon' with which he could not agree. So far, however, Newman's 'Letter' was a real justification of Pusey's demand for some kind of authoritative repudiation of extreme language; but its open hostility [1] to the dominant form of Roman teaching brought no little trouble upon the writer from his 'co-religionists' in England. These attacks naturally drew out an expression of Pusey's sincere sympathy; at the same time he asked him to join in the common use of prayer for the reunion of Christendom. Manning had objected to any union in prayer, but Mgr. Dupanloup had promised to circulate for use in his diocese the forms of devotion which were being used by some members of the English Church. Newman replied as follows:—

REV. J. H. NEWMAN TO E. B. P.

The Oratory, Birmingham, April 2, 1866.

... Thank you for your sympathy about the attacks on me—but you have enough upon yourself to be able to understand that they have no tendency to annoy one—and on the other hand are a proof that one is doing a work. I hail the article in the *Times* [2] with great satisfaction as being the widest possible advertisement of me. I never should be surprised at its comments being sent by some people to Rome, as authoritative explanations of my meaning, wherever they are favourable to me. The truth is, that certain views have been suffered without a word, till their maintainers have begun to fancy that they

---

[1] 'The spirit of Newman's letter is most offensive.' Mgr. Talbot to Abp. Manning, Apr. 19, 1866. 'Life of Cardinal Manning,' ii. 308, note.

[2] This article appeared on March 31, 1866. It is now known to have been from the pen of Dean Church. See Church's 'Occasional Papers,' vol. ii. pp. 398–440.

are *de fide*—and they are astonished and angry beyond measure, when they find that silence on the part of others was not acquiescence, indifference or timidity, but patience.   My own Bishop and Dr. Clifford, and I believe most of the other Bishops are with me.   And I have had letters from the most important centres of theology and of education through the country, taking part with me.   London, however, has for years been oppressed with various incubi ; though I cannot forget, with great gratitude, that two years ago as many as a hundred and ten priests of the Westminster diocese, including all the Canons, the Vicars-general, the Jesuits, and other Orders, went out of their way (and were the first to do so) to take my part, before the 'Apologia' appeared.

I am sorry the Jesuits are so fierce against you.   They have a notion that you are not exact in your facts, and it has put their backs up, but we are not so exact ourselves, as to be able safely to throw stones.

As to union in prayer, it is not allowed.   Not that it is positively unlawful, but any application to Rome is answered in the negative. The Jesuits used to allow converts to go to family prayers in Anglican houses :—whether they do so now, I do not know : but I have heard those, who had received leave, express their regret afterwards that they had availed themselves of it, under the feeling that the practice had put them in a false position, as regards their friends, out of which they could not get without inflicting pain.   And most people feel that it is honestest and most straightforward, not to smooth over difficulties which really exist.

What is prayer but communion ?  to pray together is to be in the same Communion.   If the two bodies form one Communion, all controversy ceases : differences become little more than pious opinions, or incidental defects : and for three hundred years the whole world has been under an enormous hallucination.   This few people will grant : they will think it not common sense.   And at Rome, as in Cardinal Patrizzi's letter, they call it 'indifference.'

At this moment, when both Pusey and Newman were, in their respective Communions, alike exposed to attack from various quarters, their dearest mutual friend Keble was lying on his deathbed at Bournemouth.   He had gone there for the health of Mrs. Keble, when on March 22 he was seized with a paralytic stroke, which, after a momentary rally, terminated fatally a week later.   'It is to me a stunning blow,' Pusey wrote when the news of the serious illness reached him.   'I had so hoped that we should have had him by God's mercy, for years to come, if I should see years myself.'   On Easter Eve, on receiving the news of Keble's death, he could only write of it that 'it is past words.' On the Thursday following he started for the last of his many visits to Hursley to be present at the funeral. Liddon had arrived there earlier in the day, and the following extracts from his diary will best describe the sad but eventful evening and morning that followed :—

'At 8.15 we [those who had already arrived] went out on the Southampton Road to meet the hearse, coming from the Chandler's Ford Station. It left Bournemouth at four, and came *via* Christ Church, Ringwood, and Bishopstoke. It was a beautiful and starlight night, and the silent movement along the road in front of the hearse, filled me with wonderful thoughts ... Dr. Pusey arrived last of all from Ampthill [? Ampfield] where he had left the Bishop of Brechin. He wishes the College at Oxford to be the Memorial, and to be called Keble College. I trust that this will be so.

'Before going to bed, we (Dr. Pusey, I and Tom Keble) went into the Study where the Body is laid out with a Cross of white primroses stretching the entire length of the coffin, and a Cross and candles at the end. We remained there in prayer for an hour.'

On the next day, April 6, he writes :—

'The "Body" was taken to the Parish Church and placed in the Chancel before the early Celebration. The Celebration by Mr. Richards at 8 a.m. Afterwards I found Dr. Pusey in his bedroom ... quite overcome, unable to speak. With great difficulty could I persuade him to take any food. We went up to the Park and saw the Bishop of Salisbury, and the plan of a College at Oxford, which I had started the night before at Hursley Vicarage, was agreed upon. It is to be called the Keble College. Matins at 11.30 followed by the actual Burial Service. The Dr. again nearly broke down when the Coffin was lowered into the grave. After the funeral a fuller meeting of ten persons at Sir W. Heathcote's at which a series of resolutions were drawn up. I never saw Dr. Pusey so broken as to-day. He seemed to feel quite terribly the weight of responsibility which had devolved on him. I had much talk with Butler of Wantage[1].'

As soon as he returned from the funeral, Pusey wrote briefly to Newman. 'The Church was full of mourners, as you will think. But there is nothing to add. For *he* was away. . . . When *he* was wandering, he spoke of the reunion of the Churches, and I think that he spoke as if he were present at it. But I will ask more accurately.'

---

[1] For another interesting account of this funeral, see Dean Church's 'Life and Letters,' pp. 172, 173.

Thus passed away the simple, retiring, holy man who had exercised more influence on the history of the English Church than any other man of his generation. Pusey and Newman naturally filled a larger space in the popular view of the Oxford Movement; but, as has already been described [1], Keble was 'the true and primary author' of it. 'I compared myself with Keble,' Newman used to say when speaking of his work before 1845, 'and felt that I was merely developing his, not my, convictions.' Pusey also always held that the real source of the Movement was to be found in 'The Christian Year.'

More than thirty years had elapsed since these three friends had embarked on a work, which had changed the whole aspect of the English Church, and the two who were now left behind were outwardly separated by the barriers of religious differences, and in open, if friendly, conflict on matters of vital importance. They differed on that which had been the first principle of the Movement; to the one the claims of the Catholic Church seemed to give an imperative summons to complete submission to the See of Rome, while the same claims kept the other steadfast in his allegiance to the Anglican Communion. The last meeting between the three friends in the preceding October was now remembered with special pleasure. 'I feel,' wrote Pusey to Newman, 'that it was very good of God to bring about our meeting at his house. It is a bright spot.' But to Pusey Keble's death was of necessity a far more serious blow than it could have been to Newman. To the latter, except in deep personal affection, Keble had been as it were dead ever since the great separation in 1845; while to Pusey it was the loss of one who had been throughout the whole period the wise and keen-sighted counsellor and guide, the 'dearest father' as he always addressed him in his letters. And outside the circle of these most intimate associates, his influence as an adviser, if not a guide, in all kinds of difficulties—ecclesiastical, parochial, theological, and personal—had been felt up to the end. 'When all else

[1] Vol. i. pp. 270, 271.

had been said and done, people would wait and see what came from Hursley before they made up their minds as to the path of duty [1].'

Pusey returned to his ordinary work, and his answers to Newman and the recent Pastoral of Archbishop Manning. But all went slowly; and in his loneliness he grew weary of the distasteful controversies which were inevitably stirred up by his project for Reunion. It was while he was in this frame of mind that Newman told him, in confidence, that, after all, he would probably be sent to Oxford to found a Roman Catholic College. Pusey's reply reflects his feelings at the moment.

E. B. P. TO REV. J. H. NEWMAN.

Christ Church [April 21, 1866].

Thank you for the information which you have given me. The one thing which I have desired is not to be in collision with you. Perhaps before you come, I shall be gone. A little more than four years will complete the threescore and ten.

The memorial of dearest J. K. seems likely to take the shape of a College for diligent students living simply (100 of them). I took a part in promoting it. Had I known the intention of your authorities, I don't think I could have done it, i.e. had the heart to do it [2].

But an unexpected work in the Long Vacation of 1866 turned for a time the whole current of his thoughts. There was then a severe visitation of cholera in the East End of London; and in the beginning of August, Pusey took a lodging at No. 18, City Road, to see if he could be of any help in tending the sick in Bethnal Green. He had intended to stay there only a week: but October finds him still writing from the same address, for he found there abundant occupation. He divided his time between working at his Answer to Newman in the British Museum and nursing his ' cousins in Spitalfields [3] ' as he called them.

---

[1] Dr. Liddon's ' Sermons on Clerical Life and Work.' p. 350. The sermon from which these words are taken was preached at the opening of Keble College Chapel in 1876, and expresses throughout Dr. Liddon's estimate of Mr. Keble's work and character.

[2] For the further account of this plan of a Roman Catholic College and the causes of its failure, see ' Life of Cardinal Manning,' vol. ii, chapters xiii and xiv.

[3] This was an allusion to his descent from one of the Walloon refugees in the sixteenth century, many of whom had found a home in Spitalfields.

'Those I have visited,' he tells his brother, 'have been all such nice people—all better than I. They have been very happy visits.' Later on he was joined by his son Philip and by the Hon. C. L. Wood, the present Lord Halifax, who stayed and helped him in his work for three months.

Dr. Sutton, the physician at the Cholera Hospital, recalls how Pusey busied himself first in establishing the Cholera Hospital, and then in visiting the patients.

DR. SUTTON TO VISCOUNT HALIFAX.

May 4, 1889.

One incident I well remember. I had just finished, as physician, going round the wards, when he came up to me, and in his own gentle, encouraging manner, asked me how the different patients were progressing. I answered that I could not lead some Jewish patients to do what was necessary: and he smiled and said, "I will go and speak Hebrew to them, and then perhaps we shall succeed better." That was only one of the many occasions in which he showed his heartfelt desire to assist in their relief.

A graphic account of some incidents in his life there, as also in a similar work at Ascot, is given in a letter to Liddon from the Rector of Bethnal Green, written soon after Pusey's death :—

REV. S. HANSARD TO REV. H. P. LIDDON.

Rectory, Bethnal Green, Nov. 18, 1882.

In your letter to the *Times* you make mention of Dr. Pusey's 'practical kindness.'

It will more than interest you to read my reminiscences of him sixteen years ago, when there came upon the East End of London what may be called a sudden explosion of cholera in a more virulent and 'plague' like form than had hitherto been experienced in England. It became my duty as official chairman of the Vestry of Bethnal Green to seek for a building which would serve the purpose of a temporary cholera hospital.

The members of my Vestry were giving time and trouble ungrudgingly to the work in which I found I could give them but little substantial help.

The cholera was raging round the Parish Church and Town Hall where the Vestry, under the Rector, assembled daily. Within a few yards of the Rectory and Town Hall, there were six sudden seizures and deaths in one morning.

My curates were ill, unable to do any duty—I had been up for several nights running to two or three in the morning, attending to the sick, and more especially to the timid and fearful,—who would not go to bed for fear of 'the pestilence that walketh in darkness.'—Wearied and at my wits' end as to how I could possibly help my Vestry through their arduous duty, I had come down to a late breakfast at nine o'clock, when my servant announced Dr. Pusey. He had with him a letter of introduction from the Bishop (the present Archbishop) [Dr. Tait]. His pleasant smile, his genial manner, his hearty sympathy expressed in a manner so winning and sincere, at once introduced him. He needed no letter. He not only put me at my ease at once, but he made me feel at one with him directly. During breakfast he said he had heard of my working single-handed just then, and as I must give a great portion of my time to my Vestry, upon whom fell all the sanitary work of the Parish and this special work of providing doctors, medicine and hospital, &c. as well, he offered to act as my assistant Curate to visit the sick and dying whom I could not visit in my stead, and to minister to their spiritual wants. And he did so. Quietly and unobtrusively this true gentleman, this humble servant of Christ, assisted me in this most trying duty of visiting the plague-stricken homes of the poor of Bethnal Green.

But this is not all—He came with the offer of a large temporary hospital for cholera patients. Miss Sellon, the Mother Superior of that most excellent Sisterhood, the Devonport Sisters, to whose wise beneficence and unweariness in well-doing, it is a lasting pleasure to be grateful, would take charge of the hospital with her Sisters,—and so she did; as she had done at Devonport, so she did at Bethnal Green.

Well practised skill, unremitting energy, and self-sacrifice in little as in great things, of the Devonport Sisters under the Mother Superior, and of their wise and skilful physician, Dr. Sutton, saved scores of lives which would otherwise have perished miserably, and they stayed the plague from our people. I served on the committee of the hospital with Dr. Pusey, and very often I met him at the bedside of the patients—simple, tender-hearted, and full of sympathy; he was always ready at the committee meetings with practical advice on such matters as raising and managing funds, and always cheerful, always hopeful. If the word 'sweet' had not become somewhat canting—I should say that there was something inexpressibly sweet in the smile and quiet laughter which so brightened his face when he was pleased and hopeful. I remember going with Dr. Sutton to Ascot hospital, previously to my writing a short appeal in the papers for that excellent institution.—After our work was over the Sisters would not hear of our leaving without giving us dinner. How well I remember that simple, hospitable and comfortable meal in the picturesque guest-chamber. We were wearied and hungry, and while Miss Sellon was entertaining us, Dr. Pusey waited on us. I remonstrated and made efforts to wait on myself. No, he said, he must wait on me; when I said, perhaps somewhat conventionally, that that was an honour I must not let *him* pay me, he said, No, it was an honour, a pleasure to him to wait on a clergyman who, &c. &c. &c. And so he handed me the potatoes and the bread, and poured out the beer, and made it froth, and helped me to the cutlets &c. &c., smiling all the time, and saying all sorts of little playful things of kindness to us, which made us all the more refreshed and encouraged; and then he walked home with us to the station, talking with us as to the best way of supporting the Hospital in which he took so great interest, and where I am told he died.

I hope I am not wearying you with these reminiscences. I am sorry to say I can only find one letter of those I had from him, and that relates to a suggestion I made him of compiling an account or history of Sisterhoods in the English Church, such as would enlighten and encourage Churchmen.

This time last year I went to Christ Church to see Dr. Pusey. He received me with outstretched hands, shaking mine most cordially. His voice trembled with emotion as he referred to the danger I had recently incurred from a virulent attack of typhoid. I need not repeat the encouraging words he used about my ministry to the poor, past and present. I can only say that the interest he showed in the work of the Clergy of the East End of London, the sympathy he had for them in their discouraging work, and the respect and esteem he expressed for those many East-End clergymen who work on year by year without the slightest acknowledgment or recognition from any respected authority, I thought far more encouraging than all the Charges and Visitations of Bishops and Archdeacons that it had been my duty to listen to. My letter is too long or I would tell of what he said about the Atheists and the Salvation Army, which are both at work in my parish—and of his request that I would always do what I could to help the Devonport Sisters and the Ascot Hospital. His *bequest* to me, his last hearty shake of my hands, his last words to me, so full of sympathy and truest kindness, and the sweet expression of his face, I shall ever remember.

From this congenial work of succouring the poor and suffering, Pusey had to return to the work of controversy about the Eirenicon, which was still pressing on him. In fact the difficulties of his position were increasing daily. Current Roman gossip, claiming first-class authority, denied Pusey's pacific intentions, and represented him as desiring only to attack Rome so as to prevent conversions; and hence the printed replies to the Eirenicon from the Roman side began to take a personal form and to be tinged with a bitterness which promised ill for peace. And this was made still worse by the widespread rumour that the Eirenicon had been placed upon the Index [1]. At the same time, the movement in the Convocation of Canterbury against 'Ritualism' was rapidly gathering force, and loud voices were identifying Pusey with the ceremonial which they denounced, openly accusing him of having written the Eirenicon as part of a conspiracy to Romanize the country. Pusey found himself between two fires. On the one hand, there was the hostility of one section of English Roman Catholics which nothing could appease; on the other, there was the unreflecting Puritanism which learns nothing and forgets nothing. The accusations which were hurled recklessly at him by these opponents, although mutually destructive and flagrantly untrue, must needs have been perplexing and galling. He laboured for peace, but when he spake unto them thereof they made them ready for battle. Yet he still pursued his plans of peace, and there is a touch of humour as well as of pathos in the allusion to both classes of his assailants, in a letter to Newman about this time.

E. B. P. TO REV. J. H. NEWMAN.

May 2, 1867.

Yesterday I was in London about a new Association for prayer for the Reunion of Christendom, the well-being of the Church, especially the English. Of course R. C.'s cannot join it; but prayers which go up apart may meet in Heaven.

I saw my name 'P—ism' on large placards carried about the streets, charging us with a 'conspiracy to bring England under the Pope.' So the *Dublin* and *Weekly Register* might be a little more merciful. However it is all one: only I wish they loved us a little better.

Thank you for your Easter blessing. All good be with you alway.

Throughout 1867 he was engaged in helping Bishop Forbes in his 'Explanation of the Thirty-nine Articles,' a work

---

[1] It was six months before Newman was able to discover for Pusey that this rumour was entirely untrue. In the meanwhile, on the supposition of its truth, the French and German translations had been abandoned, after considerable expenditure of time and money.

which was intended as a further contribution to the cause
of Reunion in the way of simplifying difficulties. It
followed in the main the lines of Tract XC, but Pusey
revised the Bishop's work throughout, correcting it minutely,
besides himself writing the explanation of some of the
Articles. He supplied almost the whole of the passages
which under the head of Article XXII deal with the
subject of Purgatory and the Invocation of Saints; and it
was arranged that he should also contribute the section on
Transubstantiation. With a view to this work he had somewhat earlier in the year begun to correspond with Newman
on the subject. A few of the letters that passed between
them are reproduced in the Appendix to this chapter,
both as being theologically important in themselves, and
also as being closely bound up with the Eirenicon and the
'Explanation of the Thirty-nine Articles.'

When the book was printed, the Bishop of Brechin paid
a visit to Rome, and was not a little distressed at the un-
compromising attitude of those to whom he was introduced.
Newman explained to Pusey that this was natural. Rome
itself can only speak to individuals 'according to the
strictest rules of ecclesiastical principle and tradition': to
a large body she might perhaps lend a more appreciative
ear. The right procedure for individuals, he said, is to
approach the Roman Church through the Roman Bishops
*in England.* Pusey had had some hopes that this 'Explanation of the Thirty-nine Articles' might at least win
a hearing from these Bishops; but instead of this, everything had been done to increase difficulties rather than
to soften them. He soon found that, although Roman
Catholics of authority, like Newman, Lockhart, and others,
were willing to listen and assist, nothing whatever could
be looked for as helping towards Reunion so long as Ward
used his powers as proprietor of the *Dublin Review* in
propagating extreme Ultramontanism, and so long as
Archbishop Manning was the official counsellor of the
authorities at Rome.

Very different was the reception of this work by the

most distinguished German theologian in the Roman Church.

DR. DÖLLINGER TO BISHOP (FORBES) OF BRECHIN.

Munich, Oct. 5, 1868.

MY DEAR LORD BISHOP,

It is high time to let you know that I have received two months ago your second volume [1]. I would have acknowledged your kindness before, but a lengthened absence from Munich prevented me from writing.

The impression which your work left on my mind is, that you have given the best and certainly the most Catholic Commentary on the Articles. I wish only that it may be read, or rather studied and pondered in wide circles.

I think, and by several communications I am confirmed in the opinion, that the *binding* authority of those Articles, which were evidently framed to favour or to introduce the Protestant system, will be weakened, loosened, more and more, and that the rising generation of the clergy of England will not be prevented by those three or four Articles from adopting views which, under God's gracious dispensation, may lead to a future reunion. On the other hand, if that 'consummation devoutly to be wished' is to be made possible, several important changes or reforms must take place in the Roman Catholic Church of the West. The declaration of that Article of yours, which says that 'the Church of Rome' (evidently only that particular Church) 'has erred,' will not then be a real difficulty; for it is historically certain, and no one familiar with ecclesiastical history can deny, that the Church of Rome (meaning the Popes and their Roman advisers) has erred, and erred in very serious matters: for instance, in declaring the deposing power as a doctrine of faith, in prescribing, as Eugene did, false definitions of the Sacraments, their materia and forma, &c. I could wish that our friend Pusey had mentioned more distinctly those serious stumbling-blocks, for the Ultramontane party (particularly in France and England) refuse to see the beam in their eye, and talk constantly as if they were invulnerable and immaculate, and as if the Oriental and the Anglican Churches had only to say with contrite heart and mien, 'mea culpa,' and to submit unconditionally to every error in theory and every abuse in practice.

If you think it worth while to let our friend Pusey see these lines, you are perfectly free to do so.

The approaching Council fills many reflecting sons of the Church with anxious dismay, for there is a mighty power at work, which intends to use the Council as an engine for the corroboration of their favourite views.

---

[1] i. e. vol. ii. of 'Explanation of the Thirty-Nine Articles.'

L 2

My hope and consolation is, that a small but resolute knot of bishops who will make resistance is quite sufficient to frustrate their designs; but there must be some moral courage.

Believe me, yours sincerely,

I. DÖLLINGER.

On June 26, 1867, Pius IX had made the momentous announcement that he had decided to call a Council of all the Roman bishops. Newman told Pusey that this was his opportunity 'if a large and strong body of united Anglicans would address the Council, being willing to be reconciled.' But the growing attack on Ritualism was distracting attention so greatly that Pusey despaired of getting the ear of any number of English Churchmen. Even his Answer to Newman had been put aside for nearly twelve months. As an alternative, if he was unable to get many to join him he himself was urged to make strong representations to the Council; such a course might even prevent that declaration of Papal Infallibility which it was expected one party at the Council would unscrupulously push forward. At any rate, Newman, as the following letter shows, expected that such an appeal from a number of Anglicans might have a deterring effect on the Ultramontanes.

REV. J. H. NEWMAN TO E. B. P.

July 21, 1867.

. . . As to what you could do, I fear the Council is called too soon for any effect you might produce on the minds of the assembled Bishops. No one or two men, however great, could expect to have any answer made them, but 'Submit to the Church, become one of us —that is your duty—and nothing more has to be said.' But, as there have been always great concessions, when some great obvious object was to be accomplished, so now too they would put themselves out of the way, and go as far as ever they could, if great questions depended on their determination. I don't suppose the Infallibility of the Pope would have a chance of being defined, if the alternative lay between defining it and the reconciliation of the Anglican Church. Nay, I do not think it would be defined if a large body of men pledged themselves to submit to the Church, on condition that it would not be defined in the Council. I am not going into the question of the logical consistency of men who thus conducted themselves— some people would think them consistent, others not—I only say, that if as a matter of fact a thousand Anglican priests of reputation and influence said to the Council, ' It will make all the difference whether we consider the Roman communion the Church or not, that you profess the Pope to be infallible,—or that you do not—we are so firmly persuaded that the Papal Chair is not the seat of infallibility by itself, that we think that your ruling it to be such will be a proof, a critical test, that the Roman Communion is not identical with the Church ; we will join you if it is not defined, we will not if it is,'—well, I don't think this would be a satisfactory way of entering the Church, not a generous way, and it certainly would give a weight and prominence to the doctrine that the Pope is *not* infallible which it never has had, and many Bishops and theologians certainly would repudiate such transaction, independent of this accidental accession of probability to a doctrine which it is difficult to think probable ; still I think it would make a number of them pause and consider whether it was *expedient* to define a doctrine which nevertheless they considered true. And so of other points which are difficulties to Anglicans, points of ritual or discipline or devotion, everything would depend on the number and characteristics of the body presenting itself, and the definiteness, and firmness of their representation. But in saying this, you must not suppose, (as I have implied,) that I could myself ever have been induced so to act— I should say myself, ' The Roman Communion is either the Church or it is not ; if it is not, don't seek to join it,—if it is, don't bargain with it—beggars must not be choosers.'

I am disappointed at your not bringing out your Letter to me [1]— certainly as regards *the subject* of the Appendix, which you told me. Those who do not love you, give out that you ought either to answer your opponents or to allow you cannot—and they give out that they are suspicious of you. The first step at negociation is mutual confidence. I should add too, that, as to such 'grievances' as you might be supposed to prefer against our teaching or acting, I consider that the longer you all considered them, the less they would appear, and at length they would quite fade away from your minds, as worth little or nothing, and you would see that you had no reserve or condition to make in becoming one with us.

Pusey gathered from this letter that Newman supposed that there was a desire on his part to be admitted into the Roman Church, if only certain doctrinal difficulties could be cleared up. He wrote at once to remove such a misunderstanding. He did not desire to enter the Church of Rome : he wished for her union with the Church of England.

---

[1] i. e. Eirenicon, Part II.

E. B. P. TO REV. J. H. NEWMAN.

Chale, I. of Wight, Vigil of St. James, 1867.

. . . My feeling is just the same as yours. If I believed the Roman Church to be *the* Church, I should not dream of making an inquiry or a condition. I should submit as a little child. And here lay my difficulty, 'Would the Pope or Bishops of weight, or any who could speak with authority, consider any questions as to doctrine put by any body of men, unless it was understood that the submission of that body would follow upon a satisfactory answer?' I felt this when Mgʳ. Dupanloup so kindly offered to take any proposition from myself and other Anglican clergy to Rome [secret, you remember]. I feel no individual need to be in union with Rome, but I do feel the evils of division; and so I wanted a ποῦ στῶ to work from. I should have been glad to say to the English people, 'On such terms the division might be ended. You dread this and that; but you see that all which you need accept, all which is practically required of you, is to believe that and that. Look at it and see whether you object to it.'

Newman had expressed his sorrow that Pusey had not finished a reply to his 'Letter,' and had urged the necessity of answering other Roman attacks. The summoning of the Council made Pusey decide to finish his Letter to Newman, but as for the Appendix in answer to Father Harper he says,—

'I cannot feel the slightest interest about it. Man's opinion is not worth a breath with the Judgment-seat of Christ before one. I hate personal controversy. It is so petty and unprofitable. Of course, if I believed that I had made grave blunders I ought to own it as matter of good faith. I have not yet seen that I have. I went carefully through the parts of the book on the Immaculate Conception, and found partly that Fr. H. had misunderstood me, partly that he made blunders himself; e. g. his own statement as to the meaning of the active and passive Conception is, I believe, wrong: certainly his translation of Pope Innocent III whom he quotes against me is flagrantly wrong. But Fr. H.'s book has not shaken people's confidence in me among my own people; and the English R. C.'s who write, except yourself and Lockhart and Oakeley, have been writing against me ever since the Eirenicon. So there seemed to me no good in any defence.

'Some few slips I have, I suppose, made. . . . But as for the impression which Fr. H. gives or states that "nearly all his [my] quotations from Scholastics, Theologians, and Fathers have been gathered together from other second-hand sources and not from the authors themselves"

(Contents, p. xxvii), and that "without my being at the pains to verify them," it is simply untrue. I think too that it is very unfair to represent a book which was written in defence of the doctrine of the Real Presence, which (as being the last) has the fullest collection of Patristic testimonies to it (in addition to the common sources and my own knowledge of the Fathers, I went through such books as the Spicilegium Solesmense, Cardinal Mai's different collections, Cramer's Catenae, in fact what ἀνέκδοτα I knew of, and I looked through St. Ephrem's Syriac works), as if it were a mere attack on the doctrine of Transubstantiation, which, moreover, I did not attack, since I professed not to know whether the dispute was not a question of words, and expressed my own opinion that it was.

' I see other mistakes in references. Fr. H. makes the most of these. His charges of *suppressio veri* are grossly unfair. I suppose that he is not a Hebraist, and so that he does not know the valuelessness of what he produces upon Gen. iii. 15 ; but as far as " suppression " goes, it is all (I think) in De Rossi (the great Catholic critic) whom I quoted, and who attaches no weight to it. Again, he calls me guilty of a suppression because I did not mention the names of those later great names who believed in the Immaculate Conception. If the question had been decided the other way (as those who employed Cardinal de Turrecremata to write hoped) there would have been occasion to name them. All which I said was, " A matter is made a point of faith which even at a late period was disbelieved by such men as A. and B. and C. (some of them Saints)." It did not seem to me to come into the question whether the contrary was believed by D. and E. and F., because I did not speak against it as matter of "pious belief" ; but I thought it hard that it should be made a dogma *against* such and such authorities, who were thus in fact adjudged to have spoken against the truth, though innocently. He finds fault with me for mis-stating the number of the Bishops who answered the Pope about the Immaculate Conception. I counted very carefully all those in the Pareri. It was, anyhow, no fault of mine that I did not know that they were [? not] all ; however Perrone came to the fact that there were, he states, 150 more.

' I give you these as specimens, my dearest friend, but *cui bono*, to spend a life, which must be ebbing out, in pointing out such things? Fr. H. says I " probably stole a barrowful of quotations from the Calvinist Blondel," whom I never looked at, " and discharged one cartload from the Calvinist Albertinus and another cartload [from] the Lutheran Gerhard." Albertinus (Calvinist as he was) was a really learned man ; so was Gerhard. I looked into Aubertin for two things, (1) to see whether he had any passages in support of the Real Presence which he combated, and which I had missed, and (2) I took from him what I thought a really remarkable collection of passages as to the words μεταβάλλω, μετασκευάζω, &c., [showing that they] did not necessarily mean a physical change. But I both verified and acknowledged them, and omitted (I think) certain which I could not verify.

'I give you, my dearest N., all this explanation : but I do not in the least care about giving it to the world. If your people would listen to me more, it might be another matter.'

Newman persisted in urging that Pusey should complete his work.

REV. J. H. NEWMAN TO E. B. P.

Aug. 4, 1867.

Your character is not your own, nor does it cease to be after your lifetime : and though you do not find that others are alive to the arguments of Fr. Harper now, they may and will be so years hence, when to-day's doings are matter of history. I have already implied that in being silent you are unfair to your own people : but further, you are thereby unfair to your own cause. It is very desirable that the large question you have entered on, so far as opponents have taken up your glove, should be worked out—desirable in the cause of truth. If you have strong points, let them be put forward ; for myself I do not sympathize at all in the policy of suppression. I have no fear that it will harm the cause of what I think truth, that some things, nay, strong things, can be adduced against it. There are objections, and grave objections, to the simplest truths, and the cause of truth gains by their being stated clearly and considered carefully. Lastly, for myself personally and others of my own friends on my side of the question, I don't like you to be thought of as a man who had said things rashly and at second hand, and then by his silence had virtually admitted that he had done so. . . . As to your question, whether it would be worth while to publish a statement of points of doctrine which are touched upon in the Thirty-nine Articles, e.g. in Art. xxii, all would depend upon the number of persons who signed it. Did a thousand of the Clergy, headed by the Bishops of Salisbury and Brechin, sign a Latin profession of faith, it would attract the attention of many influential persons at Rome and elsewhere —though I don't know enough to say more. The Bishop of Orleans would certainly welcome it, and I am told there is a reaction beginning in the French Episcopate which would tell at a Council. The Cardinal most likely to be interested in you is Cardinal de Luca : he is at the head of the Congregation of the Index—he reads and almost speaks English. He was secretary or something of the sort to Cardinal Acton ; he has been about four years a Cardinal, and so prominent a member of the Sacred College already that men talk of him as likely to be the next Pope. He is sixty-two years old. St. John, who was lately at Rome, formed a high opinion of him. He has far larger views than Manning has.

However, as to all statements, I fear I must repeat what I have said before, that it is a first principle with us, which no one can hope to put aside, that the Pope is the centre of unity, 'totius Ecclesiae caput et omnium Christianorum Pater et Doctor,' and that he has a universal jurisdiction.

A few days later, alluding to a question that he had been asked about Pusey's relation to the Roman Church, Newman wrote again.

REV. J. H. NEWMAN TO E. B. P.

Aug. 9, 1867.

. . . It is a question often asked me, and I have one answer. I am accustomed to say that you never have felt that the Pope is the necessary centre of unity, or that the Church of England is outside the Catholic Church because it is out of Communion with the Holy See. But if you saw *that*, that I did not doubt you would join us without hesitation.

Several months passed, however, before Pusey's many engagements allowed him to resume the Reply to Newman. Since Pusey's visit in 1865 to Monseigneur Darboy, the Archbishop had kept up the liveliest interest in the Eirenicon and the hopes that it represented. Many letters of the greatest interest were received both from him and from Bishop Dupanloup; but unfortunately all the letters of the Bishop of Orleans and nearly all from the Archbishop of Paris have been destroyed or mislaid. Of one of them, Bishop Forbes writes to Pusey: 'Thank you for the perusal of this most interesting letter which I return. You have got much more from the Archbishop of Paris than I expected you would get from any R. C. Bishop in view of the terrorism of the Jesuits. So far as I see, the Archbishop takes the place of Du Pin. The Archbishop and the Presbyter only have changed places.'

When in March, 1868, the Bishop of Brechin was about to go to Italy, he took with him a letter of introduction from Pusey to the Archbishop of Paris. His visit was the cause of the only letter to Pusey from the Archbishop which has survived; it gave him new hopes by its promise of an assistance which he had good reason to regard as of great value.

THE ARCHBISHOP (DARBOY) OF PARIS TO E. B. P.

Archevêché de Paris.

Paris, le 21 Mars 1868.

Monsieur,

J'ai vu, à son passage à Paris, Mgr. l'Evêque de Brechin : sa visite m'a fait beaucoup d'honneur et de plaisir. Je vous remercie de m'avoir procuré l'avantage de connaître ce prélat, qui m'a paru un homme considérable par sa science et sa droiture de cœur. Il s'est mis en route pour Rome, où je lui ai ménagé l'entrée de notre Ambassade, qui pourra l'adresser à des personnages éminents de la Cour pontificale.

Je ne crois pas que le Concile puisse se réunir aussi promptement qu'on l'avait d'abord annoncé. Vous aurez encore le temps de discuter vos affaires et de préparer mieux le résultat que vous avez en vue.

Il ne me semble nullement difficile d'obtenir la chose spéciale dont vous parlez dans votre lettre, à savoir qu'une Congrégation Romaine se prononce sur la valeur doctrinale des propositions qui lui seraient soumises et qui représenteraient le *maximum* de vos concessions possibles. Si cela peut vous être agréable, je me chargerai très volontiers de mener très discrètement l'affaire à bonne fin et de vous faire avoir une réponse authentique. Voyez si vous voulez rédiger à votre point de vue les propositions et me les adresser : je les présenterai en mon nom et sans rien dire qui fasse penser que vous ou les vôtres y soyez pour quelque chose, et je serai heureux de vous transmettre la décision qui me sera donnée.

Veuillez, Monsieur, agréer l'assurance de mes sympathies pleines de respect et d'affection et me croire tout à vous en N. S.

† G. ARCHEV. DE PARIS.

Thus encouraged, Pusey attempted to draw up a sketch of some propositions, and submitted them to Newman, who in reply addressed himself to the previous question of the chance of an audience.

REV. J. H. NEWMAN TO E. B. P.

The Oratory, Birmingham, Sept. 4, 1868.

. . . I don't think that at Rome they will attend to anything which comes from one person, or several persons, however distinguished. If the Archbishop of Canterbury were to say, 'I will become a Catholic if you will just tell me whether what I have drawn up on paper is not consistent with your definitions of faith,' the only question in answer would be, 'Do you speak simply as an individual or in the name of the Anglican Church?' If he said 'as an individual,' they would not even look at his paper.

Therefore I do not think the Bp. of Orleans, &c., could get the Bishops of an Ecumenical Council to listen to any proposition from you as such. The initial step would be an address to the Council signed by a great show of names. Say you could present a petition from three or four Bishops of the Church of England, fifty Professors (Fellows of Colleges would count as such), 200 clergy, stating that they, the undersigned, with certain congregations of the Church of England, say 150, were desirous of coming into communion with the Holy See, that they were willing on the question of the Anglican Orders to submit to the decision of the Council, and that they presented statements of some of their articles of belief in the hope and belief that they would be found consistent with the definitions of former Councils, including the Council of Trent, and that in the sense of those statements they accepted what was there defined: moreover, that they received the doctrine of the Im. Conc. B. M. V. provided so-and-so was to be reckoned a right explanation of it, I think your cause must be taken up. But I think you will be putting yourself to bootless trouble, if you draw up statements which are to be presented in the name only of half a dozen, however eminent.

You will say perhaps that the conditions which I have set down are simply impossible—both the number of signatures and the admissions to be made in the Address. Of course I grieve if this should be the case; but consider how full a Council is of work, and whether it can be expected to go out of its way except for some great end. The reconciliation of the Church of England would be such an end, but then you must bring proof that it *is* the end of the conversion of a certain number of individuals. It must be recollected too that such an Address as I have supposed cuts off the subscribers to it from the existing Establishment, and, if it were listened to, would gain that attention for *its own* sake, from the actual body of men it spoke for, not as leading to the reconciliation of the Church of England. But not only a Council, but the ordinary ecclesiastical bodies at Rome, have not time except for great objects. All large systems fall into routine, and at Rome the Sacred Congregations go by rule, by precedent, by law, by reason, but not by that fine attention to individuals, particular cases, actual combinations, which is implied in the φρόνησις, ἀγχίνοια, σύνεσις, and γνωμοσύνη of Aristotle. In this age of the world individual greatness and self-action is superseded by routine. The routine at Rome is the routine of 1,000 years—nay, Rome, except in the case of some great Popes, has never shown any great gift of origination. It has (I believe surely) a divinely imparted instinct and a promise of external guidance as regards *doctrine*, but while it listens to practical plans brought before it, it does not go and hunt for them. Cardinal Barnabò says that only three countries give him trouble—viz. the Turks much, the English more, and the French most. That is to say, routine won't do in those countries. Under these circumstances it is a great thing for him to have an Archbishop

like Manning, who makes everything easy to him by doing his best to
work by routine and to *make* routine work in England.  As I have
said before to you, the *local* authorities are they who should encourage
any aspirations in England towards unity, and the Archbishop has
taken the opposite line.

Here is another disadvantage to you—the French Bishops are not
the natural organs for your Address ; and the natural question which
would be asked at once would be, 'Why does not Dr. Pusey apply
through the Bishops of England ?'

However, that the Bishop of Orleans, &c. are willing to take up
your cause is a great point.  Could you through Döllinger interest
any German Bishops for you ?  The Archbishop of Mayence is a great
man, and, though an Ultramontane, is far from narrow in his notions
and measures.  But Döllinger would tell you all about Germany.
Professor Reusch (I forget his name, he is Professor of Exegetics) at
Bonn is also a moderate man.  Your knowledge of German would
almost be a reason for your going there on this matter, if Döllinger
gave you any encouragement.  The state of religion (*Protestant*) there
is so sad that they look with yearning toward England, are very kind
to me, and I am sure would listen to you.  But all depends on your
being able, even if confidentially, to show them a list of educated
people and congregations who on given terms would enter into
communion with them.  *Are* there such terms ?

You know *I* deeply despair that terms *could* be named between
you and them.  The more I think of it, the more sure I am that
unsurmountable difficulties (i. e. at present unsurmountable) would
show themselves.  E. g., you can't belong to two Communions at
once—but if you cannot promise in the name and for the Church
of England, how can you be in communion with Rome without
separating from the Anglican Church, how in communion with the
latter without coming short of the former?

Still, my feeling of these obstacles is no reason why I should not
give you as much information as I can.

Pusey explained that he was not intending to send any
propositions direct to Rome.

E. B. P. TO REV. J. H. NEWMAN.

[Sept. 1868.]

The Bp. of B[rechin]'s report of the state of the ecclesiastical mind
in Italy made me give up the idea of sending propositions to Rome.
The Bishop of O[rleans] undertook, in his great kindness, to go
himself to Rome, take the propositions, and obtain an opinion about
them—the whole in secrecy.  I do not think that my name was to be
used.  I think that he meant to ask the abstract question ; and that
he understood that what I wanted was an authoritative exposition on
certain doctrines, that I might be able to say, 'What is required for

reunion is that you should acknowledge this, and no more.' I know that the Abp. of P[aris] understood this, and he certainly offered to send the propositions to Rome in his own name, without in the least committing me. (This was his own offer, for I did not care about being committed.) But the Bp. of B[rechin] brought back the impression that those who were not Ultramontane before in Italy had been driven into Ultramontanism by the wicked proceedings of the kingdom of Italy, and that the Abp. of P[aris] was in very bad odour. So, he being indisposed to it, I gave up the plan, and yet, unwilling not to do anything, I thought that at the end of my second Letter to you[1] (i.e. in the book) I would print as an Appendix, in Latin, propositions which I thought would gain acceptance with at least a large body, and so try to get them known, or perhaps send them to the principal Archbishops and Bishops in Germany and France. If we had a Cardinal Wiseman now, a great deal might be done in England; but Manning appeals to God to avert such an evil, as he thinks 'organic reunion' to be. I should like myself to try the original plan of committing them to the Bp. of O[rleans]. It was his offer to take them; but it was to be an absolute secret. He evidently feared the counter-working of some in England; I suppose Manning.

In fact, what I wanted is what Bossuet did for the Lutherans. No one was committed but Leibnitz and the Lutheran Abbot of Lokkum. Having got such propositions accepted, I should have a ποῦ στῶ, and could set to work. This might add to the Protestant uproar, and might end in a split, to which things look very much as if they were going: those represented by the Church Association would drive it to this if they could. But then the Bishops won't let it come if they can help it.

As for inducing others to declare their adherence to any propositions, there is the extreme difficulty of getting any one, except under very imminent pressure, to adopt or agree upon any voluntary propositions. . . .

Mgr. Dupanloup entered with so much love into the plan. I loved him much; he is so marvellously sweet and tender, although possibly not with the political (I do not mean secular) grasp of the Abp. of P[aris]. . . .

As you say, any such attempt is full of untold difficulties, but, after all, truth is truth, and it must be good that truth should be known. If (as Bossuet believed) a good many difficulties could be removed on explanation, then it must be good that they should be removed. It cannot be for the glory of God that untruth should be believed for truth, and that as hiding His truth. Bossuet failed in both his attempts: (I cannot help misgivings as to the sincerity of Leibnitz:) the result was (they tell us) in France the conversion of a good many of the Calvinists through the 'Exposition.' It may be so again. With results I have nothing to do. I only see this

---

[1] i.e. in Eirenicon, Part III.

longing that there could be union in eminent persons in the Greek Church, in the United States (though there rather setting towards the Greek Church than to you), among ourselves, among some of yours. This must come from God, for thoughts of peace and love can come from Him only. So I wish to do what I can.

At this moment, it was announced in the *Weekly Register* that invitations to the Roman Council had been issued to all the Eastern Bishops, and that the English Bishops were left out. Pusey wrote to Newman at once to know if this was true.

E. B. P. TO REV. J. H. NEWMAN.

Holy Cross Day, Chale, Sept. 14, 1868.

The *Weekly Register* puts me quite out of heart as to any negotiations. For the Roman Curia has prejudged the question as to our Orders (at least if the *W. R.* is right) by inviting Nestorians and other heretics, because they own their Orders, and not our Bishops, because they are laymen. To refer the question of our Orders to it, then, is simply a way of having it decided for us that we and all our sacerdotal or episcopal acts are one great sham, indeed of owning it ourselves. And yet Roman controversialists have shown themselves ready to take up any stone, so that they had something to fling : I think, I counted over eight or nine different objections, which had been raised and afterwards abandoned. (1) The fable of the Nag's Head ; (2) Lingard (who was blamed for giving up this) said, that the words 'Receive the Holy Ghost' were not used, which (*a*) were used according to the Lambeth Register, (*b*) are said not to be required; (3) that the words, 'for the office and work of &c.' were not there at first. It is since said that they are of no use, but the designation of the office somewhere else in the Service (which there was) ; (4) that Barlow was not consecrated : though I have no doubt that he was, nothing turned on it, since all four consecrating Bishops said the words and imposed hands ; (5) that the Lambeth Registers were forged : their genuineness is confessed, being so supported by collateral and incidental evidence; (6) that there was a break in the time of the Republic, (I think) ; (7) absence of intention, but, as Bossuet says, Theologians define intention, men would be in doubt any how. . . . I forget the rest.

Now, I do not want to waste your time by a discussion. But how can we refer the question of our Orders to be decided by those who have shown this kind of *animus*, alleging what they might have known to be untrue, had they been at the pains to enquire? However, this does not discourage me from what I am about, if one does but 'arbores serit quae alteri prosint saeculo,' preparing in a far-off way for Reunion, by breaking down prejudices, if God enable me. I could not perform another priestly act, if I were prepared to accept the decision of Roman controversialists on my Orders. I do not count you, of course, among Roman controversialists : I mean, persons who take up any stone, to fling at a dog. Haddan, who is accurate, says that the first precedent of re-ordaining, or any how that now acted upon, was set on the occasion of a Scotch Bishop, who asked to be re-ordained at Rome, himself alleging the Nag's Head fable. So that the precedent was founded on mistaken facts. If that fable had been true, there would have been no more question than about Lutheran Orders. Every Absolution which one pronounces, though in good faith, is, according to them, material blasphemy. It is not the opinion against our Orders, but that readiness to take up any instrument which comes to hand, before they examine whether it is good or bad, which seems to me to disqualify any from judging. Who is to be arbiter? However, this is not for you or me to settle. I only say it, because it makes me so hopeless as things stand ; but God can bring it about in His way if we pray.

The report to which Pusey referred turned out to be true. It seemed as if in the issuing of the summons to the Council, the Pope had assumed the whole question of the status of the Anglican Church to be already settled. Besides the Bull of June 29, 1868, which commanded the presence of the Patriarchs, Archbishops, Bishops, Abbots and all others who by right or privilege are entitled to sit in general Councils, he issued two letters, one on September 8, 1868, inviting the Bishops of the East ' who are not in communion with the Apostolic see '[1] ; another on September 13, addressed ' Omnibus Protestantibus aliisque Acatholicis,' who, in place of an invitation to attend the Council, were urged to join ' the one fold.' Since no summons was issued to English Bishops, it was understood that they were included among the ' Acatholici.' In the face of these facts Pusey hardly thought it worth while to attempt to send any propositions to Rome except as an individual.

E. B. P. TO REV. H. P. LIDDON.

(Secret) Chale, I. W., Oct. 6 [1868].

You will remember that Mgr. Dupanloup offered himself to take to Rome any propositions as to our *maximum*, which I would send him,

---

[1] A most interesting account of the firm and dignified bearing, and of the Christian courtesy of the Patriarch of Constantinople towards the bearers of this document, is given in Cecconi, ' Storia del Concilio Ecumenico Vaticano,' II. pp. 14–17.

and to obtain an opinion there, whether they were Catholic. The outburst of that storm of Protestantism made me delay, I think. I hoped it might spend itself. And a year ago I hoped that the Bp. of B[rechin] would do something at Rome itself. The Abp. of P[aris] made me the offer to send any propositions in his own name, withholding mine.

Now, I suppose that, in the event of this Council, something ought to be done, and the Protestant storm seems increasing. The Bishop returned from Rome utterly discouraged. The wickedness of the Italian Government had made even his friends at Mte. Cassino Ultramontanes. They said, 'The only question is, whether you will submit or no; if you will, you won't want propositions : if you won't, propositions will do you no good.' So, as he was indisposed to move, and rather dissuaded me from moving, I stayed. But you know how out of heart he always is. However, I did not like to act alone. So I settled to publish them [the Propositions] in Latin as an Appendix to my Second Letter to Newman 'on Corporate Reunion.'

Now the question is between these two plans. I explained to Mgr. Dupanloup that I did not want these explanations for my own satisfaction; that I was at rest in my own Communion; but that I felt that this state of disunion was very weakening and injurious; that our Lord's prayer was not fulfilled as it should be; and that therefore I wanted them in order to act upon my countrymen : that they thought that, in order to be in communion with Rome, they must believe this and that, and that I wanted to tell them that they need only believe that and that. In fact, it would be authenticating such statements as those of Veron or the De Walenburch. He evidently thought that there would be efforts on this side the water to prevent it. For he enjoined repeatedly *absolute* secrecy; and spoke of the different position of French and English (R. C.) Bishops. I think too he was afraid of the Jesuits, whose organ I suppose M[annin]g is.

Now then the *pros* on this side are (1) the gaining of time; (2) a certain probability that it would be done in a period of comparative leisure, whereas it [was] said that, during the Council itself, nothing could be done which did not promise an immediate result, as if a certain number of bishops, priests, and people promised to submit, if such and such propositions should be accepted ; (3) that such men as the Abp. of P[aris] and Mgr. Dupanloup think it practicable ; and the ecclesiastic who spoke to C. (whose letter you showed me) seemed to suggest overtures on our side.

Now I do not think that many would subscribe to all these propositions beforehand. But I think that they might accept them afterwards. I should send them on my own responsibility.

I shall see you, I suppose, please God, on Monday week. I am to arrive by the 11.30 train. So I do not want you to write, only to think it over. I have written most part of that Second Letter to Newman. It consists mainly of extracts from Bossuet and Molanus.

I have not seen the Pope's Bull, and only know that we are lumped in under the general title of ' Protestants.' Your Bishop said that he should go, if invited. If you think well to see him and show or send him this, I should be glad that he should see it, only as an absolute secret. I have scarcely spoken to any one for fear of their letting it out : I think only to dear J. K., the Bp. of Brechin, and yourself as to the propositions. I did not like to trust even G. W[illiams].

This attack on our Orders is a great difficulty. How can we submit the question to those who have prejudged the question? The R. C. Bishop of Chicago told De Koven that it would be proposed to have the question examined by a commission, half theirs, half ours.

The two propositions on the Seven Sacraments and Purgatory, one of theirs (whose name I offered not to quote) accepted ; and on the Invocation of Saints he only suggested an addition about their merits. The explanation of *substantia* and *species* had also been said to be adequate to the Catechism of the Council of Trent.

I see to-day that the *Times* is willing to make a present of us all to the Pope ; but his present would be more large and costly than, I imagine, he thinks.

What an absorbing and anxious move this is of the Pope's. It throws every other anxiety into the shade.

Liddon recognized with regret that the whole claim on behalf of Anglican Orders had been treated as settled in an adverse sense. But he thought it possible that the Pope might yet issue a third Letter to English Bishops, as such : if this were not done, Pusey might circulate his propositions at the conclusion of his Letter to Newman. But if none of the English Bishops were present, what would be the use of the propositions? 'The Council would not take up propositions with no one to back them. The only question seems to be whether they would do privately beforehand what they would not do publicly.' Pusey then thought that Newman might help, if he went to Rome ; but Newman explained that he was not going : Mgr. Dupanloup had asked him to go as his ' theologian ' ; and more recently the Pope sent a message offering him the office of ' Consultor,' but he declined both offers. ' I am not a theologian, and should only have been wasting my time in matters which I did not understand.'

Pusey was at least certain of one step. He would send to the press the Answer to Newman's Letter which he had

all but finished when helping the cholera patients in
Bethnal Green.   Hitherto he had left the work incomplete,
because of the 'disdain or condemnation' with which
English Roman Catholics had received 'the far-off sugges-
tions of reconciliation,' and because of the storm which the
Low Church party were attempting to raise against the
Ritualists.   He thus alluded to these reasons in the first
page of his last Eirenicon :—

'The disdain has not been mitigated ; the effort to raise a storm has
been aggravated. What will be the issue?  He alone knows Who
"ruleth the raging of the sea, and the noise of the waves, and the
madness of the people." Yet, in view of the Council which is to be
held among you at the close of next year, I have thought it not amiss
to continue to put together the evidence on the Immaculate Conception
which Cardinal de Turrecremata was prevented, by the confusion of
the times, from presenting to the Council of Basle, and which, although
originally published with the sanction of Pope Paul III, is, I suppose,
now with difficulty to be procured, though at Rome, I suppose, you
have access to everything.  But, in order to do justice to the evidence
at all, it has been necessary to produce it at such length (considering
also what has been opposed to it) that what, in its commencement,
I intended to be only "a brief explanation" to yourself, has become
a volume, and necessarily wears a controversial appearance [1].'

These words really describe the Second Part of the
Eirenicon, which was issued in Lent, 1869, under the title
'First Letter to the Very Rev. J. H. Newman, D.D.   In
explanation, chiefly in regard to the reverential love due
to the ever-blessed Theotokos, and the Doctrine of her
Immaculate Conception.'   It will be remembered that
Pusey's treatment of the Roman popular teaching with
regard to the Blessed Virgin was the main point of
Newman's objection to the first Eirenicon : Pusey, he
complained, had touched them, like an Exeter Hall controversialist, on a very tender point in a very rude way.
In his reply, Pusey explained that he had not said a single
word in derogation of the honour due to the Mother of
our Lord ; he had spoken only of the offices assigned to
her in the popular Roman teaching which went so far
beyond what was required *de fide*, and was contrary to the

[1] Eiren. III. 'Is Healthful Reunion impossible ?' pp. 1, 2.

language of antiquity. This popular system represented her as Mediatrix with her Son, as the Channel of all grace, as the only Gate of Heaven, as the Hope of sinners, as restraining her Son that He might not inflict chastisements[1].

At very great length, Pusey shows the Scriptural and Patristic position on this subject, and reproduces the enormous mass of evidence contained in Cardinal de Turrecremata's comparatively unknown but most valuable work on the Immaculate Conception. He maintains that in itself the Bull 'Ineffabilis,' which decreed that doctrine, needs explanation, for it appears to assert only one side of the doctrine. If it means more than what it asserts, it will have to be in acknowledged contradiction to the whole teaching of the universal Church in all ages, with the exception of the Roman Catholic Church at that moment.

In arguing thus, no one knew better than Pusey that he was appealing to one of the causes of disunion among Roman Catholics. He was fully aware (and the discussion on Reunion had given abundant evidence of the fact) that there was an irreconcileable 'Marian' party within the Church of Rome[2], and it was a delicate matter to write about them to Newman. They would give no explanation, and evidently wished that much which had hitherto only been taught as part of the popular system might henceforth be made of obligation *de fide*. Still he appealed to Newman to help him in the effort to bring the English and Roman Churches to a mutual understanding by ' requiring of one another the least which fealty to our God requireth ' :—

'We have one common enemy. His instruments on earth are banded together at least by one common hatred of the truth, which Jesus revealed or sealed ; which Apostles, taught by the Holy Ghost, proclaimed ; which the Church has, by a continuous succession, taught ; and which the Holy Ghost teaches in her. Satan seems to have organized his armies more, and to have learned from the Church the necessity of union. Devil does not cast out devil. And shall not we, who hold together the same body of faith, who believe

---

[1] Eirenicon II, pp. 41, 42.     [2] Eirenicon II, p. 43.

the same mysteries of the All-Holy Trinity, of the Incarnation of our Lord and God, of the operations of God the Holy Ghost in man's regeneration and restoration, the same Word of God, inspired by Him; the same offices of the Ministry instituted by Him; the same authority given to the Church to bear witness to, uphold, maintain, transmit the same truth; the same Real Presence of our Lord's Body and Blood; the same Atoning Sacrifice of the Cross; the same pleading of that one Meritorious Sacrifice on earth, as He, our Great High Priest, evermore pleads it in heaven—shall we not seek to be at one in the rest too[1]?'

The book was sent to Newman on May 14, 1869: and on June 9, Newman thanked him from his heart for the affectionate words it contained about himself, and acknowledged the research which the book showed. He declined to recognize the positive value of it; but still he had himself suggested to his Bishop (Dr. Ullathorne) some words of explanation on the doctrine of the Immaculate Conception of the Blessed Virgin which he thought would satisfy Pusey if the Vatican Council would accept them.

This, however, in no way inclined Pusey to modify his position.

E. B. P. TO REV. J. H. NEWMAN.

[June 10, 1869.]

I published the book because I thought that your people had not the case fully before them, and that those who prepared for the decision were one-sided. The grave question now seems to me the tradition. The decision, unless it can be explained, seems to me a heavy blow upon the '*quod semper*,' which concerns you as much as it can us.

I stated the difficulty fully, in case the Council should consider the question, that it might qualify the statement in whatever way God the Holy Ghost should teach them, so as to get rid of this seeming contradiction. I have no prejudice against the supposition that Almighty God infused grace into the soul of the Blessed Virgin at the first moment of its creation. On the contrary, considering what He did for Jeremiah and St. John Baptist, it seems the most likely. My only difficulty is the counter-tradition.

Pray thank the Bishop preliminarily for this kind thought of me.

It would certainly be a great gain if the Council could declare that, although *the B. V. had, by reason of the mode of her conception, original sin in the cause,* yet Almighty God, for the foreseen merits of her Son, infused grace into her soul at the same time that He created and infused it into her body.

[1] Eirenicon II, pp. 421, 422.

Newman in his reply, while suggesting Bishops to whom the book might be sent, described the effect produced upon Roman Catholics by the evidence that Pusey had amassed.

REV. J. H. NEWMAN TO E. B. P.

July 4, 1869.

I should not be acting as a friend if I did not say that I have not found any one (I think) who has not been repelled by what has been thought your hostile tone. I know how different this is from your intention. Since your new book came out, a priest, who is more hostile to Ward, Manning, &c., than perhaps any one I know, has written to me about your part in the controversy in quite violent, and I know most mistaken, terms. Men seem to think that you are not really seeking peace, but indoctrinating Anglicans how to accost, to treat with, to carry themselves towards, the Roman see ; what points to make, what to concede, what not to concede ; also, as saying to the Evangelical body, ' You see, we don't agree with, and don't mean to give in to, the Romanists.' In a word, that your books are really controversial, not peace-making. You may be sure I take your part— without any merit of mine, because I know how loving your heart is— but it has sunk deep into the minds of all Catholics, ' He has got an *arrière pensée.'*

It seemed to Pusey almost hopeless to think of Reunion with the Roman Catholic Church when the vast majority of their number were not inclined to believe his single-hearted desire for peace. Yet he still intended to publish a third, and he hoped a more successful, Eirenicon, in the form of a second Letter to Newman.

E. B. P. TO REV. J. H. NEWMAN.

Chale, I. of W. [July 19, 1869].

. . . What pity that people should waste time in judging one another. People compliment my abilities at the expense of my sincerity, which is alone of value. I never had organizing talent, and am very thankful for not having any talent which I have not. I never was in any sense a party-leader. People used my name ; but I never had any influence with them, else in many ways things would not be as they are or were.

I hear the *Dublin Review* and *Month* are angry with me. I expected it, and was sorry to publish my Letter I to you without Letter II, which is, please God, the Eirenicon.

# APPENDIX TO CHAPTER V.

### E. B. P. TO REV J. H. NEWMAN.

March 4, 1867.

*We* say that Transubstantiation is only rejected in the Articles in one specific sense, viz. that, in which there would be no outward visible sign, only something which has no objective existence, but is an illusion to the senses. This lies, as the only difficulty to all who believe the Real Objective Presence. When I stated to Mgr. Dupanloup that we believe the Real Objective Presence and that our difficulty related only to the desition of the natural substances, he said that the Real Objective Presence was the main point, and that the rest could easily be arranged, and he hushed a young priest who was rather eager on the controversy. To me the question of '*substantia*,' &c. is not of any moment, except that I do not (as R. Wilberforce thought too) see what we can be taken to mean by the 'natural substances' (which we state to remain), which you do not mean by 'accidents,' (which you state to remain), and so I am puzzled as to what '*substantia*' means.

### E. B. P. TO REV. J. H. NEWMAN.

Aug. 9 [1867].

. . . I know you won't grudge time and patience about Transubstantiation. You say that you do not understand anything about the way in which God nourishes. I say that I do not [at] all understand what the *substantia*, οὐσία of anything is. I understand what an Englishman means by 'natural substances,' i. e. that he means that there are the same particles of matter (whatever matter is) that there were before. But *substantia* or οὐσία is an abstract thing. The Church does not commonly (does it?) take up terms of philosophy in their strict philosophical sense. Why are we necessarily to take *substantia* in the Aristotelian sense? Mr. Harper says that there is one *substantia* of the little child. If there is, it must be something very abstract, something which is neither its body, nor its soul, but its personality, I suppose. Again, of any material substance, what is its οὐσία? Chemists tell us all the component parts of things material, grass, bread, flesh, &c., and how the same things which there are in the grass reappear in the animal which eats it. These are what we practical Englishmen mean by substances, but not what can be meant by so abstract a term as *substantia*, οὐσία. Again, what the Council of Trent speaks of as present, is the substance of our Lord's Body, but still in a way distinct from that way in which He is present at the Right Hand of God. . . . I suppose it would hardly be said that because our Lord's Body was present really, substantially, sacramentally, therefore It was present materially.

But then, if when it says that 'the substance of bread is changed into the substance of our Lord's Body,' it is not meant that the bread is changed into something material, then it would seem to follow, that nothing material is meant by the substance of the bread. For the two terms substance are correlatives. Plainly, we must all believe that there is a change. It was mere bread (ψιλὸς ἄρτος), it *is* the Body of Christ. Whether the term used is 'becomes' or is 'transubstantiated' is so far alike. If what it becomes is called (so to speak) *à fortiori*, that which one may call its essence, It is the Body of Christ, as Isaac the Great wrote so beautifully : 'Faith gave me the pen of the Spirit and bade me write, This is the Body of God.' But why should simple faith be troubled with Aristotelic discussions about *substantia*, or physical discussion about nutrition, or be told about miracles of which Scripture and the Church say nothing, about 'new matter' being created, or the old brought back, &c. &c.? The Schoolmen seemed to me successful in overthrowing each other's way of accounting for nutrition : no one to succeed in establishing his own. Again, you do not like putting Theology against Physical Science. But these Aristotelians (who, I suppose, understood very little of Physics) lay down that the matter returns when the Sacramental species no longer retain their character so as to be a veil for the Body and Blood of Christ (at least, so I understand them). And this they do, it seems to me, in order to escape the supposition that our Blessed Lord's Body and Blood are there while the matter of bread and wine is there. But the physicist says that that change in the species is in fact a re-ordering of the atoms of which the material thing consists, and so that the matter was there all along. And again, as to that physical effect, which corresponds to the 'gladdening of the heart of man,' it takes place instantly in many cases. So that, according to the Schoolmen, the matter returns when, according to the Physicist, it had already changed its form.

Now why should faith have these intricacies, which follow upon those scholastic explanations of the word '*substantia*'? If the doctrine of the Real Objective Presence is propounded to me, I understand not the 'how,' but I understand what it is which is proposed to me, and, of course, believe it. So in regard to *substantia* I can [believe], as I have twenty-three years or more implicitly believed, what the Church believes; but I can get no idea what the substance or, it may be, the essence of a material thing is, while I can adore and say, ' Under these outward veils is the Body of God.'

For myself, I believe whatever the Church believes, and I am not concerned what it believes in this. For my faith as to the Presence of my Redeemer is not affected by it. But if I am to teach others what Transubstantiation means, I am at a loss, since I do not know what substance is.

REV. J. H. NEWMAN TO E. B. P.

The Oratory, Birmingham, Aug. 12, 1867.

Gladly would I talk on Transubstantiation if I knew how. What I shall say, I say under correction—for I think the subject altogether beyond us, and never have felt an interest to pursue it into its scholastic ramifications.

With this *proviso*, I say that οὐσία or *substantia*, in my idea, is not an abstract idea, but a real, concrete thing. Two men have not one and the same *substantia*, each of them has his own. It is not capable of being made the predicate of a proposition, except in the way of an identical proposition, as when we say, ' Caesar is the conqueror of Pompey.' The substance of a man's body is a *res*, so is the substance of a piece of bread. (Whether a man's body or[1] a piece of bread is made up of as many substances as it has crumbs, is a further question, which I will not enter upon.) That *res* is beyond our senses : we only know bread subjectively, in its phenomena—as white, sweet, dry, &c., &c. These phenomena are produced upon our senses by what are called its accidents, which are real things too, and beyond the senses too. I have called them *forces* in a former letter by way of giving them a name. Sometimes they are called ' *natura*.' The forces and the phenomena are as little abstract as the substance. The *res ipsa* of bread, its forces, their impressions on our senses, are all concrete things. When the *res ipsa* of bread is succeeded by the *res ipsa Christi*, then the *res* or substance of Christ is represented by the forces, and through them by the phenomena of bread. As to the word ' matter,' I do not see that comes into the doctrine of the Eucharist at all, except when we begin to speak of concomitance, viz. that where the body of Christ is, there is His Soul, i. e. where the *material* substance, there is the *spiritual*. Material is contrasted to spiritual, but is in no other way necessary. Whether chaos still is supposed to exist at all or no, I do not know. I suppose it does not. If not, then ' matter' *is* now an abstract word, as denoting something, not existing in fact, but which would exist if substance could be divided into its constituents.

Holding the above, I go to no questions such as whether ' new matter be created' or ' old brought back.' I am not aware I need

[1] The words 'a man's body or' were inserted between the lines in the original.

hold that the *substance* of our bodies is nourished by the *substance* of bread. I think the accidents of our bodies are nourished by the accidents of bread. That I cannot make a perfect theory I know very well, for it is beyond me—but I have not read anything to make me think I ought not to hold what I have been saying. If I ought not, which I do not suspect, then I can only say I shut up the whole subject, and believe what the Church declares on the word of the Church. Whether what physical philosophers call 'atoms' be phenomena or accidents or substances, I do not know; perhaps they are accidents or forces. But, to tell the truth, I cannot get beyond the words of the Tridentine canon, that the substance of the bread is changed into the substance of the Body of Christ, and that the species remain. And I do not think we know anything more, nor can answer any questions safely.

I wish I could speak more to the purpose.

E. B. P. TO REV. J. H. NEWMAN.

Christ Church, Oxford, Nov. 8, 1867.

I had a long conversation with Renouf the other day, and what I gathered from him was, that modern philosophy, as he believed, was converging to the notion that the 'substantia' of any physical object was something, incognizable by any human faculties, about =τὸ νοούμενον. Now this, I suppose, would make the 'substantia' immaterial, and matter would come under the 'phenomena.' So, I am told, that Kant uses the νοούμενον to signify the real nature, which is one of relation to our faculties, holding that all our faculties are cognizant only of phenomena.

Now, would it be thought an unevasive or admissible acceptance of Transubstantiation to say 'but by "substance" I mean "essence," something incognizable by any human faculties; and under "species" I include all the natural properties of bread and wine, not excluding those which affect our human organization'?

Some one told me that you had written a kind letter to the writer of 'The Kiss of Peace,' approving, so I understand, of his book. But perhaps it was only your kindness. He speaks of the change as 'sacramental, spiritual, heavenly, not sensible, *natural*, earthly,' p. 60. Now when I wrote about the change being 'not physical but hyperphysical' (by which I meant, not a change in the natural substanc*es* in the popular way in which we speak of substanc*es*), Harper writes that the change is hyper-physical, as being a miracle, physical in its effects.

Now when we speak in our unphilosophic way about 'substanc*es*,' it is plain that we do not mean '*substantia*.' *Substantia* and *substantiae* would be contradictories. For *substantia* must, I suppose, mean a simple 'essence'; anyhow, it is *one* thing. It cannot mean the component parts of a thing, such as we mean by substanc*es*, which are many. Bread has a certain unity. Chemists tell us that its component parts are manifold—oxygen, hydrogen, carbon, nitrogen, sulphur, phosphate of lime, &c. But these manifold things have each a *substantia* of its own. Certainly they would if they were separated by analysis. The *substantia* then must be something beyond them.

Now, if the Church of Rome, by the word Transubstantiation, means only to preserve the exactness of our Lord's words, and (as Cardinal Wiseman says) it is simply the same as γίνεται, if it is not to involve us in anything which contradicts our physical knowledge or, as an alternative, involves miracles as to the removal or new creation of matter, of which no authority tells us anything, I think that a great stumbling-block would be removed. For Transubstantiation is the great bugbear to prevent people owning to themselves that they believe a Real Objective Presence.

The power of nourishing seems to stand *per se* distinct from all the accidents, and has, I suppose, never been formally included among them. I forget the number of the accidents, but some of them may be changed without changing a single property, or only by adding something, as size by compression, or colour by something external or, it even seems to be, without light, or touch is affected, at least in its nature (hard, soft) by compression. But the effects on our animal organization are not seemingly produced without a real change. But might one include 'power of nourishing' under *species*? If this were so, then the English Article would mean, so far, trans-accidentative, i.e. the change of this accidental property, which I think the Schoolmen and Harper included under substance.

Is there not a certain correlation in the terms 'change of the *substance* of the Bread and Wine into the *substance* of the Body and Blood of Christ?' I mean, since the 'substance,' as to His precious Body and Blood, is something spiritual, i.e. with no relation to material laws, would it not correspond to this that the *substantia* of the Bread and Wine should also be something not belonging to those laws?

REV. J. H. NEWMAN TO E. B. P.

The Oratory, Birmingham, Nov. 14, 1867.

I am puzzled to write, for I have nothing to say that I have not said before, and therefore I conclude you must have some radical differences of thought, which makes further writing useless.

There is hardly a point in your letter which is not (to me) either indisputable or inadmissible.

1. I agree with Renouf that modern philosophy is converging to the notion that *substantiae* are incognizable by human faculties.

2. I think this *substantia*, or rather those innumerable independent *substantiae*, of which we see the phenomena, are actual things.

3. I think they are material *substantiae*, not immaterial, as the soul is.

4. Till better informed, I don't believe in the existence of matter as a thing ; what is commonly called [a][1] matter or matters, is to me specimens of matter and material *substances.*

5. By matter is meant chaos ; and I suppose chaos no longer exists, if it ever did in fact, in the *ordine chronologico.*

6. I don't deny that the things which physical philosophers are apt to call matter are the same as what modern metaphysicians call phenomena.

7. To my mind substance and essence express the same thing, *substantia* expressing it relatively to its phenomena, essence expressing it positively.

8. Under the word ' *species* ' are included all the phenomena of bread and wine, including nourishment, i. e. phenomena nourish phenomena—the species of bread and wine nourish our (phenomenal) flesh and bones.

9. *Physis* is synonymous with phenomena, accidents, species ; transubstantiation is of course hyper-physical.

10. Every particle of the phenomena of bread may have its own *substantia*—that is, its own ultimate *res* or thing to which belongs the particular phenomena of that particle.

11. In spite of physicists using the word 'matter,' I do not think it is a theological word.  As I said before, I think it hardly occurs in the Catechism of the Council or in the Thirty-nine Articles.  Our words are substances and accidents.

12. Our Lord's Body and Blood are material substances though they have spiritual properties.

13. *What* the difference is, though there *is* an essential difference, between material substance and spiritual or immaterial substance, no man knows.

PS.—My upshot is this—viz. why do you use a word (matter) which is recognized neither by our Catechism or your Articles?

PS.—Mind, I do not write as a theologian, which I am not—but according to my measure of knowledge. . .

This last letter enabled Pusey to draw up the following explanation of the meaning of 'substance' and 'species,' which he submitted to Newman, as being both his own belief and also what he held to be the meaning of the Council of Trent.

Nov. 15, 1867.

By 'substance' I mean the essence of a thing, that which it is, its *quidditas* (if I am right as to the term).

---

[1] So written in the original.

By 'species' I mean the *physis* or *natura*, all those properties of which the senses are cognizant, including the natural powers of supporting and nourishing our bodies.

REV. J. H. NEWMAN TO E. B. P.

The Oratory, Birmingham, Dec. 4, 1867.

I ought long before this to have written a line to you to say that what you said in your last letter about Transubstantiation seemed to me quite to come up to the account of it taught in the Catechism of the Council.  I don't think anything needed to be added to it.

# CHAPTER VI.

CORRESPONDENCE WITH DE BUCK — THE THIRD
EIRENICON—THE VATICAN COUNCIL—DISAPPOINTED
HOPES.

1869–1870.

WHILE Pusey was engaged on his second Letter to
Newman, other events happened in connexion with Roman
Catholics on the continent, the exact value of which it was
very difficult then, as it is now, to estimate : still they
undoubtedly coincided opportunely with Pusey's sanguine
desire that the claims of the English Church should obtain
a hearing at the Vatican Council.

It will be remembered that the Archbishop of Paris,
and the Bishop of Orleans, had both suggested that
definite proposals should be made on behalf of Anglicans
to the Council. The Bishop of Brechin was as active as
Pusey in the matter; and there was also a small body of
laymen of influence and ability, who felt that the summoning
of the Council was an occasion which laid on the Church of
England a certain moral obligation of doing something
towards union, whatever might be the probabilities of
success. These laymen and the Bishop of Brechin both
entered into correspondence with Victor De Buck, a Jesuit
priest who had written a favourable review of the 'Eirenicon'
in the *Études religieuses, historiques et littéraires* of March,
1866.

De Buck, it appears, had lost an opportunity of an interview with the Bishop of Brechin from a bashful timidity lest he should be meddling with matters which were more suitable for his superiors. On mentioning this to Mgr. Dupanloup, he received a sharp rebuke, and was told that no effort was to be spared in trying to get Anglicans to the Council, that it was a moment for risking not a little, and that God would prosper his efforts ; if he was still timid, he should suggest to the Bishop of Brechin a visit to Orleans. Thus exhorted, De Buck seized the opportunity of acknowledging a present of Bishop Forbes' 'Explanation of the Thirty-nine Articles' to write a most urgent letter begging the Bishop to attend the Council. Three Bishops, he wrote, who would there play important parts had said in his hearing that the English Bishops ought to receive all honour. A Scotch Bishop would be treated as was Macarius of Thessalonica at the Council of Trent : he would only have to profess the creed of Pius IV, and all disciplinary difficulties could be easily arranged afterwards. His presence with Dr. Pusey as his 'theologian' would fill with joy the hearts of the Bishops. If he could not do this, the Bishop of Orleans would receive him, as he had received Pusey, and would give him every help. If neither plan were convenient, a scheme for Reunion at least should be submitted, clearly stating difficulties. With these practical suggestions there were intermingled many compliments and lavish promises as regards the facility of Reunion, and warnings against the sin of wilful schism. To another friend in England the same writer sent a sketch of what he thought Rome would allow : conditional re-ordination, Communion in both kinds, the English Prayer-book with a few doctrinal modifications might be conceded ; married clergy might retain their wives, and either a statement might be accepted setting forth the minimum of allowable belief about the *cultus* of the Blessed Virgin Mary, or extreme developments might be condemned. Pusey's comments on these suggestions show how fully he appreciated the practical difficulties of a plan for Reunion.

E. B. P. TO REV. H. P. LIDDON.

[Chale, March 24, 1869.]

I have already seen a full and confidential letter of M. Buck. He is kind, earnest, truthful. But, like most R. C.s, he looks upon individuals only and what may facilitate their reunion with the Church. He would let down individuals as easily as he could. But he cannot throw himself into our position, with whom the past is of more moment than the future. Conditional reordination would suffice for us individually; but we should, at the same time, be throwing (as we are satisfied) an unmerited and perplexing slur on all our past priestly acts, and on all of all besides in our Communion. It would be an admission on our part that everything was doubtful. I would far sooner, in Oxenham's position, act as Oxenham, retain my own belief in my Orders, and do what I could as one of the *clerus*, though inhibited all priestly acts. I had rather be a monk.

This, then, is an excessive difficulty. We are satisfied about our Orders; we are exercising our priestly offices; we are satisfied that we are in the Catholic Church: we have nothing to gain. But we wish the broken intercommunion to be, if possible, healthfully restored. Yet what a condition at the outset—to have to act as if we had been no priests, or as if very possibly we had been no priests, while consecrating and absolving and teaching our people that we had the power from Christ to consecrate and absolve. It would make everything like a troubled dream.

Their side is, I suppose, that they wish for certain, not doubtful, ordinations; and if we are to officiate among their people they have a special interest in them. Anyhow, a Council claiming to be general should not acknowledge as certain what is doubtful (if it were so).

My opinion is to wait till Haddan's book is out, and see what they make of it. M. Buck says that ten of their theologians would probably agree in holding our Orders to be null or doubtful, but on ten different grounds. My answer was, 'Then they would be nine to one against every specific objection.' He instanced one, 'a better theologian than' himself, whose only objection would be Barlow. Then he ought to acknowledge our Orders wholly, since Barlow's consecration has been shown to be *nihil ad rem*.

My own idea, ever since my visit to France, has been to formulize propositions and see whether any real authorities would accept them. But I explained that we did not put forth such propositions as terms on which we should individually join Rome—but that we wanted to be able to tell our people what they would be required to believe as matter of faith. It would be as a $\pi o\hat{v}\ \sigma\tau\hat{\omega}$.

I fear that the whole letter is framed upon something temporary. The object is to merge as many as may be in the Roman Church, without making any change. Thus, actual married clergy would be allowed to officiate, retaining their wives; but there would be no relaxation as to celibacy : those who now have the Cup would be allowed it still, but it would only be to those individuals. In the next generation things would be as before.

There is no provision as to continuance, e. g. as to the appointment of Bishops; but if our uniates were to be placed under Archbishop Manning all would soon be as before. They would have sunk in the lake and the waters would have closed over them.

I fear that the condemnation of 'certain extreme developments' would not touch what we need. They could not condemn such statements as those which I have mentioned either in the 'Eirenicon' or any of the other books. For they are over and over again in S. Liguori, and to say truth some are in S. Bernard. But we do not want to have things condemned, only to be free of [them].

I did nothing about the propositions, which I thought we might submit—because (1) of this ultra-Protestant storm which lay upon us, (2) because the Bishop of B. threw such cold water upon it. He harps always on that string 'we represent no one,' or 'a handful.' I say we represent a large number, but we cannot tell whom we represent until we have definite propositions formulized by us, accepted by them.

I have asked him again whether we should formulize statements.

Bishop Forbes too consulted Pusey with regard to his answer to De Buck, and Pusey advised him not to go to Rome in person, but to send propositions which would bring out a discussion and a formal reply : ' I suppose,' he adds, 'that De Buck tacitly calculates on the effect which the sight of so many Bishops assembled from different parts of the world would have upon some two or three, and that they would give way.' Bishop Forbes therefore assured his Jesuit correspondent that he entirely under-estimated the difficulties of Reunion, and that formal propositions should be submitted through Mgr. Dupanloup. In replying on April 14, 1869, De Buck assured him of ' ce fait immense, qu'un des motifs déterminants de convoquer le concile a été d'essayer d'opérer une réconcilia-tion avec l'Église haute d'Angleterre,' and further that Mgr. Dupanloup, beyond all others, influenced the Pope during the negotiations previous to the summoning of the Council. In his next letter he announces that Mgr. Dupanloup is almost blind.

M. DE BUCK TO THE BISHOP OF BRECHIN.

April 27, 1869.

. . . Dieu nous conserve ce grand évêque! Vous ne sauriez croire combien il est préoccupé des Anglais et des Orientaux. Avant sa maladie, il avait enlacé toute l'Allemagne dans une correspondance qui avait pour but de promouvoir la grande œuvre de la réconciliation. Quand je l'ai vu, il était prêt à tous les sacrifices qui ne fussent pas une trahison de l'Église catholique.

In the same letter the writer represents that moderate principles are in the ascendent at Rome, that there is no longer any chance of the definition of Infallibility, and on all practical questions 'nulle part on n'est plus modéré qu'à Rome.'

Pusey was not a little afraid that Bishop Forbes would be misled by the fair-seeming representations of these plausible letters. He urges the Bishop to confine his replies strictly to the one point of 'explanations before negotiation about union': if the Church of Rome would make authoritative explanations, then there would be a definite object to work for. It would be enough for this Council to lay the foundation of union by way of explanation: English people would not look at things until they had definite points before them. The Bishop acted on Pusey's advice, while at the same time he felt bound to thank De Buck for the gentle and attractive tone of his letters, which contrasted so strangely with the 'torrents of scorn and sarcasm' that were poured on the High Church party by the English converts to Rome.

On May 15, 1869, De Buck announced that the General of his Order had just summoned him to Rome, and offered while there to do anything in his power for Pusey or the Bishop. But the original plan of accepting Mgr. Dupanloup's offer seemed best, and it was decided that propositions should be sent to him containing a negative and a positive statement. 'The negative will contain what we do not believe on each subject, and the positive will say what we do hold as Catholic Christians in communion with the Church of England.' On both sides the strictest secrecy was to be observed : Dupanloup alone knew of the matter from De Buck, and the Bishop and Pusey kept their own counsel.

But while he was at Rome in the summer of 1869, De Buck communicated all that had passed to Cardinal Bilio, the Grand Penitentiary, and Secretary of the Inquisition, who was regarded as the leader of the *Intransigenti* in the Sacred College, and was looked upon by many as the future Pope. He conveyed to him his estimate of the situation in a lengthy historical statement which, although drawn up from memory, was fairly accurate, at least it could not be said seriously to misrepresent any of the opinions of ' Episcopus Z. et Oxonienses,' as the ' Unionistae' were called anonymously. He carried his account up to the time when he left Brussels, the end of May, 1869, and added that the ' doctores Oxonienses ' were now busily engaged in preparing a statement of faith which was to be brought to Rome by the Bishop of Orleans. After apologizing for his ' officiosa opera ' hitherto, he expressed a hope that the negotiations would in future be carried on by some weightier authority. He ventured to make three suggestions to the Cardinal—(1) that a small committee should be appointed at Rome of men full of learning and discretion, with Cardinal Bilio at its head. This committee, he said, must be ready to put the best construction on the statements submitted to them, must remember that Anglican and Roman theological terminology are not identical, must be capable of distinguishing dogma from unauthorized opinions, and above all must be able to bear with human infirmity—' quod hominum genus Romae frequentius est quam alibi.' All converts, except, perhaps, Lockhart and Newman, ought, he thought, to be rigidly excluded from this committee, whose work might well be limited to the opening of negotiations, under a promise of a patient hearing and every possible support at the Council[1].

---

[1] It can hardly have been without any reference to these negotiations that the Pope addressed to Archbishop Manning the two published letters of Sept. 4 and Oct. 30, 1869. Cecconi, ' Storia del Concilio Ecumenico Vaticano,' ii. 167–170.

(2) Further, that all exasperating newspaper gossip and comment should be stopped on both sides, a truce which the Archbishops of Westminster and Dublin and the Bishop 'Z.' and Dr. Pusey might well arrange. (3) Above all, that no handle should be given to any assertion that the Council was not oecumenical. Cannot the Anglican bishops, he asks, be invited as *episcopi dubii*, or at least as *episcopi a multis habiti?* This would, according to Bellarmine, be within the Papal powers. A note to this most interesting document says 'Oblatus hic commentarius Em. V. Ludovico Bilio Romae, medio mense Junio anni 1869, et per eum Concilii Vaticani praesidibus.'

The writer was most anxious to preserve secrecy, and headed the copies of this document with the words 'Confido omnino typis hoc scriptum non excusum iri neque passim communicatum V. D. B.[1]'

On his return to Brussels early in July, De Buck at once wrote to Bishop Forbes, and told him that, without divulging his name, he had discussed his letter with leading men at Rome and was astonished at the welcome with which the news was received. He suggested that each of the propositions sent to Rome should have three divisions instead of the two which Pusey had intended: on each point they should define (1) *quid sit credendum*, (2) *quid credi non debeat*, (3) *quid credi non possit*; and the propositions should be ready for the first meeting of the Council.

But persistent rumours of further definitions of doctrine by the Roman Council prevented the Bishop from sharing the hopes of his kindly and sanguine correspondent. He wrote to say that if the Council was to be pressed to define any political theory that may be contained in the Syllabus, or the corporal Assumption of the Virgin Mary, or the Infallibility of the Pope, and so 'to stereotype such follies' —it would only make Reunion impossible. De Buck warmly denied the possibility of at least the two latter

---

[1] The document is alluded to by Cecconi, 'Storia del Conc. Ecum. Vatic.,' I. ii. p. 301, *n.* 2.

Definitions; he was certain that at Rome there was no wish for Infallibility, and not a word about the other subject was to be heard anywhere. It was, he said, all newspaper gossip. But the Bishop had other sources of information, on which he thought he could rely, and was sure that there was ground for his fears: above all he bitterly complained to De Buck of the cruel injustice to Anglicans in the deliberate neglect of summoning them to the Council, and of their being classed with Socinians, &c., and not even put on a level with 'the withering heretical Communities of the East.' In replying on July 27, De Buck maintained that every one at Rome was astonished to hear that the Anglican Bishops did not consider the command to attend the Council as addressed to them; the Pope in no way wished to insult them.

Other individuals were solicited to appear at Rome by this eager Belgian priest. But Pusey felt certain that no English theologian ought to accept anything short of a formal invitation to attend the Council, in connexion with a direct summons addressed to the Anglican Bishops. It was not, he felt, a moment for any concessions which would affect even indirectly the Catholicity of the English Church. Pusey addressed the following letter to one who had received an informal invitation from De Buck :—

E. B. P. TO REV. DR. LITTLEDALE.

Chale, Isle of Wight, July 17 [1869].

I have received no, even the most informal, invitation to attend, nor should I accept an informal invitation. If they invited any, it should be the Bishops. Theologians go to accompany their Bishops. They have ignored our Bishops, and ask any of us whom they may ask informally, because they will deliberately to withhold all acknowledgement of the slightest basis upon which we can treat as a Church.

I have seen a good deal of De Buck's correspondence, and there seemed to me to gleam through it a great desire of individual conversions, or of detaching us as a body, not the slightest, of organic reunion, not any indication that they would acknowledge our Orders. The utmost that they would concede would be conditional re-ordination.

I have no doubt that the invitation to Rome is given in the hope that the imposing spectacle presented by the Council may bring about individual conversions of English Churchmen more or less learned or well known.

But what can we expect when they invited the great Greek Church simply to submit ?

I expect nothing under the present Pope. Under a future Pope there may be great changes.

The difficulty of treating is this, that we have two entirely distinct objects ; we, corporate reunion upon explanation of certain points where they have laid down a *minimum* and upon a large range beyond it ; they, individual conversions or the absorption of us. Any negotiations must go off on the authority of the Pope, while Papal claims are what they are, as their conduct towards the Greek Church shows, unless we are prepared to accept Archbishop Manning's teaching, and place ourselves under him. But explanations also seem to be made to satisfy individuals. ' We mean, you see,' they say, ' this and that : if you are satisfied with our explanations, accept Pope Pius' Creed.' And so Pope Pius' Creed is accepted, and the explanation is precipitated [?].

A Council would require a *quid pro quo* at all events. They might say, ' If a large body, some thousands, are ready to submit to the Church upon such and such explanations being formally given, we will enter into the question. But why should we give our time, if nothing is to come of it, except some possible future action of an external and often hostile body ? '

Perhaps God will show us through events what is to be done. The primary difficulties are—(1) that we represent no definite body : we represent a large *x* which might in time and ultimately be gained, and the *x* might be Catholicized England ; (2) as I said, their first condition of entering into intercourse with us would be that we should leave the English Church and join them if they should satisfy us : our object would be to get a $\pi o\hat{u} \ \sigma\tau\hat{\omega}$, whence to act upon the English Church and people. But in any case I think that anything could be better done from England than at Rome.

In the meanwhile Pusey was pressing forward with two works which he hoped might in some way influence the Council. By August, 1869, the new edition of Cardinal De Turrecremata's work on the Immaculate Conception was finished. Pusey had felt that the analysis which he had published in his first Letter to Newman did not bring out the power of the original. The work of transcription for the new edition was done by two Christ Church friends, and the book was edited throughout by the then recently-appointed Regius Professor of Modern History,

Rev. William Stubbs [1]. In September Pusey sent a copy
of the book to Newman, who, in thanking him for it,
expressed his opinion that '*all* questions sink before' that
of the Pope's infallibility, and that the moderate party
would find it hard to resist extreme measures. About the
same time also he urged Pusey to visit Rome.

REV. J. H. NEWMAN TO E. B. P.

Sept. 16, 1869.

I suppose it has not entered into your mind to go to Rome yourself.
There would be no way like that to know just what the Bishops of
different countries thought. I think you would find them all of one
mind as regards the position of the Church of England—but still you
would know, as you now do not know. I am quite sure that every
one would be rejoiced to see you and that you would receive kind-
nesses on all hands.

Or is there any one else who could go instead of you? Two would
be better than one.

I don't think they would go out of their way except they were sure
that by doing so they brought important people into the Church.
They would want a *quid pro quo*.

Bp. Forbes would not do, because he is a Bishop, and it would be
unpleasant to him—so at least I think.

I do really think one or two learned Anglicans would tend to soften
the antagonism which exists in so many quarters.

But Pusey had made up his mind as to the probable
result of such a visit, and would not be moved from his
intention of stopping at home.

E. B. P. TO REV. J. H. NEWMAN.

[Sept. 17, 1869.]

. . . I know what I should find at Rome—great individual kindness, of which I am unworthy, an exaggerated belief of my personal
influence, great interest in the progress of truth, and conviction of the
duty of individual submission.

I trust that I shall be, please God, of more use in finishing my
'Eirenicon,' Part III, which I am doing as much as I can in the language
of Bossuet, though, to judge from the letter of P. Hyacinthe. or what one
guesses to be the ground of his offence, Gallicanism (I do not mean
on its political side) finds little favour now. Yet what has been may

---

[1] Consecrated Bishop of Chester, 1884, and translated to Oxford 1888.

be. I suppose some of us will send propositions to the care of
Dupanloup, which De Buck is very urgent to have done : but I suppose
it will have no result, except, please God, for hereafter.

Some details of his arrangements about the proposed
circulation of De Turrecremata's work are given in another
letter of the same time :—

E. B. P. TO REV. G. WILLIAMS.

Ascot Hermitage, Bracknell, St. Matthew's Day [1869].

. . . In view of the sale abroad I have fixed the price so low that
if all the copies sold it would not pay its expenses. I fixed it at
twelve shillings ; Parker wished it to be sixty-five shillings.

It was a venture in view of this Council, and if it falls on me, I shall
right again, in time, please God.

I fear that the R. C.s will not take any good notice of the book.
I have sent it to the Archbishops of Paris and Cologne, the Bishops
of Orleans and Mainz, and the Cardinal Archbishop of Bordeaux, six
to American bishops, and one to Bp. Ullathorne.

By the beginning of November Pusey finished also his
second Letter to Newman, which makes the third part of the
'Eirenicon,' and which was intended to be ' a real Eirenicon.'
It was published under the title ' Is Healthful Reunion impossible?'[1] It is a volume of 350 pages; and in the
elaboration of his position Pusey shows that he had profited
by the criticisms on his earlier books. He writes more
clearly and systematically, and deals alike with the obvious
objections which the Romans raised to any explanations
and with the practical difficulties of Anglicans.

He points out that if Romans claim only absolute submission, they are acting very differently from Eugenius IV at
the Council of Florence, and that such a claim can only
be substantiated by begging the whole question at issue.

Then he passes to consider and examine at great length
the difficulties which are suggested to the minds of
Anglicans when Reunion is mentioned.

[1] 'Is Healthful Reunion impossible ?
A Second Letter to the Very Rev.
J. H. Newman, D.D. Eirenicon, Part

III,' by the Rev. E. B. Pusey, D.D.
1870.

' I suppose that the most common dread among us in case of union with Rome is, that we should be involved in a belief in Justification, which would in some way substitute or associate our own works for or with the Merits of Christ; in idolatry, not only in the *cultus* of the Blessed Virgin or of the Saints, but in that of images, or in the Adoration in the Holy Eucharist, as being, they suppose, an adoration of the Eucharistic symbols; or Eucharistic sacrifice, which should in some way interfere with and obscure the One meritorious Sacrifice on the Cross; or in a belief that sin might be remitted by Absolution, though unrepented or half-repented of, or, as some imagine, even future; or in a Purgatorial fire, the same or like that of hell, in which the departed suffer torments unutterable without any consolation; or in Indulgences, which should be a great interference with God's judgments in the unseen world, taught for the sake of gain; or that *human* traditions should interfere with the supreme authority of God's Word; or that we should be arbitrarily forbidden the use of Holy Scripture, or the gift of the Cup, or the use of prayers in a language which we understand; or people dread certain moral evils which they apprehend from a constrained celibacy of the Priesthood, or some interference with Christian liberty from an arbitrary, boundless authority of the Pope; or, perhaps, some interference with the due authority of a Christian Sovereign in matters temporal [1].'

Each of these points Pusey discusses in detail and suggests some way of agreement where possible; but the greater part of the book is occupied with an examination in the light of history of the claim to Infallibility. In conclusion, he disclaimed any ulterior object except unity; he was in no way educating a party in the best form of anti-Roman arguments. As a matter of fact there was no party behind him; since Keble's death he stood, he said, quite alone: his position had been altogether exaggerated.

' I wish, in this new "Eirenicon," to be understood as speaking in the name of no one but my single self. I have consulted no one. The one whom I ever consulted, with whom I was ever one, who was deeply interested in whatever might promote healthful Reunion, to whom, in his last days, the hope was a subject of joy, can now only pray for it, but, perhaps, does more for us there. I write, then, in the name of no party. But I do write in the full confidence that I express the feelings of thousands upon thousands of English hearts, both here and in the United States, when I say that if, not individual but accredited, Roman authority could say, "Reunion would involve your

---

[1] 'Eirenicon,' Part III, pp. 39, 40.

professing your belief in this and that and that, but it would not involve your receiving such and such opinions, or practices or devotions or matters of discipline," I believe that the middle wall of partition which has existed so long in, as we believe, the one fold of Christendom would be effectually shattered. . . . We are children of common fathers, of those who, after having shone with the light of God within them upon earth, and set on a candlestick which shall never be hid,—the clear light of their inherited faith,—now shine like stars in the kingdom of their Father. Sons of the same fathers, we must in time come to understand each other's language. I need not commit this to your deep personal love and large-hearted charity. To others in your Communion I would only say through you that neither in this nor in my former work have I thought to speak against anything which is "of faith" among you; one only desire I have had, if it were possible to such as me, to promote a solid, healthful, lasting peace. Evil days and trial-times seem to be coming upon the earth. Faith deepens, but unbelief too becomes more thorough. Yet what might not God do to check it, if those who own One Lord and one faith were again at one, and united Christendom should go forth bound in one by Love—the full flow of God's Holy Spirit unhemmed by any of those breaks or jars or manglings—to win all to *His* Love Whom we all desire to love, to serve, to obey! To have removed one stumbling-block would be worth the labour of a life[1].'

As Pusey finished his work he wrote to Newman, expressing his fears and asking how he should make use of the book to the best advantage. Bossuet's opinions were, he thought, too moderate for modern Romans, and any dispassionate consideration of Infallibility had become to many only a declaration of war. Still he begged Newman to suggest some names of English and American Bishops to whom he might send copies. Following Newman's advice, the book was despatched, soon after the assembling of the Council, to several Bishops who were at Rome, as well as to Mgr. Dupanloup and De Buck. Pusey could not quite give up hope, even when the strength of the extreme Ultramontane party seemed to make hope impossible. Speaking of the low appreciation of Bossuet, which he was now convinced was current at Rome, he said to Newman just after the meeting of the Council: 'Had I known it, I should, I suppose——— no, I don't know

---

[1] 'Eirenicon,' Part III. pp. 341–343.

what I suppose I should have done. Perhaps I should not have thought it hopeless.'

Before the Council assembled the Pope had sanctioned the decision of the Supreme Congregation that De Buck should be bidden to cease his correspondence with some ' heterodox Anglicans[1].' But it appears that the General of the Jesuits must have been rather slow in forwarding this decision to De Buck, for although the decree was passed on November 17, 1869, the correspondence still continued.

On December 2 Bishop Forbes assured De Buck that he had not forgotten his promise of sending in proposi-tions, but that the turn of events had shown that De Buck had wrongly interpreted the summons to the Council. He went on, however, to express his earnest hope that something might be done to keep the position open in view of better days. De Buck's answer, dated December 13, complained of the Bishop's tardiness, which impeded his own action. On every side he had been warned, he said, especially by the General of his own Order, and a Spaniard (his old theological tutor, now on the 'Commission conciliaire papale'), 'de me tenir en dehors de tout ce qui aurait l'air d'être un parti.' The prominence of Manning at the Council, and his appointment on the Committee for receiving and considering all propositions of the assembled Bishops, was, he said, to be explained as a position of honour like that which was given to the Hellenists in the Acts of the Apostles, 'the last are the first.' He begged Bishop Forbes to come to Rome himself; Manning's position was an earnest of the treatment that would be accorded to him if he decided ' à faire enfin le pas définitif.' He wrote again on December 20, delivering a message from Cardinal Bilio, to the effect that he would make

[1] 'Feria IV die 17 Novembris 1869. Eĩni *DD*. . . . *decreverunt quod per medium Rĩni P. Generalis Societatis Jesu, sub secreto Sancti Officii, scribatur opportune P. de Buck ut ab incoepto conciliationis tractatu cum nonnullis heterodoxis Anglicanis omnino desistat.* . . . Eadem die ac feria. *SSĩnus resolutionem Eĩno-rum adprobavit.*' Cecconi, ' Storia del Concilio Ecumenico Vaticano. Ante-cedenti del Concilio.' Secunda Primae, p. 302 note.

every arrangement for their worthy reception at Rome
by Cardinal de Lucca, the first President of the Council[1];
thus putting them into communication with the person
best able to advance their interests, and avoiding the
difficulty which they apprehended in an introduction by
Archbishop Manning.

In reply to this invitation Bishop Forbes writes the
following letter; which was evidently from Pusey as well
as from himself:—

BISHOP (FORBES) OF BRECHIN TO DR. DE BUCK.

Christ Church [end of Dec., 1869].

VERY LEARNED AND DEAR SIR,

I was much gratified by the receipt of your letter conveying
to me the results of your conversation with the eminent Cardinal who
has exhibited such an intelligent interest in the position of the
Reunionist party in the Church of England. For the first time
I begin to conceive hope that something may be done in a matter
so fraught with important results to the interests of Christianity.

At the risk of repeating what I have placed before you ere this,
in order that His Eminence may not be deceived or disappointed, I shall
endeavour to lay down our present position.

That powerful section of the High Church party in the English
Church who look to the restoration of the corporate unity of
Christendom as one great remedy of the advancing and all-devouring
Rationalism of the nineteenth century stand in this relation to the
body of which they are members:

(1) They are able to accept *ex animo* all the documents which they
sign as terms of ministering in the Church, interpreting them in the
Catholic sense and as illustrated by the references to the consent
of the Early Fathers which these documents recognize.

(2) They deplore the existence of the schism which took place
at the Reformation, though they are alive to the many incidental
advantages that flowed from it, e.g. the freedom of the use of the
Holy Scriptures and the destruction of many of the superstitions
which defiled the Church and which called for reform long before
the too long delayed Council of Trent. Better had it been for all
that we had reformed along with the Council of Trent, and that both
reforms had been made more thorough. Deploring, then, the existence
of the schism, they yet accept their isolated position: they have
inherited it, not made it, having regard to the fact that they are
where the Providence of God has placed them, and where their

---

[1] Shortly afterwards Card. de Lucca
was disgraced and removed, apparently
for sympathy with Bishop Strossmayer
(*Guardian*, 1870, p. 82).

circumstances are such that they would feel treasonable to God if they did not recognize that His Spirit was working.

(3) They firmly believe that not only is salvation to be had in Anglicanism, but that they have valid Sacraments, and that grace flows to them through those Sacraments. They believe that providentially at the Reformation the forms used were sufficient to transmit the grace of the Episcopate—that therefore the Bishops confer a valid Ordination, the Bishops and Priests consecrate a valid Eucharist and convey ministerially the remission of sins to all true penitents. They believe that the English Church has had a special duty in the matter of Evidential Theology—that concerned with the proofs of natural and revealed religion—and they appeal with confidence to the general character for religion and morality of the English people, so truthful, so brave, so conscientious, as a proof that the English Church, far short as she has come of her ideal, has yet continued by God's grace to operate for good. Above all, they point with thankfulness to the mighty religious revival of the last forty years, which has filled the country with new churches, restored the old in their pristine beauty, founded religious orders, restored auricular Confession, and introduced a higher standard of faith and practice both among Clergy and laity. In fact, making allowances for the [presence] of the tolerated Calvinism, that the situation is similar to that of the great schism, when Saints were arrayed on either side.

(? 4 or 5) They have a conservative horror of what are called the extremes of Romanism. The excess of the cultus of our dear Lady and such exaggerated expressions as that of the Bishop of Geneva, that the Pope is an incarnation of God, fill their souls with dismay—the more so because not only are such expressions unchecked by authority, but there seems a gradual tendency to increasing exaggeration in these and similar respects. I would wish His Eminence to have this very strongly borne in upon his mind. I believe that in this is the real bar to what Dr. Pusey has happily termed healthful reunion.

(? 5 or 6) Against all this discouragement must be put the fact that we acknowledge that the condition of Anglicanism in reference to the great Church of the West is unsatisfactory, and that the prospects of the Church of England, politically, are not encouraging. Soon she will be emancipated alike from the trammels and the support of the State, and then most important changes are likely to occur. Reconciliation on fair terms with the Latin Church would, of course, be best absolutely for her. The Calvinistic element would incorporate itself with the Dissenters, or unite itself to the mass of political Churchmen, while it is to be hoped that God may open the way to the Catholic party, without injury to its convictions resting under the Chair of St. Peter. It is to this consummation that present efforts must be directed. We may not live to see it ; but surely to lay the foundation of such a work as this must be well pleasing to our

Gracious Saviour, Whose prayer for unity sounds forth from the Upper Chamber of Jerusalem through all time to the ends of the earth. 'Ut hi omnes unum sint, sicut tu Pater etc. Fiat voluntas Tua, Domine Iesu, Fili Mariae. Amen.'

At the same time Newman and Pusey exchanged the news which they had received from Rome. Newman told Pusey that he had heard that the power of Manning was dwindling, and that the popular estimate of the numbers of the Ultramontane party was exaggerated. Pusey replied—

E. B. P. TO REV. J. H. NEWMAN.

Jan. 28 [1870].

It is very satisfactory to find the 500 who were said to have signed the petition for the declaration of Infallibility so reduced. But what was the *Westminster Gazette* about? Manning's is a strange lot. With, I should have thought, but a very moderate share of learning, by throwing himself into the tide, to seem to be at the head of a movement which should revolutionize the Church. It is a mysterious lot, one which one should not like for one's self.

The composition of the Congregation on Dogma has discouraged us. Those whom we should have had most confidence in, Mgr. Dupanloup and Darboy, omitted, and Manning in it. It is utterly hopeless to send any propositions to a Congregation in which Manning should be a leading member. I am told that he has been impressing the Council, or at least important Bishops, with the idea that hundreds of thousands of the English would join the Roman Communion if the Infallibility were declared. I hear that he has been pressing it on this ground, from Lord Acton and Döllinger, and from D. that the Nuncio at Munich (as I understood him) was impressed with his assertion. Both wrote to ask me what I thought. Of course I wrote to Lord A. first. Their letters were not private; but it is as well not to repeat names. . . .

I have had a letter from De Buck also on the 'Is Healthful Reunion, &c.', which I have answered. He also, like the Bishop who writes to you, regards it as 'an approximation,' which is, in kinder language, to say that it is unsatisfactory. Yet the part which I suppose is most unsatisfactory, viz. that asking for the same αὐτονομία, in the ordinary course of the affairs of the Church as was enjoyed in St. Augustine's time, was in conformity to what was said to me by a very eminent French ecclesiastic.

I am glad to see that your book, of which I had heard from Copeland, is almost finished. It must be a great relief to you, and will be a great gain to us all.

You had my book, I hope. I directed it to be sent, but more than one miscarried.

I had a very kind letter from the Abp. of St. Louis, to whom Lord Acton gave a copy of my book from me (though not committing himself), and saw a letter from the Archbishop of Halifax, which in fact he said I might see, in which he too looked on it as granting much, only he said I had before 'wriggled' out of concessions which I had made. I sent it to the three English Bishops at Rome whom you named, and also to Father Häcker. But either my direction was insufficient or they are busy. I hear there is a kindly notice in, I think, *Le Français*, but I have not seen it. I did not send it to Manning, thinking it simply provocative, as so much is against the Infallibility.

But as the meetings of the Council went on, Pusey had really very little hope of any wise result. Writing to Liddon on January 13, 1870, he says: 'The Council looks as unlike any assembly guided by God the Holy Ghost as one could well imagine. All seems to be done by human policy or stayed by human fears. I fear some compromise which shall involve the principle [of Infallibility], leaving the actual affirmation until hereafter.'

Those who are familiar with the condition of Rome in 1870, and the despotic power that then prevailed in the Papal dominions, will not be astonished at the following correspondence. To Pusey it must have been a deep disappointment after the labour and the hopes of so many months.

E. B. P. TO REV. J. H. NEWMAN.

March 10, 1870.

You said that the moderate party would have enough to do to keep their own ground. So I suppose they wish to have nothing to do with us. I have just had the two copies of the 'Is Healthful Reunion Impossible?' which I sent to the Bishop of Orleans and your Bishop of Clifton returned to me from Rome with '*refusé*' written upon them. I doubt whether the Bishop of Orleans reads English; but anyhow, he could have had it read for him by one of his theologians. The cover was so far torn that he could see what the book was, and my own respectful and affectionate inscription.

It seems an abrupt ending of great kindness, the more singular in a Frenchman.

Newman hoped that the fault lay with Pusey, although he had a suspicion that the books were returned by Roman authorities.

REV. J. H. NEWMAN TO E. B. P.

March 11, 1870.

This I am sure of, that Dr. Clifford would be guilty of no incivility to you, any more than Mgr. Dupanloup.

One suspicion came on me, that the Roman police would not pass a book with your name; but I suppose *some* of your presentation copies *have* got to their destination. . . .

I am writing to Rome, and I will inquire into the fact without introducing you.

Pusey explained that he could quite understand that the friends of Reunion at Rome thought the matter so hopeless that, without any intended discourtesy, they did not think it worth while to receive his books. The anathemas attached to the *Schema de Fide*, even in their amended form, showed that conciliation was the last thing in the minds of the majority of the Council.

Newman had to wait some time before he could get an answer from Rome to his inquiry.

REV. J. H. NEWMAN TO E. B. P.

The Oratory, May 20, 1870.

I have just now received Dr. Moriarty's (Bishop of Kerry's) answer to the question I addressed to him immediately that I heard your news about the returned copies of your book. I suppose he has forgotten to give me his answer (as people do forget) in former letters.

You will see my suspicion is confirmed by his own. He says, 'Neither Dr. Clifford nor Mgr. Dupanloup received Dr. Pusey's Letter. They think it was probably stopped in the Post Office. I lent my copy to Dupanloup, and marked for him the passages which he wanted.' Of course I transcribe this in confidence.

What makes this more likely, is that the post-office or police actually hindered the Bishop of Mayence's (Ketteler's) pamphlet being brought into Rome.

I fear, from Dr. Moriarty's letter, there is no chance of the Definition being avoided.

Pusey's reply summarizes his later correspondence with De Buck.

E. B. P. TO REV. J. H. NEWMAN.

Christ Church, May 21, 1870.

Kindest thanks for your letter. I have been meaning to write to you, at the first breathing time, to mention that I had a very kind letter from Bp. Clifford, telling me that neither he nor the Bp. of Orleans had refused my book, and asking me to send it to him at Clifton.

I do not indeed know that any of my books escaped the post-office authorities, except some which it was suggested to me to send to Lord Acton and one which I sent to the Jesuit College.

But it matters little. Kind as individual Bishops are, the party which takes the hard line seems to be in the ascendent. I have written twice to De Buck about the proposed condemnation of the 'branch theory,' as people call it, explaining to him that the only principle really involved in it was that there could be suspension of intercommunion without such schism as should separate either side from the Church of Christ. This any one must admit in the case of Anti-Popes, St. Cyprian, the Churches of Asia Minor, St. Meletius: and De Buck himself admits it in the abstract. Again, I said that they allowed that invincible ignorance excused an individual. But, I said, whatever may have been the case as to Photius, to judge from all the Greeks who have come to visit us, they do labour under an invincible prejudice that the *Filioque* involves the heresy of two 'Αρχαί in the Godhead. They would, in such case, be under invincible ignorance as to the doctrine of the *Filioque*; and, as long as they believe it honestly to involve a heresy, they are of course bound not to believe it.

To my first letter, he said that the formula of the 'branch theory' would certainly be condemned, and suggested to me to submit, as *he* did as to something which *he* had held. To this I answered that it would be perfectly easy to me to withdraw any Eirenicon or Eirenica in which it was contained, but what good would that do? What we meant by it was that principle which they too would admit, and which was inseparable from our existence and our prayers and our use of the Creeds. For that we could not profess our belief in the Catholic Church, mentally excluding ourselves from it, or pray for its Bishops, excluding our own or any other orthodox Bishops, either in our weekly Prayers or those for the Ember weeks. This last letter only went last Sunday.

But the hard line seems to prevail. Manning seems to me to use his experience in our controversies to direct anathemas skilfully against us. I see that there is an anathema proposed against those who do not hold that St. Peter had jurisdiction over the other Apostles, who had equal fullness of inspiration with himself. What a multiplication of minute anathemas ! I can only turn away, sick at heart, and say, 'Though they curse, yet bless Thou.'

I am again at work on my Commentary on the Prophet Nahum, as perhaps I have said before.

God be with you.

Your most affectionate friend,

E. B. Pusey.

I fear that these decisions will be a great strain on men's faith. Anti-Christ must come, and everything which tries faith must prepare for his coming. Then those who believe must be driven together; whereas this Council seems to be framed to repel all whom it does not scare.

As every one knows, the extreme Ultramontanes succeeded in carrying all before them at the Council, and all the hopes of conciliation were rendered absolutely futile, when the decree about Papal Infallibility was adopted on July 18, 1870. In all later issues of his third Eirenicon, Pusey altered the title from 'Is Healthful Reunion possible?' to a form which embodied his future attitude towards the Roman Question—'Healthful Reunion, as conceived possible before the Vatican Council.'

No correspondence passed between Newman and Pusey when Infallibility was first defined ; but in reply to a congratulatory letter from Newman, on his seventy-first birthday, Pusey expressed his sense of the entire failure of these prolonged negotiations for the union of God's Church.

E. B. P. TO REV. J. H. NEWMAN.

[Christ Church] Aug. 26, 1870.

I knew that your love would remember the 22nd, the entrance, probably, of my last decennium. Before the Council, I wondered whether I might not live to see the union of the Churches: you will have seen and mourned how that has already repelled minds. The last Eirenicon has sunk unnoticed to its grave ; the first, as you know, was popular ; both against my expectations.

I wonder whether the Council will do anything, on its reassembling, to express the conditions of the Infallibility which it has affirmed. To me some of the lesser cases seemed more irreconcileable with Infallibility than the great case of Honorius. As to Honorius, it seemed to me (as I said) either that Honorius erred as to faith, or that General Councils and Popes bore false witness against him. Still, answers were made. But the errors of Popes as to marriage Bellarmine himself does not defend.

However, I say this, because I am writing to you; I have done what I could, and now have done with controversy and Eirenica.

For the moment the principles of Ultramontanism had triumphed, and Pusey seemed to have laboured in vain. Yet it would be a shallow estimate which would consign the Eirenicon, with all the loving work which it enshrined, to a corner in the lumber-room of costly failures and exploded Utopias. The immediate project had failed, but the cause of Reunion was not lost : rather in the end it will be found to have gained. However long God may defer the wished-for end, the contemplation of these years of patient labour will still, as they have already done, kindle others to a like self-devotion. Their history exhibits a picture of no ordinary grandeur,—a noble soul daring to believe, amidst the din of jarring controversy, that God is able to fulfil His own ideal, spreading the contagion of his faith to others, and toiling on through calumny and misrepresentation in his efforts to bring low the mountains that bar the way of the Lord. In spite of all, Pusey knew that he was on the winning side, and continued to pray, as he had prayed for thirty years, in ' The Brotherhood of the Holy Trinity[1] ':—

'Vouchsafe, we beseech Thee, O Lord, to grant to Thy faithful people, unity, peace, and true concord, both visible and invisible, through Jesus Christ our Lord.'

[1] See vol. ii. p. 135.

# CHAPTER VII.

OXFORD ELECTION OF 1865—KEBLE COLLEGE—SPEECH
ON THE DAY OF ITS FOUNDATION—RELATIONS WITH
MR. GLADSTONE.

1865-1872.

SINCE 1847 Mr. Gladstone had represented the University
of Oxford in Parliament. He had been elected six times,
on each occasion after a severe contest. The opposition
had been in the main purely political, because of Mr. Gladstone's connexion with Lord Palmerston and Lord John
Russell. For a long time the High Church party had
loyally voted for him; but it was evident now that he
could not rely much longer on their united support. The
passing in 1861 of the Universities Election Bill, which
allowed non-residents to record their votes by proxy, made
his rejection at the next election more than a remote
possibility. Accordingly already in March of that year
Mr. Gladstone had written to Pusey, to sound him on the
subject of his retirement from the wearisome contests for
the University seat; he desired to know what were his
prospects at the next election, for it was quite possible
that he might be asked to offer himself for the new
constituency which was about to be formed in the
Southern Division of Lancashire. Pusey found it hard
to forecast the future.

E. B. P. TO RIGHT HON. W. E. GLADSTONE, M.P.

March 17, 1861.

We none of us here can doubt that you would do everything loving
and thoughtful for the University which we know you love. As for
contests, I do not suppose that your retiring would put an end to them.

O 2

The Liberal and Conservative parties are, I suppose, more balanced than they used to be. The country Clergy are, I suppose too, wearied of Conservatism.

For Conservatism has long not had a principle left, and, when in power, is revolutionary. I think that the country Clergy see this more than they did. So, a good many members of Convocation being in-different, I suppose that if you should retire, whether Conservative or Liberal should be returned, the other party would dispute the seat. However, if this new Bill should pass, giving non-residents the power to vote by proxy, there will be a new element introduced which no one can calculate. My first thought was, whether it would introduce less careful voting than now, when voting involves a good deal of trouble to most. My second was, how it would affect your seat. I suppose if any recent act of yours should vex the country Clergy, the change might have a considerable effect, and probably on the first occasion the D'Israeli party would try their utmost.

One or two other letters passed between them on the subject, Pusey urging him to remain, and Mr. Gladstone showing how tired he was of the contested elections. At last Pusey ceased to urge his point.

E. B. P. TO RIGHT HON. W. E. GLADSTONE, M.P.

March 30, 1861.

. . . An uncontested seat for South Lancashire may be much better for a Minister of the Crown than a contested, though retained, seat for the University. I hoped that the opposition to you would wear itself out (but for the new Bill as to our votes). I think that a large proportion of our Clergy are weary of Conservatism, and glad to have a representative (whatever his politics) of religious principle, as your-self. But I thought that if those who dispute your seat thought that they would tire you out, they would not be tired out themselves. It was just your not being able to 'hide your weariness of the Oxford contests' which I thought likely to prolong them. For weary as an opponent may be, he will still struggle on, if he have any hope that by so doing he will gain his end.

Forgive me, but the one thing I wanted you not to do was not to balance in public.

Now, do not let me make you write any more. I do not pretend to see what is best for you. As for Oxford, I should think that your retiring would rather perpetuate contests. The days when a member was elected for life are, I should think, except in the case of some felicitous combination, over. They were the days of Toryism. Conservatism has no hold over the affections, or principles, having neither principle nor enthusiasm, in its present form. You have a hold from personal character, from the affections of a good many of us, from your having held the seat thus long, from the respect in which a good many M.A.'s hold you. Even that malicious *Times* says, that you are just the member for us.

But what is best for you is another matter: and, since I cannot judge, I have no opinion. The contests must be wearying, and yet each successive contest has only drawn out the fact that a decided majority of your constituents thinks you our best representative.

Consequently, when in July, 1861, a deputation from South Lancashire presented a memorial signed by 8,000 electors asking Mr. Gladstone to represent them, he declined the honour on the ground that he could not quit his Oxford constituents, 'except in a manner which would enable me to feel that I had exposed them to no prejudice by the act.'

When the General Election came on in 1865, feeling ran very high against Mr. Gladstone among a large portion of the Churchmen who had votes for the University, and his chances of election were from the first doubtful. An active Committee of ardent Conservatives and of disappointed Churchmen had already been working against him for twelve months. It may have been that they had expected too much from Mr. Gladstone's influence in Liberal ministries, or they may have been disappointed at the readiness of Liberal ministers to sacrifice what they themselves considered safeguards of the Church and her teaching. When then the natural results of the University legislation of 1854 were beginning to be felt, when surviving disabilities of Nonconformists were being swept away, as in Mr. Hadley's Bill, when the 'Abolition of Universities Test Act' was coming into view, their dislike in any way to support a Liberal ministry was increased. They were still further alienated by Lord Palmerston's Episcopal appointments, and the cynical manner in which Lord Westbury, as Lord Chancellor, had emphasized the Judgments of the Supreme Court of Appeal in the cases of 'Essays and Reviews' and of Bishop Colenso. As Bishop Wilberforce, writing to Mr. Gladstone on July 18, 1865, says—

'Of course if half of these men had known what I know of your real devotion to our Church, that would have outweighed their hatred of a Government which gave Waldegrave to Carlisle, and Baring to Durham, and the youngest bishop on the bench (Thomson) to York, and supported Westbury in seeking to deny for England the Faith of our Lord.'

Still Pusey and Keble both joined Mr. Gladstone's Committee. Keble was not well enough to take any active share in the canvass. It was on what proved to be Keble's last birthday that Pusey sent him the following message :—

E. B. P. TO REV. J. KEBLE.

April 25, 1865.

. . . I have said that you will be on the London Committee for Gladstone : it being understood that this is not to involve the slightest work, only to express your interest in him. I am on the resident Committee.

I am writing on purpose to-day to express my thankfulness for the many and great mercies which God gave us through giving you to us to-day and my hope for their continuance.

But Pusey did all he could to secure Mr. Gladstone's return, writing letters to any whose votes he might be able to influence. To one he writes on June 3, 1865 :—

'The more I think of it, the more it grieves and alarms me to think of what is going on against W. E. G. Besides all the rest, I think him the only statesman, so far as I see, who really understands as well as loves Church principles.'

To another correspondent, now the Dean of Chichester, he sends a fuller appeal :—

E. B. P. TO REV. R. W. RANDALL.

Christ Church, Oxford, July 4, 1865.

A friend of mine tells me that he thinks that you would not dislike to hear from me about Gladstone's election. You will have seen, perhaps, that I am deeply interested in it, and that from my personal knowledge of him, which reaches back to his Undergraduate days. We cannot expect that any statesman will fight the battles of the Church, exactly in our way. But all must be right, in the end, where there is that single-hearted loyal love of God and His Church, of His Faith and Truth, which there is in Gladstone. It would be an ill day if Oxford were to snap the relation of eighteen years of faithful service. Recently too we owe him much. Before his political weight was felt, the canon would have been altered, without any expression of the opinion of the Church[1]. In the trying days, which may be before the Church, we may be sure that he will act out of a devoted love for God and her.

In spite of the efforts of all those who still supported him, Mr. Gladstone was rejected at this election. Pusey thus expresses his thoughts on the result to an old friend, who had felt obliged to remain neutral in the contest :—

E. B. P. TO THE VENERABLE ARCHDEACON CHURTON.

Ventnor, July 25, 1865.

I think that Oxford has made a terrible mistake, which she will soon have to rue. Of course, a large accession to the support of Goschen's Bill will be an immediate fruit. But *the* mistake, I think, is, in itself, to cast away one loyal and devoted to God, the Faith, and the Church. His affecting farewell must have given a pang to many hearts, as well as to mine. The case of a bond which had lasted eighteen years is very different from the question of forming one for the first time.

It has, I think, too, gone far to commit Oxford Churchmen (for *they* turned the election) to Establishmentarianism. Some Low Churchmen, at least, held aloof because they expected Gladstone to be Prime Minister one day, and not to make Low Church bishops. So far their concern was for the Church, as they understood its interests. Some High Churchmen rejected him, because he could not see his way in all the perplexed questions about the Establishment. I could have been a Tory; but 1830 ended Toryism. I could not be a mere Conservative, i.e. I could not bind myself, or risk the future of the Church on the fidelity or wisdom of persons whose principle it is to keep what they think they can, and part with the rest. I believe that we are in the course of an inevitable Revolution ; that the days of Establishments are numbered, and that the Church has to look to her purity, liberty, faithfulness to Catholicism, while I fear that the Conservatives would corrupt her in order to increase the numerical strength of the Establishment. Gladstone did more for the Church, by gaining the recognition of the non-established Church of Scotland, and obtaining freedom for Convocation (against others in a divided Cabinet) to debate on the alteration of the canon, than any other statesman I know of. This formed a great precedent, full of important consequences (as all precedents are), that changes in the canons of the Church be not made by the State without her concurrence. Oxford requites this by rejecting him. Do not trouble yourself to answer this. You, as a member of Convocation, are in the battle, not I. Gladstone's rejection has

---

[1] The reference is apparently to the manner in which a proposed alteration in the canon about sponsors was first submitted to the Convocation of Canterbury.

severed my last link with earthly politics; I fear it has broken other links too; or rather has shown that it only wanted a pull to sever what was only seemingly held together. The High Church are broken to bits.

But if his interest in general politics was at an end, he was profoundly interested in all measures that affected the Church and the University. During this time he was regularly returned at each election as a member of the Hebdomadal Council, and took the greatest pains about all the business of the University. His letters to Liddon and Bright are full of allusions to his work as a member of that body, where he watched with eagerness everything that might affect the interests of Religion at Oxford. The decision in the Jowett case had practically convinced him that it was hopeless to attempt to enforce the old religious character of the University; but he felt that he could at least keep vigilant guard over all that promoted Religion within its walls.

It was during these years that Mr. (afterwards Lord) Coleridge's Bill for abolishing all those religious tests at the University which had been retained by the first University Commission was first brought forward. It was practically a measure of Church disendowment, for its effect would be that offices which had hitherto been tenable only by Churchmen would in future be thrown open to all candidates irrespective of their religious opinions. Two letters from Pusey, one to Liddon and one to Mr. Gladstone, will show his view of the measure as affecting the future of the University.

E. B. P. TO REV. H. P. LIDDON.

March 21, 1868.

It seems to me a marvellous proposition (to limit myself to this only) to require that the Church of England should have immediate notice to quit, and to decide either to educate her future clergy in some as yet unformed Clerical Colleges like Stonyhurst or Highbury, or to have them educated by those who need have no religious belief, not even in the God Who made them.

I have long foreseen that some form of Denominationalism must sooner or later replace Establishments. Denominationalism sacrifices money, not principle or faith. Secularism destroys all religious teaching altogether, perfect or imperfect.

It is but a little portion of the evil that the Church will have to detach itself from the Universities unless it consent to risk that its future teachers should go through the ordeal of an unbelieving teaching, when their minds are unripe to cope with it. This principle indeed occasioned the Bishops of France to obtain the emancipation of the future clergy from the University of France—we think to the disadvantage of both.

A like cause must produce consistently a like effect ; although it is not a little hard upon the Church to wrest from her the only places of education which she has for her clergy, and upon the retention of which the provisions of the last University Reform Act taught her the more to rely.

But this is only one part of a large whole. There lie before our legislators three possible lines only—(1) the continuance of Establishments, (2) Denominationalism, (3) Secularism. The experiment on the University is not *in corpore vili*, and will naturally be the precedent for the line which the other changes shall take. Denominationalism, rude as it is, has something earnest about it. Let us be in earnest, and England will be saved, though it has abundance of elements to produce a worse than the first French Revolution. But an indifferentist education can but unnerve all earnestness and energy for good.

E. B. P. TO RIGHT HON. W. E. GLADSTONE, M.P.

March 24, 1868.

I had long seen that things were driving to some sort of Denominationalism in lieu of Establishments, i. e. since the Church had lost so many of her children through her neglect, it was probable that she should be punished, at least temporally. But J. Coleridge's Bill and Bright's speech on the Irish Church (as I hear) and a saying of Mr. Lowe's, point to a much worse evil, Secularism. For rude and rough as Denominationalism is, endowing every error which can gain adherents, it still presupposes that people are in earnest ; for without some sort of earnestness they would not have adherents. But Secularism can promote only indifference. I had far rather see the money of the Colleges taken, and Socinian, Baptist, Wesleyan, Presbyterian, and of course Roman Catholic Colleges endowed with it [1], than have Coleridge's Bill, according to which our laity and future Clergy are (as a condition of University training) to be exposed to Atheistic or any sort of God-denying teaching.

If they mean by 'the Church' which they say this absence of security of any religious belief on the part of our tutors is not to injure, an undogmatic Church of the future in which persons are to believe

[1] This proposal he made in a letter to the Wesleyan Conference at Liverpool in the following August, inviting their co-operation ; and he defended the scheme at length in a letter to the *Times,* dated August 20.

anything or nothing, to deny a life to come, and count themselves Christians, while they speak of Christianity as a thing of the past, which has served its time—this would be intelligible, but it is not the sense in which the House of Commons would understand the word 'Church.' But to say that it cannot hurt the Church that her laity and future Clergy should be taught by Atheists and others who deny the claim of the Gospel as a Revelation from God, is such mockery, and that aggravated by the provision that nothing is to hinder the religious intercourse of the young men with their tutor ! As if any Act of Parliament could hinder the intercourse of any one with any one ! But what is to be the religious intercourse with one who denies God or His Revelation ?

To-morrow's *Guardian* ought to have letters from Liddon and myself avowing our preference to Denominationalism over Secularism. I fear no battle (though I believe that the party who would gain most are the Roman Catholics)—any battle, at whatever disadvantage, at whatever close quarters, rather than indifference and corruption at the fountain head of education.

I think that the measure is specially hard to the English Church, because we were taught by the Oxford Act, twelve years ago, to rely on the Universities as the place of education for our Clergy ; and now, unprepared with any Colleges like Stonyhurst or Highbury, with all our clinging to the old Universities, we are bid to take our choice, either go on with a system which necessarily involves God-denying teaching to a greater or less extent, or abandon them and all the reminiscences of the past, and try a system as yet untried by us, and which we have always been told will narrow our Clergy and diminish their influence, at least among the higher classes.

A Liberal said to me, 'Your weak point is that you have such already.' No system can bind those who accept obligations and violate them. But this is but a passing evil. Coleridge's Bill stereotypes it. It is asked for to soothe the consciences of those who are uneasy under obligations which they set at nought. But Coleridge's Bill would not only justify them in retaining their tutorships, it would justify them also in denying Christ to their pupils.

It may be understood that with such changes in contemplation Pusey threw himself with all the more zest into the work of the establishment of an institution like Keble College.

It has been mentioned that, immediately after Keble's funeral, his friends met at the house of Sir Wm. Heathcote, and Pusey propounded his scheme for a College which should emphasize the principles of religion and economy and thus advance University extension in the best way possible. It will be remembered, as described in the last volume[1], that a scheme of this kind had been discussed as early as 1845 amongst certain Churchmen—Mr. Keble, Pusey, Mr. Gladstone, Sidney Herbert, Charles Marriott, and others. It had advanced so far as a proposal being laid before the Hebdomadal Council, but it had not met with a favourable reception. Efforts were made again to facilitate the coming to the University of a poorer class of students at St. Mary Hall under Dr. Chase, the Principal. A further plan was in contemplation which Dr. Shirley had discussed with Keble himself, only a short time before his death, securing his full sympathy.

It seemed only reasonable that any memorial to Keble should be advanced on these lines; and accordingly at a meeting shortly after the funeral, held at the Archbishop's palace at Lambeth, the scheme began to assume a definite shape. A body of trustees was formed, of which Pusey was one, and committees, both general and executive, were appointed to carry on the work.

Every step of the preparation for the College was most anxiously watched by Pusey. It seemed most appropriate that the memorial to Keble should aim at securing for the Church a firmer foothold in the University at the moment when it was contemplated to secularize in great measure the endowments of the older Colleges.

On St. Mark's Day, April 25, 1868, the anniversary of Keble's birthday, the first stone was laid by the Archbishop of Canterbury. On that occasion a great meeting, at the Sheldonian Theatre, publicly inaugurated the undertaking. Pusey amongst others made a very impressive speech, and expressed his grave anxieties for the position of the University and his ardent hopes for the New Foundation :—

'Some time after I knew of the loss, in which I myself had more than a common share, the thought would obtrude itself, "They will propose a memorial to him. What memorial can befit him? What memorial would not be mere mockery?" A monument, in (which was spoken of)

---

[1] Vol. iii. pp. 79-89.

Westminster Abbey?   The two letters " J. K.," author of " The Christian Year," would speak more to the heart than any monument,
however beautiful.   For, as ἀνδρῶν ἐπιφανῶν πᾶσα γῆ τάφος, so, and
much more, a work which in words of simple beauty had awakened
and would awaken in human hearts, as long as our language shall
endure, thoughts of truth and awe and chastened love, and pure faith,
and deep reverence and spiritual devotion, was a monument *aere peren-
nius* written anew in the souls of successive generations, who would
bless him who taught them.   I should have been glad at the time that
" The Christian Year " should have been his only monument. . . .

' It was not a mere plan to bring up those who could not afford the
expenses of ordinary Colleges.   It was to extend the College system,
but it was more.   It was to found a College which would react upon
the rest of the University : which should have a character of its own,
of which all our members should, whatever their several capacities, be
real students ; in which none, except for some accident, should fail in
any examination, or fall short of that distinction for which his natural
capacity fitted him ; which should not be divided into good and bad
sets, of which the bad would be ever trying to absorb the freshmen
into itself, but whose *esprit de corps* it should be to knit in one by the
mutual intercourse and friendship of all with all ; in which the Head
and Tutors should be the friends of the undergraduates, live with
them, live for them, have all interests visibly in common with them.
I believe that such a plan would be eminently successful.   The cords
of love bind much faster than any chains of discipline. . . . It has been
said : " Found a College which must needs in some way abide when
everything is reeling around you?   Give it his loved and revered
name, when you know not into whose hands it will pass—whether the
plan of secularizing the University and its Colleges may not prevail,
and the College which you stamp with his name may not be directed
by Indifferentists, by those who believe that there is nothing to believe,
that every definite system is sure to be wrong, or that Christianity is
a thing of the past ? "   All which man or the law can do to prevent this
has been done ; and, I believe, done securely.   Parliament can, but
will not willingly, overrule a recent deed of trust.   The poverty of the
College is also a security.   Men covet wealth, not poverty ; the pomp
of Herod, not the white robe of Jesus Christ.   But the argument goes
much further.   Were such counsels to prevail, not a Church or School
could be built, for fear the Church should be alienated, the School
secularized ; every work for God would be paralyzed, and this religious
paralysis would bring about the decay which it dreads.   Let us not
part with this prerogative.   No!   Viewing steadily in the face the awful
life and death struggle around us and among us ; viewing that more
personal, yet in one way more miserable, strife whereby some who love
their Redeemer, Whom we too love, are, by an inconceivable infatua-
tion, bent, if they could, to expel from the Church of England those
who hold the Faith which Keble held and taught—our confidence is not

in ourselves, not in man, but in Him Whose Truth he taught. But be it that things around us are whirling ever so giddily, be it that all things seem to be borne swiftly on a steady and ever-swelling tide, we know not whither, yet such reeling strife is ever the time for the ventures of Faith. We remember still how it startled the Carthaginian conqueror to hear that the soil on which the camp of his victorious soldiers stood, was sold at an unbated price within besieged Rome. On higher authority we know how Jeremiah, while yet in prison. and with the certain knowledge that Jerusalem should be taken by the Chaldaeans, was taught of God to buy the inheritance of his uncle's son at Anathoth, and bury the title-deeds for many days. So now, be Oxford beleaguered as it may or by whom it may—be it that, as the writer of the " Christian Year " said, with presaging mind, some thirty years ago, viewing it from Bagley encircled by the overflowing waters,—

> " The flood is round thee, but thy towers as yet
> Are safe [1],"—

yet safe, as he thought and felt, only by prayer—the stone which has been placed this day by our Church's Primate has, we trust, been founded on the firm Rock, Which is Christ, and the College to be raised thereon will be like that far-famed beacon on our southern shores, built stone by stone out at sea, amidst the tumult of the waters, well knit together.'

It had been one of Pusey's great hopes from the time the College was first mentioned that Liddon should be its first Warden. 'The one idea I have had,' he wrote to him on June 3, 1868, 'was that you could give a stamp to it such as he would wish.' Bishop Wilberforce, Lord Beauchamp, and others who had taken great interest in the memorial joined with Pusey in urging Liddon to accept the post; but he resolutely declined. He felt that his true vocation was elsewhere, that he was unable to accept for himself a life of academical struggle such as Pusey's had been, and further, that he was unfit for many of the duties which must devolve on the first head of a new foundation. It was a profound disappointment to Pusey, and seemed for the time to damp his hopes about the whole scheme; but when in the following year, Edward Stuart Talbot was, chiefly on the urgent recommendation of Liddon, nominated Warden, Pusey warmly welcomed the appointment, and again renewed his intense interest in every detail of the preparations for the opening of the College.

---

[1] ' Lyra Apostolica,' No. cl.

It was an unfortunate circumstance that at the particular time when the College was about to be opened Pusey was somewhat alienated from Mr. Gladstone. In the early winter of the year 1869, on the death of Bishop Phillpotts, Mr. Gladstone nominated Dr. Temple, one of the writers in 'Essays and Reviews,' to the see of Exeter. Upon this, Pusey, most sorrowfully, felt it necessary to dissociate himself finally from Mr. Gladstone's actions as a politician. With our present knowledge, it is perhaps equally difficult to do justice to the courage of the appointment and to Mr. Gladstone's discerning confidence in the character of his nominee, and on the other hand to estimate the grounds of the outcry which it caused. Nearly all who had attacked 'Essays and Reviews' were loud in their disapproval. Churchmen varying as much as Pusey and Lord Shaftesbury alike protested. No doubt the agitation was founded on a mistake as to what were the opinions held by Dr. Temple; but it cannot be denied that the blame for the mistake lay really on the Essayists. A number of men cannot combine to publish their Essays in one volume, without leading others to the conviction that their union extends beyond the sewing of the pages. All the Essays were naturally judged by the tone of the volume as a whole. It must be remembered that even Dr. Tait had taken this view, and writing to Dr. Temple in 1861, had expressed himself as follows :—

THE BISHOP (TAIT) OF LONDON TO DR. TEMPLE.

Feb. 22, 1861.

. . . I shall be ready to state publicly, if you desire it, what is my opinion of your essay taken by itself. But the public appears, I must say not unnaturally, resolved to regard the volume as one whole.

Without entering on other points to which I object, I will say that when taken as a whole the teaching of the volume is in my judgment not consistent with the true doctrine maintained by our Church as to the office of Holy Scripture. I feel convinced that there is much in this volume of which you as well as others of the contributors disapprove, and I therefore the more regret that your high character and deserved influence should, as matters stand at present, seem to give weight to the volume as a whole. . . .

Mr. Gladstone, indeed, may have known that Dr. Temple was very far from sharing the opinions of the writers who had been chiefly attacked; but as a matter of fact he had never done anything during the eight years since the volume appeared to separate himself from statements which incurred the condemnation of such an intimate friend as Dr. Tait. It was only by his sermons after his Enthronement and the subsequent withdrawal of his Essay that Dr. Temple publicly reassured his friends and the main body of aggrieved Churchmen. It would seem that the misunderstanding had much apparent justification, although every allowance must be made for the extreme difficulty of retreating from such a position under such peculiar circumstances. In reply to Pusey's warm protests Mr. Gladstone contented himself with pointing out to him that he could not see the evidence for the charges which were urged against his nominee: while Pusey refused to acknowledge that there was any distinction to be drawn between the various contributors to the offending volume. And when Mr. Gladstone persisted in defending the nomination, nothing remained but to bid him farewell. Loyalty to what he believed to be the requirements of the Truth was the ruling consideration of Pusey's life. He never allowed anything to come in the way of it. A deepening friendship of forty years was sacrificed to it. It will suffice to quote only one letter on this subject.

'Oct. 7, 1869.

'I have written to Gladstone to say that I had clung to him during all those years when my friends at Oxford left him. Now I too must bid him a sorrowful farewell, until such times, if we should live to see them, when, Church and State being severed, he should be free to act according to his better conscience. . . . I should have nothing to say to any one, unsettled as to the Church of England, except to bid them hope for the time when we shall be free from the tyranny of the State at any cost. I must henceforth long, pray, and work, as I can, for the severance of Church and State. If we are to have such an infliction from Gladstone, what shall we not have from irreligious Liberal Premiers? Gladstone has ventured on what Lord Melbourne with all his wilfulness did not do. . . .

'If some vigorous resistance is not made thousands must take refuge in Rome from an "Essay and Review" Church.'

Such a separation was a deep personal sorrow to Pusey, but he thought it a duty to the Faith. For two years he seems to have had no communications with Mr. Gladstone. But at the most critical moment of the Athanasian Creed controversy he received the following letter from Liddon :—

REV. H. P. LIDDON, TO E. B. P.

Nov. 13, 1872.

Mr. Gladstone is in Oxford for one night. . . . He says, 'I cannot bear to be in Oxford without paying my respects to Dr. Pusey, if I could think that he would like to see me.' May I bring him to you at ten to-morrow morning? . . . It is of the greatest practical importance, in view of all our immediate dangers, that you should if possible be on terms of confidence with him again; and I would give anything to see this. And God seems to have given an opportunity of re-establishing such terms.

Pusey could not altogether refuse this appeal.

E. B. P. TO REV. H. P. LIDDON.

Nov. 13, 1872.

It would look like anger, or I know not what, not to see one whom I loved as I did Gladstone. I bade him farewell because I wished to separate my line from his wholly. I felt that he had inflicted a terrible wound and scandal wantonly upon the Church. As a public man, he is a lost friend; as an individual, I love him still; and we hope, by God's mercy, to meet in Heaven. On 'terms of confidence' we can never [be]. His doctrine of 'yielding to the inevitable' must lead him one knows not whither.

But, as an individual, if, in memory of old times, he has a kind wish to see me, I shall be most glad to see him, suppressing the past. The Athanasian Creed is, I trust, common ground.

The following morning, Mr. Gladstone called with Liddon and they found the common ground where Pusey had hoped. But the constant correspondence of earlier years, in which each had applied for and received the assistance and advice of the other, was never renewed.

# CHAPTER VIII.

EARLY RELATION TO RITUAL—SPEECH AT MEETING OF
ENGLISH CHURCH UNION IN 1866—EUCHARISTIC
DOCTRINE—THE BENNETT CASE—OXFORD IN 1870—
THE PRIVY COUNCIL JUDGMENTS IN THE PURCHAS
AND BENNETT CASES.

1866-1872.

AT one period during the troubles in connexion with
'Essays and Reviews,' there appeared to be reasonable
ground for hoping that the two great parties in the Church
were about to work together in defence of those common
beliefs of Christendom which appeared to be in danger.
But to some minds this union was most undesirable. It
has been noticed[1] that Dr. Tait, the Bishop of London,
regarded it as his 'own vocation[2]' to put an end to such a
combination, as being dangerous to the Broad Church party.
The progress of the movement for increased ceremonial in
public worship, and the popular outcry that was raised
against it, assisted him most effectually to realize such a
'vocation.' This 'Ritualistic' controversy, which dates from
a period before the 'Essays and Reviews' appeared, and
continued to rage so long afterwards, not only effectually
brought about the separation which he desired, it embit-
tered party spirit, it frittered away time, wasted money,

[1] See above, p. 68.
[2] 'Life of Archibald Campbell
Tait,' i. p. 325: 'I feel my own vocation clear, greatly as I sympathize
with the Evangelicals, not to allow
them to tyrannize over the Broad

Churchmen; and to limit that tendency which is at present strong in
them, to coalesce with the High
Church party for the mere purpose of
exterminating those against whom the
cry is now loudest.'

injured souls, and exposed the Church to the ridicule of her adversaries. Yet it was a controversy which involved questions of the highest moment. The doctrine of the 'Real Presence,' the Eucharistic Sacrifice and Worship, the doctrine of Absolution, the practice of private Confession, were directly involved in it : and, as if these questions were not of sufficient intricacy and importance, a proposal to discontinue the use of the Athanasian Creed was incidentally thrown in. On all these points there was a sharp severance between the two great sections of the Church. The Latitudinarian party associated itself, as a rule, with the Evangelicals ; and in the Athanasian Creed controversy the Evangelicals sided with them. The High Church party stood alone, but solidly compacted, in defence of all the doctrinal and the more important ceremonial positions : and on every point they won the day.

To a certain extent, 'Ritualism' was an inevitable result of the Oxford Movement. The Tractarians were immediately concerned with the revival of forgotten or half-forgotten truths ; but at the first the use of ritual for the expression of doctrine had not even presented itself to their minds. Some letters, written in 1839, which have appeared in a preceding volume [1], will show Pusey's earliest attitude towards any tendency to the outward expression of a devotional spirit in forms with which ordinary Churchmen were not in those days familiar. The same general position is taken in a letter written in 1851, to the Incumbent of Christ Church, Hoxton, who was involved in difficulties in connexion with some changes in ritual which he had ventured to introduce.

E. B. P. TO REV. W. SCOTT.

Jan. 1, 1851.

I am grieved to hear of your trouble about your ritual. One most grievous offence seems to be turning your back to the people. I was not ritualist enough to know, until the other day, that the act of turning had any special meaning in the Consecration. And it certainly seemed against the Rubric, that the Consecration should take place so that they

[1] Vol. ii. pp. 141–145.

cannot see it. Dear Newman consecrated to the last of his Consecrations at the North end of the altar. Everything may have a meaning· It was, as you know, in some old Roman Churches, the custom to consecrate behind the altar. This too might have its meaning; and the eyes of the people might be more directed to the Oblation.

I cannot myself think that this, or any other ritual, is of moment enough (if not essential to the Sacrament) that priests who would work in the service of the Church should give up, because the Bishop insists on his interpretation of the rubric. Beauty, ritual, music, are all helps; but if we [be] bared of all, three hundred men and the sword of the Lord and of Gideon will rout the mixed rabble. If we cannot have [the] very ritual some of us wish, we have the Faith and the Truth of God, and Holy Scripture, and the Fathers and the Prayer-book and the Holy Eucharist. 'They be more that be for us than they that be against us.'

In the light of this letter it seems a strange irony that the ignorant agitators who led the outcry against the increasing development of ceremonial should have attached the title 'Puseyism' to everything of the kind, from the wearing of the surplice in the pulpit or turning to the East at the Creed, to the most ornate celebration of the Holy Eucharist. During the disgraceful riots at St. George's in the East in the years 1859 and 1860[1], in which the scum of London was hounded on to mob the Rev. Bryan King for ceremonial usages, the cry most frequently raised was 'Down with the Puseyites'; and the Society which organized the disturbances was called 'the Anti-Puseyite League.' Dr. Tait, who was then Bishop of London, did not know Pusey well enough to understand his attitude towards ritual, and had apparently written to him about his 'friends' who were supposed to have given occasion to these disgraceful scenes. Pusey replied :—

E. B. P. TO THE BISHOP (TAIT) OF LONDON.

April 26, 1860.

In regard to my 'friends,' perhaps I regret the acts to which your lordship alludes as deeply as you do. I am in this strange position, that my name is made a byword for that with which I never had any sympathy, that which the writers of the Tracts, with whom in early days I was associated, always deprecated,—any innovations in the way

[1] See 'Charles Lowder, a Biography,' pp. 169-187.

of conducting the Service, anything of Ritualism, or especially any revival of disused Vestments.  I have had no office in the Church which would entitle me to speak publicly.  If I had spoken, it would have been to assume the character of one of the leaders of a party, which I would not do.  Of late years, when Ritualism has become more prominent, I have looked out for a natural opportunity of dissociating myself from it, but have not found one.  I have been obliged, therefore, to confine myself to private protests which have been unlistened to, or to a warning to the young clergy from the University pulpit against self-willed changes in ritual.  Altogether I have looked with sorrow at the crude way in which some doctrines have been put forward, without due pains to prevent misunderstanding, and ritual has been forced upon the people, unexplained and without their consent.  I soon regretted the attempt which the late Bishop [Blomfield] made, and which was defeated.  Had I been listened to, these miserable disturbances in St. George's in the East would have been saved. . . .

But in the next few years the position of ritual entered on a new phase.  Perhaps the change cannot be described better than in Pusey's own words, in a speech which he made when he first joined the English Church Union.  It was delivered at the seventh anniversary meeting of that Society, on June 14, 1866, in proposing a Resolution which called on all the members of the English Church Union to pray for the Church of England.

' It is well known that I never was a Ritualist and that I never wrote a single word on ritual until a short time ago, when my opinion had been quoted against it, on the strength of some particular expressions which I had used.  In our early days we were anxious on the subject of ritual.  I am speaking of days that very few here can know anything of—three-and-thirty years ago.  The circumstances of those times were entirely different from those of our own.  Then there was not the amount of evil or the amount of good that there is now.  There was then a state of apathy in which nothing was disbelieved, and perhaps very little held very deeply.  There was less of luxury and extravagance in those days, and there was very little of self-denial.  Everything was on a cold level.  What we had to do was to rouse the Church to a sense of what she possessed ; and, being ourselves as nothing, so to teach her that she should herself act in all things healthfully from herself.  We had further a distinct fear with regard to ritual ; and we privately discouraged it, lest the whole movement should become superficial.  At that time everything we did was very popular ; and we felt that it was very much easier to change a dress than to change the heart, and that externals might be gained at the cost of the doctrines themselves. To have introduced ritual before the doctrines had widely taken possession of the hearts of the people, would only have been to place an obstruction in their way. It would have been like children sticking flowers in the ground to perish immediately. Our office was rather, so to speak, to plant the bulb where by God's blessing it might take root, and grow and flower beautifully, naturally, healthfully, fragrantly, lastingly. We had also ground for fear lest it should be thought we were only engaged in a matter of external order. There used to be a painful motto, " Evangelical truth and Apostolical order "—as if *we* had not also the truth in all its fullness, and as if all that *we* cared for were matters of order.

'Again, we thought that nothing should be done by the clergy till it was asked for by the great body of the people. There was at that time a school—a somewhat stiff school—who were anxious on all occasions to bring out all the details of the rubrics, and that even in matters which were of no importance whatever, and which had no definite meaning ; though they created not only tumults, but an idea of clerical tyranny. Of course you remember how the Bishop[1] of this diocese and the Bishop of Exeter, two of the ablest prelates on the bench, endeavoured to introduce a low uniformity of ritual, and how they were successively and entirely defeated. Our own maxim was— first gain the people, and then the people will of themselves gain what we wish. . . .

'Now, in these days, many of the difficulties which we had in the first instance to contend with have been removed. In the first place, I suppose that this is from its very centre a lay movement. The clergy have taught it the people, and the people have asked it of the clergy. We taught it them ; they felt it to be true : and they said, " Set it before our eyes." There is no danger of superficialness now. Thirty years of suffering, thirty years of contempt, thirty years of trial, would prevent anything from being superficial.'

At that time the outcry against Ritualism, from the platform and the press, was so loud and persistent that there was every fear that the Bishops would commit themselves to some united action against it ; and any such action in response to mere clamour might well result in far-reaching disaster. The leading opponents of Ritual and its most weighty supporters alike understood the real point at issue. Elaborate ceremonial and costly decoration of the Altars

---

[1] Dr. Blomfield, Bishop of London. In his charge in 1842 he had enjoined the use of the surplice in preaching and some similar changes, all of which he found himself obliged to withdraw shortly afterwards. Bishop Phillpotts also tried in vain to enforce the use of the surplice in the pulpit.

of the Church were both intended to set forth the highest doctrine in connexion with the Holy Eucharist. Both the doctrine and the ceremonial were equally obnoxious to the Protestant mind ; but the ceremonial afforded a more obvious point of attack than the doctrine, and more readily admitted of the invidious charge of Romanizing. All the world knew that ceremonial was a recent reintroduction ; it was therefore taken for granted that it was contrary to the law, and a revival of what the Reformation had forbidden. In February, 1867, the Bishops, in the Convocation of Canterbury, passed a Resolution on the subject of Ritualism. In the preamble to this Resolution, they adopted the vague language of popular denunciation, and said that Ritualism was in danger of 'favouring errors deliberately rejected by the Church of England.' Such a statement, issued on the authority of the Upper House of Convocation, made it necessary to clear the doctrinal meaning of Eucharistic ritual from all ambiguity. Therefore, in the same month, Pusey took the opportunity of the publication of one of his University sermons to state quite definitely his belief with regard to the Holy Eucharist[1], and to identify himself entirely with the Ritualists in that respect. He wished it to be understood that he held and taught the doctrine which they expressed by means of ceremonial, and desired to shield them if necessary by diverting prosecution to himself. He ends his statement of faith with the following challenge[2] :—

'These truths I would gladly have to maintain, by the help of God, on such terms that, if (*per impossibile*, as I trust) it should be decided by a competent authority, that either the Real Objective Presence, or the Eucharistic Sacrifice, or the worship of Christ there present (as I have above stated those doctrines), were contrary to the doctrine held by the Church of England, I would resign my office. Extrajudicial censures, or contradictions, or opinions, if directed against faith or truth, condemn none but their authors.'

[1] In May, 1867, he joined with seventy other clergy in publishing a similar statement of belief about the Holy Eucharist. See *Guardian* (1867), p. 599.
[2] 'Will ye also go away?' A Sermon, &c., p. 28.

Two months later, the Rev. C. P. Golightly wrote and published an anonymous Letter to the Churchwardens of the Diocese of Oxford, in which he alleged charges of serious doctrinal error against Pusey. Bishop Wilberforce felt that so public a statement ought not to be overlooked ; and at his wish Pusey wrote to the local papers inviting Mr. Golightly to institute proceedings against him. He promised that he would not avail himself of any side issue that might be raised, but would confine his defence simply to the question of doctrine. He alludes to this matter when writing to Newman about the Eirenicon.

E. B. P. TO REV. J. H. NEWMAN.

Christ Church, Oxford, May 2, 1867.

. . . I am rather waiting to see whether Golightly accepts a challenge of mine which you may have seen, if you read the *Guardian*. Of course I don't care a pin for his abuse ; I only did it because he was trying to stir up the Churchwardens in the three counties [Oxford, Berkshire, and Buckinghamshire], and the Bishop of Oxford wished something done. I have staked my office on the result, if I am decided wrong by a ' competent tribunal.' . . .

I think the more seriously about Golightly's possible move, because the feeling that it was serious came over me, after I had committed the challenge to God as should be for His glory. I mean that He hears such prayers, when one offers Him one's all : and though Courts are slow to convict error, it does not follow that they will be slow to condemn truth. They have an instinct that it is against them. But perhaps G. likes hounding others on, rather than fighting himself. . . .

But Golightly never took the case into the Vice-Chancellor's Court. It is quite possible that the legal difficulties of the suit were insurmountable ; and the contest continued on the ground of ritual, in which Pusey was the least interested, instead of on doctrine, where his whole mind was engaged.

The first Report of the Ritual Commission in August, 1867, was mistakenly regarded, at first sight, as a clear attempt to put down all ritual, and as a call for legislation in that direction ; but a little later Pusey came to see that the apparently adverse recommendations of that Report were only directed against any attempt to impose ritual on unwilling congregations. At the English Church Union meeting on November 20, 1867, he warmly supported a Resolution to the effect that any proposed alteration of existing laws on the subject should be resisted by Churchmen to the utmost of their power. But at the same meeting he spoke most strongly against making any changes in the Services of a parish Church in opposition to the wishes of the communicants in that Church. This regard for the laity in ceremonial points was, he maintained, entirely different from the question of their interference in matters involving doctrine. He said :—

'The question does not in the least refer to legislation. . . . The share of the laity in legislation is one thing, and the right of an individual priest by himself, without the support of his Bishop, or of the general body of the Clergy, or of his own congregation, to introduce changes into the Services is quite another. I do wish to lay stress upon the point that no individual member of the whole body has a right to make changes by himself. . . . It has been said that we may have to wait a long time before we can introduce any change at all if we are to wait till we can win the parishioners. I believe it would be better to wait almost any time, except for the Bread of Life Itself—I mean the weekly Communion—rather than introduce changes against the wish of the communicants, especially in this matter of reviving obsolete laws[1].'

On this occasion he had great difficulty in carrying his hearers with him. He described the scene to a correspondent several years afterwards :—

'I had three-fourths or four-fifths of a meeting of the E. C. U. against me on a sentence of mine disclaiming the forcing of ritual on an unwilling congregation. They gave way when I said that if such a proposition were rejected I could be of no more use to the E. C. U. or to Ritualism. But I had only one supporter besides —— and I could tell from the scraping of feet throughout the discussion that my opponents had the hearts of the meeting; not I.'

In the following year, however, his Eucharistic doctrine was submitted to a legal tribunal in a most unexpected

---

[1] *Guardian,* 1867, p. 1280.

manner, and with every possible disadvantage. In the summer of 1868, the Church Association[1] commenced a prosecution against the Rev. W. J. E. Bennett, Vicar of Frome Selwood, for his doctrine of the Eucharist, chiefly as stated in a published Letter to Pusey[2]. In this Letter he had identified himself with Pusey, but also had used some unguarded and inaccurate language about the Eucharist. Pusey disowned these statements, and induced Mr. Bennett to amend them. At the same time he requested the Church Association to direct the prosecution against himself instead of against Mr. Bennett. After a little hesitation this request was refused, on the ground (which apparently was sufficiently correct for controversial purposes) that Pusey had already been authoritatively condemned by the University of Oxford; and the prosecution was continued against Mr. Bennett, for his earlier words, in spite of his amended statement. When the case came on for trial Pusey made several efforts to be included in the suit. In the following letter he explains the grounds for his very justifiable anxiety about it :—

E. B. P. TO RIGHT HON. W. E. GLADSTONE, M.P.

Christ Church, Oxford, Dec. 6, 1868.

Amid your many anxious duties, you are not likely to have observed minutely the charges against Mr. Bennett or to have observed how they affect me primarily, and then the whole High Church body. It is a strange part of the present condition of the law, that an accessory, so to speak, may be indicted so as to involve the condemnation of the principal, and yet that principal have no opportunity of defending himself. Except two careless expressions, which Bennett retracted at my wish, he is indicted simply for approval of language of mine, which he states to be mine in the places in which he expresses that approval. If then the Judicial Committee of the Privy Council should condemn Bennett, then I am already condemned : for they are my *ipsissima verba* for which he would be condemned. And since the Supreme Court of Appeal never reverses its decisions, I could obtain no subsequent hearing. It would be impossible for them, having

---

[1] This Association had recently been established for the special purpose of maintaining and enforcing upon others the Puritan view of the doctrine and formularies of the Church of England.

[2] 'A Plea for Toleration in the Church of England.'

condemned Bennett for expressing approval of words of mine, to acquit me whose words he approved.

Were it simply my own case I should not be troubled myself, or trouble you. It matters little where I spend the remaining years of my life. But it is the existence of the whole High Church body, which is aimed at, and which is at stake; and, with them, the possible existence of any future High Church party in England. This Judgment is to us what the Gorham Judgment would have been to the Evangelicals.

When Dr. Jackson succeeded Dr. Tait in the See of London it seemed as if the Bennett prosecution might lapse. But by the following August not only was this found to be untrue, but also it was announced that Bennett had definitely refused to defend himself or allow himself to be defended. Since he had identified himself with Pusey, this meant that Pusey was on his trial in an undefended suit, and could get no chance of a hearing. He was, as he said, in the position of Uriah, in the assault on Rabbah. He had been set in the forefront of the battle and there left without any means of defence.

The Case was heard before the Court of Arches on June 16, 17, and 18, 1870, and Judgment was pronounced on July 23. Dr. Phillimore condemned Mr. Bennett's first statements, but acquitted him on the ground of the corrected statements in his second edition. He affirmed that it was permissible in the English Church to teach that the Presence of our Lord in the Holy Eucharist was 'objective, real, actual, and spiritual,' and that Mr. Bennett's statements about the Eucharistic Sacrifice and Eucharistic worship did not exceed the liberty allowed by the Formularies and the language used by a long roll of illustrious divines who have adorned the English Universities. So far the faith of the Church was clearly defined; but the case was at once carried by the Church Association before the Final Court of Appeal, and the anxious position was indefinitely prolonged.

On the news of Dr. Phillimore's decision, Pusey thus expresses his sense of the situation in a letter to Dr. Bright :—

E. B. P. TO REV. W. BRIGHT, D.D.

[July 24, 1870.]

It is indeed a great defeat of the Church Association, they having taken what they felt to be vantage-ground on Bennett's inaccurate statements and B. not defending himself. Lord Cairns will do what he can, but he cannot reverse it. However, it is a matter of prayer that he may not be Chancellor by next October.

Dr. Bright was one of the younger generation of brilliant and learned men, who had grown up under the influences of the Oxford Movement, and was at this time beginning to take a leading place in the counsels of Churchmen in the University. He had been appointed in January, 1869, to the Regius Professorship of Ecclesiastical History, to which was annexed a Canonry at Christ Church. Pusey welcomed him to the Chapter with great joy. 'I have been here,' he said, 'forty years, and have never had any one like-minded until now.'

At this time also the growing friendship with Liddon, which has been evident in their frequent letters, was another source of great joy and real help to Pusey. He had hoped that Liddon would, as he had himself done, spend his life at the University, for he was convinced that no other place in England offered any equal opportunity for influencing the religious future of the country. But Liddon refused the Wardenship of Keble College, and in 1870 accepted a Canonry at St. Paul's, in each case in spite of Pusey's earnest entreaties. In the former case, Liddon left the decision with Bishop Hamilton; in the latter, after conditionally accepting it, he threw the final decision on Pusey himself, and Pusey decided that the acceptance had better stand. It was therefore all the greater delight to him when, on June 11 of the same year, Liddon was elected to the Ireland Professorship of Exegesis in the University. He hailed it as a means of keeping him in Oxford, there to fight the battle of the Faith by his side.

E. B. P. TO REV. H. P. LIDDON.

[June 11], 1870.

You see this is no doing of mine. I hope that you will think this is the Voice of God. It is, equally with St. Paul's, without any act of you or your friends. I had so completely given it up that I was only anxious against ——. . . . . I am sure that you have the ear and heart of the young men. . . . I thought when Scott was going, and you, as I supposed, gone, that the Oxford for which we laboured so many years was given up to the infidel. Do then, in the Name of God, accept this.

Undoubtedly the fight for the Faith in Oxford at that moment needed every soldier, and Liddon could ill be spared from a place where he had already made so great an impression. To Pusey's great happiness he accepted the Chair.

Soon afterwards Mr. Gladstone appointed another most able pupil of the early Tractarian movement, Mr. J. B. Mozley, to be Regius Professor of Divinity. As a young graduate he had lived in Pusey's house[1] and studied theology, and was for several years one of Newman's closest friends. On the day of his Ordination, in 1838, Newman had written to him the following note: '*Charissime*, I send you my surplice, not knowing whether or not you want it. It is that in which I was ordained deacon and priest[2].' As 1845 came nearer there was a suspension of this as of so many other friendships; and a little later his published opinions on the Baptismal controversy had caused him to stand somewhat aloof from the High Church party altogether. But he was well known as one of the most keen and able minds as well as a most brilliant Essayist, a reputation which he more than sustained by the great power of his later University sermons. He had been for some time holding a college living at Shoreham in Sussex, when he was appointed to the Professorship, vacated by Dr. Payne Smith's installation as Dean of Canterbury, and Pusey wrote to tell him of the change that had come over the intellectual life of Oxford since the old times

---

[1] See vol. i. p. 338, and vol. ii. p. 139.
[2] Letters of Rev. J. B. Mozley, D.D., p. 81.

when he had lived under his roof. Then it had been the day of grace for the Church in Oxford; but now her enemies were compassing her on every side.

E. B. P. TO REV. J. B. MOZLEY.

Christ Church, Oxford, Feb. 7, 1871.

How strangely different are the times, in which you return among us, from those in which you left us. Now the fight is not for fundamentals even, but as to the existence of a Personal God, the living of the soul after death, or whether we have any souls at all, whether there is or can be any positive truth, except as to Physics, &c. I asked a physical Professor about a R. C. book on Geology, and the relations of Physical Science to faith discussed in it. 'No one,' he said, 'thinks any longer of this; the question is wholly removed to Materialism, &c.;' and instanced some eminent person [or persons], who was entirely happy, having satisfied himself that he had no hereafter. Other physicists look upon Revelation as an interference with the study of physical certainties.

But we have a grand battle; I, for whatever time remains to me; you, during, I hope, many years of vigour. It is an encouragement that the battle is so desperate. All or nothing: as when the Gospel first broke in upon heathen philosophies, and the fishermen had the victory.

Mozley replied:—

REV. J. B. MOZLEY TO E. B. P.

Shoreham, Feb. 9, 1871.

I thank you much for your note, though it contains a sad disclosure of the influence now at work in Oxford. It certainly would seem that a form of Comtism was the prevailing thought of the day, and that it was the only shape in which they would admit the principle of morality and obligation of any kind. People cannot throw over morality altogether, but they imbed it in a more material system. What you mention about persons actually not *wanting* an hereafter is a horrible feature of the day, and sounds almost like a Second Fall and a descent from human nature.

About the same time Mr. Gladstone made another not less notable addition to the power of the Church in Oxford by nominating the Rev. Edward King[1], who had been for ten years Principal of the Theological College at Cuddesdon, to the Chair of Pastoral Theology, vacant by the death of Dr. Ogilvie. To the varied and brilliant abilities of the

---

[1] He was consecrated Bishop of Lincoln on St. Mark's Day, April 25, 1885.

already remarkable body of Theological Professors, Dr. King contributed, besides other high qualifications for his office, a gift of sympathy so extraordinary that it has been well described as 'nothing less than a form of genius.' As a result of this singular power, he was already in touch with a large number of clergy in every part of the country ; and soon after his arrival at Oxford he obtained an influence over the younger members of the University second only, if not quite equal to, that of the most distinguished of his colleagues.

But Pusey was obliged repeatedly to turn from the special difficulties of the Church in the University to the less congenial controversy about Ritual. On February 23, 1871, the Ritual suit against the Rev. J. Purchas, Incumbent of St. James' Chapel, Brighton, was decided by the Judicial Committee of the Privy Council. In this decision it was declared that the Rubric which enjoins that, at the time of the consecration in the Communion Service, the priest shall stand 'before the table,' does not necessarily mean 'between the table and the people '; and they condemned Mr. Purchas for having so interpreted it. A petition was made that the Case might be re-heard : but it was refused on the ground of 'the grave public mischief that would arise from any doubt being thrown on the finality of the determination' of the Judicial Committee. The Eastward Position of the officiating clergyman which had thus been declared to be illegal and penal, was by widespread consent very closely connected in the popular apprehension with the maintenance of Eucharistic truth, and certainly was most in accordance with the prevailing practice of Christendom. It was practically identified in the eyes of those congregations who had been accustomed to it, with a belief in the Sacrificial aspect of the Holy Eucharist.

This decision of the Privy Council did not stand alone. The Archbishop of Canterbury publicly stated[1] that the Bishops would be ready to enforce its observance in cases

---

[1] 'Life of Archibald Campbell Tait,' vol. ii. p. 100.

which were brought before them in a legal way; and the officers of the Church Association exhorted their members to be vigilant and unsparing, loud in an 'abundance of complaints,' while they laid special emphasis on the doctrinal meaning of what was thus condemned. In the face of such a combined attack, Churchmen felt that everything had to be risked to obtain a new hearing of this point, unless the Church of England was to stand committed to the doctrinal standard of the Church Association. They declined to say what they would do, if the Purchas Judgment was finally declared to be the lawful interpretation of the Rubrics; but for the present it was generally agreed to court further prosecution.

At the same time, the Bishop of London announced that he had no option about enforcing the Judgment on his clergy; and therefore the two Senior Canons of St. Paul's, the Rev. R. Gregory and Dr. Liddon, wrote to him stating that they would continue to say the Prayer of Consecration as ordered in the Rubric, and begging to be included in any proceedings that he thought it good to sanction. Pusey at the same time published a Letter to Liddon. He expressed regret that although he used the Eastward Position elsewhere, believing it to be in accordance with the Rubric, and most in harmony with the highest act of Divine worship, he thought himself compelled to abstain from it in the Cathedral at Oxford, where alone he could be held responsible. He proceeded to point out the gravity of the Judgment: that the Privy Council, under whose authority the greatest laxity of doctrine had been sanctioned in the 'Essays and Reviews' case, was now proceeding to enforce the most rigid stringency in matters of Ritual. He thought resistance a lesser evil than obedience, but he declined to counsel any co-operation with those who would disestablish the Church, 'in view of the sufferings and privations, temporal and spiritual, of our villages,' if that policy were carried out. But he adds, 'We may be driven (and God only knows how soon) to decide whether it be right and faithful to our God "propter vitam vivendi perdere causas," for the sake of an Establishment which has such a fleeting life to see that wrested from us which alone gives to Establishments their value.'

This Letter he published as a postscript to a Letter which Liddon wrote to Sir John Coleridge, who entirely sympathized with the opposition to the decision. Pusey added yet a few more words at the last moment about the condemnation of the Mixed Chalice.

E. B. P. to Rev. H. P. Liddon, D.D.

April 5, 1871.

When will your letter be printed? It would be worth while for me to give the proof about the Mixed Chalice, and this I would ascertain at the British Museum on Monday. It is so absurd that the Court should have laid down that the Church of England condemns our Blessed Lord's mode of celebration. But it is better not to wait a day for anything except that you write fully what you mean.

It is a grand fight and enough to make one twenty years younger.

But it is of moment that the Letter should be out as soon as it is consistent with your other occupations and the fullness of your life.

It is a sort of programme of our proceedings, which ought to stay the minds of our friends. And every word of yours will be of value, especially for the younger men and for England.

He was extremely anxious to throw in his lot with those who contravened the Privy Council's interpretation of the law by taking the Eastward position in the Cathedral at Oxford; but he refrained from doing so out of personal regard for two of the Canons who would be pained by such an action. Yet he found himself forced to adopt it by the fact that his practice at Christ Church was alleged against Liddon at St. Paul's. Therefore, from Ascension Day, 1871 and onwards, he consecrated eastwards in the Cathedral, except when either Dr. Ogilvie or Dr. Heurtley was present.

Three years later, after Dr. Ogilvie's death, he began to use the Eastward position on all occasions, as he thought that Dr. Heurtley would not object; but he received at once a letter of remonstrance on the 'breach of law.' His answer showed exactly his relation to this practice :—

Christ Church, April 25, 1874.

I do not know whether you have seen anything which I have written publicly. I have adhered to the way used at Christ Church, in order not to give pains to Canons yet older than myself, especially dear Ogilvie. I do not attach any doctrinal meaning to the position. Of course, I cannot ; since until of late I have not used it. I suppose that you have not been in Church when I have used it before, but having used it before I did not think that you minded it. I believe that in standing as I did this morning, I was obeying the law of the Church, which directs me to stand 'before the Table'; for '*before* the Table' cannot, I think, mean '*at the side of* the Table,' and Lord Cairns' Judgment cannot alter the meaning of the English word 'before.' However I have, for love's sake, disobeyed what seemed to me the obvious and necessary meaning of the Church's law, because I thought that the law of charity was a higher law. But as to setting at naught Lord Cairns' Judgment as to its meaning, there is no way of ' seeking to have the matter tried again ' (which you seem to think allowable) save by contravening it. . . . If you read the *Times*, you will see that my practice was made an argument against that of my friends (such as Liddon and Gregory at St. Paul's), and believing that you did not feel strongly about it (as in a matter of fact you do not, except that you suppose it to be a breach of law) I made the slight change from my former position. However charity is the higher law, and since it pains you, you need not fear that I should use it when you are there. . . . In law I am told that there is what is called 'judge-made law,' that is the result of the Judgments delivered, if undisputed. It is a principle I have understood in civil law that such Judgments may be contravened with a view to having the question reconsidered. Those who have contravened Lord Cairns' Judgment have been acting, I understand, on a principle recognized by law.

The far more directly important prosecution of Mr. Bennett for Eucharistic doctrine was, as has been said, not allowed to rest after the acquittal in the Court of Arches. The appeal of the Church Association to the Privy Council was heard in December, 1871, Lord Hatherley being Lord Chancellor; and on June 8, 1872, in the very crisis of the anxiety about the Athanasian Creed, the Judgment was delivered. The Final Court confirmed the decision of the Court of Arches. The news was brought by Dr. Bright to Pusey, who was far from well. He was already beginning to suffer from the illness which necessitated his going abroad in the next Long Vacation, and terminated eventually in the dangerous attack of the following January. Dr. Bright thus describes the interview with him :—

'Went to see Pusey. He is very glad, of course. But he has got a fresh cold, and he now finds he cannot work in the evening . . . He is certainly much weaker than he was in *body*. But how like him it was to say, with a sweet, eager look, after we had been talking of this failure of the attempt to get Bennett condemned, "Well now, how would it do to make one more appeal to the Evangelicals and say, ' Now that this is over, will you not join with us in opposing unbelief ?'" I answered in effect that I felt sure they would not respond to this appeal. I instanced Shaftesbury's present line about the Athanasian Creed. "Ah !" he said, "I don't understand Shaftesbury now."'

After being defeated on a point of such critical importance, it is astonishing that the Church Association could continue the childish policy of attacking the ritual which expressed the doctrine they could not touch. Those who used the ritual could not surrender it, when they had taught their people what it meant, without appearing to surrender the doctrine itself. But so long as they retained it, the Church Association was resolved to use to the utmost the weapon which the decision in the Purchas case had put into their hands, and, under the sacred plea of enforcing ' the law,' to prosecute these outward expressions of a truth which they themselves had given the Law Courts an opportunity of affirming.

At this time Pusey had to use all his influence to prevent Liddon leaving Oxford. Under the strain of the twofold work of his Professorship at Oxford and his Canonry at St. Paul's, and amid the excitement of the day, his health was breaking down. His medical adviser recommended the resignation of the Professorship, but Pusey wrote to explain that he did not think such a course would give the needed relief.

E. B. P. TO DR. OGLE.

Christ Church, Oxford, Jan. 21, [1872].

No one can influence Liddon except his physician. Have you observed the effect of that peculiar work at St. Paul's, the strain on his whole strength from that preaching under the dome, and all his lecturing? I used to be in terror at the strain of his preaching long before he was made Canon. He was ill, I think, repeatedly after a sermon. He throws his whole energy into his sermon, and speaks, I suppose, not in his natural voice, but with an exhausting force.

My own belief is, that the resignation of his Professorship would only aggravate the physical evil, and that he would only bring about what you dread, all the sooner. He imbibed from Bp. Hamilton, to whom he much looked up, the thought that Cathedrals ought to be places of very central exertion, which they could not be under the system of a three months' residence. . . .

Last year the stress was the greater, because, through a vacancy at St. Paul's, he had four months' residence, instead of three ; in those four months he was straining himself to the utmost, and then his work here was the more oppressive because he had less time in which to do it. . . .

But conceive his having no work except his Canonry, and that, with that vast Church to fill, and his idea of carrying out Bp. Hamilton's thought of what a Cathedral ought to be, and the terrific spiritual wants of London ; do you not think that the towards six months, which are spent here, would be employed in much more exhausting work in London?

I should look upon his resigning his Professorship, as consigning him to an early death, on account of the excessive strain of his multiplying and ramifying work at St. Paul's. . . .

I write this letter, because you seemed to take it for granted, that his resignation of his Professorship would be a diminution of toil. I believe that it would be an aggravation of it; and this opinion I found on all my past knowledge of his mind. But I write it, not to elicit an answer, but for your consideration medically.

The earnest wish that lay behind arguments of the '*μέγας*' as Liddon always called him, prevailed, and he retained his Professorship, at whatever cost of physical strain, until after Pusey's death.

# CHAPTER IX.

THE controversy about the Athanasian Creed was a sudden and most unexpected result of the Royal Commission on Ritual which had originally been appointed in 1867. When this Commission was engaged in preparing its fourth Report, which suggested alterations of the Rubrics throughout the Prayer-book, Lord Stanhope proposed a modification of the Rubric which stands before the Athanasian Creed; his aim was to make the use of that formulary in public worship optional instead of compulsory. The Commission under the influence of Bishop Wilberforce voted that such a proposal was *ultra vires*; but at a later meeting, when some new members had joined the Commission, this vote was treated as only a provisional arrangement; and the proposed alteration was again taken into consideration. On July 8, 1869, it was rejected; but in spite of this, other proposals were brought forward with a like object. Before any decision was arrived at, memorials for and against the innovation were sent to the Archbishops, and laid before the Commission. A memorial in favour of some kind of change was signed by a body of forty-four clergy and laymen, who, differing very widely among themselves as to the kind of change which they desired, yet agreed in wishing for some sort of alteration; and, on the other hand, the following representation, signed by upwards of twelve hundred clergy and laity, was sent to the Archbishops by Pusey in February, 1870 :—

'Of the proposals submitted to your Graces, we are of opinion, that either to use the Creed less frequently in the Church Service than at present, or to render its use in any cases optional, or to omit the mis-termed damnatory clauses, will be fraught with danger to the best interests of the Church.

'Any of these expedients would be a grave injury to the maintenance of the dogmatic principle in the Church of England in its relation to the most central truths of Faith, and a new and severe shock would be given to the confidence of many of her most attached members in the claim to teach unfalteringly the Faith once delivered to the Saints.

'If we do not suggest the insertion of an explanation of the real force of the most solemn warnings of the Creed, this is because we apprehend that every well-instructed Christian must understand them to apply only to those whom God knows to have enjoyed full oppor-tunities for attaining faith in the perfect Truth and to have deliberately rejected it.

'In the interests of the future cohesion of the Church of England we earnestly beg your Graces not to sanction any tampering with an essential portion of the Book of Common Prayer, in which under God we still recognize our most powerful bond of unity [1].'

While this subject was being discussed by the Royal Commission, together with the examination of every Rubric in the Prayer Book, another great change was being dealt with by Convocation. On Feb. 10, 1870, Bishop Wilber-force proposed the appointment of a Committee to consider the Revision of the Authorized Version of the Bible. Many years before, when Pusey was fresh from his studies in Germany, he had commenced a revision on his own ac-count [2], which he abandoned at first because of other work, and afterwards because of his own mistakes. In maturer years, he said of them in his will, dated 1875, ' I saw reason to withdraw many alterations which I made when young.' He deeply regretted that Bishop Wilberforce should now lend his weight to an authoritative scheme of the kind, and wrote to tell him so.

---

[1] Fourth Report of the Royal Commission on Ritual, p. 159.
[2] See Vol. i. pp. 118–122.

E. B. P. TO THE BISHOP OF WINCHESTER.

Feb. 12, 1870.

. . . I fear that evil will result, from the state of criticism as to the text of the New Testament and as to the language of the Old.

. . . There is a fashion in criticism, and I think that there was a good deal of truth in what the Bishop of St. David's said, that one revision would involve continued revision. For if the principle is admitted that supposed errors are to be corrected, there ought to be continual revision. Yet I have outlived a good many interpretations. I have seen their birth, their flourishing state, their death and burial and their mummy state, in which they are curiosities. I doubt not that there has been considerable increase in the knowledge of Greek as a language : in Hebrew our translators had every advantage which we have, except a very uncertain one, the comparison of cognate dialects in the illustration of obscure words.

There is also a fashion in being liberal, not insisting overmuch on orthodox interpretation. . . .

But this is nothing compared with the questions raised as to the Athanasian Creed and the Liturgy, except [so far] as the corrections of the translation will, as I fear, shake faith. The Bible, more than the Church, holds the masses of Englishmen to Christianity ; their source of Faith is, I believe, the Bible. If their confidence in the Bible is shaken, so will be their Christianity.

For these reasons he declined to join the Old Testament Revision Committee when it was formed.

E. B. P. TO REV. H. P. LIDDON.

May 30, 1870.

I have declined the Bishop of Gloucester and Bristol's invitation to join the Revision Committee, on the ground that on the verge of seventy, one must make one's choice what one would still do on earth for God, and that I hope that I am doing good by my Commentary, whereas I anticipated no good from Revision, in which I should probably only be in a minority. This is final.

He was all the more glad that he had refused when he discovered that a Unitarian minister had been asked to take part in a work which had originated with the Bishops in the Convocation of Canterbury. When Dean Stanley invited all the members of the Revision Committee to receive the Holy Communion in Westminster Abbey, and admitted the Unitarian to Communion with the others, Pusey, though he felt keenly the character of such an act, declined to regard it as one for which the Church could in any way be held responsible. He wrote about it to Liddon on July 2.

E. B. P. TO REV. H. P. LIDDON.

July 2, 1870.

Single Bishops or an association like the Revisionists do not commit the Church. . . . Dear J. H. N. said to me one day at Littlemore, ' Pusey, we have leant on the Bishops, and they have given way under us.' Dear J. K. and I never did lean on the Bishops, but on the Church. We, or rather the whole Church have had plenty of scandals as to Bishops, and always shall have them.

But there were many others who would not accept his view that all the blame lay with the Dean of Westminster, but maintained that the Bishops were really responsible for the scandal. It was the cause of great offence, and the Bishops in no way repudiated it. No protest was raised in Convocation: to many the Church seemed to have forgotten the Nicene Creed, and their faith was strained to the breaking-point. Pusey wrote to Bishop Wilberforce to beg some help from the Bishops to calm the agitation :—

E. B. P. TO THE BISHOP OF WINCHESTER.

Christ Church, Oxford, July 18, 1870.

I thank you for your letter; but you might as well say 'Stop! stop!' to an army in full rout as try to allay a panic, that the Church of England in Convocation has assented to the denial of the Faith, otherwise than by repudiation of the act which would involve it. Could not you prevail on the Bishops of Salisbury and Gloucester and Bristol to say, each, that he holds it wrong to invite to Holy Communion one who denies the Godhead of our Lord, or that Atoning Death, of which that Blessed Sacrament is the memorial and participation; I mean, to say this in the abstract?

I heard yesterday from Bennett of Frome : ' Many are preparing to secede ; but whither, they know not, but somewhere they must go rather than be against their Lord.' These are not what are called Romanisers; for Bennett says, 'they know not where to go.' It is in mere despondency and terror about the Church of England, and lest they should be involved in the guilt of this sacrilegious Communion. No one would have been disturbed by any doings of Dean Stanley. They were simply in keeping with his whole character, as a fanatic enemy of all dogma. The misery was, that so many Bishops, when appealed to in Convocation, seemed deliberately to connive at and defend it.

I do not wish those two Bishops to retract what they have said, but to say something which they have not said, and which one should have thought every Bishop could say, that it is not right to invite to the Holy Communion one who does not believe the Creed of the Church, and who denies the Godhead of our Lord, and His Atoning Death. Your Lordship will do great service if you can persuade this.

The agitation about this 'Westminster scandal,' as it was rightly called, lasted far into the following year; it was at its height when, in September, 1870, the fourth Report of the Ritual Commission appeared. In the text, the Report recommended a vast number of emendations to the Rubrics; it left the use of the Athanasian Creed as it was before, but proposed the following explanatory statement: 'Note, that the condemnations in this Confession of Faith are to be no otherwise understood than as a solemn warning of the peril of those who wilfully reject the Catholic Faith.' This would have been satisfactory enough; but any value it may have had was entirely nullified when it was found that seventeen out of twenty-seven of the Commissioners had appended to their own report a series of separate protests against the 'Note.' Foremost among the dissentients was Dr. Tait, the Archbishop of Canterbury, who openly declared against the use of the Creed in the service of the Church. A great fight was evidently at hand.

At one time, the Archbishop appears to have thought that he could carry his project with little difficulty. He wrote to the Bishop of London about it as of a question 'in which there seems to be an almost universal consent in the Church.' He urged that a clause allowing the disuse of the Creed should be added to the Bill in connexion with the new Lectionary which the Government was about to re-introduce in 1871. But the Ministry would not consent to this course. The Bill was introduced without it; and when, on April 25, Mr. (afterwards Sir) T. Chambers proposed such a clause in the House of Commons, the feeling of the Bishops was so strong against this method of procedure that the Archbishop himself was obliged to use his influence with the mover to restrain him from taking a vote on the subject.

It was obvious, however, that the battle must be fought in Convocation. In that assembly, although very few objected to the actual statements in the Creed, yet the practical difficulties raised by the common misunderstanding of its warning clauses were found to have great weight. Heated debates produced no satisfactory conclusion. At last, on June 14, on the proposal of Bishop Wilberforce, a Committee of all the English Bishops was appointed to consider the question and report to their next meeting. Pusey felt that every effort must be made to prevent other Bishops from being misled by the Archbishop, and he had many fears about the attitude which Bishop Wilberforce might take. It was advisable therefore that the Bishops, before they came to a decision, should know some of the consequences either of mutilating the Creed or of removing it from its place in the public service of the Church. He thus expressed his own position to Bishop Wilberforce :—

E. B. P. TO THE BISHOP OF WINCHESTER.

Christ Church, Oxford, Oct. 19, 1871.

I am grieved to gather an impression from different sources, that you are in favour of banishing the Athanasian Creed from our Services. I believe that it is our only safeguard against our clergy and people falling into Nestorianism and Eutychianism, some into the one, some into the other. It seems to be thought that those who have faith may always be sacrificed with impunity to those who have none. I have fought the battle of the Faith for more than half my life. I have tried to rally people to the Church when other hearts failed. But if the Athanasian Creed is touched, I see nothing to be done but to give up my Canonry, and abandon my fight for the Church of England. It would not be the same Church for which I have fought hitherto. I should not doubt myself that Liddon would do the same. Indeed, he could hardly bring himself to look at the question, which the Bishop of Gloucester and Bristol proposed to the Divinity Professors about the text and translation of the Creed, in the name of the Bishops of both Provinces.

This move of the 'old Catholic party' abroad may make an opening to many who could not have joined the Church of Rome. Or I might myself abandon our fight at Oxford, which year by year becomes more hopeful, and go to Scotland.

I cannot say what I should do. May God teach me! But one thing I cannot do—abide as a teacher in a Church which abandons a Creed which expresses the faith of Christendom, as expressed by the great Councils of Ephesus and Chalcedon, and held from the first.

As for the idea, which I hear to have been introduced, of placing it with the Thirty-nine Articles, it is merely a civil bowing it out. Hitherto, I have been able to say and to teach in sincerity, that the Church of England teaches her people through the Prayer-book in the language of the people. This has been my plea for these twenty-one years, ' Lex supplicandi lex credendi.' I could say so no more.

I cannot think that your Lordship would take upon yourself the responsibility of making this split in the Church of England. I do not think that, on that deathbed to which we are approaching, some sooner, some later, but all, year by year, nearer, you would like to have it upon your conscience. I do not think that you would like the memory that one who had long studied the human mind told you that you combined in letting loose Nestorianism and Eutychianism and Arianism upon the Church of England. I believe that the removal of the Athanasian Creed would do this, and those who contribute to it would be among the agents. Your Lordship has a right zeal for winning all to the truth, but fire and water cannot be combined. We have endured much : but we cannot endure having one of our Creeds rent from us.

I cannot believe that you would concur in it : but reports so grave are circulated, that I felt it my duty to say how deeply such a measure, as those talked of, would cut.

An entry in Bishop Wilberforce's diary of the following day, October 20 [1], informs us that he showed this letter and a similar one from Liddon to the Archbishop of Canterbury, with whom he was then staying; and although the Archbishop had openly avowed his wish to remove the Creed from the services of the Church, and only a few days before had been eager to get legislative sanction for such a course, yet to all appearance he was '*for the time* convinced that he must not' attempt to meddle with it. Pusey in the meanwhile returned to the attack, and set himself to state with even greater clearness the really critical character of the question. He therefore sent to Bishop Wilberforce another letter a few days later.

E. B. P. TO THE BISHOP OF WINCHESTER.

Christ Church, Oxford, Oct. 25, 1871.

It is strange, after above forty-six years of labour for the Faith and for the Church of England, to hold my office of teaching in her by a thread,

[1] Life of Bishop Wilberforce, vol. iii. p. 390.

the possible act of those under whom I have laboured. I do not say this publicly, because it would only stimulate some to urge the more, what would bring about my resignation. It is not for me to wish to bring this uncertainty to a close, except as I wish earnestly that our Bishops may not do what would be fatal to the Church and to faith in her. But in this state of suspense I am entirely crippled, as to any plans for the Church, which depend upon clerical income, seeing that my own may be forfeited at any time, nor could I advise any who hesitated, to receive Holy Orders, seeing I may have to cease from the office of teacher. I did not know when I last wrote to your Lordship, that Dr. Liddon had publicly stated that he should resign his office of teaching if the Athanasian Creed were tampered with. It is not for me to estimate what effects our joint resignation might produce. Liddon's influence here with the young men is only equalled by that which Newman had in his most influential days. He has been the great instrument of restoring faith. Those congregations in St. Paul's are only a specimen of his London influence : not a sermon but brings numbers of inquiring minds, seeking after faith. If it should please God that that voice should be silenced by death, every one would mourn the loss. Now they are our own Bishops, whose act would silence him. For myself, my work, at seventy-one, must be almost done : still glimpses, which I have from time to time, show me that many hearts would be a good deal shaken, if I should have to resign my office, on the ground that I could no longer keep the office of teacher in the Church of England. I have no idea who else would resign, or what people would do ; but the fact of my having stood firm during so many shocks for these twenty-six years would emphasize the more my having to give way now. Each resignation too (Liddon's and mine) would give the greater import to the other.

I have stood, and said that I would stand, so long as the Church of England remains the same. I said to Bishop Jenner, in view of people's restlessness and the talks of change, ' I have wondered whether the Church of England will last my time, or whether it will split in two.' Your Lordship will think that it would be no slight wrench to have to give up the work of all those years. But I dare not hold on, if there should be any organic change. I should gladly see any right explanation of those warning clauses in the Athanasian Creed. To abandon them would [be] to me to be ashamed of our Lord's words, ' He that believeth not shall be condemned,' ' He that rejecteth Me and receiveth not My words hath one that judgeth him : the word that I have spoken, the same shall judge him at the last day.' It is plainly (as your Lordship must feel), the same contempt of Almighty God to refuse to believe what He reveals to us, as to refuse to do what He bids us. But of disobedience men repent : of unbelief or misbelief, voluntarily contracted, scarce any.

Equally, or even more, I should think it fatal to relegate the Athanasian Creed into some corner, to be acknowledged by one knows not whom of the clergy, but to make no part of our devotions, to be banished out of the minds of the people. The Athanasian Creed has been the guide of my faith, ever since I began to think as a young man. What it has been to me it has been to all who have thought on those subjects of faith. Your Lordship must be aware, that it is the object of attack on two grounds; (1) its clear dogmatic faith, which minds like Dean Stanley's hate; (2) that it asserts the importance of definite faith to all who can have it. The contrary is the heresy of the day. 'It is of no importance what we believe,' 'one Creed is as good as another,' is the central heresy of the day. There are symptoms that if it were (God forbid) given up, the Nicene Creed would be soon a point of attack, and whatever contains a definite faith.

I am amazed, why grave persons should now be talking of giving up the Athanasian Creed.

Before the end of the month Pusey received the following letter from the Archbishop:—

THE ARCHBISHOP OF CANTERBURY TO E. B. P.

Oct. 30, 1871.

It was stated at a meeting of Bishops held last summer at Lambeth that you had suggested some explanation of those clauses in the Athanasian Creed which are supposed by certain persons to declare that no member of the Greek Church can be saved. I am of course firmly convinced myself that the Church of England does not adopt the clauses in question with any such meaning. You are probably aware of the proposal made by the Ritual Commission to add an explanatory rubric to the Creed. The Bishop of Winchester has recently informed me, that in a letter deprecating any organic change in this Creed, you have said you would 'gladly see any right explanation of those warning clauses.' There is no doubt that very many faithful minds have been and are afflicted by the clauses unexplained.

It would be a great help to me at this anxious time if you would kindly tell me what the explanatory words are which I am led to suppose would be acceptable to you. I know how strong your feelings as to the danger of touching this Creed are, and it is therefore the more desirable that I should know your mind as to any right mode of explanation.

The Archbishop's letter showed Pusey that Bishop Wilberforce had warmly and most successfully espoused the cause which he had at heart. If the Archbishop was about to be satisfied with explanatory words, the hold of the Church of England on the Catholic faith would not be loosened. Pusey wrote at once to thank the Bishop for his intervention.

E. B. P. TO THE BISHOP OF WINCHESTER.

Christ Church, Oxford, All Saints Eve, 1871.

Thanks be to God, and under God, I bless Him for your Lordship's interposition. Bright said, 'Then the Church of England is saved.' It is a heavy weight rolled off, after which one can breathe again freely.

Liddon tells me that, at the time of the Ritual Commission, you framed a very clear statement as to the Greek Church in reference to the Athanasian Creed and the inclusion of the Filioque. The clauses cannot really apply to them, since we had the Filioque from our great Greek Archbishop Theodore, St. Augustine of Canterbury's successor. It might be of great use to us here, if your Lordship could recall what that formula was and would entrust it to me.

At the same time a formal request was received from Bishop Ellicott, in the name of the Committee of Bishops, addressed to the Divinity Professors of Oxford and Cambridge, asking their advice in this matter. Some of the Oxford Professors were most unwilling to enter on the question. They had already in the Memorial to the Ritual Commission of February, 1870, declared that they did not see the necessity for alteration or explanation, and further they did not know what use might be made of anything which they might suggest. But Pusey urged them to the work, on the ground that it was the Archbishop's wish. At last, early in December, the following Note was sent to Bishop Ellicott:—

Your Lordship has addressed us severally in the name of the Bishops of both Provinces asking our aid in the revision of the original text and Prayer Book version of the Athanasian Creed, together with any 'suggestions' that might occur to us.

We have held frequent mutual consultations, and respectfully beg leave to report as follows:—

1. After examining the various readings of the Latin text of the Athanasian Creed which our translation may be assumed generally to represent, we find none of sufficient authority to warrant us in suggesting them to your Lordships with a view to the revision of the text.

With respect to certain omissions in the Commentary of Fortunatus it is evident from an inspection of that manuscript of the Commentary which is preserved in the Bodleian Library and is believed to be the oldest in existence, that the commentator cannot have intended to exhibit a complete text of the Creed since, in some cases, passages are wanting which are obviously necessary to the coherence of the text on which he comments.

It must further be observed that of the warning verses commonly, although improperly, called damnatory, the first are given by Fortunatus, while those he omits have the support of all known manuscripts of the Creed.

II. We should not have been disposed to recommend any alteration in a translation associated with three centuries of faith and devotion. But if such a proposal is entertained we would observe —

1. That the Prayer Book version of the Creed has departed from the Sarum Text in its rendering of verses 29 and 42—' *Ut incarnationem quoque Domini nostri Iesu Christi fideliter credat.*' ' *Quam nisi quisque fideliter firmiterque crediderit.*'

2. That having considered various new renderings of particular expressions, we are of opinion that the following alone are of sufficient importance to be laid before your Lordships :—

    (a) Verses 9, 12. For 'incomprehensible' 'incomprehensibles' read 'infinite' 'infinites.'

    (β) Verse 23. For 'of the Father and of the Son' read 'of the Father and the Son.'

    (γ) Verse 28. For 'He therefore that will be saved must thus think of the Trinity' read 'He therefore that would be saved let him thus think of the Trinity.'

Your Lordships will observe that we are unable to make any suggestions as to either the text or the translation which may be expected to obviate the objections popularly raised against the Creed. But on this very account we the more willingly submit for consideration the following form of a Note such as may tend to remove some misconceptions.

Note.—That nothing in this Creed is to be understood as condemning those who, by involuntary ignorance or invincible prejudice are hindered from accepting the faith therein declared.

We cannot conclude without expressing to your Lordships our deep sense of the practical value of this Creed as teaching us how to think and believe on the central mysteries of the faith. Experience has proved it to be a safeguard against fundamental errors into which the human mind has often fallen, and is ever liable to fall. For these reasons we earnestly trust that, in the good providence of God, this Creed will always retain its place in the public service of our Church.

J. B. MOZLEY, D.D., Regius Professor of Divinity.

E. B. PUSEY, D.D., Regius Professor of Hebrew.

CH. A. OGILVIE, D.D., Regius Professor of Pastoral Theology.

C. A. HEURTLEY, D.D., Margaret Professor of Divinity.
W. BRIGHT, D.D., Regius Professor of Ecclesiastical History.
H. P. LIDDON, D.D., Ireland Professor of Exegesis.

On the same day that this reply was sent Pusey wrote to the Archbishop of Canterbury to tell him of the decision [1]. He added—

E. B. P. TO THE ARCHBISHOP OF CANTERBURY.

December (? 2), 1871.

. . . Dr. Bright told us of a dictum of your Grace which he had treasured up from his Rugby days, 'That a person cannot hold what he has not received,' or to this effect. I think that this explanation removes all objections by exempting all except culpable rejection of the known Mind of God, and it is, I suppose, even greater contempt of God wilfully to reject what He declares to us, than to do what He forbids us. For it is more deliberate rejection. Anyhow it does not say any more than our Lord, St. John xii. 48.

The Bishops met at Lambeth on December 5, and the Archbishop openly declared against a material alteration of the Athanasian Creed. He gave as his reason for this, his fear lest an alteration should split the Church, and it was decided that Convocation should be asked, as soon as possible, whether legislative sanction should be sought for an Explanatory Rubric of some kind.

But the question was not to be so easily settled. A letter from 'Anglicanus' in the *Times* of December 23, showed that the writer at least had not shared the Archbishop's change of policy, and that he intended to renew his attack on the Creed itself. It was well known that the Archbishop's heart was still with this effort, even when his judgment was obliged to go against it. Upon this, Liddon wrote to the Archbishop, as he and Pusey had done two months before to the Bishop of Winchester, to state that if the offending clauses were struck out by the Convocation of Canterbury, or the Creed disused, he would resign his preferments and retire from the Ministry of the English Church. Pusey thought that all fear of the alteration was over when the Archbishop had once changed his mind ;

[1] ' Life of Archibald Campbell Tait,' ii. 133.

and he had not seen the *Times* correspondence.   Liddon
wrote to tell him of the letter of 'Anglicanus,' and of his
correspondence with the Archbishop.   He replied :—

E. B. P. TO REV. H. P. LIDDON, D.D.

[Torquay, Jan. 2, 1872.]

I hoped we had been in port.   The Archbishop knows from the
Bishop of Winchester that I stake my all on the Athanasian Creed.
Lord Beauchamp is very apprehensive about an attempt against the
Athanasian Creed as making way for the central heresy of the day,
the unimportance of definite faith to salvation.

They will send people by shoals off to Rome, and we could do
nothing to prevent it.   They will not shake Ritualists very possibly,
whom they might wish to get rid of.   These take their own line of
caring for nothing, would go on their own way ; say the Athanasian
Creed in the old way.   So the reign of lawlessness would be enlarged,
and dutiful minds would be precipitated to the Church of Rome.   It
seems to me such utter madness now, when the Vatican Council would
by its decree of Papal Infallibility have gained great rest for minds
among us, to make changes which would unhinge even quiet minds.

I only had your letter [to-day].   You may use any of this with my
name to the Archbishop.

The Archbishop called this announcement 'a threat,'
and many of Pusey's friends were unable to understand
why he should act in this way.   To one of them he wrote
a full explanation :—

E. B. P. TO REV. H. A. WOODGATE.

Oxford [Feb. 12, 1872].

The more the fact as to L. and myself distresses you, the more
essential it seems to me.   It does not matter taking one's stand
a little earlier or later.   The Athanasian Creed is only a part of a
whole ; a Metz, which, if it fell, people would march on.   It is no
secret as to L. or me.   *He* has written formally to the Archbishop ;
*I* to the Bishop of Winchester, who told the Archbishop ; but the
Juggernaut car is still driven on, and that by the Archbishop.

I think that the effect of Liddon's resignation would be to send so
many who are coming to the faith, both here and in London, adrift ;
some to go to unbelief, some to Rome.   I cannot conceal from myself,
that if, after having fought the battle for near forty years, I say I can
fight no longer, it will shake a good many.   I must say, in resigning,
' The ground is cut away from under my feet.'   ' Amid all our confusions,' I have said, ' the Prayer-book in the language of the people
is the teacher of the people : *lex supplicandi lex credendi*.   But if

you remove the Athanasian Creed, you have removed the whole teaching which protects our people against the manifold heresies about the doctrine of the Holy Trinity and the Incarnation. I have no answer left.' This is independent of the question itself that a Church, which, without a strong system of discipline to restrain heresy, gives up a teaching of sound doctrine, so far exposes her members to heresy and unbelief.

I have thought of nothing beyond ; but I think Liddon's resignation in his full strength and I as a veteran, who have stood so many storms, *would be a repetition* of the collapse of faith upon the resignation of J. H. N., &c. It would be the more so, because we have been prominent in defending the faith.

. . . The words of the Creed are only an application of our Lord's words in St. John, 'Whosoever rejecteth Me, and receiveth not My words,' &c. Of course the words cannot apply to those who do not reject His word, viz. those who never heard it. The Church is speaking to members of the Church. It is her Creed for them. She delivers to them what was delivered to her by the Apostles as the Revelation of God. Whoso rejects it, rejects Him.

It startles people to say the Anti-Trinitarian or Mohammedan and we believe in a different God ; but an Uni-personal God is altogether a different God. How could such a God be Love, with None to love?

In this controversy Pusey might have hoped that he should again have the support of the Low Church party, as in the matter of 'Essays and Reviews.' Then Lord Shaftesbury had been with him ; and again in 1869, he had really sided with Pusey against Dr. Temple's appointment to the see of Exeter, but refused to act openly in concert with him, from fear of compromising his determined attitude against Ritualism. But now Pusey had good reason to fear that he would be acting against him. He wrote to his cousin anxiously expressing these fears. The answer he received was another instance of the manner in which even distinguished members of that party can be blind to the logical consequences of a policy to which they lend the weight of their name and position and the influence of their high character.

LORD SHAFTESBURY TO E. B. P.

Feb. 22, 1872.

You may be assured that I do meditate taking a part against the Athanasian Creed. I regard it as a document almost divine, and I believe every word of it from the first to the last syllable.

But the belief and veneration are quite consistent with a desire not to thrust it on unwilling and captious congregations. The uneasiness, the surprise, the confusion, that come over all the worshippers when it is read, greatly among the educated classes, but unboundedly among artisan and rural listeners, are distressing. I am convinced that it revolts many and furnishes abundant matter for easy and effective ridicule.

Many a thinking man, who rejects it in Public Service would accept it, if not forced upon him, in the quiet of his study.

Let it remain in the Prayer-book as a very pillar of our Church. If you will insist on its use, insist on its use for every Sunday. People will then become familiar with the mighty document and submit accordingly. The reservation of it for special days, without giving it weight and conviction, only creates when it is read, an unpleasant wonder in every one's mind.

Convocation discussed the Creed during its sitting in February, but reached no conclusion. Memorials were prepared on every side for the next meeting in April. Among them was one which Pusey intended to circulate for signatures, but at Liddon's suggestion, he sent it with his own name only. It embodies, in their shortest form, Pusey's arguments on the question. It ran as follows:—

The humble petition of the Rev. E. B. Pusey, D.D., showeth—

That it has not been the custom of the Catholic Church to rule by majorities things which affect the faith, and that the contrary proceeding of the Vatican Council has given occasion to grave perplexity in the Roman Communion and to censure among ourselves.

That to withdraw, or change anything in, a Creed in which the Church has heretofore confessed its faith to God, would be a change gravely affecting the faith.

That the members of the Church are bound to one another, not only by the One Spirit and by common Sacraments, but also by the prayers and confessions of faith in which they unite and are united before God.

That no great change can be made herein without disturbing our relations to one another, and that no change can be made herein against the wish and faith even of a minority without a tyrannical abuse of power.

That your Petitioner, with tens of thousands of others, has always felt the Athanasian Creed to be an invaluable guide in his belief on matters of faith, where error, as experience shows, comes very naturally to the human mind; and we doubt not that it has to us been a safeguard, under God, against heresy, to which the human mind is prone.

That, although the same truths are embodied in the first five of the Thirty-nine Articles, yet in matter of fact it has not been those Articles, although subscribed and believed, but the clear statements of the Athanasian Creed, confessed to God in devotion, which have been the safeguard of faith.

That, amid the contradictory teaching of individual clergy, it has been a solace to thousands to be able to point out that the Church of England does teach clear definite truth through her Prayer-book in the language of the people, which Prayer-book we all, bishops and clergy, own to be superior to and above ourselves; and that the teaching, so made our own in our devotions to Almighty God, sinks deeper and becomes part of ourselves much more than any abstract statement of truth, according to the saying—*Lex supplicandi, lex credendi.*

That it could no longer be affirmed that the Church of England did teach the full truth as to the Holy Trinity and the Incarnation, if the Athanasian Creed were removed from our public services, or in any way mutilated.

That the so-called warning clauses (as to which there is no doubt but that they form an integral part of the Creed) are themselves a protection against [the] one great heresy of the day, that it is of no import to man's salvation whether he have any definite faith as to what Almighty God has revealed, contrary to what our Blessed Lord has expressly declared, St. John xii. 48, St. Mark xvi. 16.

That a Church which should withdraw from the public worship, or mutilate, the Athanasian Creed, would, in the conviction of many thousands of its members, no longer be the same Church as that in which we were baptized, and which at our Ordination we vowed to serve, and that such change would ultimately break the Church of England to pieces, besides involving at once the loss of very many devoted servants and ministers, as appears already from the hesitation of devoted young men to pledge themselves to her Orders while the grave question of the Athanasian Creed is thus agitated, or to retain the exercise of them.

That, on the other hand, there was perhaps never a time in which the prospects of the Church of England were more hopeful, if, under the guidance of God's good Spirit, we hold fast what we have, and teach, according to the light which God gives to each, the blessed truths which He has committed to us.

That your Petitioner, and those with whom he has been for near forty years associated, have studiously abstained from suggesting any organic changes, even while we have not concealed our conviction that the Church of England incurred loss by the changes in the Prayer-book arbitrarily made towards the end of the reign of Edward VI. We felt that changes should not be made by majorities, and now that a change is threatened which would vitally affect our own position, and, as we believe, dislocate the Church of England, we claim that the same forbearance should be shown towards us, which, as relates to organic changes, we ever used ourselves.

At the April sittings, the Lower House of Convocation decided that the use of the Creed should remain unaltered, but they were willing to consider any change of translation that would make the rendering more exact. The Upper House failed to reach any conclusion, until at the next session on July 4, 1872, Bishop Wilberforce carried a motion that, 'having regard to the scruples alleged by many faithful members of the Church,' a Committee of both Houses of Convocation should be appointed to consider 'as to any mode of relieving such scruples, whilst we maintain the truth which has been committed to our charge.' The Committee was appointed but was unable to meet until December.

Pusey had gone abroad for his health when this motion of Bishop Wilberforce was carried. The unwelcome news that the controversy was to be further prolonged was conveyed to him by Liddon and caused him to write at once to the Bishop of Winchester.

E. B. P. TO THE BISHOP OF WINCHESTER.

!Hotel Meurice, Calais, July 8, 1872.

I hear from Liddon that you have obtained a Committee to consider 'what measures of relief &c. were advisable.' I am afraid your Lordship has a hopeless task to reconcile what is irreconcilable—Lord Shaftesbury's petition and Dean Stanley's speeches show what they desire, the excision of the Creed from our Services. Nothing short of this will satisfy Dean Stanley. Rather he will think every measure of proposed 'relief' to be an admission that there is something really to be relieved, and use it as a vantage-ground from which to renew his attacks. ... He scorned all Explanatory Notes, and used our readiness to admit one as an argument that we thought that there was something to be explained away. Any concession will, I fear, be but the beginning of the end; it will be used as a precedent for fresh relaxations in favour of heretical clergy, at the expense of believing congregations. You will not be averse to seeing a few lines which Liddon sent me in answer to my inquiries.

'As the Bishops all consented including C. I cannot but fear mischief. Indeed the mere fact, that the question is kept open, is mischievous. If indeed the Committee were to decide, (1) upon ad-

vising the removal of penalties attaching to the disuse of the Creed ;
or (2) upon recognizing a dispensing power with the Bishops, so far
that if they used it, as part of their *jus liturgicum,* no penalties should
attach to their doing so ; or (3) upon leaving the whole thing alone,
no great harm would be done, but I fear this can scarcely be
looked for.'

The inquiries of the Bishop of Gloucester and Bristol have brought
before the Church what I always felt certain of, the high antiquity of
the Creed. But now, our Bishops would be acting with their
eyes open if they should tamper with the Creed, and going against
what the Church of England has ever reverenced, the early and
undivided Church. Your Lordship knows how strongly I feel about
it. May God guide your Lordship's Committee. I am come abroad,
for, if God will, the recovery of health, but *post equitem sedet atra
cura.* It is in vain to seek health with this gnawing care at one's
heart, what is going to be done in a matter which vitally affects all
one loves. If your Lordship should have any occasion to write,
a letter from Ch. Ch. from you would always be forwarded.

I dread having no Church to return to.

In concluding the debate in Convocation on July 4, the
Archbishop of Canterbury used words which showed the
influence which the action of Pusey and Liddon had had
on the controversy. He said :—

'My own opinion is that the whole difficulty of the question arises
from the conscientious scruples of what I believe to be a very small
body, but a body eminent for its zeal, eminent for its talent, and
eminent in some respects also for its position. Had we not had
statements from gentlemen whom we greatly respect, that, if certain
courses were not taken, they should feel it their duty to retire into lay
Communion with the Church of England, the matter would have been
settled one way or the other.'

The words were no doubt a tribute to the opportuneness
of Pusey's action, but they were inaccurate in more ways
than one. Pusey heard of them, when he paid a hurried
visit to England to consult Sir James Paget, and he
wrote at once to Bishop Wilberforce to remove any
misunderstanding.

E. B. P. TO THE BISHOP OF WINCHESTER.

Lille, July 27, 1872.

I called at Winchester House when in England for a day, wishing
to correct authentically a statement which His Grace the Archbishop
of Canterbury was reported to have made in Convocation ; viz. that it

was but 'a small number of zealous men' (as he was pleased to call us) whom the tampering with the Athanasian Creed would drive into extremities, and that the specific effect upon us would be to drive us ' into lay Communion.'

1. I do not think that any one has used the term 'lay Communion.' But to speak for myself, I have looked on only to the first step, viz. that, as my defence of the Church of England, that she is a teacher of truth through her formularies, would be cut away, I must abandon my defence of her, and with it my position in her. What my next step would be, I do not yet know. . . . It would be a very grave thing, and would involve much, to have to own that Archbishop Manning, &c., were right in asserting that the Church of England did not discharge one of the essential duties of the Church—that of teaching her members the faith once delivered to the saints. Whither I should turn, if she should abandon me, I know not. But to remain in 'lay Communion' seems to me an absurdity. It would not be my own Orders, but her character, as having abandoned the trust committed to her, which would be brought into question. She, if she tampers with the Athanasian Creed, would acquiesce in ———'s central heresy, that a definite faith has nothing to do with salvation. How a Church which does this with her eyes open (not, as the Church in the United States did, without seeing what it involved) can remain a portion of the Church of Christ, I know not. She would formally suppress the declaration, that what our Lord has revealed of Himself is essential for salvation ; and *that*, because men affect to be scandalized at this His teaching.

I cannot then see how those who believe the Church of England to have been ashamed of our Lord's words can continue to connive at her misdeeds or cast in their lot with her. I believe that the issue must be a rent of the Church of England in two. Dean Stanley looks at this in the face. He says, 'we should replace you by those whom we should gain.' But of what sort? It would be childish to think that Dissenters would be satisfied (as some one said publicly) by the removal of the Athanasian Creed. Up to the last year one never heard of any objection to it on the part of any Dissenters, except those who disbelieve in the doctrine of the Trinity and the Incarnation The real question at issue is, any definite faith. . . . It follows logically, if definite faith, such as our Lord has revealed to His Church, is not essential to salvation, what is? Or what did our Lord come upon earth to teach?

2. As to the numbers. No one could predict what would be the extent, to which such a departure from the faith, would affect men. Those whom it would move would perhaps not be those whom the Bishop of Gloucester and Bristol would gladly get rid of—the Ritualists. These seem to me absorbed in having their own way ; and they might go on, only holding your Lordship's Order all the cheaper (and *then*, I think, rightly), as having betrayed the faith. The Bishops would

herein put them in the right; they could no longer be slighted: they would in the very gravest matter be in the right, you in the wrong. You would be in their eyes a sort of necessary evil, for the performance of such offices as we, of the second order, cannot perform. . . . So very possibly the withdrawal of Liddon and myself, and the grounds of that withdrawal, would be to precipitate an avalanche of just the most dutiful, faithful minds into Ultramontanism. In any case it would be over, sooner or later, with the Church of England.

Your Lordship, though more slowly than myself, is approaching towards your end. You, I suppose, must have past three score years, as I the three score years and ten. It must be some forty-five years, I think, since I first knew you. Allow me, then, in the memory of that almost half century, to say, that not for the whole world would I, on my deathbed, have on my conscience that I had not resisted to the loss of all things earthly, the aggression on the Athanasian Creed.

But he soon saw there was a necessity for a more public declaration of his position. In the early summer Lord Shaftesbury had presented to the Archbishops an influential Petition against the Creed, and on July 23 they, in a Letter which was published in the papers, replied to the effect that they considered that no explanation could be devised which would meet all the difficulties involved in the use of the Creed, but that they were ready to suggest some scheme which would deal with the question. Pusey saw that this meant that the Archbishop had not in the least abandoned his original wish to drop the Creed out of the public worship of the Church, and that he would only yield to the strongest pressure. He therefore wrote the following letter to the *Times* :—

E. B. P. TO THE EDITOR OF THE ‘ TIMES.’

Mayence, Aug. 10, 1872.

. . . I believe that a crisis is come upon the Church of England which may move men’s minds and make a rent in her or from her far deeper than any since 1688. Whether in these days the Establishment, in which you, Sir, feel more interest than I can profess to have, would survive the shock, the event only can show.

Allow me, without entering into any theological questions beyond the bare statement of facts, to state briefly why I think so. The wish to remove the Athanasian Creed rests in different minds on two grounds :—First, the supposition that the belief therein stated is too detailed ; secondly, that the warning clauses speak of that belief as essential to salvation in those who can have it. Those, on the contrary, to whom the question of retaining the position of the Creed is a matter of life or death, hold the Creed to be the great instrument of teaching ourselves and the people how to believe and think aright on the Being of God and our Blessed Lord's Incarnation. The 'warning clauses' we believe to be the only statement in our Church services (in contradiction to the prevailing wrong opinion of the day) that a definite faith in the truths which our Lord revealed is essential to salvation in those who can have it ; in other words, that right faith as well as right life is essential to salvation, since our Lord has so declared it, and as a much greater contempt of God can be shown by rejecting what He reveals than by disobeying what He commands. Without, then, judging the Church in the United States, whose few leading Bishops, at the time of its foundation, in framing its Prayer Book, parted with the Athanasian Creed, not knowing what they did, we believe that if the Church of England were, in view of the objections raised, to tamper with that Creed, it would forfeit its character of a teacher of the people as to that which, whether we believe or disbelieve it, is more central than the belief or disbelief of any one doctrine—viz. whether it is of moment to salvation to believe what Almighty God has revealed or no.

I state these as our convictions. The result of acting upon these convictions, if the Church of England (I do not speak of the State or State interference) should tamper with this Creed (which God forbid), no one can now foresee. The Archbishop of Canterbury spoke of those who have these convictions as a handful, and of their retiring into lay communion. I believe his Grace to be mistaken as to both points. People, mostly, do not speak out beforehand. Acute politicians were utterly mistaken in their calculations on a matter of very inferior importance which gave birth to the Free Kirk. To retire into lay communion seems to me an absurdity ; for the question would be, not as to the exercise of our Orders, but as to the character of the Church of England. To resign the office of teachers in her, since she would have become a new Church, would be the first step ; what would be the next, they themselves have probably not predetermined as to a future which they hope will never be.

Allow me, in conclusion, to say that we only claim that things should remain as they are. Clergymen, at least, have no plea to demand a change ; for of their own free will and choice they received Holy Orders in a Church which recites the Athanasian Creed in her services. I believe that there is a great future for the Church of England if she remains what she is. What she would become if she made this first change no one could imagine. In principle, it would involve many more. It would content none, except as a stepping-stone to more. Our Common Prayer is the one great bond of union in the Church. I believe that the great majority of devout Churchmen are for retaining the Creed as it is. Anyhow, the change, we are convinced, if made by the Church, would constitute a new Church of England; our vows and duty remain to the old.

The Archbishop replied to this letter in his Charge in the early autumn. He acknowledged that he wished to remove the Creed, but some other alteration might be adopted, as distinct from an Explanatory Note. He had evidently returned entirely to his original plan. He adds:—

‘ Now I must state, though with much reluctance, that the greatest difficulty in the way arises from the unreasonable conduct of certain eminent persons, who declare that they will break the Church in two if we adopt any other than their own particular way of settling this grave difficulty. Such conduct, I say, is deserving of our reprobation, and I trust that, after a full consideration, those who are guilty of it will come to a better mind. All of us are anxious to maintain the great doctrine of the Trinity and that there shall be reality in our declarations ; and if we meet with great difficulties, which have long pressed on the minds of earnest men, we have a right to seek the best advice, and to request these learned and devout members of the Church to assist us, and not to commence the discussion with an unwarrantable declaration that they are prepared to break the Church in two if the decision arrived at does not meet their own particular views.’

Rarely, probably never in the history of modern controversy has any prelate in so high a position used such language of ‘ reprobation ’ with regard to ‘ learned and devout members ’ of the Church ; they are words which savour rather of the irritation of a partisan in a losing cause than of the weighty utterance of the chief bishop of a Church speaking of one who was confessedly among the most scholarly and devoted of her members. Pusey felt it necessary to explain to the Archbishop that the rent in the Church would be made by those who altered the Church’s Formularies, not by those who adhered to them. Copious extracts from his letter are given in the Archbishop’s ‘ Life[1].’ But the passage in which Pusey

---

[1] It was not to have been expected that Pusey’s action in this controversy should have been viewed with favour by the biographers of Archbishop Tait. Yet it is to be regretted that they should have been at the pains of appearing in some cases to suggest doubts of the accuracy of Pusey’s words (see notes, vol. ii. pp. 150 and 153). In each case a more complete knowledge of the full facts would have shown them that they themselves were in error.

explains the motives for his action is omitted[1]. It ran as follows:—

E. B. P. TO THE ARCHBISHOP OF CANTERBURY.

Oct. 12, 1872.

. . . Allow me to explain the grounds on which I think that any tampering with the Athanasian Creed would produce a serious rent in or from the Established Church. It would be, of course, a concession to something, whether the objection be to the truths of faith as confessed in the Creed as being untrue or uncertain, or to the assertion that the belief in those truths of the Holy Trinity and in the Incarnation is essential to salvation. Probably, in the minds of most objectors, both objections are blended together. Scepticism as to truth generally is far more common than absolute unbelief, in any who are outwardly members of the Church. Such hold nothing or scarcely anything of revealed truth to be certainly true, and even if they think anything to be true, they do not hold the belief in it to be necessary to salvation. Truth is confessed in the other Creeds; nowhere except in the Athanasian Creed is it stated to be necessary to salvation in those who can have it. This necessity is stated as clearly in the simpler words, ' Furthermore, it is necessary to everlasting salvation : that he also believe rightly the Incarnation of our Lord Jesus Christ,' as in those more strongly-worded forms upon which opponents most dwell.

The tampering, then, with the Athanasian Creed would in effect say to plain people, ' The Church of England does not hold the belief in the Holy Trinity or the Incarnation to be necessary to salvation, nor does it hold those truths, as set forth in the Athanasian Creed, to be certain.'

In a later passage he explains exactly who the authors of the division would be :—

' I used in a letter, upon which, I suppose, your Grace animadverts, the expression, "a rent in or from the Church," not wishing to express more clearly my fears as to a future, which I hoped might never be; but meaning by "a rent in the Church," a division of the Church itself; by a "rent from it," the tearing away of its members to join some other body or bodies, whether the Greek Church, or the Old Catholics, or the Roman Church. But the rent, if made, would not be of our making. The responsibility would not lie with us, who are grateful to the Church for having preserved to us the use and teaching of the Creed to which we are so much indebted. and who in all respects willingly acquiesced in the state of things, in which, by God's providence [? we were placed], and who have never wished to bring about any changes in any of our formularies, which

---

[1] ' Life of Archibald Campbell Tait,' vol. ii. pp. 151–153. The following    extract is from the rough draft of the letter that was sent.

are the common birthright of us all. We should simply remain faithful to that which we have been taught from our youth, the expression and guide of the faith of our riper years, which the Church of England upheld when we devoted ourselves to the service of God in her. The rent would be caused, not by us—who should be cast out of our homes, who would have to sacrifice all the cherished hopes of our lives—but by those (whoever they may be) who would trample upon our consciences, and the consciences of the laity who are faithful to the old belief. I doubt not that, unless encouraged by those in high places, the tornado which has been raised would spend itself, and that the result of the agitation will only be a more intelligent appreciation of the Creed.'

The Archbishop's reply[1] was to ask Pusey what kind of solution of the difficulty he would be likely to agree to, since an Explanatory Rubric seemed to find no favour with Convocation. Pusey answered that, with the exception of the proposal of an Explanatory Note, every suggestion that he had seen cast some slur on the Creed, and was therefore inadmissible. He expressed himself as not specially attached to the 'Note,' which the Oxford Professors had suggested, as he would prefer to state that the warning clauses were directed only against a culpable failure to believe. He therefore enclosed another formula, which he thought more satisfactory[2].

The meeting of the Committee of both Houses was fixed for December 3, and in preparation for it Bishop Wilberforce summoned a conference of clergy at Winchester House on November 27, which he invited Pusey to attend. Pusey was at first hopeless about it. He told the Bishop that it was a conflict of principles. He maintained that the Creed was hated by a party that did not think a definite faith to be 'necessary to salvation' in those who could have it, and who on that account considered the Creed to be uncharitable. 'We [think it] . . . the truest charity, as it would be to warn people of a precipice. They think that there is no precipice about which to warn them.' Pusey was also afraid that any suggestion that could be made would only be used as if it were a concession to the

---

[1] 'Life of Archibald Campbell Tait,' vol. ii. pp. 151, 152.
[2] Ibid., vol. ii. p. 152.

principle of change, and be treated in the same way as the suggestion by the Oxford Professors of an Explanatory Rubric had been two years before. He told the Bishop that if he attended the meeting he would say, 'anything which would be considered as a compromise would seem to me to be giving up the whole question. The warning clauses must be either true or false. Since "it is necessary to everlasting salvation that a man believe rightly" the Holy Trinity and the Incarnation (else he believes in a different God and a different Being from our Redeemer Christ Jesus), then it is the truest charity to tell people so, and it would be unfaithfulness to their souls to withdraw the statement.'

Under these conditions he consented to attend the Conference. He felt that he must continue to offer, as a relief for scruples, some explanation of the clauses; and Liddon joined him in drawing up yet another form. It was sent to Newman and amended at his suggestion, and then forwarded to Bishop Wilberforce. The Meeting seems to have adopted this Explanatory Note; for Pusey writes to Newman the day after:—

E. B. P. TO THE REV. J. H. NEWMAN.

Nov. 28, 1872.

You will see that we have adopted one of your pencil alternatives.... The meeting yesterday for which I went to London looked hopefully. I have seen so little of Church of late, and he is so modest and reserved that I was happy to find him so defined and outspoken.

The Archbishop now saw that he must finally abandon all hope of removing the Creed from the Services of the Church, and he told the Dean of Westminster that he must adopt the next best practicable course. The Dean replied:—

'Would it not be possible to put forward a declaration which should express the real facts of the case, viz.—that the use of the Creed is left, not from any concurrence in its contents, but out of deference to the scruples of certain distinguished clergymen,—specifying, if desirable, the Regius Professor of Hebrew and the Ireland Professor of Exegesis at Oxford[1]?'

[1] 'Life of Archibald Campbell Tait,' ii. 157.

On the Sunday after the Meeting at Winchester House, the first Sunday in Advent, November 30, Pusey preached before the University a sermon which he had been preparing for several weeks, and which dealt with the central point of all this controversy.    It was an Advent sermon entitled 'The Responsibility of the Intellect in matters of Faith[1].'  It passed from the thought of death, to Judgment, and especially to Judgment with regard to our relation to God's Revelation of Himself.  'The thought that each shall have to give account for his "opinions" (as people call them), or the process by which he arrives at them, seems to them as strange an imagination as if the subject-matter were some proposition of pure mathematics.'  He then passes in review the power of intellect, describing the various ways in which the intellect can sin and can intensify all other forms of sin, dwelling especially on the sinfulness of intellectual pride, and of intellectual injustice and error in judging the truths of Revelation.   These sins of intellect he traces to the sources which naturally can produce them, whether moral or spiritual, whether they spring from a careless life, or from 'mere inactivity of faith.'  He then shows the great danger of these sins from the example of the Jews in our Lord's day, who for reasons which He pointed out, rejected an unique opportunity of believing, and on that account were exposed to the Divine sentence of judgment.   Failures to believe are as sinful as failures to obey in those who have the opportunity, although no one can venture to measure the exact responsibility of any individual soul.  'The Church has its long list of saints (he quotes the words); it has not inserted one name in the catalogue of the damned.'   Then he proceeds to state the truths of the Athanasian Creed, their supreme importance, and the value of the clauses 'which press upon us our own responsibility as to truth which God has made known to us'; and in view of much of the tone of the Oxford of that day he concludes with a most earnest warning against the fashionable trifling in matters of vital moment.

[1] 'University Sermons,' vol. iii. serm. v.

The whole sermon is a very solemn and yet most tender justification of the 'warning clauses.' In view of the audience to which it was addressed and the controversy out of which it sprang, it is full of direct and pointed appeal. It was in print before it was delivered: and immediately after delivery was circulated with an elaborate and powerful note in reply to Bishop Moberly's strictures on the Creed, which he specially inserted in order to influence the meeting at Lambeth two days later.

The Committee of the two Houses of Convocation met at Lambeth on December 3. Bishop Wilberforce proposed the adoption of an Explanatory Note, or rather of a Synodical Declaration, as from this time it was called, with regard to the warning clauses of the Creed. Every other form of 'relief' was in its turn suggested as an amendment, but only to be defeated on a division. Eventually the Bishop's motion was carried, the terms of the Declaration being left for later consideration. 'Thanks,' writes Pusey to Liddon, 'for the cheering news of the Lambeth Conference, which gives good hope. I hope there will be many thanksgivings to God.'

A week later he left Oxford for a rest on the Continent. He would not delay his journey so as to join in the vote against Dean Stanley's nomination as a Select Preacher at Oxford, on the ground, as he explained in a letter to the *Times*, dated 'Genoa, December 22,' that 'opposition would only aggravate the evil by enlisting the enthusiasm of the young.' At Genoa, he strained his chest when shouting to a child who was in danger of being run over. The strain caused a serious attack of bronchitis, followed by pneumonia, and for a time his condition was critical. On January 21, 1873, Dr. Acland was summoned by telegraph from Oxford. He found him in great danger, and very prostrate; but on the 27th was able to telegraph to a meeting of the Hebdomadal Council at Oxford, 'Dr. Pusey is out of danger.'

Meanwhile preparations had for some months been going on for a public meeting in London in defence of the Creed.

At Leeds, during the Church Congress in October, 1872, a numerous and influential committee had been appointed to organize such a gathering. It was eventually held in St. James' Hall, on Friday, January 31. On the same day that Dr. Acland was able to send such reassuring news to Oxford, Pusey had dictated in a whisper to his son Philip, who was with him at Genoa, a letter, which he desired Liddon to read to that meeting. Throughout the whole evening the greatest enthusiasm had prevailed. But when Liddon rose to speak, and again when he mentioned Pusey's name, a tumult of applause followed which will never be forgotten by any who witnessed it. The whole vast assemblage rose to their feet to do them honour, and renewed their cheers again and again. Pusey's letter ran as follows :—

E. B. P. TO REV. H. P. LIDDON, D.D.

Genoa, Piazza Galeazzo Alessi, Jan. 27, 1873.

Words dictated from a very sick bed must be very true. Yes. I wish to express through you to the meeting how unchanging through sickness or health is my sense of the intensity of the crisis with which we were threatened all last year, and out of which the Church of England has, by God's mercy, been brought. However men might disguise the question themselves, I could not conceal from myself that the real issue was, whether the Church of England should virtually deny that the faith in the Holy Trinity and in the Incarnation of our Lord Jesus Christ was essential to salvation in those who could have it. As to the remarks of some in authority as to the line to which our convictions independently led us, they cannot have understood the strength of our convictions. It was no 'threat' to give up, in my case, the cherished aspirations of a past sixty years to serve God in the ministry of the Church of England, the home and the centre of one's deepest interests, to go forth not knowing whither one went. It was like a moral death ; but with my convictions of the issue of that question I dared no more hesitate than about being guilty of parricide. God be thanked for all His mercies.

During the many days of Pusey's very slow recovery, Convocation was deciding upon the form which the Synodical Declaration should take. All was settled before he returned to England in the following May, but he still heard echoes of the controversy during the days of his convalescence.

### Rev. J. H. Newman to E. B. P.

The Oratory, Feb. 15, 1873.

As you may fancy, you have been a great deal in my thoughts lately, and I should have written to you, except that I felt you could be sure of it, and had not much or anything to say besides.  Thank Philip very much for me for his acceptable letter.

I congratulate you on the present prospects of the Athanasian Creed in the Anglican Formularies.  I have cursorily read the proposed notice of the Convocation Committee; and it seemed to me unexceptionable.

Of course it won't answer the purpose of the Liberals, whose quarrel with it goes far beyond their professed difficulty.

Pusey was unable to answer, but Newman heard of his slow progress from William Pusey, who feared lest the anxieties of controversy would retard his brother's recovery.

### Rev. J. H. Newman to Rev. W. B. Pusey.

March 6, 1873.

I do hope the Athanasian Creed matter is settled, at least for our time, for that must agitate him immensely.  I am sure it would me.  I think a mere sense of tenderness to one so great a benefactor to the Church of England as your brother, should make a man like Tait suspend his hand.

It was not till after Easter that Pusey himself was able to write.  The letter shows Pusey's employments during the leisure of recovery from a serious illness.

### E. B. P. to Rev. J. H. Newman.

Genoa, Easter Tuesday, [Apr. 15], 1873.

All Easter blessings.  I knew that your love would follow me at all times and under all circumstances.  God reward you for it.

By God's blessing and mercy, I am able to work again, so I have completed (as far as I could here) the Commentary on Haggai and (Zechariah being completed all but the Introduction) am within eight verses of the close of Malachi.  Now, being allowed to be in England early in May, I am leaving Genoa, though I feel doubtful whether my chest is strong enough to lecture yet.  Still God allows me to go [on] with the Commentary without hindrance, thanks be to His mercy.

Now I want to ask you whether you think I have overstated the doctrine of invincible ignorance in the Sermon I sent you?  You have perhaps seen the line which the assailants of the Warning Clauses take of declaring our interpretation to be 'non-natural,' which is a clever weapon. But though they might say this of any private opinion of ours, they could not say it if it should be the received sense in which these clauses are taken throughout the Roman Church. For those among whom the Creed originated, and who have directed its use by all their Clergy and by all who are bound to say the Hours, must needs know in what sense they take it.

You have answered my question as far as the Synodical Declaration goes, as you thought it to contain nothing amiss. And this is the main point. But since some of the assailants of the Creed profess to approve of what I have myself written and have given it an undue prominence, but accused it of being a non-natural interpretation of the Creed, it would be satisfactory to be able to say to them privately, 'Without saying anything about this or that expression, the interpretation advocated is in the main the interpretation acknowledged in the Roman Church.'

I do not see how the doctrine of invincible ignorance, combined with that of the universal gift of grace, can come short of that interpretation of St. Peter's words that God has His own elect amid whatsoever blindness or ignorance or error, and that millions may be saved by the precious Blood of Christ, who never heard His Name or misbelieved about Him.

The meeting of Convocation is not till somewhere in May. I can give no direction abroad, as I have no certain stopping-place ; but I should be very glad to give some answer, without quoting you.

Newman answered :—

REV. J. H. NEWMAN TO E. B. P.

The Oratory, April 27, 1873.

In answer to your question, I fear I can say nothing satisfactory to you. I do not know where to look for such a Catholic limitation of the anathemas of the Athanasian Creed, as you wish to find, and for what seems an obvious reason, which I will explain.

Our writers either hold that faith in the Holy Trinity is necessary *necessitate medii* or *necessitate precepti*—in neither case does the question of invincible ignorance come into consideration. If *necessitate medii* there is no place for invincible ignorance—just as no invincible ignorance can avail to put out a conflagration instead of a fire engine. If *necessitate precepti*, as I should myself hold, then the very word *preceptum* implies the formal presentation of the Creed to the individual for his acceptance, and thus here again there can be no ignorance, vincible or invincible, for the reason that it is always directly presented to him as being one of the conditions of admittance into the Church, so that every one who is made a Christian is made acquainted with the Creed. Indeed, the very idea of a 'Creed' in itself excludes the notion of ignorance altogether, it being the very *tessera* or ticket of Church fellowship. As Baptism is necessary for salvation as a mean, so is faith in the Holy Trinity as a condition. So that there cannot be any escape from culpable unbelief in those who refuse to accept the doctrine. I don't see how there is any 'non-natural' explanation in this; nor does it oblige us to pronounce absolutely on the future state of any one, for we cannot tell what takes place on a deathbed. . . .

You also ask, whether you have gone too far in what you say of invincible ignorance. I think not, supposing what you say be coupled with the proviso that we can as little decide absolutely that a man *is* in invincible ignorance, as that he *is not*. No one has a right to be sure that he is in invincible ignorance. I think I have heard Keble say, 'Well, all I can say is, that, if the Roman Communion is the One True Church, I do not know it, I do not know it.' Indeed, you have implied this spirit of godly fear in what you say against levity in theological inquiry.

At last, on May 10, 1873, the question was settled. The Creed was retained in use and unmutilated; but both Houses of Convocation accepted the following Synodical Declaration with regard to its warning clauses :—

'For the removal of doubts and to prevent disquietude in the use of the Creed commonly called the Creed of St. Athanasius, this Synod doth solemnly declare :—

'1. That the confession of our Christian faith, commonly called the Creed of St. Athanasius, doth not make any addition to the faith as contained in Holy Scripture, but warneth against errors which from time to time have arisen in the Church of Christ.

'2. That as Holy Scripture in divers places doth promise life to them that believe, and declare the condemnation of them that believe not, so doth the Church in this confession declare the necessity for all who would be in a state of salvation of holding fast the Catholic faith, and the great peril of rejecting the same. Wherefore the warnings in this confession of faith are to be understood no otherwise than the like warnings in Holy Scripture, for we must receive God's threatenings, even as His promises, in such wise as they are generally set forth in Holy Writ. Moreover the Church doth not herein pronounce judgment on any particular person or persons, God alone being the Judge of all.'

Throughout this controversy, as also in the matter of 'Essays and Reviews,' Pusey had found more support from Bishop Wilberforce than from any other occupant on the Episcopal bench. He knew him far too well to suppose that the mistrust which the Bishop had felt and expressed in the early years of his episcopate had given way to a state of complete agreement and sympathy : but he had abundant tokens that the Bishop had materially altered his attitude towards him. In the eventful years which had elapsed since 1845 Pusey had been able again and again to justify his position by the steadfastness of his loyalty in situations of no ordinary delicacy and difficulty ; and the Bishop had gradually come to see that there was no evidence for his early suspicions, and to recognize the sincerity and depth of Pusey's character, and the value of his work for the Church. If Stanley attributed the defeat of his wishes with regard to the Athanasian Creed to Pusey and Liddon, he would have also allowed that the action of Bishop Wilberforce had not a little contributed to the same result. Humanly speaking Pusey might have had great hope for the future with such an ally among the Bishops. But their common work in this world was over. The news of the Bishop's sudden death [1] a few weeks after the close of this controversy was a great grief. When he had passed away, Pusey remembered him only as he had been in his later days.

E. B. P. TO P. E. PUSEY, ESQ.

Malvern, July 25, 1873.

. . . It is indeed a grievous loss. He was always full of kindness and a great check to persecutors. How strange to be in that world, and on the way to the Judgment throne, without knowing death, except that he found that he had died, because he was not in the body !

At this time of his life, many other gaps were caused by death in the wide circle of Pusey's friends, but of course no one of them was of such moment to the Church as this. His letters to Newman and the replies frequently mention the passing away of friends whom they had known together many years before—James Hope Scott, Henry Wilberforce, and Jelf, were among the number. To the same period belongs also his reconciliation with his old college friend Hook. They had dropped their correspondence after the

---

[1] He was killed by a fall from his horse on July 19, 1873.

difficulties at St. Saviour's, Leeds[1] ; Hook was now Dean
of Chichester, separated both in time and space from the
troubles which had perplexed and distressed him. His
brother was dying in London, and was daily visited by
Liddon. In acknowledging this kindness the Dean takes
the opportunity of asking another favour :—

THE DEAN OF CHICHESTER TO REV. H. P. LIDDON, D.D.

July 28, 1873.

Can you add to your favours ? Can you tell that saint whom
England persecuted, our dearly beloved Pusey, that I should like,
as I am passing out of this world, to be permitted to renew the
friendship with him, which in my youthful days was my joy and crown
of rejoicing ? No one prayed more earnestly for him than I did when
he was almost despaired of on the continent. No one rejoiced
more entirely than I did, when he returned to England recruited in
health.

Pusey was truly glad to find that he had lived down
another of the sad misunderstandings of which the years
between 1840 and 1860 had been so fruitful. He wrote
immediately on receiving Hook's message :—

E. B. P. TO THE DEAN OF CHICHESTER.

Sidmouth House, Malvern, Aug. 1, 1873.

Thank you much for your loving message which Liddon conveyed
to me, and for your loving prayers while I was so ill at Genoa. God
heard them, and I can now walk about (though my breath is still
weak) and write my Commentary.

What a long life of friendship it has been since 1819, when I used
to come down from my garret to your rooms in Peckwater, fifty-four
years ago ! Who could have imagined what lay before us ? I am so
sorry that some whom I sent to St. Saviour's worried you. I always
studied you, though I was misinformed in two cases.

I am grieved to hear that you are suffering, and that your brother is
passing away. Death has swept away more of those whom I love
in these last few months than for a long time before. I need not ask
you to remember me, since you do this so earnestly, as I you, during
our remaining pilgrimage.

God be with you now and ever.

Yours affectionately,

E. B. PUSEY.

---

[1] See vol. iii. pp. 112–136.

# CHAPTER X.

WHILE the public mind was full of the discussions about Ritual and the Athanasian Creed, another violent storm arose on the subject of Confession. It was caused by a lengthy Petition [1] to Convocation signed by 483 Clergy, which was presented on May 9, 1873. The Petition was intended apparently as a counterblast to the persistent and destructive assaults which had been delivered on the side of extreme Puritanism and Latitudinarianism against the Church, and advocated sundry ecclesiastical changes in somewhat startling terms. In a state of atmosphere less charged with electricity it would probably have passed unnoticed; as it was the public suspicion fastened upon one phrase, 'licensing of duly qualified confessors,' and under the leadership of the Archbishop of Canterbury an attack on Confession was delivered in force. The petition had prayed that 'in view of the widespread and increasing use of Sacramental Confession, your venerable house may consider the advisability of providing for the education, selection, and licensing of duly qualified Confessors in accordance with the provisions of canon law'; and in reply, the Upper House of Convocation had resolved itself into Committee to consider the teaching of the Church of England on Confession.

But it was very evident that the question would not be confined to Convocation. The 'Church Association' was

---

[1] The petition will be found in full in the *Guardian*, 1873, p. 711.

stirring up public feeling in the matter, and urging on
public men to some action ; and the two Archbishops were
readily playing into its hands.   In reply to a memorial
which the ' Church Association ' had presented to them,
the Archbishops sent a lengthy letter on June 16, 1873,
in which, specially alluding to the petition of the four
hundred and eighty-three Clergy, they said :—

> ' We believe that through the system of the Confessional great evil
> has been wrought in the Church of Rome, and that our Reformers
> acted wisely in allowing it no place in our reformed Church, and we
> take this opportunity of expressing our entire disapproval of any such
> innovation, and our firm determination to do all in our power to
> discourage it [1].'

Pusey and the old High Churchmen felt themselves in
a difficult position.   On the one hand, the assertion of the
Archbishops, besides being historically baseless, was another
declaration of active hostility against the Prayer-book : and
on the other, they themselves were identified in the popular
mind with the demands or suggestions of the 483, whereas
as a matter of fact they would have gladly repudiated, in
many particulars, both the language and intentions of their
memorial.   The Bishop of Brechin strongly urged that they
should put out a Declaration embodying the teaching of
the Prayer-book on this subject, which without mentioning
the Archbishops would be an answer to them.   Dr. Bright
and Pusey were not averse to doing so : but Liddon doubted
the wisdom of such a course.   It would, he thought, only
continue the controversy, and no one could seriously suppose that the wild utterances of the ' Church Association '
on this subject represented the teaching of the Prayer-
book.   Pusey, however, still thought that some simple
statement would be valuable :—

' People would be very much surprised,' he wrote to the
Hon. C. L. Wood (now Viscount Halifax) on July 4, 1873,
' if they knew how early the authority for private Confession after the Reformation is. . . . It would startle people

[1] *Guardian,* 1873, p. 838.

to find Latimer and Cranmer advocating Confession, besides Bishop Jewell who does not object to it.' But as opinions were thus divided, no declaration was at that moment put forth.

The report of the Committee of the Upper House of Convocation was presented on July 23, four days after the death of Bishop Wilberforce. It ran as follows :—

' In the matter of Confession the Church of England holds fast those principles which are set forth in Holy Scripture, which were professed by the Primitive Church, and which were reaffirmed at the English Reformation.

' The Church of England in the twenty-fifth Article affirms that Penance is not to be counted for a sacrament of the Gospel, and as judged by her formularies, knows no such words as "sacramental confessions."

'Grounding her doctrine on Holy Scripture, she distinctly declares the full and entire forgiveness of sins through the Blood of Jesus Christ to those who bewail their own sinfulness, confess themselves to Almighty God, with full purpose of amendment of life, and turn with true faith unto Him. It is the desire of the Church that by this way and means all her children should find peace.

' In this spirit the forms of Confession and Absolution are set forth in her public services. Yet, for the relief of troubled consciences, she has made special provision in two exceptional cases.

' 1. In the case of those who cannot quiet their own consciences previous to receiving the Holy Communion, but require further comfort or counsel, the minister is directed to say, " Let him come to me, or to some other discreet and learned minister of God's Word, and open his grief, that by the ministry of God's Holy Word he may receive the benefit of Absolution, together with ghostly counsel and advice." Nevertheless it is to be noted that for such a case no form of Absolution has been prescribed in the Book of Common Prayer, and further, that the rubric in the First Prayer Book of 1549, which sanctions a particular form of Absolution, has been withdrawn from all subsequent editions of the said book.

' 2. In the Order of the Visitation of the Sick it is directed that the sick man be moved to make a special Confession of his sins if his conscience is troubled with any weighty matter ; but in such case Absolution is only to be given when the sick man shall humbly and heartily desire it. The special provision, however, does not authorize the ministers of the Church to require from any one who may repair to them to open their grief in a particular or detailed examination of all their sins, or to require private Confession as a condition previous to receiving the Holy Communion, or to enjoin or even encourage any practice of habitual Confession to a priest, or to teach that such practice or habitual Confession, or the being subject to what has been termed the direction of a priest, is a condition of attaining to the highest spiritual life.'

Pusey had left Oxford for Malvern on July 14; when he heard rumours of what had happened, he wrote at once to Dr. Bright, on whose affection and help he relied so greatly during the later years of his life:—

E. B. P. TO REV. W. BRIGHT, D.D.

Malvern, July 26, 1873.

I have not seen the details of Convocation or the language of the Archbishops. I should imagine it simply impossible that they meant to deny the power, 'Whose sins ye do remit, &c.,' which they or their predecessors gave us. As you keep such documents, would you send me any? you shall have them back. I wrote to the Bishop of W[inchester] before I left Oxford, and heard from him that he agreed with me as to Confession in the English Church, that he knew the authorities, of which I reminded him, that he had lately used them to stop some ultra-Protestant (churchwarden, I think), but that which he grieves and differs from me in was—I have not his note here, and might not do him justice, but they were points in which my own practice had not been what he dissented from.

When he had seen the Report of the Bishops, he felt strongly that the Bishop of Brechin's proposed action was right; some Declaration ought to be made in order to prevent any restriction on the liberty of Confession within the English Church. And as Mr. Carter, of Clewer, also had written very strongly urging the same course, Pusey writes again to Dr. Bright about it.

E. B. P. TO REV. W. BRIGHT, D.D.

Sidmouth House, Malvern, July 30, 1873.

. . . I should think that the Bishop of Winchester had chiefly the drawing up of that Report. I think that he *bona fide* believed of Absolution as we do, but that he was timid as to its systematic use. I think that our Declaration ought to have no reference to the Bishops. We ought to assume that they meant right. As to habitual Confession, where there was deadly sin to strive with, the Bishop of Winchester thought as we do. I thought that a subject which he asked us to take for a Lenten sermon would involve my preaching on Confession, and told him so. (This was years ago.) He asked me to come out and speak with him. I said to him, *inter alia*, 'You know, my Lord, that there are some sins of young men for which habitual Confession is *the* remedy' (emphasizing the *the*). He said at once, 'Yes, it is;' and went on to instance a case which had been delivered from it by Confession[1]. But what he and Lord Salisbury and, I suppose, the mass of Englishmen are thinking of are not these cases, but those to whom the Bishop of Winchester alludes in the last clauses,—souls which never did commit a deadly sin probably, certainly do not now, and yet who, I suppose, are the greatest number of those who use confession—Christian women. These come under the clause of the Communion Exhortation, for (*you* will remember the saying accurately) 'Delicate souls feel more the slightest offence against a law of God than others do whole cartloads of sin.'

Popular excitement on the subject of Confession grew, instead of diminishing, as the summer went on: and Pusey was reminded of the old troubles of the Maskell and Allies controversy in 1850.

E. B. P. TO REV. H. P. LIDDON, D.D.

Malvern, Aug. 21, 1873.

. . . It is a tremendous storm, but not greater than 1850, with the institution of the R. C. Episcopate, the attack of Dodsworth, Maskell, and Allies, and the prevailing suspicion. As, for instance, I know not whether you know, that I was wished not to preach in the Diocese of Oxford till I should publish my letter to the Bishop of London. At St. Saviour's, Leeds, C. Marriott went over to Bishop Longley about my preaching. I suspected the result, so as he came, just as the service was to commence, like Nelson, I shut my eyes and put the note in my pocket. *Fortes, pejoraque passi.* But what with the ultra-Ritualists, Lord Shaftesbury, and the Church Association, the Declaration of the two Archbishops and the utterances of some others, the ambition of the Wesleyans taking occasion of it all, no small storm lies upon us. Will the vessel bear it, which so many wish to break to pieces? 'O Lord, Thou knowest.'

Letters continued between Pusey, Liddon, and Dr. Bright throughout the whole of that summer and autumn, first as to the advisability of a Declaration and then as to its terms. Pusey was clear on both points:—

'We have to regain the confidence of plain English people,' he writes, having in view, no doubt, his own experience in 1843, with regard to the condemned Sermon, 'and so, I think, we ought to support our proposition out of English

---

[1] See also Pusey's Sermon, 'God and Human Independence,' p. 34.

authorities—the Prayer-book or (secondarily) the Homilies, and also from common sense. English people will understand that if a thing is good for the soul, it ought not to be put off to a possible sick-bed: if a grievous matter ought to be confessed *then*, it ought to be confessed before.'

Pusey spent more thought over this Declaration than over any other work of the kind in which he had been engaged: it was not until November that he, Dr. Bright, Canon Carter, and Liddon had completed their work. In writing to ask for Copeland's signature to it he explains that it was purposely issued with only a few selected names.

E. B. P. TO REV. W. J. COPELAND.

Nov. 17, 1877.

' I send you in great haste our Declaration and the names attached. They are names of some age and standing. We have excluded mostly those of the advanced school. Mackonochie is the only Ritualist. It is, in fact, a rallying of the old school for whom the young ones have been speaking and whom they profess to represent. They mostly maintain Confession to be necessary for the forgiveness of sin. This Declaration certainly has not been hastily got up. For as we are scattered, Carter, Liddon and I have had the forms before us corrected and recorrected for four months. It was planned originally to prevent all the ignorant statements about Confession being contrary to the Church of England, &c., and unadvised speeches of Bishops. It is now too late for this, but as a document it may, I hope, be of lasting use, and may prevent some perhaps lasting mischief.'

At last, on December 6, 1873, the Declaration appeared in the columns of the *Times* with a short note from Pusey, who only described it as dealing with a subject which had of late engaged a large share of the public attention [1].

DECLARATION ON CONFESSION AND ABSOLUTION, AS SET FORTH BY THE CHURCH OF ENGLAND.

We, the undersigned, priests of the Church of England, considering that serious misapprehensions as to the teaching of the Church of England on the subject of Confession and Absolution are widely prevalent, and that these misapprehensions lead to serious evils, hereby

---

[1] This Declaration is reprinted practically as it appeared in the *Times*: it differs in some slight particulars from the version printed by Pusey in his Edition of Gaume's *Advice on Hearing Confession*, Pref. pp. clxxi-clxxiv.

declare, for the truth's sake and in the fear of God, what we hold and teach on the subject, with special reference to the points which have been brought under discussion.

1. We believe and profess that Almighty God has promised forgiveness of sins, through the Precious Blood of Jesus Christ, to all who turn to Him, with true sorrow for sin, out of unfeigned and sincere love to Him, with lively faith in Jesus Christ, and with full purpose of amendment of life.

2. We also believe and profess that our Lord Jesus Christ has instituted in His Church a special means for the remission of sin after Baptism, and for the relief of consciences, which special means the Church of England retains and administers as part of her Catholic heritage.

3. We affirm that—to use the language of the Homily—'Absolution hath the promise of forgiveness of sin [1],' although, the Homily adds, 'by the express word of the New Testament it hath not this promise annexed and tied to the visible sign, which is imposition of hands, and therefore,' it says, 'Absolution is no such Sacrament as Baptism and the Communion are [2].' We hold it to be clearly impossible that the Church of England in Art. XXV can have meant to disparage the ministry of Absolution any more than she can have meant to disparage the rites of Confirmation and Ordination, which she solemnly administers. We believe that God, through Absolution, confers an inward spiritual grace and the authoritative assurance of His forgiveness on those who receive it with faith and repentance, as in Confirmation and Ordination He confers grace on those who rightly receive the same.

4. In our Ordination, as priests of the Church of England, the words of our Lord to His Apostles—'Receive ye the Holy Ghost; whosesoever sins ye remit, they are remitted unto them, and whosesoever sins ye retain they are retained'—were applied to us individually. Thus it appears that the Church of England considers this commission to be not a temporary endowment of the Apostles, but a gift lasting to the end of time. It was said to each of us, 'Receive the Holy Ghost for the office and work of a priest in the Church of God, now committed unto thee by the imposition of our hands;' and then followed the words, 'Whose sins thou dost forgive, they are forgiven, and whose sins thou dost retain, they are retained [3].'

5. We are not here concerned with the two forms of Absolution which the priest is directed to pronounce after the general confession of sins in the Morning and Evening Prayer and in the Communion Service. The only form of words provided for us in the Book of Common Prayer for applying the absolving power to individual souls runs thus:—'Our Lord Jesus Christ, Who hath left power to His

---

[1] Homily 'of Common Prayer and Sacraments.'

[2] Ibid.

[3] 'The Form and Manner of ordering of Priests.'

Church to absolve all sinners who truly repent and believe in Him, of His great mercy forgive thee thine offences : And by His authority committed to me, I absolve thee from all thy sins, in the Name of the Father, and of the Son, and of the Holy Ghost.   Amen[1].'   Upon this we remark, first, that in these words forgiveness of sins is ascribed to our Lord Jesus Christ, yet that the priest, acting by a delegated authority and as an instrument, does through these words convey the absolving grace ; and, secondly, that the Absolution from sins cannot be understood to be the removal of any censures of the Church, because (*a*) the sins from which the penitent is absolved are pre-supposed to be sins known previously to himself and God only ; (*b*) the words of the Latin form relating to those censures are omitted in our English form ; and (*c*) the release from excommunication is in Art. XXXIII reserved to 'a Judge that hath authority thereunto.'

6. This provision, moreover, shows that the Church of England, when speaking of 'the benefit of Absolution,' and empowering her priests to absolve, means them to use a definite form of Absolution, and does not merely contemplate a general reference to the promises of the Gospel.

7. In the Service for 'the Visitation of the Sick' the Church of England orders that the sick man shall even 'be moved to make a special confession of his sins, if he feels his conscience troubled with any weighty matter.'   When the Church requires that the sick man should, in such case, be moved to make a special confession of his sins, we cannot suppose her thereby to rule that her members are bound to defer to a death-bed (which they may never see) what they know to be good for their souls.   We observe that the words 'be moved to' were added in 1661, and that, therefore, at the last revision of the Book of Common Prayer the Church of England affirmed the duty of exhorting to Confession in certain cases more strongly than at the date of the Reformation, probably because the practice had fallen into abeyance during the Great Rebellion.

8. The Church of England also, holding it 'requisite, that no man should come to the Holy Communion, but with a full trust in God's mercy, and with a quiet conscience,' commands the minister to bid 'any' one who 'cannot quiet his own conscience herein' to come to him, or 'to some other discreet and learned minister of God's Word, and open his grief ; that by the ministry of God's Holy Word he may receive the benefit of Absolution, together with,' and, therefore, as distinct from, 'ghostly counsel and advice[2];' and since she directs that this invitation should be repeated in giving warning of Holy Communion, and Holy Communion is constantly offered to all, it follows that the use of Confession may be, at least in some cases, of not unfrequent occurrence.

---

[1] 'The Order for the Visitation of the Sick.'
[2] Exhortation in the Service for Holy Communion.

9. We believe that the Church left it to the consciences of individuals, according to their sense of their needs, to decide whether they would confess or not, as expressed in that charitable exhortation of the first English Prayer Book, 'requiring such as shall be satisfied with a general confession, not to be offended with them that do use, to their further satisfying, the auricular and secret confession to the priest: nor those also which think needful or convenient, for the quietness of their own consciences, particularly to open their sins to the priest, to be offended with them that are satisfied with their humble confession to God and the general confession to the Church. But in all things to follow and keep the rule of charity; and every man to be satisfied with his own conscience, not judging other men's minds or consciences; whereas he hath no warrant of God's Word to the same.' And although this passage was omitted in the second Prayer-book, yet that its principle was not repudiated may be gathered from the ' Act for the Uniformity of Service' (1552), which, while authorizing the second Prayer-book, asserts the former book to be 'agreeable to the Word of God and the primitive Church.'

10. We would further observe that the Church of England has nowhere limited the occasions upon which her priests should exercise the office which she commits to them at their Ordination; and that to command her priests in two of her offices to hear Confessions, if made, cannot be construed negatively into a command not to receive Confessions on any other occasions. But, in fact (see above, Nos. 7, 8), the two occasions specified do practically comprise the whole of the adult life. A succession of Divines of great repute in the Church of England, from the very time when the English Prayer-book was framed, speak highly of Confession, without limiting the occasions upon which, or the frequency with which, it should be used; and the 113th Canon, framed in the Convocation of 1603, recognized Confession as a then existing practice, in that it decreed, under the severest penalties, that 'if any man confess his secret and hidden sins to the minister for the unburdening of his conscience, and to receive spiritual consolation and ease of mind from him . . . . the said minister . . . . do not at any time reveal and make known to any person whatsoever any crime or offence so committed to his trust and secrecy (except they be such crimes as by the laws of this realm his own life may be called into question for concealing the same).'

11. While, then, we hold that the formularies of the Church of England do not authorize any priest to teach that private Confession is a condition indispensable to the forgiveness of sin after Baptism, and that the Church of England does not justify any parish priest in requiring private Confession as a condition of receiving Holy Communion, we also hold that all who, under the circumstances above stated, claim the privilege of private Confession, are entitled to it, and that the clergy are directed under certain circumstances to ' move' persons to such Confession. In insisting on this as the plain meaning

of the authorized language of the Church of England, we believe ourselves to be discharging our duty as her faithful ministers.

ASHWELL, A. R., Canon of Chichester.

BAKER, HENRY W., Vicar of Monkland.

BARTHOLOMEW, Ch. Ch., Vicar of Cornwood, and Rural Dean
of Plympton.

BENSON, R. M., Incumbent of Cowley St. John, Oxford.

BUTLER, WILLIAM J., Vicar of Wantage, and Rural Dean.

CARTER, T. T., Rector of Clewer.

CHAMBERS, J. C., Vicar of St. Mary's, Soho.

CHURTON, EDW., Rector of Crayke, and Archdeacon of
Cleveland.

DENISON, GEORGE A., Vicar of East Brent, and Archdeacon
of Taunton.

GALTON, J. L., Rector of St. Sidwell's, Exeter.

GILBERTSON, LEWIS, Rector of Braunston.

GREY, FRANCIS R., Rector of Morpeth.

GRUEBER, C. L., Vicar of St. James's, Hambridge.

KEBLE, THOS., jun., Bisley.

KING, EDWARD, D.D., Canon of Christ Church, Oxford.

LIDDELL, ROBERT, Incumbent of St. Paul's, Knightsbridge.

LIDDON, H. P., D.D., Canon of St. Paul's, London.

MACCOLL, M., Rector of St. Botolph, Billingsgate, London.

MACKONOCHIE, A. H., Perpetual Curate of St. Alban's,
Holborn.

MAYOW, M. W., Rector of Southam, and Rural Dean.

MEDD, P. G., Senior Fellow of University College, Oxford.

MURRAY, F. H., Rector of Chislehurst.

PUSEY, E. B., D.D., Canon of Christ Church, Oxford.

RANDALL, R. W., Incumbent of All Saints, Clifton.

SHARP, JOHN, Vicar of Horbury.

SKINNER, JAMES, Vicar of Newland, Great Malvern.

WHITE, G. C., Vicar of St. Barnabas, Pimlico.

WILLIAMS, G., Vicar of Ringwood.

WILSON, R. F., Vicar of Rownhams, Southampton.

The hasty and somewhat ill-advised petition of the 483
had been both misunderstood and overrated, and had been
a cause of serious distress and perplexity in more quarters
than one. But its publication and the storm which ensued
cannot be regarded as all loss if it resulted in nothing else
than eliciting so weighty a document as this, which sets
forth in terms so concise and clear a careful and complete
statement of the position of the Church of England on the
very important subject of Confession.

# CHAPTER XI.

ATTITUDE TOWARDS RITUAL DEVELOPMENT.

1873-1877.

THE events described in the last chapter caused Pusey to feel very keenly the growing separation between himself and the more extreme 'Ritualist' wing. In letters of this period he allowed himself occasionally to express his thoughts in language which represented only one side of his attitude towards Ritual. For instance, writing to Dr. Bright on the subject shortly after the presentation of the Report of Convocation he expresses himself in the following somewhat unmeasured terms.

E. B. P. TO REV. W. BRIGHT, D.D.
[July 28, 1873.]

I have a thorough mistrust of the Ultra-Ritualist body. I committed myself some years ago to Ritualism, because it was unjustly persecuted, but I do fear that the Ritualists and the old Tractarians differ both in principle and in object. I hear that there is a body, called 'the Society of the Faith,' or some such name, which desires that none except Ultra-Ritualists should belong to it.

Dr. Bright greatly feared that Pusey would allow his irritation against the injudicious action of a few of the younger Ritualists, to make him forget his own earlier statements in defence of the principle of ritual.

REV. W. BRIGHT, D.D. TO E. B. P.
July 29, 1873.

I do not belong to [that Society] and have not the slightest intention of doing so. Nor am I as you know an 'Ultra-Ritualist,' but I cannot quite go with all you say about 'ritualism.' I believe that within limits (everything can be abused)—within limits it is simply the providential, inevitable outcome of the Movement now just forty years old. You yourself, you remember, threw your shield over it as being the response to the people's demand or desire—'Set these truths visibly before us.' It has made Catholicism intelligible to masses of men, it has brought together a great force of enthusiasm, energy, corporate feeling—all of course needing careful management, and not always receiving it. I fully own that some of the Ultra-Ritualists are in excess, grave excess in more ways than one . . . still the principle is not compromised by foolish or headstrong representatives.

Pusey replied: 'It is true I did use those words about Ritualism. There was Ritualism in the Oakeley School, and the old Margaret Street Chapel, all along co-existent for many years with ours. But they have developed since. . . . I do not break with the Ritualists, because of the good work which some are doing.' He then went on to complain, almost with bitterness, of the extravagance and ignorance of some of those who called themselves by that name, although he never forgot or denied that there were other Ritualists who were not so indiscreet, and whose loyal self-sacrifice in winning souls had endeared them to him.

Pusey, however, felt most strongly the great disadvantage of the position in which even the moderate High Churchmen were placed with regard to ritual. So long as they refused to obey the Purchas Judgment, they were regarded by the public as men who set 'the law' at defiance. The passing of the new Judicature Act in 1873, which established another and better Final Court of Appeal, seemed to offer some hope that that Judgment might be reversed by this newly constituted body. He writes on this subject to Liddon.

E. B. P. TO REV. H. P. LIDDON, D.D.

Dec. 29, 1873.

. . . It certainly would be a great gain (if we lawfully could) to have the points raised in the Purchas Case reconsidered, after hearing. Theoretically it would only be seeking the reversal of the decision of one Civil Court by a fairer Civil Court. But it would seem unreal, if the Case should be dispassionately considered, to appeal to a Court and not abide by its explanation of the Rubric. We are in a disadvantageous position. Englishmen love what is legal, and of course, in itself, the feeling is right; and we are breaking judge-made law, and cannot make it popularly clear that we are contradicting *bad* law, still less, why being members of an Establishment, we do not comply with the laws of the Establishment. . . .

While matters were in this state it was announced that the Archbishop of Canterbury was about to bring in a Bill for the purpose of speedily and economically enforcing 'the law,' or, as Mr. Disraeli described it, of 'putting down Ritualism.' The differences between the so-called 'Ritualists' and the old High Churchmen effectually deprived the leading laymen on their side of any firm ground of defence. It was asked, if the Purchas Judgment was not to be obeyed as a fair interpretation of the Rubrics, what kind of interpretation would the majority of the High Church party accept? Pusey and Liddon could have spoken for themselves; but they could not speak for the 'Ritualists.' They therefore appealed to the Rev. A. H. Mackonochie[1], the well-known vicar of St. Alban's, Holborn, as one who was most prominently associated in the public mind with the development of ritual, and as one in whose judgment, as was shown in the last chapter, they had special confidence.

E. B. P. AND REV. H. P. LIDDON TO REV. A. H. MACKONOCHIE.

March 14, 1874.

You will have seen from the newspapers that we are threatened with legislation having for its object the summary enforcement of recent disputed decisions of the Judicial Committee of the Privy Council. If, as is apparently the case, we can trust the articles which have appeared in the *Times*, the Episcopal authority is to be shared—in the work of the diocesan administration—with laymen elected by the nominees of the ratepayers and therefore not necessarily Churchmen or Christians; while it is proposed that those directions of the Prayer-book which are notoriously disregarded by the Low Church and Broad Church clergy shall no longer have the power of law.

We will not characterize this project as it deserves. But we wish to submit to you, that even if, as we trust will be the case, it should be defeated, it points to a permanent source of danger to the progress of Church work and life among us.

[1] 'Life of A. H. Mackonochie,' p. 221.

There are, of course, opponents whom [nothing] that we can do or say will ever conciliate, since, unhappily for themselves, they reject the revealed doctrines of Sacramental grace, and, not infrequently, the more central truths of Christianity from which these doctrines directly radiate. But if such persons are assisted by others who seriously believe what God has revealed, or wish to do so, we have reason to ask ourselves whether we ever act or speak in a way calculated to cause needless 'offence,' and so to retard that very work of God which we have at heart.

Must it not be acknowledged in view of the exaggerated ceremonial and ill-considered language, which are sometimes to be found among (so called) 'Ritualists,' that there are grave reasons for anxiety on this head? We at least cannot help thinking so, and we are therefore writing to ask you to use your great influence with many of our brethen, in favour of a course which appears to us to be recommended alike by charity for souls, and by loyalty to the common Truth.

Would it not be possible to take some early opportunity of considering how much of recent additions to customary ritual could be abandoned without doing harm? We will not attempt to go into details. But surely matters of taste or feeling, not necessarily or of long habit associated with the enforcement or maintenance of doctrine, yet calculated to alarm the prejudiced and uninstructed, ought, on St. Paul's principle, to be at least reconsidered. If we could show that we have unity and humility at heart, as truly as we have at heart the loyal maintenance of the Church's faith and worship, much of the existing opposition would be disarmed, and we might hope by God's mercy to escape from dangers which are more imminent and serious than appearances would suggest.

You will, we are sure, understand this appeal in the sense in which it is addressed to you, viz. that of a sincere wish to secure whatever has really been gained of late years in the way of faith and reverence, to the glory of our Lord and the good of souls.

Mackonochie's reply to this appeal is given in his 'Life' almost at full length[1]. He acknowledged his inability to answer the question, or to influence those who were more advanced in ceremonial than he was himself; and he pleaded most warmly against being obliged to give up any of that Ritual which had become dear to his people as the expression of their faith. It was a vigorous, warmhearted letter, but useless for Pusey's purpose. It was obviously impracticable to suggest to the Archbishops as a standard of Ritual that measure of ceremonial which the congregation of St. Alban's had been taught to desire.

---

[1] 'Life of A. H. Mackonochie,' pp. 222–226.

Meanwhile, Pusey wrote a powerful letter to the *Times*, on March 13, against the scheme of Church legislation which had been foreshadowed in a leading article in that paper. He pleaded for delay in the creation of any new facilities for enforcing the existing Judgments, on the ground that the new Final Court might possibly be found to reverse previous decisions : and urged a reconsideration of the whole object of the proposed Bill. Two other letters followed in reply to leading articles in the same paper, and yet a third, in answer to a challenge that he should formulate his own remedy, in which he pleaded that the real cure lay in a better understanding between the Bishops and their clergy. He went on to say :—

E. B. P. TO THE EDITOR OF THE 'TIMES.'

March 28, 1874.

I speak from personal knowledge when I say that the Bishops might have guided the Movement of 1833, &c., if they would. There was nothing that we who were young then, so much wished. The battle-cry of the early Tracts was, ' Let us rally round our Fathers the Bishops.' I believe that now, too, things would come right, if the Bishops would be to us 'Fathers in God.' . . . Some of our Bishops have been in an unnatural position towards us. When they shall no longer be constrained by their own respect for a judicial sentence, and when that ill advised petition of the 483 shall be forgotten, the Bishops will, I doubt not, be influenced by their own feeling, and by a sense of their spiritual office, to resume their fatherly relation to all their Clergy, and we shall again rejoice to think and speak of them as ' Fathers in God.' God, the great Father of all, will, I hope, turn the hearts of the fathers to the children, and of the children to the fathers.

When the Archbishop of Canterbury had introduced his Bill for the Regulation of Public Worship, these letters were republished from the *Times* at the request of Dean Church, with a preface restating the arguments. In it Pusey contended that the Bill was in no way adequate to meet the difficulties of the moment ; that even supposing all ritual to be abolished, the tumults would not cease, inasmuch as the attack of the ' Church Association ' was really directed against belief in the Sacraments. He pointed out further that, seeing that the direct attack in the Bennett case had conspicuously failed, and that the doctrine of the Holy Eucharist, which the obnoxious ritual was intended to express, had thus been admitted to be in accordance with the teaching of the Church of England, the next most obvious step would be more clearly to define the legitimate limits of that ritual as ordered by the Prayer-book.  The Ritualists, he trusted, would be satisfied when so much of ritual had been conceded as should elevate the Holy Eucharist to its proper position as the centre of Christian worship.  And the laity would cease to be alarmed when they know that changes would not be made against their wishes.

But the Archbishop's Bill went forward, and its promoters were able to count on the support of the Conservative majority in the House of Commons.  Pusey saw that this was not the time for any separation in the ranks of those who were being attacked.  The Archbishop was being urged on by men who hated the whole High Church position.  In such a crisis Pusey readily laid aside all his irritation about acts which he could not himself defend, and endeavoured to rally round him all the Ritualists.

He made a stirring speech at the crowded anniversary meeting of the English Church Union in St. James' Hall, on June 16.  But he made use of the opportunity to make some suggestions which he hoped might restrain excessive Ritual.  Having shown the doctrinal value of Ritual, he added :—

'Now there is special danger lest the love of the beautiful should interfere with the inward spiritual life.  This is of course what our enemies say.  But *fas est et ab hoste doceri.* . . . of course I am not speaking of the devoted leaders of the Ritual movement, who have given their lives to the recovery of the lost sheep for whom Christ died. But every movement has its defects, and I believe that this love of Ritual for its own sake is one of the weak points which Almighty God means by this check to correct.'

He went on to dwell on the danger of arbitrarily reviving obsolete usages, which the people were ill-prepared to receive, and concluded with an appeal for union, on the ground of the experience of the later Tractarian days.

'I believe that one great end of this check is to consolidate us. There has been too much of guerilla warfare of late—every one doing what was right in his own eyes. One secret of our strength in the early days of this great Movement was our union. What one thought, all thought; what one said, all said. We taught what we inherited from those before us, deepened by the study of the Fathers to whom the Church of England sent us. Other days came, and extreme articles (as they then seemed, I forget what was in them) were written in our common organ by one now an extreme Ultramontane, by another who has withdrawn from theology. The storm was raised as now. People were maddened. You will have heard how it broke upon a Tract which taught nothing but what we all held and hold, and upon its author, and cost us him who, with John Keble, was one of the two bright jewels of the English Church, John Henry Newman. Yet when the storm was at its height, he said to me, "If I had had my way, those articles would never have been written." I trust that those who think themselves most advanced in this day will profit by that experience, and retiring into the main body, will neither expose themselves nor us, nor the Church, nor what we hold dearer than life— the Truth of God—to perils, the extent of which they cannot well estimate ; but by union will give strength to the whole.'

Soon after the meeting Pusey wrote to Mackonochie a very warm and hearty letter, dealing with a suggested reform in Convocation. He added :—

E. B. P. TO REV. A. H. MACKONOCHIE.

June 28, 1874.

. . . Your strength is and will be in the hearts of your people. These you have won wonderfully. Courts cannot really move you while you have them. . . . If the younger clergy will but win their people first as you have. . . . It was a grand Roman boast, '*Volentes per populos dat jura.*' . . . The tone of the St. James' meeting was delightful. If we could but remain as one, as we were that evening.

These last words expressed Pusey's great hope at the time. Ritualism and Puseyism were identical in the popular mind ; but as a matter of fact Pusey was not a Ritualist, and he greatly doubted the wisdom and disliked the abruptness with which much of the ceremonial had been introduced into the parish churches. They had indeed a large common ground in doctrine ; the question was, would the most advanced Ritualists, in view of anxieties of the moment, accept such a limitation of their Ritual that Pusey could continue to work with them and defend them? He hoped they would; in fact he hoped they had already done so at the St. James' Hall meeting, and on July 22, asserted that hope in a letter to the *Times*. But he was soon undeceived; a long course of unwise treatment from those in authority had made the Ritualists chafe under any sort of restraint. To Pusey himself, the charge of 'lawlessness' was most repulsive; he was bound to endure it as regards disobedience to the Purchas Judgment, for he maintained that he could only obey the law by disobeying the judge's version of it. But 'the lawlessness' and arbitrary self-will which was charged against some of those who were unjustly called by his name, he would have nothing to do with; and before the end of the year, he gave up their defence. 'I have made up my mind,' he writes on October 25, 'not again to come forward in any meeting, nor to mix myself up with them.' It was to him, as he confided to Liddon, a repetition of the history of 1841 and the following years.

E. B. P. to Rev. H. P. Liddon, D.D.

Dec. 31, 1874.

. . . The High Church have entrusted themselves to the extreme Ritualists, who are now their representatives, as the extreme party always is. Ward, &c. were in their time of the High Church, the extreme Ultramontanes [are] of the Church of Rome, the extreme Ritualists of us. They are like stragglers from an army, who have got into a defile, and finding themselves embarrassed, instead of retreating to the main body, beg the main body, at whatever cost, to support them. I mistook in my time (J. H. N. was too far-sighted), and the High Church are mistaking now. I hoped (as I said at St. James' Hall) that they would profit by the check and fall back on the main body. I was mistaken in them, and have told Denison that I cannot fight *their* battle. But I do stick to the battle, 'Don't alter the Prayer-book.'

His meaning was that so far as Ritual was the expression of the doctrine for which he had fought for so many years, he would gladly contend for it: but points of ritual were being insisted on which caused offence without symbolizing any vital doctrine. Further, he could not attempt to defend ceremonies which were introduced against the will of the congregation; while he found it impossible to work with those who laid, as he considered, undue stress on unmeaning points of Ritual, and irritated their congregations by introducing them. For points such as the Eastward Position and the Eucharistic Vestments, he felt he could not contend too stoutly. But he earnestly desired that some of the less significant ceremonial might be dropped.

E. B. P. TO THE HON. C. L. WOOD.

West Malvern, Jan. 2, 1875.

I wish that the extreme Ritualists would take your advice, but are there any signs of it? . . . The Ultras have had their way; nothing has been abandoned, so far as I have heard, and the irritation has been kept up by acts which you too think unwise. Randall, of Clifton, said to me that he had not heard of Ritual being excepted against by the congregation when there was not fussiness or self-consciousness or some like fault. I do not think then, that it is fair to say (as so many do), that the objection is simply to the faith symbolized. Doubtless it is so in the controversialists, *Rock*, *Record*, Church Association, &c., but not, I think, in the people of England. The people of England have, I think, been moved much more by arbitrariness or the dread of it; by the expectation that changes might be made in their mode of worshipping God, without any will of their own, by rash sayings against the Reformation, by continued restlessness and change. I think that in the debates last year (except in some few speakers) they were extravagances which pointed the argument.

Even granted, that whatever is not mentioned is not prohibited, or even that what is not prohibited is allowed, this surely does not give individual priests a right to revive *mero motu* whatever is not expressly prohibited. I suppose that in no Church or body would the claim be allowed that an individual priest should, of his own mind, change the existing Ritual without ascertaining the mind of his congregation, without the sanction of the Bishop, or the concurrence of his co-presbyters. And in all the controversy, it is assumed that those who did make changes were perfectly right, and that every parish priest has a perfect right to do this, only that he ought to do it discreetly, but still according to his own individual judgment. But the English mind hates arbitrariness, the exercise of an individual will. And I think that they have had a good deal to complain of in this respect. There has been, and is, a good deal of infallibilism outside the Vatican decree. The whole extreme Ritualist party is practically infallibilist. 'We will not retreat; because we are *certainly* right.' And so they must lay the whole blame upon their opponents' hostility, as they think, to truth. Yet very much of their practice has no relation to the truth, or only so far as it makes the Eucharistic Service gorgeous. I do not know, e. g., that censing persons and things has anything to do with setting forth the Real Presence. Yet Lowder, in that meeting at Brighton, said that he had insisted upon censing persons and things, as being as important as anything. And yet to the mass of the English people (and among them to me) it is an un-understood rite. Three different explanations of it have been given me by Ritualists. (As it does not concern me, I have not looked into books.) This, and what is included in the word 'histrionic,' is, at present especially, un-understood by the English. Our service being in English, is especially addressed to the heart and conscience. Acting interferes with this. People are taken off from their devotions to see a ceremony whose meaning they do not know. They may know it by-and-by, they do not now.

Again, there has been a good deal of pedantry. 'The use of the word "Mass,"' Liddon said, 'alienated thousands who ought to belong to us.' Yet a young priest put on his church door a notice that 'there will be Mass' at such an hour in his village church. What should the villagers understand by it? The squire of course got offended.

I asked A. Bouverie (a friend of my own) why he had joined the Petition against Vestments; he appealed to me, 'you would not go along with these,' and gave an instance where a layman was repelled from communicating, because 'only the clergy communicate to-day.'

I think that, with this and so much beside, we have no right to assume the character of suffering simply for the Truth's sake.

His resolution to do battle for the Prayer-book was no mere form of words. The Synod of the Irish Church had been busy preparing a scheme for the revision of the Prayer-book, in an ultra-Protestant direction ; and Pusey had noticed, with the greatest distress, the proposal to mutilate the Athanasian Creed, even omitting the assertion of a right belief in the Incarnation as necessary to salvation, while attempting at the same time radically to alter the sacramental teaching of the Church. About such changes he had the same strong conviction as about the changes in the Athanasian Creed in England ; they would create a new doctrinal standard, and those who forced them on would be themselves creating a schism. While the Synod was sitting in 1873, he wrote to the Archbishop of Dublin most strongly with reference to fundamental changes in the matter of Eucharistic doctrine. The letter is given in full in the 'Letters and Memorials' of Archbishop

Trench[1]. Its burden throughout is precisely that of the third of the 'Tracts for the Times': 'No change in the Prayer-book.' 'The line of not changing the Prayer-book,' he writes to the Archbishop, 'avoids all controversy as to details.'

When the worst proposals were being set forward by the Irish revisionists in April, 1875, he sent to the Archbishop a closely written letter of seven quarto pages[2] commenting chiefly on the proposed new Preface to the Prayer-book; he apologized for thus intruding in the affairs of the Irish Church on the ground, '"It is our concern when the next house is on fire," and in Christ, it is not the next house but part of the same.' In the following month the Archdeacon of Dublin appealed to Pusey for an expression of his opinion as to the alterations proposed in the Irish Synod, such as he might publish; he desired to strengthen the hands of the Archbishop in his struggle against the enormous majority of Protestant revisionists.

Pusey sent him the following letter:—

### E. B. P. TO THE ARCHDEACON OF DUBLIN.

Christ Church, Oxford, Ascension Day, 1875.

I am thankful to see your appeal. It is to me exceeding strange to see how people, who really love the truth, allow dust to be thrown in their eyes, because the denial of the truth which they love is not outspoken. The proceedings of the (so called) Irish Synod remind me vividly of the Arian attempts to supplant the Nicene Creed by Creeds of their own, which should convey to the ear something sounding like the truth, but in fact denying it. If the Puritan party had nakedly proposed the denial of all sacramental truth, the conflict would have been intelligible, and the tyranny of imposing this denial upon their fellow Churchmen would have shocked men's minds. As it is, by ambiguous formulae, which do not speak out their mind, they would make the Irish Church a mere Presbyterian body in all but the name, having Bishops to convey nothing except a licence to preach what men will.

I cannot but hope that your good Archbishop must, when the time seems to him to be come, repudiate the new Prayer-book with its disingenuous misinterpretations, and *must* officiate according to the old rite. Still, the bugbear which frightens people, and hinders their

---

[1] Vol. ii. pp. 152-154.     [2] Ibid. pp. 183-191.

looking at the evil of these changes in the face, is the dread of schism ; as if this dishonest Prayer-book were not in itself schismatic and the instrument of schism. I think, then, that your movement is right to show Churchmen that, if this faith-destroying Prayer-book is insisted upon, the schism which they dread is inevitable.

But if Pusey was obliged to retire for the moment from one part of the struggle, he still had an anxious war to wage on the question of Ecclesiastical Courts. For the peace of the Church, it was very desirable that a clear understanding should be reached with regard to these Courts. The Public Worship Regulation Act of 1874 had established a new Court for the hearing of ecclesiastical cases, in place of the old Court of Arches; and the Judicature Act of 1873 had established a new Final Court of Appeal for the same cases. Objections were raised against both Courts for different reasons; and although Pusey in a manner shared the objections, he could not altogether agree with those who alleged them.

The question of the Court of Appeal was of immediate practical importance. Lord Penzance had on Feb. 3, 1876, given his decision in the new Court created by the Public Worship Regulation Act, in the suit against the Rev. C. Ridsdale: he had condemned him on every one of the twelve charges alleged against him. On four of these points, Mr. Ridsdale appealed to the new Court of Appeal, which had taken the place of the Judicial Committee of the Privy Council. Lord Penzance had felt himself obliged to accept earlier Judgments of the Judicial Committee of the Privy Council as binding interpretations of the Rubrics, and had without argument condemned Mr. Ridsdale on the points which contravened those decisions. It was hoped that the new Court of Appeal would be more independent and would reconsider those decisions. The Court was to consist of Lay Judges, with a certain number of Archbishops and Bishops as Assessors. The two Archbishops had already taken part in the decision against the Eastward Position in the Purchas case : their presence on the bench at the Ridsdale appeal was most undesirable if the decision was to be independent. It was in these circumstances that the Archbishop of Canterbury wrote a letter to Pusey about the Episcopal Assessors: the following is Pusey's answer:—

### E. B. P. TO THE ARCHBISHOP OF CANTERBURY.

Nov. 21, 1876.

I did not understand those in common with whom I thought that the presence of your Graces as Assessors was not in conformity with our usual judicial proceedings, to have any ground except that you had (as they supposed) already expressed an opinion unfavourable to them. Your Grace thinks that the opinion which you have expressed does not amount to this, since you only insisted on the duty of obeying the law. In our minds this is tantamount to saying that the interpretation of the law given in the Purchas Judgment was right. The law which we are bound to obey (your Grace knows) is the Rubrics, as laid down by the Church. A misinterpretation of these Rubrics is not law. If acquiesced in, it would be acknowledged as the right interpretation of the law and be identified with it, as your Grace has done in reproaching us, as disobeying the law because we disregard its interpretation some in more points, some in fewer. I understand that something of this sort takes place in Civil Courts, and gives rise to what is called 'judge-made law.' And these interpretations become in time as much law as the original law, of which they are undisputed interpretations. If we did not in act and considerable numbers contravene the Purchas Judgment, we should fasten what we think a misinterpretation of the law around our own necks. Opponents can afford to wait till a few opponents die out.

Your Grace will allow me to say that we are not always the best judges of the strength of our own expressions, especially if we have a thing much at heart. However right or wrong, this was our ground in excepting against your two Graces as Assessors, that the decision which we sought to have reversed was reported to have been drawn up by his Grace the Archbishop of York, and to express his mind, and that your Grace's language amounted to agreement with it.

Your Grace seems to ask me whether those with whom I am interested in obtaining an impartial review of the Purchas Judgment would decline pleading before the new Court unless they thought the Assessors to be favourable to them. I have not been at their discussions, but all which I have heard from Mr. C, Wood amounts to an exception against Assessors who have committed themselves or who seem to them to have committed themselves against them. This would apply to some Bishops as well as to your Graces.

Altogether, the relation of your two Graces' suffragan Bishops to yourselves would make their position as Assessors an embarrassing one, since if they decide in our favour, they would have to assist in reversing the Judgment of one Archbishop, in which the other is thought to concur.

My conviction is that the Court most likely to command acquiescence would be a purely Civil Court. It is not like a matter of faith, in which Bishops ought to express the mind of the Church, and yet they might (as in the *Essays and Reviews* case), and the Judgment might be delivered contrary to their conviction of the truth. . . . The quasi-ecclesiastical element in those decisions was what shook people's minds through and through, lost us many who might have done the Church good service, and who have since done her great harm. Could we have thought early in 1850 of the Court as we now do, it might have saved great harm and loss.

I believe then that the best way out of the difficulties into which the Purchas Judgment has plunged us would be to make the Court of Appeal a purely Civil Court. I trust that the impartiality of the Judges would produce a decision which, although it might please neither party, would yet bring peace. Else I see no prospect except of continued prosecutions and condemnations in undefended suits until the arm would be more tired of smiting than we of being smitten. And yet it would be unjust to leave any of us, since myself and Canons Gregory and Liddon contravene the Purchas Judgment as distinctly, though not upon so many points, as the Ritualists.

In the meantime the Rev. A. Tooth, Vicar of St. James', Hatcham, had been prosecuted in the Court of Lord Penzance for Ritualism. From the very first he had refused to acknowledge the jurisdiction of the Court, and had declared that he would not obey its decisions. Lord Penzance gave judgment against him, and, on further complaint, suspended him on December 2, 1876, from performing Divine service for three months. Pusey had all along defended Lord Penzance's Court as a Court which had jurisdiction over temporalities; but its judge had now passed a sentence which deprived a clergyman of the exercise of his spiritual functions. But he wished to understand the position which the advanced party took on this subject; he therefore wrote to Mr. Wood, who as President of the English Church Union would be most likely to be able to give him the desired explanation :—

E. B. P. TO THE HON. C. L. WOOD.

Christ Church, Oxford, Dec. 4, 1876.

I do not understand the line of the Ritualists about the new Court. I could understand their objecting to it, because it is bound by a wrong decision (the Purchas Judgment) of a Superior Court. But I do not see how the appointment by Act of Parliament vitiates the authority of the Court in which Lord Penzance provides. The Act of Parliament does not give, or profess to give, any spiritual authority to it ; it gives it power only to inflict temporal penalties, which of course it could not have, simply as the Archbishops' Court.

But Lord Penzance holds his appointment from the Archbishops, whereas the former Court of Arches represented one only. It does not vitiate the fact that he holds his authority from the two Archbishops; that, if they did not appoint, the civil power would nominate a judge. He holds his appointment from the Archbishops, and this is not affected by any other possible mode of appointment, in default of their appointing. Some of us, I think, got into the habit of thinking lightly of the Archbishops' Court, because it was at times administered by a prejudiced layman. Of course there ought to be an appeal to the Bishops of the Province, but this is not urged.

Now, what I think we have to make clear to ourselves is, what we *do* mean ; that we may not seem to use arguments whose validity we do not recognize, or reject particular authority because we reject all authority except our private judgment. There ought to be an answer to the Bishop of Lichfield's question, 'Whom, or what would you obey ?' I suspect that most of the Ritualists would be at a loss for an answer. Their line seems to me to be—'We are certainly right, we shall obey our own consciences and what we think to be right, and shall obey no authority, spiritual or temporal, which contravenes this.'

This is something tangible; but then it is not acting openly, to except against the mode of appointment of a particular judge, if all authority alike is rejected. I am not arguing the case. I only desire openness.

Archbishop Tait urged it as an argument for the present spiritual element in the Supreme Court, that the Ritualists only wished to eliminate it in order then to disclaim the authority of the Court as a purely secular Court.

To me it has seemed the safe line to acknowledge the authority of the Supreme Court in temporals and (as Mill, Manning, R. Wilberforce worded it) 'the temporal accidents of spiritual things,' viz. our temporalities.

While he was still hoping to be able to act with his friends in this matter of the Courts, Pusey was confronted with the following Resolution which it was proposed to submit to a general meeting of the English Church Union early in 1877 :—

'That this meeting declares that in its judgment any sentence of suspension or inhibition pronounced by any Court sitting under the

Public Worship Regulation Act is *spiritually* null and void, and that, should any priest feel it his duty to continue to discharge his spiritual functions, notwithstanding such sentence, he is hereby assured of the sympathy of this meeting, and of such support and assistance as the circumstances of the case may allow.'

This resolution Pusey only felt able to interpret as a declaration that the English Church Union, of which he was a Vice-President, considered that the clergy were not bound by the decision of any existing Courts. He at once sent in his resignation, because, as a Vice-President of the Union, he would be considered to be responsible for it. He privately explained the reason for this act in the following letter to Mr. Wood :—

### · E. B. P. TO THE HON. C. L. WOOD.

Christ Church, Oxford, Feast of Holy Innocents, 1876.

What compels me to leave the E. C. U. is that they propose to put forth propositions which I do not think honest, and yet, as a member of it, and having taken a prominent part in the defence of the Ritualists, I should seem to agree with them.

In these last Resolutions, the E. C. U. shifts its ground from the Purchas Judgment to the Public Worship Bill. The ground against the Purchas Judgment was, on a matter of fact, that it was bad law : the ground against the Public Worship Bill is against the Ecclesiastical Court. I do not see any difference which the P. W. B. makes, except that it makes shorter work (they say). Lord Penzance was appointed by the two Archbishops, Sir Robert Phillimore by one. The Supreme Court is so far better than the old Committee of the Privy Council in that it has no episcopal members. I should prefer (and so would you, I suppose) a purely Civil Court.

The Resolution to which I objected, and against which I wrote, about the P. W. Bill, was carried by a large majority. Carter wrote to me that he thought that it would be a relief to me, that it was delayed till the ‘ Branches ’ should be consulted, but, he added, that he had no doubt that the Branches would agree with it. Thus I have been already tacitly recommending what I do not agree in.

The Resolution, as I read it, declares the clergy not bound by any decision of the existing Courts. But the existing Courts make absolutely no difference. It shifts, as I said, the question from a particular wrong decision, to all authority. A clergyman writing to the Bishop of Lichfield ‘ on the disobedience of the clergy ’ justifies this.

These are different principles from those with which we began our work forty-five years ago, and I must free myself from them. I assign no reason for ceasing to be a member of the E. C. U. (Liddon, more wisely, never, I think, became one[1]). I shall leave people to find it out for themselves. Carter will make a better Vice-President. . . . I withdraw at the same time from all Church politics, and return to my former state of neutrality. My only regret (and it is a *great* regret) is being outwardly separated from you.

Mr. Wood, however, felt it to be of vital importance that Pusey should not thus sever his connexion with the Union. He begged him to retain his position and continue to assist them with his advice and criticism. Pusey replied that he would have preferred to retire quietly. He thought it absurd that he should remain on condition of reserving to himself a quasi-censorship of the Resolutions proposed to the Society. ' Yet,' he adds, ' there is a large body of real High Churchmen outside, whom I must not seem to compromise by allowing myself to appear to agree to what I do not think. . . .'

In consequence, however, of this correspondence the original terms of the Resolutions were altered, and the following Resolutions were drafted in their place, to be discussed at a general meeting of the English Church Union summoned for January 16, 1877, at the Westminster Palace Hotel :—

' 1. That the English Church Union, while it distinctly and expressly acknowledges the authority of all Courts legally constituted in regard to all matters temporal, denies that the secular power has authority in matters purely spiritual.

' 2. That any Court which is bound to frame its decisions in accordance with the Judgments of the Judicial Committee of the Privy Council or any other secular Court, does not possess any spiritual authority with respect to such decisions.

' 3. That suspension *a sacris* being a purely spiritual act, the English Church Union is prepared to support any priest not guilty of a moral or canonical offence, who refuses to recognize a suspension issued by such a Court.

' 4. That "the Church" (not the State) "having power to decree rites and ceremonies and authority in controversies of faith," this Union submits itself to the duly constituted synods of the Church ; and in regard to the legality of matters now under dispute, appeals to the rubrics of the Book of Common Prayer, and to the interpretation put upon those Rubrics in 1875 by the resolutions of the Lower House

[1] This was not correct. Dr. Liddon had become a member some years previously.

of Convocation of Canterbury in regard to the Eucharistic Vestments and the Eastward Position.'

Pusey wrote at once to the President to express his complete satisfaction with this form of the Resolution, and withdrew his resignation, and the amended proposals were enthusiastically adopted by the meeting.  In fact, he continued to belong to the Union until his death, and through the affectionate loyalty of the President, he enjoyed practically a right of veto on all their public proceedings.  He was unable to attend their meetings, but carefully examined every Agenda paper that was sent to him, and wrote his opinion on any question on which he feared a wrong decision.  The influence of the President was sufficient to prevent anything being carried of which Pusey did not approve.

In anticipation of the Judgment of the Court of Appeal in the Ridsdale case, there were many rumours afloat. Mr. Tooth was lying in prison for disobedience to Lord Penzance, whose jurisdiction he could not recognize, and other clergy, whose parishes loyally supported them, were threatened with a similar fate at the instigation of those who were not really parishioners.  Ritualists were being persecuted mercilessly by the application of the Purchas Judgment.  It was now currently asserted that the Court would in the coming Judgment condemn the Eucharistic Vestments, although it would allow the Eastward Position.

At this moment of anxiety Pusey ventured to write to the Archbishop and to Lord Selborne to urge the common-sense view of a case which seemed to be going forward through a one-sided interpretation of law to widespread disaster.  He only wished to point out how impossible it was to read a negative into the positive language of the Ornaments Rubric, by which many practical people believed that the Vestments were enjoined. ' When a body of men of very different minds agree in taking simple words as a simple direction, I think that there is a strong probability that they are right.'  At the same time Dean Church headed a memorial to the Archbishops and Bishops urging that the great troubles that afflicted the Church might be cured by the living voice of the Church, but would only be made worse by a series of legal actions. Pusey declined to join in this public manifesto, because he thought that any public statement before the decision was delivered would imply suspicion of the Judges, or suspicion of the weakness of the cause of those who signed it. He always felt sure that an unbiassed Court. i. e. a Court that was free to weigh the simple meaning of language and was not overruled by any preceding interpretation, must decide in favour of the essential points of Ritual.

The Judgment in the Ridsdale case was delivered on May 12, 1877: it forbade the Vestments, but allowed the Eastward Position of the celebrant. Pusey writes at once to Liddon :—

E. B. P. TO REV. H. P. LIDDON, D.D.

Christ Church, Oxford, May 13, 1877.

Is anything being resolved on or prepared in consequence of the Judgment?

I see a statement that 1,000 clergy have given in their adherence to Disestablishment as the only remedy. They must be very short-sighted or blinded by self-contemplation, if they do not see that Disestablishment would leave them a small minority or *ecclesiola*. It is best to remain with our hands tied, until we can keep them from striking one another. Disestablishment would be hopeless disruption, in which the only gainer would be Rome.

In the next month he joined in a petition against the Judgment as being a non-natural interpretation of the Ornaments Rubric; but accompanied his signature with the following characteristic letter :—

E. B. P. TO THE HON. C. L. WOOD.

Christ Church, Oxford, Eve of St. Barnabas, 1877.

. . . I signed that petition, but we ought to understand what we are defending. Is it ritualism *en masse*, i. e. what any one may think right? or is it what can fairly be understood to be prescribed by the Ornaments Rubric? For such outsiders, or High Church men as I, ought not to be seeming to be defending one thing, while we mean to defend another.

The late Judgment has given a $\pi o\hat{v}\ \sigma\tau\hat{\omega}$, 'the natural interpretation of the Ornaments Rubric and the honesty of our Prayer-book.' I think that the straightforwardness of the English people would go along with this, 'You don't mean that when the English Prayer-book says "Such ornaments are to be used," it meant they are *not* to be used?'

We should also have a good deal of support in mixing water with the wine quietly beforehand, since it was that which our Lord consecrated. 'Wine,' of which Scripture speaks, meant wine with water: and with our brandied wines we may well claim to mix it. The Court of Arches allowed the mingling beforehand; it could not come under the name of 'additional ceremony,' because being done beforehand (as it was in the old English Church, sometime, and is in the Greek Church). I suppose it might conciliate those who feel scruples about intoxicating liquors. Our wine is not the $o\hat{i}\nu o s$ of the N. T. It would at best be the $o\hat{i}\nu o s\ \mathring{\alpha}\kappa\rho\alpha\tau o s$, which one stigmatized as 'drinking like a Scythian.' It is much more like that condemned by Isaiah (v 22).

I think what sets people against Ritualism is chiefly that the service for the Holy Eucharist is in many churches really a different service. Taking into account what is left out and what is put in, is not half adscititious? The Commandments are left out, and the prayer for the Queen and the exhortation (how much more I don't know); then hymns are put in. Would it be in the proportion half left out and as much put in?

But I want to be honest. I am not honest, if under the plea of attacking the Privy Council Judgment as non-natural, I am really defending a great deal behind : such as censing persons and things. &c.

If the Ritualists would content themselves for the time with (*a*) the Eastward Position ; (*b*) the mingling the water with the wine out of the service ; (*c*) hymns not interpolated but (if the congregation liked) sung while others were communicating or at the end; (*d*) whatever is really meant by the Ornaments Rubric,—I think that the battle would be easily won. They could say, 'We do not want to enforce on others the revival of an obsolete Rubric: we only wish to be allowed to do, what (though it has fallen into disuse) the Church of England bids us do.' Sooner or later, I must say in honesty, this is what I mean by attacking the late Judgment.

In the honesty of his position and the certainty that it would eventually triumph, he was joyous and confident. Immediately after the decision, the Vicar of one of the most advanced churches was about to resign in despair. Pusey wrote to beg him to change his mind, and with success.

E. B. P. TO THE REV. ——.

Christ Church, Oxford, May 18, 1877.

MY VERY DEAR FRIEND,

Liddon tells me that you speak of resigning. Pray do not. The battle is not lost. But it would be lost, if those who are to fight it, resign. Each individual encourages or discourages. You have a prominent post. I would gladly go to prison for you. But I can't.

'O fortes pejoraque passi
    Mecum saepe viri . . .
Nil desperandum Christo duce et auspice Christo,'

has been my motto for many years of trouble.

Yours very affectionately,

E. B. PUSEY.

# CHAPTER XII.

## 1875-1876.

'THE thought of "Eirenica" had been a dream and interest of my life,' Pusey stated in a letter to the *Times* at the end of February, 1876: but he for ever laid aside all hope of those dreams being realized in his lifetime when his great efforts for reunion with the Church of Rome were brought to naught in 1870. Union with the 'Old Catholics' who had seceded from the Church of Rome at that date because they could not accept the Vatican decrees, was to many others a tempting proposal; but Pusey would not do anything to assist it. He was no mere enthusiast for unity: the Faith was to him the primary consideration. Even when he was in Germany at the time of the second Old Catholic Congress at Cologne in 1872, and was invited to attend, he declined, from a well-founded fear of committing himself to connexion with a body whose principles had not been stated clearly enough to rescue their name from an obvious ambiguity. He explains his refusal to Liddon :—

E. B. P. TO REV. H. P. LIDDON, D.D.

Reichenhalle, Sept. 13, 1872.

I let Dr. Wingerath see that my main ground for not going to the Congress was that they did not make clear their own position. Their title of 'Old Catholics' seemed at first to mean that they were on the same basis as they were before the Vatican Council, believing everything which they believed before. [But] 'Old Catholics' might mean those who, like ourselves, believe all that was matter of faith to 'the undivided Church,' an expression which the Bishop of Lincoln notices that they had used. This would be a position such as, there seems reason to think, the Latin Church was ready to take at the Council of Florence, ignoring all mere Latin Councils. But then what was held of faith by 'the Undivided Church' would be open to different questions which might be answered differently. The Greek Church, I think, had them at advantage, saying that if they were Old Catholics they must go up higher; for the Vatican Council only developed what *might be* the meaning of previous Councils. . . . But then what is the ground of the Old Catholics on all those subjects, as of grace or the sacraments, which the Council of Trent laid down so elaborately? I thought it best not to advance towards the Old Catholics, if afterwards one has to withdraw. I wished to know their position. Dr. W. might have told me. Perhaps he had not time. I had no answer either from him or from Döllinger. I softened my answer by saying that, '*under these circumstances*, I thought it best to stay here, whither I had come for health.' Had I had a satisfactory answer, I should not have minded the loss of a week's quiet or the journey.

The same resolve not to encourage any movement that appeared to him in the least to imperil the Catholicity of the English Church caused him to stand somewhat aloof from the projects for reunion with the Eastern Church. Since the establishment of the Eastern Church Association in 1864, he had been a member of it, and had not unfrequently contributed papers which were published by the Association. But the bright hopes of the possibility of Reunion with the Churches of the East, which at that time he had entertained, and had expressed in some of the closing pages of the First Eirenicon [1], had now faded away before the impracticable attitude of the Russian Church. He also began to feel that the hold of English Churchmen upon the truth expressed in the *Filioque* clause of the Nicene Creed was being undermined by the language which some of the ardent advocates of Reunion allowed themselves to use with regard to it. He was so firmly convinced that it was impossible for the Western Church to remove that word from their Creed without serious danger to the faith, that when he thought it clear that the action of the Eastern Church Association was endangering that clause,

[1] Eirenicon, Part I, pp. 262–267.

he quietly ceased to be a member of it, and expressed his fears to the Secretary.

E. B. P. TO REV. G. WILLIAMS.

Nov. 5, 1872.

I think that we are doing mischief to our own people by accustoming them to the idea of abandoning the *Filioque*, and to the Russians by inflating them. They look upon every longing for unity as so much incense offered to them as the one true Church. So they answered the 'Old Catholics.'

When however the Reunion Conferences between Old Catholics, Anglicans, and the Eastern Church were held at Bonn in 1874 and 1875, Pusey followed the discussion with great interest, especially on the second occasion, when the *Filioque* clause of the Nicene Creed was under discussion. This clause, 'and the Son,' which occurs in our form of the Nicene Creed, was not in that form of the Creed which was accepted by the Undivided Church at the Council of Chalcedon in A. D. 451. It is found only in the Western forms of the Creed; its earliest recorded use being at a Council at Toledo in 589. With regard to this later addition, the Eastern Church maintains that the West had no right to add anything to a Creed which had been sanctioned by the whole Church, and further that this additional statement is theologically inaccurate, because, they maintain, it implies the existence of two 'Principles' (ἀρχαί) in the Godhead, which would be incompatible with a belief in the Unity of God. The Westerns acknowledge that the words are an addition, but hold them to be true, always explaining that they were never intended to assert or imply the existence of two Principles.

Pusey was very anxious lest the Western position should be incautiously surrendered by the more ardent promoters of Reunion; especially he feared lest Döllinger's strong anti-Roman feeling should prejudice his mind in favour of the Eastern form. Both he and Bishop Forbes sent communications to the Bonn Conference on the question. The Bishop's letter was a short and clear suggestion of a basis for agreement; Pusey sent the Preface to his son's translation of St. Cyril's Commentary on the first eight chapters of St. John, which he had written in the preceding year; this contained a large number of quotations from the Greek Fathers expressing the truth which the disputed words were intended to convey though in different terms.

At the Conference in 1875 a formula was drawn up which all who were present found themselves able to accept. Pusey saw that it was practically a surrender of the position for which the Western Church had contended for so many centuries. He writes anxiously to Liddon :—

E. B. P. TO REV. H. P. LIDDON, D.D.

West Malvern, Aug. 19, 1875.

. . . I do not see any occasion for any formula in which the Greeks and we should agree. We are content to let them alone. They have all along been on the aggressive. I fear that it has been their way of keeping off the question of the Papal authority. On one or two occasions it has been owned by writers on their side that the real question was about the θρόνοι.

We ask nothing of them, in case of reunion, but to go on as we are. We do not ask them to receive the *Filioque,* but only not to except against our expressing our belief in the way in which their own great writers St. Epiphanius, St. Cyril, and others did. Why should they refuse our communion on the ground of our using doctrinal language, used so freely by the great *Doctor Ecclesiae,* who presided over the Third General Council? . . . If ever there is to be an agreement, and we are not to be simply merged in the Greek Church and to embrace false doctrine, I am sure that this is the only way that they should (as Wassilief did) accept our rejection of the heresy which they impute to our formula and leave us in possession of it. But I fear that they are animated now by an evil spirit of ambition; and that they are unwilling to have their old battle-cry against Rome 'You are heretics as believing two ἀρχαί in the Godhead,' taken from them.

This correspondence, with regard to the Bonn Conference, was the last occasion on which Pusey and the Bishop of Brechin acted together. In spite of sixteen years' difference in age between them, they had been on terms of most intimate friendship since 1846, when the Bishop was curate of the parish of St. Thomas the Martyr, in Oxford. Pusey was attracted to him by his simplicity of life and deep piety, as well as by his intellectual ability, courageous loyalty to revealed truth, and keen theological insight ; others saw in him a great likeness to Pusey both in these characteristics and also in his unstinted charities and his self-sacrificing labours for the sick and poor. Throughout the troubles of the early years of his episcopate, Pusey and Keble had been his chief advisers ; after Keble's death, no one entered with greater eagerness than the Bishop into Pusey's sanguine efforts towards the Reunion of the Western Church. Whenever he came to Oxford, Pusey's house was his home, and he had been staying there towards the end of May, 1875. Four months later his health began to fail, and he passed away suddenly on the evening of Friday, October 8. Liddon, knowing full well how keenly Pusey would feel his loss, and fearing the effect of the shock on him in his weak state of health, wrote to him immediately. 'Kindest thanks,' was the answer, 'for your loving letter. It chokes one ; and it seems unnatural to do anything but follow him with prayer to those worlds unknown.' About two months later in a letter to Liddon he gives the following sketch of the Bishop's character :—

E. B. P. to Rev. H. P. Liddon, D.D.
Dec. 5, 1875.

. . . What strikes me most about the dear Bishop in looking back are his great love, tenderness, simplicity, and self-forgetfulness, and his sensitiveness about whatever bore on doctrinal truth. That trial[1] was like the piercing of a sword to him, for fear the truth should be compromised, or in the defence lest he should any way compromise it. He did not recover the physical effects of it, in any degree, for two years. I saw his nervous system gradually tranquillize : but during those two years it was preternaturally alive. His happiest time was that which he spent in the hospitals by the sick, or in the alleys of Dundee, if so he might minister to souls or bodies. Then there was his utter want of self-consciousness. He had, as you know, brilliant conversational talents, yet one never could detect the slightest perception that he was aware of it. So also as to his theological knowledge. He had a large grasp of mind, devoted loyalty to truth, sorrow for those who had it not, tender feeling for them ; but for himself utter unconsciousness of his gifts. It was all a matter of course. Of his humility to God . . . I can only say the Day of Judgment will show how deep it was.

[1] See vol. iii. pp. 448-459.

But in the meanwhile Pusey had gone steadily on with his defence of the Western form of the Creed, endeavouring for this purpose to remodel his Preface to St. Cyril.

### E. B. P. TO REV. J. H. NEWMAN.

Christ Church, Oxford, Oct. 11, 1875.

How death has been sweeping all around one! What memories T. Keble's departure brings vividly back, and now Bp. Forbes, whom I never imagined myself surviving! Will you say Mass for him? It is a great gap to me; he was so tender and loving.

I am recasting that little Preface to my son's St. Cyril, which I sent you: so many stupid prejudices against the *Filioque* seem rising; and now that the Vatican decree has so scared people, they are looking to the Greek Church for reunion, and seem ready to part with the *Filioque* from the Creed. Do you know any book which would throw light on the use of the Athanasian Creed in early Breviaries? My impression is that the *Filioque* came into the Nicene Creed through the Athanasian[1], in that, through the Athanasian, as being devotionally recited, it became our Western formula and so crept unawares into the Nicene, which seems to have been little known in the West until the Third Council of Toledo directed it to be sung at Mass. . . . My question is, whether there are traces of the *Quicunque* being said so widely at Prime on Sunday that it was probably an integral part of the Breviary at an early time?

In December he found that the Eastern Church Association was petitioning Convocation to take the Resolution of the Bonn Conference into consideration. This light-hearted method—as it seemed to him—of treating an extremely difficult and profound theological question was a cause of astonishment to Pusey. He immediately wrote to the *Times* a popular and untechnical statement of his reasons for objecting to these propositions.

### E. B. P. TO THE EDITOR OF THE 'TIMES.'

Christ Church, Dec. 27, 1875.

Having been formerly a member of the Eastern Church Association and having publicly taken part in its proceedings, but having silently quitted it, on the ground of the aggressive line as to the English Church adopted by Russian ecclesiastics and of some other apprehensions, may I ask you to allow me, through the *Times*, to disclaim any connexion with the petition to the Convocations of Canterbury and

---

[1] This interesting point is discussed at length in his Letter to Dr. Liddon, 'On the clause "And the Son,"' pp. 51–67.

York now being circulated by the Committee of that Association, and that on the following grounds:—

1. That (although not in the minds of the framers) it really prepares the way for the abandonment of the expression of our belief in the mode of existence of Almighty God—i.e. in God as He is.

2. That the question of abandoning the expression of our belief, which we have had for at least 1,200 years, would very much distract the minds of our people, and its abandonment would, in the practical English mind, be followed by the abandonment of the belief itself.

3. That one of the propositions to which we are requested to express our consent is misleading, and calculated to raise prejudices against the truth, since the reception of the Niceno-Constantinopolitan Creed in the Western Church for itself, together with the addition of the *Filioque*, is no more ecclesiastically irregular than the additions to the Nicene Creed by the Council of Constantinople, wholly a Greek Council, for its necessities in the East. The Creed, also with this addition, was notoriously received under the impression that it was the Creed enlarged by that Council.

4. That another of these propositions is contradictory to our Creeds and Articles in that it states *absolutely* that 'the Holy Ghost goes not forth out of the Son,' whereas *they* declare that He proceedeth from the Father and the Son, and furthermore St. John of Damascus, in the passage quoted, meant to reject our Western mode of expressing our faith, which in earlier times was the predominant language of Eastern Fathers also.

5. That any proceedings on the part of the English Church with regard to the Creeds on this great truth would be utterly useless as to the object alleged, 'the removal of our unhappy divisions,' since there are other grave points which would hinder the Eastern Church from accepting our communion, the more so since we are still so divided among ourselves.

6. That whereas it ought to be a first principle that in religious matters nothing ought to be done by majorities, and it is one charge against the late Vatican Council that the majority overrode a considerable minority in enacting a new matter of faith, it is manifest that in the English Church also even the majority is not now prepared to enter into communion with the Eastern Church, not knowing what consequences it would involve as to ourselves. Particular questions are therefore better left to the discussion of private theologians than to bodies speaking in behalf of the Church, as the Convocation, of which the Lower House of this province inadequately represents the clergy, however adequate for ordinary practical purposes.

7. That even if such negotiations did not end (as I myself think probable) in the disruption of the English Church, they would, while pending, increase divisions among ourselves rather than promote unity with the Eastern Church, and that while grasping at a shadow we should, like the dog in the fable, lose the substance.

In deprecating such authoritative negotiations I do not mean to throw any slur on the pacific endeavours of the theologians assembled at Bonn, although, in regard to this great doctrine, I think that the results are unhappy, and that it would have been much better simply to claim, in case of reunion, the possession of our hereditary Creed (with which our faith is practically bound up), while disclaiming any error which the Greeks have erroneously imputed to it, or any wish that they should adopt it.

I think it also a misstatement that the words 'and the Son' have for so long a time divided the East from the West. Writers on the Greek side have said that 'the dispute was not about the Creed, but about the sees,' i. e. the absolute authority claimed by the See of Rome over the Eastern patriarchates, so different from the relation of earlier times.

It was hinted in reply that the Lambeth Conference of 1878 might remove the *Filioque*, and that Pusey was the only theologian of reputation in England who thought that its insertion could be justified. Certainly the American deputies at Bonn, as was well known, were eager to drop the clause, and Döllinger also had spoken strongly against it. But Pusey still fought the matter in the press without a sign of shrinking. In the *Times* of January 10, 1876, there is a second letter reasserting his previous position, although admitting a slight modification. He still maintained that the Eastern and Western forms of the Confession, if rightly understood, now confess the same truth under different language: but if we, after using the *Filioque* for so many centuries, were to abandon it, we should forfeit part of the truth. We could not give up a portion of the Creed, and repeat the remainder with unaltered meaning. He ends, ' I write this simply as an individual, never having been a "leader," and having now survived almost all in harmony with whom I once acted.' Two days later he heard from Newman.

REV. J. H. NEWMAN TO E. B. P.

The Oratory, Jan. 10, 1876.

. . . I have read with great interest your letters in the *Times.* To-day's is particularly good. Your last sentence is very sad. I hope it does not mean that there are any who are differing from you on the point on which you write, whom you have hitherto acted with.

Pusey explained his allusion at once.

E. B. P. TO REV. J. H. NEWMAN.

Jan. 11, 1876.

The last sentence did not allude to any defalcations: it was a tacit answer to one who taunted me with writing as a 'leader.' We never had one. It would have been better for us had you allowed yourself to be one. As it was, the tail always guided. There are no apparent defalcations. But now that the Vatican Council seems to us generally to have shut the half-open door in our faces, there is a prominent feeling, 'Union at any cost'; and so, since the Greeks set their faces against being in communion with those who retain the *Filioque* in the Creed, there is the disposition to abandon it.

Döllinger, of course, attempted an impossibility—to squeeze the principle of our Western Confession into the words of St. John Damascene, who rejected it. But people do not yet see this, and are carried away by his name; but our English people are not prepared, God be thanked, to give up the *Filioque*.

There is, as I said, an active party in the United States who are ready to give up the *Filioque*, retaining, as they think, the faith contained in it. It was for them that I wrote that Preface.

The attitude which Pusey assumed toward the Bonn propositions caused a good deal of anxiety among those who had consented to them. Explanations of a reassuring character were addressed to him; and the public correspondence ended with the insertion in the *Times* of a private letter from Pusey to Liddon dated Feb. 8, showing the nature of these assurances. They had removed some of his fears about the Conference; it was clear that the English representatives at least were more like-minded with him than the proceedings seemed to suggest. He concluded :—

'With your object of promoting the restoration of communion with the East I, of course, with my whole heart, sympathize. Great as the difficulties may be, they are not insuperable by prayer. It has been my conviction for above forty years that since the Latins believed in the Monarchia and the Greeks of old believed in the Eternal Procession through the Son, their belief must be the same. And this must have been the mind of the Westerns generally, since Roman writers (as far as I know) did not call the Greeks 'heretics,' but 'schismatics' only. I should be very glad of any explanation to the Greeks, as promoting the great cause of unity, if only we do not therewith give up that which has been the expression of our faith for 1,200 years at least and which could not be replaced.'

He had been attempting to recast the Preface to his
son Philip's translation of St. Cyril on St. John, so as
to suit the exact form of this discussion; but Liddon
begged him to write a public Letter instead, stating how
the Bonn propositions could be amended so that they
would not, to his mind, involve any sacrifice of truth.
This letter was greatly delayed, and was not completed
until the middle of July, 1876, when it appeared under
the title of 'On the clause " And the Son," in regard
to the Eastern Church and the Bonn Conference.' This
valuable treatise consists of about 200 pages, and is the
fullest discussion of this clause, historically and doctrinally,
in the theology of our Church. The Bonn propositions
are asserted to be too ambiguous and incomplete to be
considered by Convocation, and in an Appendix several
amendments are suggested. But, on the whole, it seems
that the difficulties[1] which Pusey found in the actual wording
of the propositions arose rather from inaccurate language
or inadequate translation, than from fundamental divergences in doctrine. The 'Letter' is on a subject too
technical to be widely appreciated; but the clearness of
its thought, and its theological insight, show that neither
ill health nor old age were diminishing the keenness of his
mental powers.

Pusey interrupted the preparation of this book for the
press by another piece of work which proved to be a solid
contribution to Biblical literature. Some years earlier,
whilst he was preparing one of his sermons on the Jewish
interpretation of the prophecies about the Messiah, he had
felt that the difficulty of the subject was increased by the
scantiness of the accessible materials. Most of the books
in which the statements of Jewish Commentators were to
be found, were beyond the reach of the ordinary student.
To remedy this, in 1874, he requested Dr. Neubauer to
undertake the task of editing a complete catena of Jewish
Commentaries on the Fifty-third Chapter of Isaiah—'the

---

[1] Dr. Liddon discussed Pusey's objections at length in his preface to the
English translation of the Report of
the Second Bonn Conference.

remarkable chapter which has for ages formed one of the
principal battlefields between Christians and their Jewish
opponents.' This collection was, at Pusey's request, translated into English by the united labours of Mr. Driver,
who afterwards succeeded to Pusey's Professorship, and
Dr. Neubauer. Pusey himself contributed to the volume [1]
an Introduction of thirty-five closely printed pages, which
are dated December, 1876. This Introduction contains
incidentally a learned defence of the valuable work of
Raymond Martini, entitled 'Pugio Fidei,' a collection of
Jewish interpretations which had been made in the thirteenth century, and which had been recently denounced
as containing important and audacious corruptions of the
text. But one of the most interesting points in this Preface
is his apology for the apparently paradoxical attempt to
defend the Christian faith by reprinting at length the
anti-Christian interpretations of Messianic predictions.
His reply is that he hoped that these attempts to avoid
the Christian appeal to the Old Testament Scriptures
would enable Christians to appreciate more vividly the
difficulties of the Jews of the present day, while at the
same time they would illustrate, rather than overthrow,
the truth of the Christian interpretation. Jews of the
greatest ability had for centuries tried to find some other
satisfactory interpretation, but had been unable with all
their labour and ingenuity to discover any person, or body
of people, who could be said to be the object of this great
prophecy. Their continued failure Pusey regarded as of
great evidential value; it contributed some further cogency
to the general argument from the fulfilment of predictions,
on which he always, especially in the later years of his
life, laid so much stress.

---

[1] 'The Fifty-third Chapter of Isaiah according to the Jewish Interpreters.' Translations by S. R. Driver and Adolph Neubauer; with an Introduction to the Translations by E. B. Pusey.

# CHAPTER XIII.

GAUME'S MANUAL — LAMBETH CONFERENCE ON CON-
FESSION—PUSEY AND THE 'CHURCH ASSOCIATION.'

1877–1878.

As time went on, the troubles of the English Church
seemed to increase rather than to be removed. Even if
the Ridsdale Judgment had been of such a character as
to suggest hopes of peace, there were some who would
effectually prevent their realization. Almost before it was
pronounced, another storm was raised, and again on the
subject of Confession. For many years Pusey had advertised,
in his series of 'Adapted Devotional books,' an edition of
a 'Manual for Confessors,' by the Abbé Gaume : the greater
part had been long in type, but the completion of the book
was repeatedly delayed. Such a manual was thought
to be greatly needed, because of the increased use of
Confession throughout the Church of England, and the
great dearth of English works on the subject. While
Pusey was still delaying the issue of this work year after
year, a book [1], entitled 'The Priest in Absolution,' had been
compiled, and was being privately circulated among the
clergy, dealing with questions of practical casuistry for
the guidance of those called upon to exercise the ministry
of hearing Confessions. It was a book intended only for
the Clergy, and, on account of the difficulty of some of the

---

[1] For a full statement of the origin
and purpose of this book, and its
relation to the 'Society of the Holy
Cross,' see the letters from the Rev.
A. H. Mackonochie, which were published in the *Guardian* for July 4,
1877, p. 925.

questions which the compiler felt himself bound to handle, every care was taken to guard it from a more general circulation. At this moment it is not necessary to consider whether the book was wise in its conception or sufficiently guarded in its language. A copy of it was produced in Parliament, and certain expressions were laid hold of in such a manner as to lash to fury the suspicions of those who were already only too eager to denounce the whole doctrine and practice of Confession as taught in the Church of England. Great use was made of this opportunity in the summer of 1877 ; sweeping denunciations were levelled against the clergy who taught Confession, and by implication against those who used it for the health of their souls. No instance of misuse or scandal was ever alleged, but a general distrust and uneasiness was created in the public mind. In one respect the position was like that which gave rise to the Bennett case ; Mr. Bennett's inaccurate language had endangered true Eucharistic doctrine in the same way that some expressions in this book had now reopened the question of Confession in the most invidious form.

With the controversy so far as it refers only to ' The Priest in Absolution,' Pusey had no direct concern. He had not even seen the book when Lord Redesdale brought it to the notice of the House of Lords in June, 1877 ; but since suspicion was thrown on a practice in which he was so deeply interested, he felt that the moment called for the publication of a trustworthy guide for those who heard Confessions, and a clear restatement of the Anglican authorities for the practice. He therefore completed the preparation of Gaume's Manual, and wrote a lengthy Preface of an historical and apologetic character. He first traced the growth of the habit of voluntary Confession during the preceding forty years, and briefly touched upon ' the hateful subject[1] ' of the calumnious attacks which ' ill-informed and inconsiderate ' people had brought against it. He then proceeded to quote the statements of leading

[1] Preface to Abbé Gaume's Manual, p. 62.

Anglican Divines on the value of Confession, beginning with the emphatic language of Cranmer, Latimer, and Ridley, and ending with Keble; this he thought only 'a work of charity, to bring before those who *would* hear some portion of the evidence that the very chief of our Divines have recognized Confession and Absolution as a provision of our Church for the healing of our infirmities and the cure of diseases which might otherwise fester and bring death upon the soul.' At the end of the Preface he discussed the frequency of Confession as permitted by the Church of England, and the nature and extent of the 'ghostly counsel and advice' which may in some cases accompany it. On the former point he insisted that there must be freedom : 'we cannot make one unvarying law for souls which God has made so varied and forms so variously;' while universal experience contradicted the *a priori* theories of those who describe habitual Confession as 'enfeebling,' 'injurious,' 'formal,' and 'perfunctory.' On the other subject, he pointed out that 'Direction' is quite distinct from Confession, and is only given in Confession to those who wish for it. At the same time he claimed that the clergy ought to be able to guide souls, and cautioned both clergy and laity against laying so much stress on such direction as in any way to diminish the sense of the personal responsibility of each individual, or to damage the sensitiveness and impair the health of their consciences. As a postscript to this preface he reprinted the Declaration on Confession, which he and a few others had drawn up with such great pains four years earlier.

Pusey sent this preface to Liddon, stating the reasons which made him publish the book in opposition to the earnest entreaty of some who had a claim to great consideration.

E. B. P. TO REV. H. P. LIDDON, D.D.

Ascot Hermitage, Bracknell, 13th S. after Trin. [Aug. 26], 1877.

I do not wish to do anything which shall commit my friends. I have put off the publication of the manual for ten years ; but I find that

'Rusticus expectat dum defluat amnis ; at ille
Labitur et labetur.'

1. I had before this an earnest entreaty that I would put off the publication; when the persons had seen the Preface they were just as earnest that I should publish at once.

2. The battle is about Confession itself. Are we to seem to give this up or carry it on *sub rosâ*? This would be very un-English and give a great and real handle against us.

3. If we do not maintain the system of Confession plainly and unreservedly, quiet, gentle people will go to Rome for it and it alone.

4. If I do not publish the Manual, others will; and if they do, they will publish it with all the penances of Ave Marias, devotions to the Blessed Virgin, &c., which I have systematically omitted. There is nothing distinctly (? distinctively) Roman, as I have printed it. . . .

If I had published Gaume in those former years, 'The Priest in Absolution' never would have been compiled. Chambers asked me to put out Gaume, and it was only on my continual delay that he published the first part and prepared 'The Priest in Absolution.'

The *Church Times* has committed itself to my edition completely and with much satisfaction. If I drop the reins, now that I have them for once in my hands, I am sure that some one else will pick them up, probably Phaeton.

Gaume is, as *you* probably know, not an ordinary Manual. They are the *very words* of such as S. Charles Borromeo and S. François de Sales. The only name which is blown upon is S. Liguori, but I have left out every hint of devotions which are so associated with his name. I have lately gone through the book and, although it was stereotyped, have left out all the expressions implying the necessity of Confession.

Liddon strongly advised the publication; but Pusey yet delayed for two months before sending it to the press, and it was only published just before Christmas. It was soon attacked.

REV. H. P. LIDDON, D.D., TO E. B. P.

Jan. 13, 1878.

In the *Rock* of Friday there is a long notice of the 'Advice for Confessors.' The *Rock* is angry, but disconcerted. You should see it, though there is no reason for dissatisfaction. The providential purpose of the *Rock* seems to be to advertise good books by abusing them.

A member of the House of Commons also endeavoured to make some use of the book in the same way as a member of the House of Lords had used 'The Priest in Absolution,' and Pusey had to defend himself in the *Times* against many absurd charges.

But early in 1878, he was for a time removed from the

strife of tongues by a serious illness. He began to show evident signs of failing health and of the exhaustion of brain which was natural after so long a life of ceaseless activity. In the middle of March he was taken ill; at first the only symptom was listlessness, 'sitting still in his chair and doing nothing for the greater part of the day.' This was followed by faintness, helplessness, and a distressing cough. Liddon heard from day to day of his state; and on March 29, he sent Newman an anxious letter from Pusey's daughter, Mrs. Brine, which showed the real seriousness of the attack. Newman immediately answered; the reply recalls his visit to what was expected to be Pusey's deathbed, at Tenby, in July, 1846 [1].

REV. J. H. NEWMAN TO REV. H. P. LIDDON, D.D.

The Oratory, March 31, 1878.

Your letter, so kindly sent me, has of course troubled me much. I fear Pusey cannot last long, and I am troubled, first on that account, and next as to my own duty under that anticipation.

I know you will give me credit for honesty and simplicity of purpose, as I do you.

If his state admits of it, I should so very much wish to say to my dearest Pusey, whom I have loved and admired for above fifty years, that the Catholic Roman Church solemnly lays claim to him as her child, and to ask him in God's sight whether he does not acknowledge her right to do so.

Were I now writing to an ordinary Anglican, I should expect you to answer, 'If I do ask him for you, he will be sure to make a strong declaration of his fidelity to the Church of England, and so you would be baulked, as you ought to be.' This would be the answer of a controversialist, but you will understand me quite otherwise. Should he make a simple avowal of his confidence in the Anglican Church, as part of the Church Catholic, at least I should gain this comfort from it, that he died in simple good faith.

I cannot let him die, if such is God's Will, with the grave responsibility lying upon me of such an appeal to him as I suggest; and, since I cannot make it myself, I must throw that responsibility on some one else who is close to him as you are: and this I do.

Oh! what a world is this, and how piercing are its sorrows!

With this letter Liddon received an alarming bulletin from Oxford, which caused him to go immediately to see Pusey: on his return that evening he wrote to Newman.

---

[1] See vol. ii. p. 512.

Rev. H. P. Liddon, D.D., to Rev. J. H. Newman.

3, Amen Court, St. Paul's, April 1, 1878.

This morning I received the enclosed letter from Mrs. Brine. So I went off to Oxford as soon as I could ; and I have spent more than an hour with Dr. Pusey this afternoon. I found him on the whole much better than I had expected. He looked reduced by illness ; but he was very bright and joyous, and even energetic. He spoke of his illness as a great subject for thankfulness, and, when I alluded to his difficulty in breathing, said that each hard breath, like the flakes of snow to St. Francis when he was shut out of his convent, was part of the Will of God. He talked chiefly about unfulfilled prophecy, and especially about Damascus, which ' George Williams used to cite as a difficulty,' of which Dr. Pusey thought lightly.

I told him that you had asked for him, and he desired me to write ' a loving message.' But I did not say more about the contents of your letter.

He has not a shadow of doubt as to the entire consistency of his position with the Revealed Will of God. Only two days before he became ill (he told me to-day) he 'quieted' a person who was unsettled about the Roman question ; and on Saturday last, when he was in bed and too ill to see any one, he sent another for the same purpose to Dr. King.

Only the week before last he told me how completely Mr. Allies appeared to him to have failed to answer his own book, ' The Church of England cleared from the charge of Schism ' ; and how inconsistent the history of the African Church, under St. Cyprian and St. Augustine, was with the modern claims of Rome.

I mention these things only, as you will believe, to show you how completely his mind is at rest on the main question ; though he is of course very keenly alive to the evils which result from the language and action of living authorities in the Church of England. When the Athanasian Creed was attacked, four years ago, he had made up his mind, if it was withdrawn from use, to resign his preferments ; but he had no thought, so far as I know, of secession.

He always of late spoke as though the Definition of the Immaculate Conception and the Vatican Council had made that step *impossible*.

You will, I am sure, forgive the explicitness with which I write this ; but you would, I think, say yourself that his clear and strong convictions were inconsistent with his being anything else than an English Churchman.

Yet his vivid sense of the fundamental unities which bind the whole Body of Christ into one, always made him speak of Rome in tender and respectful language, and without the conventional asperities of Anglican controversialists.

He is certainly somewhat better, and may rally for a time if the weather should improve. But I feel that he cannot be with us for long, and that each opportunity of seeing him is increasingly precious.

Dr. Acland says that his unwillingness to move is quite a new feature. In all previous illnesses he has tried to get up too soon. Dr. Acland attributes this to brain exhaustion.

Newman made no further allusion to the subject, although his notes show the sympathy with which he read the daily accounts from the sick bed. A week later Liddon paid another visit to Oxford, and sent a report from Christ Church.

REV. H. P. LIDDON, D.D., TO REV. J. H. NEWMAN.

April 8, 1878.

Dr. Pusey is looking rather more reduced by illness than was the case last week. And he is quite unable to talk. The deafness has increased, so that when I proposed to say some prayers, he said. ' I shall not hear what you are saying, but I shall be sure that you will pray for me.' . . . His life is now a life of prayer, so far as he is conscious. He told me last week that he had made a kind of 'Litany' out of the Epistle for the Fourth Sunday in Advent, which he found it a great comfort to repeat. And Mrs. Brine tells me that almost the only questions that he asks are about *the hour* of day or night; which is, *I know*, with a view to a scheme of prayers which he observes as regularly as he can. His face is quite beautiful, though thinner than last week.

As strength slowly returned, the correspondence with Newman ceased: and after a while Newman returned all Liddon's letters, saying, ' I should have contented myself with burning that private letter of yours, but it struck me that you might like them all as memorandums to look back upon.'

When Liddon returned to Oxford in the beginning of May. he found Pusey convalescent but still very weak. ' The shadow of a great loss ' through which he had passed made him feel how uncertain was the life of his revered friend, and how great a treasure of experience and intimate acquaintance with the life of the Church during the past fifty years would pass away with him. From that date he took every opportunity of getting Pusey to dictate to him the story of the great events in which he had taken so conspicuous a part: and the book in which he wrote it down has supplied many facts for these volumes.

In July Pusey went away to the Hermitage at Ascot.

where he now regularly spent the Long Vacation since he gave up his house at West Malvern. The work of the Sisters at the Convalescent Hospital, the young children whom they had brought from London slums, and the fresh air and the pines of Ascot, were a constant delight to him and made all his work easier. 'What a peaceful life I have here,' he writes, 'amid convalescents, children glad and bright, the pines, the rooks, and Commentators on the Psalms.' When he had completed his Commentary on the Minor Prophets in 1877, after eighteen years' persistent labour at every spare moment, he at once began a similar work on the Psalms. This was his last great plan for Hebrew study: he worked at it continuously until his death. In Term time he lectured on these Psalms: in Vacation he increased his notes on them. But the interruptions were so frequent and so serious that progress was very slow.

In July also he had to resume his defence of Confession. In that month the second Lambeth Conference met, under the presidency of Archbishop Tait. Its deliberations were awaited with great anxiety by many Churchmen. A body of a hundred Bishops, gathered from every portion of the Anglican Communion, can utter an opinion which must carry great weight, and yet they may be called upon to deal with subjects on which some of them have little practical knowledge. It was greatly feared that the Archbishop of Canterbury would endeavour to draw this great assembly to some pronouncement on such subjects as Ritual and Confession. No formal notice of any attempt to deal with these burning questions appeared among the Agenda of the Conference; but a place was easily found for them among 'the questions submitted by Bishops desiring the advice of the Conference.' One of these questions was about 'difficulties arising in the Church of England from the revival of obsolete forms of ritual and from erroneous teaching on the subject of Confession.'

On the Ritual question, the Conference desired 'to affirm the principle that no alteration from long accustomed ritual

should be made contrary to the admonition of the Bishop
of the Diocese.' The question of Confession was far more
difficult to handle. It will be remembered[1] that the
Upper House of the Convocation of Canterbury had passed
a Resolution on the subject in 1873. In 1877, when the
virulent agitation against 'The Priest in Absolution' was
at its height, the Bishops sent this Resolution to the Lower
House of Convocation to be accepted or rejected by them
as a whole. The Lower House endeavoured in various
ways to avoid this somewhat extraordinary demand ; but
after a long discussion, in which great dissatisfaction was
expressed at such an unusual proceeding, a motion was
passed asserting 'general concurrence' in the wording of the
Resolution. But now the Conference of all the Bishops
could not be dealt with in the same way. Many protests
were raised by English, Colonial, and American Bishops
against the introduction of the subject ; but these were
overruled. The Resolution of 1873 suffered considerable
mutilation at the hands of the Conference, and reappeared
at last in the following form :—

'Having in view certain novel practices and teachings on the subject
of Confession, your Committee desire to affirm that in the matter of
Confession the Churches of the Anglican Communion hold fast those
principles which are set forth in the Holy Scriptures which were professed
by the Primitive Church and which were reaffirmed at the English
Reformation ; and it is their deliberate opinion that no minister of the
Church is authorized to require from those who may resort to him to
open their grief a particular or detailed enumeration of all their sins,
or to require private Confession previous to the Holy Communion, or
to enjoin or even to encourage the practice of habitual Confession to
a priest, or to teach that such practice of habitual Confession, or the
being subject to what has been termed the direction of a priest, is
a condition of attaining to the highest spiritual life. At the same
time your Committee are not to be understood as desiring to limit in
any way the provision made in the Book of Common Prayer for the
relief of troubled consciences.'

Only a Committee, and a very divided one, could ever
have put forth such a clumsy Resolution. Clearly no one
person could have written it ; but when a certain verbal

[1] See p. 263.

agreement had been reached after a heated discussion, it
was felt best to issue it as it was in all its vagueness and
self-contradiction. It mixed up in indiscriminate condemnation the enforcement of compulsory Confession (which few
even of the most advanced 'Ritualists' ever attempted to
require) with the practice of habitual Confession which all
High Churchmen believed to be clearly sanctioned by the
Church of England. And after thus very strictly limiting
the language of the Prayer-book, its concluding sentences
permitted the widest construction of which that language
was capable. In fact, the opposition to Confession worked
itself out on the same self-destructive lines as the opposition
to Ritual had already done : in each case the opponents
interpreted a positive statement by words which practically
denied it. The Lambeth Conference was now endeavouring
to insert a 'not' into the Church's rule for Confession,
as the Ridsdale Judgment had already succeeded in doing
into the Ornaments Rubric ; and after insisting on their
gloss, were obliged to refer to the text, which practically
contradicted it. The Resolution nevertheless at first sight
seemed to condemn the practice of thousands of the most
loyal members of the Church.

Pusey thought it good to write at once to the Archbishop
to obtain, if possible, some explanation of this ambiguous
utterance.

E. B. P. TO THE ARCHBISHOP OF CANTERBURY.
South Hermitage, Ascot Priory, July 30, 1878.

MAY IT PLEASE YOUR GRACE,

In the draft of the report which Your Grace is reported to have
presented to the Lambeth Conference, there are two expressions which
I do not clearly see the force of, but which personally affect myself.
They are the words 'authorized' and 'encourage' in the statement
about Confession.

The statement declares that it is the deliberate opinion of the Conference that no minister of the Church of England is 'authorized'– even
'to encourage the practice of habitual Confession.'

It seems to me that by our 'not' being 'authorized,' you may only
mean that we have no direct sanction from the Church of England.
This we have never claimed. It is a detail upon which the Church of
England has given no directions, leaving it to people's consciences.

'Habitual Confession' did, in fact, as I have often said publicly, originate with the laity. Having once used Confession, in consequence of something which was a burden on the conscience, and derived benefit from it, they continued to apply to be again received to Confession. And so they continued on and on, until it became habitual. Even Bishop Phillpotts, who was averse to habitual Confession, said, in his letter to the Dean of Exeter, 'I do not think that the clergy can refuse the habitual application to them to receive Confession' (p. 24).

But your Grace may mean much more, and, without explanation, I should fear that people in general would suppose that your Grace, and the Conference in adopting your Grace's formula, meant much more; that we who receive habitual Confessions are doing what would be called an 'unauthorized' act—an expression which would always be used in blame.

In regard to the other expression, 'encourage,' I should think that any clergyman who does not 'discourage,' but receives Confessions habitually, does, in fact, 'encourage' them. We are (the Ordination Service says) 'called to teach and to premonish, to feed and to provide for the Lord's family.' Those who come to us must look up to us; if then we receive their Confessions habitually, we do *ipso facto* 'encourage habitual Confession.'

Your Grace will not think it a captious question, that I ask what your Grace disowns under the word 'habitual Confession.' Some might use Confession once a fortnight; some once in a year. If repeated year by year, Confessions made once in the year would come to be habitual.

These questions have been forced upon me by the adoption of your Grace's Resolution by the Lambeth Conference. I do not remember how far the terms of that Resolution coincide with that of the Upper House of Convocation some years ago; but since that Resolution was not adopted by the Lower House, it was only an inchoate measure, not a Canon of a Synod of Bishops.

I do not know what the authority claimed for this Resolution is; whether it is an opinion accepted by the hundred Bishops who met at the Conference, or whether it is a judgment which is meant to have a binding force upon us the inferior Clergy.

With all respect to your Grace, I do not think that the Bishops of the United States or of Ireland had any office to pass an opinion about our way of hearing Confessions. For the first Bishops of the United States consented under pressure to have their Prayer-book altered in this respect, as did the Irish Bishops in their recent revision of the Prayer-book. They are, then, no judges as to our practice who retain the former Prayer-book.

But it is a grave matter that your Grace has obtained the concurrence of about a hundred Bishops in an apparent condemnation of the practice of thousands or tens of thousands,—which I myself have continued for some forty years, in the belief that I was, in so doing, acting according to the mind of the Church of England.

The Church of England has certainly not given to the Bishops of the United States or of the Colonies any authority over us, the second Order in England. And yet the right of censure is a very grave power; and I trouble your Grace with this letter, that I may know what my position is, whether I am one with a brand-mark placed on me by a hundred Bishops, as contravening the mind of the Church of England.

It would, I am sure, be a great relief to thousands if your Grace would inform me that, under the words, 'encouraging habitual Confession,' your Grace did not mean to censure those Clergy who receive the habitual Confessions of those who wish to make Confession by virtue of the invitation, 'let him come to me or some other and open his grief,' but only to say that the Church of England does not give any *direct* sanction to it, but left it to the discretion of priests and people, leaving them liberty of conscience.

The Archbishop replied :—

ARCHBISHOP (TAIT) OF CANTERBURY TO E. B. P.
*Private.*

Lambeth Palace, S.E., August 3, 1878.

I have your letter of yesterday's date this morning.

The statement respecting Confession was prepared by a large and influential Committee consisting of ten members, of whom nine attended. It was presented by me to the assembled Bishops, and after discussion was taken back to the Committee and materially altered. It was afterwards very fully discussed in the Conference itself as revised, and before it was finally adopted by the Conference especial attention was called to the words 'authorized' and 'encourage.' I have of course no authority to explain the words which received the sanction of the assembled Bishops.

All I can say in answer to your letter is that the words used, which have been very carefully prepared, must be taken to mean neither more nor less than they express, and that the degree of weight to be attached to them must be judged of by Churchmen according to their conscientious convictions.

If I can be of any use to you, pray employ my services.

Many anxious minds, however, on both sides assumed that authority which the Archbishop disclaimed, and held that the words condemned what Pusey and others had been for a long time 'encouraging.' As Pusey said of it himself, ' To act against the apparent mind of a hundred Bishops is a hard thing. I know they think me loyal at heart; but to take the literal meaning of the words, I have for some forty years been teaching people to do unauthorized acts.

Such an act as theirs would have driven dear J. H. N. out
of the Church of England, if he had not been driven
out before.' On the other hand, Bishop Alford [1] had quoted
the Resolution of the Conference as prohibiting Confession
altogether. This gave Pusey the opportunity of publishing
a Letter to the Archbishop in September, 1878, which he
entitled, ' Habitual Confession not discouraged by the Resolution accepted by the Lambeth Conference.' He stated
that he had received Confessions habitually from some
people for thirty-five years, and desired to know whether
he was to consider himself censured by the Resolution, as
Bishop Alford supposed. He could not believe that he
was censured : he avowed he was puzzled by the words,
but was satisfied that, notwithstanding the ambiguity and
apparent self-contradiction of the Resolution, he and all
others who acted with him did not lie under this censure.
Incidentally he made a strong protest against any interference in the disciplinary order of the Church of England
by the Bishops of the United States and of Ireland. On
this question they were especially bad judges. In the one
Church all allusion to private Confession and Absolution
had been removed from the Prayer-book : and in the other,
the English form of the Absolution in the Order for the
Visitation of the Sick had been extruded. He concluded
his letter in the following words :—

'Nothing will satisfy the Puritan mind except our extirpation ; but
as Confession began in the renewed earnestness worked by God the
Holy Ghost in this century, so it will grow with the growth of that
earnestness. It may be directed, but it cannot be extinguished.'

Pusey had no word of reply from any of the Bishops of
English sees. As he said,—

'Our Bishops seem paralyzed by our Presbyterianizing Archbishop of Canterbury. Not one breath to soften the Declaration of
those hundred Bishops at Lambeth. However, no one has excepted
against my minimizing of their words, and for this I am thankful. . . .
I have good hope that I hindered some tender souls from leaving our
Communion, out of which Archbishop Tait would have driven them.'

[1] He had been Bishop of Victoria, China, from 1867 to 1872.

Voluntary habitual Confession had already by this time taken deep root as part of the authorized system of the Church of England. Most of the objections against it were based on the supposition that it was compulsory and not voluntary. It would be useless to deny that some clergy may have endeavoured to make this system compulsory; but the leaders of the High Church party never did so. The uniformity of their teaching on this and on other important questions is shown by the answers independently given to a correspondent, who addressed the following questions to Pusey, Liddon, and Canon Carter of Clewer: (1) Whether a clergyman of the Church of England had a right to require Confession before Communion? (2) Whether it was wrong for members of the English Church to attend Roman Catholic services in England?

The answers were as follow:—

E. B. P. TO E. A. TUGMAN, ESQ.

[Ascot], August 19, 1878.

An English clergyman would do very unjustifiably if he ventured to 'tell communicants that he would rather they (the communicants) did not go to Communion unless they had first been to private Confession.' I hope that such a case (which I fear from your letter must have happened) is very insulated. Such things make it impossible to defend the new school as a body. It is beyond Roman doctrine. For even the Romans do not confess of necessity before each Communion. There are hundreds of thousands of pious English communicants who never felt any occasion for Confession. And God only can tell who are nearest to Him, those who use it or those who do not. I cannot conceive how any English clergyman can say such things.

It is quite wrong for a member of the Church of England to worship in Roman Churches in England.

REV. H. P. LIDDON, D.D., TO E. A. TUGMAN, ESQ.

3, Amen Court, E.C., Aug. 19 [1878].

The Church of England *offers* the relief of Confession before Communion to those whose consciences tell them that they need it. She gives no authority to her clergy for *insisting* on Confession, as a necessity before Communion. If a clergyman expresses a wish that people would use Confession, it does not necessarily follow, I suppose, that he says that they *must* use it. Everything indeed turns upon the exact language which is employed: but the line between the *offer* of

Confession, if felt to be needed, and the compulsory enforcement of it, is plain enough. The latter is the system of the Roman Church; but a clergyman may say that he thinks confession a good thing before Communion without saying that it is a *sine qua non*. It is, as I have said, a question of the terms employed.

Certainly I do think it schismatical to join in Roman Catholic worship in England. It is impossible to do so without denying by implication that the English Bishops have a true jurisdiction from Christ our Lord, since the existence of R. C. worship is a contravention of that claim.

REV. T. T. CARTER TO E. A. TUGMAN, ESQ.

Rothesay, N. B., Aug. 20 [1878].

Your letter has followed me to Scotland which has caused some delay in replying. I willingly say what my own opinion on the points that you mention, is.

Let me first observe that the point about Confession is not quite clear to me. You ask whether a priest of the Church of England can rightly tell a communicant 'he would rather he did not go to Communion if he did not go to private Confession previously.' It is not clear whether you speak of a particular case, or generally.

Supposing a communicant to be under some priest's guidance, and the priest knew the communicant to have committed some grievous sin, the priest might very properly advise the person in question to seek Absolution before Communion, and even press the person to do so.

But if you speak generally, as I suppose you do, and if you mean whether a priest of the Church of England can rightly *require* persons to go to Confession before Communion, it is clear that he cannot rightly do so. It would, I answer, be contrary to Church of England rule, to put on any one such a pressure that he could not without disobeying the priest communicate without Confession, when he was not himself desirous of it. Confession is with us dependent on the free will of every one, however much it may be advised, and in some cases pressed.

With regard to English-Church people attending Roman services in England, I feel strongly that it is wrong to do so. I suppose you to mean worshipping at their Services. It is not I think too strong a term to use, to say that to do so in England is schismatical.

Copies of Gaume's Manual were sent to all the Bishops who attended the Lambeth Conference; some of the letters of acknowledgment expressed a hope that on some future occasion leisure would be found for a study of its contents, while others entered at some length upon the practical question at issue.

In November, 1878, a lecturer at Oxford, on behalf of the Church Association, brought various charges against Pusey, based upon this book : the only interest in his oratory comes from a correspondence that ensued between Liddon and the Rev. A. M. W. Christopher, the Rector of St. Aldate's, Oxford, who had presided on that occasion. In reply to a letter expressing surprise that Mr. Christopher should have lent his name to such a meeting, and suggesting that prosecution in a court of law, for which Pusey had so often asked in vain, would be a preferable course, Mr. Christopher wrote as follows :—

REV. A. M. W. CHRISTOPHER TO REV. H. P. LIDDON, D.D.

St. Aldate's Rectory, Oxford, Dec. 7, 1878.

More than twenty years ago, before the formation of the Church Association, a small committee of theologians and lawyers met in London to consider the duty of prosecuting Dr. Pusey in the Ecclesiastical Courts. It seemed to them that from him, as the directing mind, the stream of doctrinal error, which has since risen to such a height, was invading the Church. Every one of his theological writings was carefully perused and considered, and a case was eventually laid before very eminent ecclesiastical counsel. The then movers were distinctly advised that though much written by Dr. Pusey was so repugnant to the formularies of the Church of England as to ensure judicial condemnation, yet his peculiar position rendered him unassailable by any process of law. His Canonry is only an incident of his Professorship which he holds under Letters Patent. The foregoing I have received from one of the lawyers concerned, but it is pretty widely known, and long has been so.

The legal advisers of the Church Association and its committee are conversant with these facts.

Liddon communicated this unexpected information at once to Pusey.

E. B. P. TO REV. H. P. LIDDON, D.D.

Christ Church, Oxford, Dec. 12, 1878.

I was as much surprised as you are, that any one can think, that I should not be amenable to a Court for any false doctrine (if unhappily I had fallen into it) because my Canonry is united, by Act of Parliament, to my Professorship. I certainly for many years acted repeatedly on the contrary conviction. I sought prosecution. Indeed I thought the Church Association guilty of great injustice to me in prosecuting Mr. Bennett, and not joining me in the prosecution (as I requested it to do), or not prosecuting me directly, since two of the counts against Mr. Bennett were that he quoted with approbation what I had written, and I was (as Mr. Christopher calls me) the chief offender. For if, in consequence of Mr. Bennett's not defending himself, the case had gone against him (which I held to be impossible, if it were defended) then I should have been, virtually, condemned without a hearing. I forget to whom I wrote, whether it was the Secretary; but I did write, requesting whoever was the real prosecutor of Mr. Bennett to include me in the prosecution. I told them that they were afraid to do so, because they knew that I should defend myself. They declined; but neither then, nor on any other occasion when I invited prosecution, was any hint given me, that those who declined did so because they held my position to be ' legally unassailable.' I certainly should not have thought that any Englishman could commit any wrong, and be legally irresponsible. Our proverb, ' The king can do no wrong,' implies the contrary. It implies certainly that the Sovereign is the only person irresponsible to man. But it is also held that his constitutional advisers are responsible ; so that even for his acts, if wrong, some one may be prosecuted.

If the Church Association should wish to challenge the lawfulness of any of my writings, I should raise no technical objections to its doing so, as I have indeed said, whenever I have invited prosecution. As far as I am concerned, they should have no difficulty, except that of making out their case.

Pray show this to Mr. Christopher and ask him to show it to his friends.

I am sorry that he thinks as he does, as I have always thought him an earnest and loving man ; and I have ever supposed that I held as matter of faith all which he holds as such; only I have been taught more.

Mr. Christopher forwarded this letter to the Church Association; it was kept for six weeks, and then returned without comment. But the suggestion that Pusey took advantage of a position that he knew was technically safe, and challenged a prosecution that he knew was impossible, was again made by the Secretary of the Church Association shortly before the end of Pusey's life. Pusey repudiated the suggestion in the following letter to the *Times* :—

E. B. P. TO THE EDITOR OF THE 'TIMES.'

Christ Church, Jan. 24, 1881.

I did not expect that my simple statement addressed to yourself would bring you a small snow-shower of letters, but there is only one statement to which I need ask you to do me the favour to admit any reply of mine. It is an official statement by the Secretary of the Church Association :—' Dr. Pusey is well aware of the valid reasons for which his writings have not yet been submitted to a judicial consideration.' I am not in the least aware of them. It may be that he gave me reasons which I did not think 'valid' and so forgot them. I thought myself hardly used in the prosecution of Mr. Bennett, in that the first two charges against him were his expression of agreement with doctrinal statements of mine. As Mr. Bennett did not think well to defend himself, I was left to take my chance in an undefended suit.

I endeavoured to goad the Association in some way to substitute me for Mr. Bennett, or, anyhow, to sue me, in a letter which I published. In this letter, published, I believe, in the *Guardian* on July 20, 1868, I said :—

'I would renew to you that same invitation which I have given at different times to others who have impugned my good faith at public meetings, or have otherwise uttered calumnies against me. You accuse me of teaching doctrine contrary to that of the English Church. Substantiate your charge, if you can, in any Court. If you do, I will resign the office which I hold by virtue of my subscription. I will oppose no legal hindrances, but will meet you on the merits of the case.'

To this I had the answer, dated July 30 :—

'The council cannot entertain the idea of advising Mr. Sheppard to discontinue the action against Mr. Bennett ; but if in the progress of the case it should appear necessary to take proceedings in order to vindicate the Church of England from the false dogmas of the Church of Rome, they will hold you to the offer made in your letter.'

I answered, in a letter which was also published :—

'I deeply regret your wasting against us—who, in all which you hold of faith (i. e. as many of you as are not Lutherans or Calvinists), are at one with you (for denials of faith are not faith)—energies which had better have been directed to gain those who deny the Saviour Whom we both adore. But since you will have it so, I shall not need to be held to the offer which I have made, but should at any time gladly defend against you Primitive and Catholic truths, which, if the Church of England denied, she would forfeit her claim to be a portion of the Church of Christ.'

I do not know that I had any answer to this letter, or any further information why they did not accept my challenge. Perhaps their failure in the undefended suit 'Sheppard *v.* Bennett' deterred them.

So far as Mr. Christopher was concerned, the incident in 1878 was closed by his sending a very friendly note to Pusey on New Year's Day, 1879, with a copy of Dr. Bonar's 'God's Way of Holiness': Pusey replied in the same tone of personal respect, and asked his correspondent to accept a volume of Keble's 'Lenten Sermons.'

# CHAPTER XIV.

RETIREMENT FROM THE HEBDOMADAL COUNCIL AND
KEBLE COLLEGE COUNCIL—OPENING OF KEBLE COL-
LEGE CHAPEL—LETTER ON EDUCATION—PROPOSED
PORTRAIT FOR THE HALL OF CHRIST CHURCH.

1876–1879.

PUSEY was of the same age as the century: and the
infirmities of old age naturally began to show themselves
in a body which never had been strong, but had been
consistently presented as a living sacrifice to the work of
the Church of God for nearly fifty years. The indomitable
force of his will, the concentration of his energy, and the
unsparing devotion of his whole life to God had enabled
him to labour on and to throw off illnesses in a way that
would hardly have been possible to any mere strength of
constitution. But when 'the leaves were falling thickly
round him,' and the weight of sorrows was added to the
weight of years, it was evident that his strength was
beginning to fail. Ever since his illness at Genoa in 1873,
he had been an old man; but the shock of Bishop Forbes'
sudden death in 1875, and the death of Miss Sellon, the
Foundress of the Devonport Sisterhood, in 1876, had
brought on a sudden great increase of deafness. 'It is an
odd life,' he writes to Liddon in December, 1876 :—

'God grant that I may be the more driven inwards. I passed
three and three-quarter hours in the Hebdomadal Council to-day, not
hearing a voice: but learning from my neighbour, the kind President
of St. John's, what was to be voted on. I have once only said a few
words this term, because I do not know the right time to say them.
It is such an odd contrast to former eagerness. Thank God that my
books can speak to me ; and He too, I hope.'

For upwards of twenty years Pusey had been continuously re-elected to this position on the governing body of the University. He held it as he did all his appointments, not as a piece of academical work, but as a position in which he could fight the Cause of God and His Truth against the dominant liberalism of the University. It was often weary work; and he sometimes had been tempted to regret what seemed to be a spending of strength in vain. Now, however, he began to feel that it was his duty to make room for a younger man. Yet he still held his place on the Council as long as health would allow. The last meeting that he attended was on December 10, 1877 : the prolonged illness described in the last chapter prevented him from attending the Council in the Lent and Easter Terms of the following year, and he did not offer himself for re-election in the Michaelmas Term.

For some time longer he retained his place on the Council of Keble College. although he was rarely able to attend their meetings. All that concerned the welfare of this great memorial to his dear friend appealed to him most strongly; he was specially interested in the munificent gift of a Chapel by Mr. Gibbs—'indeed. a gift of God.' One of his letters about the plans has a value of its own. Mr. Butterfield, the architect, proposed to place over the Altar a Mosaic, representing our Lord as He appeared to St. John in Patmos, and the Council had accepted his design. Pusey was ill at Genoa, when the design was discussed ; soon after his return to Oxford, he wrote to express his disapproval of it.

E. B. P. TO THE WARDEN OF KEBLE COLLEGE.

Christ Church, June 18, 1873.

It is only lately that I heard of this Symbol, which the Council, at Butterfield's instance, acquiesced in for the East end of Keble College. I think that there are some symbols which may be represented in words, but cannot in material form. We have probably, most of us, been pained by representations of the 'Ancient of Days,' because old age is, with us, necessarily associated with decay. So the symbol from Rev. i. cannot be really represented ; no *material* form can represent Eyes which should be a flaming fire, or Feet like fine brass which burned in a furnace, or the seven stars in one Hand.

But I chiefly object :—

1. To the great austerity of it over the Altar. The representation of Rev. i. is our Lord in the midst of the Church as Judge. It says, ' Judge yourselves, that ye be not judged.' It is the opposite to, ' Come unto Me, all that are weary and heavy laden, and I will give you rest.' At the West end is to be the Judgment : at the East our Lord as Judge. It gives great prominence to the austere side of truth.

2. Since there are visible representations, I much miss the Crucifixion, which is relegated (I understand) to a side quasi-transept where it will be scarcely seen.

It might be represented (without destroying Butterfield's plans) either by inlaying the figure of our Lord upon the Cross, which, I understand, is to be behind the altar, or by painting it upon the Cross after the manner of those devout pictures of Giotto at Florence.

I should wish, then, to be allowed to give notice of a motion on Monday—That it be represented to the Donor of the Chapel of Keble College, that it is desirable that there should be some conspicuous monument of our Lord's Death fronting the Communicants, and that such representation be not relegated to the side.

Mr. Gibbs had a very strong feeling against making any change after the design had once been accepted. Yet he was willing, because of 'the very great reverence' that he felt for Pusey, to accept his suggestion, if he were to press it. Pusey could only thank Mr. Gibbs for his kindness, and decline to press any unwelcome change upon such a generous benefactor of Keble College.

When the Chapel was opened on St. Mark's Day, 1876, Mr. Keble's birthday, Pusey preached the first Sermon, on the Beatitude pronounced upon the Meek. After speaking in general on the meaning of this Beatitude, he explained why he had chosen the text. Meekness, he said, which is the rarest of all graces, was ' eminently possessed by him in memory of the gift of whom to us, on this day, this day has been chosen for the dedication of this magnificent chapel.' He glowingly sets forth as an example to the students of the College, the beautiful lowliness of character, and the lifelong low estate of one of Oxford's greatest scholars, and of the Church's wisest teachers [1].

[1] The issue of the second edition of this sermon, with some alterations, was Dr. Pusey's last piece of work for the press. It was finished in the latter part of August, 1882.

In connexion with the working of Keble College, he left on record some of his latest anxieties about University education. He was very anxious that a more thorough training in Theology should be given to the future clergy. This was his hope when he had assisted the foundation of the Theological School in the University, and he deeply regretted the continued predominance of classical studies to the exclusion of the accurate and systematic study of Theology, which was so essential a part of the education of the clergy.

E. B. P. TO THE WARDEN OF KEBLE COLLEGE.

Advent Sunday, 1876.

I suppose that there is no one solution as to the course of intellectual education here. People look at the two sides of the shield. One party asks, ' When is our (simply intellectual) education to be broken off?' The other (of whom I am one), ' When are the studies of our life to begin? *Is any solid foundation ever to be laid?*' You have the advantage in the one question, I (I think) in the other. If life were long enough and the possible length of education had no limits, nothing could be said against your side. Make the preliminary education as long and as solid as you can: extend it on and on until the young mind and the activity of intellect have reached their fullest development. When you have gone on and on, I ask, ' Jurisprudence and Theology are real studies, what room will you leave for them?' Both will develop the fullest faculty of mind. St. Paul (granted that a person is fit to read him, but Aristotle requires the same) will develop a person's reasoning power as well as Aristotle. It is reasoning as close.

The history of the Early Church and its struggles into recognition, or with heresy, is as instructive as that of Grecian independence in Herodotus or the selfishness and ambition of the Peloponnesian war. Human nature can be studied as well in its conflict and submission to faith as to Sparta. . . .

Do not trouble yourself to answer this, but think how you can solve the problem,—how are our young men to learn solidly, or lay the foundation of solid knowledge of God and His truth? If they are not laid here there will be no building.

But old age compelled him to give up this office also: for the sake of the College, and of the memory of ' dearest J. K.,' he was very anxious about his successor. Nine years' experience had shown how extremely difficult was the task of maintaining the stamp of definite Churchmanship in an Oxford College in the presence of the almost purely academical tone of the rest of the University. The letter in which he resigned his office and expressed his earnest wish about his successor is a very careful statement of this deep anxiety.

### E. B. P. to the Warden of Keble College.

South Hermitage, Ascot Priory, Oct. 19, 1879.

My increasing and now (for a time at least) total deafness makes me a useless member of the Keble College Council. I am extremely anxious about my successor. . . .

Members of Council affect very indirectly the character of the training of the young men, which is, by the Charter, wholly lodged in the hands of the Warden. Still, the only pledge of the fidelity of the College, as a foundation, to the teaching which characterized John Keble and which is stamped by the Charter on the College, lies in the soundness of the Council. Higher duties might by God's Providence be imposed upon you. The character of the successor who should carry on the lamp of truth would depend upon the then Council. If a majority of members of the Council should once be unfriendly or even indifferent to the claims of Catholic truth, or should make the office of Keble College to train good soldiers of Christ Jesus subordinate to Academic distinction, all would be lost, and that irretrievably. What would become of it, God only knows.

My own part with Keble College relates to my successor in the Council. I, with one other, am mainly responsible for the existence of the College and the name which it bears; great as the enthusiasm was, with which that name was received, and the pecuniary sacrifices made for it. I have then a responsibility for it, which one only shares besides. I am then intensely anxious that my successor should be one who should intelligently and definitely, with whatever influence a member of the Council has, maintain the principles upon which it was founded. Mine is an anxiety which no other can have, since at that meeting of mourners, on the day when his earthly remains were parted with out of sight, I gave the impulse, at Hursley Park, to the foundation of the College.

I am very anxious that that successor should be one whom I have known intimately for many years, who is one of singular moderation as well as wisdom, who can discriminate with singular sagacity what is essential from what is not essential—C. Wood. I do not think that I was ever more impressed than by a public address which I heard him deliver now many years ago, in which Theology of necessity largely entered, in which, without controversy or anything which could have offended any one, he expressed his own faith on deep subjects with a precision, which reminded me of Hooker's wonderful enunciation of the doctrine of the Holy Trinity and of the. Person of our Lord Jesus Christ.

His future secular position will make him a useful member of the Council secularly also.

As to his being President of the E. C. U. he is the sense and moderation of it, and, in the eyes of the *Rock*, he would only replace one much blacker.

Five, I know, of the members of the Council strongly wish that he should be my successor. I myself, when the election occurs, can of course only give my earnest wishes and prayers. You, I hope, will not object to it.

His earnest recommendation was accepted, and Mr. Wood succeeded to his place on the Council.

As his life was drawing to a close, his friends greatly desired that a good portrait of him might be painted, so that future generations might not have to ask in vain 'what manner of man was he in aspect?' The request had often been made before, but always met with the same answer. In 1843, soon after the Vice-Chancellor of Oxford had suspended him from preaching before the University, Keble forwarded to him a request of this kind from Mr. Justice Coleridge. He answered, on July 27, 1843: 'There is no likeness of me, and I have put off my brother's wish to have one, because people give me such an undue place already, and I wish to sink back.' A last attempt was made in 1878. Early in that year, just before his serious illness, Dr. Acland mentioned that Dean Liddell would in a few days present him a paper signed by all the resident members of the Governing Body of Christ Church, requesting that he would allow his portrait to be painted and placed in the Hall. As soon as his health permitted, he anticipated the Dean's intention by writing to decline.

E. B. P. TO THE DEAN OF CHRIST CHURCH.

Christ Church, Oxford, May 13 [1878].

Acland told me, before I became so ill, that you and he and some others kindly wished that some likeness of me should be preserved. People, with much more modesty than I, have acceded to the expression of such a wish, so much as a matter of course, that it seems almost a piece of conceit in me to shrink from it. When Newman and Keble and C. Marriott and Bishop Selwyn have done it, what am I that

I should make a fuss about it? To explain this, I must give you a little piece of autobiography. From the time when I began to work hard at Theology, as a young Fellow of Oriel, and people spoke kindly of me, I always thought, 'Well, they will see one day how much they have over-rated me.' And then I resolved never to do anything to put myself forward. When my future patron, Bishop Lloyd, asked me what was the end of all my reading, whether I was thinking of this corner of the quadrangle (i. e. the Hebrew Professorship), I remember simply shrugging my shoulders and saying, 'Quid valeant humeri.' A religious book, which instanced having a likeness taken of one's-self as implying that one thought well of one's-self, fixed me, and I settled with myself not to have it done. It surprised me when Newman, Keble, &c., one by one did it, but I declined all wishes of relations, friends, &c. ; and it became to me a part of my religion not to have it done. At times it pained me to decline, when I was asked affection-ately, and the more so because some whom I respected and loved did it. And now it has gone on for some forty years.

It might naturally seem strange to you, that I who have been (as censured or praised) so much before the world, should think of not putting myself forward. However, if people put me forward, it was no doing of mine. I only followed the rule, 'Whatsoever thy hand findeth to do, do it with all thy might.' ... When in early days (Sir R. Peel's) people spoke of 'Dr. Burton's and my stocks rising,' the thought only crossed me, how it might be an occasion of putting any real power into the hands of another. In later years, when it[1] was spoken of, I prayed it might not be offered me, but determined not to accept it. When the new school was rising, though I thought it mistaken in many things, I could not meddle, without taking the office of a leader of a party ; so I went on my way, they theirs. In Newman's day, I looked at things mainly as they would affect him.

Now all this egotism is in order to ask you not to ask me to do, what it would pain me to decline, yet what I must decline, because it has been a religious ground personal to myself, upon which I have declined before, and all my past declinings would look like a piece of mock-modesty.

Accept, my dear Dean, my warmest thanks for the kindliness which has made you take part in this, and for all your other kindness ; but, pray, do me one kindness more, to express to any who have joined you in this, or to whom you have given the weight of your name, my earnest wish that they would not by asking me put me to the pain of declining the wish of persons whom I respect or love.

The Dean replied that in spite of Pusey's 'very interesting and touching letter,' he was bound to present the memorial with which he had been entrusted, and he begged him to

[1] i. e. a Bishopric.

consider the strong claims of a request which expressed
the goodwill and interest of the great foundation to which
he had belonged for more than half a century. Accordingly
a few days later, the Dean and Dr. Acland called at Pusey's
lodgings, presented the address, and urged every argument
to induce him to yield. They specially pointed out that, if
he persisted in his refusal, a few caricatures would be the
only answer to the natural desire of future generations to
know what he was like. 'With a peculiarly winning smile
and gentle manner,' the Dean writes, 'he took up the
address and said how much he was gratified by the loving
wish of so many members of the House, and that he greatly
desired to comply with their kind wishes.' He went on,
however, to explain that nearly forty years before, he had
announced, in a conversation with Keble, his solemn
determination never to have his portrait painted: and on
this resolution he had always acted. His visitors still
continued to press him with arguments. 'All was of no
effect,' the Dean writes. 'He shook his head, smiled
gently, and said, "It is a matter of religion with me"
(I remember this phrase distinctly) "and I cannot go back
from it." We expressed our great regret at his decision,
and parted with a friendly shake of hands.' On the next
day he wrote the following formal reply to the request :—

E. B. P. TO THE DEAN OF CHRIST CHURCH.

Christ Church, Oxford [May, 1878].

I hope that I have not seemed ungrateful to the love and kindness
and goodwill of the members of the Governing Body, and others whose
wish you and Dr. Acland made me acquainted with, with your usual
kindness. To them it might be enough to say, that an old man verging
on seventy-eight does not get over a rooted repugnance of thirty-nine
years.

To you, my dear Dean, I may give another glimpse. I was much
shocked to see that a Roman Catholic writer of controversy opened
with some such sentence as this, 'We are told that Dr. P. is a vain
man. This would account for' &c. We are all agreed that vanity is
a most absurd thing, that no one could be vain who had not a low
ideal; besides being very ungrateful to Almighty God Whose gift
everything is, however little. I, of course, know that I have nothing
to be vain about. However, I had seen, in the care of souls, that

people often are brimful of a leading fault of which they have no
suspicion. So my not suspecting it was no proof that I had not it.
A caricature often suggests the truest likeness. Chantry got his
suggestion for Dean Jackson's statue from one. Himself he had
never seen. Anyhow, proud flesh needs a caustic. I fear that
I have not applied it near enough. Nobody could accuse Newman
or John Keble of being 'vain,' however sharp they may have written
against either.

And now having our Lord's words sounding in my ears, 'Whoso
exalteth himself shall be abased,' I cannot withdraw a precaution
which I have acted upon for thirty-nine years. I have an instinctive
repugnance against it. J. H. N. and J. K. of course did naturally what
they did. They had no need to take precautions against conceit. And
now, when just passing out of the world with all my failures, self-
confidences, mistakes and mischiefs, I cannot expose myself to any
temptation or rescind my desire to make myself nothing. *Hæret
lateri lethalis arundo.* Rather, in the days of memorials, when
people begin planning memorials before a person's remains are hid
out of sight, I must add a codicil to my will requesting that none may
be made of me.

In sending these letters and an account of the interview,
Dean Liddell added, 'The portrait that now represents
him in Christ Church Hall was painted after his death
by Mr. George Richmond. Mr. Richmond had known
Dr. Pusey well, and had of his own accord executed a fine
bust of his departed friend. Three of these busts were
taken in terra cotta. . . . The painted portrait is not
equally successful. It gives the sentiment and general
bearing of Dr. Pusey, but fails, I think, to represent his
countenance and expression. But it was the best thing to
be got. Dr. Pusey suffers still from his unshaken resolution
not to have his portrait taken. Perhaps we ought not to
have attempted it. But it was undertaken in accordance
with the earnest desire of a great number of friends, and
I did not think it right to disregard their wishes.'

# CHAPTER XV.

1878-1879.

DURING the Long Vacation of 1878, Pusey was engaged
in preparing two sermons, the last that he ever wrote for
the University pulpit. They were both apologetic in their
character, and were calculated to guide his hearers amidst
the difficulties of the day. The former was on the supposed conflict between the truths of Revelation and the
facts of Physical Science, and was published under the title
'Unscience, not Science, adverse to Faith.' The latter
was in reply to several recent publications which had most
unduly minimized, if not entirely overlooked, the definite
predictions of the Old Testament. He called this sermon
'Prophecy of Jesus—the certain prediction of the [to man]
impossible.'

On the former sermon especially he spent great pains,
because it dealt with a subject which in its details was to
a great extent new to him. His true delight in the beauties
of Nature, and his deep reverence for God as Creator of the
world, gave him always a lively interest in Science. 'It
teaches us,' he used to say, 'with a minuteness of which we
had no idea, the minute wisdom of our God. What a varied
preacher Nature is! One great delight of the "Christian
Year" used to be to me, that dear J. K. so listened to

Nature and interpreted it to us.' From this point of view he had from the first steadily encouraged the legitimate study of Science in Oxford. Sir Henry Acland, who, as Regius Professor of Medicine at Oxford for nearly forty years, took an important part in the promotion of the study of all departments of Physical Science, vividly recalls the following recollections of Pusey's attitude towards his own great work :—

' In 1845 I was offered by the Dean the Lee's Readership of Anatomy at Christ Church ; and before entering on my duties, I called on Dr. Pusey, to whom I had been introduced by my brother ten years before, and asked his leave to put to him two questions.

' 1. "Am I right in believing that you, Mr. Newman, Mr. Keble, and your friends disapprove of Physical Science as a branch of education in Oxford ? "

' He said, " Yes, we do ; and you would not hold up . . . as persons whom you would wish young men to imitate in many ways."

' I then put to him my second question.

' 2. "Am I to understand that you, who with the Dean and Chapter have appointed me a teacher in a great department of Science, will consider me a mischievous and dangerous member of society, when I endeavour to do my duty in my office ? "

' Dr. Pusey, who, whatever may be considered his faults by those who did not know him, was a strong, true man, and endowed with a sense of humour, threw himself back in his chair and laughed aloud. He then sat upright, and earnestly said : " The desire to acquire such knowledge, and the power to obtain it, are alike the gift of God, and to be used as such. As long as you discharge your duties in the manner which this implies, count on my support in whatever you do." He always attended the meetings of the Chapter in the Museum, and paid great attention to the Reports on the progress of the Biological Collection, which was being made with the help of Victor Carus, Beale, and others. He also at one time lent me his stables for a whole long vacation, to carry on part of my work for which I had not room in Lee's Building.

'When the British Association was about to meet at Oxford in 1847, he wrote to me as local Secretary to say that he should not be in Oxford then, but that he placed his house in Christ Church at my disposal for any members I should place there, being strangers, adding all necessary details as to the numbers and the accommodation and the entertainment which the servants could provide. Van der Hoeven, Joseph Henry Green, and five others were there for a week.

'In the year 1855 the final vote for £30,000 for the construction of the Museum would have been lost without the votes of Dr. Pusey, Charles Marriott, and their friends. I might add that Charles Marriott, Church (afterwards Dean of St. Paul's), and Mr. Wilson (afterwards Professor of Moral Philosophy), were serious students at Christ Church in advanced practical Physiological Histology some years before.'

But although Pusey was interested in Science and ready to assist its study, he had naturally not been able to keep up with the later discoveries of Science; in the midst of his theological and controversial work he would from time to time read a work which had occasioned special difficulties to some one who sought his advice, but his time was so fully occupied that he had made it a rule never to read anything that was not directly on the lines of the work which immediately lay before him. Still the difficulties that Darwinism raised were keenly felt by a very large number of people. It had already led many away, in England as in Germany, into unbelief; and Pusey was frequently asked to show its due relation to Revealed Truth. To him a pulpit seemed hardly the place for such a discussion; it was, however, the only opportunity of a hearing that offered itself, and the battle with unbelief was the work of his life.

When he reached Ascot in July, 1878, his health seemed for the time quite restored. 'Altogether I am very bonny,' he writes. 'Acland thinks that I may very well preach one sermon early in November. Whether I preach the second depends, I suppose, on how I get through the first.'

He carefully read several eminent authors on the side of Evolution. The notes at the foot of the pages of his sermon refer to a large number of works, but they represent only a portion of his studies during that summer. His desire was to discover exactly and estimate aright what was being taught under the name of Physical Science, and to suggest the terms of a lasting peace between Theology and Science by showing the lawful frontier between them. He had always abstained from confusing the two studies. At the Norwich Church Congress in 1865 he had pointed out the lines for the right interpretation of the Bible with reference to Geology. Now he wished to do a similar work in connexion with the later discoveries; he was convinced that scientific men made as many mistakes as theologians about the relation of Theology to Science. In his sermon he warily keeps off all scientific detail, and confines himself to theology, standing simply on the defensive. He says that he meant it to be 'an Eirenicon. Theology does not interfere with Science as it reads the book of God's works: let not Science interfere with the book of God's Word.'

Two days before the sermon was to be preached, Dr. Acland forbade him to deliver more than half of it. He therefore thought it best to ask Liddon to take his place.

E. B. P. TO THE REV. H. P. LIDDON, D.D.

Nov. 1, 1878.

Acland is decided that I must not even attempt to preach the whole sermon. He proposes only half. The sermon is a dissertation rather than a sermon, which I should not have thought of delivering from the pulpit, but for the hope of arresting the minds of some of the young ones. Else I have no interest in it, except in the peroration. But breaking off deliberately in the midst is like making a scene, or making too much of myself ... or clinging to preaching when beyond my strength. Apart however from any reasons, I should be much more comfortable if you would deliver the whole.

On the morning of November 3, to the astonishment of the crowded congregation at St. Mary's Church which

had assembled to hear Pusey, Liddon was seen entering
the pulpit instead of Pusey, carrying the bulky manuscript
of Pusey's sermon. It was a strange, perhaps a unique,
scene. A sermon, written by one of the greatest preachers
of one generation, equalling, at least in range, intellectual
force, and moral power, any sermon that he had ever
prepared, was being read for him by the greatest preacher
of the next. Elisha was wearing Elijah's mantle, yet the
master was still with him, though Israel would never again
see his face. He begins by asking the question why, in
the present day, in sad contrast with the past, the study of
Physical Science is so often adverse to continued belief in
God and in His Revealed Truth. The sphere of Science
is material fact, the sphere of Theology spiritual fact. Why
should they be in conflict? True genuine Theology has no
preconceived opinions in the province of Science: it has
room for all the facts, and even for the most romantic
imaginations of Science, if those imaginations are confined
to its own region. The danger to faith has arisen first
from the study of the phenomena of matter to the rigid
exclusion of the phenomena of the spiritual world, and in
a forgetfulness of the Existence of God, more contemptuous
than positive denial; and, secondly, from the intrusive
attempt on the part of material Science to explain from
beneath spiritual facts about the soul's existence, about
religion and about morals. Theories of the evolution of
the world and of animal forms may or may not be true.
' Theology does not hold them excluded by Holy Scripture,
so that they spare the soul of man.' The powers of the
human soul, especially its power to know God and be in
communion with Him, and above all, its powers as shown
in the Mind and Life of Jesus Christ, His attractive beauty,
His wondrous reign, and His continued daily miracles, attest
its true origin.

A bare analysis of this remarkable sermon can give no
idea of its solid strength, or of its impressive insight into
the great questions at issue. The great age of the writer
and the veneration with which his words were listened to

made them all the more effective.  At the moment it opened
up fresh lines of thought, and pointed to the right solutions
of painful difficulties which some had regarded as inexplicable.  But beyond that, it is no exaggeration to say that
it is a permanent and most valuable contribution to the
right understanding of the relations between Religion and
Science.  When published, it was dedicated ' with truest
affection' to Dr. Acland, the Regius Professor of Medicine
at Oxford, ' who devoted the prime of life to the revival of
the study of the book of God's works in Oxford, and
through whose kind care and skill God restored to the
author the strength to write it.'

The publication of the sermon entailed much correspondence.  His statement of the position between Theology
and Physical Science was to many of his readers entirely
new ; the line of demarcation had been sadly blurred by
ignorant attacks on Revealed Religion, and equally ignorant
attempts to defend it.  Several well-known men of Science,
some of whom could by no means be reckoned on the side
of Christianity, thanked Pusey heartily for it.  ' We have
no right,' one says, speaking as a scientific teacher, ' to
complain of dogmatism, for the scientific men of the day
surpass the theologians in this.  Haeckel indeed speaks like
the Pope.  The earlier part of your sermon pleased me
most, as an important step towards peace, which every
one wishes for provided it may be obtained without the
sacrifice of truth.'  Another welcomed the sermon as ' an
Eirenicon, as the preliminaries of peace between genuine
science and genuine theology.'

In writing to Dr. Rolleston, the well-known Professor of
Physiology in Oxford, who had complained of one ex-
pression in the Sermon which, he said, had caused him pain,
Pusey says :—

E. B. P. TO PROFESSOR ROLLESTON.

Easter Tuesday, 1879.

. . . I had no idea that anything in it could have pained any one.
I went to the utmost verge, to which I lawfully (as I thought) could.
to make out limits of Theology and Physical Science, so that no

physical philosopher could think that Theology invaded his territory, while I remonstrated with him, if he invaded that of Theology.

I have now looked at the passage in my sermon which you referred to as giving you pain. I hesitated about it, in that one could scarce bear to put into an assailant's mouth such an hypothesis. I consulted Liddon about it. He thought I might venture to say it, because, on their hypothesis, it would be true. So I wrote it, to scare others from blasphemy.

But I do not see what could pain you, except the terribleness of the words. *You* do not believe that *our* souls and minds are from the ' pithecoids.' I thought and hoped that the terribleness of the expression, or rather of the fact implied, might open the eyes of some and scare back others.

The theory of Evolution seems to me one of the threatening clouds of the day. I fear that it will wreck the faith of many. It is very fascinating to a certain class of minds, and seems already to be a sort of gospel. A young man wrote to me on occasion of that sermon, that he believed in Evolution and in Genesis also, and supposed that they could be reconciled somehow; although he did not see how. I fear that, with most, Genesis would have to give way.

Darwin's ' Descent of Man ' was very distressing to me. Hitherto, Darwin had, in all his illustrations, kept himself to scientific facts, the variations or, if so be, fresh species of animals or plants of the same kind. In the ' Descent of Man,' he claims to have done good service in ' aiding to overthrow the doctrine of separate creations ' (p. 61). He accepts (as you know) in principle all Haeckel's genealogy of our ancestors, ' still more simply organs than the lancelet or amphioxus ' (p. 609).

To me, it would seem to stultify the whole of the Darwinian theory, to suppose a mere natural development up to man, including man's body, and then to suppose that this descendant from its ape-ancestors was, at once, endowed by God with all those magnificent gifts with which the Bible says He endowed us.

I can only hope that, in days which I shall not see, God may raise up some naturalists who may, in His hands, destroy the belief in our apedom.

I do not myself see the slightest difference between Darwin and Haeckel, except that Darwin assumes a First Cause, who, all those aeons ago, infused the breath of life into some primaeval forms, and has remained inactive (if, indeed, He is supposed to be a Personal Being) ever since.

I am thankful for any admission which may be a ποῦ στῶ for something better, and so would not depreciate the belief in a First Cause, even if any one acknowledged nothing else. I can hardly understand a ' First Cause ' being the object of love or adoration, or hope or trust.

Pusey was not even allowed to read the second sermon

on the following Sunday; it was 'delivered by a young friend of the writer, the Rev. F. Paget,' now Dean of Christ Church. It was a protest against the current depreciation of the predictive element of the Old Testament. He pointed out that the astonishing events which the prophets distinctly foretold should take place, such as the Birth, Life, Death, Atonement, Resurrection, Ascension of the Messiah, His world-wide kingdom, and His work in winning souls— events which 'human wisdom could not foresee and human power could not accomplish'—are now matters of history. 'I wished to put before you, that the impossible, i.e. to man, is the actual and the real. One Event, one Form, is the centre of the Universe.'

Shortly afterwards Liddon was using some of the arguments of this sermon in writing to a clergyman who had ventured to suggest that the use of the Old Testament in the first two chapters of St. Matthew was somewhat arbitrary. Pusey sent him the following interesting note on St. Matthew's use of the earlier Scriptures.

E. B. P. TO REV. H. P. LIDDON, D.D.

Christ Church, Jan. 20, 1879.

I wonder whether if St. Matthew could come again to this earth your correspondent would begin to teach him, or to ask him what he meant. It is sorrowful, for those small beginnings so spread. It struck me many years ago that these quotations were made to teach us how to understand the Old Testament, not as proofs; to show his readers the deeper harmony of the Old and New Testaments. Ἐρευνᾶτε τὰς γραφάς our Lord says, but ἐρευνᾶτε is not a superficial glance at the surface. The text, upon which this struck me, was St. Matthew's quotation of Isa. liii. 4 of our Lord's healing diseases. Rationalism objects, 'The writers of the New Testament do not quote Isaiah liii. of our Lord's vicarious suffering.' Perhaps one explanation may be that they did not quote what we should be sure to understand for ourselves. Alas! it is not so far off to extend it to Him Who taught St. Matthew. For if St. Matthew were wrong either he was a bad learner or——

Do you know Claudius' lines?—

> Es kam mir ein Gedank von Ohngefähr,
> So spräch' ich, wenn ich Christus wär',

which I roughly translated—

> There came to me a random thought,
> Had I been Christ, so had I taught!

I suppose that there is no alternative but that either we must be taught of God, or His creatures must teach Him.

You could make a sermon on 'The two teachings.'

He had been busy also at another piece of work during the Long Vacation of 1878. In 1851 he had preached a valuable sermon on the Rule of Faith. The Gorham Judgment had at that time shaken so many in their allegiance to the English Church, that he thought it good to state clearly, for the younger members of the University, the principles recognized by the English Church as the groundwork and rule of faith. This sermon had been for some time out of print. In re-issuing it in 1878, he wrote a long preface to show how entirely the Vatican Council had changed the whole Roman system, inasmuch as it had substituted the Infallibility of the Pope for the consent of Antiquity. The preface would itself have been a complete answer to the appeal which Newman had wished Liddon to make to Pusey in the preceding March[1]; but it was probably written for other reasons, especially from the fear that in the troubles of the English Church, many, who knew not the character of the modern Church of Rome, might in their ignorance look in that direction for a Church which ruled its faith by the voice of Catholic antiquity.

At this time Pusey was constantly urging upon those who were best qualified to write an account of the Oxford Movement—the necessity for an accurate history of its stirring events, its chief characters, and its real aims. In a correspondence about Keble College in the *Times* during May, 1878, he had dwelt on the influence of Keble in the Movement, as being one of the reasons why those who loved him united to perpetuate his memory. He had for several years hoped that the history would have been written by the Rev. W. J. Copeland; but he feared that even if Copeland should ever finish his work, it would not be rightly focussed. His devotion to Newman would blind his eyes to the effect on Newman's mind of the friendship and guidance of Keble, which made him what he was until 1839.

[1] See above, p. 307.

The publication of Dean Hook's 'Life' made Liddon also see that a book was needed which would put in right proportion the history of the origin of the Church Revival.

REV. H. P. LIDDON, D.D., TO E. B. P.

Jan. 9, 1879.

Have you seen Dr. Hook's 'Life'? I have been reading parts of it, and think it likely to attract a great deal of attention. One loves him for his courage and affectionateness : his work at Leeds was very noble. . . . The perusal of this book has made me greatly wish that I could resign my Professorship and set to writing a life of you. Pray forgive me. But I foresee great troubles, hereafter, in the questions which *will* be raised, and which it will be hard or impossible to answer after you are gone. This notion of Mr. Christopher that you challenged the Church Association out of what you knew to be an unassailable fortress is a specimen. If the interests at stake were only personal I should think less about it. But in reality the whole past, and, humanly speaking, the future of the Oxford Movement, turns upon it.

Pusey would not hear of such a proposal ; he never thought that Liddon would do what he said.

E. B. P. TO REV. H. P. LIDDON, D.D.

Jan. 10, 1879.

You frighten me by what you say about the life of one who only wishes to sink into his own nothingness. Mr. Christopher has scared you unduly. What signifies it if the Church Association and its advisers thought me in 'an impregnable castle'? In one sense I am, because I hold the truth by God's mercy, and no weapon that is framed against it shall prosper. But the idea that I could not be prosecuted, if I had unhappily taught false doctrine, is too absurd. As for me, people have made too much of me, so that a little moderate abuse is a relief to me. It adjusts the balance a little.

It will all come right. As for me, if you thought of anything of the kind, I should cut and run and hide myself in some cave.

Liddon, however, fully intended what he said : the past must be rightly recorded. 'Its value,' he maintained, 'is not merely or chiefly personal or biographical. It will govern the future ; and if we do not give our version of it, others will, I fear, give theirs.' Pusey, in reply, promised to assist him to collect materials for a history of the Oxford Movement. 'But the central figure,' he said, 'should be J. K. . . . I should be glad to see it brought out, for J. K.

was a mainspring. He published the " Christian Year," while Newman was just emerging from Evangelicalism, and I was busy with Arabic, in hope of counter-working, with God's help, German rationalism on the Old Testament. The *quod ubique* seemed to me the strong bulwark of faith ; when hearts had failed, I fell back on my Hebrew criticism.'

It was but a short time after this that an announcement appeared in the *Times* of February 18, 1879, that Pope Leo XIII had intimated his desire to make Newman a Cardinal, but that he had excused himself from accepting the purple. The 'Life of Cardinal Manning' has lately made known part of the story of this extraordinary announcement. The truth was that this honour had been offered to Newman through his ecclesiastical superiors, Bishop Ullathorne and Cardinal Manning. and had been accepted on February 5. Ten days later Cardinal Manning started for Rome bearing Newman's answer, having in some strange manner persuaded himself that Newman had declined it. Three days after his departure. he allowed the supposed refusal to be published in the *Times*. It was of course at once accepted as a statement of the facts. Pusey did not write for some days ; he waited to see whether the offer would be pressed in a form that would oblige Newman to accept it. But as no other announcement appeared, Pusey wrote ten days later, sending a copy of his last Sermon on Prophecy :—

E. B. P. TO REV. J. H. NEWMAN.

Christ Church, Oxford, March 1, 1879.

I was silent while every one was speaking of the token of confidence shown to you where you would most value it. I am glad both of it and of your declining the outward expression of it. But I did not like to say anything for fear it should be pressed upon you, so that you would not think it right to decline it. But I thought in my inward heart that your place would be higher in heaven for declining all on earth. So I was glad.

As for your popularity with the Liberal papers, the words came into my mind, ' Your fathers killed the prophets, and ye build their sepulchres,' and I thought, ' O that there [had] been a little of this feeling thirty-four years ago ! '

Newman had good reason to be annoyed at what had happened, and his reply to Pusey gives full expression to his feelings. He pointed out how unnatural and ungrateful his conduct would have been had he refused an offer so full of generosity and confidence, which wiped away for ever the stigma of thirty years' suspicion and misrepresentation. Pusey could only explain that he would not have written as he did had he not supposed himself to be falling in with Newman's own deliberate choice as expressed in the paragraph in the *Times*. 'I supposed you had a hidden reason for it, and thought that it was the sequel of "I have been honoured and obeyed" [1].'

This correspondence gave rise to the report that Pusey had written to Newman most earnestly begging him to refuse the offer of a Cardinal's hat : this misstatement he contradicted in a letter to Father Belancy, dated May 20, 1879, which was afterwards published in the *Weekly Register*.

During the later years of Pusey's life, there was hardly any work in which he was more deeply interested than in the affairs of the Convalescent Hospital at Ascot, to which allusion has been already made. This Hospital was a branch of the work of the Devonport Sisterhood : it was established by Miss Sellon as a private Hospital for convalescents from London, and had done much good work. The Sisters who were at work in the back streets of the East End had no difficulty in finding many who sorely needed the fresh air and good food which could be had at Ascot. After Miss Sellon's death at the end of 1876, Pusey took the affairs of the hospital to a great extent into his own hands. Many anxieties crippled the institution : Pusey threw himself into every, even the smallest, detail as if he had no other work to do. He used to spend the Long Vacation in a small house near

---

[1] 'Lyra Apostolica,' No. xix. 'Obscurity,' written by Newman.
> 'I have been honoured and obeyed,
> I have met scorn and slight ;
> And my heart loves earth's sober shade,
> More than her laughing light.'

the Hospital called 'the Hermitage.' A visitor describes his life there in the summer of 1877 :—

'I went to stay at Ascot in July, but he was still quite an invalid, and he used to sit on the heath for a long time most days, never tired of talking of his hopes and plans for Ascot. He seemed very happy that summer. . . . He was scarcely indoors from morning to night; he used to bring his writing out. He was pleased at many taking an interest in Ascot, and looked forward to a grand future for it. . . .

'He spent a great deal in planting trees on each side of the drive up to the Priory door, because he said he thought they would make the place more attractive to Novices. Else he had the greatest dislike to anything being touched which possessed for him associations with the past. He used to tell me of the pain it was to him when his brother made what were thought improvements at Pusey, and of how he used to get up at night and look out of the window because the horizon looked the same as when he was a boy and the darkness hid the changes. One day I asked him if some Deodaras in a clump at Ascot were not crowding each other, and he said " No," that he had planted them so on purpose, one in the middle and three or four round it, because it had been done at Pusey, and the whole had grown into what looked like one huge tree.'

He was most anxious to put this work on a sound financial basis. 'It is a pity,' he says, 'that this beautiful air should be wasted.' A large annual subscription had been withdrawn, and a heavy mortgage had to be paid off. He exerted himself to obtain assistance to meet this need, and was most deeply touched by the affectionate act of some personal friends who collected £2,000 for the Hospital and presented it to him as a 'memorial of love.' He himself sought also to enlist sympathy with the work on all sides: influential names were obtained to form a committee, including the Earls of Devon, Carnarvon, and Glasgow, Sir William Gull, Dr. Acland, and Dr. Sutton; Dr. Mackarness also, the Bishop of Oxford, after some hesitation and a personal visit of inspection, heartily consented to be Visitor. The greatest happiness of all was when Mr. Wood undertook to ask the Princess of Wales to be a Patroness, and she graciously consented. The following letter of thanks to him gives some details of the life there :—

E. B. P. TO THE HON. C. L. WOOD.

South Hermitage, Ascot Priory, Bracknell, Aug. 1, 1879.

It is indeed a bright dawn, after the struggles in which you have, under God, been our helper. It has been an anxious time, in which a Hospital, which had so long been a Private Hospital (except in great emergencies, like that visitation of the smallpox), which had sought no friends except among the poor, the maxim of whose foundress was 'Don't boast,' had all at once to make its way, amid the thousand claims which are now crying for help.

What it wanted especially was some names, in which those who had means might have confidence. Other Societies have their long lists of Patrons and Patronesses. They have their connexion amid the rich and the great. This convalescent hospital is away from all in this wonderful air of heath and pine, but doing its quiet work unobserved and unnoticed, save by Him for Whom it is done.

Its range of relief is of necessity small, for it has but forty beds as yet, though with large capacities, yet what is done is, by God's blessing upon the wonderful air and the care, done solidly. . . . It is a bright place to live and work in, everybody looks happy. From my own 'Hermitage' I can see them walking in twos or threes. The young women become friends after being here a little while. There must be so much thanksgiving to God and increased love of Him; and though Religion is not forced on them, they are glad to hear about God.

But the characteristic of the hospital, as I said before, is that 'the Sisters of Charity' working in the East of London can find those whom none else can find; sometimes they hear from a parish doctor that 'the only hope of recovery is going for a few weeks into the country'; sometimes the eyes of a Sister, quickened by long practice, sees the necessity, and can anticipate the coming illness.

It would gladden Her Royal Highness's heart if she could see as I do, while recruiting here, the joyous happiness here, and that in contrast with the close unhealthy air in which they pass their days in London. But one must observe them when one's self is unobserved to see the ever-varying brightness, ever forming new combinations, like the toy of my boyhood, a kaleidoscope, or like the ever-varying hues of a summer evening.

God bless you and yours;—and Her Royal Highness, whom I hope to remember the more, where we all remember her and hers.

# CHAPTER XVI.

DR. FARRAR'S 'ETERNAL HOPE'—PHILIP PUSEY'S DEATH
—REPLY TO DR. FARRAR.

1879-1881.

In November, 1864, Pusey had preached a sermon
before the University in defence of the doctrine of Everlasting Punishment, which was impugned by the Judgment
of the Privy Council in the 'Essays and Reviews' case.  It
was of course earnest and impressive, but expressed in
carefully measured terms throughout; the argument was
based on the nature of sin, of God's judgments, and of
the eternal world, as well as on the express words of our
Lord; and it concluded with a wistful exhortation to each
of his undergraduate hearers, 'My son . . . listen not to
those who repeat to you the tempter's words, "Thou shalt
not die."'

In 1877 the Rev. F. W. Farrar, Canon of Westminster,
preached a course of Sermons, which he published under
the title of 'Eternal Hope.'  These Sermons contained
a passionate attack upon 'the common belief in hell';
and whatever were the intentions of the preacher or the
exact force of his language, his words were commonly
understood to include in one sweeping denunciation every
form of belief in Everlasting Punishment.  When a preacher
of such high position in the Church, and great reputation
for learning, and undoubted rhetorical ability, threw in his

weight on this always popular side, it was no wonder that his words were caught up with ready acquiescence, and obtained a wide circulation.

Pusey felt himself called upon to write an answer to this teaching : not only because of the harm that he found was being done to souls on all sides, but also because of a special challenge to himself which was contained in them. In an excursus at the end of the volume which contained these sermons he was made to appear as a teacher of doctrine so awful that Dr. Farrar could say, ' I would here, and now, and kneeling on my knees, ask God that I might die as the beasts that perish, and for ever cease to be, rather than that my worst enemy should endure the hell described by . . . Dr. Pusey[1] . . . for one single year.'

In the winter of 1878 Pusey began to prepare his answer. ' I am shut up,' he wrote to Newman, ' if one is to call it being shut up, to be enclosed in the magnificent walls in which I have lived nearly one-seventh of the time which has passed since Cardinal Wolsey built them. It is strange to be exempt from all the sufferings which this cold inflicts on the poor ; my comfort is that I could not work for God otherwise.' Then he went on to ask Newman many questions about the ' terrible subject,' as he calls it, apologizing for saddening Christmas by writing about it at all. Shortly afterwards also, writing to Dr. Bright, he alluded to Dr. Farrar's book and its numerous inaccuracies of statement, saying that a ' solid answer ' would be very valuable.

His letters give glimpses of his work on this subject from time to time. He devoted to it a large portion of the Long Vacation of 1879 at Ascot. The Rev. J. Skinner, the chaplain of the Hospital, who was Pusey's nearest neighbour there, wrote of him at this time[2] :—

'August 1, 1879.

. . . ' The dear doctor comes to me and I to him. . . . He is all sweetness and love, and I never saw him more vigorous in mind, nor

---

[1] The reference may have been, in part, to a parochial sermon in 1856, which was never published because of its sternness.

[2] 'Memoir of James Skinner,' p. 352.

do I find him so deaf as last year. He is very keen just now on an
answer he is preparing to Farrar. . . . No one seems able to hold up
against the atmospheric troubles, except the dearest old E. B. P., who
is perfectly well and works all day.'

During this summer he spent a long time, so he tells
Liddon, in the minute investigation of what Dr. Farrar
called his 'palmary argument,' namely the assertion that
the Jews of our Lord's day did not use the word 'Gehenna'
in the sense of everlasting punishment; and he came to
the conclusion that the argument from the Jewish writers
at the commencement of the Christian era went entirely in
the opposite direction to that which Dr. Farrar supposed.
In such an inquiry Pusey was on ground peculiarly his
own. One of the greatest living authorities on Rabbinical
writing is reported to have said that the only two Christians
of this century who thoroughly understood Rabbinical
literature were Delitzsch and Pusey.

But the work was repeatedly delayed by weak health
and heavy correspondence, or rather, as he described it,
'God sent him other things to do.' And there was yet
another message on its way. On January 5, 1880, he
returned to Christ Church from Ascot, and nine days later
his only son was suddenly taken from him. For the last
twenty-five years, since the marriage of his youngest
daughter, Mrs. Brine, Pusey's son, Philip, had been the
only member of his family to share with him 'the large
house, once so full' at Christ Church. His continued
illnesses had brought the once healthy active child to
a physical condition which was a perpetual trial of fortitude
and patience: besides other infirmities, he was deaf and
a cripple, and was thus excluded from a large portion of
ordinary life. But he inherited from his father indomitable
energy, deep religious earnestness and singleness of eye, and
had learnt from him entire self-devotion to the cause of
the Church. He took his degree in 1854, having obtained
Second Class Mathematical Honours, both in Moderations
and in the Class List of the Final School. To his great
regret, his bodily infirmities compelled him to forego his

life-long hope of being ordained ; he therefore gave himself
up to theological study, so that he might be of as much
help as possible to his father. As was most truly said
of him in a review of one of his books [1] :—

'Piety, in the most comprehensive sense, was indeed the motive
power of Philip Pusey's life, and the source of all his strength, active
and passive. In him the Fifth Commandment was linked most closely
to the First. The profound adoring earnestness with which he would
mentally follow the Cathedral services of which he could not distinctly
hear a word, was of a piece with the beautiful devotedness which
made him accept absolutely his father's directions as to the line in
which he was to work for Him, Whom, in the notes to his volume, he
repeatedly calls "our Master".'

The special tasks that he undertook at his father's
suggestion, 'in his uniform filial love,' were a critical
edition of what Pusey called 'that much undervalued
critical authority, the Peshito,' and a carefully revised edition
of the works of St. Cyril of Alexandria, with an English
translation of them for the Oxford Library of the Fathers.
In this work, with rare self-devotion and true scholarly
thoroughness, he compelled his weak deformed body to
labours which many an able-bodied student would have
declined. In the hope of discovering and collating manuscripts, he had visited libraries in France, Spain, Italy,
Germany, Russia, Mount Athos (of the nineteen monasteries
on Mount Athos he visited all in which he had any reason to
expect to find Greek manuscripts), Cairo, and Mount Sinai,
and had thus formed the completest collection extant of the
fragments of St. Cyril. These he had already published with
expressions of heartfelt gratitude to God for His continued
protection and preservation. At this time he considered
that he had still fifteen years' work before him, if his life
should be spared so long. But, to use his father's words
at the end of the preface to his translation of St. Cyril's
treatises on the Incarnation, 'Almighty God was pleased
to break off the work "in the midst of the years."' On the
morning of Jan. 15, 1880, Liddon received the following
note :—

[1] *Church Quarterly Review*, xxx. p. 258.

Jan. 15, 1880.

Your loving heart will grieve that it has pleased God to take my son. Yesterday he was doing things as usual for me : went to the Bodleian to get a book for me. After a cheerful evening and being at family prayers, he went upstairs. A fit of apoplexy was God's messenger ; and about 3 he was on his way to the Judgment-seat of Christ. You will pray for him. I was there, but he could not hear a sound.

Under the shock of the loss and the exhaustion caused by the strain of watching at the side of the death-bed in the long hours of that night, Pusey's feeble health entirely gave way, and for three days Dr. Acland thought that he would have been buried in the same grave with his son. On the next Sunday, in a sermon at Christ Church, Dean Liddell touchingly alluded to this heavy sorrow in the following words :—

'While I am writing this, tidings reach me of the sudden death of the only son of our oldest and most honoured Canon. Most of you must have seen that small emaciated form, swinging itself through the quadrangle, up the steps, 'or along the street, with such energy and activity as might surprise healthy men. But few of you could know what gentleness and what courage dwelt in that frail tenement. . . . In pursuing his studies, whenever it was necessary to consult manuscripts at a distance, he shrank from no journey, however toilsome. Everywhere on those journeys he won hearts by his simple, engaging manner, combined with his helplessness and his bravery. He was known in Spain, and Turkey, and Russia : at Paris, or Madrid, or Moscow, the impression was the same. The first question put by the monks of Mount Athos to their next Oxford visitor, was significant, " And how is Philippos ? " One might speak of the pleasant smile with which he greeted his friends, his brave cheerfulness under lifelong suffering, and what seemed in him an absolute incapacity of complaining— his delight in children, the sure sign of an innocent and happy temper—his awe and reverence for Almighty God, and constant desire to serve and please Him. When it was brought home to him that his infirmities disabled him from taking Holy Orders, as he had desired to do, he only said, that his wish then was to do what he might be able for God's service at any time and in any way. To such a one, death could have no terror : death could not find him unprepared. . . . I need not say how many prayers have been and are breathed that God Almighty and our Lord Jesus Christ would comfort the bereaved and honoured father, who, just forty years ago, saw her who was truly the half of his being interred beneath the pavement of this church, and will now have to see his only son carried to the grave before him. . . . God will comfort him, we trust; God has comforted him, we know.'

The Funeral was on the 20th of January. Through the great kindness of the Dean of Christ Church, the body was laid in the small graveyard on the south side of the Cathedral; the Burial Service was said by Dr. King. It was nearly the end of the month before Pusey had sufficiently recovered to ask where the grave was and for some particulars of the funeral. During these days Liddon was almost the only visitor. Pusey's talk was at first entirely about Philip's life of conformity to the Will of God and devoted work for the Church in the only way that lay open to him when Ordination was found to be impossible. As for his own illness, he expressed a hope that it was not caused by any want of conformity to God's will in taking his son, but that it was only natural in such a case.

His strength very slowly came back, and he resumed his answer to Dr. Farrar as soon as possible. But the loss of Philip was indeed very great, although his grandson, the Rev. J. E. B. Brine, came to be his companion in his large empty house at Christ Church. 'I am returning,' he wrote to Mr. Wood, 'to my work again. Life is changed for the last time. I thank God that He has retained to me such a son for nearly fifty years.'

At last, in June, eighteen months after he had commenced his work, he was able to announce its completion.

E. B. P. TO REV. R. F. WILSON.

Christ Church, June 26, 1880.

. . . I have finished at last my little answer to Dr. Farrar's challenge. It has been hard work and will be very dry. The old [original] plan was to make a Catena of Fathers and to put the proofs together that Origenism was condemned by the Fifth General Council. So it is an odd mish-mash. I have tried to answer Dr. Farrar sentence by sentence and hint by hint. I would not leave one out nor conceal it. . . . I hope that I have not made many slips. But after my illness, I had to work against time.

The reply is a book[1] of nearly three hundred pages, the last book of any size which came from his pen, and one of the most well-timed and powerful. It is characterized by the minute accuracy and richness of detail that mark all his work. There is no sign of failure of eye or diminution of spiritual force: rather it might be said that in grasp of the full meaning of the position, in cogency of argument and clearness of statement, it equals and perhaps surpasses anything he ever wrote.

The body of the book is the direct answer to Dr. Farrar. In it, he first sets forth the wide difference between what Dr. Farrar had called 'the common opinions respecting hell' and the belief of the Church on the subject. According to Dr. Farrar, the 'common opinions' included the belief that 'the majority of mankind will incur everlasting punishment and are doomed to it by absolute predestination'; this Pusey showed is the teaching of Calvin and unwarranted by Scripture. The assertion that the 'fire' of hell is 'material' fire is by no means an essential part of the Church's interpretation of our Lord's words, and to maintain that 'the vast mass of mankind die in a state of sin' implies that we know a great deal more about the secret things of God than is the case. In the following twelve propositions he sums up the arguments which to his mind showed that the Revelation of Everlasting Punishment is the correlative of the fact of human freewill :—

1. Without freewill, man would be inferior to the lower animals, which have a sort of limited freedom of choice.

2. Absolute freewill implies the power of choosing amiss and, having chosen amiss, to persevere in choosing amiss. It would be self-contradictory that Almighty God should create a free agent capable of loving Him, without being capable also of rejecting His love.

3. The higher and more complete and pervading the freewill is, the more completely an evil choice will pervade and disorder the whole being.

[1] 'What is of Faith as to Everlasting Punishment? in reply to Dr. Farrar's challenge in his " Eternal Hope," 1879.' By Rev. E. B. Pusey, D.D. 1880.

4. But without freewill we could not freely love God. Freedom is a condition of love.

5. In eternity those who behold Him will know what the bliss is, eternally to love Him. But then that bliss involves the intolerable misery of losing Him through our own evil choice. To lose God and be alienated from Him is in itself Hell, or the vestibule of Hell.

6. But that His creatures may not lose Him, God, when He created all His rational creatures with freewill, created them also in grace, so that they had the full power to choose aright, and could not choose amiss, except by resisting the drawing of God to love Him.

7. The only hindrance to man's salvation is, in any case, the obstinate misuse of that freewill, with which God endowed him, in order that he might freely love Him.

8. God wills that all should be saved, if they *will* it, and to this end gave His Son to die for them, and the Holy Ghost to teach them.

9. The merits of Jesus reach to every soul who wills to be saved, whether in this life they knew Him or knew Him not.

10. God the Holy Ghost visits every soul which God has created, and each soul will be judged as it responded or did not respond to the degree of light which He bestowed on it, not by our maxims, but by the wisdom and love of Almighty God.

11. We know absolutely nothing of the proportion of the saved to the lost, or who will be lost; but this we *do* know, that none will be lost, who do not obstinately to the end and in the end refuse God. None will be lost, whom God *can* save, without destroying in them His own gift of freewill.

12. With regard to the *nature* of the sufferings, nothing is matter of faith. No one doubts that the very special suffering will be the loss of God (poena damni): that, being what they are, they know that they were made by God for Himself, and yet, through their own obstinate will, will not have Him. As to 'pains of sense' the Church has nowhere laid down as a matter of faith, the material character of the worm and the fire, or that they denote more than the gnawing of remorse. Although then it would be very rash to lay down dogmatically, that the 'fire' is *not* to be understood literally, as it has been understood almost universally by Christians; yet no one has a right to urge those representations, from which the imagination so shrinks, as a ground for refusing to believe in Hell, since he is left free not to believe them.

Passing to the discussion of the word αἰώνιος, and of the Jewish belief in Gehenna, on which great stress had been laid, he maintains by means of lengthy quotations that there is no trace of any doubt among the Jews of our Lord's day that punishment would be eternal for those who incurred it, that is, for those 'who to the end would

not have God as their God.' The main argument concludes
with some striking thoughts about the state of the departed
which seem to have been suggested by the recent passing
away of so many of his friends. The discussion of the doctrine of Eternal Punishment seemed to him likely to bring
out into far greater prominence the value of a right belief
in the intermediate state, the comfort of believing in some
purifying process after death, the happiness of that opportunity of preparing for the final Beatific Vision, and the
value of prayer for the departed. In the following passage
he briefly states his own 'hope' as regards the eternal
world, for himself and for those whom he loved :—

'Our own consciences may tell us that, our repentance for our sins
having been very imperfect, and our own longings for the sight of
God, amid this whirl of duties and religious interests, such as we do
not like to think of, we are not fit to behold Him. This, perhaps, more
than the direct dread of hell, is the source of the fear of death to
many. They trust in God's mercy in Christ, that they shall be saved ;
but they feel themselves unfit to enter into His Presence. To be
admitted into any vestibule of His Presence,—where they can sin
no more, and, by longing for that Beatific Vision, may be ever freed
from the. slough which has clung to them in this life—this is not too
high for their hopes ; the thought of this unspeakably allays their fears.

'So, as to others also, instead of being haunted with the thought
as to some one loved as one's self, "Was he saved?" and longing
that God would in some way reveal to us that he *was* saved, we may
commend our departed ones to their Father's care, sure that if they
have not, by an obstinate rejection of Him to the last, shut out His
grace and love, they are, in whatever mansion of His, still under the
shadow of His Hand, longing for their consummation both of body
and soul, and prepared and perfected the more by that intense
longing [1].'

The rest of the book is an Appendix containing the
proofs that Universalism was condemned at the Fifth
General Council, and that the early Church undoubtedly
could not be claimed on the side of the novel negative
teaching.

Pusey felt more misgivings as to the effects of this book
than of any other that he ever wrote : but he was relieved by
numerous letters expressing the warmest gratitude. The

[1] ' What is of Faith as to Everlasting Punishment ?' pp. 121, 122.

correspondence showed how great the anxiety of Churchmen was, and how necessary it was to expose the crude
assumptions and the current misrepresentations of the
Church's teaching, which had combined to recommend
Universalism to so many minds. The book is marked by
simple loyalty to Revelation, and anxious longing to save
souls, and the earnest refusal of false teaching and all that
could endanger souls; but it exhibits. more than any writing
of his early years, the true character of an apologetic work.
Its pages show that he is able to combine a very clear
knowledge of the sin of man and of the love of God with
the most vivid realization of the awfulness of the Judgment-seat of Christ; and that he can state truths which
rouse the very deepest feelings with fearless sincerity, and
yet with a recollectedness and self-restraint which measures
every word.

As soon as the book appeared, Dr. Farrar wrote to the
*Guardian* expressing his agreement with its conclusions on
almost every point.

E. B. P. TO THE REV. F. W. FARRAR.

South Hermitage, Ascot Priory, Bracknell, July 30, 1880.

I beg to thank you for the courtesy and kindness with which you
have spoken of me in your letter to the *Guardian* [1], so far beyond what
I deserve.

On two points you have thought that I was expressing my own
personal belief when I did not mean to say anything of it. My object
was to remove hindrances to the belief in God's awful judgments.
I had no occasion to speak of myself. But as you have spoken of my
faith, let me say

1. I was glad to be able to urge, after Divines of undisputed authority,
that the belief that there are 'pains of sense' in Hell is not essential
to the belief in Hell itself, so that those, who have a strong feeling
against the belief in them, need not, on that account, disbelieve
Hell itself. There was no occasion to say, that I do myself believe
that there will be 'pains of sense,' although unutterably less than the
'pain of the loss' of God. So I said nothing about myself: but it
seems to me to have been the Christian belief from the first, and
so I believe it.

2. I do strongly hope that the great mass of mankind will be saved,
all whom God could save without destroying their free-agency. He

_____
[1] *Guardian* of July 28, 1880, p. 1000.

does not draw us like stocks and stones, but as beings whom He has endowed with the power freely to love Him. But since God has only spoken of His Will to save us, and has not said whether mankind will accept that Will for them I could have no *belief* on the subject. I left it blindly in the Hands of God (p. 281).

If I had had time, I would have rewritten my book, and would have said, 'You seem to me to deny nothing which I believe. You do not deny the eternal punishment of "souls obstinately hard and finally impenitent." I believe the eternal punishment of no other. Who they are, God alone knows.' I should have been glad to begin with what we believe in common, and so to say, There is no need then to theorize about a new trial.

But I heard, on different sides, that the absence of any answer to your book was perplexing people's minds or destroying their belief in Hell. The answer to what you called your 'palmary argument' about the belief of the Jews in our Lord's time belonged to my office as Hebrew Professor. Very much time had been lost through my different illnesses. So I dared not delay any longer, and was obliged to leave my book in a shape which I regretted, as a personal answer to yourself, instead of simply removing the objections against belief, which the Church (I wished to show) inherited from our Lord.

Dr. Farrar replied, expressing his agreement with Pusey excepting only on one point :—

REV. F. W. FARRAR TO E. B. P.

July 31, 1880.

I am much obliged to you for your kind letter. My own letter to the *Guardian* was only the sincere expression of my respect and esteem, and also of the deep gratitude with which I find that my views are not so widely opposed to those of Churchmen like yourself, as some have angrily asserted. Your twelve theses I accept unreservedly. My main divergence from the view commonly supposed to be the sole orthodox one, lies in this point—that whereas you and others hold that God may reach many souls, as He reached the soul of the penitent malefactor, in the hour of death, I have rather believed that the moment of death was not necessarily, and for all, the final irreversible moment of determination respecting the endless years beyond. I do not think that I have ever dwelt on the conception of a new 'probation'; and I am perfectly willing to substitute for it the conception of a future 'purification' for those who have not utterly extinguished the Grace of God in their hearts, if that be the more Catholic view.

Of course there are points of criticism, detail, and exegesis on which I must examine with some care the powerful arguments which you have brought forward, especially as to the view of 'Gehenna' in our Lord's day. Whether I shall have leisure for this, I do not know; for it has pleased God to give me a life burdened with so many daily cares and occupations that I have never had any leisure for the thoroughness of exhaustive research at which, by His aid, I should otherwise aim. But meanwhile I am very sure that your statement of what is NOT *de fide* on this solemn and awful subject, will bring comfort to thousands who have been taught from childhood that they are bound to believe a far more merciless set of opinions than those which you maintain are solely essential to Christian faith on this subject.

With a view to Dr. Farrar's reply, Pusey thought it good to direct his attention to the main errors of his book.

E. B. P. TO THE REV. F. W. FARRAR.

South Hermitage, Ascot Priory, Bracknell, Aug. 3 [1880].

It is a great relief to me that you can substitute the conception of a future purification for those who have not utterly extinguished the grace of God in their hearts. This, I think, would put you in harmony with the whole of Christendom.

Forgive me, but I think that in your eagerness to overthrow the narrow (I suppose, Calvinistic) opinions in which you were educated, you took up the arguments which came to hand without weighing them. I wish that you had not written in such haste. Apart from the question of R. Akiba's Jewish Gehenna having been subsequent to the time of our Lord, you did not observe that a Gehenna of at most twelve months is entirely at variance with any meaning which could be attached to the word αἰώνιος, and which you yourself attach to it. Then, also, I think, that you did not observe that the passages of Holy Scripture, which you alleged were all Universalist [1], included Satan, whose case you wished to leave on one side, or were nothing. Indeed, the aeonian fire, if a purifying fire, would, according to our Blessed Lord's words (St. Matt. xxv. 41), have been expressly created for Satan and his angels to save them. I think too that you have fixed your eyes exclusively on the one side of the question, the exceptions which you thought could be found, and did not take time to think, on Whose word the awful doctrine, as believed by the incomparably larger body of Christians, rested. We have got so into the habit of bandying about arguments as to the meaning of the word αἰώνιος, that we lose sight, for the time, Whose word it is. If our Lord had been a mere human teacher, it would have been a great mistake to use a word which His disciples would for the most part take, if so be, in a wrong sense. A Socinian would find no difficulty in this: but for us who believe our Lord to have been God, it would be inconceivable. I neglected this argument in my book [2]. As you have borne so kindly with all which I had said before, I venture to send you the pages of the second edition in which I have urged this (pp. 46, 48).

---

[1] I. e. suggestive, *taken by themselves*, of the Universalist conclusion.
[2] I. e. in the *first* edition.

I did not send you the book in the first instance, because I thought it would be provocative. I published it, thinking it a dry book, to do whatever God might employ it for.

Newman acknowledged a copy of the book in the following letter.

CARDINAL NEWMAN TO E. B. P.

The Oratory, Aug. 4, 1880.

I have been writing to you every day to thank you for your volume. It is, as all you do, thorough in its research, and sure to be useful to docile and humble minds, and those, I trust, are many. Your arguments, as addressed to them, are strong. For these I conceive the book is adapted and intended.

There are intellectual men, thoughtful, earnest, self-relying, for whom I conceive it is not intended. 'Nothing can make me believe it—it is against my nature. What is a score of Fathers to me? What is a dozen generations? I rather believe St. Matthew wrong than such a doctrine true.'

Thank you for making use of me once and again. I wish one could do something to make the doctrine less terrible to so many minds; but its being terrible is its very profit.

In spite of many reassuring answers Pusey was still afraid that he might be misunderstood, and that some readers might interpret his language about Purification so as to justify moral indifference, or diminish the fear of the Hell of the lost. He expresses these fears to the Warden of Keble College.

E. B. P. TO THE WARDEN OF KEBLE COLLEGE.

South Hermitage, Ascot, August 12, 1880.

. . . I must correct in some note to the third edition of my book (which I am expecting) two statements of Dr. Farrar: 1. that I believe that the worm and the fire are figurative. I myself believe the fire is *poena sensus* (the belief is so uniform, from St. Polycarp downwards). I only say that those who do not, need not think that on that account they disbelieve hell, since they are not bound to believe it.

2. I say nothing about the proportion of the saved and the lost, except that we *know* nothing about it.

I enclose a sheet of the second edition, which I hope will have more effect than all besides. Some will say, 'I'd rather think St. Matthew wrong than believe such a doctrine,' who would yet shrink from rejecting the doctrine, if they saw that that rejection involved that our Blessed Lord did not foresee the effect of His own words.

I suppose that this generation has been wiser than Almighty God, that whereas He used those two most powerful motives, love and fear—fear to drive us back to His love—we have thought that we could do His work with one only.

I was so busy in answering Dr. Farrar's book, step by step, that I myself omitted to ask, 'What do those who disbelieve Eternal Punishment think that God became Man for?' Eternal Punishment and the Incarnation cast light upon each other. God did not, we must think, become Man to remedy a passing evil.

Our Lord says, 'In My Father's house there are many mansions.' As Cardinal Newman said, 'There are (almost) infinite degrees of holiness and nearness to God.' Only not infinite because number (and so the numbers of our race) is finite. Whatever mansion the Aztecs may be placed in, or those who never heard of the love of Jesus, it does not follow that they will be placed in the same mansion as the Seraphim, or those who have most grown in that love. But those who have 'resisted law or power or a high ideal' resist also the workings of God the Holy Ghost, and would probably resist His working by an appeal through His love. How for centuries was the Cross the special scandal of the heathen! 'Him, you mean, who was crucified?' was their taunt. The Jews still have a special hatred of the Cross.

Must we not suppose that very many who disbelieved Noah's preaching, and so went on marrying and giving in marriage till the Flood came, may still have repented, so as to escape the eternal punishment, though too late to escape the temporal? These (I have supposed) were they who were kept in ward for those millennia until our Lord went to announce to them their deliverance.

I think that it is generally supposed that Sodom in Ezekiel is a symbolic name, though it is not agreed for what, but that it relates to some future conversion on this earth.

It seems a very prosaic explanation of our Lord's words, 'it would have remained unto this day,' of a partial conversion of these cities. Yet they seem to me to refer back to God's saying to Abraham, that He would spare it, if even ten righteous should be found in it. It would have remained; for that temporal judgment would not have fallen upon it.

The next year Dr. Farrar issued a reply entitled ' Mercy and Judgment.' Pusey did not think it good to write again : he did not desire a controversial victory : he had already stated the truth as he held it. As he often said, he greatly disliked arguments of the ' I said,' ' you said,' ' I meant.' ' you suggested ' order. Statements of this kind had to do with personal matters, he thought, not with the assertion of the truth.

July 10, 1881.

I would not disturb your short holiday about Dr. Farrar. So I told him I should write for advice from one whose opinion I valued; that, at almost eighty-one, I must concentrate what I would do for God; that I had written what I wrote because, although he declared himself not to be an Universalist, his arguments, I thought, were, and were used as an encouragement in sinful living. but that there was no good in a see-saw, and that I should not read his book unless advised. I said, too, that I had been advised to leave Mr. Oxenham's book alone, and meant to leave it. . . . As Dr. Farrar claimed to believe what I believe, I just began looking at his summary, but I did not see anything more definite than before, so I left it.

The reply to Dr. Farrar was Pusey's last great public contribution to the defence of the Faith. The battle with unbelief in Oxford and elsewhere was frequently the subject of his later letters and of his private conversations. Two such letters to one of his oldest surviving friends in the University are here given, as representing his way of regarding the struggle in his latest days.

E. B. P. to Professor (now Sir H. W.) Acland.

Nov. 1879.

As for this place I trust that things are at their worst now. I have given up struggles which I once made; the battle as to all outward things is lost. Well, then we are in the state of which Zechariah was told 'Jerusalem shall be inhabited as towns without walls, for I, saith the Lord, will be unto her a wall of fire round about her, and the glory in the midst of her.'

There never was so much unbelief as now. I dread the compromisers much more than the antagonists. But there is also a rising set of men who have hearts on fire, and will do much, please God. So I leave people to go their own way, and I quote the words

'I do the little I can do
And leave the rest to Thee.'

So I am in good heart and we may the more work God's Will,—the more because we cannot work our own.

[1880.]

Your last words to-day were that there were 'very great difficulties.' I see but one, insoluble in this life, 'Why did God create us?' Why did God will to create beings with free wills to accept or reject Him? All the evils and difficulties around one, in time and in eternity, are from man's free agency. I can only look on the bright side of the question—How God must love us and our free love that He should create us for His love, notwithstanding all the miserable consequences of rejecting Him.

As for doctrines about which people tormented themselves last century,—as the Being of God, Three Persons in One God,—they, to me, remove difficulties. To me the abstract Deity of the Deists or Theists, existing isolated, in a dreary solitude, would be absolutely unintelligible. We cannot of course understand Three in One. But we can understand Eternal Infinite Love, which God the Father is, loving eternally the Co-eternal Son, Who is Love Infinite, in the Holy Ghost, Each inexisting in Each. We cannot understand here why God endowed us with a free will like His own ; that He has made us free, as He is free ; that He will not force our will which is the finite image of His own ; that He, so to say, respects it, even while, through sorrow or through joy, or through the aching of the heart, He teaches us that He made our soul for Himself, and that nothing but Himself can content it.

This is a wonderful picture. The soul in its unfettered free will (not a stick or stone, to be dragged) whom God, in each man, woman, child, cares for, loves, and would draw to Himself, even if in this life it knows Him not, yet feels after Him.

> O then, Sursum corda, Sursum corda.
> Lift your faces to the skies
> God Himself shall be your prize.

The source of all the unbelief, misbelief, and half-belief around us is that the minds have not brought to themselves this conception. All [difficulties] disappear when one believes God and Jesus, and minds believe in Jesus as they know Him.

THE HERMITAGE, ASCOT PRIORY.

# CHAPTER XVII.

1880–1882.

IN his eightieth year Pusey was no longer able to take
that prominent part in public events which has caused the
record of his life to be, to a great extent, an account of the
more salient facts of the recent history of the English
Church.   But from the thick walls of Christ Church in the
winter, and from the pine woods of Ascot in the summer,
he still watched what was going on, and, so far as his
health permitted, gave advice and encouragement to those
dear friends who in their turn were now fighting the good
fight.   This result of advancing years has necessitated
a corresponding change in the form of the last few chapters :
a full account of the events to which they refer would have
taken the reader too far away from Pusey himself.   Still
more in the two years that remain, his letters must be
given with only enough introduction to make them
intelligible.

The Public Worship Regulation Act of 1874 had been
designed to exterminate the Ritualists: but Mordecai is

not always hanged on the gallows which Haman erects
for him. The ruthless application of this measure tended
insensibly, as Pusey had always predicted, towards the
toleration of that Ritual which it was intended to destroy.
The 'Church Association' had mercilessly used its summary
methods to enforce an inaccurate interpretation of the
Rubrics, and consequently at the end of 1879 Mr. Mackonochie was under a sentence of suspension, and three
other clergymen were on the way to prison for refusing
to disobey the grammatical meaning of the Prayer-book.
Public opinion began to regard this state of things as
intolerable, and the High Church party was consolidated
by such persecution, more thoroughly than they had ever
been since the early days of the Ritual movement. In
Advent, 1879, Pusey, while the persecution was at its
height, was urged to issue an address to the English
Church Union : he took the opportunity of giving them
the counsels most needful for the persecuted and irritated ;
—warning them to distinguish between a mere partisan zeal
for a good cause and a sincere love of God Himself, and
bidding them not to be censorious towards their opponents,
or forgetful of the need of self-abasement. If they would
contend for Sacramental truth and the freedom of Confession, he told them that one of the best weapons they
could select would be careful preparation for, and thanksgiving after, the Holy Communion combined with a growth
in real penitence. The old Tractarian times were ever
vividly present to his mind, and the robust reality of those
early healthful days of stern self-discipline.

The troubles of the political world made less direct
appeal to him ; but he noted them with sorrow and
distress. Of some he writes :—

E. B. P. TO THE HON. C. L. WOOD.
April 3, 1880.

. . . What a turmoil poor England is in, and how fierce the words !
I fear that there must have been a good deal of wood, hay, stubble
built up. . . . With the politics themselves, I, of course, have nothing to
do. But people seem [either] to forget that our Lord ever said anything
about idle words, or to think that the Apostle said, 'Speak evil one of

another. brethren.' They would keep it most diligently, if he had. I often think that if the 'not' had been left out, it would have been one of the best kept of all God's commands. A very superior and self-observant spiritual daughter of mine said to me, some thirty-five years ago, 'I have changed the question which I put to myself. I used to ask myself, "*May* I say this, to the disadvantage of another?" and I *always* found a reason for it. Now I ask myself, "*Must* I say this?" and I never find a reason for it.' I only tell this as a striking rule, for it is of course a duty to keep God's commandments unless some higher duty of love makes an exception. You yourself are always oil on the waters.

Again, on being asked by the same correspondent to join in an expression of sympathy with the Church in France in her sufferings at the hand of the State, he replies:—

E. B. P. TO THE HON C. L. WOOD.

July 2, 1880.

The majority of the Vatican Council crushed me. I have not touched any book of Roman controversy since. Pope Pius IX devised and carried two new articles of faith ; and the absolute personal infallibility of the Pope, to which they sacrificed Döllinger, stands in my way, contradicting history. All other questions sink into nothing before this. Our Creeds must be reformed : 'I believe in the Pope,' instead of ' I believe the Holy Catholic Church.' I have no heart left. I could not, the other day, read some Encyclical of the present Pope because I did not know whether I was to read it as a third or a thirtieth general Epistle of St. Peter.

My only hope is that Antichrist will somehow drive the Church into one. . . .

I never read a paper. Of course the persecution of the Jesuits in France is Antichrist. It used to be said that 'St. Ignatius prayed that his Order might always be persecuted.' He thought persecution so good for it. I have verified the statement.

But the present Ultramontane Archbishop of Paris could only make an Address to him an occasion of telling us that he hoped that we should soon return to the fold. You are young and sanguine. . . .

Thirty years earlier, at a great public meeting in St. Martin's Hall, when some of his friends wished him to commit himself to some ambiguous statements in opposition to the Roman Church, Pusey had said [1] that in preference to any merely verbal anti-Roman declaration he would give one satisfactory proof of his conviction that he was already in the true Fold—a proof that would admit of

[1] Vol. iii. p. 282.

no contradiction—by dying in the bosom of the Church of England : the time for that evidence was now very near.

As the struggle about Ritual went on, Pusey threw in his lot more and more definitely with those who were being persecuted. In a letter to the *Times* in January, 1881, he expressed himself in terms of much clearer accord with them than he would have done ten years earlier. He was writing to identify himself with the Memorial which Dean Church had presented to the Archbishop of Canterbury, claiming toleration in Ritual. It was arranged that Pusey should not sign it ; his separate support it was thought would have greater weight.

E. B. P. TO THE EDITOR OF THE 'TIMES.'

Jan. 14, 1881.

. . . Whatever mistakes any of the Ritualists made formerly, no Ritualist would now, I believe, wish to make any change without the hearty goodwill of the people. But all along those who have closely observed the Ritual movement have seen that it has been especially the work of the laity. While the clergyman has been hesitating, his parishioners have often presented him with the Vestments which they wished him to wear. Mr. Enraght and Mr. Mackonochie have not been struggling for themselves but for their people. St. Alban's was built by a pious High Church layman, in what was one of the worst localities in London. It is now full of a religious population, who join intelligently in the service provided for them and love it. Agents of the Church Association tried in vain for years to find a third parishioner in the Mission at the London docks, to disturb the ritual of the priest who had won them to God, and whom, with the ritual which he had taught them, they loved—Mr. Lowder. . . .

What the Dean of St. Paul's asks for, is simply that toleration which is accorded to every one else. The toleration granted to the Broad Church is so large that it has publicly been said to be an anachronism when a clergyman parted from the Church of England because he disbelieved the Incarnation and Resurrection of our Lord. The Low Church pain many communicants by the administration of the Holy Communion to 'railfuls'; but this requires the alteration of the words with which it is given, not of a rubric only. The Ritualists do not ask to interfere with the devotions of others—only to be allowed, in their worship of God, to use a Ritual which a few years ago no one disputed, and that only when their congregations wish it. Of the Judgment which forbade it, the Lord Chief Baron Kelly said that it was 'a Judgment of policy, not of law.'

The Memorial to which the letter refers was a formal

reply of a large number of influential clergy to the question
of the Archbishop of Canterbury, 'What do you want?'
The Memorial said that peace could only be obtained by
the toleration of divergences in Ritual.    In a Letter to
Liddon, which he published early in 1881, under the title
of ' Unlaw in judgments of the Judicial Committee and its
remedies,' Pusey sketched the remedy that he would suggest.
The Letter is a valuable *résumé* of the history of the High
Church party in their struggles in the courts of law.    In
a review of all the cases since 1850, he shows that his
friends had been in a state of continuous protest against
the Final Court of Appeal, and that there could be no
peace until that Court was reformed, the moderate ritual
of our Prayer-book tolerated. and the indefensible decisions
in the Purchas and Ridsdale cases superseded.    This
pamphlet is not only his last, but also one of his most
effective utterances on the subject : he himself was well
aware that his opponents would find difficulty in dealing
with its statements ; he described it as ' something like
a hedgehog.'

Pusey sent a copy of this Letter on ' Unlaw ' to
Mr. Gladstone among other friends.    In reply, Mr. Gladstone informed him confidentially that it had been arranged
that the Archbishop should apply for a Royal Commission
to inquire into the whole of the troubled question about
Ecclesiastical Courts.    He added that in the correspondence
on this proposal. he had noticed a most conciliatory spirit
on the part of the Archbishop, and that his whole tone,
judging from a recent Charge and private conversation and
conference, seemed entirely changed.    Mr. Gladstone further
assured Pusey that he was convinced that the Archbishop
was now honestly bent on a work of peace in the Church ;
' When I think of the days of the Public Worship Regulation Act,' he added, ' I can hardly believe him to be the
same man.'    Pusey sent on the note to Liddon ; it seemed
an answer to all his prayers for peace for so many years,
but he was unable in this case, as in many others, to
understand why the Archbishop had been so slow to see

the strength of the position of those whom he had so doggedly opposed.

Soon after this, on July 18, 1881, Dr. Stanley, the Dean of Westminster, passed away. Throughout all his active life he had been the most ardent and consistent champion of the Broad Church party. His conception of the nature of the Church of Christ and its doctrine, and of the true policy for the Church in England, was in direct contradiction to all that Pusey held to be most vital. Every one must have felt the charm of his high character and personal attractiveness, even when they most disagreed with him. But the differences which separated him from the High Church party were wide and fundamental; they were, in fact, bound up with the very first principles of Religion. It is necessary to keep this in mind when seeking to estimate the attitude which Pusey adopted towards him, as for instance in the controversy described in the earlier part of this volume. His words may often seem stern, and even wanting in Christian charity. But the questions at stake could never be to him mere academical points to be discussed, they were vital truths to be maintained; truths moreover, which each in his several way was bound to defend at all costs, and for which they must severally give account before the bar of a Just Judge, Who knows no respect of persons. It may well be, that as he now reflected on the life of his brother Canon, whose career had been suddenly arrested, and recalled their common life, as members of the same Chapter, and the frequent controversies which had separated them on matters of the deepest importance, he would cast about for some hidden causes, which all unconsciously might have turned that brilliant intellect into those channels which seemed to him so divergent from the Faith, and set himself to think whether in any way he himself was to blame, in want of sympathy or faithful proclamation of the Truth. For Death is a stern end to controversy. They are thoughts such as these, which crowd into a letter which he wrote the day after the Dean's death :—

E. B. P. TO REV. H. P. LIDDON, D.D.

July 19, 1881.

The leaves have been dropping so fast that nothing startles me. They fall according to God's law, whatever it is; only one is sure that it is one which one does not understand. One only thinks of the Judgment seat of Christ and accompanies each there. . . . How overwhelming that sight must be! One can only say, 'Lord, remember me in Thy kingdom,' with the dying thief, though without his excuses. ' Rock of ages, cleft for me, let me hide myself in Thee.' . . . I trust he was taken away from the evil to come. He was, alas! a Hebrew pupil of mine own, and I did nothing for him.

When the efforts to obtain the release of the Rev. S. F. Green, Vicar of Miles-Platting, one of the imprisoned Ritualists, had for the time failed, he wrote to Mr. Wood:—

E. B. P. TO THE HON. C. L. WOOD.

Aug. 6, 1881.

Lord Penzance's jurisdiction is made then as stringent as human law can make it. Our efforts to obtain Mr. Green's freedom and restore him to the people whom he loves and who love him, and some of whom must owe their souls to him, have failed : and he lies a State prisoner in a felon's gaol. It might have been my own case, if the persecuting party had been consistent. For the same Judgment which forbade wearing and using what the letter of the Prayer-book directs, forbade also our celebrating the Holy Eucharist as our Blessed Lord celebrated it, in wine mingled with water. I did it, and called the attention of the persecuting party to my doing it. I had not the same strong ground, as Mr. Green, for there is no direction in our Prayer-book to mingle water with the wine, but only a custom since our Lord instituted it. No Church Court, no Consistory, no jury of twelve honest Englishmen could have said that a clergyman ought to be sent to prison, for doing what the letter of the Prayer-book bids him do. Had the persecutors obtained a sentence against me for celebrating Holy Communion as our Blessed Lord did, in wine mingled with water, I must have been writing this in the Castle at Oxford. I challenged them to do their worst.

I only mention my own case, because it looks so selfish to talk quietly about Mr. Green's remaining in Lancaster Castle, while one's self is in God's free air, unless one had had to face the same result; and not I only, but he too, to whom throngs are listening in hushed silence in St. Paul's.

Hampden and the Shipmoney will be a proverb as long as English history shall last. Ungrateful as the Government of William and Mary were to the Seven Bishops, who were imprisoned in the Tower of London, they did their work – by suffering first, at the hands of James;

and then, as Nonjurors, they remained long the salt of the English Church.

In the Gospel, suffering is the royal road to victory. For it is the road which our Master's sacred feet trod, and consecrated it by their blood. 'Yourselves know,' St. Paul says, 'that we are appointed thereunto.' True, our prisons are pleasant places which cannot be named in the same breath with those loathsome places in which St. Paul approved himself 'by imprisonments.' But every trial has its own weight. We all love liberty and free air, and power to work for our Lord. And Mr. Green must lie, deprived of the power of working directly for souls and for his Lord, unless he will own, in fact, that he did amiss in following a distinct direction of the Prayer-book, and giving to his people a service which they loved.

We can do nothing. The prison is shut with all safety and men's wills are more iron than the locks. But 'the Lord Who dwelleth on high is mightier.' He 'looseth men out of prison.' Only let us ask Him earnestly, and He will either open the prison doors, or make this prolonged imprisonment be, in what way He willeth and knoweth, to His Glory.

The issue of the Revised Version of the New Testament in 1881 was very far from a pleasure to him. It seemed to warrant all the fears that he had expressed when the Committee was originally appointed. He used to say that he could not read it devotionally because of the number of changes and uncertainties that were to be found in its pages : they were a continual source of distraction. He wrote the following letter about it in view of the approaching discussion at the Newcastle Church Congress.

E. B. P. TO DEAN LAKE OF DURHAM.

Ascot Priory, Oct. 1, 1881.

I see that the Revised Version of the New Testament is to be a subject at the Congress. Its merits will, of course, be impressed upon the Congress. I know not whether any one will draw attention to any drawbacks in it. To me the Revisers seem to have paid more attention to the Greek than to the English, and to have been over-particular in retaining the same English word for the same Greek word. Yet how many English words does e. g. Liddell and Scott's Lexicon give for the same Greek word, which implies, of course, that the same English word will not always suffice.

But a formidable evil has passed unnoticed, except by Dean Stanley.

This relates not to the revision of the Version as such but to the changes in the text of Holy Scripture, which is the basis of the translation.

The evil is, the uncertainty which it throws on most passages, bearing upon the Divinity of our Lord. On most passages which declare it, there is an 'or,' substituting some other reading which does not contain it. The Θεός in 1 Tim. iii. 16 is peremptorily dismissed, although St. Ignatius is an older authority than the Codex Sinaiticus. Two texts only remain, upon which a doubt is not thrown, St. John i. 14 and Heb. i. 8. Of course one text is quite enough; but to those who hold that 'the Bible and the Bible only is the religion of Protestants,' it will, I fear, be a great shock.

The revisers, I believe, do not say in what sense they use the word 'or.' In our present translation it means, I believe, that they balanced the two renderings, but on the whole preferred that which they inserted in the text. If the 'or' in the Revised Version means, that those who settled the text which the revisers adopted, were really in doubt, or leave the two readings as optional, then, thus far, everything is left to each reader according to his bias, or he is left to think that everything is uncertain.

If the revisers of the Old Testament shall proceed on the same plan, there will be an 'or' upon every passage in the Old Testament which teaches the Divinity of Christ. For in these days, of course, everything is disputed, and so there will be an 'or' on Psalm xlv. 6. And then there will be the question as to one of the two remaining passages in the New Testament, and it will be asked, 'Did the writer of the Epistle to the Hebrews argue from a mistranslation?'

I cannot imagine how any one who knew Greek, and the use of εὐλογητός and ἐπικατάρατος in the LXX, could have imagined the constructions in Rom. ix. 5, mentioned in the margin, to have been right. Hitherto they have been counted Socinian glosses. To me they seem absolutely dishonest.

Of Greek, those acquainted with the language can judge for themselves. Few can estimate so intricate a subject as the revision of the text. Another generation may no longer have the preference for a certain class of MSS. which are the favourites now. Alas for England! Everything seems let loose against the Faith now. Some will be driven back to the *quod semper, quod ubique*, &c., and will regard texts of Scripture in their office of proving the Faith already delivered. Some will seek refuge in the Church of Rome from all this chaos. More will go to scepticism.

For I have mentioned only the uncertainty thrown upon the proof of one great doctrine. The effect of this and more is brought out by Dean Stanley in the article inserted in the *Times* of July 20. 'Doctrine' and 'heresy' are to lose their meaning which they have had since the Apostles' time and to become mere 'teaching' and 'party spirit.' All the modern fancies which have congregated round the words 'hell,' 'everlasting,' and 'damnation' have, from different causes, been exploited in this Version. And so as to 'inspiration.'

My only hope is that this 'revision' will be revised: that there will be less antipathy to words expressive of doctrine, and that the show of alternative texts without any ground of judging between them will be withdrawn.

Just before he left Ascot in October, 1881, the Chaplain of the Priory, Mr. Skinner, was obliged by his rapidly failing health to give up his work. It was a great loss to Pusey, who rejoiced in his companionship; they lived next door to one another within the Priory grounds and met frequently. He wrote to him the following letter of farewell :—

E. B. P. TO REV. J. SKINNER.

South Hermitage, Ascot Priory, Oct. 13, 1881.

It is very, very sad, as all partings are. I had so hoped that this would have been your home, until God should call you to your ever-lasting home. I had such bright dreams of your future usefulness here when —— told me of your thinking of work in a Convalescent Hospital, and I said of your coming here, 'It is too good to be true.' It is very, very sad; and although my loss of hearing cuts me off from much intercourse with those whom I love, yet it is pleasant to be under the same roof with one who loves one, and whom one loves. But God's will is clearest there where it 'triumphs at our cost,' and His will has acted by conforming yours to it.

God knows whether I shall come here another year or whether I shall see another year. The two houses will be different, in that there will be not one whom I love, as for these many years I have loved you, next door; and the likelihood of your coming to Oxford must be very small. So it will be a loving out of sight.

Nine months later, Mr. Green was still in prison, and Pusey was asked to write an address to the English Church Union on the anniversary of his being shut up in gaol. He was already feeling sure that the battle for toleration in Ritual was now nearly won.

E. B. P. TO THE HON. C. L. WOOD.

Christ Church, March 8, 1882.

Mankind in the year 1892 will, I think, be much ashamed of us in 1882.

The panic which produced the P. W. R. Act is not yet over, and panics are always unreasoning and unreasonable. All evil is growing (as is good also, but silently—good makes no noise); crimes are more atrocious than they were some years ago; Atheism flaunts itself; all unbelief is more aggressive; and the exterminating party, as a remedy to all this—does what ? It keeps in prison one who (to use the words of the Bishop of Chichester in Convocation) ' is the anxious and diligent Pastor of a large congregation in a parish now numbering nearly 5,000 souls,' who ' is shown to live in the affections of his people.'

And for what? For wearing a garment which was worn in the English Church in the reign of Edward VI ; for having a Vestment, as both East and West have, for the Eucharistic Service—a Vestment which was first enjoined by Cranmer, and the direction to wear which stands in our present Prayer-book. . . .

The exterminating party have, I trust, now run too wild a race. Three priests whom it imprisoned were delivered. The fourth, whom we cannot extricate from its fangs, will, I hope, preach to the hearts of the English the tolerance which the intolerant will not exercise towards him. It was said by a Bishop in Convocation : ' There are hundreds of clergy who are disobeying rubrics (of the meaning of which there is not the shadow of a doubt), who are not only left unmolested, but are taking part in the action which led to the imprisonment of Mr. Green.'

The English have a great reverence for law ; but they love also honesty and fair play. They will not, in the end, I trust, endure ' law-breakers,' invoking the aid of the law, to imprison those who do in reality keep the law, and contravene only unlaw.

One of the earliest English laws extant, nearly twelve centuries ago (A.D. 697) ordains that the Church shall enjoy her own judgments (Spelman's ' Concilia,' i. 194). For maintaining this Mr. Green is imprisoned. Hard must it be for a zealous lover of souls to be cut off from the people whom he loves, and by whom he is loved. Hard must it be for one who had fought the good fight to lie inactive while the evil one is busy in capturing souls for whom Christ died. But, as in the days of martyrdom the blood of Martyrs was the harvest seed of the Church, so every trial borne meekly for the Faith of Christ, and the cause of Christ, is a pledge of final victory ; and on this anniversary of Mr. Green's imprisonment we may respectfully congratulate him in the words of one put to death in the Marian persecution, that the fire so kindled will not easily be put out. Through his imprisonment the Church of England will, I trust, be freed.

In May, 1882, Pusey sent the following letter to Lord Dalhousie, who had charge of the Bill for legalizing marriage with a deceased wife's sister, who had written to ask Pusey whether he considered such marriages were prohibited by the Levitical law.

E. B. P. TO LORD DALHOUSIE.

Christ Church, Oxford, May 16, 1882.

I fear that your Lordship will live to regret the change in the marriage-law which you are now proposing to your Lordship's House.

Things are very much changed, since forty years ago a firm was employed to solicit signatures to petitions in favour of legalizing those marriages. The agitation was then, in favour of this particular marriage, from some known individuals who wished to marry their deceased wives' sisters. Now it has spread (as all such questions do spread) consistently, to the whole subject of affinity. Now the question is raised whether *any* affinity is a hindrance to marriage. If marriage with the deceased wife's sister is legalized, I do not see how any other marriage with one connected by affinity can be consistently maintained to be illegal. The principle is one, and as the question has been discussed, people have come to see that the whole subject of affinity is one, that the sisters, mothers, daughters (if there be any by a former marriage), are sisters, mothers, daughters to him, with whom the wife is become one flesh. I think that it would startle your Lordship's House (in which the reality of the tie of affinity has recently come home through the consciousness of the reality of the connexion with one recently snatched from them) to be told that the relations of their wives were nothing to them.

The social effects of the permission in Protestant Germany were said to be frightful, and, before they were limited by the Code Napoleon, in France also. May I ask your Lordship to take the trouble to look at my evidence before the Commission, of which I take the liberty to enclose a copy, pp. 5–56; and of France, p. lxxxi?

I have ventured beyond the question proposed to me by your Lordship, on account of the terrible evil resulting from any relaxation of the sacredness of the law of marriage. We are already suffering so fearfully from the new Divorce Court, in which it is said to be notorious that every undefended suit is a case of collusion.

In regard to your Lordship's question whether I believe marriage with the deceased wife's sister to be prohibited by the Levitical law, I have no doubt that it is prohibited by Leviticus xviii. 6. The literal translation of the words is, ' None of you shall approach to any flesh of his flesh to uncover their nakedness, I am the Lord.' They were universally understood to include the near relations of her who by marriage had become one flesh with her husband. This continued on from the earliest times of which we have any notice, before the Council of Nice, to the dispensation of Alexander VI (Borgia) at the close of the fifteenth century. For 1,500 years the unlawfulness of this marriage was unquestioned, until it was violated by the dispensations of a Pope, stained by almost every vice. . . .

The law of the Church was rested on Lev. xviii. 6. The omission of the daughter among the cases specifically prohibited shows that the specific prohibitions were not meant to be exhaustive.

In regard to details, your Lordship, if you thought it worth while, would I believe find them in my evidence, which consisted in fact of answers to a somewhat strict cross-examination.

Oriel College had recently obtained, for their Common Room, a portrait of Cardinal Newman, by Mr. Ouless. The Provost of Oriel sent it over to Christ Church for Pusey to see. This act of thoughtful kindness touched him deeply.

E. B. P. TO THE PROVOST OF ORIEL.

Christ Church, Feb. 8, 1882.

Kindest thanks for your great kindness in enabling me to see the portrait of my old friend. The eyes have still their wonted sweetness ; the deep lines in the cheek betoken many a care and sorrow since those old days when we took sweet counsel together. Alas for poor Oxford, which would not have him !

I have now every line of his later countenance impressed upon me as well as his former. . . . It is his resting countenance, full of thought, I suppose, about evils curling round the ark of God and threatening human souls.

On Mr. Thomas Mozley's 'Reminiscences, chiefly of Oriel College and of the Oxford Movement,' he wrote many very lengthy letters. He found it almost as difficult to correct the misstatements of that book as he had found it to suggest what replies should be written to 'Essays and Reviews'; the inaccuracies were so numerous, the subjects so varied, and the whole point of view and tone of mind so entirely different from his own that he hardly knew where to begin or where to end. Only one portion of one letter can be given. It is selected because it contains the only possible answer to the often-quoted story of a sermon on 'Sin after Baptism' which this inaccurate and gossiping writer attributed to Pusey.

E. B. P. TO REV. H. P. LIDDON, D.D.

South Hermitage, Ascot, July 1, 1882.

I am afraid that I can be of very little use to you about poor T. Mozley's book, because I was always living in the present, or the proximate, and not looking back, and so things left no impression upon me, so soon as they were past. I remember —— saying to me, when James Hope was taking all that pains about my Suspension, that he (J. H.) cared far more about it than I. T. Mozley has a chapter upon a sermon of mine on Heb. vi. 1-6. I had utterly forgotten that I had ever preached one on that text, nor does his account of it bring me back the slightest memory of it. He mentions the impression upon himself, that I dwelt upon sin being irreparable. He himself says, I suppose, much what I meant to say. I suppose that the great difference was, that I insisted that all things done in the body, would appear in the Day of Judgment. The Day of Judgment was very much passed over at that time. Some Evangelicals spoke of great deadly sins before their conversion as quietly as if they had been done by some one else, without expression of any compunction for them. My sermon, 'The Day of Judgment,' preached later at Brighton, astonished people, because I insisted on every act being brought into judgment. But this is about myself, not about T. Mozley.

To me, T. Mozley's book looks like a mere string of anecdotes without the power of appreciating what he is writing about.

The statement at the beginning of this letter that he had always lived in the present, occurs frequently in letters of this period. It is his own reflection on one aspect of his life. Another interesting use of it will well bear quotation. He is writing to a friend who had asked him to furnish a list of books on a certain subject.

Christ Church, Oxford, Jan. 25 [? 1882].

Thank you much for your kind wishes. In these solid walls, I have passed the winter very comfortably with my books, only ashamed of all the comfort which I have been living in.

I have, all my life, so lived in the present, that, if I could make up my mind to try to make a list of books for ———, I should not know how to set about it. But I never could make a list for different people, who kindly asked me, and I have thrown the papers into the fire. I suppose that it will be true of my books, as of myself, that they served their generation and fell asleep.

Mozley's 'Reminiscences' were most painful to him in every way. He again and again recurs to them. He longed to get some one who had lived through the whole Movement to write an accurate, sympathetic, and discriminating account of it. Exactly a month before his death he begs Liddon to ask Dean Church to undertake the task, or at any rate a portion of it :—

E. B. P. TO REV. H. P. LIDDON, D.D.
August 16, 1882.

. . . He showed power of historical writing on St. Anselm, and one who could write so discriminatingly and so graphically must have his eyes about him. . . . I am sure, if he has time, he could revive any knowledge which he has parted with. . . . He might not like to publish it yet, because he might not like to tell of my blunders.

At the same time the prevailing tone of Mozley's work induced Pusey to lose no time in destroying all old letters in which 'any one said anything of fault of any one.' His sense of his own near approach to the great Judgment Seat, and his deep realization of the Love of God, made all such criticisms jar upon him. In the record of the busy years of his ceaseless activity, there has of necessity been little opportunity of alluding to the deep calm that lay behind it : only a collection of his spiritual letters could reveal aright this inner peace. But two or three glimpses of it, as unveiled in his correspondence of this period, will not be thought inappropriate, before the account of his passing away to his rest. The secret life seems at this time to shine through his ordinary letters.

In acknowledging an Easter gift of a picture representing some flowers, which he had received from a little girl in whom he was specially interested, he wrote as follows :—

Christ Church, Oxford, Easter Monday, 1881.

Your loving little painting reached me this morning. I love flowers very much. They tell one such histories of the love of God. He seems to have given them all that varied beauty for no other end than to give His creatures pleasure. And there they are in deep dell or mountain top, 'where mortal foot hath ne'er or rarely been.' I have often thought that they must be for the Blessed Angels to gaze upon and thank God for. The Daisy, as it spreads itself out as wide as it can, seems to be drinking in the love of Heaven ; and the Rose, which opens itself to that glow from above and gives out all its fragrance, seems to be giving back love for love. It gives back all which it has in return for the warmth which opens it. You, my very dear Beatrice, are the rosebud which no force could open (as children sometimes try to force an opening rose with their little fingers and only spoil it), but which the glow of God's love will open as time goes on, more and more. And the white of the lily of the valley tells of purity, and its low-hanging head of tenderness and humility. And then by the name of that lovely flower the 'Forget-me-not' God tells you 'Forget not Me,' and then He says that great word which you have chosen, 'Thine for ever.' For God will be as much your own as if He had never made Angel or Archangel, or Cherubim or Seraphim : quite your own ; quite belonging to your own individual tiny self: for St. Paul says, 'Who loved *me* and gave Himself for *me*,' as if there had been no one besides to die for. So the Psalmist says, 'O God, Thou art *my* God.' He is the very own God of every one who will have Him as his. And

God changes not, so He will be your very own God for ever and ever and ever. So He teaches us to say, 'I am my Beloved's, and my Beloved is mine.'

May He keep you as His very own for ever.

In another letter he is acknowledging a New Year's gift from the brother of the same little girl. Here quite unconsciously, Pusey sketches a vivid picture of his own life :—

Christ Church, Oxford, Feast of the Epiphany, 1882.

It was a very pretty picture which your dear Mother chose for you to send me. She told you perhaps that it is a knight in complete armour from head to foot. What that armour is St. Paul tells us Eph. vi. 13–17. Mama or Grandpapa will explain to you by-and-by what it is. I do not know whether you have begun yet to hear or read about knights and chivalry. There was a great deal grand about those old knights. They thought nothing of any hardships, they were very devoted and fearless, they never thought of themselves, or feared any reproach in a good cause. They were men, and so did, some of them, unwise things. Still they have left the name of 'chivalry' behind them as a name for devoted self-forgetful fearlessness in a good cause. We (St. Paul tells us) are 'soldiers of Jesus Christ.' He says of himself, 'I have fought the good fight.' God enlisted you in this warfare when He made you His child and a member of Christ, and I hope that you will be a good soldier and fight His battles bravely. It is strange that it should be hard not to be a coward. But people are cowards if they are afraid of ridicule for doing what is right. But among the young, those who do wrong laugh at those who do right because they feel *themselves* in the wrong, and wish to shame people out of what is good because it is a reproach to them. Then is the time to remember that you are 'a soldier of Jesus Christ,' and if you are brave, those who laughed will be ashamed of themselves. You will remember how, in the picture, the Guardian Angel points upwards to the height, reminding him where his strength lies, as St. Paul says, 'I can do all things through Christ strengthening me.'

This has been all about war and fighting. I thought what little picture I could send you as a token of my love. This is another side of our Christian life. I do not know why in these pictures they represent our Lord as a little Child. Perhaps it was because at this time He became a little Child for love of us. You see while He has His own Cross in one hand, how tenderly He holds the little lamb with the other (for He calls Himself the Good Shepherd) ; and how trustfully the little lamb leans its head against His Bosom ; which is what Isaiah foretold of *Him* (Is. xl. 11). That little lamb, dear, is you. For Jesus, being God as well as Man, loves each one as tenderly as if there were no Angel or Archangel, Cherubim or Seraphim ; and this thought will be a treasure for you for your whole life. 'Jesus loves *me*,' and in the little picture He tells you how to be like Him: 'Learn of Me, for I am meek and lowly of heart.' He does not say, 'Do great things'; but be like Me, lowly.

On his birthday, two days before his last illness, he wrote the following letter in reply to a friend's greetings on that anniversary. It recalls and illustrates Newman's affectionate description in a conversation with his own sister, Mrs. Mozley. 'He spoke,' we are told, 'of Dr. Pusey with deep affection and admiration—"so full of the love of God." . . . The tone and action with which the words "so full of the love of God" were spoken live in memory to this day[1].'

E. B. P. TO ——

South Hermitage, Ascot Priory, August 22, 1882.

God bless you for all your love. Love is indeed a wonderful thing, and yet it would be more wonderful if it were not; since love is of God, a spark out of the boundless, shoreless ocean of His Fire of Love.

What you say of this past near-half-century has been wonderful. It was often on my lips, 'This is the Lord's doing, and it is marvellous in our eyes.' There was a little seed scattered, and what a harvest of souls! But God had prepared the soil, and the fields were white to harvest. There was, however, a great deal of heart's devotion before which never talked, but acted. I remember it in those before me of whom I learned.

You, I hope, are ripening continually. God ripen you more and more. Each day is a day of growth. God says to you, 'Open thy mouth and I will fill it.' Only long. He does not want our words. The parched soil, by its cracks, opens itself for the rain from heaven and invites it. The parched soul cries out for the Living God.

Oh! then, long and long and long, and God will fill thee. More love, more love, more love!

---

[1] 'Letters and Correspondence of J. H. Newman,' vol. ii. p. 475.

# CHAPTER XVIII[1].

LAST ILLNESS AND DEATH—THE FUNERAL—
THE MEMORIAL.

## 1882.

IF any man ever lived with the thought of death constantly present to his mind, that man was Pusey. The
two truths on which throughout life he constantly fell back
were the nothingness of this world, and the enduring love
and magnificence of God. He sometimes quoted Burke's
well-known exclamation, 'What shadows we are, and what
shadows we pursue!' But he more often repeated St. Paul's
words, 'We know that if our earthly house of this tabernacle
were dissolved, we have a building of God, an house not
made with hands, eternal in the heavens.'

As each friend of his earlier days had been called to pass
beyond the veil, Pusey had gazed after him with a wistful
longing, which had only been kept in check by his habitual
submission to the Divine Will. As years passed on he felt
these losses less acutely, not because old age was bringing
with it any failure of natural sensibility, but because he
knew that the separation could not be long. No sorrow of
this kind, in his whole life, equalled the loss of his wife:
perhaps the greatest in his later years was that which he
felt when in April, 1866, he stood by Keble's grave in
Hursley churchyard. But when his son Philip died,

---

[1] The earlier part of this chapter was written by Dr. Liddon.

in January, 1880, he rarely expressed himself as if they were separated. 'Philip says,' was a more frequent form of quoting his departed son than 'Philip used to say': it was as though they were living in adjoining rooms. 'At my age we cannot, you know,' he observed with his bright smile, 'be very long without seeing each other again.'

Pusey's life had been for more than half a century a preparation for death : and he seems to have been granted something of the nature of a presentiment as to the time at which his summons might come. One day in the autumn of 1880 he was talking with a friend on the probable future of Religion in Oxford, and a reference was made to measures which might be expected after October, 1882, when, in the due course of succession, the Master of Balliol would become Vice-Chancellor. 'Ah,' said Pusey, suddenly and decidedly, 'that may concern you and others. I shall have nothing to do with it.' His death occurred within one month of the Master's entering on his office.

On Trinity Sunday, June 4, a friend called to see him, and found that he was keeping the day, as he had kept every Trinity Sunday since 1839, as the solemn anniversary of his wife's death. In a short talk, Pusey mentioned that this was the first summer term in the more than fifty years that had elapsed since he became Professor, in which he had stopped his lectures before the end of full Term. He had only done so now because those who had been attending them were leaving Oxford. He spoke of it with tears in his eyes, as if it were presentimental.

When all the other work of the Term was over, Pusey left Oxford for Ascot Priory on the morning of June 16. As usual, two or three large boxes, filled with books of reference, went with him : and Channing, his faithful servant, was not neglectful of any provisions which would enable her master to bear the fatigue of the journey. For the last time he looked round the rooms in which he had lived for fifty-three years, and for the last time walked from his door to the steps on the south side of the great gateway, where Dr. Acland was awaiting him with his brougham to take him to the station. Although wearied by his effort to attend a meeting of the Governing Body on the previous day, he talked cheerfully about his plans and hopes for work up to the last moment, and left the Oxford station by the twelve o'clock train.

As usual, when he was at Ascot, the change of air appeared to do him good, and throughout July he was 'remarkably well.' He walked a great deal in the pine wood, among the rabbit holes and in the heather; in this, it was noticed, returning to an old habit, which he had dropped since the great shock of his son's death. At times he was even in buoyant spirits. 'It seems,' he said one day, 'as if Almighty God were going to take away my cough'—the cough which he had been unable to shake off for six months.

At the end of July those who watched him narrowly observed something like the beginning of a change. The Sister in charge of the Penitentiary at Plymouth became suddenly and seriously ill. As a rule Pusey never showed symptoms of surprise at anything that came from the Hand of God. 'One learns,' he used to say, 'as life goes on, to hope for nothing, to be surprised at nothing, and to try to make the best of everything.' But the news of the Sister's illness came to him as a shock; it affected him very deeply. He at once took a desponding view of the case, and of its probable consequences. Even when, on the following day, a hopeful report from Plymouth arrived at Ascot, he did not recover his cheerfulness.

However, he appeared to be in his wonted health during the first three weeks of August. He used to sit out in front of his little house for several hours of the day, and occupied himself in reading and dictating. Before he left Oxford a friend had asked him his opinion of Mr. T. Mozley's 'Reminiscences,' then recently published. His opinion was that the clever writer had not been able to resist the temptations which beset a good story; and that the book was inaccurate, and sometimes illnatured. In particular, he was greatly concerned by a story about the way in which Dr. Routh, the venerable President of Magdalen, had received a story of the death of a Fellow of his College under very distressing circumstances. Pusey had a correspondence with Dr. Bulley, then President of Magdalen, which satisfied him of the baselessness of the story. But the book took possession of him in a manner which would not have been the case in his days of health, and the friend who had mentioned it to him has always regretted that he had done so.

August 22 was Pusey's eighty-second birthday. It found him still, to all appearance, in his wonted health. He had heard the confessions of the Sisters during the three or four previous days. In discharging this duty, he had not been quite equal to himself: one Sister said that he had detained her for a long time, and had repeated himself unnecessarily. But on his birthday he was cheerful ; and acknowledged the congratulations which he received with his wonted courtesy and tenderness.

His last illness really began two days later, on the night of St. Bartholomew's Day, August 24. On the 23rd he had heard that a lady who had intended to join the Sisterhood had lost the relative, whose claims upon her time and duty had hitherto made it impossible for her to carry out her purpose. On the 24th he was told that she did not now intend thus to consecrate her liberty. The report strangely agitated him : and he wrote her a very earnest letter. The report, as it afterwards proved, rested on a misapprehension.

The post of that morning also brought a letter from a person who had been visiting the Rev. S. F. Green, who was still confined in Lancaster gaol, on account of his conscientious inability to obey the Privy Council's interpretation of the Prayer-book. In his days of health Pusey would have dwelt on the high privilege of suffering for conscience sake. Now his own depressed physical condition coloured his thoughts. 'Here,' he said, ' we have all our comforts and this beautiful air to breathe, and all around us is happy and peaceful; while he, poor man, is in prison.' The letter had described Mr. Green as 'wasted and gaunt'; locked up in 'a room which looked like a very large dungeon with a huge fire.' Pusey forwarded to the *Times* an extract from this letter, and added a short note of his own.

To the Editor of the 'Times.'

August 24, 1882.

The character of the Rev. Mr. Green has been so entirely misrepresented as if he wilfully remained in Lancaster gaol, 'keeping the door locked on the inside,' that it occurred to me that the following account of his condition from one who saw him lately might open the eyes of some who would not jest at suffering.

But Pusey was no longer in a condition to write or talk on subjects which deeply moved him: and there can be little room for doubt that in his critical state of health, the slight effort which he thus made contributed to precipitate his illness. On the evening of the 24th he went to bed without complaining of anything serious. When he was called at seven o'clock as usual on the morning of the 25th, he could not rise. Evidently he had had some kind of seizure. On that and the following day he remained in bed: but he got up at nine on Sunday the 27th, read his letters, and those about him hoped that his getting well was only a question of days. He had often been worse before and had regained his strength.

For a week he seemed to maintain the level which he had reached on Sunday, August 27. He tried several times to resume reading for his Hebrew Lectures. But each time he had to put the books away, saying that he could not get on. It was now becoming clear to those about him that he was not to be long in this world. But letters were received as usual, and some were still written day by day.

His note to the *Times*, as was inevitable, had reopened the floodgates of controversy. It was supposed, greatly to

Pusey's annoyance, to reflect upon the Archbishop of York, and it entailed a correspondence with his Grace, who expressed himself as perfectly satisfied with Pusey's explanations. Then a correspondent of the *Times*, who signed himself 'a Vicar-General,' made fun of the account of Mr. Green's condition in Lancaster gaol; and proceeded to allude in similar terms to a piece of heartless and indelicate gossip which was utterly without foundation. As soon as Pusey had ascertained from Mr. Green that the story was false, he wrote to the *Times* once more, and for the last time, on Thursday, August 31. He enclosed Mr. Green's letter, and added—

E. B. P. TO THE EDITOR OF THE 'TIMES.'

August 31, 1882.

... The supposed fact which the Vicar-General states to rest on very good authority, and on which he comments with so much flippancy, is absolutely and entirely untrue. ... Idle words have to be given account of at an unerring tribunal[1].

These were the last words he ever addressed to the world at large. The week which ended on September 2 was the last week—in any sense active—of Pusey's life.

On Sunday, September 3, he was in low spirits; but he said through the Evening Service for the day with Miss Kebbel, who made the responses. She specially noticed with what repressed energy he repeated the first words of the eighteenth Psalm—'I will love Thee, O Lord, my Strength.' After he had gone to bed, he repeated aloud the Litany from memory: when he could not recall one petition, he asked Miss Kebbel to write it in large characters that he might see it, and then went on.

Monday, September 4, was the critical day on which the illness entered on its second and, as it proved, its fatal stage. Up to that date it might have seemed likely that he would recover. He had recovered from much worse

---

[1] The *Times*, Sept. 1, 1882. The Vicar-General made an ample re- tractation of his statement in the *Times* of Sept. 12, 1882.

illnesses more than once ; and his constitution seemed, humanly speaking, to have vast reserves of vital power. But after that day there was no real prospect of any issue but one. During the morning of that day Pusey remained in his little bedroom reading the Hebrew Bible. He observed on coming out that he had spent a long time over a single botanical term without being able to satisfy himself as to its exact meaning. In his days of health, when he had come to the conclusion that the sense of a word was uncertain, he would have weighed the probabilities, decided, at any rate provisionally, in favour of one meaning, and gone on to something else. Now the word haunted him ; he talked about it at luncheon to the kind friends who waited on him, and who, of course, did not understand Hebrew. Still, in the middle of the day, Mr. Fagge, the doctor, called, and thought him so much better that he begged him to go out and take the fresh air in the afternoon.

About an hour later he was seen trying with evident pain and difficulty to move across his room, resting on the back of a chair, and almost immediately afterwards he fell forward in a state of unconsciousness. He was lifted into a chair, and when he opened his eyes, seemed to know no one ; and after a short time was, by his own request, moved to his bed. He never left it again.

Dr. Acland, his old friend, was at once summoned from Devonshire. He of course saw the full gravity of the situation. ' If it were any one but Dr. Pusey, a man in this condition would not be likely to live for twenty-four hours.' But on the morning of the 7th, he pronounced him to be even ' surprisingly better.' He had seen Dr. Pusey in worse illnesses from which he had recovered, and he hopefully promised that when the time came for the return to Oxford, he would himself come and take him home.

It was not to be. There was another partial rally on the morning of Friday the 8th ; but his strength was now giving way, and from that date, the downward progress was unrelieved by any hopeful symptoms. The characteristics of illness in its later stages now began to display themselves: the increasing restlessness, the difficulty in taking any nourishment, the weariness of weakness, the long periods of apparent unconsciousness or stupor, during parts of which, however, there is reason to think he was engaged in constant prayer or keenly alive to what was going on in the room. On Monday and Tuesday it was quite evident that the end was near. His daughter and her husband were sent for and reached Ascot late on Tuesday. On Wednesday, at 8.30, Mrs. Brine visited her dying father. He received her with a bright, cheerful smile: 'Well, you see, dear, I am soon down, and soon up again.' Then he asked about his grandchildren, one after another, especially the absent soldier-boy, Percy Brine. Then he added, 'What brought you here?' Mrs. Brine wrote an answer in large letters: and Pusey put on his spectacles to read it, but he could not see anything. Dr. Fagge came at 10.30. 'Well, Dr. Pusey,' he said very slowly, 'how are you this morning?' Pusey looked hard at the mouth of the speaker, and then answered with a bright smile, 'Is it not your business to tell me how I am, rather than mine to tell you?' Dr. Fagge then felt his pulse, and, wishing his patient to understand the grave character of his illness, said slowly, 'Your strength seems to be failing.' He wrote the words in large letters on a piece of paper. Pusey again put on his spectacles and tried hard to read them: but it is doubtful whether he did more than guess at their meaning.

He was now exhausted; and begged that he might be undisturbed. After some hours he roused himself to ask after the Archbishop of Canterbury, who was seriously ill. In the middle of the day his grandson, the Rev. J. E. B. Brine (who had lived with him since 1880), Dr. King, and Miss M. Milner came over from Oxford. Dr. King's presence roused Pusey: he looked at him with his clear blue eye, and put out his hand, while his face lighted up with a beautiful smile. But he could say nothing. Soon after-

wards it seemed as if the end was very near; and
Dr. King, who had been saying prayers at his bedside,
read the Commendatory Prayer.

But he rallied at night, and on the following day, Thursday,
the 14th, recognized with delight his brother, the Rev. W. B.
Pusey, who had now arrived. He was, however, only able to
speak at intervals. When Mrs. Brine handed to her uncle
the Prayer-book which had belonged to his mother, Lady
Lucy, Pusey said in quite a strong voice, ' The dear old
book.' During Friday, the 15th, he was for the most part
wandering, and in his delirium his mind moved continuously round the solemn ministerial acts which had been
his greatest practical interest in life. He repeated again
and again the words, ' The Body of our Lord Jesus Christ,
Which was given for thee, preserve thy body and soul unto
everlasting life.' When a cup containing some food was
brought him, he clutched it with reverent eagerness, thinking
that it was the Chalice. When he saw some of those who
were around kneeling at the bedside, he raised his hand,
with the words, ' By His authority committed unto me,
I absolve thee from all thy sins.' Mrs. Brine was anxious
that he should receive the Holy Communion, and the
question was written on paper in large characters, which
he succeeded in reading. He paused and then said, ' If
I am to receive the Holy Communion I must administer it
myself.' It was clear to his brother that his mind was
too overclouded ; and the subject was dropped.

But as death came near his thoughts were clearer, while
bodily weakness hourly increased. From time to time in
the morning of Saturday, September 16, faint words escaped
him, which appeared to show that he was repeating the
Te Deum mentally, in accordance with the advice which
he had often given to the sleepless and the sick. The
death-sweat was on his brow when he was heard to sigh
out a last aspiration, which summed up his life—' My
God.' He passed away at twenty minutes after three in
the afternoon.

His Hebrew Bible still lay on a little table near his bed,

open—as he had left it on the previous Sunday—at 1 Chron. xvi, which describes David's triumphant restoration of the Ark of God to its place in the reverent worship of Israel.

All present remained for some time kneeling round the bed ; when they rose, the Rev. T. T. Carter was standing just outside. They all went into the open air : it was an autumn afternoon of cloudless beauty; and some of those present looked up into the clear blue sky, not without many thoughts of the Blessed Angels who were just carrying the departed soul into the Presence-chamber of the Judge, and earnest prayers that nothing might be wanting to his eternal rest [1].

Dr. Liddon was abroad when the illness began: the first news of its seriousness reached him at Turin. He tried to start back the same night, but all the places in the sleeping-carriages were engaged. When at last he got to Paris, on the 18th, he bought an English paper, and his eye fell first of all on an obituary notice headed 'Dr. Pusey.' The following words are from his own diary :—

'I had not the heart to look on, but walked about the streets rapidly for an hour before I came back to the hotel. . . . So he has left us— most dear and revered of friends, of whose friendship I have been all along so utterly unworthy. How little I can realize it, though I have been looking forward to this day for twenty years. Now that dearest Dr. Pusey is gone, the world is no longer the same world. . . . He Who created and trained Dr. Pusey, can train successors if He will. Requiescat in pace amicus dilectissimus.'

On the following Monday, September 18, the Body was taken by road to Oxford. The Canons of Christ Church were at the gate of the College, to receive it, and it was laid in the room which he had used as his study for so many years ; here sorrowing friends kept continual watch by its side day and night. On Thursday, St. Matthew's Day, September 21, a very large gathering assembled for the Funeral, although it was in the quietest part of the Long Vacation. The procession of clergy, five or six

---

[1] Dr. Liddon's manuscript ended with these words.

abreast, reached round three sides of the Great Quadrangle ; the fourth, between Dr. Pusey's house and the Cathedral, being kept clear. As the Coffin was brought out of the well-known door in the south west corner of the quadrangle, the Cathedral Choir came to meet it. By the sides of the Coffin there walked as pall-bearers those who represented the friendships and the labours of his life : the Archdeacon of Oxford and three Canons who were also Theological Professors (Dr. Heurtley, Dr. Bright, and Dr. King), Mr. Gladstone, the Hon. C. L. Wood, the Earl of Glasgow, the Hon. and Rev. C. L. Courtenay, the Warden of Keble College, and Dr. Acland. As they passed towards the Cathedral the Choir sang the hymn, 'A few more years shall roll,' recalling his own often-repeated solemn words about the life which he had left and that to which he had passed. At the west door of the Cathedral the procession was met by the Dean of Christ Church, the Bishop of Oxford, and Dr. Liddon, who read the opening sentences of the Burial Service. After the Dean had read the Lesson, Newman's hymn, 'Lead, kindly light,' was sung, and Dr. Liddon then said the concluding part of the Service, committing 'his dear body' to the grave beneath the floor of the central aisle 'in sure and certain hope of the resurrection to eternal life.' Before the Bishop of Oxford pronounced the final Benediction, the well-known hymn · Jerusalem the Golden' rang out, lifting up the hearts of all the mourners from the thoughts of death and separation to that Holy City where the Lord God is the Light and the Life of the Saints, and to the time, as he so often used to say in the solemn farewells of his later years, of 'that coming in where there is no going out, in life everlasting.'

He was laid to his rest to await that Day in the same grave with his wife and two eldest daughters. A large white marble slab in the floor of the central aisle of the Cathedral marks the spot. The inscription on it, so far as it refers to those who had gone before Pusey, was written by himself; Dr. Liddon wrote the rest.

IN SPE
BEATAE RESURRECTIONIS AD VITAM AETERNAM
PER MERITA D. N J. C.
HIC DEPOSITUM EST QUICQUID MORTALE FUIT

### MARIAE CATHERINAE
UXORIS E. B. PUSEY S. T. P.
LINGUAE HEBRAICAE PROFESSORIS
ET HUIUSCE AEDIS CANONICI
OBDORMIVIT FESTO SS. TRINITATIS MDCCCXXXIX
VIXDUM EXPLETIS ANNIS
AETATIS SUAE XXXVIII
IN AMORE CONJUGIS XI
DECURTAVIT ANNOS MEOS
TU AUTEM IDEM ES ET ANNI TUI NON DEFICIENT
FILII SERVORUM TUORUM HABITABUNT
ET SEMEN EORUM CORAM TE PERMANEBIT

### EDWARDI BOUVERIE PUSEY S. T. P.
LINGUAE HEBRAICAE PROFESSORIS
ET HUIUSCE AEDIS CANONICI
QUI IN PACE ET MISERICORDIA JESU
OBDORMIVIT D SEP. XVI MDCCCLXXXII
NAT. ANNOS LXXXII DIES XXIV

BENEDICTUS DEUS QUI NON AMOVIT
ORATIONEM MEAM ET MISERICORDIAM SUAM
A ME

### LUCIAE MARIAE NAT. EOR. MAX.
PUELLAE JAM IN VOTIS CHRISTO DESPONSATAE
OBDORMIVIT FER. II INF. HEBD. II POST OCT. PASCH. MDCCCXLIV
ANNO XV NONDUM EXPLETO

QUOD CONCUPIVI JAM VIDEO QUOD SPERAVI JAM TENEO
ILLI SUM JUNCTA IN CAELIS
QUEM IN TERRA TOTA DEVOTIONE DILEXI
CATHARINAE AEMILIAE FILIAE EORUM OB. D NOV, VII MDCCCXXXII
NAT. MENSES X
REQUIEM AETERNAM DONA EIS DOMINE
ET LUX PERPETUA LUCEAT EIS

INSCRIPTION ON THE MARBLE SLAB OVER DR. PUSEY'S GRAVE.

The following words, spoken in the University pulpit at Oxford on the first Sunday of the next Term, by Dean Church, may well be quoted here. They are the words of one who from the beginning had his hand on the pulse of the Movement, and whose minute knowledge and singular capacity for judgment enabled him to speak as no one else could :—

'Many, I suppose, are thinking this morning, among the changes since the University was last assembled, of one name which since then has disappeared from its roll of members—a great and illustrious Name, a Name which was the special possession of Oxford, but belonged scarcely less to England and to Christendom. One of our Great Men has passed away from us. I hope it is pardonable, even when I cannot be sure of all sympathies, if I allow myself to remember that only within the last month we were many of us standing about the grave where the toils of his long life ended, and where he still sleeps among us, in the Oxford which he so deeply loved. Merely as the end of a career, without its match in modern Oxford, the ceasing from among us of that long, familiar life must touch us all. Few here present saw the outset of it in the Oxford Honour Schools, just over sixty years ago ; few of those who saw its beginning could look forward to its surprising and eventful course. They could not imagine through what vicissitudes it would pass—all that it would see of what stirs and tries the soul—what persistent, unwearied industry, what unabated energy of public interest and sympathy, up to the very week of death, what deep, inconsolable sorrows, what piercing wounds, what profound disappointments, what strange chequered successes, what unlooked-for revolutions, what alternations of disgrace and honour, of unchecked obloquy and wanton insult, of boundless reverence and trust. No man was more variously judged, more sternly condemned, more tenderly loved. Of course that means that his was a time of great and prolonged conflict, of great changes and great reverses ; that in it all he took a foremost part ; that he had to deal largely with foes as well as with friends. But now, all is over—hardly yet weary, hardly exhausted, he rests from his labours of more than half a century. What is the judgment upon him—not on the representative of ideas, or the champion of a cause, or the worker in the field of knowledge, but on the man ? I think that there is but one answer from those whose hearts thrill at the memory of all that he was to them, and from most of those— from many, I am sure—who stood against him, disapproved, resisted him. First and foremost, he was one who lived his life, as above everything, the Servant of God. He takes rank with those who gave themselves, and all that they had, and all that they wished for—their unsparing trouble, their ease, their honour, their powers, their interests, to what they believed to be their work for God; who spared nothing, reserved nothing, shrank from nothing, in that supreme and sacred ambition to be His true and persevering Servant. The world will remember him as the famous student, the powerful leader, the wielder of great influence in critical times, the man of strongly marked and original character, who left his mark on the age. Those who knew and loved him will remember him, as long as life lasts with them, as one whose boundless charity was always looking out to console and to make allowance, as one whose dauntless courage and patient hopefulness never flagged, as one to whose tenderness and strength they owed the best and the noblest part of all that they have felt and all that they have done. But when our confusions are still, when our loves, and enmities, and angers have perished, when our mistakes and misunderstandings have become dim and insignificant in the great distance of the past, then his figure will rise in history as one of that high company who really looked at life as St. Paul looked at it. All who care for the Church of God, all who care for Christ's Religion, even those—I make bold to say—who do not in many things think as he thought, will class him among those who in difficult and anxious times have witnessed, by great zeal, and great effort, and great sacrifice, for God and Truth and Holiness; they will see in him one who sought to make Religion a living and mighty force over the consciences and in the affairs of men, not by knowledge only and learning and wisdom and great gifts of persuasion, but still more by boundless devotedness, by the power of a consecrated and unfaltering will [1].'

Pusey had made a will on November 19, 1875. The whole of the document is in his own handwriting. It begins:—

' I, Edward Bouverie Pusey, make this as my last will and testament. I die in the faith of the One Holy Catholic and Apostolic Church, believing *explicite* (as I have for many years declared) all which I know Almighty God to have revealed in her; and *implicite* anything which He may have revealed in her which I may not know. I give my soul into the Hands of Almighty God, humbly beseeching Him to pardon all my sins, known to me or unknown, for the sole Merits of the Blood of my Redeemer, Jesus Christ (one drop of Whose Precious Blood might cleanse the whole world), and interpose His Precious Death between me and my sins.

' I desire that my body should be buried quite simply and in the churchyard of the place in which it shall please God to call me, unless I should die in term-time within the precincts of Christ Church, and then, too, as privately as the customs of the place may permit.'

The Will then goes on to leave everything to his son Philip, with special injunctions not to reprint the two

[1] Dean Church's ' Cathedral and University Sermons,' pp. 267–270.

volumes on the Theology of Germany, nor any of his
earlier corrections and notes on the English translation of
the Hebrew Scriptures [1]. He never drew up another Will,
after Philip's death ; 'in a case like mine,' he said, 'the Law
is the best Will-maker,'—so he really died intestate, and
his Library, which represented the studies of his life,
passed to Mrs. Brine, his married daughter and only
surviving child.

On the afternoon of the day of the funeral, a meeting
was held at Dr. Bright's house in Christ Church, to consider
the form which his Memorial should take. Dr. Liddon
advocated a College of Clergy in Oxford, to be a centre of
religious faith, theological learning, and personal sympathy,
as the most fitting Memorial of one whose whole heart was
devoted to the preservation of the Faith, and whose days
had been spent in fighting its battles in Oxford. This
proposal was then provisionally adopted ; and on Thursday,
November 16, a very large meeting was held in London, at
the house of the Marquis of Salisbury, in Arlington Street,
to settle finally the form that the Memorial should take.
At that meeting, Dr. Liddon's proposal was finally accepted. It was decided that the Memorial was to be in
Oxford, and that a fund of £50,000 should be raised to
purchase his Library and provide a suitable building for
it. and also an endowment for two or more clergy to act
as librarians, who should aim at promoting in every way
the interests of theological study and religious life within
the University.

The words of Lord Salisbury at the opening of that
meeting set forth the claims which may rightly be made
on Pusey's behalf to the gratitude of even a wider circle
than English Churchmen :—

'It was Dr. Pusey's fate to be engaged in a double task—to have
before him two duties, differing very much in their immediate interests,
and differing, though in an inverse direction, with regard to their ultimate importance to the Church. He was deeply mixed up, I need not
say, with the controversies of the day, and it was probably owing to his

[1] See vol. i. pp. 117-122.

connexion with those controversies that the only authority in the Church which he enjoyed was given him before his fame and his merits became known.　But there was another aspect of his character, another goal to his efforts—he was above all things a Christian apologist. His most earnest aims were not associated with the controversies, deeply interesting though they were, with which his name in public estimation was specially bound up.　His mind was chiefly bent upon one thing, that in an age when Christian faith was exposed to many and dangerous attacks, the first duty of her sons and of those whose learning could give her support, was to defend it in all its integrity.　It was as a defender of the Christian Church as a whole—as a defender of the Faith once given to the Saints, and as a champion of the Church of eighteen centuries—that he lived and worked ; not, as many have thought, simply as a fighter in one of the transient conflicts which from time to time divide the Church. . . . Already it seems as if the fervour of old differences were passing away, and as if men were turning from the narrow disputes in which many years ago they were engaged, in order to prepare themselves for that great struggle which is coming upon us—the struggle with the spirit of general unbelief.　It is with the efforts which he made, with the instruments which he furnished for combating this danger, that, in my belief, the name of Dr. Pusey will be ultimately bound up.'

To the clear-sighted and statesmanlike discernment of these words, it is only necessary to add that they express what was throughout Pusey's view of his own work.　To the defence of the Christian Faith he had solemnly devoted himself in his early days at Göttingen, when he first realized to what an extent 'the spirit of general unbelief' had in Germany shattered loyalty to Jesus Christ.　In England he saw that, as apologists for the Creed of the Catholic Church, there was little to choose between the Evangelical School of Cambridge and the Broad Church School of Arnold.　Both of these schools had a zeal for holiness ; but they were both in danger of disparaging, and even seemed ready to surrender some vital portions of that 'deposit of faith' which was the heritage and the strength of Christendom.　The Tractarians—and Pusey was a Tractarian till the day of his death—were convinced that Christian Apology could only be successful in the hands of those who held the whole of the Faith once delivered to the Saints.　They maintained that the Creeds, the Sacraments, and the Apostolical Succession are not unessential outworks of the Church; they are parts of a unity which has logically been surrendered when one portion has been

INTERIOR OF MEMORIAL CHAPEL AT ST. SAVIOUR'S, LEEDS.

abandoned. With this clear conviction, Pusey spent his life first in reasserting the Truths which were in danger of being overlooked, then in proving that the Church of

England had ever taught those Truths and in straining
every nerve to prevent their forfeiture, and afterwards in
showing how the Faith thus recovered in its completeness
was able to impart new spiritual energy to the English
Church, and in its strength to welcome without fear all those
discoveries of Science which were thought by others to
contradict it. When his share of this great work was
finished, very much still remained to be done. But under
God he had laid the foundation, and now others in grateful
remembrance may build upon it. He could well have
chosen for himself the motto selected for his Memorial in
Oxford, *Deus Scientiarum Dominus :* and he would have
always gone on to add the motto of the University which
he loved so truly, *Dominus illuminatio mea.*

MEMORIAL CROSS IN THE PINE WOODS OF ASCOT CONVALESCENT HOSPITAL.

# APPENDIX A.

THE following list has been compiled chiefly from the copies of Dr. Pusey's works contained in the British Museum, and in the Bodleian, Keble College Library, and the Pusey House Library at Oxford. It is intended to embrace every separate printed book and paper of which Dr. Pusey was author or editor, arranged in chronological order, the several editions of a book being connected by cross-references. Wherever a full collation (including the number of pages) is given, the volume has been seen. The order in each year is roughly according to the importance of the books. The sizes given only indicate the ordinary publisher's idea of folio, quarto, octavo, and duodecimo. An obelisk precedes a work edited, not written, by Dr. Pusey. An attempt has been made to subjoin to each year a list of printed letters (whether addressed to newspapers or to private persons) and of public speeches, which have not been separately issued. Imperfect as this supplementary list is, it would have been impossible to form it, but for the extensive collections of Miss Hughes, Lady Superior of the Convent, Woodstock Road, Oxford, and of Miss Kebbel, also of Oxford : to whom, as well as to Mr. C. J. Parker, of Broad St., Oxford, my best thanks are due. It must be understood that the titles of these letters are not meant to be exact, but sufficient for their identification : but the main entries are intended to be verbatim transcripts. The Rev. J. O. Johnston has kindly criticized and improved the whole Appendix, and Miss Milner of Oxford has also given much welcome assistance. The only papers issued by Dr. Pusey which have been knowingly omitted are the formal notices of lectures issued from term to term by him as Regius Professor of Hebrew, the first of which is dated Jan. 25, 1830, and the last June 6 (or perhaps June 13), 1882.

It would have been impossible, within the necessary limits of this List, to include literary pieces addressed to or commenting on

Dr. Pusey. The aim of the writer will be fulfilled if the following pages serve as a touch-stone by which a reader of this Life may test his own collection of the printed works therein referred to. Any corrections and additions will be gladly received.

FALCONER MADAN.

BRASENOSE COLLEGE, OXFORD :
*September,* 1897.

## 1824.

1. COLONIARUM APUD GRÆCOS ATQUE ROMANOS INTER SE COMPARATIO. Oratio Cancellarii præmio dignata, et in Theatro Sheldoniano habita die Jun. 30º. A.D. 1824. . . .

> Pp. [4] + 36 : [Oxford, 1824], 8ᵘ. Signed at end ' E. B. Pusey, e Coll. Oriel.'

## 1828.

1. AN HISTORICAL ENQUIRY INTO THE PROBABLE CAUSES OF THE RATIONALIST CHARACTER LATELY PREDOMINANT IN THE THEOLOGY OF GERMANY, to which is prefixed, a Letter from Professor Sack, upon the Rev. H. J. Rose's Discourses on German Protestantism ; translated from the German. By E. B. Pusey, M.A. Fellow of Oriel College, Oxford. [Part I.]

> Pp. xvi + xvi + 186 : London, 1828, 8º. See 1830, 1.

## 1830.

1. AN HISTORICAL ENQUIRY INTO THE CAUSES OF THE RATIONALIST CHARACTER LATELY PREDOMINANT IN THE THEOLOGY OF GERMANY. Part II. containing an explanation of the views misconceived by Mr. Rose, and further illustrations. By E. B. Pusey, M.A., Regius Professor of Hebrew in the University of Oxford and late Fellow of Oriel College.

> Pp. xvi + 436 : London, 1830, 8º. See 1828, 1. Part of a letter from Mr. Pusey to H. J. Rose, dated Oct. 10, 1828, is printed at pp. 175-80 of the latter's Letter to the Lord Bishop of London in reply to Mr. Pusey's work (Lond., 1829, 8º).

## 1832.

1. A SERMON [on Haggai ii. 9] PREACHED AT THE CONSECRATION OF GROVE CHURCH ON TUESDAY, AUGUST 14, 1832. By Edward Bouverie Pusey, B.D., Regius Professor of Hebrew, and Canon of Christ Church ; late Fellow of Oriel College.

> Pp. 38 : Oxford, 1832, 8º. See 1856, 4. The titles as above were the common ones used by Dr. Pusey on his titlepages till 1851 : in that year he began to omit the reference to Oriel College, which is not found after 1855. The 'B.D.' was of course changed to ' D.D.' after Feb. 25, 1836.

## 1833.

1. REMARKS ON THE PROSPECTIVE AND PAST BENEFITS OF CATHEDRAL INSTITUTIONS, IN THE PROMOTION OF SOUND RELIGIOUS KNOWLEDGE, OCCASIONED BY LORD HENLEY'S PLAN FOR THEIR ABOLITION. By Edward Bouverie Pusey, B.D., . . .

> Pp. [4] + 136 : London, 1833, 8°.

2. ——[as above, omitting 'occasioned—abolition.'] Second edition.
Pp. xii + 184 : London, 1833, 8°.

3. THE PHARISEE AND THE PUBLICAN [sermon on St. Luke xviii. 14].

> Pp. 169–184 of 'Original Family Sermons,' vol. 1 (London, 1833, 12°).

## 1834.

1. THOUGHTS ON THE BENEFITS OF THE SYSTEM OF FASTING, ENJOINED BY OUR CHURCH.

> Pp. 28 : Oxford, [1834], 8°. No. 18 of 'Tracts for the Times,' signed 'E. B. P.,' dated 'the Feast of St. Thomas' = Dec. 21 [1833]. See no. 2 ; 1835, 1 ; 1838, 5 ; 1839, 4 ; 1845, 7.

2. —— [as above : second edition].
Pp. 28 : London (Oxford), [1834], 8°.

3. QUESTIONS ON THE SUBJECT OF SUBSCRIPTION TO THE ARTICLES, SIGNED 'A BACHELOR OF DIVINITY,' i.e. Mr. Pusey. (23 questions beginning '1. Is the University willing,' preceded by a sentence beginning '☞ The expediency of substituting.')

> Pp. 4 : (Oxford), [circulated in the Oxford Common Rooms in November, 1834], folio. See 1835, 5.

## 1835.

1. SUPPLEMENT TO TRACT XVIII. On the benefits of the system of Fasting prescribed by our Church.

> Pp. 16 : London, [1835], 8°. No. 66 of 'Tracts for the Times,' signed 'E. B. P.,' dated July 25, [1835]: observations caused by a letter of 'Clericus' to the *British Magazine* of April, 1835 : but the postscript is dated 'Passion Week,' [1835]. See 1834, 1 ; 1839, 5 ; 1840, 3.

2. TRACTS FOR THE TIMES. SCRIPTURAL VIEWS OF HOLY BAPTISM.

> Pp. 208 : Oxford, 1835, 8°. Nos. 67 (pp. 1–48), 68 (pp. 49–104), 69 (pp. 105–208), of the 'Tracts for the Times,' unsigned, dated Aug. 24, Sept. 29, Oct. 18, [1835]. See 1836, 1 ; 1839, 6 ; 1840, 4 ; 1842, 7.
> The bibliography of Tracts 67–70 is a little intricate. The first edition of Nos. 67–69 is as stated above, and a note on No. 69 shows that the Notes to the three Tracts were intended to form No. 70. But the number 70 was given to an abridged reprint of Bp. Wilson's Meditations on Saturday, and the Notes were probably not issued at all in the year 1835. In 1836, Nos. 67–69

were reissued, with the Notes (pp. 209–296) and a general title-page bearing the writer's name and some prefatory matter, as an independent work, but still called Nos. 67–69. In 1839, No. 67 is issued revised and enlarged and called the second edition, but Nos. 68–69 were never reissued, and No. 70 has disappeared, having been printed in an unabridged form as an addition to the original Friday Meditations (by Bp. Wilson) in No. 65. So that practically Nos. 68–70 disappear entirely, and in and after 1839 no edition of the Tracts which seems to want them can be called imperfect.

3. BIBLIOTHECÆ BODLEIANÆ CODICUM MANUSCRIPTORUM ORIENTALIUM CATALOGI PARTIS SECUNDÆ VOLUMEN SECUNDUM ARABICOS COMPLECTENS CONFECIT ALEXANDER NICOLL, J.C.D. .... EDIDIT ET CATALOGUM URIANUM ALIQUATENUS EMENDAVIT E. B. PUSEY, S.T.B. .... [There is also a general title to the 'Pars secunda,' of which the present work is vol. 2: and also an original titlepage, dated 1821, of the 2nd vol. as it first began to be issued.]

> Pp. [2] + xii + 730, with nine plates of facsimiles: Oxonii e typographeo academico, 1835, fol. Edited by Mr. Pusey from p. 389 on, with additions and corrections to the whole: his contributions are more important than would appear from the title. The Uri Catalogue is the 'Pars prima' of the work and was published in 1788.

4. CHURCHES IN LONDON. Past and present exertions of the Church and her present needs. Reprinted from the British Magazine for November, 1835 [by E. B. Pusey].

> Pp. 16: Oxford, [1835 ?], 8°. See 1837, 1.

(Nos. 5–12. Papers about Subscription to the Articles, see 1834, 3 :—)

5. (CIRCULAR LETTER TO NON-RESIDENT MEMBERS OF CONVOCATION, beginning 'Sir, I am requested (as a Member of a Committee ...': no doubt by Mr. Pusey: dated April 3, 1835.

> Pp. 4: (Oxford, 1835), 8°.

6. —— (Another issue of the above, with variations, dated April 4, 1835.)

> Pp. 4: (Oxford, 1835), 8°.
> \*\*\* Nos. 5 and 6 above introduce no. 7 and are connected with it.

7. QUESTIONS RESPECTFULLY ADDRESSED TO MEMBERS OF CONVOCATION ... [27 in number, beginning 'Is the proposed substitution ...,' signed 'A Bachelor of Divinity,' i.e. E. B. Pusey.]

> Pp. 8: [Oxford, April, 1835, 8°.]

8. OXFORD MATRICULATION STATUTES. Answers to the 'Questions ... by a Bachelor of Divinity' with brief notes by A resident Member of Convocation [Dr. Edw. Hawkins: the original Questions are here reprinted as they stand in art. 7].

> Pp. 32: [Oxford, published May 7, 1835], 8°.

9. A second edition of the QUESTIONS ... with some additional queries suggested by the foregoing ones. [In this the 27 Questions

are reprinted and opposite to them in a parallel column 27 others *not* by Mr. Pusey.]

> Pp. 12 : [Oxford, published May 9, 1835], 8⁰.

10. SUBSCRIPTION TO THE THIRTY-NINE ARTICLES. Questions . . . with answers by a resident Member of Convocation, and brief notes upon those answers by the Bachelor of Divinity. [Mr. Pusey's answer to the 'Answers' of Dr. Hawkins.]

> Pp. 38 : [Oxford, published May 13, 1835] 8⁰.

11. (CIRCULAR LETTER TO NON-RESIDENT MEMBERS OF CON-VOCATION, beginning 'Sir, I beg to inform you . . .': no doubt by Mr. Pusey : dated May 5, 1835.

> Pp. 4 : (Oxford, 1835), 8⁰.

12. (A reprint of 1834, 3, issued as No. 5 in *both* issues of ' Pamphlets in defence of the Oxford usage of Subscription . . .': the first issue being on May 30, the second June 26, 1835).

> Pp. 8 : [Oxford, May–June, 1835], 8⁰.

## 1836.

1. TRACTS FOR THE TIMES. Nos. 67, 68, 69. SCRIPTURAL VIEWS OF HOLY BAPTISM, WITH AN APPENDIX. By the Rev. E. B. Pusey, B.D., . . .

> Pp. xx + 296 : London, 1836, 8⁰. See 1835, 2 : this may be re-garded as a reissue with additions rather than as a second edition, for the 1839 edition bears the words ' Second Edition, enlarged.'

2. AN EARNEST REMONSTRANCE TO [Dr. Charles Dickinson] THE AUTHOR OF THE 'POPE'S PASTORAL LETTER TO CERTAIN MEMBERS OF THE UNIVERSITY OF OXFORD': with a postscript noticing the Edinburgh Review, and other pamphlets, and an ap-pendix on Apostolical succession. By the Rev. E. B. Pusey, D.D. . . .

> Pp. 104 : London, 1836, 8⁰. Dated Apr. 25, (1836). The ap-pendix is a first reprint of No. 74 of ' Tracts for the Times' perhaps by J. H. Newman : pp. 1-36 were reprinted as No. 77 of ' Tracts for the Times': see no. 3.

3. —— [A reprint of the EARNEST REMONSTRANCE, headed by the following 'Note to the Advertisement':—] 'The following is Dr. Pusey's answer to an anonymous pamphlet, reflecting on these Tracts, which appeared in the end of March, 1836. The pamphlet professed to be a "Pastoral Epistle from the Pope . . ." Dr. Pusey's answer was entitled "An earnest Remonstrance . . . ." Tract 74 was added to it as an Appendix.'

> Pp. 36 : London, [1836], 8⁰. No. 77 of ' Tracts for the Times'; a reprint of the ' Earnest Remonstrance,' no. 2 above. See 1837, 4; 1839, 7; 1840, 8.

4. DR. HAMPDEN'S THEOLOGICAL STATEMENTS AND THE THIRTY-NINE ARTICLES COMPARED. By a resident member of Convocation.

With a preface [by Dr. Pusey] and propositions extracted from his works. . . .

> Pp. 42 + 62 : Oxford, 1836, 8°. The Preface and Propositions occupy the first 42 pages, and are signed 'E. B. Pusey,' March 12, (1836).

5. DR. HAMPDEN'S PAST AND PRESENT STATEMENTS COMPARED [by Dr. Pusey].

> Pp. 24 : Oxford, 1836, 8°. Signed 'E. B. P., March 21, 1836': on p. 23 is an 'Erratum in part of the impression,' in some copies.

6. — — [as above, adding] a Sequel to 'Dr. Hampden's Theological Statements and the XXXIX Articles compared.' Second edition, revised and enlarged.

> Pp. 36 : Oxford, 1836, 8°. Signed 'E. B. Pusey, Mar. 26, 1836.'

7. (A PETITION TO PARLIAMENT ABOUT CATHEDRALS, signed 'E. B. Pusey,' July 21, 1836.)

> Pp. 4 : 1836, folio.

8. †MAKE VENTURES FOR CHRIST'S SAKE. A Sermon [on St. Matth. xx. 22].

> Pp. 16 : Oxford, 1836, 8°. The sermon is by J. H. Newman : the preface (on p. 2) was written, and the motto (on p. 1) was suggested, by Dr. Pusey. Very rare.

## 1837.

1. CHURCHES IN LONDON, with an Appendix containing answers to objections raised by the 'Record' and others to the plan of the Metropolis Churches' Fund. By the Rev. E. B. Pusey, D.D.

> Pp. 40 : Oxford, 1837, 8°. See 1835, 4.

2. PATIENCE AND CONFIDENCE THE STRENGTH OF THE CHURCH. A sermon [on Ex. xiv. 13] preached on the fifth of November before the University of Oxford, at St. Mary's, and now published at the wish of many of its members. By the Rev. E. B. Pusey, D.D., . . .

> Pp. xvi + 58 : Oxford, 1837, 8°. See 1838, 3, 4, and 6 ; 1841, 9 ; 1864, 9.

3. CATENA PATRUM NO. IV. Testimony of writers of the later English Church to the doctrine of the Eucharistic Sacrifice, with an historical account of the changes made in the Liturgy as to the expression of that doctrine. [Compiled by Dr. Pusey, dated Nov. 1, 1837.]

> Pp. 416 : London, 1837, 8°. No. 81 of 'Tracts for the Times.' See 1839, 8 ; 1840, 5.

4. [A reprint of the EARNEST REMONSTRANCE, exactly as 1836, 3, with the following addition to the Note 'Two extracts have been added by the Author in the second reprint.']

> Pp. 36 : London, [1837], 8°. This is part of the Second Edition of vol. iii of the 'Tracts for the Times,' being itself No. 77 : the additions are on pp. 26-7 and 33-4.

## 1838.

1. THE ROYAL AND PARLIAMENTARY ECCLESIASTICAL COMMISSIONS. From the British Critic and Quarterly Theological Review, No. xlvi, April, 1838 [by Dr. Pusey]. Reprinted for private distribution.

> Pp. 112: London, [1838], 8°.

2. THE CHURCH THE CONVERTER OF THE HEATHEN. Two sermons [on Ps. lxxvii. 3–5 and Eph. iv. 12–14] preached in conformity with the Queen's letter in behalf of the Society for the Propagation of the Gospel, at St. Mary's Church, Melcombe Regis, Sept. 9, 1838. By E. B. Pusey, D.D., . . . Published by request.

> Pp. 148: Oxford, 1838, 8°. See 1839, 9; 1859, 3; 1864, 7.

3. PATIENCE AND CONFIDENCE . . . [&c., as 1837, 2, omitting ' now ']. Second edition.

> Pp. xvi + 152: Oxford, 1838, 8°.

4. PATIENCE AND CONFIDENCE . . . [&c., as 1837, 2, omitting ' now ']. Reprinted by permission of the author.

> Pp. 58: Glasgow, 1838, 8°.

5. THOUGHTS ON . . . FASTING . . . [&c., as 1834, 1]. Third edition.

> Pp. 28: London, 1838, 8°.

6. APPENDICES TO THE SERMON PREACHED BY THE REV. E. B. PUSEY, D.D., ON THE FIFTH OF NOVEMBER, 1837. Containing I. An explanation of points mistaken by the author of ' Passive Obedience contrary to Holy Scripture ' ; II. Remarks on the Revolution of 1688, and the principles involved or not involved in its condemnation, in answer to an article of the Edinburgh Review ; III. The Oxford Decree of 1683.

> Pp. 96: Oxford, 1838, 8°. See 1837, 2.

7. †THE CONFESSIONS OF S. AUGUSTINE. Revised from a former translation [by W. Watts], by the Rev. E. B. Pusey, D.D., with illustrations from S. Augustine himself. [Preface dated Aug. 24, 1838.]

> Pp. [8] + xxxvi + 364: Oxford, 1838, 8°. See 1853. 9; 1876, 8.
> (Vol. 1 of the ' Library of Fathers of the Holy Catholic Church, anterior to the division of the East and West, translated by members of the English Church,' in forty-eight volumes, 1838–85, which were superintended by the Rev. E. B. Pusey, the Rev. John Henry Newman, the Rev. John Keble, the Rev. Charles Marriott, and others. Pusey contributed several prefaces to separate volumes : see vol. i, pp. 445–7 of the present work.)

8. †S. AURELII AUGUSTINI CONFESSIONES POST EDITIONEM PARISIENSEM NOVISSIMAM AD FIDEM CODICUM OXONIENSIUM RECOGNITÆ, ET POST EDITIONEM M. DUBOIS EX IPSO AUGUSTINO ILLUSTRATÆ [ed. by Dr. Pusey: the preface is signed 'E. B. P.,' Aug. 24, 1838].

> Pp. xvi + 324: Oxonii, 1838, 8°. See 1872, 8. Vol. 1. of the ' Bibliotheca Patrum ecclesiæ Catholicæ qui ante Orientis et Occidentis schisma floruerunt. Delectu presbyterorum quorundam Oxoniensium.' A second ed. was published before 1846.

The ten volumes of the 'Bibliotheca Patrum,' 1838-70, were superintended by Pusey, Newman, Charles Marriott, and others. Dr. Pusey contributed a short note by way of preface to Theodoreti Comm. in B. Pauli Epistolas, pars ii (1870).

## 1839.

1. A LETTER TO THE RIGHT REV. FATHER IN GOD RICHARD LORD BISHOP OF OXFORD, ON THE TENDENCY TO ROMANISM IMPUTED TO DOCTRINES HELD OF OLD, AS NOW, IN THE ENGLISH CHURCH. By the Rev. E. B. Pusey, D.D., [with an 'Appendix. Extracts from the "Tracts for the Times," the "Lyra Apostolica," and other publications; showing that to oppose Ultra-Protestantism is not to favour Popery'].

> Pp. 240 + 24 : Oxford (London), 1839. 8°. See 1840, 1 and 2. The Letter is sometimes found without the Appendix.

2. —— A LETTER . . . [&c., as above].   Second edition.

> Pp. 240 + 24 : Oxford (London), 1839, 8°. Apparently a simple reissue : this edition was reprinted in America in this same year.

3. —— A LETTER . . . [&c., as above].   Third edition.

> Pp. [?] (1839 or 1840), 8°.

4. THOUGHTS ON . . . FASTING . . . [as 1834, 1].   New edition.

> Pp. 28 : Lond., 1839, 8°. No. 18 in 'Tracts for the Times,' vol. 1, Lond. 1839, 8°. See 1834, 1.

5. SUPPLEMENT TO TRACT XVIII . . . [as 1835, 1].   New edition.

> Pp. 16 : Lond., 1839, 8°. No. 66 in 'Tracts for the Times,' vol. 2, Lond., 1839, 8°. See 1835, 1.

6. TRACTS FOR THE TIMES. SCRIPTURAL VIEWS OF HOLY BAPTISM, as established by the consent of the ancient Church, and contrasted with the systems of modern schools . . . Part 1. [At head :—]   Second edition, enlarged.

> Pp. 398 : Lond., 1839, 8°. No. 67 in 'Tracts for the Times,' but two chapters only. See 1835, 2.

7. [A reprint of the EARNEST REMONSTRANCE, exactly as 1837, 4].

> Pp. 36 : London, [1839], 8°. See 1836, 3. The third edition of Tract 77 : part of the New Edition of vol. iii of the Tracts, 1839.

8. CATENA PATRUM, IV. . . . [as 1837, 3].   Second edition.

> Pp. 424 : Lond., 1839, 8°. No. 81 in 'Tracts for the Times,' vol. 4, Lond., 1839, 8°. See 1837, 3 ; 1840, 5.

9. THE CHURCH THE CONVERTER OF THE HEATHEN. . . [&c., as 1838, 2].

> Pp. 24 + 28 + 74 : Oxford, 1839, 12°. The two sermons were also issued separately. The cover sometimes bears the date 1842.

10. THE DAY OF JUDGEMENT. A sermon [on Joel ii. 11] preached on the twentieth Sunday after Trinity in S. Peter's Church, Brighton. By the Rev. E. B. Pusey, D.D., . . . Published by request.

> Pp. 32 : Oxford, 1839, 8°. See 1840, 6 and 7 ; 1854, 4 ; 1872, 6 ; 1884, 2.

## 1840.

1. A LETTER . . . [&c., as 1839, 1] with a preface [dated July 25, 1840] on the doctrine of Justification . . . Fourth edition.

> Pp. lx + 240 + 24 : Oxford (London), 1840, 8°. See No. 2.

2. —— PREFACE TO THE FOURTH EDITION OF THE ' LETTER . . .' [as 1839, 1] ON THE DOCTRINE OF JUSTIFICATION. . . . By the Rev. E. B. Pusey . . .

> Pp. 60 : Oxford (London), 1840, 8°. A separate issue of part of the preceding art.

3. SUPPLEMENT . . . [&c., as 1835, 1]. Fourth edition.

4. . . . HOLY BAPTISM [as 1839, 6]. Third edition, enlarged.

> Pp. 400 : London, 1840, 8°. No. 67 of the ' Tracts for the Times ' : identical with the second edition : see 1835, 2.

5. CATENA PATRUM IV [as 1837, 3]. Third edition.

> Pp. 424 : London, 1840, 8°. No. 81 of ' Tracts for the Times.'

6. THE DAY OF JUDGEMENT . . . [as 1839, 10]. Second edition.

> Pp. 32 : Oxford, 1840, 8°.

7. —— THE DAY . . . [&c., as above]. Third edition.

> Pp. 46 : Oxford, [no date, 1840?], 8°. See 1865, 2.

8. [A reprint of the EARNEST REMONSTRANCE, exactly as 1837, 4.]

> Pp. 36 : London, [1840], 8°. The fourth edition of Tract 77 : part of the New Edition of vol. 3 of the Tracts, 1840.

## 1841.

1. THE ARTICLES TREATED ON IN TRACT 90 RECONSIDERED AND THEIR INTERPRETATION VINDICATED IN A LETTER TO THE REV. R. W. JELF, D.D., CANON OF CHRIST CHURCH. With an appendix from Abp. Ussher on the difference between ancient and modern addresses to Saints. By the Rev. E. B. Pusey, D.D., . . .

> Pp. [4] + 218 : Oxford, 1841, 8°.

2. THE ARTICLES . . . [&c., as above]. Second edition.

> Pp. [4] + 218 : Oxford : 1841, 8°. A reissue with an alteration on p. 115.

3. PLAIN SERMONS BY CONTRIBUTORS TO THE ' TRACTS FOR THE TIMES.' Vol. III [entirely by Dr. Pusey].

> Pp. [4] + 320 : London, 1841, 8°. Sermons 73-92, Series 13-18 : probably their first publication. The same as ' Parochial Sermons, vol. 3 ': see 1873, 1 ; 1878, 3 ; 1883, 3. The ' Plain Sermons ' consisted of ten vols. issued in 1839-48.

4. CHRIST, THE SOURCE AND RULE OF CHRISTIAN LOVE. A sermon [on St. John xiii. 34-35], preached on the feast of S. John the Evangelist, MDCCCXL., at St. Paul's Church, Bristol, in aid of a new Church to be erected in an outlying district in that parish ; with a preface on the relation of our exertions to our needs. By the Rev. E. B. Pusey, D.D., . . . Published by request.

> Pp. 56 : Oxford, 1841, 8°. See 1865, 2 ; 1878, 10. Preface dated Nov. 21, 1841.

5. THE PREACHING OF THE GOSPEL A PREPARATION FOR OUR LORD'S COMING. A sermon [on St. Matth. xxiv. 14] preached at the parochial Church of St. Andrew's, Clifton, in conformity with the Queen's letter, in behalf of the Society for the Propagation of the Gospel. By the Rev. E. B. Pusey, D.D., . . . Published by request.

Pp. [4] + 32 : Oxford, 1841, 8°. See 1864, 10.

6. (The 'LIBRARY OF ANGLO-CATHOLIC THEOLOGY,' begun in this year, was published under the superintendence of a committee, of which Dr. Pusey was one.)

7. (THE COMMENTARY ON THE FOUR GOSPELS COLLECTED OUT OF THE WORKS OF THE FATHERS, translated from the Catena Aurea of Thomas Aquinas, published 1841–45, was superintended by the Rev. E. B. Pusey, the Rev. John Keble, and the Rev. John Henry Newman.)

8. †PRAYERS FOR UNITY AND GUIDANCE INTO THE TRUTH [' published (not compiled)' by Dr. Pusey].

Pp. 19 : Lond., 1841, 24°.

9. PATIENCE AND CONFIDENCE . . . [&c., as 1837, 2]. Third edition.

Pp. xvi + 60: Oxford, 1841, 8°. See 1859, 1.

10. (PAPER IN FAVOUR OF THE REV. ISAAC WILLIAMS, a candidate for the Professorship of Poetry. Signed 'E. B. Pusey,' Nov. 17, 1841.)

Pp. 4 (pp. 2–4 blank): [Oxford, 1841], 4°.

11. —— (LETTER TO DR. GILBERT, PRINCIPAL OF BRASENOSE, on the same subject, signed 'E. B. Pusey,' Nov. 25, 1841.)

Pp. 4 (pp. 2–4 blank: [Oxford, 1841], 4".

---

12. LETTER TO A FRIEND, dated Mar. 27, 1841, printed in the *Record* of April 5, 1841 : on the inspiration of Holy Scripture. Two more followed on the same subject, dated April 10 and 22, and printed in the *Record* of April 19 and 26, 1841.

13. LETTER TO THE REV. H. V. ELLIOT (1841) on sorrow.

14. LETTER TO A FRIEND, dated Sept. 7, 1841, on a passage in Dr. Miley's sermon about Dr. Pusey's supposed leaning towards Rome: apparently printed in the *Herald* of Sept. 25.

15. LETTER IN CONTINUATION OF THE ABOVE, dated Sept. 20, 1841 : also in the *Herald*.

## 1842.

1. A LETTER TO HIS GRACE THE ARCHBISHOP OF CANTERBURY, ON SOME CIRCUMSTANCES CONNECTED WITH THE PRESENT CRISIS IN THE ENGLISH CHURCH. By the Rev. E. B. Pusey, D.D., . . .

Pp. [4] + 172 : Oxford, 1842, 8°. There is a German translation of this Letter (1843) in the British Museum.

2. —— A LETTER ... [as above]. Second edition.
> Pp. [4] + 172 : Oxford, 1842, 8⁰.

3. —— A LETTER ... [as above]. Third edition.
> Pp. [4] + 164: Oxford, 1842, 8⁰.

4. —— A LETTER ... [as above]. Fourth edition.
> Pp. [4] + 166: Oxford, 1842, 8⁰.

5. —— NOTES ADDED TO THE THIRD EDITION OF A LETTER TO HIS GRACE THE ARCHBISHOP OF CANTERBURY by the Rev. Dr. Pusey.
> Pp. 24 : Oxford, [1842], 8⁰. A separate issue of part of No. 3, above.

6. A LETTER ON THE PROPOSED CHANGE IN THE LAWS PRO-HIBITING MARRIAGE BETWEEN THOSE NEAR OF KIN. Reprinted from the British Magazine, November, 1840. By the Rev. E. B. Pusey, D.D. . . .
> Pp. 24: Oxford, 1842, 8⁰. With a prefatory note dated ' Lent, 1842.'

7. . . . HOLY BAPTISM [as 1839, 6]. Fourth edition.
> Pp. 400: Oxford (London), 1842, 8⁰. No. 67 of 'Tracts for the Times.'

8. †TERTULLIAN, TRANSLATED BY THE REV. C. DODGSON. . . . Vol. [?]. Apologetic and practical treatises.
> Pp. viii + xx + 536 : Oxford, 1842, 8⁰. Part of the *Library of the Fathers*. Dr. Pusey contributed the Preface and notes of this volume, signing the former 'E. B. P.', June 24, 1842. See 1854, 7.

THE CHURCH THE CONVERTER : see 1839, 9.

## 1843.

1. THE HOLY EUCHARIST A COMFORT TO THE PENITENT. A sermon [on St. Matth. xxvi. 28] preached before the University in the Cathedral Church of Christ in Oxford on the fourth Sunday after Easter. By the Rev. E. B. Pusey, D.D., . . .
> Pp. viii + 96: Oxford, 1843, 8⁰. The appendix of 'Extracts' is by the Rev. W. J. Copeland. This is the well-known sermon for which Dr. Pusey was inhibited from preaching in the University pulpit for two years. See 1859, 1 ; 1865, 1 ; 1879, 2.

2. —— [another ed.] with an American appendix . . .
> Pp. vi + 80: New York, 1843, 8⁰. In the British Museum. There are also two German translations, 1843 and 1844, both in the British Museum.

3. †THE GOLDEN GROVE: A GUIDE TO DEVOTION. To which is added, the Guide for the Penitent. Also, Festival Hymns. By Jeremy Taylor, D.D. . . . A new edition with a notice [by Dr. Pusey] on the Guide for the Penitent.
> Pp. [4] + xvi + '232' [but 149–176 occur twice] + [8] : Oxford, 1843, 12⁰. The Notice (pp. 149*–176*) is signed 'E. B. P., Advent, 1842,' but there is nothing to prove that the rest of the book was edited by Dr. Pusey.

4. PROTEST [against suspension, addressed to the Vice-Chancellor, signed 'E. B. Pusey,' June 2, 1843].

> Pp. [2] : [Oxford, 1843], 4°.

5. —— (SUPPLEMENT TO THE PROTEST, signed by Dr. Pusey, beginning 'When I drew up', June 6, 1843.

> Pp. [2] : [Oxford, 1843], 4°.

------

> 6. LETTER TO THE REV. E. CHURTON, printed in the *English Churchman* in June, 1843, on the English Reformation.

> 7. LETTER TO THE 'IRISH ECCLESIASTICAL JOURNAL,' dated Oct. 14, 1843, on Dr. Newman's consistency.

## 1844.

1. THE SEARCHING OF THE HEART. By the Rev. E. B. Pusey, D.D., of Christ Church, Oxford.

> Pp. 12 : Lond., 1844, 12°.  No. 2 of 'Tracts for Englishmen.'

2. GOD IS LOVE. WHOSO RECEIVETH ONE SUCH LITTLE CHILD IN MY NAME RECEIVETH ME. Two sermons [on 1 St. John iv. 16–17 and St. Matth. xviii. 5] preached (with the sanction of the Lord Bishop) in the Church of the Holy Trinity, Ilfracombe, in behalf of a new church, and of the parochial schools, on the tenth and twelfth Sundays after Trinity, 1844. By the Rev. E. B. Pusey, D.D. . . . Published by request. The profits to be given in aid of the new Church.

> Pp. [4] + 48 : Oxford, 1844, 8° : see 1864, 11.

3. —— [as above].  Second edition.

> Pp. [4] + 50 : Oxford, 1844, 8°.

4. †A GUIDE FOR PASSING ADVENT HOLILY. . . . By Avrillon [translated and edited by Dr. Pusey, who signs the preface 'E. B. P.'].

> Pp. lxiv + 286 : London, 1844, 12°.  An inserted notice of Nov. 28, 1844, states that the frontispiece, not being ready, will be issued later.  See 1847, 6 ; 1872, 7.  There is also an undated edition (pp. lxiv + 306 : London (Oxford), 12°) probably after 1890.

5. †A GUIDE FOR PASSING LENT HOLILY. . . . By Avrillon.  Translated from the French and adapted to the use of the English Church [by Dr. Pusey, with a preface, also by him, signed 'E. B. P.,' Sexagesima, 1844].

> Pp. [2, frontispiece] + lxiv + 396 : London, 1844, 12°.  A second edition was issued before 1847 : see 1864, 18 ; 1872, 8 ; 1878, 14 ; 1884, 14.

6. †THE FOUNDATIONS OF THE SPIRITUAL LIFE : drawn from the book of the Imitation of Jesus Christ.  By F. Surin.  Translated from the French and adapted to the use of the English Church [by Dr. Pusey : the preface is also by him, signed 'E. B. P.,' July 24, 1844].

> Pp. [2, frontispiece] + lxxii + 252 : London, 1844, 12°.  See 1847, 8 ; 1874, 7.

7. †THE EPISTLES OF S. CYPRIAN, BISHOP OF CARTHAGE AND MARTYR, WITH THE COUNCIL OF CARTHAGE ON THE BAPTISM OF HERETICS. To which are added, the extant Works of S. Pacian, Bishop of Barcelona. With Notes and Indices. [Translated by the Rev. H. Carey, with a preface by Dr. Pusey signed ' E. B. P.,' Ember Week after Whit-Sunday, 1844].

> Pp. [4] + xxxiv + 422 : Oxford, 1844, 8⁰. See 1868, 12. Part of the ' Library of the Fathers '; the St. Cyprian has also a separate titlepage.

8. †SERMONS ON SELECTED LESSONS OF THE NEW TESTAMENT. By S. Augustine ... Vol. I.

> Pp. xii + 486 : Oxford, 1844, 8⁰. See 1854, 6. Part of the ' Library of the Fathers ': the preface is signed ' E. B. P.' The translation is by R. G. Macmullen.

## 1845.

1. ON THE RECENT JUDGEMENTS IN THE COURT OF ARCHES. Three letters to the English Churchman, 1845. By the Rev. E. B. Pusey, D.D., ... I. The Stone Altar case. II, III. Mr. Oakeley's case. Privately reprinted.

> Pp. 56 : Oxford, [1845 ?], 8⁰. The letters are dated Sept. 25, Oct. 5, Oct. 11, 1845.

2. A LETTER TO ONE PERPLEXED ABOUT HIS DUTIES TO THE ENGLISH CHURCH. Reprinted and revised from the English Churchman newspaper, No. 148 [Oct. 30, 1845].

> Pp. 8 : Leeds, [1845], 8⁰. The letter is dated August. In another issue of this, dated Nov. 3, 1845, there is no title (pp. 8 : Leeds, (1845), 8⁰).

3. LETTER TO THE REV. J. KEBLE, M.A. By the Rev. E. B. Pusey, D.D. .... [Reprinted] from the English Churchman, Nov. [really Oct. 16] 1845.

> Pp. [2] + 4 : [Oxford, 1845 ?], 8⁰. This is a reprint of about the year 1860, but is placed here for convenience of reference. It also bears the words ' To the Reverend J. K.', i.e. Keble, and Dr. Pusey did not correct this, but as a fact the letter was not addressed to any one person, see Vol. ii, p. 459.

4. A COURSE OF SERMONS ON SOLEMN SUBJECTS, CHIEFLY BEARING ON REPENTANCE AND AMENDMENT OF LIFE, PREACHED IN ST. SAVIOUR'S CHURCH, LEEDS, DURING THE WEEK AFTER ITS CONSECRATION ON THE FEAST OF S. SIMON AND S. JUDE, 1845. [Chiefly by, and all edited by, Dr. Pusey, who signs the preface ' E. B. P.,' Advent Ember Week, 1845.]

> Pp. [4] + xvi + 352 : Oxford, 1845, 8⁰. The editor explains that his own sermons, out of the nineteen, are the first and eleventh to nineteenth, but he delivered seventeen of them, and made some additions. See 1847, 1 ; 1877, 3.

5. THE BLASPHEMY AGAINST THE HOLY GHOST. A sermon [on St. Matth. xii. 31] preached at Margaret Chapel, on the feast of S. Peter, 1845. By the Rev. E. B. Pusey, D.D., ... Published by request.

The profits, if any, to be offered for the fund for rebuilding Margaret Chapel.

Pp. 24 : Oxford, 1845, 8º. See 1875, 4.

6. —— THE BLASPHEMY . . . [as above]. Second edition.

Pp. 28 : Oxford, 1845, 8º. See 1865, 2.

7. THOUGHTS ON . . . FASTING . . . [&c., as 1834, 1]. New edition.

Pp. 28 : London, 1845, 8º.

8. †PARADISE FOR THE CHRISTIAN SOUL. Compiled by J. M. Horst. Part IV.

See 1847, 5.

9. †THE YEAR OF AFFECTIONS . . . by Avrillon. Translated from the French, and adapted to the use of the English Church [by Dr. Pusey, who signs the preface ' E. B. P.,' Jan. 25, 1845].

Pp. lii + 336 : London, 1845, 12º. See 1847, 7.

10. (PRAYERS, signed J. K(eble), E. B. P(usey), C. M(arriott).)

Pp. 16: Oxford, (1845), 12º.

---

11. LETTER TO DR. HAWKINS, Provost of Oriel College, printed in the *Morning Post*, dated Jan. 8, 1845 : on Dr. Pusey's suspension from preaching.

12. LETTER FROM DR. PUSEY, on the case of Mr. Oakeley, printed in the *English Churchman* of Oct. or Nov.

## 1846.

1. ENTIRE ABSOLUTION OF THE PENITENT. A sermon [on St. John xx. 21–23] mostly preached before the University in the Cathedral Church of Christ, in Oxford, on the fourth Sunday after Epiphany. By the Rev. E. B. Pusey, D.D., . . . [Sermon I.]

Pp. xx + 76 : Oxford (London), 1846, 8º. See 1859, 1 ; 1865, 1 ; 1866, 6.

2. ENTIRE ABSOLUTION OF THE PENITENT. Sermon II. Judge thyself, that thou be not judged of the Lord. A sermon [on 1 Cor. xi. 31] preached before the University in the Cathedral Church of Christ, in Oxford, on the first Sunday in Advent, 1846. By the Rev. E. B. Pusey, D.D., . . .

Pp. 40: Oxford, 1846. 8º. See 1857, 5.

3. †THE LIFE OF JESUS CHRIST, IN GLORY ON EARTH ; a series of meditations for each day from Easter to Ascension Day. Adapted for members of the Church in England, from the French of Nouet. [Edited by Dr. Pusey, who signs the preface ' E. B. P.,' Easter, 1846].

Pp. xvi + 292 : London, 1846, 12º. See no. 4 ; 1847, 4 ; 1872, 7.

4. †THE LIFE OF JESUS CHRIST, IN GLORY IN HEAVEN ; daily meditations, for three weeks, from Ascension Day to the Wednesday

after Trinity Sunday. Adapted for members of the Church in England, from the French of Nouet. [Translated and edited by Dr. Pusey.]

> Pp. [2] + '293'—'478': London, 1846, 12°. The pagination connects this with No. 3; and an additional general titlepage, dated 1846 (otherwise exactly as 1847, 4), is appended, with a leaf of dedication.

5. †THE SPIRITUAL COMBAT, by ... Lawrence Scupoli ... with the Path of Paradise, by the same. Translated (with the additional chapters) from the Italian, for the use of members of the English Church. [Edited by Dr. Pusey, who signs the preface 'E. B. P.,' Quinquagesima, 1846].

> Pp. [2, frontispiece] + xxxii + 240: London, 1846, 12°. See 1849. 3; 1868, 11; 1883, 15; 1891, 2.

6. BUNSEN ON THE CHRONOLOGY OF HOLY SCRIPTURE: a letter signed 'E. B. P.,' pp. 298-324 of the *Christian Remembrancer*, xii, July, 1846.

CONVERSATION IN 1846: *see* 1866, *ad fin.*

# 1847.

1. A COURSE OF SERMONS ... [&c., as 1845, 4]. Second edition.

> Pp. [2] + xvi + 352: Oxford, 1847, 8°.

2. ROMANISM IN THE CHURCH, ILLUSTRATED BY THE CASE OF THE REV. E. G. BROWNE, AS STATED IN THE LETTERS OF REV. DR. PUSEY AND REV. A. B. ROWAN, A.M. Republished from the '*Standard*' and '*Morning Herald*' newspapers. With observations.

> Pp. 48: London, 1847, 8°. Letters of Dr. Pusey dated Sept. 4, 1847 (*Morning Herald*, copied by the *Standard*), Sept. 9, and Sept. 16 (both *Morning Herald*) are reprinted, with other matter.

3. CHASTISEMENTS NEGLECTED FORERUNNERS OF GREATER. A sermon [on Joel ii. 12–13] preached at Margaret Chapel on the vigil of the Annunciation, being the day appointed 'for a general fast and humiliation before Almighty God ...' By the Rev. E. B. Pusey, D.D., ... Published by request. Any profit to be given to feed poor Irish children.

> Pp. 32: London, 1847, 8°. See 1859, 2; 1872, 5.

4. †THE LIFE OF JESUS CHRIST, IN GLORY: daily meditations from Easter Day to the Wednesday after Trinity Sunday. Adapted for members of the Church in England, from the French of Nouet. [Translated and edited by Dr. Pusey, who signs the preface 'E. B. P.,' Easter, 1846.]

> Pp. 16 + 478: London, 1847, 8°. See 1846, 3 and 4.

5. †PARADISE OF THE CHRISTIAN SOUL, ENRICHED WITH CHOICEST DELIGHTS OF VARIED PIETY. By J. M. Horst. Adapted to the use

of the English Church. In two volumes. [Translated and edited by Dr. Pusey, who signs some of the prefaces 'E. B. P.'.]

> Pp. [4, frontispiece and title] + viii + 112 : [part 3] [2] + ii + 68 : [part 4] [4] + 92 : [Vol. 2, part 5] [4] + xxxii + 136 : [part 6, 2nd ed.] [2] + vi + 128 : [part 7] [4] + 88 : London, 1847, 12°. The separate issues of these parts are too intricate to be here followed out. Part 2 of the original was omitted. See 1845, 8; 1848, 4; 1869, 12. There is also an undated edition (pp. xlii + 246 : Oxford, 12°).

6. †A GUIDE FOR PASSING ADVENT HOLILY, . . . by Avrillon. Translated from the French, and adapted to the use of the English Church. [By Dr. Pusey, who signs the preface 'E. B. P.,' Nov. 17, 1844.]

> Pp. [2, frontispiece] + lxiv + 288 : London, 1847, 12°. See 1844, 4.

7. †THE YEAR OF AFFECTIONS, by Avrillon . . . [&c., as 1845, 9].

> Pp. lii + 336 : London, 1845, 12°.

8. †THE FOUNDATIONS OF THE SPIRITUAL LIFE, . . . by F. Surin [ . . . as 1844, 6].

> Pp. [?] : Oxford, 1847, 12°.

9. †SELECT WORKS OF S. EPHREM THE SYRIAN, translated out of the original Syriac. With notes and indices. By the Rev. J. B. Morris. . . . [With an Advertisement of 4 pp. by Dr. Pusey, signed E. B. P.,' Lent, 1847.]

> Pp. [2] + xviii + 450 : Oxford, 1847, 8°.

---

10. LETTER TO THE 'MORNING HERALD,' dated Sept. 4, 1847, on the Rev. G. Browne, followed by one dated Sept. 9 : and one to the *Guardian*, dated Sept. 16.

## 1848.

1. SERMONS DURING THE SEASON FROM ADVENT TO WHITSUN-TIDE. By the Rev. E. B. Pusey, D.D., . . .

> Pp. xxviii + viii + 376 : Oxford (Littlemore), 1848, 8°. This is 'Parochial Sermons, vol. 1.' See no. 2; 1852, 1; 1864, 6; 1883, 2. One of these sermons, on 'Increased Communions' (on 1 Cor. xi. 28) was reprinted at Aberdeen (pp. 28 : n. d. : 12°).

2. —— [as above]. Second edition.

> Pp. [4] + xxviii + viii + 376 : Oxford (Littlemore), 1848, 8°.

3. LITANIES FOR PENITENTS. In the words of Holy Scripture.

> Pp. [?] : n. pl., 1848, 12°. Edited by Dr. Pusey?

4. DEVOTIONS FOR HOLY COMMUNION.

> Pp. [?] : n. pl., 1848, 12°. Taken from Horst's 'Paradise for the Christian Soul,' as edited by Dr. Pusey (1847, 5). There is also an issue of the entire work in two volumes, with titlepage dated 1848. See 1856, 1.

## 1849.

1. MARRIAGE WITH A DECEASED WIFE'S SISTER PROHIBITED BY
HOLY SCRIPTURE, AS UNDERSTOOD BY THE CHURCH FOR 1500
YEARS. Evidence given before the Commission appointed to inquire
into the state and operation of the Law of Marriage, as relating to the
prohibited degrees of affinity, with a Preface by E. B. Pusey, D.D., . . .
To which is appended, a speech . . . by Edward Badeley, Esq. . . .

> Pp. xciv + 174 (pp. ' 3 '—' 176 ') : Oxford (London), 1849, 8°.

2. DO ALL TO THE LORD JESUS. A sermon [on Col. iii. 17]. By
the Rev. E. B. Pusey, D.D., . . . Published by request.

> Pp. 18: London, 1849, 12°. See 1853, 8 ; 1855, 3 ; 1875, 5.

3. †THE SPIRITUAL COMBAT . . . by L. Scupoli [&c., as 1846, 5].
Second edition.

> Pp. [2, frontispiece] + xxxii + 246 : London, 1849, 12°. See 1846, 5.

## 1850.

1. THE ROYAL SUPREMACY NOT AN ARBITRARY AUTHORITY BUT
LIMITED BY THE LAWS OF THE CHURCH, OF WHICH KINGS ARE
MEMBERS. By the Rev. E. B. Pusey, D.D., . . . Part I. Ancient
Precedents.

> Pp. iv + 260 : Oxford (London), 1850, 8°.

2. —— THE ROYAL SUPREMACY . . . [&c., as above]. Second edition.
> Pp. iv + 260 : Oxford (London), 1850, 8°.

3. THE CHURCH OF ENGLAND LEAVES HER CHILDREN FREE TO
WHOM TO OPEN THEIR GRIEFS. A letter to the Rev. W. U. Richards,
Minister of All Saints, St. Mary-le-Bone. By the Rev. E. B. Pusey,
D.D., . . .

> Pp. iv + 200 : Oxford (London), 1850, 8°. Dated July 25, 1850.

4. —— THE CHURCH . . . [&c., as above]. Second edition, with
a postscript, in answer to the letters of the Rev. W. Maskell.

> Pp. iv + 312 : Oxford (London), 1850, 8°. A reissue of the fore-
> going art. with pp. 201–312 (the Postscript) added, dated Nov. 30,
> 1850. Some copies of the first ed. have the Postscript (which
> was issued also separately) bound with them.

5. THE DANGER OF RICHES : SEEK GOD FIRST, AND YE SHALL
HAVE ALL. Two sermons [on St. Luke xviii. 24–27 and St. Matth. vi.
33] preached in the parish church of St. James, Bristol. By the
Rev. E. B. Pusey, D.D., . . . Published by request.

> Pp. [4] + 48 : Oxford (London), 1850, 8°. See 1865, 2 ; 1880, 6.

6. GOD WITHDRAWS IN LOVING KINDNESS ALSO. [A sermon on
the Song of Solomon v. 2–8] preached by E. B. Pusey, D.D.

> Sermon xiv in ' Sermons preached at S. Barnabas, Pimlico, in . . .
> 1850,' London, 1850, 8°, p. 379. There is also a separate reprint
> of this sermon, entitled ' A sermon preached . . .' (pp. [2] + 30 :
> n. pl., n. d., 8°). In the later issues (see App. B) some passages
> are omitted.

7. London Union on Church Matters. Address of the Rev. E. B. Pusey, D.D. . . . At a meeting of the London Union on Church Matters, held in St. Martin's Hall, October 15, 1850. Published at the request of the Meeting. (Reprinted from the Guardian.) With a Postscript.

> Pp. 16: Oxford (London), (1850), 8°. The postscript is dated Oct. 21, 1850. See no. 12.

8. 'Christ in us and we in Him' the Bond of Catholic Unity. [Extracted from the Preface to 'Sermons . . . from Advent to Whitsuntide: by the Rev. E. B. Pusey, D.D.' First edition, pp. v–xix: together with the Advertisement to the second edition.]

> No. 5 of 'Tracts on Catholic Unity, by Members of the Church of England,' London, [about 1850], 8°.

---

9. Letter to the 'Guardian,' dated March 4, 1850, on the Court of Appeal in ecclesiastical causes: followed by another, dated 5th Friday in Lent, 1850, on the Royal Supremacy.

10. Letter to the 'Guardian' (of April 30?, 1850), not dated, in reply to Mr. Goode's Letter to the Bishop of Exeter.

11. Letter to the 'Guardian,' dated June 17, 1850, in answer to Mr. Dodsworth.

12. Speech at a Supplementary Meeting held at the Freemasons' Tavern, London, to consider the Judgement in the Gorham Case: from the *Times*, July 24, 1850. The *Guardian* report of the meeting was reprinted with an appendix, see no. 7.

13. Letter to the 'Guardian,' dated Aug. 27, 1850, on the Royal Supremacy.

## 1851.

1. A Letter to the . . . Bishop of London, in Explanation of some Statements contained in a Letter by the Rev. W. Dodsworth. By the Rev. E. B. Pusey, D.D., . . .

> Pp. viii + 268: Oxford (London), 1851, 12°.

2. A Letter . . . [&c., as above]. Second edition.

3. A Letter . . . [&c., as above]. Third edition.

4. A Letter . . . [&c., as above]. Fourth edition.

> Pp. viii + 196: Oxford (London), 1851, 16°.

5. A Letter . . . [&c., as above]. Fifth edition.

> Pp. viii + 196: Oxford (London), 1851, 12°.

6. A Letter . . . [&c., as above]. Sixth edition.

7. A Letter . . . [&c., as above]. Seventh edition.

> Pp. viii + 196: Oxford (London), 1851, 12°. An edition printed at Hobart Town in this year is in the British Museum.

8. —— Renewed Explanation in consequence of Rev. W. Dodsworth's Comments on Dr. Pusey's Letter to the Bishop of London. By the Rev. E. B. Pusey, D.D., . . .

> Pp. 56: Oxford (London), 1851, 8°. There should also be a small additional slip referring to p. 29.

9. —— (DR. PUSEY'S REPLY to some Remarks of Mr. Dodsworth's on the above letter.)

> Pp. [?] : n. pl., 1851, 8⁰. This is different from the 'Renewed Explanation.'

10. THE RULE OF FAITH, AS MAINTAINED BY THE FATHERS, AND THE CHURCH OF ENGLAND: a sermon [on 2 St. Tim. i. 13, 14] preached before the University in the Cathedral Church of Christ, in Oxford, on the fifth Sunday after Epiphany. By the Rev. E. B. Pusey, D.D., . . .

> Pp. [4] + 72 : Oxford (London), 1851, 8⁰. See 1859, 1 ; 1865, 1 ; 1878, 8.

11. A LECTURE DELIVERED IN THE TEMPORARY CHAPEL, TITCH-FIELD ST., PREVIOUSLY TO LAYING THE FOUNDATION STONE OF THE CHURCH OF ALL SAINTS, IN MARGARET ST., MARYLEBONE, ON ALL SAINTS' DAY, MDCCCL. By the Rev. E. B. Pusey, D.D., . . . Published by request.

> Pp. 16 : London, 1851, 8⁰.

12. HINTS FOR A FIRST CONFESSION [by Dr. Pusey]. Privately Printed.

> Pp. 16 : Oxford, 1851, 12⁰. This also appears as pp. 67–77 of 'The Ordinance of Confession. By William Gresley . . .' (Lond., 1851. See 1884, 8 and 9.

13. ON THE PROPOSED VOTE OF £53,100 [a paper on the proposal to build the New Museum at Oxford, signed 'A Doctor of Divinity,' i.e. Dr. Pusey, June 14, 1851].

> Pp. 4 : [Oxford, 1851], 4⁰.

14. CORRESPONDENCE BETWEEN THE CAMDEN PROFESSOR AND THE REV. DR. PUSEY [about the Camden endowment, dated June 18, 1851].

> Pp. 4 : [Oxford], (1851', 4⁰.

---

15. LETTER TO THE 'GUARDIAN,' dated Mar. 12, 1851, in answer to Mr. Palmer.

16. LETTER TO THE 'GUARDIAN,' March, 1851, in answer to Mr. Dodsworth.

17. LETTER TO MR. SKINNER, dated Dec. 17, 1851, on Dr. Pusey's editions of Avrillon.

## 1852.

1. PAROCHIAL SERMONS. By the Rev. E. B. Pusey, D.D. Vol. I. For the season from Advent to Whitsuntide. Third edition.

> Pp. xxviii + viii + iv + 376 : Oxford, 1852, 8⁰. See 1848, 1 ; 1868, 3.

2. LETTERS OF THE REV. DR. PUSEY TO THE EARL OF SHAFTES-BURY AND SIR JOHN ROMILLY, ON THEIR IMPUTATIONS AGAINST THE TRACTARIANS, WITH SIR JOHN ROMILLY'S ANSWER. (Reprinted from the Morning Chronicle.)

> Pp. 12 : Leeds, 1852, 8⁰. The letters are dated June 23, July 21 and 27, 1852.

3. LIBRARY OF THE FATHERS [an account of the state of the series, volumes published and proposed, &c., signed 'E. B. Pusey,' Nov. 17, 1852].

> Pp. 8: [Oxford], (1852), 8°. Another undated issue, beginning with the same words as the dated account, viz., 'The Library of the Fathers has now been continued . . . for fourteen years' (in ten 8vo pages), must have been issued in 1851 or 1852.

4. †LENT READINGS FROM THE FATHERS. Selected from 'the Library of the Fathers.' [Edited by 'W. I. E. B[ennett],' with an additional prefatory note by Dr. Pusey, signed 'E. B. P.']

> Pp. viii + 272 : Oxford, 1852, 12°. See 1853, 10; 1872, 3.

---

5. LETTER TO THE 'MORNING CHRONICLE,' dated March 15, 1852, in answer to the Rev. R. Ward.

## 1853.

1. PAROCHIAL SERMONS. By the Rev. E. B. Pusey, D.D. Vol. II.

> Pp. xii + 400 : Oxford, 1853, 8°. See 1848, 2; 1862, 2; 1868, 4; 1869, 2. An 'Advertisement' deplores the loss of sermons on Dan. iv. 27, St. James v. 19-20, and St. John xx. 21, at Reading Station. They were probably not recovered, or at any rate have never been printed. The sermon on Humility was reprinted in New York in 1871 (pp. 24, 12°): and that on Patience had also some years before been reprinted in the same city: both by 'H. H.'

2. —— PAROCHIAL SERMONS . . . [&c., as above]. Vol. II. Second edition.

> Pp. xii + 400 : Oxford, 1853, 8°.

3. (LETTER TO W. G. COOKESLEY from Dr. Pusey, July 7, 1853, about a lady who joined the Church of Rome.)

> Printed at p. 1 of a letter to Dr. Pusey by W. G. Cookesley, with no title or titlepage, but dated July 16, 1853: pp. 12: n. pl., [1853], 8°.

4. A LETTER TO HIS GRACE THE ARCHBISHOP OF DUBLIN ON . . . MISS SELLON'S ESTABLISHMENT AT DEVONPORT . . . By Rev. W. G. Cookesley. . . Fifth edition. To which is added a Letter from Dr. Pusey and W. G. Cookesley's Reply.

> Pp. 78: London, 1853, 8°. The letter of Dr. Pusey is on pp. 69-71, and first appeared in this edition.

5. THE PRESENCE OF CHRIST IN THE HOLY EUCHARIST. A sermon [on 1 Cor. x. 16] preached before the University, in the Cathedral Church of Christ, in Oxford, on the second Sunday after Epiphany, 1853. By the Rev. E. B. Pusey, D.D., . . .

> Pp. viii + 74: Oxford (London), 1853, 8°. See 1859, 1; 1865, 1; 1871, 5.

6. JUSTIFICATION. A sermon [on St. James ii. 22] preached before the University at S. Mary's, on the 24th Sunday after Trinity, 1853, by the Rev. E. B. Pusey, D.D., . . .

> Pp. 50: Oxford, 1853, 8°. See 1859, 1; 1865, 1; 1879, 2.

7. EVIDENCE FROM THE REV. E. B. PUSEY, D.D., Regius Professor of Hebrew and Canon of Christ Church.

> Pp. 1–174 of Evidence in ' Report and Evidence upon the recommendations of Her Majesty's Commissioners for inquiry into the state of the University of Oxford . . .' (Oxford, 1853, 8°.)

8. DO ALL TO THE LORD JESUS . . . [&c., as 1849, 2]. Fourth edition.

> Pp. [2] + 16 : London, 1853, 12°.

9. †THE CONFESSIONS OF S. AUGUSTINE . . ., [&c., as 1838, 7].

> Pp. xl + 364 : Oxford, 1853, 8°. Part of the 'Library of the Fathers.'

10. †ADVENT READINGS FROM THE FATHERS. Selected from 'the Library of the Fathers.' [Edited by 'W. I. E. B(ennett)': probably supervised by Dr. Pusey: see 1852, 4.]

> Pp. viii + 228 : Oxford, 1853, 12°.

## 1854.

1. COLLEGIATE AND PROFESSORIAL TEACHING AND DISCIPLINE, IN ANSWER TO PROFESSOR VAUGHAN'S STRICTURES, CHIEFLY AS TO THE CHARGES AGAINST THE COLLEGES OF FRANCE AND GERMANY. By the Rev. E. B. Pusey, D.D. . . .

> Pp. viii + 216 (' 3 '—' 218 ') : Oxford, 1854, 8°.

2. A CORRESPONDENCE BETWEEN THE REV. E. B. PUSEY, D.D.. . . . AND THE REV. R. H. FORTESCUE, M.A., LATE CURATE OF BIGBURY, DEVON, ON THE PRACTICE OF AURICULAR CONFESSION. AS EVIDENCED BY THE INQUIRIES AT LEEDS AND PLYMOUTH : edited, with a Preface and Notes, by the latter of the Correspondents.

> Pp. xvi + 48 : Plymouth, 1854, 8°. Dr. Pusey's letters are dated Dec. 27 and 31, 1852.

3. SUMMARY OF OBJECTIONS AGAINST THE PROPOSED THEOLOGICAL STATUTE. By the Rev. E. B. Pusey, D.D., . . . [dated June 5, 1854].

> Pp. 16 : Oxford, 1854, 8°.

4. THE DAY OF JUDGEMENT . . . [&c., as 1839, 10, adding '1839' after 'Trinity']. Third edition.

> Pp. 48 : Oxford, [1854?], 8°.

5. †FAMILIAR INSTRUCTIONS ON MENTAL PRAYER ; from the French of Courbon : with a preface by the Editor [Dr. Pusey, who signs the preface ' E. B. P.,' Jan. 6, 1854] Second Part.

> Pp. viii + 100 : London, 1854, 12°. See 1856, 9. Only this second part is edited by Dr. Pusey, the first being edited by W[illiam] U[pton] R[ichards].

6. †SERMONS . . . By S. Augustine . . . [as 1844, 8]. Vol. I.

> Pp. xii + 486 : Oxford, 1854, 8°.

7. †TERTULLIAN . . . [&c., as 1842, 8]. Second edition.

> Pp. [2] + iv + lvi + 548 : Oxford, 1854, 8°.

## 1855.

1. THE DOCTRINE OF THE REAL PRESENCE, AS CONTAINED IN THE FATHERS FROM THE DEATH OF S. JOHN THE EVANGELIST TO THE FOURTH GENERAL COUNCIL, VINDICATED, IN NOTES ON A SERMON 'THE PRESENCE OF CHRIST IN THE HOLY EUCHARIST,' PREACHED A.D. 1853, BEFORE THE UNIVERSITY OF OXFORD. By the Rev. E. B. Pusey, D.D., . . .

> Pp. xii + 724 : Oxford (London). 8º. Dated April 5, 1855. See 1883, 4. Another work, entitled 'The Doctrine of the Real Presence as set forth in the Works of Divines and others in the English Church since the Reformation,' was published in two parts in this same year, but had no connexion with Dr. Pusey. The first part was by Dr. William Wright.

2. ALL FAITH THE GIFT OF GOD. REAL FAITH ENTIRE. Two sermons [on 1 Cor. iv. 7 and Rom. i. 4] preached before the University of Oxford on the twenty-third and twenty-fourth Sundays after Trinity, 1855. By the Rev. E. B. Pusey, D.D., . . .

> Pp. viii + 96 : Oxford (Bristol), 1855, 8º. See 1856, 5 ; 1864, 8.

3. DO ALL TO THE LORD JESUS. . . [&c., as 1849, 2]. Fifth edition.

> Pp. 24 : Oxford, 1855, 8º. See 1865, 2.

## 1856.

1. DEVOTIONS FOR HOLY COMMUNION.

> Pp. [?] : Lond., 1856, 12º. Privately printed : ' The Thanksgiving after Holy Communion, &c., to end were by Dr. Pusey, and were previously published separately : the first part was by the Rev. [W.] U. Richards.' See 1848, 4 ; 1869, 5.

2. BEDELL'S STATUTE [a paper on the proposed alteration in the position of the Bedells at Oxford : anonymous, but by Dr. Pusey : undated, but Feb. 1856].

> Pp. 4 : [Oxford, 1856], 4º.

3. SERMON [on Rev. xxi. 6] by the Rev. E. B. Pusey, D.D., Regius Professor of Hebrew in Christ Church College, Oxford. THE END OF ALL THINGS.

> Pp. 222–40 of 'Sermons by eminent living Divines of the Church of England' (London, 1856, 8º), 'British Eloquence. Sacred Oratory, first series.' See Appendix B.

4. A SERMON . . . [&c., as 1832, 1]. Third edition.

> Pp. 30 : Oxford, 1856, 8º. See 1865, 2 ; 1884, 2.

5. ALL FAITH . . . [&c., as 1855, 2]. Second edition.

> Pp. viii + 96 : Oxford (Bristol), 1856, 8º. See 1859, 1.

6. (DECLARATION on the Real Presence, first form, drawn up by Dr. Pusey, beginning '[*Private and Confidential*] We the undersigned Priests.')

> Pp. 4 : n. pl., [1856], 8º. With a passage from Bp. Poynet.

7. —— (Declaration as published, with the title PROTEST AGAINST THE BATH JUDGEMENT.)

> Pp. [?] : n. pl. [Oct. 1856], 8°.  See Vol. iii, p. 440.

8. †MEDITATIONS AND PRAYERS . . . by S. Anselm, sometime Archbishop of Canterbury.  [Edited, but not translated, by Dr. Pusey, who signs the preface 'E. B. P.' Sept. 1856.]

> Pp. xx + 280 : Oxford, 1856, 12°.

9. †FAMILIAR INSTRUCTIONS . . . [&c., as 1854, 5].  Second edition.

> Pp. xxviii + 188: London, 1856, 12°.  In this edition both parts are included.

---

10. LETTER TO THE 'GUARDIAN,' dated Oct. 20, 1856, on the Doctrine of the Holy Eucharist.

### 1857.

1. THE COUNCILS OF THE CHURCH FROM THE COUNCIL OF JERUSALEM, A.D. 51, TO THE COUNCIL OF CONSTANTINOPLE, A.D. 381, CHIEFLY AS TO THEIR CONSTITUTION BUT ALSO AS TO THEIR OBJECTS AND HISTORY.  By the Rev. E. B. Pusey, D.D., . . .

> Pp. xvi + 356: Oxford (Bristol), 1857, 8°.

2. THE REAL PRESENCE OF THE BODY AND BLOOD OF OUR LORD JESUS CHRIST THE DOCTRINE OF THE ENGLISH CHURCH, WITH A VINDICATION OF THE RECEPTION BY THE WICKED AND OF THE ADORATION OF OUR LORD JESUS CHRIST TRULY PRESENT.  By the Rev. E. B. Pusey, D.D., . . .

> Pp. xxx + 354 : Oxford (Bristol), 1857, 8°.  See 1869, 3 ; 1885, 3.

3. —— THE REAL PRESENCE . . . [&c., as above].  Second edition.

> Pp. [?] : Oxford (Bristol), 1857, 8°.

4. REPENTANCE, FROM LOVE OF GOD, LIFE-LONG.  A sermon [on St. Luke xxii. 61–62] preached in the Church of St. Mary-the-Virgin, Oxford, on Thursday, April 2, 1857.  By Edward Bouverie Pusey, D.D., . . .

> Pp. 28 : Oxford, 1857, 8°.

5. ENTIRE ABSOLUTION OF THE PENITENT.  Sermon II. . . . (&c., as 1846, 2).  Third edition.

> Pp. 48 ; Oxford (Bristol), 1857, 8°.  See 1859, 1 ; 1865, 1 ; 1879, 2.

6. †EXPOSITIONS ON THE BOOK OF PSALMS BY S. AUGUSTINE, BISHOP OF HIPPO, translated with notes and indices [by C. Marriott(?) and H. Walford].  In six volumes.  Vol. VI.  Psalm cxxvi–cl.

> Pp. [2] + vi + 548: Oxford, 1857, 8°.  Part of the 'Library of the Fathers.'  The Advertisement is signed 'E. B. P.', Advent 1857.

### 1858.

---

1. LETTER TO THE 'GUARDIAN,' dated Dec. 7, 1858, on the action of the Scotch Bishops.

## 1859.

1. NINE SERMONS PREACHED BEFORE THE UNIVERSITY OF OXFORD AND PRINTED CHIEFLY BETWEEN A.D. 1843-1855. Now collected into one volume. By the Rev. E. B. Pusey, Regius Professor of Hebrew, and Canon of Christ Church. [Preface dated 'Easter 1859.']

> Pp. [8, i.e. 5 + 'xxii' + 'xxiii' + 1] and viii + 94 (= 1843, 1), and xx + 76 (= 1846, 1), and 48 (= 1857, 5), and viii + 74 (= 1853, 5), and 50 (= 1853, 6), and [4] + 70 (= 1851, 10), and viii + 94 (= 1856, 5), and xvi + 60 (= 1841, 9): Oxford, 1859, 8°. See 1865, 1; 1879, 2. Afterwards issued as 'University Sermons, Vol. I,' see 1872, 1; 1878, 4.

2. CHASTISEMENTS . . . [&c., as 1847, 3]. Third edition.

> Pp. 32: Oxford (Bradford on Avon), 1859, 8°. See 1865, 2.

3. THE CHURCH THE CONVERTER . . . [&c., as 1838, 2]. Fourth edition.

> Pp. 68: Oxford (Bradford on Avon), 1859, 8°. See 1865, 2.

## 1860.

1. THE MINOR PROPHETS, with a Commentary explanatory and practical and introductions to the several books, by the Rev. E. B. Pusey, D.D., Regius Professor of Hebrew, and Canon of Christ Church.

> Pp. viii + 624: Oxford, 1860, 4°. Issued in six parts (1860 (2nd ed. 1861: tenth thousand, 1863), 1861, 1862, 1871, 1875, 1877) and with an additional titlepage, 'The Holy Bible, with a Commentary explanatory and practical and introductions to the several books, by Clergymen of the Church of England,' Oxford, 1860, with Preface dated Easter, 1860. See 1877, 2. The parts were re-issued without modification in various years. An index to this work was published in 1891.

2. GOD'S PROHIBITION OF THE MARRIAGE WITH A DECEASED WIFE'S SISTER, LEVITICUS xviii. 6, NOT TO BE SET ASIDE BY AN INFERENCE FROM A RESTRICTION OF POLYGAMY AMONG THE JEWS, LEVITICUS xviii. 18. By the Rev. E. B. Pusey, D.D., . . .

> Pp. 44: Oxford (London), 1860, 8°.

3. ON THE 'HONORS' PROPOSED TO BE CONFERRED BY THE NEW THEOLOGICAL STATUTE. [Signed 'E. B. P.,' i.e. Dr. Pusey: undated, but May, 1860.]

> [Oxford, 1860,] 4°.

## 1861.

1, 2. See 1860, 1 ('Minor Prophets,' pt. 1, 2nd ed., and pt. 2).

3. A LETTER ON THE 'ESSAYS AND REVIEWS,' by Dr. Pusey. (Reprinted from *the Guardian* [of March 6, 1861].)

> Pp. 4: n. pl., (1861 ?), 8°. The letter is dated 'Lent, 1861.'

4. WITH WHOM LIES THE RESPONSIBILITY OF THE APPROACHING CONFLICT AS TO THE GREEK CHAIR? [Signed 'Pacificus,' i.e. Dr. Pusey: undated, but Nov. 1861.]

Pp. 4: [Oxford, 1861], 8°.

5. ON WHOM LIES THE RESPONSIBILITY OF THE PRESENT CONTEST? Answer to M.A. [Signed 'Pacificus,' i.e. Dr. Pusey: undated, but Nov. 1861.]

Pp. 2: [Oxford, 1861], 8°.

6. ANSWER TO PROFESSOR STANLEY'S STRICTURES [on the subject of the endowment of the Greek Chair at Oxford: signed 'E. B. Pusey,' Nov. 25, 1861].

Pp. 8: [Oxford], (1861), 8°.

7. THE THOUGHT OF THE LOVE OF JESUS FOR US, THE REMEDY FOR SINS OF THE BODY. A Sermon [on 1 Cor. vi. 15] preached to younger members of the University, at St. Mary's Church, Oxford, on Friday evening, March 1, [1861]. By the Rev. E. B. Pusey, D.D., . . . Published by request.

Pp. 20: Oxford, 1861, 8°.

8. GROUNDS OF OBJECTION TO DETAILS, AT LEAST, OF THE STATUTE, AS NOW PROPOSED, FOR MIDDLE CLASS EXAMINATIONS. [Signed 'E. B. Pusey.']

Pp. 8: [Oxford, April, 1861], 8°. Another issue of this paper is identical except that it bears Messrs. Parker's imprint, and the price.

9. VINDICATION OF GROUNDS OF OBJECTION TO DETAILS, AT LEAST, OF THE STATUTE, AS NOW PROPOSED, FOR MIDDLE CLASS EXAMINATIONS, AGAINST A LEADING ARTICLE IN THE 'GUARDIAN.' [Signed 'E. B. Pusey,' May 6, [1861]

Pp. 8: Oxford [1861], 8°.

10. †THE WORKS NOW EXTANT OF S. JUSTIN THE MARTYR, translated, with notes and indices. [Preface revised by Dr. Pusey, who signs it 'E. B. P.': the Editor was the Rev. C. Marriott.]

Pp. [8] + xxiv + 286: Oxford, 1861, 8°. Vol. 40 of the 'Library of the Fathers.'

---

11. LETTER TO THE 'GUARDIAN,' dated Dec. 9 (?), 1861, on the Greek Chair at Oxford.

## 1862.

1. See 1860, 1 (' Minor Prophets,' pt. 3).

2. PAROCHIAL SERMONS, Vol. II. Third edition. See 1853, 1.

---

3. SPEECH AT THE CHURCH CONGRESS AT OXFORD, JULY 9, 1862. See pp. 141-3 of the *Report of Proceedings* (1862).

## 1863.

1. THE SPIRIT COMFORTING. A sermon [on St. Matth. v. 4] preached in the Church of St. Mary-the-Virgin, Oxford, on Wednesday, March 18, 1863. By the Rev. E. B. Pusey, D.D., . . .

> Pp. 22 : Oxford, 1863, 8°.　See 1877, 4.　One of the Oxford Lenten Sermons, 1863.

2. See 1860, 1 (Minor Prophets).

---

3. LETTER TO THE REV. G. WILLIAMS, dated Jan. 27, 1863, printed in the *Guardian* of Feb. 4, 1863, on Inspiration.

4. LETTER TO THE 'TIMES,' dated Feb. 17, 1863, on the 'persecution of Prof. Jowett' : followed by others dated Feb. 20, 23, 25, March 3, 16, and 20.

5. LETTER TO THE 'GUARDIAN,' dated Apr. 2, 1863, on the living of Whitwoods.

## 1864.

1. DANIEL THE PROPHET.　Nine lectures, delivered in the Divinity School of the University of Oxford, with copious notes.　By the Rev. E. B. Pusey, D.D., . . .

> Pp. xl + 628 : Oxford (Plymouth), 1864. 8°.　See 1868, 1 ; 1883, 6. A few copies of a privately printed ' Index to Dr. Pusey's Daniel the Prophet ' by the Rev. G. R. Adam were issued in 1892 (?).

2. —— [As above].　Second thousand [or ' Third thousand '].

> Pp. xl + 628 : Oxford (Plymouth), 1864, 8°.

3. †CASE, AS TO THE LEGAL FORCE OF THE JUDGMENT OF THE PRIVY COUNCIL *in re* FENDALL *v.* WILSON ; with the Opinion of the Attorney-General and Sir Hugh Cairns, and a preface to those who love God and His truth, by the Rev. E. B. Pusey, D.D. [The Opinion is dated June 7, 1864.]

> Pp. 36 : Oxford (London), 1864, 8°.

4. —— CASE . . . [as above].　Second edition.

> Pp. 36 : Oxford (London), 1864, 8°.

5. DR. PUSEY ON THE PRIVY COUNCIL JUDGEMENT.

> Pp. 4 : n. pl., n. d., 8°.　A reprint of a letter by Dr. Pusey, dated Feb. 17, (1864), which appeared in the *Record* of Feb. 19.

6. PAROCHIAL SERMONS, Vol. I.　Fifth edition.

> Pp. [4] + xxiv + viii + 480 : Oxford (Plymouth), 1864, 8°.　The title is not quite certain : the only copy I have seen had the 1852 titlepage.　This edition has a dedication ' To the Congregations. . . .'　See 1848, 1.

7. THE CHURCH THE CONVERTER . . . [&c., as 1838, 2].　Fifth thousand.

> Pp. 58 : Oxford (Plymouth), 1864, 8°.　See 1865, 2 ; 1884, 2.

8. ALL FAITH . . . [&c., as 1855, 2].　Third thousand.

> Pp. viii + 94 : Oxford (Plymouth), 1864, 8°.　See 1865, 1 ; 1879, 2.

9. PATIENCE ... [&c., as 1837, 2]. Fourth thousand.

> Pp. [4] + 52 : Oxford (Plymouth), 8⁰. See 1865, 1 ; 1879, 2.

10. THE PREACHING OF THE GOSPEL .., [&c., as 1841, 5]. Third thousand.

> Pp. [4] + 28 : Oxford (Plymouth), 1864, 8⁰. See 1865, 2 ; 1884, 2.

11. GOD IS LOVE ... [&c., as 1844, 2]. Third thousand.

> Pp. [4] + 50 : Oxford (Plymouth), 1864, 8⁰. See 1865, 2 ; 1884, 2.

12. EVERLASTING PUNISHMENT. A sermon [on St. Matth. xxv. 46] preached before the University in the Cathedral Church of Christ, in Oxford, on the twenty-first Sunday after Trinity, 1864, by the Rev. E. B. Pusey, D.D., . . .

> Pp. 32 : Oxford (1864), 8⁰. See 1865, 6 ; 1878, 11 ; 1880, 8.

13. DAVID IN HIS SIN AND HIS PENITENCE. [A sermon on Ps. li. 4.] By the Rev. E. B. Pusey, D.D., . . .

> Pp. 161–188 of 'Sermons preached during Lent in Great St. Mary's Church, Cambridge' (Camb., 1864), 8⁰.

14. FOR THE HEBDOMADAL COUNCIL ONLY [a paper addressed to the Vice-Chancellor, about the Middle Class Examinations, signed ' E. B. Pusey ' : undated, but apparently 1864].

> Pp. 8 : [Oxford, 1864?], 4⁰.

15. ANSWER TO THE OBJECTIONS TO THE MIDDLE CLASS EXAMINATION STATUTE, AND REASONS FOR ITS ACCEPTANCE. (Signed ' E. B. Pusey ' : undated, but April or May, 1864.]

> Pp. 8 : [Oxford, 1864], 4⁰.

16. WILL THE PLAN OF THE DELEGATES PROMOTE OR DISCOURAGE THE STUDY OF THE BIBLE, OR WILL THE PROPOSED STATUTE DISCOURAGE ESSENTIAL SECULAR KNOWLEDGE? [Signed ' E. B. P.' : undated, but April, 1864.]

> Pp. 2 : [Oxford, 1864], 4⁰.

17. (A FORM OF STATUTE, 'for the Hebdomadal Council only,' to give the Greek Professor £360 a year, with an anonymous preamble composed by Pusey : undated, but probably Oct. 1864 : a single sheet quarto : there is another form omitting the words about the Hebdomadal Council.)

18. †A GUIDE TO PASS LENT ... [&c., as 1844, 5]. Third edition.

---

19. LETTER TO A FRIEND, dated Jan. 4, 1864, printed in the *Guardian* : on the Burial Service.

20. SPEECH IN CONGREGATION, AT OXFORD, ON FEB. 4, 1864, printed in the *Guardian*, Feb. 10, 1864, p. 136 : about the Endowment of the Greek Chair.

21. LETTER TO THE ' RECORD,' dated Feb. 17, 1864, on the Privy Council Judgment on *Essays and Reviews.*

22. LETTER TO THE ' RECORD,' dated Feb. 23, 1864, on the same.

23. LETTER TO THE ' TIMES,' dated March 2, 1864, on the endowment of Professor Jowett.

**24.** LETTER TO THE 'TIMES,' dated March 7, 1864. on Mr. Maurice and the Oxford Declaration: followed by another, not dated, beginning 'Sir, As before, I will not trouble you': and another, undated, printed in the *Times* of March 15, 1864, beginning 'Sir, Mr. Maurice, from a charge.'

**25.** LETTER TO THE REV. H. B. WALTON, dated April 5, 1864, printed in the *Guardian* soon after: on the Oxford Declaration.

**26.** LETTER TO THE 'TIMES,' dated Dec. 13, 1864, on Mr. Keble and 'Anglicanus': followed by another, not dated, beginning, 'Sir, As "Anglicanus" does not wish.'

**27.** LETTER TO THE 'TIMES,' not dated, on Dr. Pusey's preface to the Opinion of the Attorney General: beginning 'Sir, Accidentally I have only seen,' followed by a similar one, not dated, beginning 'Sir, It would be very unreasonable.'

## 1865.

1. NINE SERMONS ... [&c., as 1859, 1].

> Pp. xxii and as 1859, 1, except that the last two sermons are pp. viii + 94 (= 1864, 8) and [4] + 52 (= 1864, 9): Oxford (Plymouth), 1865, 8⁰.

2. PAROCHIAL SERMONS PREACHED AND PRINTED ON VARIOUS OCCASIONS, NOW COLLECTED INTO ONE VOLUME. By the Rev. E. B. Pusey, D.D., ...

> Pp. viii and 46 (= 1840, 7) and 56 (= 1841, 4) and [4] + 30 (= 1864, 10) and [4] + 50 (= 1864, 11) and 32 (= 1859, 2), and 28 (= 1845, 6) and 24 (= 1855, 3) and [4] + 48 (= 1850, 5] and 68 (= 1859, 3) and 58 (= 1864, 7!) and 30 (= 1856, 4): Oxford, 1865, 8⁰. See 1884, 2.

3. THE CHURCH OF ENGLAND A PORTION OF CHRIST'S ONE HOLY CATHOLIC CHURCH, AND A MEANS OF RESTORING VISIBLE UNITY. An Eirenicon, in a Letter to the Author of 'The Christian Year' [John Keble]. By E. B. Pusey, D.D., ...

> Pp. xiv + 410 ('3'—'412'): Oxford (London), 1865, 8⁰. Part I of the Eirenicon: see 1866, 7; 1869, 1; 1870, 1. The 'Fifth' 'Sixth' and 'Seventh thousand,' in the same year, do not differ. The title on the label on the back is 'The Truth and Office of the English Church.'

4. TRACT XC. ON CERTAIN PASSAGES IN THE XXXIX ARTICLES. By the Rev. J. H. Newman, B.D., 1841. With a historical preface by the Rev. E. B. Pusey, D.D., and Catholic subscription to the XXXIX Articles considered in reference to Tract XC by the Rev. John Keble, M.A., 1841.

> Pp. xxviii + 88 + 26: Oxford (London), 1865, 8⁰. See 1866, 5; 1875, 7; 1893, 2. There is an undated edition: 'Sixth thousand' (pp. xliv + [?]: London, 8⁰). Tract XC is reprinted from the stereotypes of the 4th ed.

5. SERMON X. THE CONFLICT:—IN A SUPERFICIAL AGE [a sermon on Ps. xxxix. 6–7 by Dr. Pusey].

> Pp. 137–156 of 'The Enduring Conflict of Christ with ... Sin ... Sermons preached during ... Lent, 1865, in Oxford ... with a preface by Samuel, Lord Bishop of Oxford' (Oxford, 1865, 8⁰).

**6.** EVERLASTING PUNISHMENT . . . [&c., as 1864, 12].

Pp. 32: Oxford (Plymouth), 1865, 8°.

**7.** THE LOCAL EXAMINATION STATUTE [signed 'E. B. Pusey.' March 6, 1865].

Pp. 2: [Oxford], (1865), 4°.

**8.** UNIVERSITY EXAMINATION STATUTE [a paper signed 'A Member of Council,' i. e. Dr. Pusey: undated, but March, 1865].

Pp. 2: [Oxford, 1865], 4°.

**9.** AN ANSWER TO THE PAPER 'AN IMPORTANT PRINCIPLE IN DANGER' [signed 'E. B. Pusey,' issued soon after March 10, 1865. The subject is the Local Examination Statute].

Pp. 2: [Oxford, 1865], 4°.

**10.** THE SPIRIT IN WHICH THE RESEARCHES OF LEARNING AND SCIENCE SHOULD BE APPLIED TO THE STUDY OF THE BIBLE. By the Rev. E. B. Pusey.

Pp. [?]:    [1865?], 8°. A Norwich Church Congress Paper: it occupies pp. 181–190 of the *Report of the Proceedings* (London, 1866, 8°) and was read on Oct. 5, 1865. The paper was also 'Privately reprinted . . .' (pp. 24: n. pl., n. d., 8°).

---

**11.** TWO LETTERS TO THE 'GUARDIAN' (?), on the Colenso Judgment, the first undated, beginning 'Sir, Friends and foes,' the second dated March 29, 1865.

**12.** LETTER TO THE 'GUARDIAN' (?), dated April 26, 1865, on the Oxford University election.

**13.** LETTER TO THE 'GUARDIAN,' dated Oct. 9, 1865, on Dr. Newman.

**14.** LETTER TO THE 'TIMES,' dated Dec. 4, 1865, on the Confirmation of Archbishop Parker: followed by one, perhaps to the *Times*, dated Dec. 16, 1865, in answer to Mr. Gurney.

**15.** TWO LETTERS TO THE 'JOHN BULL' in answer to Mr. Gurney, dated Dec. 7 and 18, 1865. (Dr. Pusey also wrote a letter to the *Morning Post*, on the same subject, at about the same time, not dated, beginning, 'Sir, Having already answered.')

**16.** LETTER TO THE 'TIMES,' Dec. 12, 1865, on Anglican Orders.

**17.** LETTER TO THE 'WEEKLY REGISTER,' Dec. 20, 1865, on the same.

## 1866.

**1.** OCCASIONAL PAPER OF THE EASTERN CHURCH ASSOCIATION. No. II. THE ESSENTIAL UNITY OF THE CHURCH OF CHRIST. Extracted from 'An Eirenicon' by E. B. Pusey, D.D., . . . with the sanction of the author.

Pp. 20: London, 1866, 8°. The preface reprints a letter from Dr. Pusey to the Rev. G. Williams, of King's College, Cambridge, dated Dec. 23, 1865.

**2.** A REVIEW OF DR. PUSEY'S EIRENICON, reprinted from the 'Weekly Register,' with two letters to the Editor from Dr. Pusey on his hopes of the reunion of the Church of England with the Catholic Church, . . .

> Pp. 36 : Lond. [1866?], 8°. See 1867, 3 : the second letter is dated Dec. 6, 1865.

3. The Miracles of Prayer. A sermon [on St. Matth. xxi. 22] preached before the University, in the Cathedral Church of Christ, in Oxford, on Septuagesima Sunday, 1866. By the Rev. E. B. Pusey, D.D. . . .

> Pp. 36 : Oxford (Plymouth), 1866, 8°. See 1878, 4 ; 1880, 1. The ' Sixth thousand ' issued this year is identical.

4. Sermon V. The Kingdom of Light set up.—The Conflict and Victory of its Faithful Children. [A sermon on St. Luke xxiv. 49, by Dr. Pusey].

> Pp. 61–80 of 'The Conflict of Christ' . . . Sermons preached during . . . Lent, 1866, in Oxford . . . with a preface by Samuel, Lord Bishop of Oxford (Oxford, 1866, 8°).

5. Tract XC. . . . [&c., as 1865, 4, adding after ' 1841 ':—] Revised edition of the Preface. Fourth thousand.

> Pp. xliv + 88 : Oxford (London), 1866, 8°.

6. Entire Absolution . . . (&c., as 1846, 1). Sixth thousand.

> Pp. xx + 64 : Oxford (London), 1866, 8°. See 1879, 2.

7. The Church of England. . . . [&c., as 1865, 3]. Ninth thousand

> Pp. xiv + 410 : Oxford (London), 1866, 8°.

---

8. Letter to the 'Guardian,' dated Jan. 20, 1866, in answer to Dr. Wordsworth.

9. Letter to the ' Weekly Register,' dated Jan. 21, 1866, a reply to Mr. Allies.

10. Letter to the 'Guardian,' dated June 26, 1866, correcting Mr. Gurney.

11. Two Speeches to the English Church Union, in June, 1866 : reported in several newspapers.

12. Letter to the ' Weekly Register ' of July 28, 1866, in answer to Mr. J. M. Rhodes.

13. Letter to the ' Weekly Register,' dated Sept. 12, 1866.

14. Letter to the 'Weekly Register,' dated Sept. 22, 1866.

15. Letter to the 'Times,' dated Nov. 13, 1866, on Confession. (At least seven more letters from Dr. Pusey on this subject appeared about this time in the *Times*).

16. Letter to the 'Times,' dated Dec. 12, 1866, on the alteration of a line in ' The Christian Year.' See 1867, 8; 1878, 12.

(Conversation in 1846 between Dr. Pusey and Mr. ' G.,' then an Anglican clergyman, printed in the *Weekly Register* of March 17, 1866.)

## 1867.

**1.** WILL YE ALSO GO AWAY? A sermon [on St. John vi. 67-69] preached before the University of Oxford, on the fourth Sunday after Epiphany, 1867. By the Rev. E. B. Pusey, D.D., . . . Published by request.

> Pp. x + 30 : Oxford (London), 1867, 8°. See 1878, 4 ; 1880, 7.
> Copies marked 'Third' and 'Fourth thousand' do not differ.

**2.** LIFE, THE PREPARATION FOR DEATH: a Sermon [on Heb. ix. 27] preached at Great St. Mary's, Cambridge, on the first Friday in Lent, 1867. By the Rev. E. B. Pusey, D.D. . . .

> Pp. 28 : Oxford (London), 1867, 8°.

**3.** LETTERS ON THE 'EIRENICON': addressed to the *Weekly Register* by M. J. Rhodes, Esq., M.A., and now reprinted with the replies of the Rev. Dr. Pusey . . . and additions.

> Pp. iv + 48 : London, 1867, 8°. Dr. Pusey's letters to the *Weekly Register* bear date 1866, July 28 (date of publication), Sept. 12, 22. See 1866, 2, 12–14.

**4.** † ESSAYS ON THE RE-UNION OF CHRISTENDOM . . . edited by the Rev. Frederick George Lee, . . . with a preface by the Rev. E. B. Pusey, D.D. . . .

> Pp. lxxxviii + 310 : London, 1867, 12°.

**5.** —— ESSAYS ON RE-UNION. The introductory Essay by E. B. Pusey, D.D.

> Pp. 62 : London, 1867, 8°.

---

**6.** LETTER TO THE 'LITERARY CHURCHMAN,' dated Jan. 12, 1867, on Legislation as a remedy for Dissensions within the Church.

**7.** LETTER TO THE PRESIDENT OF THE ENGLISH CHURCH UNION, dated Jan. 12, 1867, read at the meeting on Jan. 14.

**8.** LETTER TO THE 'LITERARY CHURCHMAN,' dated Jan. 21, 1867, on the alteration in the Christian Year, see 1866, 16.

**9.** SPEECH TO THE ENGLISH CHURCH UNION, Feb. 21, 1867.

**10.** LETTER TO THE 'OXFORD CHRONICLE,' dated March 26, 1867, about supposed tendencies in Dr. Pusey towards Romanism, and including one to Mr. Golightly.

**11.** SPEECH TO THE ENGLISH CHURCH UNION, in March, 1867, on Ritual.

**12.** LETTER TO THE 'OXFORD CHRONICLE,' dated April 13, 1867.

**13.** SPEECH TO THE OXFORD BRANCH OF THE ENGLISH CHURCH UNION, June 11, 1867.

**14.** LETTER TO THE 'CHURCH REVIEW,' dated June 13, 1867, on the 'Index.'

**15.** SPEECH TO THE ENGLISH CHURCH UNION, June 19, 1867.

**16.** LETTER TO THE 'GUARDIAN,' dated July 29, 1867, on the English Church and the Scandinavian bodies.

17. LETTER TO THE 'GUARDIAN,' dated Aug. 5, 1867, on the Confessional, in answer to the *Globe*.

18. LETTER TO THE 'TIMES,' dated Sept. 9, 1867, about Dr. Colenso.

19. SPEECHES TO THE ENGLISH CHURCH UNION, Nov. 20, 1867.

## 1868.

1. DANIEL THE PROPHET . . . [&c., as 1864, 1, substituting for 'Second thousand'] Second edition, fourth [or fifth] thousand.

Pp. civ + 652 : Oxford (Plymouth), 1868, 8º.

2. DANIEL THE PROPHET . . . [&c., as above]. Third edition, fifth thousand.

Pp. [?] : Oxford, 1868, 8º.

3. PAROCHIAL SERMONS . . . Vol. 1 [as 1852, 1]. Third edition, sixth thousand.

Pp. [4] + viii + 480 : Oxford (Plymouth), 1868, 8º.

4. PAROCHIAL SERMONS . . . Vol. 2 [as 1853, 1]. Second edition, fifth thousand.

Pp. [?] : Oxford, 1868, 8º.

5. ELEVEN ADDRESSES DURING A RETREAT OF THE COMPANIONS OF THE LOVE OF JESUS, ENGAGED IN PERPETUAL INTERCESSION FOR THE CONVERSION OF SINNERS. By the Rev. E. B. Pusey, D.D.

Pp. viii + 136 : Oxford (Plymouth), 1868, 8º. A second edition was published subsequently. See 1878, 9; 1882, 4.

6. OUR PHARISAISM : a sermon [on St. Luke xviii. 11] preached at St. Paul's, Knightsbridge, on Ash-Wednesday, 1868. By the Rev. E. B. Pusey, D.D., . . . Published by request.

Pp. [2] + 22 : Oxford (Plymouth), 1868, 8º.

7. SERMON V. THE VICTOR ON HIS THRONE, THE OBJECT OF DIVINE WORSHIP. [A sermon on Rev. v. 11–13, by Dr. Pusey.]

Pp. 73–98 of 'The Victor in the Conflict. Sermons preached during . . . Lent, 1867, in Oxford. With a Preface by Samuel, Lord Bishop of Oxford' (Oxford, 1868, 8º).

8. THE BOARD OF EXAMINERS FOR THE PROPOSED THEOLOGICAL SCHOOL. [Signed 'E. B. Pusey,' June 10, 1868.]

Pp. 4 : [Oxford], (1868), 4º.

9. THE DIVINITY SCHOOL. [A paper signed 'E. B. Pusey,' Nov. 19, (1868).]

Pp. 4 : [Oxford, 1868], folio.

10. THE WORSHIP OF MARY IN THE CHURCH OF ROME. (Extracted from Dr. Pusey's 'Eirenicon.') With a few words to Ritualists and Protestants.

Pp. 8 : London, [1868?], 12º. Compiled by 'Veritas': an attack on Dr. Pusey's doctrines.

11. †THE SPIRITUAL COMBAT . . . [&c., as 1846, 5]. Sixteenth thousand.

> Pp. xxxii + 246 : Oxford, 1868, 12°. The 'Seventeenth thousand' does not differ.

12. †THE EPISTLES OF S. CYPRIAN . . . [&c., as 1844, 7].

> Pp. xxx [(2) + ' x '–' xxxvi '] + 422 : Oxford (London), 1868, 8°.

---

13. LETTER TO DR. LIDDON, in a postscript to a letter of Dr. Liddon's to the *Guardian* (?), dated Mar. 21, 1868: on the Oxford Tests Bill.

14. SPEECH AT KEBLE COLLEGE, OXFORD. Pp. 40–46 of ' Proceedings at the Laying of the First Stone of Keble College, Oxford, . . . Apr. 25th, 1868 ' (Lond., 1868, 4°).

15. SPEECH TO THE ENGLISH CHURCH UNION, June 16, 1868.

16. LETTER TO THE HON. C. L. WOOD, dated July 9, 1868, on the English Church Union : published in the *Guardian*.

17. LETTERS TO THE 'GUARDIAN,' dated July 20 and Aug. 10, 1868, about the Church Association.

18. LETTER TO THE PRESIDENT OF THE WESLEYAN CONFERENCE at Liverpool, printed from the Proceedings of the Conference in the *Guardian* of Aug. 19, 1868.

19. LETTER TO THE 'TIMES,' dated Aug. 20, 1868, on the above letter. This was reprinted in the *Guardian* of Aug. 26.

20. LETTER TO MR. BURGON, printed in the *Guardian* of Sept. 2, 1868 : on the Tests Bill.

21. LETTER TO THE 'TIMES,' dated Dec. 26, 1868, on the Mackonochie judgment.

## 1869.

1. FIRST LETTER TO THE VERY REV. J. H. NEWMAN, D.D., IN EXPLANATION CHIEFLY IN REGARD TO THE REVERENTIAL LOVE DUE TO THE EVER-BLESSED THEOTOKOS, AND THE DOCTRINE OF HER IMMACULATE CONCEPTION; with an analysis of Cardinal de Turrecremata's work on the Immaculate Conception. By the Rev. E. B. Pusey, D.D., . . . [Half-title :—] Eirenicon, part II.

> Pp. xiv + 526 [' 3 '—' 528 ']: Oxford (London), 1869, 8°. See 1865, 3.

2. PAROCHIAL SERMONS. Vol. II. . . . [&c., as 1853, 1]. Seventh thousand.

> Pp. xii + 400 : Oxford (Plymouth), 1869, 8°.

3. THE REAL PRESENCE . . . [&c., as 1857, 2]. Third thousand.

> Pp. xxxii + 350 : Oxford (Plymouth), 1869, 8°.

4. PERSONAL RESPONSIBILITY OF MAN, AS TO HIS USE OF TIME. [Sermon on St. John ix. 4, by Dr. Pusey.]

> Pp. 69–85 of ' Personal Responsibility of Man. Sermons preached during . . . Lent, 1868, in Oxford . . . ' (Oxford, 1869, 8°).

5. DEVOTIONS ... [&c., as 1856, 1]. Second edition.

Pp. [?]: London, 1869, 12°.

6. THE PROPOSED STATUTE FOR A THEOLOGICAL SCHOOL. [Signed 'E. B. Pusey,' May 12, (1869).]

Pp. 4: [Oxford, 1869], 4°.

7. THE PROPOSED SCHOOL OF THEOLOGY. [Signed 'E. B. Pusey,' Whit-Monday, May 17, 1869.]

Pp. 4: [Oxford], (1869), 4°.

8. SKETCH OF A CASE PREPARED BY DR. PUSEY. [A paper on technical points connected with the Statute constituting a new Theological School: unsigned and undated, but apparently May, 1869.]

Pp. 4: [Oxford, 1869 ?], 4°.

9. †THE SUFFERINGS OF JESUS ... Composed by Fra Thomé de Jesu ... Translated from the original Portuguese [edited by Dr. Pusey, who signs a note on p. iv. of Part I 'E. B. P': in two parts].

Pp. xxiv + 500 and vi + 416: Oxford (Plymouth), 1869, 12°. See 1884, 15.

10. †VILLAGE SERMONS ON THE BAPTISMAL SERVICE. By the Rev. John Keble ... Third thousand. [With a 'Notice' of 2 pp. by Dr. Pusey, signed 'E. B. P.,' June 7, 1868.]

Pp. [2] + xii + 310: Oxford (Plymouth), 1869, 8°.

11. †TRACTATUS DE VERITATE CONCEPTIONIS BEATISSIMÆ VIRGINIS ..., ANNO DOMINI MCCCCXXXVII ... COMPILATUS PER ... FRATREM JOANNEM DE TURRECREMATA ... [edited by Dr. Pusey, who signs the preface 'E. B. Pusey,' July 25, 1869: but the Rev. R. W. Stubbs prepared the text].

Pp. 44 + 808: Romæ, 1547, repr. Oxford (London), 1869, sm. 4°.

12. †PARADISE OF THE CHRISTIAN SOUL ... [&c., as 1847, 5]. Fifth thousand.

Pp. xxxii + 112 and 68 and [2] + 92 and [2] + 136 and [2] + 128 and [2] + 86 leaves: Oxford (Plymouth), 1869, 12°. Vol. 1 has sometimes an 1870 titlepage, and Vol. 2 an 1871 one. Part V has also sometimes a titlepage (London, no date), 'Devotions for Holy Communion. ...'

---

13. SPEECHES TO THE ENGLISH CHURCH UNION, Feb. 17 and June 15, 1869; and to the Oxford Branch, May 18, 1869.

14. LETTER TO THE 'GUARDIAN,' dated July 26, 1869, on the Tests Bill.

15. LETTER TO THE 'GUARDIAN,' dated Oct. 10, 1869, on the appointment of Dr. Temple to the Bishopric of Exeter.

16. LETTER TO 'JOHN BULL,' on the same.

17. LETTER TO THE 'TIMES,' dated Oct. 25, 1869, on the same: followed by another, not dated, in answer to Dr. Pusey's critics, beginning, 'Sir, Will you allow me.'

18. LETTER TO THE 'GUARDIAN,' in seven parts, on the same.

19. LETTER TO THE 'GUARDIAN,' on Disestablishment: beginning, 'Sir, I did not say.'

## 1870.

1. IS HEALTHFUL REUNION IMPOSSIBLE? A second letter to the Very Rev. J. H. Newman, D.D. By the Rev. E. B. Pusey, D.D., . . . [Half-title : —] Eirenicon, part III.

> Pp. xii + 354 : Oxford (London), 1870, 8°. See 1865, 3 ; 1874, 4 ; 1876, 4.

2. ISAIAH. [Sermon on Is. vi. 8–10, by Dr. Pusey.]

> Pp. 75–93 of 'The Prophets of the Lord . . . Sermons preached during . . . Lent, 1869, in Oxford . . .' (Oxford, 1870, 8°).

3. †PARADISE OF THE CHRISTIAN SOUL : see 1869, 12.

---

4. LETTER TO THE 'TIMES,' dated Feb. 10, 1870, on the opposition to Dr. Temple.

5. LETTER TO THE 'TIMES,' undated, on Dr. Temple's explanation : beginning, 'Sir, I gladly would have remained.'

6. LETTER TO THE REV. A. R. FAUSSET, on Biblical revision : included in one from Mr. Fausset to the *Record*, dated Mar. 23, 1870.

7. LETTER TO THE 'ROCK' (April ?, 1870), about the *Record* and the *Rock* : beginning 'Sir, Allow me, in reference.'

8. SPEECH AT THE OPENING OF KEBLE COLLEGE, June, 1870.

9. LETTER TO THE 'TIMES,' dated Nov. 15, on Mr. Voysey's appeal : followed by one to the *Standard*, dated Nov. 20, on the same subject.

## 1871.

1. THE PURCHAS JUDGMENT, a letter of acknowledgment to the Right Hon. Sir J. T. Coleridge . . . by H. P. Liddon . . . together with a Letter to the Writer by the Rev. E. B. Pusey, D.D., . . .

> Pp. 72 : London, 1871, 8°. Dr. Pusey's letter occupies pp. 53–71, and is dated April 3 and 10, 1871.

2. —— [as above]. Second edition.

> Pp. [4] + 76 : London, 1871, 8°. Pusey's letter has a postscript, dated April 29, 1871, which was also separately printed (pp. 4, 8° : 'Note on a Letter . . .').

3. See 1860, 1 ('Minor Prophets,' pt. 4).

4. THIS IS MY BODY. A sermon [on St. Matth. xxvi. 26] preached before the University at S. Mary's, on the fifth Sunday after Easter, 1871. By the Rev. E. B. Pusey, D.D. . . .

> Pp. 48 : Oxford, 1871, 8°. See 1878, 4 ; 1880, 1.

5. THE PRESENCE OF CHRIST . . . [&c., as 1853, 5].

> Pp. viii + 74 : 1871, Oxford (London), 8°. See 1879, 2.

6. DOCTRINAL OR UNDOCTRINAL INSTRUCTION of the Undergraduate Members of the University belonging to the Church of England.

> Pp. [2] : [Oxford, 1871], 4°. Signed 'E. B. P.,' 'Nov. 21.' About the study of the XXXIX Articles, in connexion with a proposed amendment of the Statute.

7. (Dr. Pusey issued a paper reprinted in the London papers, dated Nov. 30, (1871), about TOLERATION, addressed to Members of Congregation at Oxford.)

8. (The 14th Occasional Paper of the Eastern Church Association issued in 1871 or 1872 contains five LETTERS from Dr. Pusey to the Rev. Geo. Williams, dated —, Feb. 20, —, Feb. 21, March 10, 1870: on the subject of the Filioque clause.)

9. †PARADISE OF THE CHRISTIAN SOUL : see 1869, 12.

10. LETTER TO A FRIEND, published in *Saunders's News Letter*, and reprinted in the *Guardian* (?), dated April 23, 1871, on Auricular Confession.

11. LETTER TO MR. W. BROOKE, dated May 23, 1871, published in the *Dublin Daily Express*, in reply to Mr. Maskell.

12. SPEECH TO THE OXFORD BRANCH OF THE ENGLISH CHURCH UNION, May 30, 1871.

13. LETTER TO THE 'RECORD,' dated June 12, 1871, on Dr. Pusey's Sermon on the Holy Eucharist.

14. LETTER TO THE MEMBERS OF THE CATHOLIC UNION FOR PRAYER, dated Nov. 5, 1871, printed in the *Guardian* (?).

15. LETTER TO THE MEMBERS OF THE CATHOLIC UNION FOR PRAYER, undated, enclosing a Petition from Dr. Pusey to be presented to the Lower House of Convocation, about the Athanasian Creed: printed in the *Guardian* (?).

16. LETTERS TO THE 'TIMES,' dated Dec. 2, 14, and 16, 1871, on Dr. Pusey's Suspension in 1843.

## 1872.

1. SERMONS PREACHED BEFORE THE UNIVERSITY OF OXFORD BETWEEN A.D. 1859 AND 1872. By the Rev. E. B. Pusey, D.D., . . .
    Pp. xvi + 496 : Oxford, 1872, 8°. This volume counts as 'University Sermons, Vol. II': see 1859, 1; 1884, 1.

2. —— SERMONS . . . [&c., as above]. Second thousand.
    Pp. xvi + 492 : Oxford, 1872, 8°.

3. LENT READINGS . . . [&c., as 1852, 4].
    Pp. viii + 270: London, 1872, 12°.

4. EVE. [Sermon on Gen. iii. 4–5, by Dr. Pusey.]
    Pp. 69–87 of 'The Typical Persons of the Pentateuch . . . Sermons preached during . . . Lent, 1870–71, in Oxford . . .' (Oxford, 1872, 8°). There is a separate edition of this sermon (20 pages) marked 'Sermon viii' and 'Lenten Sermon, 1870, Eve,' without title-page or author's name: probably a proof-copy issued for the author's use in 1871 or 1872. The sermon is No. v as published.

5. CHASTISEMENTS . . . [&c., as 1847, 3]. Fourth edition.
    Pp. 32: Oxford, 1872, 8°. See 1884, 2.

6. THE DAY OF JUDGMENT . . . [&c., as 1839, 10]. Fifth edition.
    Pp. xii + 32: Oxford, 1872, 8°. See 1884, 2.

7. †A GUIDE FOR . . . ADVENT . . . [&c., as 1844, 4].
> Pp. lxiv + 306 : Oxford, 1872, 12º.

8. †A GUIDE FOR . . . LENT . . . [&c., as 1844, 5]. Fourth edition.
> Pp. xiv + 394 : Oxford, 1872, 12º.

9. †THE LIFE OF JESUS . . . [&c., nearly as 1846, 3, 4]. Third thousand.
> Pp. xvi + 478 : Oxford, 1872, 12º.

10. †. . . AUGUSTINI CONFESSIONES . . . [&c., as 1838, 8]. Editio secunda.
> Pp. viii + 326 : Oxonii (London), 1872, 8º.

---

11. LETTER TO THE 'TIMES,' dated Aug. 10, 1872, on the Athanasian Creed : followed by another dated Aug. 22.

12. LETTER TO THE 'TIMES,' dated Dec. 22, 1872, on the Oxford Select Preachers.

## 1873.

1. PAROCHIAL SERMONS, Vol. III . . . [&c., as 1841, 3]. Revised edition.
> Pp. xii + 482 : Oxford, 1873, 8º.

2. THE RESPONSIBILITY OF INTELLECT IN MATTERS OF FAITH : a sermon [on St. John xii. 48] preached before the University of Oxford, on Advent Sunday, 1872. With an Appendix on Bishop Moberly's Strictures on the warning clauses of the Athanasian Creed. By E. B. Pusey, D.D., . . .
> Pp. 84 : Oxford (London), 1873, 8º. See 1876, 6 ; 1879, 4.

3. SINFUL BLINDNESS AMIDST IMAGINED LIGHT. A sermon [on St. John ix. 41] preached before the University of Oxford, on the twenty-third Sunday after Trinity, 1873. By the Rev. E. B. Pusey, D.D., . . .
> Pp. 34 : Oxford, 1873, 8º. See 1878, 4 ; 1879, 5 ; 1880, 1.

---

4. LETTER TO DR. LIDDON, dated Jan. 27, 1873, read at a meeting in defence of the Athanasian Creed, Jan. 31, 1873.

5. LETTER TO THE ' TIMES,' about July 21, 1873, on a petition to Convocation.

6. LETTER TO MR. GROVE, dated Nov. 28, 1873, printed in the Quarterly Statement of the Palestine Exploration Fund Committee, Jan. 1874.

## 1874.

1. LENTEN SERMONS, preached chiefly to Young Men at the Universities, between A.D. 1858–1874. By the Rev. E. B. Pusey, D.D., . . .
> Pp. xii + 488 : Oxford, 1874, 8º. The ' Conclusion to " The Losses
> of the Saved " as preached at All Saints, Margaret St., Ash-
> Wednesday, 1867,' which is omitted in this volume, though the
> rest of the sermon is there, was printed separately (pp. 4, n. d., 8º.).

2. THE PROPOSED ECCLESIASTICAL LEGISLATION. Three letters to the *Times* (reprinted by request): with a Preface. By the Rev. E. B. Pusey, D.D. . . .

> Pp. 40 : Oxford, 1874, 8°. The Letters are dated 1874, March 13, 20, 28.

3. (LETTER FROM DR. PUSEY TO THE MEMBERS AND ASSOCIATES OF THE ENGLISH CHURCH UNION, dated Jan. 31, [1874 ?], followed by a prayer written by John Keble, modified.)

> Pp. 4 : London, [1874 ?], 12°.

4. IS HEALTHFUL REUNION IMPOSSIBLE ? . . . [&c., as 1870, 1].

> Pp. [?] : Oxford (London), 1874, 8°.

5. PUBLIC-WORSHIP-REGULATION-BILL. Speech at the meeting of the English Church Union, held at St. James's Hall, June 16, 1874, by the Rev. E. B. Pusey, D.D., . . .

> Pp. 12 : n. pl., 1874, 8°.

6. †COMMENTARY ON THE GOSPEL ACCORDING TO S. JOHN BY S. CYRIL, ARCHBISHOP OF ALEXANDRIA. Vol. I. St. John i-viii. [Edited by Philip E. Pusey, but a large part of the preface, see p. ix, is by his father Dr. Pusey.]

> Pp. lx + 684: Oxford, 1874, 8°. Part of the 'Library of the Fathers.'

7. †THE FOUNDATIONS OF THE SPIRITUAL LIFE . . . [&c., as 1844, 6].

> Pp. [2] + lxxiv + 252 : Oxford, 1874, 12°.

---

8. LETTER TO THE 'TIMES' of July 24, 1874, on Dr. Pusey and the Ritualists.

9. ADDRESS TO THE ASSOCIATES OF THE CATHOLIC UNION FOR PRAYER, Aug. 18, 1874 (printed in the *Guardian* of Sept. 23, 1874, and *Times* of Sept. 17).

10. LETTER TO ARCHDEACON JOHN ALLEN, dated Nov. 2, [1874], on the Rubrics (printed in the *Guardian* of Nov. 11, 1874).

## 1875.

1. See 1860, 1 ('Minor Prophets,' pt. 5).

2. LETTER TO THE ARCHBISHOP OF DUBLIN.

> Pp. 16: [Oxford, 1875], 8°. On proposed changes in the Prayer-book of the Irish Church. 'Not published': dated April 2, 1875: signed 'E. B. Pusey.'

3. CHRISTIANITY WITHOUT THE CROSS A CORRUPTION OF THE GOSPEL OF CHRIST. A sermon [on St. Luke ix. 23] preached before the University of Oxford, on Septuagesima Sunday, 1875. With a note on 'Modern Christianity a Civilised Heathenism.' By the Rev. E. B. Pusey, D.D., . . .

> Pp. 44: Oxford, 1875, 8°. See 1878, 4; 1880, 1. The third thousand was issued in this same year unaltered.

4. THE BLASPHEMY ... [&c., as 1845, 5]. Third edition.

> Pp. 24: Oxford, 1875, 8°. See 1884, 2.

5. DO ALL ... [&c., as 1849, 2]. Seventh thousand.

> Pp. 20: Oxford (London), 1875, 8°. See 1884, 2.

6. †SERMONS FOR THE CHRISTIAN YEAR. By the late Rev. John Keble ... [edited by Dr. Pusey]. 11 vols.

> (Vol. 1) pp. xvi + 480, 1875: (vol. 2) pp. xvi + 492, 1875: (vol. 3) pp. xviii + 444, 1879, with Advertisement by Dr. Pusey signed 'E. B. P.': (vol. 4) pp. xxiv + 458, 1875, with similar Advertisement: (vol. 5) pp. xviii + 488, 1876: (vol. 6) pp. xviii + 488, 1876: (vol. 7) pp. xvi + 404, 1876: (vol. 8) pp. xvi + 488, 1878: (vol. 9) pp. xvi + 496, 1878: (vol. 10) pp. xvi + 464, 1877: (vol. 11) pp. xvi + 536, 1880: Oxford, 1875–80, 8°. The volumes are not numbered, and vol. (10), Sermons on Saints' Days, was issued before vols. (8–9).

7. Tract XC ... [as 1865, 4]. Fifth thousand.

> Pp. xliv + 88 + 26: Oxford (London), 1875, 8°. See 1865, 4.

---

8. LETTER TO MR. DAVIDSON, dated April 16, 1875, printed in the *Guardian* early in Oct. 1882: on divorce.

9. LETTER TO ARCHDEACON JOHN ALLEN, dated May 6, 1875, printed in the *Guardian* (?) soon after: on Church matters in Ireland.

10. LETTER TO THE 'TIMES,' dated Dec. 27, [1875], about a petition to Convocation by the Eastern Church Association.

## 1876.

1. ON THE CLAUSE 'AND THE SON' IN REGARD TO THE EASTERN CHURCH AND THE BONN CONFERENCE. A letter to the Rev. H. P. Liddon ... By the Rev. E. B. Pusey, D.D., ...

> Pp. viii + 188: Oxford, 1876, 8°.

2. GOD AND HUMAN INDEPENDENCE. A sermon [on St. John xx. 12], preached before the University of Oxford, on Sexagesima Sunday, 1876. By the Rev. E. B. Pusey, D.D., ...

> Pp. 36: Oxford, 1876, 8°. See 1878, 4; 1880, 1.

3. 'BLESSED ARE THE MEEK.' A sermon [on St. Matth. v. 5] preached at the opening of the Chapel of Keble College, on St. Mark's Day, 1876. By the Rev. E. B. Pusey, D.D., ...

> Pp. 32: Oxford, 1876, 8°. See 1878, 4; 1880, 1; 1882, 2. This sermon also occurs at pp. 6–34 of 'An Account of the Proceedings at Keble College on the Occasion of the Opening of the Chapel ... 1876' (Oxford, 1876, 8°).

4. HEALTHFUL REUNION AS CONCEIVED POSSIBLE BEFORE THE VATICAN COUNCIL. The Second Letter to the Very Rev. J. H. Newman, D.D. By the Rev. E. B. Pusey, D.D., ...

> Pp. xii + 354: Oxford (London), 1876, 8°. See 1870, 1.

5. THE SEARCHING OF THE HEART. A sermon. By the Rev. E. B. Pusey, D.D., . . . Reprinted.

> Pp. 12: Oxford, 1876, 8°. On St. Luke xviii. 11, but not the same as 1868, 6.

6. THE RESPONSIBILITY OF INTELLECT . . . [as 1873, 2]. Third edition.

> Pp. 84 : Oxford (London), 1876, 8°. See 1878, 4.

7. †See 1875, 6 (Keble's Sermons).

8. †THE CONFESSIONS OF S. AUGUSTINE. Revised from a former translation by the Rev. E. B. Pusey, D.D., with illustrations from S. Augustine himself.

> Pp. xl + 364: Oxford, 1876, 8°. See 1838, 7.

---

9. LETTER TO THE 'TIMES,' dated Jan. 8, [1876], a sequel to that of Dec. 27, 1875.

10. LETTER TO THE 'TIMES,' dated Jan. 18, 1876, in answer to Mr. Meyrick : on the Eastern Churches.

11. LETTER TO CANON LIDDON, Feb. 8, [1876], on the 'Filioque' clause : printed in the *Times* soon after.

12. LETTER TO THE 'TIMES' of Feb. 24, 1876, in reply to Mr. Orby Shipley.

## 1877.

1. OBJECTS OF THE SOCIETY OF THE LOVE OF JESUS.

> Pp. 4: n. pl., [1877], 12°. Dated Jan. 25, 1877.

2. See 1860, 1 (' Minor Prophets,' pt. 6).

> The issue of the entire work in this year bears a title exactly as 1860, 1, but is pp. vi + 624, and a note dated 1877 is added to the preface.

3. TEN SERMONS DURING A RETREAT FOR CLERGY AND A MISSION FOR THE PEOPLE AT S. SAVIOUR'S CHURCH, LEEDS, IN THE OCTAVE OF ITS CONSECRATION 1845, by the Rev. E. B. Pusey, D.D., with Eight Sermons . . . [by others]. Third edition.

> Pp. xvi + 396: Oxford, 1877, 8°. See 1845, 4. In this edition the sermon by the Rev. William Dodsworth is omitted.

4. THE SPIRIT COMFORTING [&c., as 1863, 1].

> Pp. 22: Oxford, 1877, 8°.

5. LOSSES OF THE POOR through the losses of the Devonport Sisters of Mercy in 1876.

> Pp. [2] + 14: n. pl., (1877), 8°. Signed ' E. B. Pusey, Warden,' Easter 1877. An appeal for help. An account of the result of this appeal headed ' To the Companions and Associates' (pp. 4, n. pl., [1877], 12°) includes a Letter from Dr. Pusey, dated Easter Eve (March 31), 1877, beginning ' My dearest Child, God bless you,' thanking the subscribers of a first instalment of £70).

6. †THE FIFTY-THIRD CHAPTER OF ISAIAH ACCORDING TO THE JEWISH INTERPRETERS. II. Translations . . . with an introduction to

the Translations by Rev. E. B. Pusey, Regius Professor of Hebrew, Oxford.

> Pp. lxxvi + 574 : Oxford, 1877, 8°. The introduction is dated ' Dec. 1876 ' : the first part containing Texts appeared in 1876, but seems to contain nothing directly contributed by Dr. Pusey.

7. †OCCASIONAL PAPERS AND REVIEWS BY JOHN KEBLE, M.A. [edited by Dr. Pusey, who signs the preface].

> Pp. xxiv + 508 : Oxford, 1877, 8°.

8. †See 1875, 6 (Keble's Sermons).

---

> 9. LETTER TO THE 'DAILY EXPRESS' of May 21, 1877, on Vestments.
>
> 10. LETTER TO THE 'TIMES' of May 28, dated May 25, 1877, on the Ridsdale case. (The *Times* of May 24 seems to have also contained a letter from Dr. Pusey.)
>
> 11. LETTER TO Mr. H. McNEILE, dated May 31, 1877, printed in the *Guardian* early in June : on the same subject.
>
> 12. LETTER TO THE 'DAILY EXPRESS,' dated June 14, 1877, in answer to Mr. McNeile.
>
> 13. LETTER TO THE 'ROCK' of June 6, 1877, on the 'Manual of Confession.'
>
> 14. LETTER TO THE 'DAILY EXPRESS' of July 21 (?), 1877, containing a long quotation from Dr. Pusey's preface to a translation of the Abbé Gaume's ' Manual of Confessors' adapted : ' the book is not quite ready for publication.'
>
> 15. LETTER TO THE 'DAILY EXPRESS,' dated July 24, 1877, on Confession.
>
> 16. LETTER TO THE 'RECORD,' dated Dec. 17, 1877, on Confession.

## 1878.

1. †ADVICE FOR THOSE WHO EXERCISE THE MINISTRY OF RECONCILIATION THROUGH CONFESSION AND ABSOLUTION, being the Abbé Gaume's Manual for Confessors or his extracts from the works of . . . spiritual writers, abridged, condensed, and adapted to the use of the English Church, with a preface embodying English authorities on Confession, by the Rev. E. B. Pusey, D.D., . . .

> Pp. clxxxiv + 428 : Oxford, 1878, 8°. See 1877, 13 ; 1879, 1 ; 1880, 2. This work may be said to be Dr. Pusey's, rather than Gaume's.

2. —— †ADVICE . . . [as above]. Second edition.

> Pp. [4] + clxxxiv + 428 : Oxford. This edition seems also sometimes to bear the date 1880.

3. PAROCHIAL SERMONS, Vol. III . . . [&c., as 1841, 3]. Revised edition.

> Pp. xii + 482 : Oxford, 1878, 8°.

4. EIGHT SERMONS PREACHED BEFORE THE UNIVERSITY OF OXFORD BETWEEN 1864–1876. Now collected in one Volume, and

a Sermon preached at the opening of the Chapel of Keble College by the Rev. E. B. Pusey, D.D. . . .

> Pp. viii, and 36 (= 1878, 11) and 36 (= 1866, 3, fifth thousand) and x + 28 (= 1867, 1) and 48 (= 1871, 4) and 84 (1876, 6) and 34 (= 1873, 3) and 44 (= 1875, 3) and 36 (1876, 2) and 32 (= 1876, 3) : Oxford, 1878, 8°. On the half title is ‘ University Sermons, Vol. III ’, see 1859, 1 ; 1880, 1.

5. HABITUAL CONFESSION NOT DISCOURAGED BY THE RESOLUTION ACCEPTED BY THE LAMBETH CONFERENCE. A letter to his Grace the Lord Archbishop of Canterbury. By the Rev. E. B. Pusey, D.D., . . .

> Pp. 48 : Oxford, 1878, 8°.

6. UN-SCIENCE, NOT SCIENCE, ADVERSE TO FAITH. A sermon [on St. John i. 27] preached before the University of Oxford on the twentieth Sunday after Trinity, 1878. By the Rev. E. B. Pusey, D.D., . . .

> Pp. 56 : Oxford, 1878, 8°.

7. —— UN-SCIENCE . . . [&c., as above]. Second edition.

> Pp. 58 : Oxford, 1878, 8°. See 1880, 1.

8. THE RULE OF FAITH . . . [&c., as 1851, 10, adding after ‘ Epiphany,’ ‘ 1851. With a preface on Papal Infallibility from Bossuet,’ omitting ‘ late —— College,’ adding ‘ Third thousand ’].

> Pp. xlviii + 68 : Oxford, 1878, 8°. See 1879, 2.

9. THE LOVE OF GOD AND OF JESUS FOR SOULS, AND THE BLESSED-NESS OF INTERCESSION FOR THEM. Addresses . . . [&c., as 1868, 5]. Third edition. Fifth thousand.

> Pp. viii + 136 : Oxford, 1878, 8°.

10. CHRIST THE SOURCE . . . [&c., as 1841, 4 : new edition].

> Pp. 48 : Oxford, 1878, 8°. See 1884, 2.

11. EVERLASTING PUNISHMENT . . . [as 1864, 12].

> Pp. 36 : Oxford [1880 ?], 8v°. See no 4.

12. (LETTER TO DR. LIDDON on the alteration of the words in Keble’s ‘ Christian Year ’ ‘ Not in the hands,’ of the Holy Communion. Signed ‘ E. B. Pusey,’ May 20, 1878.)

> Pp. [8] : n. pl., [1878 ?], 8°. See 1866, 16.

13. †See 1875, 6 (Keble’s Sermons).

14. †A GUIDE FOR PASSING LENT HOLILY . . . [&c., as 1844, 5]. Fifth edition.

> Pp. [2, frontispiece] + pp. xiv + 352 : Oxford (London slip pasted over, in some copies), 1868, 12°.

---

15. LETTER TO THE ‘ TIMES,’ dated May 8, 1878, on ‘ Why was Keble College built ? ’

16. —— a similar letter, dated May 11, 1878.

17. LETTER TO DR. LIDDON, dated June 7, 1878, published in the *Guardian* soon after : on Dr. Pusey’s letter to Bishop Bagot.

18. LETTER TO DR. LIDDON, dated June 13, 1878, printed in the *Guardian* in the same month : on the Real Presence.

19. TWO LETTERS TO THE 'TIMES' of July, 1878, on Concession, in comment on Mr. Jenkins's statements in the House of Commons : the first is dated July 6, 1878, the second begins, 'Sir, I did not intend.'

20. LETTER TO DR. LIDDON, dated Dec. 12, 1878, on Dr. Pusey's immunity from persecution. Printed in the *Times*, apparently early in Feb. 1881.

## 1879.

1. CORRECTION OF SOME CRITICISMS ON THE 'MANUAL FOR CONFESSORS.' By the Rev. E. B. Pusey, D.D., Canon of Christ Church.

Pp. xxxii : Oxford, 1879, 8°. See 1878, 1.

2. NINE SERMONS . . . [&c., as 1859, 1]. New edition. [Half-title :— 'University Sermons, Vol. I.']

Pp. 24 and viii + 94 (= 1843, 1) and xx + 64 (= 1866, 6) and 46 (= 1857, 5) and vi + 74 (= 1871, 5) and 50 (= 1853, 6) and xlviii + 68 (= 1878, 8) and viii + 94 (= 1864, 8 : two sermons), and [4] + 52 (= 1864, 9).

3. PROPHECY OF JESUS THE CERTAIN PREDICTION OF THE (TO MAN) IMPOSSIBLE. A sermon [on 1 St. Pet. i. 10–11] preached before the University of Oxford on the twenty-first Sunday after Trinity, 1878. By the Rev. E. B. Pusey, D.D., . . .

Pp. 56 : Oxford, 1879, 8°. See 1880, 1.

4. THE RESPONSIBILITY . . . [&c., as 1873, 2]. Fourth edition.

Pp. 84 : Oxford (London), 1879, 8°. See 1880, 1.

5. SINFUL BLINDNESS . . . [&c., as 1873, 3]. Fourth edition.

6. TO THE MEMBERS AND ASSOCIATES OF THE ENGLISH CHURCH UNION (corrected), November, 1879.

Pp. 8 : n. pl., (1879), 8vo.

7. (LETTER TO ONE IN GRIEF, beginning ' My dear Mr. —— Your loving wife' : signed 'E. B. Pusey,' Dec. 1879.

Pp. [4] : n. pl. : 12°.

---

8. LETTER TO THE 'CHURCH OF ENGLAND PULPIT AND ECCLESIASTICAL REVIEW,' dated Feb. 7, 1879, in reply to a review of ' Un-science, not Science, adverse to Faith.' See 1878, 5.

9. LETTER, apparently printed in the Literary Supplement of the *Agricultural Gazette*, March 3, 1879: about Dr. Pusey's elder brother.

10. LETTER TO MR. BELANEY, dated May 20, 1879, printed in the *Weekly Register:* on Dr. Newman's Cardinalate.

11. LETTER TO DR. KING, dated June 13, 1879, read at the meeting of the Oxford Branch of the English Church Union on the same day.

12. LETTER TO MR. J. W. WOOD, dated Dec. 21, 1879, printed in the *Church Times* of Jan. (?) 1880: on Communions.

## 1880.

1. TEN SERMONS PREACHED BEFORE THE UNIVERSITY OF OXFORD BETWEEN 1864-1879. Now collected into one volume. And a sermon preached at the opening of the Chapel of Keble College on S. Mark's Day, 1876. By the Rev. E. B. Pusey, D.D., . . .

Pp. viii and [2] + 36 (= 1880, 8) and 36 (= 1866, 3, sixth thousand) and x + 30 (= 1880, 7) and 48 (= 1871, 4) and 84 (= 1879, 4) and 34 (= 1873, 3) and 44 (= 1875, 3) and 36 (= 1876, 2) and 58 (= 1878, 7) and 56 (1879, 3) and 32 (= 1876, 3): Oxford, 1880, 8°. This counts as 'University Sermons, Vol. III': see 1878, 4.

2. †ADVICE . . . [&c., as 1878, 1]. Second edition.

Pp. [?]: Oxford, 1880, 8°.

3. WHAT IS OF FAITH AS TO EVERLASTING PUNISHMENT? In reply to Dr. Farrar's challenge in his 'Eternal Hope,' 1879. By the Rev. E. B. Pusey, D.D., . . .

Pp. [?]: Oxford, 1880, 8°.

4. —— WHAT IS . . . [&c., as above]. Second edition.

Pp. [?]: Oxford, 1880, 8°.

5. —— WHAT IS . . . [&c., as above]. Third edition.

Pp. xvi + 290: Oxford, 1880, 8°.

6. THE DANGER OF RICHES . . . [&c., as 1850, 5]. Fourth thousand.

Pp. 46: Oxford, 1880, 8°. See 1884, 2.

7. WILL YE ALSO . . . [&c., as 1867, 1]. Fifth thousand.

Pp. x + 30: Oxford, 1880, 8°. See no. 1.

8. EVERLASTING PUNISHMENT . . . [&c., as 1864, 12].

Pp. [2] + 36: Oxford, [1880?], 8°. See no. 1.

9. TO THE MEMBERS OF THE E. C. U., OXFORD BRANCH.

Pp. 4: n. pl., (1880), 8°. Dated May 18, 1880.

10. LETTER beginning 'My dear Mr. ——, I said, now some time ago.'

Pp. 8: n. pl., (1880), 8°. 'Unpublished': dated Nov. 18, 1880.

11. †See 1875, 6 (Keble's Sermons).

---

12. LETTER TO MR. H. A. BROWNE, dated Nov. 2, 1880, printed in the *Guardian* soon after : on Mr. Dale's imprisonment.

13. LETTER TO THE HON. C. L. WOOD, dated Nov. 17, 1880, on the Dale judgment : read at the meeting of the English Church Union in London, on Nov. 18. Printed in the Supplement to the *Church Union Gazette*, Dec. 11, 1880.

14. LETTER TO THE 'TIMES,' dated Nov. 23, 1880, in reply to 'A Diocesan Chancellor.'

15. LETTER TO MR. SHAW-STEWART, dated Nov. 29, 1880, read at the meeting of the Oxford Branch of the English Church Union soon after.

16. LETTER, read at a meeting in Birmingham Town Hall on Dec. 8, 1880, about Mr. Enraght's imprisonment.

## 1881.

1. UNLAW IN JUDGEMENTS OF THE JUDICIAL COMMITTEE AND ITS REMEDIES, a letter to the Rev. H. P. Liddon, D.D., Canon of St. Paul's, by the Rev. E. B. Pusey, D.D., . . .
>Pp. viii + 72 : Oxford, 1881, 8º.

2. —— UNLAW . . . [&c., as above].  Second edition, with an appendix.
>Pp. viii + 88 : Oxford, 1881, 8º.

3. (LETTER beginning ' My dear Sir, It *was* a grave charge,' on the bias of the Ecclesiastical Courts.)
>Pp. 2 : n. pl., (1881), 8º.  Dated April 19, 1881.

4. TO THE MEMBERS OF THE E. C. U., OXFORD BRANCH.
>Pp. 4 : n. pl., (1881), 8º.  Dated June 9, 1881.

5. TO THE MEMBERS OF THE C. E. W. M. S.
>Pp. 4 : n. pl., (1881), 8º.  Dated July 29, 1881 : to the Church of England Working Men's Society.  See no. 12.

6. (LETTER TO THE HON. C. WOOD, beginning 'My dearest C. Wood, Lord Penzance's jurisdiction.')
>Pp. 4 : n. pl., (1881), 8º.  Dated Aug. 6, 1881.

7. (LETTER TO A LADY, beginning 'My dear Madam, I guessed the object of your enquiry' : on the descent of man.)
>Pp. 4 : n. pl., (1881), 8º.  'Not to be published' : dated Nov. 9, 1881.

8. †LATER TREATISES OF S. ATHANASIUS, ARCHBISHOP OF ALEX-ANDRIA, with notes ; and an appendix on S. Cyril of Alexandria and Theodoret. [Dr. Pusey contributed the preliminary Observations, signed ' E. B. P.,' Oct. 21, 1881.]
>Pp. 12 + 238 : Oxford, 1881, 8º.  Part of the ' Library of the Fathers.'

9. †THE GOSPELS DISTRIBUTED INTO MEDITATIONS FOR EVERY DAY IN THE YEAR ... by l'Abbé Duquesne.  Translated from the French and adapted to the use of the English Church [edited by Dr. Pusey].  Vols. 1, 2 [for the 3rd volume see 1884, 13].
>Pp. [4] + 534 and [2] + 626 : Oxford, 1881, 12º.  See 1885, 5.

10. †S. CYRIL, ARCHBISHOP OF ALEXANDRIA.  Five tomes against Nestorius : Scholia on the Incarnation : Christ is one : Fragments against Diodore of Tarsus, Theodore of Mopsuestia, the Synousiasts. [The translation is by Dr. Pusey's son Philip, and parts of the preface : the rest of the preface, pp. xxxvii–cv, is by Dr. Pusey, who signs it ' E. B. P.,' Dec. 24, 1881.]
>>Pp. 108 + 408 : Oxford, 1881, 8º.  Part of the ' Library of the Fathers.'  The translation of St. Ambrose's Letters, issued in the same Library in this year, contains a very short introductory notice by Dr. Pusey, signed ' E. B. P.,' Lent, 1881.

---

11. THREE LETTERS TO THE ' TIMES,' dated Jan. 12, 24, and 27, 1881, on Ritualism.

**12.** Letter to Members of the Church of England Working Men's Society, read at their meeting in London on Aug. 6, 1881. Another to Sir John Conroy, dated Oct. 15, was read at a similar meeting at Reading, on Oct. 19 or 20, 1881. Another read at a similar meeting in London, Nov. 7, 1881 : all three are about Mr. Green. See no. 5.

**13.** Letters to the 'Times' of Aug. 15 and 22, 1881, on Mr. Green's imprisonment.

**14.** Letter to Mr. Packman, dated Oct. 7, 1881, read at a meeting of the S. W. Yorkshire District Union of the English Church Union, Oct. 11 : on Mr. Green's imprisonment.

## 1882.

**1.** Parochial and Cathedral Sermons.

Pp. [2]+xvi+524 : Oxford, 1882, 8°. See 1883, 5; 1887, 1. At first Dr. Pusey intended this volume to begin with a Sermon entitled ' Hell,' on St. Matth. iii. 10, preached at Frome in 1856 : but subsequently decided not to issue it. A proof of the first two sheets is in existence, in which the sermon occupies pp. 1–23.

**2.** Blessed are the Meek . . . [&c., as 1876, 3]. Second edition.

Pp. 32 : Oxford, 1882, 8°. A reprint, with an alteration on p. 24.

**3.** (Letter to Dr. Acland, beginning ' My dear Acland, Of course no Christian,' on the subjects required in the School of Natural Science at Oxford.)

Pp. 4 : n. pl., (1882), 8°. Dated May 1, 1882.

**4.** Eleven Addresses . . . [&c., as 1868, 5].

Pp. viii+176 : (Oxford), privately printed at Holy-Rood : 1882, 12°. Only eight copies printed : two prayers are added on pp. 174–5.

**5.** [Unpublished Letter to Lord Dalhousie.]

Pp. 4 : n. pl., [1882?], 8° : signed ' E. B. Pusey,' May 16, 1882 : about the marriage law.

### [Dr. Pusey died Sept. 16, 1882.]

**6.** A Daily Text-book gathered from the writings of the Rev. Edward Bouverie Pusey, D.D., late Canon of Christ Church, Oxford, and Regius Professor of Hebrew. By E. H. and F. H. With a preface by the Rev. Edward King, D.D., . . .

Pp. viii+200 : London, 1882, sq. 12°. See 1884, 12; 1896, 1.

**7.** Letter to the Hon. C. L. Wood, dated March 8, 1882, printed in the *Church Times* of March 10, 1882 : on Mr. Green's imprisonment. There were letters also on the same subject to the *Times*, dated August 24 and August 31, 1882.

**8.** Letter to the 'Spectator,' dated March 21, 1882, on the same subject.

9. LETTER TO MEMBERS OF THE OXFORD BRANCH OF THE ENGLISH CHURCH UNION, read at their meeting in Oxford on June 1, 1882.

10. LETTER TO CANON LIDDON, dated July 11, 1882, printed in the *Guardian*, July 26, 1882: about the Rev. T. Mozley's estimate of Keble.

11. SIMILAR LETTER, dated Aug. 18, 1882, also printed in the *Guardian*.

## 1883.

1. SERMONS FOR THE CHURCH'S SEASONS FROM ADVENT TO TRINITY, selected from the published sermons of the late Edward Bouverie Pusey, D.D., Canon of Christ Church and Professor of Hebrew in the University of Oxford. [Preface signed 'R. F. W.,' i.e. Rev. R. F. Wilson.]

Pp. xii + 424: London, 1883, 8°.

2. PAROCHIAL SERMONS, Vol. I, for the season from Advent to Whitsuntide. By the Rev. E. B. Pusey, D.D., ... Seventh thousand.

Pp. xxxii + 480: London (Oxford), 1883, 8°. See 1848, 1.

3. PAROCHIAL SERMONS, Vol. III. Revised ed.

Pp. [?]: London (Oxford), 1883, 8°. See 1841, 3.

4. THE DOCTRINE OF THE REAL PRESENCE ... [&c., as 1855, 1].

Pp. xii + 724: London, 1883, 8°.

5. PAROCHIAL AND CATHEDRAL SERMONS. By the Rev. E. B. Pusey, D.D., ... Third thousand.

Pp. [4] + xvi + 524: London (Oxford), 1883, 8°. See 1882, 1.

6. DANIEL THE PROPHET... [&c., as 1864, 1]. Seventh edition.

Pp. civ + 652; London, 1883, 8°.

7. MAXIMS AND GLEANINGS FROM THE WRITINGS OF E. B. PUSEY, D.D., selected and arranged for daily use by C. M. S[adler]..., with an introduction by the Rev. M. F. Sadler ...

Pp. xii + 140: London, 1883, 12°. See 1885, 1.

8. —— Second edition.

Pp. xii + 140: London, 1883, 12°.

9. SELECTIONS FROM THE WRITINGS OF EDWARD BOUVERIE PUSEY, D.D., late Regius Professor of Hebrew, and Canon of Christ Church, Oxford.

Pp. viii + 344: London, 1883, 8°. See 1885, 2.

10. CHRISTUS CONSOLATOR. Short readings for the sick and sorrowful, from the sermons of Dr. Pusey. Selected by a Lady. With a preface by George E. Jelf, ... Canon of Rochester.

Pp. xii + 44: London, 1883, 12°.

11. PRIVATE PRAYERS, by the Rev. E. B. Pusey, D.D., edited with a preface by H. P. Liddon, D.D.

Pp. xii + 276: London, 1883, 24°. The Prayers were chiefly composed in about 1853-55. See 1884, 5.

12. PRAYERS FOR A YOUNG SCHOOLBOY, by the late E. B. Pusey, D.D.

> Pp. xx + 28 : London, 1883, 12°. The Prayers were chiefly composed in 1839 for the use of the writer's son : the preface, by Dr. Liddon, contains a letter from Dr. Pusey to his son, Oct. 29, 1843. See 1884, 11.

13. PART III. PREPARATION FOR FIRST COMMUNION (published by permission) WITH INSTRUCTIONS FOR HOLY COMMUNION, gathered from the writings of the Reverend Edward Bouverie Pusey, D.D., by E. H. and F. H. With a preface by the Rev. H. S. Holland . . .

> Pp. xx + 88 : London, 1883, 12°. See 1884, 10.

14. DEVOTIONS FOR HOLY COMMUNION, compiled from various sources, with an introduction gathered from the writings of the Rev. Edward Bouverie Pusey, D.D., late Canon of Christ Church, and Regius Professor of Hebrew ; and a preface by the Rev. George Edward Jelf, . . . Canon of Rochester.

> Pp. viii + 160 : London, 1883, 12°. See 1884, 6. Compiled by Dr. Pusey's daughter.

15. †THE SPIRITUAL COMBAT . . . [nearly as 1846, 5].

> Pp. xxviii + 276 : Oxford, 1883, 8°.


## 1884.

1. SERMONS PREACHED BEFORE THE UNIVERSITY . . . [&c., as 1872, 1]. Second thousand.

> Pp. xvi + 496 : London (Oxford), 1884, 8°.

2. PAROCHIAL SERMONS . . . [&c., as 1865, 2].

> Pp. xii + 32 ( = general title + 1839, 10 without its title) and 48 ( = 1878, 10) and [4] + 28 ( = 1864, 10) and [4] + 50 ( = 1864, 11) and 32 ( = 1872, 5) and 24 ( = 1875, 4) and 20 ( = 1875, 5) and 46 ( = 1880, 6) and 58 ( = 1864, 7) and 30 ( = 1856, 4) : Lond., 1884, 8°. The volume is lettered 'Occasional Sermons . . . 1832-50,' and is made up of separate sermons with a general title. I have seen another edition made up of:—pp. [2, title-page] and xii + 32 ( = 1872, 6) and 48 ( = 1878, 10) and iv + 28 ( = 1864, 10) and iv + 50 ( = 1864, 11) and 32 ( = 1872, 5) and 24 ( = 1875, 4) and 20 ( = 1875, 5) and 46 ( = 1880, 6) and 58 ( = 1864, 7).

3. OCCASIONAL SERMONS selected from published sermons of the Rev. E. B. Pusey, late Canon of Christ Church and Regius Professor of Hebrew. With a preface by the Rev. R. F. Wilson . . .

> Pp. 8 + 400 : London (Oxford), 1884, 8°.

4. 'FOR ALL TIMES AND ALL SEASONS.' Readings selected and arranged by C. M. S[adler], from the writings of John Keble, M.A., and E. B. Pusey, D.D.

> Pp. viii + 208 : London (Bungay), 1884, 12°.

5. PRIVATE PRAYERS . . . [&c., as 1883, 1.]

> Pp. 16 + 276 : London, 1884, 24°. See 1883, 11, of which this is substantially a reprint.

**6.** DEVOTIONS FOR HOLY COMMUNION . . . [&c., as 1883, 14].
Second thousand.

> Pp. viii + 160 : London, 1884, 12°.

**7.** (I.) PRAYERS GATHERED FROM THE WRITINGS OF THE
REVEREND EDWARD BOUVERIE PUSEY, D.D., together with others
from his unpublished MSS., by E. H. and F. H. With a preface by
the Rev. R. F. Wilson . . .

> Pp. xvi + 92 : London, 1884, 12°. The 'Third thousand' was
> issued in this year, and omits the '(I).' See next art. and
> 1883, 13.

**8.** (PART II.) PENITENCE, WITH RULES FOR GUIDANCE AND
HINTS FOR A FIRST CONFESSION. (Now published by permission.)
Gathered from the writings of the Reverend Edward Bouverie Pusey,
D.D., by E. H. and F. H. With a preface by the Rev. C. W. Furse . . .

> Pp. xvi + 64 : London, 1884, 12°. The 'Third thousand' was
> issued in this year, and omits the ('Part II'). See 1893, 1.

**9.** HINTS FOR A FIRST CONFESSION. By the Rev. E. B. Pusey,
D.D.

> Pp. 40 : London, 1884, 16°. Edited with a preface by Francis
> H. Murray, who added some questions from W. E. Scudamore's
> 'Incense for the Altar.' See 1851, 12 ; 1892, 1.

**10.** PREPARATION FOR FIRST COMMUNION . . . [&c., as 1883, 13].
Third thousand.

> Pp. xx + 88 : London, 1884, 12°.

**11.** PRAYERS FOR A YOUNG SCHOOLBOY, by the Rev. E. B. Pusey,
D.D. Edited, with a preface by H. P. Liddon, D.D. Second edition.

> Pp. xx + 28 : London, 1884, 12°. See 1883, 12, of which this is
> almost a reprint.

**12.** A DAILY TEXT-BOOK . . . [&c., as 1882, 6]. Fourth thousand.

> Pp. viii + 198 : London, 1884, squ. 12°.

**13.** †THE GOSPELS DISTRIBUTED INTO MEDITATIONS . . . [&c.,
as 1881, 9]. Volume III.

> Pp. viii + 694 : London (Oxford), 1884, 12°.

**14.** †A GUIDE FOR PASSING LENT HOLILY . . . [&c., as 1844, 5].

> Pp. xlvi + xiv + 352 : London, 1884, 12°.

**15.** †THE SUFFERINGS OF JESUS . . . [&c., as 1869, 9 : in two parts].

> Pp. xxiv + 500 and vi + 416 : London (Plymouth), 1884, 12°.

## 1885.

**1.** MAXIMS AND GLEANINGS . . . [&c., as 1883, 7]. Third edition.

> Pp. xii + 140 : London, 1885, 12°. ——

**2.** SELECTIONS . . . [&c., as 1883, 9]. Second edition.

> Pp. 8 + 344 : London, 1885, 8°.

3. THE REAL PRESENCE . . . [&c., as 1857, 2]. Third thousand.

> Pp. xxxii + 350 : London (Oxford), 1885, 8°.

4. †SERMONS ON THE LITANY . . . by the late Rev. John Keble . . . with introductory notice by the late Rev. E. B. Pusey, D.D.

> Pp. viii +172 : London (Oxford), 1885, 8°. The short advertisement is signed ' E. B. P., Epiphany, 1879.'

5. †THE GOSPELS DISTRIBUTED . . . [&c., as 1881, 9]. With an introductory notice by the Rev. H. Montagu Villiers . . . Volume I. Second edition.

> Pp. xvi + cxii + 530 : London (Oxford), 1885, 12°. Apparently no more of the 2nd ed. was issued.

## 1886.

### [*Nothing.*]

## 1887.

1. PAROCHIAL AND CATHEDRAL SERMONS [as 1882, 1]. Third thousand.

> Pp. [4] + xvi + 524: London (Oxford), 1887, 8°.

## 1888.

1. EXTRACTS FROM LETTERS by the Rev. E. B. Pusey, D.D. On the Illness and Death of his eldest Daughter (April, 1844). Pp. 112–122 of the 'Convent Magazine,' April 1888 (Oxford, 8°.)

2. LETTERS &c. from the Rev. E. B. Pusey, D.D. Pp. 265–7 of the 'Convent Magazine,' Aug. 1888 (Oxford, 8°). The two letters are dated Aug. 22 and 29, 1882.

## 1889.

### [*Nothing.*]

## 1890.

### [*Nothing.*]

## 1891.

1. NOTES AND QUESTIONS ON THE CATHOLIC FAITH AND RELIGION. The Notes and Answers compiled chiefly from the works and in the words of Dr. Pusey. With a Preface by the Rev. Thomas Thellusson Carter . . .

> Pp. xxiv + 356 : London, 1891, 8°.

2. †THE SPIRITUAL COMBAT . . . [&c., as 1846, 5].

> Pp. xxviii + 274: London, 1891, 8°.

## 1892.

1. HINTS FOR A FIRST CONFESSION.
> Pp. 40 : London, 1892, 16°. A reprint of 1884, 9.

## 1893.

1. PENITENCE, WITH RULES . . . [&c., as 1884, 8].
> Pp. xvi + 64 : London, 1893, 12°. 'Part II' is only on the binding.

2. TRACT XC . . . [&c., as 1865, 4, adding the word ' (revised)' after Dr. Pusey's name].
> Pp. xliv + 88 + 26 : London, 1893, 8°.

## 1894.

*[Nothing.]*

## 1895.

*[Nothing.]*

## 1896.

1. A DAILY TEXT-BOOK . . . [&c., as 1882, 6]. Sixth thousand.
> Pp. viii + 200 : London, 1896, 12°.

## No date.

1. READING IN PREPARATION FOR HOLY ORDERS [by Dr. Pusey, but unsigned and undated].
> Pp. 4 : [Oxford, about 1875 ?], 8°.

2. Some Sermons by Dr. Pusey (chiefly addressed to Sisters of Charity) were privately printed without date at Oxford ; of which I have seen the following :
> (*a*) On Acts ii. 37-8 (1864 ?) : pp. [2] + 6, 8°.
> (*b*) On Cant. ii. 10 : pp. 8, 8°.
> (*c*) (Begins ' The Feast of the Holy Angels ') : pp. 4, 8°.
> (*d*) On St. John xiii. 34 : pp. 8, 8°.

3. (ANSWER to begging letters, beginning ' My dear       I am sorry' : signed ' E. B. Pusey.'
> Pp. [2] : [Oxford], 12°.

4. A PRAYER for the Grace of a Religious Life.
> Pp. [2] : n. pl., 12°.

5. COMMENTARY ON THE HOLY SCRIPTURES, for the unlearned.
> Pp. [2] : Oxford, [1847], 8°. A prospectus of a series, drawn up by Dr. Pusey, but unsigned.

**6.** [RULES AND REGULATIONS] OF THE COMPANIONS OF THE
LOVE OF JESUS.

> Pp. 8 + 8 : n. pl., 12°.  With nine Offices.  This was revised and
> sanctioned by Dr. Pusey, who signs a note on p. 1 of the second
> part ' E. B. P.' . . . The Offices were also printed by lithography
> on twelve pages of parchment, in a shorter form, 12°.

**7.** (Dr. Pusey drew up several papers describing and recommending
Ascot Hospital for convalescents and incurables, from 1878 to 1882
and perhaps earlier.)

**8.** (The Devonport Society, when at Bradford on Avon, was in the
habit of reprinting passages from Dr. Pusey's works on one side of an
octavo leaf, with more or less ornamental borders, as tracts.)

# APPENDIX B.

When a date and number is given, the sermon so marked will be found in Appendix A at the given reference. The dates given above in the list of Abbreviations are those of the edition which happened to be used for giving the pagination below.

FALCONER MADAN.

BRASENOSE COLLEGE, OXFORD :

*August*, 1897.

---

[1] Vol. 3 is the same as Plain Sermons, Vol. 3, 1841.

*Psalms* xxvii. 1 God is our Light in all knowledge, natural or super-
               natural.            U. S. ii. p. 32.
    „      xxxi. 16 Hope.           P. S. ii. p. 21.
    „     xxxix. 6–7 The conflict, in a superficial age (1865, 5). L. S. p. 278.
    „      xl. 9–10 Each has his own vocation.      U. S. ii. p. 437.
    „      li. 4   . David in his sin and his penitence (1864, 13).
                                           L. S. p. 237.
    „      li. 10  . Re-creation of the penitent.      P. S. ii. p. 181.
    „ lxxxvii. 3–5 The Church the converter of the heathen (1838, 2).
                                             O. P. S.
    „    cxviii. 34 Christian joy.           P. S. iii. p. 439.
    „   cxix. 59–60 Review of life.     P. S. i. p. 140; S. O. S. p. 142.
    „ cxxxix. 15–16 Daily growth.          S. S. L. p. 330.
*Prov.* i. 24–28 . Irreversible chastisements.       P. S. i. p. 172.
    „    xvi. 6  . Value of almsgiving in the sight of God.
                                          U. S. ii. p. 359.
*Eccles.* xii. 13–14 Every thought, word, deed shall be judged.
                                          P. C. S. p. 345.

*Song of Sol.* ii. 10. (*n. d.*, 2 *b.*)
      „     v. 2–8 God withdraws in lovingkindness also (1850, 6).
                      P. C. S. p. 300; S. C. S. p. 92.

*Isaiah* vi. 8–10 Isaiah, his heaviness and his consolation (1870, 2).
                                        L. S. p. 466.
    „    xlix. 5–7 The Christ the Light of the world to be rejected by
              His own, &c.        U. S. ii. p. 108.
    „     l. 6–7  . On human respect.       U. S. ii. p. 411.
    „     liii. 1  . Causes which blinded the Jews to the prophecies that
              Jesus should suffer.     U. S. ii. p. 161.
    „     liii. 12 . The prophecy of Christ our Atoner and Intercessor.
                                          U. S. ii. p. 78.
*Jer.* xxiii. 6 . . Christ, the Lord our Righteousness.   U. S. ii. p. 263.
*Hosea* ii. 14  . God's presence in loneliness.
                           P. S. i. p. 190; S. C. S. p. 196.
*Joel* ii. 11  . . The Day of Judgment (1839, 10).      O. P. S.
    „   ii. 12–13 . Chastisements neglected, forerunners of greater
              (1847, 3).           O. P. S.
*Haggai* i. 7 .  . Whither art thou going?     P. C. S. p. 352.
    „    ii. 9  . (Consecration of Grove Church) (1832, 1).    O. P. S.
*Zech.* xii. 10  . Power of truth amid untruthfulness, in Jewish inter-
              pretation of prophecy.    U. S. ii. p. 133.
*Ecclus.* xix. 1  . Peril of little sins.       P. C. S. p. 118.

---

*St. Matt.* i. 23 . God with us.      P. S. i. p. 47; S. C. S. p. 54.
    „   iii. 10 .  . Hell (1882, 1).
    „   iv. 1–2  . Fasting.           P. C. S. p. 391.
    „   iv. 21 .  . Obeying calls (St. James).    P. S. iii. p. 392.

*St. Matt.* v. 4 . Continual comfort the gift of God on continual sorrow
 for sin (1863, 1). L. S. p. 387.
 „ v. 5 . . Blessed are the meek (1876, 3). U. S. iii.
 „ vi. 10 . . God advances His kingdom through man.
 P. C. S. p. 319 ; S. C. S. p. 43.
 „ vi. 22–23. Man's self-deceit and God's omniscience. L. S. p. 128.
 „ vi. 33 . . Seek God first and ye shall have all (1850, 5). O. P. S.
 „ x. 42 . . Good of little acts to please God.
 P. C. S. p. 144 ; S. C. S. p. 31.
 „ xii. 31. . The blasphemy against the Holy Ghost (1845, 5).
 O. P. S. ; S. O. S. p. 225.
 „ xv. 28 . Prayer heard the more through delay. P. S. ii. p. 167.
 „ xvi. 15–17 Faith in our Lord, God and Man. P. S. ii. p. 283.
 „ xvii. 1–2 . The Transfiguration of Our Lord the earnest of the
 Christian's glory. P. S. iii. p. 413.
 „ xviii. 3 . Conversion. P. C. S. p. 17.
 „ xviii. 5 . 'Whoso receiveth one such little child in My Name,
 receiveth me' (1844, 2). O. P. S.
 „ xix. 18 . Murder of souls. P. C. S. p. 363.
 „ xx. 6–7 . God calleth thee. P. S. i. p. 107 ; S. C. S. p. 33.
 „ xx. 16 . . The fewness of the saved. P. S. i. p. 122.
 „ xx. 22 . . Self-knowledge. P. S. ii. p. 98 ; S. O. S. p. 61.
 „ xxi. 22 . The miracles of Prayer (1866, 3).
 U. S. iii ; S. O. S. p. 295.
 „ „ . Prayer. P. C. S. p. 273 ; S. C. S. p. 373.
 „ xxiv. 14 . The preaching of the Gospel a preparation for our
 Lord's coming (1841, 5). O. P. S.
 „ xxiv. 40–42 Sudden death. P. S. iii. p. 1.
 „ xxv. 31–46 The merciful shall obtain mercy. P. S. i. p. 16.
 „ xxv. 46 . Everlasting punishment (1864, 12).
 U. S. iii ; S. O. S. p. 245.
 „ xxvi. 26 . This is My Body (1871, 4). U. S. iii.
 „ xxvi. 28 . The Holy Eucharist a comfort to the penitent
 (1843, 1). U. S. i.
 „ xxvi. 39 . The Will of God the cure of self-will.
 P. S. i. p. 359 ; S. C. S. p. 67.
 „ xxvii. 3–5 The sin of Judas. P. S. ii. p. 197.
 „ xxvii. 21 . Barabbas or Jesus. P. S. i. p. 204 ; S. C. S. p. 274.
*St. Mark* x. 13–14 Baptism the ground and encouragement to Christian
 education. P. S. iii. p. 287.
 „ xvi. 9 . . Our Risen Lord's love for penitents.
 P. S. i. p. 257 ; S. C. S. p. 340.
*St. Luke* ii. 21 . The value and sacredness of suffering. P. S. iii. p. 116.
 „ iv. 1–2 . Victory over the besetting sin.
 P. S. ii. p. 146 ; S. O. S. p. 93.
 „ iv. 22 . . Christ's words of love the reproof of detraction.
 P. C. S. p. 215.

*St. John* xvi. 23 Conditions of acceptable prayer. P. S. p. 239.
  „ xviii. 37–38 The Gospel could not be true, unless it had certain
                 truth. U. S. ii. p. 186.
  „ xx. 12 . . God and human independence (1876, 2). U. S. iii.
  „ xx. 21 . . True peace and false peace.
                 P. C. S. p. 418; S. O. S. p. 351.
  „ xx. 21–23 Entire Absolution of the penitent, I (1846, 1). U. S. i.

*Acts* ii. 37–38 . (*n. d.,* 2 *a*).
  „ iv. 36–37 Christian kindliness and charity. P. S. iii. p. 366.
  „ vi. 15 . . Character of Christian rebuke. P. S. i. p. 76.
  „ ix. 6 . . Conversion. P. S. iii. p. 19.
  „ xvii. 27–28 The Being of God, in Whom we are. P. C. S. p. 503.
  „ xvii. 28 . Our being in God. P. S. ii. p. 372.
  „ xxvi. 27–28 'Almost thou persuadest me to be a Christian.'
                 L. S. p. 44.

*Rom.* i. 4 . . Real faith entire (1855, 2). U. S. i.
  „ iii. 26 . . The doctrine of the Atonement. U. S. ii. p. 232.
  „ iv. 25 . . Christ risen our Justification.
                 P. S. i. p. 216; S. C. S. p. 326.
  „ „ . . The Resurrection of Christ, the source, earnest,
                 pattern of ours. P. C. S. p. 451.
  „ vii. 22–23 Victory amid strife. P. S. ii. p. 327.
  „ vii. 22–25 Christian life a struggle, but victory. P. S. iii. p. 93.
  „ viii. 9 . . Actualness of the indwelling of God. P. C. S. p. 472.
  „ viii. 16–17 The witness of the Spirit. P. C. S. p. 175.
  „ viii. 22–23 Groans of unrenewed and renewed Nature.
                 P. S. ii. p. 304.
  „ ix. 1–3 . Christian zeal. P. C. S. p. 257; S. C. S. p. 81.
  „ xi. 24 . . Natural good and evil. P. C. S. p. 74.
  „ xii. 2 . . Obedience the condition of knowing the truth.
                 P. S. iii. p. 184.
  „ xii. 12 . Pray without ceasing. P. S. iii. p. 211.

I *Cor.* ii. 2 . . Jesus the Redeemer and His redeemed. L. S. p. 421.
  „ iii. 11–13 Loss through little sins. P. C. S. p. 103.
  „ iii. 11–15 The losses of the saved. L. S. p. 89; S. O. S. p. 276.
  „ iii. 16 . . God's condescending love in restoring man by His
                 own indwelling. P. C. S. p. 459.
  „ iv. 4 . . False Peace. P. C. S. p. 1.
  „ iv. 4–5 . The terror of the Day of Judgment as arising from
                 its justice. U. S. ii. p. 313; S. C. S. p. 14.
  „ iv. 7 . . All faith the gift of God (1855, 2). U. S. i.
  „ vi. 15 . . The thought of the love of Jesus for us, the remedy for
                 sins of the body (1861, 7).
                 L. S. p. 364; S. O. S. p. 195.
  „ ix. 26 . . Life a warfare. P. S. ii. p. 113.
  „ ix. 27 . . Fasting. P. S. i. p. 140.

| | | |
|---|---|---|
| *Heb.* xii. 2 . . | Looking unto Jesus, the groundwork of penitence. | |
| | | S. S. L. p. 173 ; S. C. S. p. 241. |
| „ „ . . | Looking unto Jesus, the means of endurance. | |
| | | S. S. L. p. 192; S. C. S. p. 257. |
| „ xii. 6 . . | Suffering the gift and presence of God. | L. S. p. 404. |
| *St. James* i. 2–3 | Benefit of temptations. | P. C. S. p. 185. |
| „ ii. 10 . . | Real obedience in all things. | P. S. iii. p. 70. |
| „ ii. 22 . . | Justification (1853, 5). | U. S. i. |
| 1 *St. Pet.* i. 10–11 | Prophecy of Jesus the certain prediction of the (to man) impossible (1879, 3). | U. S. iii. |
| „ ii. 16 . . | Free-will. | P. C. S. p. 431. |
| „ ii. 22 . . | Patience. | P. S. ii. p. 80 ; S. O. S. p. 22. |
| 2 *St. Pet.* i. 18–19 | Prophecy a series of miracles which we can examine for ourselves. | U. S. ii. p. 53 ; S. O. S. p. 325. |
| 1 *St. John* i. 4 . | The mystery of the Trinity, the revelation of Divine Love. | P. C. S. p. 493. |
| „ iii. 2 . . | Bliss of heaven, ' We shall be like Him.' | |
| | | S. S. L. p. 255 ; S. C. S. p. 106. |
| „ „ . . | Bliss of heaven, 'We shall see Him as He is.' | |
| | | S. S. L. p. 272 ; S. C. S. p. 120. |
| „ iii. 2–3 . | The Holy Trinity. | P. C. S. p. 479. |
| „ iv. 7–8 . | The power and greatness of Love. | P. S. ii. p. 356. |
| „ iv. 16–17 | God is Love (1844, 2). | O. P. S. |
| „ iv. 19 . | The love of God for us. | P. C. S. p. 439. |
| „ v. 3–4 . | Victory through loving faith. | P. S. ii. p. 342. |
| „ v. 4 . . | Victory over the world. | |
| | | P. S. iii. p. 164 ; S. C. S. p. 312. |
| *Rev.* iii. 14–16 | Lukewarmness. | P. C. S. p. 90. |
| „ „ . . | do. | P. C. S. p. 377. |
| „ iv. 8 . . | The rest of Love and Praise. | P. S. ii. p. 259. |
| „ „ . . | The adoration of Heaven. | |
| | | P. C. S. p. 513 ; S. C. S. p. 414. |
| „ v. 11–13 . | Jesus at the right Hand of God the object of Divine worship (1868, 7). | L. S. p. 437. |
| „ xiv. 4 . . | God's glories in infants set forth in the Holy Innocents. | |
| | | P. S. iii. p. 463. |
| „ xxi. 6 . . | The end of all things (1856, 3). | |
| | | P. S. i. p. 1 ; S. C. S. p. 1. |
| *No text* . . . | The love of God the Holy Ghost for individual souls. (Really an ' Address.') | S. C. S. p. 404. |

# INDEX TO VOL. IV.

THE END.

OXFORD: HORACE HART
PRINTER TO THE UNIVERSITY